P9-CEK-995

# A Feeling for Books

# A Feeling for Books

## THE BOOK-OF-THE-MONTH CLUB,

## LITERARY TASTE, AND MIDDLE-CLASS DESIRE

## Janice A. Radway

The University of North Carolina Press

Chapel Hill and London

© 1997
The University of North Carolina Press
All rights reserved
Manufactured in the United States of America
Set in Janson
by Tseng Information Systems

The paper in this book meets the
guidelines for permanence and durability
of the Committee on Production Guidelines for
Book Longevity of the Council on
Library Resources.

Library of Congress Cataloging-in-Publication Data
Radway, Janice A., 1949–
A feeling for books: the Book-of-the-Month Club, literary taste,
and middle-class desire / by Janice A. Radway.
p.   cm.
Includes bibliographical references and index.
ISBN 0-8078-2357-0 (cloth : alk. paper)
1. Book-of-the-Month Club—History.   2. Books and reading—United
States—History—19th century.   3. Books and reading—United States—
History—20th century.   4. Popular culture—United States—History—19th
century.   5. Popular culture—United States—History—20th century.
I. Title.
Z1003.2.R33   1997
028'.9'0973—DC21       96-52037
CIP

Portions of this work appeared earlier, in somewhat different form, as "The
Book-of-the-Month Club and the General Reader: On the Uses of Serious
Fiction," *Critical Inquiry* (Spring 1988): 516–38; "The Scandal of the
Middlebrow: The Book-of-the-Month Club, Class Fracture, and Cultural
Authority," *The South Atlantic Quarterly* 89 (Fall 1990): 703–36; and "On the
Gender of the Middlebrow Consumer and the Threat of the Culturally
Fraudulent Female," *The South Atlantic Quarterly* 93 (Fall 1994): 871–93, and
are reprinted here with permission.

01  00  99  98  97  5  4  3  2  1

*For my teachers*

*and*

*my students*

*and especially in memory of*

*Russel B. Nye*

# CONTENTS

# ACKNOWLEDGMENTS

Scholarly research and writing produce many pleasures, not the least of them a rich network of relationships and friendships and a deep sense of indebtedness to the many who have offered assistance, commentary, and encouragement along the way. When you live with a project as long as I have with this one, those networks grow ever larger and the debts pile up because, inevitably, you ask all those around you to live with your project, too. I want to thank my family, my students, my friends, my colleagues, and the many others who have generously expressed interest in my research on reading and on the Book-of-the-Month Club. It was their curiosity, advice, and support that sustained me throughout the last twelve years, especially when I couldn't imagine that the work would ever end.

This book could not have been written without the help of the people who are and have been the Book-of-the-Month Club. I am especially grateful to Al Silverman and to Bill Zinsser for their early interest in my work and for making this entire project possible. My debt to the in-house editors at the club who welcomed me into their offices and their working lives is also enormous. Not only did they willingly submit to my endless questions, but they, too, offered me their friendship and supported me with their own curiosity and concern. For our wonderful, exploratory conversations about reading and other matters, I want to thank, in no particular order, Robert Riger, Lorraine Shanley, Jill Sansone, Larry Shapiro, Phyllis Robinson, Alice van Straalen, Susan Weinberg, Marty Asher, Maron Waxman, Eve Tulipan, Elizabeth Easton, Ann Close, Lucy Rosenthal, Nancy Evans, and Victoria Skurnick. I also want to acknowledge the help of the incomparable Joe Savago, whose life at the club and much too early death have had a profound effect on the way I think about my own life and my work with my students. What I regret most is that Joe couldn't read what I have written here. Additionally, I want to thank Clifton Fadiman, Gloria Norris, and Wilfrid Sheed for sharing their reflections about the role of the judges at the Book-of-the-Month Club. And I am especially grateful to Joanne Paternostro and Sophie Yatrakis. They generously made room for me within their crowded offices, and they did everything they could to facilitate my work. I consider the friendship I shared with them one of the greatest pleasures of the many months I spent at the club. I also want to thank Mary Idoni for her help in assembling and organizing the hundreds of reader's reports that I read. And thanks to all those others at the club who assisted in ways too numerous and diverse to mention here.

My students and former students at the University of Pennsylvania and at Duke University have also had a tremendous impact on this project from the beginning. Although I can't name all of them now, I want them to know how much I have appreciated their questions and commentary and how much I have enjoyed our innumerable discussions about reading and middlebrow taste. I would be remiss, though, if I didn't acknowledge the intellectual and material support provided by a few in particular. Barry Shank was there at the beginning and at the end. As my research assistant at Penn, he unearthed most of the early commentary on the club that serves as the basis of Chapters 5, 6, and 7. Later, as a newly employed colleague, he pushed me to think ever harder about consumer culture, about the power of the culture industry, and about the nature of the pleasures we all take from the books, images, music, and films dearest to us. Barry also read the entire first draft of this manuscript with unparalleled and scrupulous attention, and his fifteen, passionately engaged pages of commentary and questions have made this a better book.

Additionally, I want to thank Barbara Will, Deborah Chay, Susan Hegeman, Rosanne Kennedy, Samira Kawash, Katie Kent, Erin Smith, Gillian Silverman, Mark Simpson, and Jennifer Parchesky for the example of their own work on books, reading, and identity, and I want them to know how much I have learned from them about how to think about subjectivity. I thank Jonathan Flatley, too, for our rich, exploratory conversations about reading and affect, modernism and mass culture, as I worked on the final draft of the manuscript. Even if those expansive talks didn't resolve my ambivalence about the Book-of-the-Month Club, they certainly helped me to understand more precisely the particular form it has taken. Nayeli Garci-Crespo was wonderfully helpful as my research assistant during the final stages of preparing the manuscript. I want to thank my other research assistants as well, including Rich Yeselson, Jane Winston, Lucía Suárez, Anita Gutiérrez, Ted Friedman, and Hank Okazaki. In thanking my students, I also want to remember and express my gratitude to all those who taught me. I am deeply grateful for the benefit of their learning and counsel. Most especially, I want to honor the memory of Russel B. Nye's infectious curiosity, generosity, and dedication.

Colleagues near and far have provided immeasurable support and assistance. I thank Fred Jameson for the many ways he has offered encouragement and for his generosity with leave time and, especially, for the continuing inspiration of his own work. I am particularly grateful to Barbara Herrnstein Smith for her shrewd and insightful questions about an early draft of Part II. Those questions prompted helpful self-reflection, a process that ultimately pushed me to write the more autobiographical sections of the book. I send special thanks to the members of my writing group, Betsy Cox, Cathy Davidson, Alice Kaplan, Jane Tompkins, and Marianna Torgovnik. They asked me to join the group at a key stage in the writing of this manuscript, and I will always be grateful for the many ways in which they supported me as I tried to compose in a new voice and a new mode. I feel as if I have learned more from them about the wondrous, variegated pleasures of language than in all the years of my education thus far. This is a much more readable book for their insight and assistance.

Toril Moi read an early version of the manuscript and asked extremely helpful questions about where I was going with it. George Lipsitz has engaged in so many thoughtful conversations about this project over the years that it is hard for me to single out any one way in which he has been influential. I thank him especially, though, for his commentary on the first draft because his observations helped me to clarify what I was trying to do and enabled me to see how far I still had to go. I am grateful, too, to Joy Kasson for her generous and helpful reader's report on the manuscript. Her sensitive comments about form were especially useful as I tried to integrate better the disparate parts of the book. At a very early stage in my research, Dick Ohmann, Alan Trachtenberg, Paul DiMaggio, and Roland Marchand asked the hard questions that pushed me to begin my historical inquiry into the origins of the club. Their questions were then added to and extended by others at the many universities where I presented some of my preliminary findings. I thank everyone involved who organized and attended those lectures, but I especially want to acknowledge how helpful I found the comments of Joan Rubin, Nancy Armstrong, Christina Crosby, Ann Cvetkovich, Evan Watkins, Gordon Hutner, David Hall, Bob Gross, Carl Kaestle, Andrew Parker, Eric Lott, Jay Fliegelman, Peter Rabinowitz, Barbara Sicherman, Meredith McGill, Mary Poovey, Robin Kelley, and Phil Wegener. I want to thank Sandy Swanson for her heroic efforts at transcribing my interview tapes, and I want to acknowledge as well all the support I have received from Sandy Mills, Joan McKay, and Priscilla Lane. I would also like to thank my copyeditor, Stephanie Wenzel, and, at UNC Press, Ron Maner, Kathy Ketterman, and Rich Hendel.

This project has been supported generously by summer research grants from the University of Pennsylvania and Duke University. I have also benefited enormously from fellowships granted by the John Simon Guggenheim Memorial Foundation and the National Endowment for the Humanities. Additionally, I want to acknowledge the assistance of Bernard Crystal and Jean Ashton in the Rare Book and Manuscript Library at Columbia University as well as that given by the Oral History Research Office, also at Columbia. I am grateful, too, for the assistance I received with the Dorothy Canfield Fisher Collection at the Special Collections Department of the Bailey/Howe Memorial Library at the University of Vermont.

My greatest debts are to my friends and family. Drew Faust and Charles Rosenberg are so much a part of my intellectual life that it would be impossible to list the ways they have supported, encouraged, and assisted me over the years as I have worked on this project. I thank them for talks various and far reaching and for our many Philadelphia and Wellfleet dinners, for the mornings at Newcomb Hollow, and for our innumerable, often befuddled conversations about child-rearing. Sharon O'Brien, Barbara Harris, Nancy Hewitt, Ken Wissoker, and Jean O'Barr have listened to me whine and worry about this project for so long that I am sure they are as glad as I am to see it finished. I want them to know how much their encouragement has meant to me. I owe a special debt to Kate Torrey. As my good friend and editor, she has supported this project in ways too numerous to mention. I am especially grateful, though, for her encouragement when I first began to write in a more personal way. I am grateful, too, to Scott Radway, for the many ways in which he has offered support. I also want to thank my mother, Dorothy M. Stewart, for understanding so well the role my work plays in my daily life. She has been immensely supportive and always understanding of its claims on my time. And I thank her, too, for reading to me and for introducing me to the magic of the library.

Last but certainly not least, there is the matter of my debt to the two people with whom I have shared the most—Kathy and Kate. Without their sustaining presence in my life, this book would never have been completed. In the years since I began this project, Kate has grown from a toddler bouncing along at my side into a funny, assured, and very strong young woman. I simply cannot imagine what life would be like without her cartoons, her astute fashion advice, her basketball wisdom, or her thoughtful way of seeing the things around her. She knows how to make me laugh better than anyone, and I want her to know that my world is more joyous because she shares it with me. My partner, Kathy Rudy, has enriched our life together in so many ways that it's impossible even to begin to encompass them here. Perhaps more than anything, though, I value our endless talk about books and ideas, about living and dying, about animals and people, and about the claims of the world and the puzzle of spirituality. In the times when I doubted most that I could ever complete this project, I learned to lean on her and take strength from her matter-of-fact belief that writing and reading are easily integrated into daily existence. Without the gift of Kathy's intensity, her love of stories, her commitments and convictions, and her constant openness to the possibilities of change, my life and this book would be much impoverished.

# A Feeling for Books

# INTRODUCTION

I finally joined the Book-of-the-Month Club in 1975 as a graduate student in English. Before that, throughout high school and in college, I had imagined becoming a member every Sunday morning as I pored over the club's full-page ads on the back of the *New York Times Book Review*. Four books for a dollar. Every week I would mentally fill out the coupon with the numbers of the four books I would select could I afford to join. I assumed that as a high school student, though, and later as a work-study undergraduate, I hadn't the resources to take up the club's offer, even though the required future commitment of four books a year seemed entirely reasonable. So I contented myself by imagining what it would be like to acquire those four new books, to hold them, to smell them, to possess the unmistakable treasure they certainly contained. The books offered to me by the Book-of-the-Month Club were no less promising, no less magical than those that had lined the shelves of the Englewood Public Library, where my mother had taken me every week from the time I was three or four. If anything, their representation in postage-stamp size suggested that their power might be even more concentrated. The alchemy they would perform on a suburban girl from New Jersey might be even more thorough, more permanent, more deeply transformative than that effected already by the plain, sturdy, library-bound books of her early childhood.

Significantly enough, it was not the offer of the four "free" books that eventually enticed me to become a club member once I was more solvent financially. By the time I actually mailed the coupon three years into graduate school, I had learned to disparage the club as a middlebrow operation offering only the come-on of free bestsellers to people who wanted only to be told what to read in order to look appropriately cultured. What I coveted was the *Concise Edition of the Oxford English Dictionary*. I had learned of its existence from a professor whom I particularly admired, the faculty member responsible for teaching the history of literary criticism, a course newly prestigious in 1975 as the first wave of what became known as continental theory made its way across the Atlantic. When he referred to it familiarly as "the *OED*" and everyone else in the seminar seemed to understand what he was talking about, I recognized that here was another mark of the distance that separated me from those more authentically cultured. When someone in the class observed with exaggerated incredulity that he had actually bought the *OED* as a premium from the Book-of-the-Month Club for $39.95, I made a mental note to look for the offer. I returned the coupon, finally, not to keep up with what the club touted as "the most talked about books," but in order to acquire this obviously indispensable accouterment of the cultured, intellectual self. It did not occur to me then that the organization my academic peers and I were all so eager to dismiss had ingeniously managed to turn our snobbery to its own purpose. It had secured our financial consent to buy four more books at full price by gratifying our desire to appear even more intellectual, to exhibit higher taste than that of the typical book club member by acquiring an arcane dictionary so compact and dense with cultural history that you could only read it with a magnifying glass.

At the time I had no idea that my act was being duplicated by countless other would-be academics because I was too embarrassed to admit that I did not already own the *OED*. So I read the monthly catalog in private, regularly refused the monthly selection, and thereby exercised what I would later learn the Book-of-the-Month Club called my negative option. But I also bought a lot of books. In fact, at one point I had amassed something like fifty-odd bonus credits, credits offered by the club to encourage me to purchase discounted dictionaries, art books laden with color prints, and huge, coffee-table books about gardens, exotic cities, animals, and home decorating styles. Although I rarely used those bonus points, they continued to mount up because I bought a large number of the alternate selections offered in lieu of the designated book of the month. I bought cookbooks, novels by women writers, Kate Millett's *Sexual Politics*, an arty edition of *Moby Dick* with fancy woodcuts, and even a copy of *Roget's Thesaurus*. In truth, I had no trouble finding books to buy. But as I made my way eagerly into the literary branch of the academy, I also deliberately mastered its daily routines, participated in its habitual forms of gossip and self-discipline, and internalized its conceptual grids and evaluative hierarchies. As a consequence, when the *OED* was mentioned (as it frequently was) and we admitted with staged irony that we all had acquired our copies through the Book-of-the-Month Club, I concurred (I thought matter-of-factly) with everyone else in the additional, dismissive observation that of course it was impossible to find anything else good to buy from the Book-of-the-Month Club. In my case, though, this was not true.

I tried hard to keep my voracious taste for bestsellers, mysteries, cookbooks, and popular nature books a secret—a secret from everyone, including the more cultured and educated self I was trying to become. I told myself I only read the stuff because one of my fields of specialization was American popular culture and I needed to be familiar with the most widely read books of the time. With grim determination I restricted this reading to late at night just before bed and devoted long daylight hours to the business of learning to describe the aesthetic complexities of true literature. What I thought I was doing was acquiring the language and repertoire of analytic techniques called for implicitly by the inherent features of self-evidently great works of literary art. But I was troubled by my clumsiness. This was not a language I felt very comfortable with or wielded naturally with any sort of grace or independence. Even more artificial than the second language of French I had mastered somewhat successfully as an undergraduate, the language of aesthetics and taste seemed a lifeless, abstract set of rules to memorize rather than a supple collection of expressive tools for elaborating my responses to good books. Although I inferred from seminar discussions that I ought to prefer Henry James to Anne Tyler, Faulkner to John Le Carré, Pound to Carlos Castañeda, and *Gravity's Rainbow* to *The Thorn Birds*, I could not always discipline my preferences as I thought I should. I still liked the books I read at night a lot more than the books I read for my classes.

I continued to read that high literature, though, and endeavored diligently to duplicate the particular styles of reading displayed by the English Ph.D.'s I saw all about me. Gradually I managed to acquire a new set of interpretive moves—techniques, really—for rendering the difficult and obscure language of the books I was reading comprehensible, if not entirely transparent. When those texts yielded to my efforts, efforts which included the supplying of intertextual references, the tracing of symbolic patterns, and the provision of a rationale for the narrative structure of the piece, I took a kind of reserved pleasure in my own mastery. Eventually I developed an appreciation for literary modernism, especially that of Henry James, William Faulkner, F. Scott Fitzgerald, Eugene O'Neill, William Carlos Williams, and Wallace Stevens. But that appreciation, no matter how intense, was always combined with an intellectual distance connected to the manner in which I had acquired this new competence, that is, in school classrooms and under the sway of authoritative experts. As a consequence, my new tastes somehow failed to duplicate precisely the passion of my response to those other, suspect, supposedly transparent, popular books. Those books prompted physical sensations, a forgetting of the self and complete absorption in another world. The books that came to me as high culture never seemed to prompt the particular shudder, the frisson I associated with the books of my childhood, because they carried with them not mere promise alone but also a threat, the threat that somehow I might fail to understand, might fail to recognize their reputed meaning and inherent worth. I developed, as a consequence, an aloof, somewhat puzzled relationship to "Literature" and to the ways of reading required and rewarded in my graduate seminars. I recorded that puzzlement, finally, in a highly academic, theoretical dissertation titled "A Phenomenological Theory of the Differences between Popular and Elite Literature." Those differences I could only conceive at the time as inherent to the texts themselves, as a function of particular textual properties. When that dissertation won for me official entry into the profession and a job at an Ivy League university, I knew it was time to let my Book-of-the-Month Club membership lapse. I sent in my resignation.

At the time I had no idea that the first half of my professional life would be spent attempting to comprehend and to explain the nature of the distance I had traveled between a small tract house in suburban New Jersey, furnished with only one small bookcase and *Time*, *Reader's Digest*, and *Woman's Day* on the coffee table, and a lectern in front of a literature class at the University of Pennsylvania, an institution founded by Benjamin Franklin. Neither did I recognize that what had fostered that journey, my own cultural education in town libraries, public schools, and the classrooms of a land-grant university in the American Midwest, was the actual subject of my dissertation. It took me the better part of fifteen years to articulate that what I had wanted to understand was not how some books were necessarily better than others. What I was really after was why some people, people like me, failed to recognize naturally and effortlessly the supposedly obvious differences discussed so confidently by professors who appeared genuinely moved by Ishmael's damp November of the soul and by the epiphanies of Stephen Daedalus but utterly disdainful of the trials of Silas Marner and Clyde Griffiths, not to mention Scarlett O'Hara or Marjorie Morningstar. In fact, my dissertation would remain unrevised and unpublished, wholly inadequate to the feelings of cultural exclusion, longing, and legitimation I wanted to explain. I abandoned it for another, more manageable way of approaching the topic of books, reading, and literary taste; I turned to the study of why women read romances. I did not take up the subject of the dissertation again until I had crossed paths with the Book-of-the-Month Club once more in an encounter I insisted at first on calling serendipitous, the chance discovery of an interesting subject and a useful body of data.

Only in the long effort to write of the history and people behind those magical, talismanic, postage-stamp books have I come to recognize why this subject, particularly, and at that moment, especially, seemed intellectually compelling and fraught with possibility. For in attempting to explain the remarkable longevity of a club that uses sophisticated marketing techniques to sell not only individual books but the very idea of taste itself, I have found myself unable to condemn the organization in any simple way for commodifying what I was taught in graduate school should never have been commodified by the market in the first place, that is, literature, art, and culture. Instead, in attempting to reconstruct the motives and intentions driving not only the club's founders but its subsequent judges, editors, *and* subscribers, I have continually encountered not merely the insistent desire to rise socially through any means available but also deep-seated longings for the possibilities of self-articulation and the search for transcendence promised by education and by art. Of course, those desires, here excavated through the use of ethnographic techniques and historical methods, may be little more than the ventriloquized projection of my own desires, which propelled me to renounce my passion for bestsellers, detective stories, and novels about women in favor of the approved tales of Isabel Archer, Jay Gatsby, Benjy Compson, Thomas Sutpen, Thea Kronborg, and Oedipa Maas. Even projected desires have a history, however, and it is the larger social history of the desire to display the tasteful signs of learning and education that I have been moved to tell as a consequence of my reencounter with the Book-of-the-Month Club. This book, then, is the result of my effort to understand the origins, the substance, the particular promise, and the multiple effects of what has been called middle-brow culture in the twentieth-century United States. That culture was aimed at people like me who wanted desperately to present themselves as educated, sophisticated, and aesthetically articulate.

The original impulse behind this book also had something to do with my own imperfect conversion to the secular religion of great literature. My conversion was imperfect, I suspect, not only because I selected popular culture as my area of specialization but also because I continued to harbor a secret but suppressed desire to read in a less cerebral, less aesthetically focused way than the one I was taught in graduate school. My inchoate doubts about the universal value of the touchstones we were encouraged to revere first began to coalesce into an idea during my work with the romance readers I was interviewing for my first book. Those readers eloquently defended *their* preference for a genre that literary critics dismissed as simple, formulaic, and among the most debased of all popular forms. Slowly they demonstrated to me that, for them, romances were not only subtle and varied but immediately relevant to the conditions of their daily lives. They showed me that romance fiction constituted a complex, living literature in the context of their day-to-day concerns, and this only increased my doubts about the intrinsic status of textual complexity and the purported universality of the sacred literary canon. Those doubts, in fact, were the source of my first, early desire to investigate the Book-of-the-Month Club and its membership. Recalling from my days as a member that the club sent out many different kinds of books, I surmised that its subscribers might be used as a way to study the possibility that different people evaluated books differently because they came to them with different backgrounds, different tastes, and different needs. My goal initially was to search for what I called variable literacies, that is, divergent ways of reading, using, and evaluating books.[1]

I found myself soon sidetracked from this concern with the club's members as I began to focus more insistently on the organization itself and on the day-to-day process of selecting books to be sent out. This happened, I now think, because I found the individuals who worked within the organization both oddly familiar and significantly different from the group of literary intellectuals I admired who constituted my academic peers and whose approbation I sought professionally. The Book-of-the-Month Club's editors proved compelling to me because they talked about books with a kind of intense fervor and expansive pleasure I had not heard since my conversations with the librarians of my childhood. They were enthusiastic and openly passionate about books, not deliberately reserved or self-consciously ironic about their own tastes as were so many of my academic friends. I was haunted, in fact, by the elaborate and eloquent reader's reports written by the club's editors about every manuscript they evaluated for selection and that they gave me to read as a way of understanding what they were about. Those reports constituted the very heart of the Book-of-the-Month Club operation. Not only did they facilitate the day-to-day business of selecting books for distribution, but more important perhaps, they fostered the definition of an imagined community of general readers, both within and without the club, who were fascinated not by the aesthetic intricacies of verbal compositions or by the challenge of a unique figural language or even by a new way of representing experience. Those readers, rather, were understood to be captivated by books in all their immense diversity and by the manifold pleasures of buying them, owning them, reading them, and using them. For the Book-of-the-Month Club editors, the world of the literary encompassed much more than the category of belles lettres that the word "Literature" had marked off in graduate English. Less pieces of textual criticism and exegesis than highly personalized accounts of what might be called "experiences with books,"

6 { *Introduction* }

their reader's reports exhibited a remarkable evaluative generosity and an appreciation for all kinds of printed products and the different uses to which they could be put. Those reports constituted my first window on the internal operations of the Book-of-the-Month Club.

It is essential to acknowledge here that the Book-of-the-Month Club reader's reports came to me not simply as documents in a research project but also as the evocative emissaries of a personal past. That past, deeply marked by the pleasures of constant reading, generated my desire to immerse myself in what my graduate student friends called "serious literature." However, because I read the kind of books I did *before* I set my sights on the high literary, I was expected to disparage and to abandon that past by my chosen profession, deeply invested as it was in constructing and enforcing the boundaries of cultural hierarchy. That profession sought to maintain not only its right to specify what constituted literary excellence but also its particular, highly technical conception of the literary itself.[2] What I have been allowed to revisit, then, with the assistance of the editors at the club, is a time before my entry into graduate education in English, a time when I read fiction and nonfiction, genre books and bestsellers, and fashion magazines and *Reader's Digest* indiscriminately and all for the particular pleasures they promised and the sensations they might convey. More than the subject of a distanced and analytical scholarly history, the Book-of-the-Month Club stands for me as the symbol of an earlier moment in a personal past and equally as evidence that the literarily trained, professional self I thought I had become is, in fact, still ambivalent and profoundly marked by the resolutely heterogeneous components of a contradictory past.

I have heard echoed in the reader's reports at the Book-of-the-Month Club my own early preference for the rush of a good plot and for the inspiration offered by an unforgettable character as well as an appreciation for the physical properties of the book as a treasured object. Similarly, in the editors' and outside readers' unselfconscious enthusiasm for the expression of deep sentiment and for the information, illumination, and enlightenment offered by individuals specially skilled as authors, I have recalled a time in my past when the act of reading was propelled more by a driving desire to know, to connect, to communicate, and to share than by the desires to evaluate, to explicate, to explain, to discriminate, and to judge. Books, then, stood for me as signs of longing for absent things, for the thrill of wider experience and the promise of greater knowledge, rather than as the occasion for an accomplished performance of the self in the act of delivering an assured interpretation or judgment. It was the Book-of-the-Month Club's reader's reports, therefore, with their emphatic focus on the variegated promises and pleasures of reading as a temporal act that gradually but insistently turned my attention away from middlebrow literature as an aesthetic object alone to a consideration of the subject of reading—to its texture, its variability, its uses and effects—and to the significance it holds for those who involve themselves in it. What preoccupies me now is the effort to understand the peculiar cultural power associated with a particular constellation of behaviors, that is, the activities of acquiring, owning, reading, and talking about books in the United States in the twentieth century.

Of course this revision and even the narrative offered here as a personal prologue to it are equally the product of a cataclysmic upheaval in the world of literary studies, an upheaval whose effects had only just begun to emerge in 1985 when I embarked on this project. That upheaval has produced profound challenges to older ways of conceiving literature as an honorific category and to related ways of justifying its professional study. I suspect, in fact, that the disputatious, stringent, recalcitrant voices behind movements such as feminist criticism, reader response theory, psychoanalysis, a revivified Marxist criticism, and cultural studies solicited my identification in part because they duplicated the sense of distance I already felt from high culture in spite of all of my efforts to seek access to its mysteries. These various contemporary critical discourses have provided me with a set of useful but often contradictory languages that I have drawn on in my ongoing effort to give material form to what had only been an inchoate feeling before, the puzzlement I felt in the face of valorized texts I could only labor through, the sense of distance I experienced from the very high culture that my English Ph.D. had declared, at least officially, to be mine. I stress the plural "languages" here as a way of underscoring the fact that I have *not* managed to construct a single, coherent intellectual perspective or method out of my particular reading of these disparate literatures. This introduction is not a theoretical manifesto describing, legitimating, and recommending a particular master code or a single set of objectively existing, automatically duplicable, or universally applicable procedures for analyzing cultural institutions and their consequences. Rather, it is an effort to provide some materials for a genealogy of a self-divided narrator, who can, and often does, recount both the receding events of her past and her most immediate situation from different and differently fruitful perspectives.

In fastening initially on my subject as a way to study the possibility of multiple literacies, it now seems to me that what I was after at the Book-

{ *Introduction* }

of-the-Month Club was the very ground on which I myself habitually but unconsciously stood when I maintained that small measure of critical distance from high culture and secretly wondered why it was necessary to evaluate every book according to a single set of aesthetic criteria. This realization about the nature of my interested investment in my subject developed only gradually, however, in the course of the ten years or so it has taken to complete this project. To begin with, I discovered that the nature of daily practice at the Book-of-the-Month Club was itself implicitly constructed with an eye toward academic ways of evaluating books. Middlebrow culture, apparently, defined itself, first, against academic ways of seeing. Then I learned later that my history of reading with the Book-of-the-Month Club was a good deal longer than I had suspected. In effect, I discovered that my education *through* middlebrow culture and *to* its particular preferences may well have provided the source of my skepticism about the secular religion of high culture. It took much longer, however, to understand the consequences of that fact and to find a way to use that recognition here.

When I first began to travel regularly to the editorial offices of the Book-of-the-Month Club in midtown Manhattan, I was struck by the similarity between the editors and the literary professors who were my colleagues. In addition to the fact that the editors dressed more like professors than the lawyers and accountants in three-piece suits who filled their building's elevators, they also displayed very similar vocabularies and ways of talking and conversed with knowledge about literary traditions, the standard canon, and well-known "serious writers." I was taken aback, then, when attending my first editorial meeting where alternates to the official book of the month were to be discussed and selected, by the fact that several of the editors dismissed different books under consideration as "much too academic for us." Not only was this criticism repeated regularly thereafter, but the editors occasionally embellished what was, for them, a kind of epithet, by using it in conjunction with modifiers such as "desiccated," "too technical," and "highly specialized." The academic, it gradually became clear, was something the people at the Book-of-the-Month Club defined themselves against. They used the word "academic" to dismiss books they did not like in much the same way my academic colleagues and I had used the word "middlebrow" to dispense with texts we judged inadequate.

It began to occur to me, then, that despite the traditional claim that middlebrow culture simply apes the values of high culture, it is in fact a kind of counterpractice to the high culture tastes and proclivities that have been most insistently legitimated and nurtured in academic English departments for the last fifty years or so. More than anything else, it may be a competitor to English departments for the authority to control reading and to define the nature of literary value. I also realized that the ubiquitous subject called "the general reader," who surfaced again and again in editorial discussions at the Book-of-the-Month Club, was integral to its self-understanding as an organization and to its daily practice. Moreover, I also began to suspect that the very term "general reader" had perhaps evolved historically precisely as a rejection and critique of some other reader, presumably a reader not general but focused, professional, technical, and specialized. The general reader was most obviously *not* the academic reader. At that point I began to suspect that the Book-of-the-Month Club looked so interesting to me in part because it enabled me to express in displaced fashion my own disaffection with the professional reading required of a literary academic.

This conjecture was strengthened by my growing sense of identification with the editors at the club. Listening to them talk of the visceral pleasures of being immersed in a book reminded me of intensely resonant scenes of reading from my own past. When they groped for the right words to describe the peculiar state that reading could induce in them, the abstract words they settled on, such as "absorption," "escape," or "captivation," evoked not ideas but highly specific and richly realized moments from my own history with books. The walls of the club offices would give way imperceptibly, then, onto the high-ceilinged, adult reading room of the Englewood Public Library. The straight-backed desk chair I was sitting in would become the rickety, yellow chaise lounge on our back patio that I sought out again and again on long, humid summer evenings after dinner in order to read. The titles they recalled and the way they recalled them would set in motion a kind of internal whispering. What I heard murmured in the background was a private litany of titles that had once deeply moved me in the ways they were describing—*Lorna Doone, Death Be Not Proud, Gone with the Wind, The Miracle Worker.* I was puzzled by all this remembering and worried about what it all meant. I was especially troubled by the peculiar, triumphant feel of these memories, a sense of vindication almost, as if the editors' talk suddenly justified a past of which I had learned to be ashamed.

It was easy enough to discount my private meditations as irrelevant to the scholarly project that engaged me until a moment about midway into my fieldwork year. In trying to read systematically sixty years' worth of the club's catalog, the *Book-of-the-Month Club News*, I discovered that I had actually read more than fifty of the titles sent out by the Book-of-the-

Month Club in the years between 1950 and 1963. Clearly, my history with the club was much more extensive than I had supposed. I may not have belonged officially to the club, then, but I had read an awful lot of what it recommended. Some of the titles I encountered in the *News* had been among my childhood favorites.

Until I remembered these specific titles in the context of studying the Book-of-the-Month Club and middlebrow culture, I had no idea that they had done anything other than simply propel me forward into a different future, a future marked by educational transformation and therefore by the evolution of a different self with different tastes, beliefs, and values. I had thought, in other words, that what those books had done was to enable me to leave them behind. Recovering them, however, while simultaneously reading the editors' reports and while trying to think systematically about reading and cultural hierarchy, it occurred to me that although those books may well have launched me into a future, they must also have left a heretofore undetected sediment, a silt of desires, preferences, and tastes. Those particular preferences, perhaps, had not been eroded or absorbed into the foundations of the educated self I had managed to build on those sands. As I raced through catalog descriptions of book after book, it seemed disturbingly clear that the expectations they had cultivated within me had not simply been thrown over or replaced by the taste for the exclusively aesthetic complexity, irony, and ambiguity I had cultivated in graduate school mainly by imitating the reading strategies and evaluative practices of those professors I admired. It now seemed that those expectations and desires may well have persisted. Those books and their reading had left what Michel Foucault has called the "stigmata of experience," marks both on and in a sentient body that forever after bears within it the capacity to respond, to react as that first act of marking had called forth.[3] Taste, as the French sociologist Pierre Bourdieu has tried to explain, may not simply be figuratively corporeal but may be quite literally so. As such, it may be only minimally open to transmutation.[4] Conceivably, my experience with so many of the books the Book-of-the-Month Club had selected had produced a set of tastes and expectations that were not fully engaged or completely met by the reading I did as a professional.

My intensifying sympathy with the views expressed so thoughtfully by the Book-of-the-Month Club editors made me aware of how much I was a product of middlebrow culture. But what, I wondered, did that mean? Critics of the club traditionally suggest that it either inspired consumers to purchase the mere signs of taste or prompted them to buy a specious imitation of true culture. Was that all I had garnered from the club? I did not think so. But what exactly had those books conferred on me? The elaborately detailed nature of my recollections suggested that some of the books at least had changed me profoundly. But in what ways? And did I want to defend middlebrow culture as a result?

From this moment of crisis on, I was intensely aware of the intricate nature of the connection between my private past and my effort to make sense of the public history of the Book-of-the-Month Club. The specific itinerary of that private past, I think, has ensured that this book about the Book-of-the-Month Club is the work of an ambivalent narrator. That ambivalence is born of the fact that the "I" I feel myself to be is, more accurately, a divided subject. Sometimes I can view the operations of the club and the tastes of the middlebrow critically, from the outside and at a distance. At other times I see them from the point of view of someone who once understood them as a participant. What results is an account that oscillates continually between critique and appreciation.

What the reader will find here is an inquiry into the nature of middlebrow taste that attempts to give middlebrow culture its due. In trying to establish it as something other than a watered-down version of a more authentic high culture, I have tried to present the middlebrow positively as a culture with its own particular substance and intellectual coherence. I have thus tried to take seriously the Book-of-the-Month Club's middlebrow critique of narrow academicism and professional elitism and to understand why that critique proved generative enough in the 1920s to found a new constellation of tastes, preferences, and desires. I have also tried to provide an account of the pleasures of a characteristically middlebrow way of reading. Finally, I have tried to delineate the promises hidden within middlebrow books and to understand the context within which those promises appeared irresistible.

The reader will find, however, that this more positive view and the approving voice within which it is couched do not always dominate here. Rather, they are shadowed throughout by a different, sometimes hectoring voice, the voice of someone who is critical, finally, of some of the founding assumptions and claims of middlebrow culture. What I am after in this context is the particular ways in which middlebrow culture managed and controlled those it addressed so successfully. I try to explain just what middlebrow culture taught us to think, to desire, and to do. For it seems clear to me that middlebrow organizations such as the Book-of-the-Month Club helped acclimate us to the business of consumer culture and ushered us into a particular life world still too complacent about certain social hierarchies. Middlebrow books may have endowed us with an ample and refined vocabulary for articulating and achieving affective states, but too often the solution they ventured with respect to serious social problems involved the moral, ethical, and spiritual rehabilitation of the individual subject alone.

But to write of these perspectives as if they give rise to two clearly defined projects is to imply that I have more control over these voices than I have. It also suggests that I have managed to develop a third perspective that can adjudicate between them in balanced, equable fashion. In fact, neither is true. My ambivalence is persistent and real. The effect of the resulting dual perspective is more like that produced by newly acquired bifocals that render the world in fractured form across a disjunctive, arbitrary line. Just when you feel you have things in focus, a swift tilt of the head or an inadvertent dip in the gaze alters your perspective and places the world at a different, disorienting distance. That happens often here as these points of view jostle for attention, interrupt each other, and counsel caution about the confident assertions of the other. Although I make some effort to signal to the reader when major adjustments to the lens of vision have been made, I also want to acknowledge that the shifting focus is not something I have been able to control fully.

The tension in my treatment of middlebrow culture is further complicated by my efforts to capture something else about reading that my experiences at the Book-of-the-Month Club taught me to recognize and to appreciate. There are moments for me now when books become something other than mere objects, when they transport me elsewhere, to a trancelike state I find difficult to describe. On these occasions reading, or what Marcel Proust has called "that fruitful miracle of a communication in the midst of solitude," manages to override my rational, trained approach to books as crafted objects.[5] When this occurs, the book, the text, and even my reading self dissolve in a peculiar act of transubstantiation whereby "I" become something other than what I have been and inhabit thoughts other than those I have been able to conceive before. This tactile, sensuous, profoundly emotional experience of being captured by a book is what those reading memories summoned for me—in the manner of Proust's madeleine—an experience that for all its ethereality clearly is extraordinarily physical as well.

Critical, analytical languages fail to do justice to the extreme specificity and idiosyncratic character of this experience, which I have heard the novelist Reynolds Price describe as a state of "narrative hypnosis," a phrase that underscores the deep involvement of the body in the act of reading. No matter the number of explanations I can generate linking the reading choices and preferences of the Book-of-the-Month Club editors to their class position, to their professional training, or to the determining nature of earlier historical events, there remains something in their sentient, affective responsiveness to particular books that always manages to escape the categorizing imperative to fix, to pin down, and to control. Like a lepidopterist who misses the beauty and magic of lilting, living flight in the appreciative act of preserving a remarkable example of the species, in my effort to explain the preferences of the Book-of-the-Month Club editors as a function of cultural events and ideological assumptions I have no doubt failed to capture completely the distinct resonance of the particular desires and fears endured with and *through* the body that have wedded individual readers to their most treasured books.

Still, I have tried to remember that just as the editors I encountered in 1985 read amidst the overwhelming and contradictory welter of detail in impossibly complex and embodied social lives, so too did the club's founder, Harry Scherman, and his early colleagues, judges Henry Seidel Canby and Dorothy Canfield Fisher. They encountered the books they eventually chose for the membership in the context of particular friendships, the birth and death of children, funerals, marriages, publishing feuds, and so on. The materials they selected to create what later became known as middlebrow culture were chosen not only because they were members of a new professional, literary elite addressing the needs and worries of a new class, but also because those books addressed them in highly concrete, deeply resonant ways as persons moving through life in embodied form, that is, as bodies crisscrossed by innumerable, minute stigmata, some highly visible and therefore traceable to past events and earlier conditions, others invisible and undetectable with the clumsy tools of perception and interpretation we have available to us.

※

I have divided the narrative of my encounter with the Book-of-the-Month Club into three separate parts. Each is told somewhat differently. Part I, "In the Service of the General Reader," is presented as an ethnographic account of the editorial practices employed by the in-house editors at the club during the years 1985 to 1988. It is also narrated autobiographically and chronologically as a story about my interactions with those editors. Because this project became as much my story as it was theirs, I place myself within the tale as a character inhabiting the same world occupied by the people and institutions I was trying to understand. What I try to provide in this section is a sense of the process through which I came to recognize that the impingement of my own history on my present activity had everything to do with what I saw and could begin to say about it.

The reader will find that the process was unsettling. It was so unsettling that it prompted me to question my ability to keep on doing what I was doing without first understanding not only more about my own past but also more about the past of the Book-of-the-Month Club. I broke off the ethnography when I felt the need to search for some of the causes that might help to explain the intensity of my emotional and intellectual collision with the club and the middlebrow culture it championed so consistently.

Part II, "On the History of the Middlebrow," situates the Book-of-the-Month Club historically by positioning it as a characteristically modern cultural institution. I argue that as a highly specific response to massive economic and social change, the club was intricately bound up with the refashioning of forms of work in the United States and with the reorganization of class in a consumer society. I also suggest that middlebrow culture and the particular configuration of taste it cultivated developed as a kind of social pedagogy for a growing class fraction of professionals, managers, and information and culture workers as well as for those who aspired to the status of this class, to its work routines, and to its privileges. I argue that even as the club taught its subscribers how to desire a world in which technical, specialized knowledge would reign supreme, it also implicitly attempted to counter some of the social costs and individual losses that would obtain in such a universe. Middlebrow culture was riven internally by certain key tensions, and it therefore addressed in contradictory ways the readers who found it so engaging.

The history I develop here also implicitly attempts to account for the ambivalence I brought to all my interactions with the Book-of-the-Month Club, whether in person or through the mediation of historical documents. My account alludes frequently to the ways in which middlebrow culture constituted itself implicitly, and sometimes quite explicitly, in opposition to both emerging literary modernism and the avant-garde and to the growth of an institutionalized, more thoroughly professionalized group of literary specialists, some employed by highbrow magazines, others in the fast-developing university English departments. I look carefully at the nature of the criticism leveled at the club and discuss why it originated among certain salaried literary reviewers who were deeply troubled by the intensifying effect of marketplace concerns on literary production. I suggest that the debate over the book clubs was an internal dispute among competing literary professionals about how much autonomy the literary field could manage and ought properly to maintain in a thoroughly commercialized and commodified society. Finally, I try to suggest that my own personal ambivalence about the Book-of-the-Month Club is the understandable result of the way I was caught up in these public historical debates. I have narrated this account in the conventional, third-person voice of narrative history as a way of placing my reactions at a distance and in an attempt to see them as a consequence of powerful forces that controlled me as much as I was able to control them.

Part III, "Books for Professionals," returns to the autobiographical mode and attempts to make more explicit the connections between the public history of the Book-of-the-Month Club and my more intimate past with it as a reader of its selections. I offer a reading of certain selected books that I devoured appreciatively as a young adolescent, books that had been chosen and sent out by the Book-of-the-Month Club between 1950 and 1963. Through them I try to provide a description of what might be called the content of middlebrow culture in the 1950s and 1960s, which is to say, the collection of beliefs, investments, and hopes the club attempted to communicate to its readers. I try to recall what those books looked and felt like, what they sounded and smelled like, and what they enabled me to think and to dream. I try to capture the shape of the future those books painstakingly carved out in the unknown that lay before me as a young, white, middle-class girl in 1963 and 1964. I have done this for two reasons.

Very little information survives about the historical subscribers to the club. Even though certain demographic statistics can be compiled, it is almost impossible to say for sure what those subscribers made of the intensely conflicted and contradictory middlebrow books they purchased from the club. Consequently, it is equally difficult to specify what the final effects of middlebrow reading might have been for those who made it a major part of their daily lives. I offer my own experience as a way to broach the question of what a reader could have taken from middlebrow culture at a particular historical moment. My own past allows me to ask what such a reader could have used her middlebrow books to do.

I draw on three genres—autobiography, literary criticism, and ideology critique—in my effort to capture the texture and tone of one reader's way of reading with the Book-of-the-Month Club. The book discussions I provide in this section are hybrid in form, at once uniting memorial knowledge of my own past readings, critical analysis of the aspects of those books that prompted those readings, and an assessment of how they might have produced the experiences they did. I have also included within each of those readings an account of certain features in those texts, invisible to me then, but which cry out now for analysis and commentary. It may have been those features, I suggest, that exerted the most powerful because unconscious effect on me. They may have acclimated me (and others) to certain deeply embedded assumptions about the nature of subjectivity, the shape of the social, and the appropriate forms for desire. What I am after, finally, is the character of the sentimental education offered by the Book-of-the-Month Club in the form of the middlebrow books it selected and recommended to readers like me.[6]

# PART ONE

# In the Service of the General Reader

## CHAPTER ONE

# A Certain Book Club Culture

## A DESIRE CALLED NEW YORK

It may have been simple anxiety. Or the weight of layered memories evoked by the familiar geography. Whatever the cause, I was not thinking about my impending appointment at the Book-of-the-Month Club as the 7:32 Amtrak commuter from Philadelphia crawled across the marshy plain outside Newark on its journey into New York's Penn Station. What I was thinking about, I recall, was New York itself. My memories were triggered by the train's slow progress past the park-and-ride lot my dad and I had used the summer we commuted together into "the city." I was twenty then and working at TWA as a reservations agent. Remembering those companionable journeys, I recalled countless other Hudson River crossings that had punctuated my New Jersey childhood. Each conjured intense, highly sensuous memories: the spangled magnificence of the New York skyline at Christmas, the city dazzling, as if deliberately bedecked for the season; the ripe, fetid smell of the fruit stands on Eighth Avenue on a hot August afternoon; the deeply shadowed midtown canyon looking up Broadway from Macy's; the recollected shock of happening on a single maple turned scarlet on an October Saturday, triumphant amidst miles of concrete. The images now seem impossibly romantic. The predictable result, I suppose, of a suburban childhood defined in countless ways by a desire called New York.

Significantly, each image was connected in my mind with an exhilarating pilgrimage to the city at the side of one of my parents or grandparents to see the Christmas pageant at Radio City Music Hall; Broadway musicals such as *My Fair Lady*, *Funny Girl*, and *The Sound of Music*; the Museum of Natural History; or my father's office in the building that housed the *New York Daily News*. In the lobby of the building an enormous silver globe was suspended, meant to be a symbol, I suppose, of the paper's reach and importance. For me New York was something other than the financial capital of the world; it was, quite simply, its cultural center—a magnet whose irresistible force captured my youthful attention and forever after defined my ambition.

At the time of that particular train ride from Philadelphia, though, to talk with people at the Book-of-the-Month Club, I did not connect these memories with the task at hand. They seemed mental distractions only, ways of controlling my mounting apprehension about the impending meeting with company officials. I was traveling to the club's Manhattan offices in April 1985 to try to persuade its executives to allow me to investigate the way their members bought and read books. The task seemed simply professional, lacking any clear connection to the private details of my personal past. However, countless conversations over the next three years with Executive Editor William Zinsser, the man I was scheduled to meet, and with his editorial colleagues at the club would teach me to recognize that the project was deeply tied to these intensely resonant memories of the city. Those conversations would teach me to see in the editors' cultural sophistication and in the understanding they accorded their aspiring "general readers" the meaning of my own desire to possess the promise held by New York. The defining power of a longing for the knowledge secreted away in New York's museums and libraries, on its stages, in its skyscrapers, in "the Village," and on the East Side revealed itself to me gradually in the mirror of the editors' similar desires, which apparently also drew each of them to New York's publishing houses and eventually to the Book-of-the-Month Club. Six more years in dusty archives and hushed libraries on the ghostly trail of Harry Scherman, the club's founder, would additionally reveal the precise historical sources of our shared wish for cultural mastery and the prestige that seemed to accompany it—a wish, I discovered, the Book-of-the-Month Club itself had been created to address. When I finally saw myself and the editors most clearly in the reconstructed image of Scherman's first subscribers, who had responded with hope and no doubt a certain amount of insecurity to his 1926 promise to deliver to them automatically "the best new book published each month," I understood fully for the first time that this project was defined as much by my own earlier longing for a life marked by books and the mysterious promise of Culture, with that authoritative and daunting capital *C*, as it was by the analytic impulse to make sense of an institution called the Book-of-the-Month Club.

I carried with me neither this self-knowledge nor this reflexive understanding of what was still an inchoate project as the Silver Meteor eased its way into Penn Station that crystalline morning in April. My thoughts focused rather more nervously on what I might say to William Zinsser about my academic credentials and about my interest in the organization. What had led me to take the train that morning was an essay on reading written by the club's chairman, Al Silverman, which he had engagingly titled "The Fragile Pleasure."[1] I was impressed by the way Mr. Silverman evoked the particular magic of being immersed in worlds etched by words. But I was also pragmatically alerted to the fact that the Book-of-the-Month Club might harbor a lot of information about readers and reading, a topic that had become the focus of my academic research. Having just published a book about how a group of women read romances differently from the way those books were read by their many critics, I wanted to know more about divergences in the ways people acquired, read, and used books. The Book-of-the-Month Club looked like the perfect site for my next research project.

I remember mentally rehearsing this explanatory narrative and self-justification as I searched for the club's offices in midtown New York at Lexington Avenue and Forty-sixth Street. Expecting only the typical mauve, gray, and glass corporate reception area of 1980s New York as the elevator doors slid open, I was momentarily stunned to find myself in a room clearly designed to evoke a book-lined study. Too neat, ordered, and regimented to be the library of an actual reader, it reminded me of a stage set or of that restaurant across the Hudson in Tenafly, New Jersey, that my parents liked, which accompanied its English prime ribs with lots of wood, a few strategically placed, fake books, and the kind of reading lamps you see in pictures of old libraries. Although the books in the club reception area were real, they, too, seemed to have been assembled for effect. When I was asked by a young woman partially hidden behind an obviously tasteful bouquet of spring flowers to wait for Mr. Zinsser, I made a mental note of the deliberate symbolic care with which the room had been organized. Callers to this establishment were obviously meant to be impressed by its understated elegance, by its attention to the literary, and by the meticulously displayed collection of every Book-of-the-Month Club selection since 1926. Bill Zinsser emerged quickly, greeted me cordially, and then escorted me back to his office past a Norman Rockwell-like portrait in oils of the club's first judges. The picture's prominent placement seemed meant to establish that here was a Cultural institution, and one with an illustrious past at that.

My notes from that first exploratory conversation with Bill Zinsser are not terribly detailed. I wrote only that he was "fiftyish," distinguished-looking, and dressed "like an academic in tweed coat and dress slacks." I noted as well that he was in charge of "special projects" and that he edited the club's catalog, the *Book-of-the-Month Club News*. Perhaps I thought the interview wouldn't amount to much. Zinsser certainly didn't promise me the access I was seeking. Or perhaps I was too afraid to hope that it had gone as well as I thought it had. I didn't record much else except to say that I liked Bill Zinsser immediately and that I thought it surprising that we seemed to have so much in common. We were, after all, from different worlds, weren't we?

Looking back, I see more clearly that despite my effort to be open-minded and receptive, unquestioned assumptions about the separation between "academics" and people in publishing had led me to assume that Zinsser and I would necessarily be very different. I had been surprised to discover that before his arrival at the Book-of-the-Month Club in 1979, Zinsser had taught writing at Yale and served as master of the one of the residential colleges there. More strikingly, he also fully understood the kind of ethnographic research I was proposing, since his wife was at that moment completing a Ph.D. in education at the University of Pennsylvania, with an ethnographic dissertation on the acquisition of literacy. Still thinking of myself as an academic and of those at the book club as somehow fundamentally different—less intellectual perhaps, and more involved in commerce, certainly—I had been surprised that he did not seem at all wary about my motives or intentions. It would take many more discoveries of similar convergences between my own past and those of the club's editors before I began to see how similar we were in certain key ways and to recognize that those similarities had a good deal to do with what we had all made of the middle-class educations we were privileged enough to receive. In time those similarities would also point up the significance of the fact that our habitual treatment of books differed in crucial ways.

During this particular conversation, however, Zinsser managed to convey to me his own enthusiasm for what he called the Book-of-the-Month Club's important educational work and to suggest that our jobs were not that different. Known for his influential book, *On Writing Well*, Bill had been brought to the club by Al Silverman to be the in-house editor of all the organization's publications. He was also to oversee special projects of an educational and public-spirited nature that he and Al felt

{ *In the Service of the General Reader* }

were important to the club's role as a cultural institution. The two men shared the same high aspirations for the club, and it was obvious that Bill greatly admired Al's values. In this particular conversation, Bill observed with a slightly ironic note of institutional pride and simultaneous self-deprecation that they liked to think of themselves as "the book club of record." I thought later on the ride home that this seemed to be a reference to the *New York Times*, and as such, it was meant to suggest that the club possessed parallel cultural authority.

Despite this transparent effort on my part to maintain the slight disdain and distance of traditional academic analysis (wasn't I intellectually clever enough to recognize pretentiousness and too-deliberate tastefulness when I saw them?), my notes nonetheless enthusiastically convey the sense of rapport I felt with Bill Zinsser and a quite fervent hope that the whole thing might work out. Zinsser promised only that he would talk to Al Silverman in order to explain to him what I was proposing and to suggest that he meet with me himself sometime in the future. I returned to Philadelphia wondering only what I could do next if this research initiative failed.

Within a week I received a letter from Al Silverman inviting me back to New York for lunch with him and Lorraine Shanley, the executive vice-president of the Book-of-the-Month Club and one of the founders of the Quality Paperback Book Club. That meeting, at a remarkably formal East Side restaurant serving huge steaks and whole broiled fish to business lunchers, also seemed to go well, at least from my perspective. I found I could talk as easily to Al Silverman and to Lorraine Shanley as to Bill Zinsser, in large part because words and books occupied a central place in all our lives. We talked a good deal, I recall, about recent bestsellers, about changes in the publishing business, and about the continued prominence of the Book-of-the-Month Club.

Prompted by Al to explain what I had in mind, I suggested that although I eventually wanted to investigate the many ways in which their subscribers read, first I would need to conduct an exploratory, pilot study of the club's editorial organization in preparation for writing a grant proposal. I would need a grant, I observed, to underwrite the costs of a full year's worth of work in the Manhattan editorial offices, at the club's distribution operation in Camp Hill, Pennsylvania, and with some of the membership. At that point, I conceptualized the larger study as focusing on the intersection between the club and its membership, with the ultimate goal of assessing the different ways Book-of-the-Month Club members used and read their books. Wryly suggesting that he, too, would like to find out what their members actually did with their books—the first, disturbing hint that the club did not know as much about its readers as I had hoped— Silverman noted that he was predisposed in my favor by his conviction that cultural institutions had a social responsibility to be open to scholarly research. He promised to think about my project and to get back to me.

Almost immediately he extended an invitation to visit the club's offices throughout the summer of 1985 for purposes of studying the in-house editors' evaluation and selection of alternate books for its membership.[2] He promised further that if I received a grant, I could continue my research in the future. Bill Zinsser, Silverman explained, would serve as my contact at the club. He would be the one to introduce me to others, the one I should apply to with specific requests. Thrilled that gaining access had proved to be so easy, I called the next day to set up my first research appointment with Bill Zinsser. I had no idea, at that point, that matters were a good deal more complex than they appeared on the surface, nor did I see that the issue of access was not then, or ever would be, fully settled.

Looking back on the course this project has taken, I realize how utterly dependent it has been on Al Silverman's genuine sense of social and cultural responsibility as well as on Bill Zinsser's openness to establishing some sort of relationship with me. I suspect that it was their intellectual interest, curiosity, and commitment to what they were doing that prompted them initially to become advocates for my project. For advocates they clearly became. Al Silverman impressed this upon me in extending the invitation to spend the summer in the club's offices. Bill's enthusiasm for what I wanted to do, as well as his ability to explain its academic purposes, Al suggested, had convinced him that my aim was not to write an exposé of the Book-of-the-Month Club. Nor was I likely to take up a simple, dismissive position on the club's selections, given the nature of my first book on romances. Bill apparently had explained to Al and to Lorraine Shanley that *Reading the Romance* had taken popular literature seriously. As a consequence, Al asked Bill to introduce me to his colleagues and to make suggestions about who I should approach first for information.

At the time I had no real idea of what Bill thought of me. Later we developed a relationship close enough to enable us to reveal to each other at least some of our hopes, worries, and fears about our professional lives. I think Bill enjoyed talking to me as much as I enjoyed talking and laughing with him. In fact, like virtually everyone else I met at the Book-of-the-Month Club, Bill Zinsser was very, very funny. He delighted in turning a crisp, witty eye on books, authors, cultural habits, and anyone who might

{ *In the Service of the General Reader* }

take herself too seriously. He had no patience with pretentiousness and pomposity, especially among academics.

In spite of the discomfort Bill's stories sometimes provoked, I developed great affection for him and for his ability to expose the foibles of the academic world. Despite the warmth that developed between us, however, I would characterize the relationship as collegial rather than as intensely personal. It seems important to acknowledge this openly here because I think the nature of the somewhat formal but affectionate friendship that developed between us set a pattern for the connections that evolved later with other editors at the club. My relationships with them were confined to, and limited by, our professional connection over the nature of *their* daily work. The fact that those interactions necessarily developed amidst endlessly ringing telephones and in short intervals between the recurrent meetings and conferences that comprise upper middle-class professional work in the contemporary United States both controlled the nature of our relationship and constantly underscored the fact that it was entirely dependent on the editors' willingness to be interrupted.

In spite of the developing goodwill, though, certain things worried me. I fretted in my field journal about my growing affection for Bill, Al, and Lorraine. Mistrustful of my feelings of identification with them, I wondered how this sense of connection would affect my ability to be analytical about what I saw. The thing that gave me real pause, however, was a copy of the memo Bill circulated to the rest of his colleagues introducing me and explaining my impending presence at the upcoming Thursday morning editorial conference. I was grateful that Bill was willing to share it with me. But I was also puzzled by an allusion I could not explain. I quote the memo here in its entirety:

July 10, 1985

TO: The Editors

FROM: Bill Zinsser

I'll be bringing to this Thursday's meeting Janice Radway, professor of American Studies at the University of Pennsylvania, who is embarking this week on a scholarly study (eventually to be a book) of reading habits in America, using the Book-of-the-Month Club and its methods as her model. Her last book, "Reading the Romance: Women, Patriarchy and Popular Literature," a study of women who read romance novels, got an admiring full-page review in the NYTBR last winter. Anyone interested in the book can borrow my copy. She is also editor of "American Quarterly," the scholarly journal in her field.

I've talked with Janice at length about her project (Al and Lorraine have also talked with her) and I think the collaboration will be a pleasant and fruitful one for all of us in a number of ways. She will want to talk with you about your work as she gets into her research. You will enjoy the quality of her mind; her questions, unlike some that have been asked of you lately, are enjoyable and even understandable.

BZ[3]

Clearly, Bill had positioned me on the side of the editors, but against whom? Who else had been asking questions of them and why? Also, he had suggested that the editors themselves might get something out of their interaction with me. But what did he have in mind? Definitely troubled that Bill's move clearly compromised my distance from them — I was more confident then about my ability to maintain this — I worried that I was being presented as their ally in a conflict I had neither detected nor understood. His memo summoned an ill-defined yet adversarial presence, an inquisitor like me, but one Bill defined as irritating and obscure. When I asked him about the identity of this individual, he said only that he was referring to managers from Time, Inc., the corporate owner of the Book-of-the-Month Club, who had been sent to the club's offices recently to gather information about its structure, operations, and profitability. When he referred to them as "MBA-types," I relaxed some and acquiesced a little too happily at being ranged against them.

Time, it seemed, had purchased the Book-of-the-Month Club in 1977 but had done nothing to integrate the club into its own massive bookselling operation. Bill worried out loud that these interviews suggested that something new was afoot. He assured me, though, that this would not have an impact on my own research. Comforted, I did not react with the alarm I should have. Instead, I thought a good deal about the suddenly obvious difference between talking with a group of romance readers, whose education and access to writing was quite distinct from my own, and this new situation of "studying up," that is, working within an organization peopled by individuals with linguistic, social, and communication resources comparable to those of the academic investigator.[4] Evidently I would have to deal much more regularly with my interlocutors' characterizations and manipulations of me as well as, possibly, with their outright disagreements and opposition to what I might write. A little more wary then than I had been only a few days before, I sat in on my first editorial meeting at the Book-of-the-Month Club on July 11, 1985.

These editorial meetings were held every Thursday morning in the club's elegant conference room.[5] Like the reception area, this room was lined by polished wooden bookshelves laden with club selections. At the entrance, enshrined in a small, lighted cabinet, were a few volumes from founder Harry Scherman's Little Leather Library, twenty-five-cent copies of the classics that Scherman sold at Woolworth's and by mail order before he created the Book-of-the-Month Club. The organization's institutional awareness of its history and position was further demonstrated by framed prints of several *New Yorker* cartoons gently gibing the club and its social-climbing members. More often than not, a lavish floral centerpiece graced the table, testimony to the fact that the club's official judges, the individuals responsible for the monthly main selections, had recently dined in the room at a catered lunch as part of their own judicial deliberations. Always referred to collectively at the club as "The Judges," at the time I started this research the group included Clifton Fadiman (a member of the panel since 1944 and its chairman), David McCullough, Gloria Norris, Wilfrid Sheed, and Mordecai Richler. The judges did not attend the Thursday morning conferences, which were dominated by the ten to fifteen in-house editors whose chief responsibility was to select the books offered as alternates in addition to the club's main selection. They were joined by several other individuals, including those in charge of subsidiary book clubs, such as Cooking and Crafts, Fortune, Dolphin, and Quality Paperback Book Club; the heads of production departments associated with the creation of the club's catalog; and assorted other employees who needed to keep up on what the editors said about the books they were offering in order to do their own work within the organization. Thus, copywriters, editorial assistants, artists, and miscellaneous others attended this July meeting, which was presided over by Joseph Savago, at that point an executive editor of the Book-of-the-Month Club who reported directly to its editor in chief, Nancy Evans, who was out of town.

Savago was young, I noted—in his early forties probably—and impeccably dressed. In fact, he was dressed much more formally than the other men at the table, who arrived casually attired in shirtsleeves and ties or in sport coat and slacks. They looked the counterpart to most of the women there, who dressed much as my academic colleagues did at the time, in longish skirts, blouses, and distinctive jewelry. Savago, on the other hand, was wearing an extraordinarily well-cut, three-piece, midnight blue, pinstriped suit. I wondered to myself if he intended this, consciously or not, as the mark of his position, as a reference to his status as a business professional, or as the mark, simply, of his difference from others. Whatever the rationale for the suit (which he duplicated in slight variations day in and day out), when combined with the showy verbal display he subsequently put on in conducting the meeting, it spoke to me of a New Yorker's sophistication, of style, of self-confidence, and, of course, of cultural mastery. Joe spoke not merely the language of sartorial style with his own distinctive accent but also fluently commanded the high aesthetic language of literary evaluation, criticism, and commentary. He had a mordant wit as well, sharper than Bill Zinsser's, a bit wicked and waspish even, but one capable of summing up cultural fads, peculiarities, and aspirations with the perfect phrase set off in rhetorical caps and quotations to mark its status as a cultural category surely everyone understood. "The Hungarian *Gone with the Wind?*" he taunted one of the editors who was fumbling for a way to describe the family saga she had read and liked but that was clearly too popularly written to be a club selection.

I am surprised now when I look back at my notes from that meeting to see that I did not register more of Joe's sardonic commentary. I remember being astonished by his ability to pronounce so confidently on so many different kinds of books. From cookbooks to cyberpunk fiction, from medical reference books to the exquisitely turned-out first novels of unknown writers, he seemed thoroughly assured of his ability to declaim at length on the merits and demerits of every one of them. I was impressed by the shrewdness of his assessment of the book reading public and by his ability to condense into a single, pointed observation an astute analysis of the cultural moment, of the anxieties of different subgroups within the population, and of the reasons why a particular book might take off in the next couple of months. Here is a cultural critic, I remember thinking, who has found the perfect use for his abilities.

It seems clear that I was entranced by what I took to be Joe's savoir faire as a New Yorker, by his remarkable cultural sophistication. Indeed he lives vividly in my imagination even now. At the time I was dazzled by his self-confidence and envious of his ability to pronounce assuredly on all things literary. He pulled off what I strove for in my classes, but with the kind of brio and finesse I had always associated with those more culturally adept than I. In fact, Joe made me feel clumsy and inarticulate again, that parvenue from the suburbs.

Later that same day, when I was given a packet of reader's reports, I

encountered Joe for the first time in writing. His command of the written language was as assured and passionate as his virtuoso verbal ballet. I
was particularly taken by the ease with which he created and manipulated
a persona in words, almost like a puppeteer who, in marshaling his alter
ego, also winks slyly over his head at the audience, acknowledging all the
while that "of course we're all in on the joke together." My first encounter
with Joe Savago, master of the Book-of-the-Month Club reader's report,
a genre that stands at the heart of the whole enterprise, was occasioned by
his commentary on Carl Sagan's book *Contact*. I quote Joe at some length
here both as a way of attempting to do justice to his confident yet gaudy
style and as a way of exploring the complex, often contradictory attitudes
about books and literature expressed at the club. For even as Joe ratified
the selection of *Contact* and admitted his thorough enjoyment of it, he
subtly revealed that he knew he was not supposed to like it and that, most
important, he knew why.

> Forget about "novel" and all the things we expect from novels and
> whine about when they're not there — *Contact* (to be billed a novel, and
> it sure as hell ain't nonfiction) is an enchanting book which does in its
> way what literature is, acc. to some, spozed to do, Instruct and Delight.
> When you've said that the protagonist/heroine, the astrophysicist Ellie,
> is a good hearted, fiercely professional, feminist woman, you've said all
> there is to say, and you can say even less, much less, about anyone else in
> the book — forget "characters," in other words. You can therefore forget
> "dialogue" too, in the usual sense of character-revealing speech, full
> of individual coloration and perspective — there's dialogue here, but it
> mostly takes the form of polemic and position-paper: Ellie argues with
> a fundamentalist, a Defense Dept, bureaucrat, etc. and each clearly
> and eloquently states his/her position and premises — not unlike (if we
> want literary precedents) the sort of "dialogue" Mann and Huxley and
> other novelists-of-ideas used to write when the idea was to dramatize
> an intellectual climate (*Magic Mountain*, eg) rather than a heroical per-
> sonal destiny.[6]

I loved Joe's roguish insubordination. "*I* know this can't be judged a fine
literary novel," he seemed to say. "*I* know you'd dismiss this — and I know
how, too." I imagined him replying to a skeptical professor, crafting the
perfect retort to a dismissive rejection of Sagan's wooden characters and
stilted dialogue. "*I* know these aren't fully realized characters and this isn't
highly colored dialogue, but that doesn't matter." "Character and con-

versation," Joe argued vigorously, "aren't always the mark of an engaging book, and besides," he seemed to add, "in the past, people we now supposedly respect, wrote this way, too." He continued:

> Let's call *Contact* a scenario, if we must call it anything, a scenario drenched in a humane and hopeful writer's humane hopes for the human future and a humane and hopeful speculator's humane and hopeful speculations as to what They might be like should They decide to get in touch with us. . . . The scientific details are fascinating because the writer is Sagan the Scientist and we trust (and learn, as we trust) his details concerning how a message might be sent and how we might decipher it. The political details are amusing and insightful and ring true because the politics are plausible in the world-as-it-is, yet gentled by an imagination of a coming detente, an imminent easing in world tensions which is not *im*plausible and accords with all of our deepest hopes for this planet. The imagination of The Contact—what They will be like, Their history—is pure imagination, no science is possible here of course, nor extrapolation, this is the Purest Sagan, and it is a beautiful imagination, very moving. And WHY NOT???

Why not, indeed? What *is* wrong with being moved? I secretly applauded Joe's refusal of the familiar, ironic pose of caustic disdain for all things sentimental and of the implicit superiority that goes with declaring oneself above such easy pleasure. I also loved the way he used caps and obvious repetition to call attention to the fact that Sagan's own authorial stance was itself a performance, a deliberate evocation of sentiment and affect. In Joe's imagination, this did not seem to be an indictment of his crass manipulation but rather a love for theater, an appreciation of a writer who could make him part of a participatory audience. He elaborated:

> We read *noir* without flinching or declaiming "Cynic!!!", we read worst-case and we read post-nuke wasteland/stone-age and we read Death Battle of the Galaxies junk so why not remember the rapture we all felt, youngest and oldest, watching *E. T.* (didn't we? I did.) and allow Sagan a lovely and mind-boggling conception of The Alien and what He will want from us. . . . It is also, to borrow a phrase from My Era (duh Sixties,), "mind expanding" in its pervasive assumptions—assumptions we all "know," but which we have probably never "assumed" ourselves for the space of hundreds of pages—about the size and the antiquity . . . of the universe, the more than likelihood of other lifeforms out there, of zones and sciences which turn all the "laws" of our planet on our head.

I was moved beyond words by *Contact*, the way we were all supposed to be moved by the satellite pictures of the Earth from the heavens or the Moon Landing, but I was not, not then. I declare myself now, at last, moved. I think this is a lovely book and I think it's going to be huge and I'm glad we already own it and I think we should play it to the hilt.

I loved the sheer energy and campy exuberance of Joe's flamboyant, operatic excess. I was impressed by his ability to keep the balls of literary analysis and judgment spinning in the air even while he juggled others—accounts of what it felt like to read this book and cultural commentary on why Sagan's offering might capture the attention of a large audience—all the while managing the de rigueur nod to the cynical sophistication of the literary aesthete even as he defiantly asserted his willingness and desire to be moved. Here was a stance, I recorded in my notes after reading this and other reports, that was informed by the formalist principles that had governed literary criticism for more than forty years or so, but one that was also attentive to the experience of reading, to the feel and the sound of it, and to the emotional weather set off by the interaction between book and reader. I grinned surreptitiously when Joe thumbed his nose at those nagging, superior authorities whom I also could conjure with such ease, schoolmasterish types who demanded the dismissal of everything popular because it was too sentimental, too crude, or too earnest. Joe did not seem to be afraid of feeling, and neither did any of his colleagues. For them, reading was completely suffused by feeling and affect; it was an experience of reply, response, and reaction. Joe's willing indulgence in emotion seemed refreshing. In fact, it came as a relief.

But there is something else in Joe's report that attracted my attention, and that has to do with the particular way in which he displayed his learning and cultural knowledge. In fact, when I pushed him later about his own tastes, I found that they were not all that different from those of the professorial critics who had educated both him and me. Joe had an eye for narrative complexity, an ear for poetic song, and an abiding appreciation for the ability to create unique aesthetic worlds. Although he responded to and appreciated many different kinds of books, he took his greatest pleasure from those self-consciously "literary" ones that foregrounded the careful and precise way they used language to construct a world. His taste, then, was profoundly modernist in that it celebrated the virtues of compression and condensation, of intricacy and complexity, of minimalism and spareness.

Yet Joe did not assume that to value works like these he had to deny the different pleasures offered by quite different books. His taste seemed not to be threatened by the existence of other tastes. In fact, what I liked best about Joe's display of his own cultural preferences, wit, and learning was the exaggerated, stagy way he expressed all of them. He did not seem to cling to them in a self-righteous, defensive way, as if he alone was the "real" critic and everyone else lacked his perception and discernment. His taste, like everyone else's, he seemed to say over and over, was an acquired performance, a pose, a deliberate adoption of beliefs about what books should do, like the belief that some are "spozed to . . . Instruct and Delight." Just as he could call attention to the kind of performance involved in Arnoldian high-mindedness with his use of that strategically chosen "spoze," so, too, did his ebullient, effervescent display of his own mastery seem to expose it as the fun of the quintessential puppet-master. Less a strategy for demonstrating his superiority and power over others, taste, for Joe, seemed more like a spirited declaration about his own peculiar and quite particular pleasures, those of someone who had lived through the passions and the inanities of "duh Sixties."

The exaggeration involved in wearing a different three-piece suit every day, I began to think, was Joe's way of indulging in the pleasures of "beautiful things" while taking what they supposedly said about him not entirely seriously. There was a kind of distance between Joe and his self-presentation, a gap, if you will, between who his tastes and preferences declared him to be and some other self he also recognized and appreciated. Perhaps it had something to do with his own class mobility. Raised in the suburb of South Salem, New York, rather than in New Jersey, he once admitted to me that "the city" had been a major Mecca in *his* childhood geography also. He, too, had excelled in school, had loved to read above all, and had eventually made his way to Cornell University, where he pursued a Ph.D. in English. Clearly, he had been deeply marked by that experience. Indeed he once observed that "if I had stayed in the academic world, which I would have if I had ever gotten my thesis written and if it hadn't been at a very bad crunch in the early seventies when there were a zillion more people with Ph.D.'s than there were jobs, I'd be doing what you're . . . ," and yet, something held him back. Something kept him from moving into that world completely. Perhaps it was his refusal to give up his appreciation for sentiment. Or perhaps it was his refusal to take on the trappings of the taste offered to him by his professors with the appropriate measure of seriousness and purpose. Maybe it was the siren call of New York. I don't know. But it was Joe's exuberant cultivation of himself as a persona that fascinated me and set me to thinking about the meaning involved not simply in the content of certain tastes but more significantly in the particular manner in which they were asserted and indulged. What I liked initially about Joe and his colleagues was that they did not seem to invest so much in cultural snobbery. Although I would soon have to revise this perception—there *were* limits to what they could support—my first reaction was one of appreciation for their willingness to be open to all sorts of books and for their love of feeling and emotion.

## RITUALS OF INSTITUTIONAL SELF-DEFINITION

Joe Savago became my most important early guide to the native terrain and the in-house maps employed by the editorial community at the Book-of-the-Month Club. I use the word "community" deliberately, for what struck me most about the group was its tightly knit, clearly defined character. Virtually all of the people responsible for reading and discussing the books had been discovered, hired, and promoted by Al Silverman, who himself set the tone for the organization through his expressed interest in particular books and their potential audiences. Thursday morning editorial meetings were characterized by a rapid-fire repartee that proceeded effortlessly but with a certain momentum because everyone relied on a peculiar lingua franca or aesthetic shorthand composed of generic tags, literary categories, and identifying handles. "Popular history at its best," "right-to-left narrative," "autistic fiction"—this last phrase Joe threw out to expose the mannered and self-involved obfuscation of a too-literary writer. Comments like these recurred again and again, and no one was asked to explain them. At the same time, editors frequently concluded their reports on books they had read for the meeting with the observation, "This is clearly *our* kind of book." On the other hand, they would go on appreciatively and somewhat sheepishly about the "trashy" pleasures of a particular celebrity biography or a long-winded women's novel only to conclude with regretful resolve, "But still, this is clearly not for *us*. Let's leave it for the Guild." The Book-of-the-Month Club, too, trafficked in the business of distinction, however much I wanted to believe otherwise.[7]

All of the editors included themselves within the "we" and the "us," pronouns with an entirely clear but unspecified antecedent and identity. And they never explained that "the Guild" referred to the Literary Guild, their chief mail-order competitor. Yet it was obvious from the way this and other terms were rhetorically wielded to make decisions and to give them institutional weight that the very idea of the Guild crystallized for them a crucially important boundary. The Book-of-the-Month Club, it was taken for granted, the "we" of which they were so proud to be a part, was everything the Literary Guild was not. I picked up very quickly that, from their point of view, the Guild's literary province was the inferior world of women's reading, romances, books on forming relationships and rehabilitating marriages, make-over manuals, and the most salacious celebrity biographies—the publishing equivalent of Phil Donahue and Oprah Winfrey. The Book-of-the-Month Club, they would tell me later, was PBS and the Smithsonian. Their tolerance, clearly, had its limits. And the limits were familiar.

By the end of the summer, after I had attended many of these meetings and could predict with a fair degree of accuracy which titles would be taken by the club and which would be dismissively rejected, I began to wonder why so much time was devoted to these meetings.[8] Generally, at least an hour and a half each week was given to the discussion of about fifteen to twenty titles. The discussions themselves were not merely amicable but high spirited and filled with pointed, sharp observations about books, writers, and readers: "The Hungarian *Gone with the Wind*," on that dubious family saga; "*I'm Dancing as Fast as I Can* for the middle-aged," on Betty Ford's memoir about her drug addiction and alcoholism; "the kind of thing you see on graph paper," of the plotting of a new mystery; "she doesn't invite you in," on a Nadine Gordimer novel the editors loved but were afraid they could not sell to their members. I was amazed by their ability to condense complex analysis into sparkling aphorisms and epithets. The meetings were also extraordinarily rich intellectually, seminars, almost, in contemporary cultural study. Disagreements were rare. What was produced—and relatively easily at that—I began to understand, was a strong consensus about the appropriateness of a book for the Book-of-the-Month Club's list. But if the process of identifying appropriate books was so simple, why the ritual of the meeting? For ritual it clearly was. And as ritual, as a kind of public performance, I wondered, what was displayed and dramatized in those discussions?[9]

The key, I think, is in the constant invocation of the Literary Guild throughout the conversation. By differentiating themselves so cleanly from a similar, yet supposedly vastly different organization, they performed a kind of boundary work, a process of self-definition that has been described by sociologist Michele Lamont, who herself has written on the aesthetic preferences of social elites in both France and the United States, as "the process by which individuals define their identity in opposition to that of others by drawing symbolic boundaries."[10] In effect, each Thursday morning the editors were saying, "*We* are different from the Literary Guild because *we* appreciate 'good writing' and feature 'serious fiction'; *we* are the 'book club of record.' " The Literary Guild, they repetitively reassured themselves, strives for the merely popular, for that which simply sells the most. "We, on the other hand, are after quality." The editors affirmed collectively, then, that they knew who they were, that they knew what position their organization occupied in the publishing hierarchy, and most important, that they knew *why* they did what they did. When they gestured dismissively in the direction of the Guild's offices across the street, they drew an imaginary line between what was acceptable to them and what was not. Their constant surveillance of the boundary between approved celebrity biographies and those beyond the pale—Vivien Leigh is "our" kind of movie star, an editor once observed at a meeting, Dolly Parton is not—created an inside and outside and thus marked the limits of acceptable space that people like themselves ought to occupy. At the same time, it offered a kind of emotional tutelage, a sense of what it feels like to be the sort of person who appreciates good writing, high quality, and serious books. By formulating again and again the principles of discrimination that they already had internalized, they constructed and reconstructed a vision of their community as one with a certain distinction.

This tendency to define the self by dismissing the tastes and preferences of others was disturbingly familiar to me. Academic high culture, after all, constantly defines itself against the suspect pleasures of the middlebrow. In fact, at roughly the same time that I was attending these meetings, I discussed book clubs and my research with one of my colleagues at the University of Pennsylvania. He disparaged the Book-of-the-Month Club particularly and told me that the club *he* belonged to, the Quality Paperback Book Club, was much more substantial and serious. When I mentioned that QPB was actually owned by the Book-of-the-Month Club and run by the very same people, he pronounced himself "shocked." I was not sure he was kidding when he added, "I guess I'll have to discontinue my membership." I remember feeling irritated by what I called "his elitism" and more generally disappointed to discover that taste at the Book-of-the-Month Club also seemed to be a way of establishing social superiority. I wanted the club and its editors to be different somehow, and I suppose I wanted to think myself different as well.

But I had to admit that I, too, had obviously used my own taste and cultural knowledge in exactly the same way in the past. Whatever else New York signified in my youth, I certainly thought that an association with it was a mark of social distinction. I suddenly remembered how much my brother disapproved of my penchant for saying I was from New York rather than from New Jersey when I was in college in Michigan. "Why don't you tell the truth?" he once asked with disgust. So perhaps my interest in the Book-of-the-Month Club and in the nature of aesthetic value was a product of guilt: guilt at leaving *Reader's Digest, Woman's Day,* and the suburbs behind; guilt at the consequences of my own social mobility; guilt at the feelings of superiority I had worked so hard to achieve.

My image of the Book-of-the-Month Club as non-elitist and tolerant was more wish than reality. And yet there seemed to be more to it than that. Something about the club *was* different. But what? True, the club's approach to culture and to value looked a lot like the game of social distinction I had become so familiar with in the academy. The editors dismissed the Guild in exactly the same way that some of my peers had recently dismissed as "banal" and "formulaic" the home decoration schemes, love for colonial domestic architecture, and suburban planting schemes of the nineteenth-century middle class. The scholarly speakers at a conference I had attended on consumption and the middle class delivered their analytical pronouncements with no apparent awareness that their own homes undoubtedly displayed very similar, eclectic collections of museum exhibition posters, oriental rugs, nonrepresentational works of art, a mix of antiques and contemporary furniture, and an assortment of "museum-quality crafts" and pottery. Just as the Book-of-the-Month Club editors felt superior to the inferior readers they conceded to the Literary Guild, so did these scholars place themselves above the plebeian tastes of those who supposedly could only follow the dictates of bourgeois fashion as codified in the Sears catalog because they could not recognize aesthetic quality or originality when they saw it.

And yet, as I read further in the club reports and attended more meetings, and as I began to question the editors themselves, it gradually became clear that although the larger game of taste and aesthetic display functioned similarly in the world of the Book-of-the-Month Club and in the academic world I myself occupied, the club editors adopted a stance toward books and reading that was also distinctly different from the one with which I was most familiar. The editors quickly made it very clear that they were wary of academic ways of reading and writing, and that wariness was closely bound up with an articulate critique of academic habits of evaluation. It was also tied to their desire to assert against such academic strictures the validity of their own competing recommendations and professional expertise. "Typically academic," they disdainfully observed about many university press books—"too dry, too specialized, too self-absorbed for us." In their world, the word "academic" was as much a term of opprobrium as the word "middlebrow" was in mine. Where the world of my peers was defined, in part, by the fact that it was not "middlebrow," the editors' world was marked by its distance from the "dryasdust academic."

The issue of our competing tastes and competencies came more forcefully to the fore as I began my interviews with the Book-of-the-Month Club editors. I was struck, in particular, by how differently they responded to my questions from the way the romance readers had reacted when I asked them why they read. Although the editors answered my questions willingly, straightforwardly, and to the point, those answers were offered in clipped, carefully crafted sentences, parsed precisely as if to fit the space on a printed survey. Neither voluble nor long winded, the editors never expanded on their initial thoughts in a self-revealing or expansive way as the romance readers had. If I asked about the role or function of the club, I received terse answers that assumed a great deal and therefore obscured as much as they offered. "I think it's a combination of middle-class leisure entertainment and uplift," I was told by one editor. Period. Pause. "There's always been a strong didactic element in the self-image of the club and in the way it's perceived by its members, a strong element of self-improvement."[11] I wanted to probe and to inquire after the specific meaning of a term like "leisure entertainment." I wanted the editor to expand on what might constitute "self-improvement." But frequently I did not ask, and the editors almost never volunteered additional information. A certain wariness and distance on their part put me off and produced self-censorship on mine.

They were right to be chary. They well knew what academic investigators did. Products of the same system of higher education as I, they were conversant with its practices and protocols, its ways of generating information.[12] They knew I meant to analyze what they said and would write about what they "really" meant. Their reserve, I thought, was a form of subtle resistance, an unconscious strategy, perhaps, for thwarting my purposes and project. What the Book-of-the-Month Club editors impressed on me in these first, early responses to my queries and probes was their comparable power as members of a professional community. Not only did they possess the knowledge and experience to make sense of what I was doing, but they had at their command the linguistic and social resources to resist politely all my efforts to get them to lay bare the basis of their own status and prestige, that is, their professional expertise, the specialized knowledge that presumably only they possessed.[13]

Their very manner of answering my questions exposed the way we were positioned as professional competitors in what might be called the literary field. The club's success as a commercial enterprise is entirely dependent on its ability to persuade potential subscribers that the advisory service it offers is actually worth something. As one of the club's executives put it to me, "Essentially, as an intellectual exercise, it is our minds that you buy. And our taste."[14] Because the Book-of-the-Month Club had successfully managed this task of persuasion for over sixty years when I encountered it, it was an important force on the publishing scene. The club imprimatur on a book almost inevitably guaranteed higher sales and a greater level of publicity and book talk. The editors and judges performed a kind of consecratory act every time they selected a manuscript from the stacks in the mailroom and decided to feature it in their catalog.

This is little different from what literature professors and academic literary critics do when we select books to present to our students in classroom discussion or to write about as complex exemplars of contemporary literary discourse. Our authority to define what this society takes to be great literature is as dependent on getting others to buy our minds and our tastes as the Book-of-the-Month Club's is. Both are constituted as literary authorities by our professional knowledge. The difference, perhaps, is that the commercial nature of the exchange involved is more masked in the case of academics. We are not paid so directly for our services but retained through the sinecure of tuition and institutional fund-raising. In returning my inquisitorial gaze as they did, the editors exposed the conditions of possibility for my own authority and for the very fact that I was there to query them about their professional knowledge in the first place. Implicitly, as well, their reticence demanded of me that I face the difficult question that sits uneasily at the heart of all ethnographic research, the question of what I intended to do with the information I hoped to generate with their help.

I recall a number of disquieting conversations with friends and colleagues at the time about what it would mean to write about some of the marks of class and intellectual privilege I had begun to detect in the editors' procedures for dismissing books. I worried that it would be unfair to presume on their good faith only to debunk, to deconstruct, and to disapprove of what they did. And yet it also seemed clear that if I erred in the other direction and presented them in unqualified fashion as an antidote to academic asceticism and snobbery, I would ratify and legitimate their expertise and power as professional purveyors of leisure reading to the middle class. I dealt with the dilemma by avoiding it. I deferred its resolution to another time. What I did actively was to throw myself into the business of describing how the editors at the Book-of-the-Month Club read.

## READING AS RESPONSE

The editors and their reading practices moved imperceptibly to the center of my attention even though I still thought I was using them as a way of getting at the more important club subscribers. In fact, I persisted in asking questions about readers and reading in the abstract even though I was very often misunderstood. When I asked, for instance, what sorts of experiences the editors thought their readers were looking for, they paused in puzzlement and queried in return, "Do you mean the editors or our subscribers?" "Reader," it quickly became clear to me, was another term for "editor" at the Book-of-the-Month Club. Subscribers, on the other hand, were usually referred to as "members." While editors *read*, Book-of-the-Month Club subscribers *bought*. Although the act of purchase certainly implied subsequent reading, I thought it significant that the club had never assembled the resources or thought it necessary to conduct extensive research into the *reading* behavior of its members. The research that had been done had focused instead on the act of purchase itself, on all the things that might motivate a reader to buy a book. This was the case, obviously, because the club was a commercial enterprise, but it also happened in this way because the in-house editors assumed—or at least hoped—that their own reading of a manuscript could stand in for or represent the likely reading behavior of their subscribers.

It was precisely their role as informed yet nonetheless representative readers that the editors at the Book-of-the-Month Club fastened on as the key element in their professional self-definition. They thought of themselves primarily as readers of books, and they prided themselves on their ability to read with sensitivity, intelligence, and attention. What they were doing in those long, ritualized conversations about books was not just constructing social boundaries or defining their difference and distance from others. They were also engaging in a performance of their professional identity; they were displaying for themselves and each other the substance of their subjectivity as a particular kind of reader. Their reader's reports were only more formalized versions of these performances—in a sense, scripts for gala theatrical events. Those reports, together with their full-dress delivery at the Thursday morning editorial meetings, staged a performance of reading and, importantly, called attention to the character of the individual engaging in the reading in the first place.

It is important to acknowledge in this context that the reports the editors wrote were not unmediated transcriptions of acts of reading. They were carefully crafted pieces of writing that attested to another of their constitutive skills as Book-of-the-Month Club editors, their ability to write about reading in a highly particular and specific way. Like their academic competitors, the editors were constituted as literary professionals by the particular ways they read and wrote about their reading. I noticed early, however, that two features especially marked their writing about reading as different from the academic practice of critical writing I had learned in graduate school. Their reports were much more personal than the style of writing I had been taught. At the same time, they conceptualized the books they wrote about not solely as occasions for extended analysis but, rather, as opportunities for experience and response.

As Joe Savago's report on *Contact* makes clear, the Book-of-the-Month Club's reader's reports were highly self-referential, constantly mentioning the familiar "we" and a highly specific "I," the unique individual who was the author of the report. As performances, therefore, the reports mutually and simultaneously constructed an individual writing "I" and a community of others assumed to be reading the report. The "I" was given specific weight and character by the inclusion of personal anecdotes and by describing previous experiences of reading as well as by careful delineation of the highly specific feelings those readings aroused. Joe told his readers that his era was "duh Sixties," that he was not moved by the satellite pictures of the earth, that he *was* moved by the book under discussion, and that he had read Thomas Mann, Aldous Huxley, and myriad other books about "the contact." His references to his previous reactions to these latter books also highlighted the fact that he had responded to these books in particular ways, thus raising the possibility that his readers might respond differently.

This gesture was very common in Book-of-the-Month Club reader's reports. It was the editor's way of warning the rest of the group that she or he was a very particular sort of reader with a highly specific taste and thus that the account in question, as well as its accompanying judgment, might be held suspect, which is to say, idiosyncratic or biased. In such a case the reading could not be held to be representative of how the members might read. Reading, therefore, was ironically construed within the Book-of-the-Month Club (given the emphasis on the usefulness to others of the editors' expertise) as a highly subjective experience. In corollary fashion, books were treated not primarily as well-crafted artifacts, as objects of knowledge, but as occasions of feeling, as opportunities for experience and emotional response. Writing was judged to be good, therefore, whether it occurred in a book or in an editor's report about a book, if it managed to provoke an intense reaction within the reader. One of the worst things that could be said about a piece of fiction at the Book-of-the-Month Club when I was doing this research was that the writer failed to make the reader care about the characters.[15] Similarly, a favorable reader's report had to convey to the other editors just why the writer of the report cared so intensely about the book under discussion. There was an important conjunction, finally, between the kind of writing the editors circulated among themselves and the kind they chose to circulate to their subscribers.

The reports the editors wrote, circulated, and discussed almost daily were part book review, part letter to a trusted friend. Their raft of personal references underscored the intimate nature of the community to which the editors belonged, and they emphasized writing as an expressive practice intricately tied to subjectivity. To read Joe Savago's reports, or Alice van Straalen's, Larry Shapiro's, or Jill Sansone's, was both to read about a particular book and to serve as audience for their singular, highly accomplished presentation of self. When the editors read their colleagues' reports, they informed me again and again, they read them always as expressions of personal opinion, as exercises in self-revelation. "I hear Joe," said Larry Shapiro. I knew what he meant. So did I.

In reading their colleagues' reports, the editors explained, they always attended first to the way a particular book had made the individual in question feel. Subsequently, like readers who follow up the book recommendations of a friend, they ratified the positive judgments of those colleagues if they had been tantalized by their observations about a book, if they had wanted to read the book themselves, and if they had been made to care. The reports themselves underscored the fact that the editors conceptualized reading as social encounter and interaction, as the occasion for a particular affective response to the ideas, the sentiments, and the preoccupations of the writer. It became clear to me that the editors thus conceived of reading as an individual and simultaneously nonspecialized process. That is to say, although they assumed that the general reader was fully capable of reading many different kinds of books, they also expected that she or he would not necessarily enjoy every one of them. Where the academic view of literature I had learned in graduate school stressed the value of writing in disciplined fashion about certain special books as intricately formed and structured objects, the Book-of-the-Month Club view and supporting protocols foregrounded the reading of many different books as a process of rejoinder, as an individual, deeply personal reaction or response to the textually embodied particularities of others.

Oddly enough, despite the fact that I had already established my career by writing almost exclusively about books that were notorious for the response they evoked in their readers—those popular romances that the university tenure committee had suggested to my department chair were beneath scholarly notice—I still found the Book-of-the-Month Club editors' emphasis on reading as a complex intellectual, emotional, and physical activity something of a revelation. It was lovely to eavesdrop on people talking with considerable enthusiasm among themselves about books they "devoured," "detested" or dismissively rejected as "nothing special." What the editors conveyed to each other and to me, amidst their particular observations and nuanced evaluations, was the underlying passion for books and for reading that had propelled them into the world of publishing. Although their talk was analytical and even judgmental, it was also enlivened by their use of an elaborated language of emotional and bodily response. I was amazed by the sheer number of expressions they found at every turn to describe how a particular book had made them feel: "captivating"; "engrossing"; "distasteful"; "it made my heart race"; "my toes tingled"; "I couldn't put it down."

The phrases evoked memories not of my study or my office where I did most of my professional reading, but of my bedroom at home where I had read as a child, often between six and seven in the morning as my Dad was getting ready to commute into the city and before I had to dress for school. The editors' way of reading seemed to have much more to do with that delicious experience of simultaneous security and adventure that I associated with my reading in the half-light of early dawn. They made me wonder what had happened to my capacity to read in this way. Perhaps, as Al Silverman had suggested in his title, reading really *is* a fragile pleasure. Fragile not only because it can be crowded out of adult life by the thousand and one responsibilities that make up its almost irreducible busyness, but fragile also because the many disparate authorities, from teachers to reviewers, who teach reading and control access to it in our society frown with particular dourness on those books that exist solely to produce the pleasures of laughter, tears, shudders, and sexual arousal.

The connection that the editors drew between reading and pleasure leaped out at me again and again during their deliberations. Not only did they talk of the projected pleasures they envisioned for their subscribers, but they also detailed with appreciation the particular nature of the feelings specific books had given them. It proved no surprise, therefore, when

{ *In the Service of the General Reader* }

I asked the editors what they most liked about their work, when they pointed out with a certain amount of wonder—indeed with an implied exclamation point—that they were being paid to read. They assumed that I would understand implicitly why this seemed so surprising. Reading, they suggested, is so pleasurable, so unlike work, that it seems absolutely astonishing to be paid to do it. But at the same time the editors also stressed the fact that they enjoy an added privilege because they worked within an organization that possessed what Marty Asher called "a certain book club culture." That is to say, they loved their jobs also because they were given the opportunity to read what they themselves most wanted to read. Their jobs were pleasurable, they impressed on me again and again, for the added reason that a real congruence existed between their personal taste and that which the club marketed as "the best." Once again, despite their appreciation for many different kinds of books, reading experiences, and pleasures, the Book-of-the-Month Club editors resorted to drawing distinctions between good and bad books. They, too, it seemed, were caught up in the game of taste, in the business of discriminating between approved pleasures and those they considered more suspect or base.

For instance, when asked to explain how he had been lured away from a senior editorship and his own imprint at a prominent trade house in order to work at the Quality Paperback Book Club, Marty Asher noted, "You know, basically, you have to publish ten bad books in order to do one good one." He continued, "And I just found that I was spending an inordinate amount of my time reading and buying books I had very little interest in in order to justify the ones that I did. I wasn't terribly familiar with book clubs and actually Lorraine very shrewdly just gave me a bunch of QPB reviews and said why don't you go home and look at these. I called her the next day and I said, 'Wow!' Suddenly I was going to be paid for reading the kinds of books that I would want to read." [16] Editor Maron Waxman observed in quite similar terms that "I didn't want to be a trade editor anymore. I felt it was just pointless, time-consuming. I was spending my time on things I didn't think were valuable. Being a trade editor, especially for a smaller, not particularly competitive house, is kind of thankless." She concluded much as Asher had, "And if you don't much like having lunch with agents, you just find your time is being frittered away reading basically not worthwhile submissions. Here people read. . . . The readers read . . . and everything they're reading is, at least in someone's view, publishable." [17]

Observations like these echoed throughout my early conversations with the Book-of-the-Month Club editors. Many worried explicitly that current trends in publishing were beginning to make their jobs much more difficult. It was becoming harder and harder, they complained, to find the kinds of books they liked to read. The editors cited the centralization of the industry, trade house buyouts by media conglomerates, and the growing emphasis on bestsellers and "blockbuster books" as the key factors transforming the kind of material making its way into their mailroom. A new "attention to the bottom line," they asserted repeatedly, had made many more publishers wary of doing what they called quality books. Pleasurable reading at the Book-of-the-Month Club was not simply allied to some notion of entertainment literature, to what the club's early judges often referred to as "hammock reading" and what the editors sometimes disparagingly referred to as the kind of thing you would read at the beach or on an airplane. Pleasure reading, for the editors, was bound up in complicated ways with notions of quality. And the standards against which such quality was to be measured, they believed, set them apart as an organization from the rest of the industry. Like academic literary critics, their expertise was staked, finally, on their ability to separate dross from gold, to discriminate between the good and the less good. A hierarchy of taste animated judgment at the Book-of-the-Month Club even though that judgment was meant to produce particular instances of emotional and corporeal response.

Editor Marty Asher elaborated on his own views about trends in the industry and the threat they posed to quality in a later interview when he observed, "I think the notion that every book published has to make money is a relatively recent one, and I don't think publishers used to feel that way. They were a special kind of business." Now, he continued, things are different:

> And you know, when you get a large corporation taking over, they're interested in the bottom line. And some of them are smart and take a long-range view, and some of them, you know, are just merciless. You know, "if it doesn't make money, we don't want it." Of course, if you applied that logic, you'd probably eliminate half of the most successful books ever published, because it takes a while. And nobody wants to wait. . . . The house I came from, if you couldn't get out fifty thousand copies, they didn't want to bother. It just wasn't worth it. And in mass market now you're talking a hundred thousand copies.

Asher clearly believed that the Book-of-the-Month Club was different. He noted that "I think we all feel that we're doing something important in the sense of maintaining a certain level of literacy standards for people in a trade market that's increasingly full of garbage." His sentiments were echoed by Gloria Norris, who observed that "there's a very unusual, supportive, warm, noncompetitive feeling [at the club]." She continued, "I think part of it is the job continuity, and the sense of shared values, and the sense that the company is not day-by-day grasping every profit, that there's a sense, more perhaps than in other companies, of a long-term profit base."[18] Club purpose and morale are maintained, finally, by distinguishing what the editors do from the more meretricious, commercially motivated practices of the larger trade houses. This form of boundary work was related to that carried out with respect to the Literary Guild. It aligned the trade with the Guild and positioned the club against, but also above, both. The editors continually reassured me and, in so doing, I suppose, also reassured themselves, that as an institution the Book-of-the-Month Club was driven by attention to "standards" and the search for quality as much as it was by the search for corporate profit. They assumed, just as they expected I would assume, that to manage this was to achieve the nearly impossible feat of balancing two mutually exclusive principles.

Focused as I was on getting these assumptions "right," on figuring out how the editors ordered their literary world, I did not attend very carefully to the emotional nuance surrounding their repetitious boundary work. As a consequence, I missed the significance of the barely repressed anxiety that surfaced around their narratives about the decline of the industry and the club's position in a changing publishing arena. I thought they were simply engaging in a general process of self-definition when they set themselves off so distinctly both from the Literary Guild and from academic writers and readers. It did not occur to me that their need to map the literary universe again and again might be tied more specifically to the particular moment at which I had encountered them than to anything else. Preoccupied with the Book-of-the-Month Club editors' understanding of reading and with what that said about my own academic ways of reading, I ignored completely the specificity of the historical moment that structured, limited, and controlled our interaction. Although I did not know it, that had been the ultimate referent of Bill Zinsser's memo introducing me to his colleagues. In fact, his last, cryptic sentence about other inquisitors was a concrete reference to the specific, anxious conditions under which he and his colleagues were operating, conditions that threatened to upset the precarious balance between the commercial and the literary which they labored so carefully to maintain. I remained unaware of the fact that I had been granted access to the club at a particularly fraught historical moment until the following June. At that point I returned to continue my research only to discover that the issue of my access had been reopened. Although the question would eventually be settled in my favor, the conditions that prompted that reconsideration would have major effects from that moment forward.

## CHAPTER TWO

# A Business with a Mission

## AN ORGANIZATION IN CRISIS

I returned to New York on June 10, 1986, with the intention of spending a year studying the club and its operations. A grant from the Guggenheim Foundation had freed me from teaching by providing support for my research. Although I spoke that day with all the editors I had come to know well the previous summer, it was my conversation with Joe Savago that prompted troubled note-taking on the train ride home. Joe "seems worried," I scribbled, "disgruntled about the 'changes.' " His exact words were " 'They' don't understand the book business." "They," Joe made it clear, were the people from "Time, Inc." In fact, he informed me portentously, in the ten months since I had been at the editorial offices the corporate owners of the Book-of-the-Month Club, Time-Life Incorporated, had made moves to become much more involved in directing business at the club. Although he was wary of saying too much—my first real indication that the anxiety level was high among the editors—he stressed the fact that, as far as he was concerned, they were "making the operation into a machine." Joe told me that Time apparently wanted to increase the size of the membership, a strategy that he felt had the potential to push the club in a more commercial direction. When I asked whether this meant that they would be competing for the Guild's audience, he said no, because he thought it would require too substantial a financial outlay. Still, Joe added, larger numbers of a different kind of subscriber might fundamentally alter the familiar Book-of-the-Month Club editorial mix.

In the next several days I tried to get a better sense of what was going on by asking exploratory questions of some of the other editors. To check whether Joe's worries were shared, I asked only a general question about what was new around the editorial offices. Every person I spoke with recognized immediately that this was a question about the appearance of Time executives in their midst. Like Joe, though, everyone I talked with was hesitant about saying too much. I could not tell whether they thought their jobs were on the line. It was clear, however, that they did not want to be too critical about the recent management restructuring. Nonetheless, I managed to learn that Time had installed as the new president of the Book-of-the-Month Club a man named Lawrence Crutcher, who had previously worked in Time's magazine division. Al Silverman now was required to work closely with him. At the same time, Crutcher had brought in a new vice-president in charge of marketing. The editors told me that this individual was young, an MBA, and someone who had no previous experience in the book business. It became increasingly clear, in fact, that few of the editors were pleased by the management changes and that they worried a good deal about what they might portend for the future of the club.

My own alarm was compounded two days later by a strange interaction at the regular Thursday morning editorial meeting. Not only was Al Silverman present—something that had occurred rarely the previous summer—but so, too, was Lawrence Crutcher. In fact, he himself opened the meeting and almost immediately introduced Al as "our keeper of the image." Al, he explained, had recently written a "mission statement" for the club, and he was there to discuss it with the editors. I wondered about the practice of writing mission statements, a strategy I knew was often taught in business schools as a way to clarify organizational goals, and I wondered whether this manner of opening the meeting was designed to establish Crutcher's authority despite Al's longer history with the club. It was clear from Al's first remarks, in any event, that the editors had previously been given copies of his statement, which he had titled "What We Stand For: A Message from the Chief Executive Officer." He was there, apparently, to make a public occasion of the statement's distribution. I wondered why.

"The Book-of-the-Month Club," Al began, "must continue to proclaim the company's priceless name and reputation. It must tell the American book reading public—our constituency—that this company is more youthful, more vital and more valuable to book readers than ever before." He continued, "The reaffirmation of our youth . . . derives from unshakable principles that form the core of the company's strength." Foremost among those principles, he observed, is the fact that "*we* are the source for serious book readers to find the best new books being published, and if we cannot find them we will invent them."[1] When Silverman later insisted that "we have to be what *we* are and resist like hell going downscale. . . . We have to resist like hell going down even midscale," I recognized that Al's statement was something of a conversational gambit, an intervention designed to counter something that had previously been said. And obviously, what had been whispered throughout the corridors and behind closed doors was that Time was going to take the club "downscale."

As Al talked, it became clear that his statement had been crafted carefully to allay the anxieties surfacing among the editorial staff about the personnel changes that had taken place. He was there to declare officially that the club would continue to do what it had always done and that, as a consequence, the editors would continue to look for the kinds of books they had searched for in the past. I felt very uneasy about what this now obvious unrest might mean for my own research. Still, I was happy to receive a copy of the mission statement, which Al immediately shared with me, because it seemed to set forth so explicitly and in no uncertain terms the organization's self-understanding and definition of its purposes. It seemed especially useful because it also contained the first substantive information I was able to obtain about the character of the club's membership.

The mission statement focused centrally on what Silverman called the most important component of the club's operation, "the upscale, affluent, informed, serious book reader, the reader willing to buy the books he or she clearly wants."[2] To support his claim, Al revealed that a recent survey of 10,000 members had demonstrated that a sizable segment of the club's membership was composed of so-called strong performers, people who bought hardback books without worrying about price. Although he did not reveal statistics, he referred to this group as "the core" of the Book-of-the-Month Club's membership and noted that these strong performers were less likely to be Literary Guild or Doubleday Book Club members. Significantly, they also bought more hardcover books and fewer paperback books than weak performers, and they tended to be older and more affluent than those who only bought one or two books a year. They also apparently acquired books from many different sources, including the club, other mail-order catalogs, bookstores, and the library. What the club needed to do as a consequence, he argued, was to "concentrate on them and enhance the income we get off them."

In commenting more informally on these written observations, Al made it clear that the club discriminated carefully among readers. Where some read only sporadically, others who wanted to read could not necessarily afford to buy hardcover books regularly. And still others, the core of the club's own membership, were so committed to their reading and well enough off financially that they could afford to feed their "book habit" by relying on the regular distribution mechanisms of the Book-of-the-Month Club. These were the ideal readers the club liked to serve, the "serious" readers they imagined perusing their catalog, the individuals they pictured making decisions about the various options offered to them each month, choosing the book or books that best suited their needs. Al's discriminations tended to confirm my half-formed hunch that, despite appearances to the contrary, the business of evaluating books at the club was coordinated very closely with the business of distinguishing among types of readers. It seemed clear that judgment could not be exclusively literary, as the editorial meetings seemed to suggest, but had to be pegged in some way to an assessment of what readers might want and could be persuaded to buy.

I was particularly struck during Al's presentation by his frank admission in this semipublic setting of the commercial aims of the organization. Although financial issues had previously been mentioned to me by individual editors in private interviews, they had been almost completely absent from Thursday morning editorial discussions, which focused much more resolutely on the books themselves than on their projected readers. I had been puzzled the previous summer by the fact that financial matters were rarely mentioned except in the most abstract and general way at those Thursday morning meetings. Discussion was focused so intensely on the strengths and failings of the books themselves that I had sometimes found it difficult to discern what decision had been arrived at during the meeting. I wondered where and when the final decision about selecting a book was made if it was not at the editorial meeting. Financial calculations had to enter the process at some point since someone had to decide what to bid for the book club rights for each manuscript. But these matters were never discussed at the editorial meetings. It seemed odd that editorial deliberations about the content of books were kept so separate from the financial end of the operation. The editors rarely referred to statistics about how an author's last book had performed for the club. Although I later discovered that many of them had tracked down this information by calling the club's distribution center in Camp Hill, Pennsylvania (at this point, the two separate headquarters were not linked by computers at the editorial level), few of them actually introduced these figures into the discussions. The editorial meetings were conducted in such a way as to suggest that decisions about the books were essentially literary in nature.

Despite its explicit endorsement of the importance of higher, literary matters at the Book-of-the-Month Club, the tenor and details of Al's mission statement suggested that I ought to pay more attention to how aesthetic and economic issues were coordinated. Al went on to suggest that the club was facing a substantial new problem in the fact that a declining percentage of the membership was accepting the club's main selection each month. More individuals were exercising their "negative option," he pointed out, requesting an alternate or indicating that they wanted no book at all that month.[3] Although Al claimed that this development testified to their readers' greater sophistication about books, he also noted that it was a cause for concern since it potentially reduced the size of the predictable income the club could count on each month. In response, he explained to the editors, the club was going to try three things: it would try to find more members; it would attempt to get those members to spend more of their disposable income with the club; and it would focus on member retention. Finally, he noted, the club would continue with its recent cost management strategies. Al concluded with the reassurance that "Larry and I are in full agreement on the necessity of these moves but . . . we will not cross the barrier where potential savings threaten to erode the quality nature of our business."[4]

Evidently Al Silverman and Larry Crutcher considered it necessary to reaffirm the club's commitment to quality at the particular meeting where the issue of literary excellence was always the preeminent concern because a perception had developed at the club suggesting that commercial interests were about to impinge more directly on the discussion of literary issues. Al's statement corroborated my earlier suspicion that at some level at least the editors at the club tended to see literary and commercial goals as contradictory and thought their separation both commonsensical and necessary. And yet it also suggested that this separation might have been unconsciously enforced as a way of denying what everyone knew to be true, the fact that, at the Book-of-the-Month Club, matters of literary judgment were tightly bound up not only with financial considerations but also with a commitment to an elaborated and finely articulated view of readers and reading. Al Silverman's mission statement underscored the fact that the Book-of-the-Month Club was and always had been a commercial organization. At the same time, it exposed its work as that of a consumer- and service-minded business. It revealed the ways in which the club's literary decisions, despite their ritual presentation as such, were in fact designed not to serve only the abstract cause of culture or "the literary," but rather were pragmatically oriented to meet the needs of book buyers, people looking for books to display, to give as gifts, or to read.

In focusing on the way economic imperatives drove the operation as a whole, Al's statement made clearer the nature of the obligatory norms that governed the editorial community. His statement clarified the fact that although a concern for literary quality was clearly a factor in individual decisions, that concern could not override in a general way the preeminent assumption that the operation as a whole must remain profitable. The editors probably did not discuss the fundamental assumption grounding their work in the Thursday morning editorial meetings because it was such an unquestioned part of their self-understanding. Although it would take me some time to discover the precise manner in which this commercial imperative ordered their daily practices and interacted with their commitment to literature and literary quality, I found out very quickly that it would have a powerful, determining impact on my own day-to-day activities at the club.

In fact, the very next week Bill Zinsser called me into his office to discuss what he called "a disturbing development" that had taken place several days before. This had occurred at one of the meetings of the newly instituted Executive Committee, which brought together, from the editorial staff, Al, Lorraine Shanley, Robert Riger, and Editor in Chief Nancy Evans and, from the management staff, Larry Crutcher and the new vice-presidents in charge of marketing and finance. This group had begun meeting regularly to facilitate better the coordination of the many different aspects of the operation and to plan implementation of new policies. Time, evidently, had found the apparent separation of editorial and financial matters peculiar, if not counterproductive as well. My reflections about this were short-circuited, though, by Bill's next observation. He said that in response to my request to continue my research at the club, Al had invited Bill to join the Executive Committee meeting in order to explain to the others the nature of my planned study. Since only Al, Lorraine, Robert, and Nancy had worked at the club the previous summer, none of the others knew about the project. I got the point quickly. Access now had to be cleared with Larry Crutcher. Bill reported that he had made his presentation and that both Al and Lorraine had then spoken eloquently on my behalf. They argued vigorously, he noted, that it was the duty of the club as an important cultural institution to be open and available to scholarship. Larry Crutcher and the marketing people objected nonetheless. They were worried that I might disclose important information and thus render them vulnerable to their major competitor, the Literary Guild. Bill reported that, at the same time, they kept asking about what was in it for the club. Although Al stressed that they would learn from my study, the others voiced strong doubts that "an English professor" could tell them anything that might be useful in the business of running the corporation.

If those book-lined shelves in the reception area and the character of the editorial meetings had lulled me into believing that I was studying an institution merely literary and cultural in nature, the skepticism of the club's new executives reminded me starkly that the Book-of-the-Month Club was indeed a commercial establishment, and as such it had its own interests to protect. My questions, together with my plans to publish the answers I intended to develop, posed a potential threat, it seemed, not just to the professional expertise of the editors but also to the economic viability of the organization. Still, I needed to follow through on a project for which I had just received a major grant. I began to think of new ways to justify what I was doing, and I even began to think about how I might reconceptualize the study. At this point Bill reported back that I would need to think carefully about justification, since Larry Crutcher wanted to meet with me to discuss the project.

Even before that meeting took place, however, Bill called to relay the contents of a memo Crutcher had sent Al Silverman after reading materials I had prepared for the meeting. Al later gave me his copy of the memo. "Radway's outline seems so very academic," Crutcher wrote, "and the lead-time so long (we'll all be gone!), that it's hard to have any immediate concern about it." Rereading eight years later and with wry amusement this comment, which I thought exaggerated at the time, I have greater respect for Crutcher's analysis of the situation. Not only has the lead time been a good deal longer than I think even he suspected, but in fact both he and Al Silverman have long since left the club. At that time, however, I was more preoccupied with the way his perception of me and my research was going to limit the nature of my study. Crutcher informed Al that "it would seem to me that we should be guarded about special editorial/regional/demographic insights, if their publicity would help the owners of the Lit. Guild." He continued, "And I think we should keep Marketing and Finance off-limits; based on her outline, she isn't interested in the business anyway."

Crutcher's characterization was accurate. Despite my growing suspicion about the primacy of commercial matters, I had subordinated an interest in the economics of the operation to my preoccupation with literary and aesthetic issues. Thus did a disciplinary habit I had learned in graduate school, the habit of assuming that the literary world is always ordered first by aesthetic distinctions, unconsciously persist in structuring my initial contact with the Book-of-the-Month Club. It was this supposition, actually, that kept me from pursuing my earlier insight that the club's day-to-day operations probably proceeded from the founding premise that people bought and read books for different reasons. The editors knew that some books were bought specifically for display and some were purchased as objects to own. Still, they usually began with the assumption that their job was to manage readerly desire. They were to find books that potential readers could actually be persuaded to buy. This much I understood. What I had not yet thought to pursue in any depth was how this starting point functioned as a distinct enabling device. It empowered the club to recognize that reading is an extraordinarily complex and variegated social activity and thus a practice to which different readers bring different tastes and different evaluative criteria because they bring to it, first and foremost, different needs. What I began to see at this point was that the editors' commercial orientation had made them into accomplished theorists of reading *and* book buying.

Still, while these events made it impossible to avoid the determining significance of economic concerns at the Book-of-the-Month Club, I thought it best not to push too hard about acquiring concrete information about marketing or contract issues. I was worried that the matter of my presence at the club would be reopened. The economic interests of the club operated externally to limit my access, but they also operated internally in the form of self-censorship. Sensitive always to signals that I was pushing too hard in certain situations or interviews, I backed off at times when I would have liked to probe. When it became clear later in the year, for instance, that the Time management was thinking of restructuring the panel of judges (rumors abounded both in-house and throughout the industry that some were going to be asked to resign), Bill and Al both advised me to hold off on a request to interview the panel. Although I eventually spoke with Clifton Fadiman and Gloria Norris at some length, the management's protective instinct at such an unsettled time to shield people whom they treated with great respect worked to limit my access in very important ways. A key limitation of this study, therefore, is its inability to compare the book selection procedures of the editors with those used by the judges. Although I have been told by many that the two groups thought about books in similar ways, I was not able to talk with the judges in the same leisurely and exploratory way I enjoyed with the editors.

It must also be remembered that I was not given detailed financial data about contracts, book sales, or the marketing operations of the organization. Consequently, what I have to say here largely concerns the conceptual structure and principles of priority governing the editorial operations of the Book-of-the-Month Club. I have tried to account in a general manner for the way financial constraints exerted an impact on the club's day-to-day operations. I have also tried to discern and to explain both how and why literary concerns continued to demand attention at the club. What I have not been able to do, however, is to address the specific details of individual decisions to buy or reject certain books. I can say little about how those general principles actually played themselves out in the concrete bidding for the book club rights to specific manuscripts. To do that, I would have had to have access to contracts and other financial data but also to the phone conversations in which those deals were negotiated.

I want to point out that while functioning within the limits set by club officials was very difficult, it also had its advantages. Because the threat of institutional change provoked great anxiety about the future of the Book-of-the-Month Club, those conditions tended to render even more explicit the structuring principles of the operation. From this moment on, I was acutely aware of how worried Bill, Joe, and the others were about the prospect that the tenuous but successful balance between literary and commercial objectives that had been established at the club was about to be disrupted. Day after day they returned to the question of balance and impressed on me the significance of the fact that the club was an organization poised between two opposing sets of interests and, finally, between two different ways of thinking about value. It was the editors' obsessive preoccupation with the future of the club's characteristic ability to weigh the commercial against the literary that gradually enabled me to see that my focus could not simply be on their aesthetic principles if I wanted to render their selection procedures with the kind of complexity they deserved.

I began to think that I would need to focus in depth on the fact that decisions about books at the club were always pegged to a highly elaborated conception of book buying and book reading. The Book-of-the-Month Club editors, I began to understand, could not privilege aesthetic issues in any simple way because the commercial nature of the operation enjoined on them careful attention to the motives of book buyers and to the needs, desires, and intentions of readers. They had to recognize that their members turned to them not only to learn about the latest fiction titles that might pique their interest, but also to find a good chicken cookbook, a useful field guide to the birds of the Midwest, the latest comprehensive medical reference book, and appropriate books to give Aunt Lynn or

Uncle Jim for Christmas. Books were conceived as useful objects at the Book-of-the-Month Club, and they were evaluated differentially according to how well they performed their intended function.

And yet, even as I was beginning to recognize the determining significance of the club's commercial aims and their impact on the way the editors mapped the world of book publishing, the stubborn intransigence of "the literary" in their minds impressed itself on me again and again. No matter what kind of book they were considering, the editors demanded always that it be "well-written." Attention to language was still accorded persistent importance at the Book-of-the-Month Club. Although the editors insisted that books could perform many different functions, they also seemed to believe that books were nonetheless always constituted in and through their use of words. As specifically literary objects, books were expected to exhibit particular respect for the suppleness, complexity, and richness of language itself. Despite their apparent subordination to commercial concerns, issues of linguistic and aesthetic quality were still never very far from the minds of the Book-of-the-Month Club editors even when they were discussing the merits of books such as *Billyball*; *Brainfood: Nutrition and Your Brain*; *Quarrels That Have Shaped the Constitution*; *Man of the House: The Life and Political Memoirs of Speaker Tip O'Neill*; and *My Name Is Anna: The Autobiography of Patty Duke*. In the end, the intensity of the editors' investment in maintaining the importance of the literary even within an organization devoted to the pursuit of corporate profit propelled me to investigate more thoroughly the precise nature of the relationship between the literary and the commercial at the club and to inquire into its sources, its rationale, and its effects.

### BALANCING THE COMMERCIAL AND THE LITERARY

Shortly after the issue of my access to the club was resolved, a long, confusing conversation with Joe Savago confirmed that the relationship between the literary and the commercial was an extraordinarily fraught one at the Book-of-the-Month Club. I was attempting to follow up on my decision to concentrate on the editorial practices of the editors themselves in response to the questions about the extent of my access. I asked Joe to clarify how the alternates offered each month were different from the main selections. Still expecting him to focus on certain features in the books themselves, I was puzzled when he answered somewhat obliquely. He observed flatly that the club would never pay more than $75,000 for the book club rights to an alternate. When I looked perplexed, he explained that alternates were thought of as books that would never prompt selection by a big enough group of readers to recoup a large financial outlay. Main selections, he elaborated, appealed to many different kinds of readers, and thus the club could afford to pay huge sums of money for the book club rights to them. Joe noted further that the alternate operation existed to enable the club to reach more particular, perhaps more specialized readers who would not place themselves in the audience for a blockbuster title. What this meant for the editors, he concluded, is that "this gives us the freedom to take some books small," that is, "to offer books of high quality" that "will appeal to only a small number of readers."[5] These books, he concluded, are bought for a small sum.

Joe seemed to be saying that the difference between main selections and alternates was not a simple matter of different content or qualities but, first and foremost, a difference in the nature of their appeal to readers. A book was chosen as a main selection by the editors because they theorized that it would assemble a very large audience. Concomitantly, other titles were relegated to the alternate list because the editors believed that they would appeal only to smaller groups of quite specific readers with particular needs, tastes, and desires. Joe seemed to assume that literary quality correlated closely with small audiences who had a more particular, more demanding taste. While the editors preferred to offer books of this type, he seemed to imply, they were willing to include obviously commercial books even though they displayed little other merit simply because the organization was a profit-minded business.

But then Joe continued in an odd way. He observed that even when the club decided to buy a title as a main selection—because the editors had already decided it would perform well commercially—they always worried about whether the book had some kind of literary merit. To illustrate how this worked, he recounted the club's discussion of a first novel by Texas housewife Karleen Koen, *Through a Glass Darkly*, for which the club had recently paid a surprisingly high sum. He explained that virtually every editor at the club had read and loved the book. He had deliberately decided not to read it when more and more editors were urging its selection because he wanted to play devil's advocate. Although he did not say so explicitly, it was clear that at the time he had assumed that the novel could not be any good. His reservations were overridden by the group's enthusiastic discussion of the novel's gripping plot, however, and the decision was made to acquire the book club rights to the title. When negotiations hit a snag and Editor in Chief Nancy Evans could not decide how high to bid, Joe jumped in with what he thought to be a key question. He asked Nancy, he said, "Was there any page where you felt guilty or gloomy or bad for reading this?" When she said no, he advised her to pay the higher price then being demanded by the publisher.

When I asked him why he posed this particular question, Joe explained that the issue was whether the subscriber could be proud of having read the book. "The issue of being good for you," he pointed out, "is very important to the Book-of-the-Month Club." What the organization tends to offer its subscribers, he added, are books that "are well-crafted but entertaining." "We like it best," Joe continued, "when we find something that does both but adds a distinctive, literary voice." Here Joe seemed to suggest that even when highly commercial fiction was offered, the club still required that the book exhibit some form of literary merit. It was the book's literary merit, clearly, that marked it as "something good for you." The literary, apparently, could not simply be subordinated to the commercial, just as the commercial could not finally be subordinated to the literary. The Book-of-the-Month Club editors themselves recognized the worth of both commercial and literary imperatives, they vacillated frequently in the privilege and priority they accorded to each, and they sought books that vibrated productively with a tension produced by an author's willingness to serve both sets of concerns.

When Joe and I continued the conversation, he went on to say that the club's editors think of themselves as providing, above all else, leisure reading for their subscribers. Those subscribers, he suggested, turn to the club because they are looking for books that will be pleasurable and entertaining to read. At the same time, he noted, the editors realize that their subscribers choose to read for pleasure rather than watch television because the act of reading itself makes them feel they are engaging in something productive and educational. The club tries to identify what they think of as "the worthwhile" from among the welter of manuscripts offered to them. And they do this, Joe pointed out, with both fiction and nonfiction. What their readers want is a kind of "super-Michener," the kind of book by Umberto Eco or Barbara Tuchman that will entertain them at the same time that it plies them with useful and intriguing information. As Joe put it, "It will tell you all you ever wanted to know about medieval monasteries and the fourteenth century."

Thinking that I had finally gotten the point, I asked Joe, "So all books have to be instructional—even fiction?" "No, that's not it," he replied, "because there are different kinds of fiction." Joe proceeded to delineate three different types, all of which were sent out occasionally by the

{ *In the Service of the General Reader* }

club. "Commercial fiction," he observed "appeals to conventional, established sets of satisfactions. It is not a personal self-exploration but a job of work." "Serious fiction," or "fiction as personal quest," on the other hand, "explores the world from the author's point of view within familiar, accessible plot terms." Finally, Joe noted, there is "autistic fiction," "fiction written autistically from a writer's individual sense of truth . . . gibberish when done badly, but literature when it works." The job of the editors, Joe explained finally, was to identify good books within each of these three categories. What was good in one category was not necessarily the same as the good in another. Then, when I mused in response that he did not seem to rank the categories themselves in a hierarchical fashion, Joe replied with exasperation, "Well, not as a business person. But I do myself." What he preferred, he assured me, is "literary stuff, you know, the delicious, erotic, literary experience."

Joe's tendency to draw a distinction between his personal taste for high literary fiction and the more tolerant taste he exercised institutionally on behalf of the club recurred constantly in my interviews with the other editors. For example, in exploring the question of whether her own preferences were representative of those of the club's subscribers, Phyllis Robinson hesitated. "That's a hard question, because it sounds awful to say, 'No, I think my taste is superior.' I think there are readers who share my tastes. Let's put it that way," she said. "It works the other way too," she continued. "I think that there are certain topics and certain books that don't interest me, and I know there are people out there . . ."; Robinson's response trailed off almost as if she could not bear either to acknowledge or to dismiss the taste of others. In explanation, she noted that she had just evaluated her first inspirational book, a genre she did not like because, as she put it, "I'm not a self-improver." "I had to disabuse myself of all my prejudices," she offered, "and I think this is pretty good. You know, like maybe we ought to take it." But, having granted the validity of other tastes, she returned again to the issue of her own. "And . . . well, I'll just say I think there are readers who will share my tastes." To my reply that many of the other editors also equivocated about their preferences and their relationship to those of their subscribers, she added, "We're all aware that we're here, not to show off our own erudition, or whatever it is. At the same time we are aware of a certain level of taste." She concluded, "I think maybe that's what you hope in the end that something like the Book-of-the-Month will do, and that is to raise the level of taste."[6]

Clearly, a familiar evaluative hierarchy continued to suffuse much that was said at the club despite the structural imperative to offer a varied selection of reading material. Although the editors labored diligently to choose books in any number of different categories, from popular history to cookbooks to commercial fiction, they did so always with a certain amount of ambivalence. On one hand, they seemed to have profound respect for the diversity of functions that books could fulfill. They recognized, for instance, that reference volumes and self-help books have their distinctive uses and that some provide the requisite information in a more sensible and readily usable form than others. On the other hand, they also seemed to reserve a special place for one kind of book above all others, that is, literary fiction. Not only did they situate this category at the top of a hierarchy, but they themselves acknowledged that what made their job particularly pleasurable were those rare moments when they came across as-yet unheralded books of high literary quality that they could introduce to their subscribers.[7] As Marty Asher put it, they enjoyed their job because it enabled them to read the kinds of books they most liked to read even as they worked to select a diverse range of material for readers with somewhat different tastes. Alice van Straalen observed similarly, "I think each person has a personal sense of that balance [between the literary and the commercial]. If you've just logged three commercial books in, you'll feel freer to make a case for a book of literary distinction. And I don't think that's even a conscious thing. But I think we all have private scales, and then the company is the sum of all those private feelings."[8] In Lucy Rosenthal's words, the "complicated" role of the club "has been traditionally to mix art with commerce, to pick books that people would like to read, that they'd like to buy." When asked whether she selected books that pleased her, she corrected, "Well, I'm pleasing the self that I have brought to this function, to this sort of job, which is the self that's trying to mediate between those people out there and me."[9]

The editors returned repeatedly in our discussions to the question of the balance between the literary and the commercial, to their respect for what they called literary distinction, and to their uneasy ambivalence about the subscribers they were employed to serve. Much of what they said suggested that the active process of maintaining a finely balanced tension between art and commerce had always existed at the heart of the Book-of-the-Month Club operation. Noting, for instance, that she was the first woman to take an executive position at the Book-of-the-Month Club, former editor in chief Gloria Norris admitted to me that "different reactions came up" when she was hired in the mid-1970s.[10] She explained, "I think they thought that I would be a very dreadful person. A very commercial person, is what one person later told me. [They worried] that I would just turn everything over, but they quickly discovered that we had much in common, and I didn't really experience much resistance." Norris's comments hinted that at another moment of change within the organization, the same kind of rumors, gossip, and apocryphal stories I heard repeatedly that summer coursed through the corridors and offices of the club. I could well imagine how longtime employees might have whispered about the implications of her previous experience in "the trade" just as their successors buzzed amongst themselves about the importance of "the bottom line" at Time.

Although the Time intervention may have exaggerated the feeling that the equilibrium that had been established was precarious, Norris's observations hinted that, for some time at least, those who worked at the club had prided themselves on their ability to walk a fine line between the desire to identify and to promote literary quality and the need to make a living by selling books. The assumption, of course, was always that those goals were contradictory, that market principles were fundamentally at odds with the aims of art. In the editors' eyes, what seemed to make the Book-of-the-Month Club special was its ability to do the improbable, to sell both James Michener and John Updike, both Stephen King and Margaret Atwood, both Dick Francis and Don De Lillo. As Susan Weinberg summed it up, "There's such an extraordinary—well, tension isn't the right word—but there's a sense of issues to balance. And they're worked out." [11] "What we do," Robert Riger explained, is "the best books in proven categories and commercial books with literary pretensions." [12]

A book with obvious commercial possibilities was acceptable to the club only if it could first be demonstrated that it laid some claim to a higher purpose, either to literary excellence or to a public-spirited interest in a major issue, and hence to a more permanent, less suspect form of value. The club's editors were willing to make money, which is to say, to accrue financial capital for the institution only if they could accrue cultural capital first by reaffirming their commitment to "good writing"; classic literary genres, values, and standards; or to a disinterested desire to provide the public with important information. [13] Robert Riger did indeed sum it up perfectly when he pronounced "the best books in proven categories and commercial books with literary pretensions." Attention to literary books, literary language, and the subject matter associated with "culture" justified the commercial nature of the business both personally for the editors and institutionally for the club itself. Despite the business school provenance of the idea of the mission statement, in the case of the club the use of the word "mission" during this moment of particular crisis effectively reminded those who worked within its precincts of the larger purposes to which the club was supposedly dedicated.

Of course the language I have used here to convey the way that the equation between literature and lucre, or culture and commerce, was figured at the club is not the language used by the editors themselves. And yet an account of the club written by Bill Zinsser only a few months before, on the occasion of the club's sixtieth anniversary, focused similarly on the question of weighing the commercial against the cultural and even seemed to posit the existence of two systems for determining value and rewards. In *A Family of Readers: An Informal Portrait of the Book-of-the-Month Club and Its Members on the Occasion of its 60th Anniversary*, a small book distributed free to all members, Bill Zinsser not only recounted some of the early history of the organization but also described how the monthly selections were chosen by the judges and the editors. One of the key chapters in what might be considered a "native" ethnography was titled "Should It Be Considered? (Yes. Maybe. No)."[14] There, Bill developed his understanding of how different criteria were mobilized in the task of book selection.

Zinsser observed that although the editors feel deeply their responsibility to the club and to its members, it was his impression "that they feel one even greater responsibility: to the book."[15] The editors ask themselves, he explained, "Are we being properly attentive to what the author was trying to do? Does the book succeed on its own terms, regardless of any terms that we may be imposing on it?" He suggested that reading protocols at the Book-of-the-Month Club demanded respect for the integrity of each volume. Despite the attempt to evaluate every book on its own terms, however, Bill admitted as well that at the Thursday morning editorial meetings, "certain practical questions are also raised." The editors additionally ask themselves, "Have we recently offered a book on the same subject, or is one expected soon that may be better? How have the author's previous books been received by the members?" Despite the nod to commercial concerns, which Bill masked by not naming them as such, he continued with the key assurance: "But ultimately those aren't the decisive factors." His account of the preeminent criterion is important enough to quote in full:

If anyone in the room feels strongly that we should take a book, that book will probably be taken, even if it's likely to lose money. Quite often the reasons are public-spirited: it's an important book on an important subject (nuclear weapons, toxic waste), or it's the memoir of a former secretary of state. "We're the book club of record," someone invariably reminds us, and under that commendable rubric another worthy volume is shepherded into the fold that will bring the club its reward in heaven if not necessarily on the bottom line.[16]

Although Bill's comment did not focus specifically on the issues of literary quality, in part because he was thinking primarily about nonfiction rather than fiction, he did stress the public-spirited, disinterested nature of the club's operation. Profit was sometimes forsworn, he maintained, in the interest of advancing the public good. Bill alluded to financial gain as if it were somehow suspect, as if it were a form of dirty self-interest that must be downplayed in the cause of serving higher goals. In playfully suggesting that the club's reward would come in heaven rather than at the bottom of the ledger, he implied that the books they distributed would accrue cultural value slowly, value which would redound to the club's credit and testify to its noble public spirit and high sense of purpose.

Bill's comments echoed Al Silverman's mission statement, which also paid similar attention to the idea of a higher purpose. Significantly, Al also ranged the club's higher goals against the easy commercial pursuit of likely bestsellers. In recounting a recent conversation with "a senior person at Time, Inc.," for instance, who had asked him why the club had offered Barry Lopez's *Arctic Dreams* as a main selection, Silverman proudly recounted to his colleagues that "I told him that we took it because it was a wonderful book, that we knew it probably wouldn't sell much but that it was one of those silent, long-term investments that might pay off in member satisfaction for a segment of our audience."[17] Continuing, he noted that "every year we need our Ludlum's, our le Carres, our Kings, and our sure-fire non-fiction books. But we also need the kind of books that are not sure bestsellers, and not faddish, but that delight our audience, and surprise them, a book that members buy not just to read, but also to keep."

Like the editors I have quoted before, Silverman drew a distinction between ready, easy profit and a form of more permanent value that could only accrue over time. While some books were written to be bought, read, and discarded, he suggested, and to realize their value immediately, others were more like long-range investments. Those were the books whose full value as possessions and as assimilated cultural knowledge could only be realized in some distant future. According to Al Silverman and his colleagues, it was this commitment to a transcendent form of cultural value that made the Book-of-the-Month Club what it was, that stood at the center of its mission, and therefore that justified its existence by transforming its trade in books into something other than a simple business.

Al's mission statement and the fraught conditions surrounding its delivery foregrounded the importance of the club's status as a commercial organization. Yet when I tried to pursue the effects of this fact, I could not escape the residual importance of the literary at the Book-of-the-Month Club. Although the literary and the commercial were viewed at the club as contradictory principles, indeed as mutually exclusive systems for determining value, they operated nonetheless always in a tangle. Most obviously, the club's self-declared mission to raise the level of popular taste justified the organization's more commercially oriented practices for virtually everyone involved in the editorial operation. Hence Joe's concern that Karleen Koen's insistently commercial romance saga also display evidence of a "distinctive literary voice." And yet, at the same time, every one of the editors knew that the club could not begin to raise taste if it could not get books to buyers, if it could not interest readers in what those books offered, and if it could not get readers to read those books. The club's literary success depended on the editors' capacity to know their membership, on their ability to understand why ordinary people who were not employed in some region of the literary business turned to books in the first place. Most significantly, perhaps, the success of the club's mission depended on the editors' skill at finding books that would seem both to meet readers' preconstituted desires and to introduce them to what everyone at the club insisted on calling "literary quality."

## READING PLEASURE AND THE LIMITS OF THE LITERARY

Despite the priority accorded to the very idea of the literary at the Book-of-the-Month Club, the editors' written reader's reports also suggested that, pragmatically, the concept of literary value was never applied as a pure principle, and neither was the category of literary fiction itself so important that everything in it was deemed acceptable. Reader's reports at the club demonstrated that not all books that marked themselves as literary were deemed acceptable by the editors. In fact, the editors did not recommend every book they knew to be a literary achievement. The category of the literary seemed to have certain clear, definable limits at the Book-of-the-Month Club. Those limits were significant because they established the fact that literary fiction was not sought out by the editors simply because the value attached to the category itself justified the enterprise as a whole. The club looked for "good" literary fiction because the editors also believed that this kind of fiction could provide a particular kind of reading pleasure for its members. In thinking about literary fiction as a particular kind of book with its own specific uses and pleasures, the editors were treating the literary at this pragmatic level as no different from the innumerable other proven categories they dealt with each day. The value of the literary, finally, was not so powerful as to override ways of thinking about reading that were closely tied to the service and commercial character of the business. Reading, in this view, was an act engaged in primarily for pleasure but also for additional practical reasons that helped to determine the kind of book to which the reader turned.

In keeping with this sort of practical logic, report after report established that books could fail miserably for the editors despite an initial claim to literary status. I noticed quickly that the editors often rejected books that too extravagantly foregrounded their pretension to literary value. The editors reacted particularly negatively to books that displayed any sort of literary excess, such as a language too crabbed, a plot too convoluted and self-conscious, or an approach to character too fractured. Such excess was objectionable, the editors seemed to feel, because it proved a hindrance to readers seeking specific reading pleasures. The very word used by Joe and some of the others to label the highest literary achievement recorded a fair amount of ambivalence about the category of literary writing itself. In referring to high literary fiction as "autistic," Joe and his colleagues implied that literary writing was, to a certain extent, conducted in a highly personal language and according to an idiosyncratic, individual sense of truth. When used successfully, they believed, this personal idiom could illuminate the world in unusual ways and endow the reader with new eyes as well as new tools for making sense of it. When done badly, however, the result was mere gibberish, in their opinion, self-referential nonsense that resisted translation and therefore comprehension. By invoking the psychological condition of autism in connection with the literary, this terminology implied that all literary writers courted the risk of remaining locked within their own peculiar and singular world. Where language and point of view were too hermetic, the editors believed, self-consciously literary writers either failed to communicate with their readers or reveled self-indulgently in verbal narcissism. They produced an unreadable text or at least one that could not be read with the right kind of pleasure. More often than not, when the editors and even the outside readers employed by the club encountered work like this, their reaction was not one of simple dismissal alone but rather one of decided irritation, annoyance, and even downright anger. They were made furious, it seemed, by literary fiction that refused to acknowledge the legitimate desires and demands of readers.

I first encountered this anger in the fall of 1986 in a reader's report about the newest offering from an acclaimed writer usually identified with late modernism or early postmodernism.[18] Outside reader Robert Mabry launched his commentary with a testy rhetorical question: "Is this to be [X]'s best-seller?" "Perhaps," he answered. "On the assumption that it may be, I suggest its consideration as a Selection." His next sentence, however, realized fully the implications of his opening, choleric tone. Mabry added, "I, personally, nearly loathe it." Why, I wondered, since this writer's work was usually described as high-spirited, comedic, and intellectually energetic? What had happened in the reading to inspire Mabry's ire? His extended commentary indicated that what he found so annoying was the self-conscious artfulness of the book, its tendency to call attention to its own literary apparatus, and, by implication, to the artist manipulating that apparatus.

After a long paragraph detailing the way stories within stories upon other stories were orchestrated by the author, Mabry wearily admitted, "I suppose all art is self-indulgent." He qualified his assertion with the added caution, "The enduring value and meaning must rest in the self that is being indulged." Meditating further, he noted, "One is, subliminally, always aware that one is reading Tolstoi or Dickens or Shakespeare, but it is Levin or Dombey or Lear who has our attention. I have never been an [X] enthusiast and this enormous ms. . . . has not converted me. For all his 'brilliance' and sophistication and theorizing, there is something smart-aleck juvenile about him, constantly calling attention to himself, a self I do not positively respond to." Continuing with the concession that the novel has "a lot of sex, 'topicality,' 'cleverness,' many characters, etc.," features that might make it a potential main selection, he nonetheless concluded, "But it also has, for me, about 500 pages of staggering boredom—perhaps more." [19]

For Mabry—an individual who wanted to meet in his reading not an arrogant, superior author but other Lears and Dombeys—the self-conscious artfulness of this book, its mannered attention to its own narrative and linguistic machinery, proved a serious obstacle. Unwilling to sustain an attention to the device, to find interest in the ways the story was constructed and told, Mabry ended up losing sight of the stories within the book; he was, quite simply, bored. Fleetingly, I recalled some of my own students' struggles the previous semester when I had asked them to read Faulkner's *The Sound and the Fury*. Although fascinated by the tantalizing whiff of scandal they detected throughout the book, they were frustrated, as Mabry apparently was, by their inability to discern that story through the screen of Faulkner's prose. Unpersuaded by my reassurance that Faulkner's meditation on the nature of storytelling was as interesting as the particulars of the Compsons' story, they tended to treat the book as a distasteful and boring exercise that I required them to complete rather than the occasion for the kind of reading experience they desired.

The Book-of-the-Month Club editors responded in much the same way. Frequently in their discussions of literary books, which they additionally called "serious fiction," they noted that "the critics" were likely to find much to like in a particular volume even though they believed it would not find a willing audience among their subscribers. They worried, as a consequence, about whether the likelihood of positive reviews should push them to take a book even though they suspected that it would be "too literary" for their subscribers. Those subscribers, they seemed to feel, would be unwilling to meet the writer's writerly demands, a feat the critics would be more inclined to undertake because it would enable them to demonstrate their own understanding of, and sympathy for, artistic practice. Those subscriber-readers would rather be entertained and instructed about certain knowable problems and truths, the editors seemed to believe, rather than be asked to duplicate the artist's own labor.

This distinction between different kinds of reading procedures and protocols figured prominently in the second report on the manuscript Mabry had read, a report that was written by senior editor Jill Sansone. The opening and conclusion to her report are worth quoting in full because they establish clearly that, for her, this manuscript failed substantially even though she recognized that it might provide the occasion for admiring critical commentary.

A maximalist novel about a minimalist writer which unfortunately offers more tedium than entertainment. Actually, there *are* some wonderful moments in this oversized ms. but since it is also stuffed with tedious tales, forced metaphors, and a self-conscious style (look at how clever I am) the end result for the average reader is fatigue ([X] fans if there are any left, may doggedly persevere). If an editor had forced [X] to make this a novel rather than an epic it might have been readable (although still self-consciously told) tale. But the excess has produced a book in which more is decidedly less.

Puns and wordplay galore; . . . and yes this is amusing for the most part. But I unfortunately drowned in the tedium between the cleverness. On and on [X] goes and where he stops I can't know, having bailed out . . .

just past the epic's halfway mark. Critics may have a field day; they often do with [X]. But few readers will be able to get through this.[20]

Sansone's seemingly offhand and ironic allusion to the modernist dictum that "less is more" seemed to me a shrewdly chosen rhetorical device that displayed her familiarity with aesthetics and literary criticism and therefore established her authority to pronounce on the book's failings in the first place. She was not rejecting the book because she could not detect or tolerate modernist play with the conventions of realist prose, her comments seemed to say. Rather, she was rejecting the book because it employed literary devices to excess and thumbed its nose at the average reader. Her report seemed to be written with a knowing glance over the shoulder at certain imagined critical authorities who might condemn the club for its literary conservatism. I was struck again and again by the fact that editors like Jill Sansone were wholly aware of how others might evaluate the literary books they were reading. They were aware that modernist and postmodernist fiction was generally valorized in the world of reviews and journals. They knew that, for the most part, realism was considered suspect, if not entirely bankrupt. To a certain extent the editors themselves also accepted the modernist premise that literary writing should be self-consciously *about* writing, whatever its pretensions to other stories or ends. The Book-of-the-Month Club editors tended to assume, therefore, that literary language should be taut, spare, economical, and yet highly original, and they assumed that it should call attention to itself and to its generative artifice.[21] The editors frequently pointed to the particularly effective use of formal devices in the manuscripts they read.

But, as Sansone's report also suggests, they were willing to tolerate only so much self-conscious highlighting of the artist's own dexterity and talent. An overload of literary language, no matter how deft and original, tipped the balance for them, producing a work that merely promoted the writer at the expense of what he or she intended to reveal or to say. Too much self-involved verbal cleverness worked to rebuff readers, they seemed to believe, refused to court their interests, and failed to attend to their desire for meaning and understanding. Readerly engagement, in such cases, could only deteriorate into tedious labor, frustrated incomprehension, and, more often than not, anger at the author's pose of superiority and command. Here, for instance, is Marty Asher's complete commentary on another novel by another well-regarded literary writer: "Now I can join my colleagues from around the country, from all walks of life, of all ages and say 'I tried to read a[n X] novel.' I got to page four. I'm willing to grant that it's very profound and meaningful because I didn't understand a word of it. Ten years ago I probably would have read 40 pages before coming to this same conclusion. But I'm getting on and life is too short for these intellectual indulgences anymore. Know what I mean? Can I go now?"[22]

Asher underscored his impatience with this novel by typing the word "Incomprehensible" after the report form's question "Did you enjoy reading it?" Where others might have discovered the pleasures of intellectual challenge in tracing the text's intricate metaphorical and metacritical commentary on its own construction, Asher found only impenetrable prose. Significantly, his aside, "Can I go now?" which effectively evoked the presence of the authoritarian English teacher, suggested that the reading experience was made even more unpleasant by his awareness that unnamed authorities had already anointed this writer a "literary author" and, as such, someone to be reckoned with. Asher was aware, obviously, that he ought to like this writer. However, by invoking the discomfiture of a squirming student itching only to escape a boring and wearisome exercise that had been designed for his own good, he also likened the book and its writer to ponderous adults who insist that they know the only right way to read. The very brevity of his report itself marked his defiance of those grown-up authorities and his willingness to assert the validity of his own demand that literary language not only give way almost immediately to readerly effort but that it offer particular insights and singular pleasures.

I cheered mentally, I have to confess, at Asher's refusal to be so disciplined. I loved the fact that he could defend the validity of other ways of reading. Although I was disconcerted by my reaction at the time, I did not think to pursue the reasons why I identified with his imaginary student rather than with the English teacher I was much closer to in daily life. Nor did I think in sustained fashion about why the "too-literary" generated so much anger. In any case, after encountering the reports by Mabry, Sansone, and Asher, I concluded that literary writing was judged a failure at the Book-of-the-Month Club when the editors thought that the labor it required of the reader would not pay off in terms of engagement or pleasure. Although the editors themselves were quite willing to work at the process of interpretation and were fully capable of understanding why any given writer had decided to use a certain narrative point of view, a certain trope, or a particular set of allusions, they demanded that those devices convey something more to the reader. Those devices, they believed, should do something other than simply call attention to themselves. In short, they ought to communicate in a significant way with the reader. And the reader, it appeared, ought to find some sort of pleasure or reward in that communion. The pleasure to be found was apparently not the cognitive pleasure of solving a difficult puzzle or following the trail of a difficult argument. Nor was it the pleasure of achieving critical and analytical distance on one's familiar world. Rather, this pleasure appeared to be more emotional and absorbing; it seemed to have something to do with the affective delights of transport, travel, and vicarious social interaction. Story and the traditional unities of plot and character seemed to figure centrally, still, to the kind of reading experience envisioned at the Book-of-the-Month Club as the goal of its general readers, even when those readers were selecting serious or literary fiction.[23]

One of Joe Savago's characteristically expansive reports articulated most clearly what the editors thought those traditional unities did for their general readers. His report rendered explicit the editors' unarticulated theory about why their subscribers read fiction in the first place. The particular report in question was helpful because Joe found the decision about Nadine Gordimer's *A Sport of Nature* such a hard one to call. It took him three pages to make his way through the various arguments both for and against the book.[24] Although he eventually recommended that the club buy the book as a main selection, he made it clear that he was not at all sure the book would satisfy the majority of the club's membership. Its particular kind of literariness almost disqualified it in his mind.

Specifically, Joe's report confirmed that a literary book must prove amenable to a certain kind of reading protocol. It must also produce a certain kind of reading experience. And it must provide a certain obvious meaningfulness as well as an opportunity for the reader to respond actively to the process of discovering that meaning. Despite the clarity of these propositions, however, the complexity of Joe's argument in this case suggested that the business of determining the boundary between a work whose literary properties would render it interesting to trained critics and a work, on the other hand, that would enable "the lay reader" to take pleasure from the very process of making her or his way through its pages and prose was difficult indeed.[25]

Because Joe's report focused so intently on the borderline status of *A Sport of Nature*, he was able to delineate with notable precision what he thought the novel would need if it was to garner something other than Gordimer's small, specialized, literary audience and thereby become her "break-out book." A break-out book, I was told later, was one that managed to test the limits of the usual category to which the writer's work was assigned, one that therefore appealed to a larger, more diversified audience with a less specialized taste. A literary break-out book succeeded in appealing to more readers, the editors suggested, when its literary excellence was tempered by the presence of features usually associated with more commercial fiction.[26] Joe's report suggested that the outer limits of the literary as a usable category of fiction at the Book-of-the-Month Club were determined by the countervailing pull associated with the demands of the average, general reader. And those demands, he made it clear, were bound up with the desire to indulge in a reading event that could supply specific pleasures.

Joe opened his report by establishing, first, that the success of literary break-out books was usually a function of context, at least to a certain degree. Some books managed to capture the concerns of a specific historical moment with particular urgency. "It's impossible to describe the story-line of this new Nadine Gordimer novel without making it sound like a real Break Out book," he wrote, "a possibility in which circumstances could not better conspire. Here's South Africa in the news everyday, and a slew of South Africa books, fiction and nonfiction, published every season, none of them hitting, none of them emerging as the South Africa book." Joe continued, "And here's Nadine Gordimer, easily the most distinguished South Africa writer, producing what surely sounds like her most commercial novel ever, a book with the plot and the shape of a Krantz, a Taylor Bradford."[27] Joe clearly assumed that "serious readers" turned to fiction in order to acquire familiarity with topical issues and current events. They read fiction as a way of thinking about key issues in their world and in their personal lives.

A certain kind of plot, Joe's report further implied, was apparently the second key ingredient if a literary book was to break away from its usual niche audience. By venturing onto this ground, he suggested, Gordimer had written a novel that could very well make a bid for popular success. After two drawn-out paragraphs enumerating the long list of improbable events that constituted the narrative bones of Gordimer's sensational story, he pronounced conclusively, "That's the trajectory of this novel, and in outline like that, it's pretty damn commercial—. . . a Sensuous, Arresting Woman Finding Her Way, Through Sexual Feeling, to Politics and Her Destiny." In addition to topicality, the literary break-out book needed to exhibit a tendency to rely on a repertoire of familiar formulas, traditional storylines that combined sex and power, portent, and resolution. Much as children love to hear beloved fairy tales told and retold, book club subscribers, the editors believed, also longed for the comfort of twice-told tales. Traditional story lines could not be present as formal features only; they also had to provide a particular sense of recognition for the reader, a sense of being immersed in a comprehensible world.

Joe presented Gordimer's handling of these formulas as a potential problem. Her mode of narration, which he termed "relentlessly intelligent," failed to provide what he took to be another necessary ingredient in highly successful fiction, a capacity to engross the reader completely, to engage her or his attentions fully. "The problem with this book," Joe continued, "from a commercial point of view, is that it does not convey its conventionally full-blooded, saga-esque, 'commercial' story in a conventionally realistic, full-blooded way." He continued, "The writing here is supremely intelligent but also elliptical, almost telegraphic—more, at times, an outline of a story, with notes and comments by the author, than a traditionally 'absorbing novel.' Gordimer throws no sops to the reader who wants, in a traditional way, to get 'lost' in her novel." Although he added that this kind of "brilliant" narration would be "very satisfying to a more sophisticated reader of fiction who doesn't demand 'absorption,'" Joe suggested that most leisure readers of serious fiction turn to the genre precisely to be immersed in a tale with its own sensuous weight and atmosphere. What they seek in their books is what he called "full-bloodedness," apparently a corporeal density and texture that enables readers to inhabit lives vicariously as if wholly abstracted from their own. Gordimer's novel could not provide this sort of pleasure for its reader because it was too distant, according to Joe, too intellectualized, and too cerebral, an ideational exercise alone.

As if this were not enough, Joe concluded his report with one final observation about another problem in Gordimer's literary treatment of her subject. He noted that the book might also disappoint its reader because it refused to provide yet another expected feature in successful popular fiction: it failed to instruct the reader even as it provided conventional delight. Joe seemed to suggest that Gordimer's highly intellectual approach to key issues in the book might be palatable if that book delivered another form of satisfaction traditionally associated with more commercial fiction. He worried, however, that it did not. "Reference is made to such events as Sharpeville, to the rise and fall of the African National Congress' fortunes, the rise of the Black Consciousness movement—indeed, Hillela's life revolves around the innumerable shifts in policy of the various resistance and liberation groups. But no effort has been made to expatiate, to lay-it-all-out in a Micheneresque fashion, so that one can 'learn' history even as one follows Hillela's fortunes." In Joe's mind, apparently, the typical lay reader would pick up a book of serious fiction, in part, to learn. Gordimer's novel worried him because it refused to detail that distant world and its determining history and events with the full sentience and attention to particular detail that would make it live for the curious reader. He worried that, far from immersing that reader in a strange world in order to persuade him or her of its pressing significance, Gordimer's distant treatment would produce only alienation, incomprehension, and resentment on the part of that lay reader.

After such a long disquisition on the limitations of the novel as a commercial possibility, it was a shock to arrive at Joe's contradictory yet decisive recommendation. His final two sentences ignored the negative case he had just set forward, abruptly wheeled, turned, and advised authoritatively, "We must own this, of course. To the judges." In this case the combination of the book's excellence, the writer's literary stature, and the obvious topicality of Gordimer's subject was enough to override Joe's clear sense that this book would very likely not please all of the club's lay readers. He could recommend Gordimer's book despite its refusal to subordinate itself to its putative reader precisely because the club understood its mission as one of balancing distinct and contradictory goals. Gordimer's novel could be judged a clear fit because the club was so invested in reconciling competing pressures, in resolving the tension between culture and economy, the literary and the commercial.

In concluding so confidently, "We must own this," after having laid out the many ways in which Gordimer refused to bow to her readers, Joe acknowledged her undisputed standing in the realm of contemporary letters and in world politics. However, in describing the club's necessary response to that stature as a move to "own" the book rather than a move to "offer" it to their readers, Joe inadvertently testified to the status of the club as a corporation defined by its own property, by the cultural capital it had amassed as the book club of record, as the proponent of readable yet literary fiction. Joe knew, finally, as did his colleagues, that even though the club might not be able to assemble a larger audience for Gordimer than she usually enjoyed, the critical acclaim her book would almost certainly enjoy would undoubtedly reflect back on the club itself and add to its reputation. Even if they had to pay dearly for the book club rights to such a manuscript, they conceived of this outlay as a long-term investment in the cultural status of the organization.

It might be said, finally, that the category of literary fiction was treated in two quite distinct ways at the Book-of-the-Month Club. On one hand, the editors treated it as a high-class sort of loss leader. Books within the category might not make money immediately, but in the long term they might contribute to the ongoing construction of the club's literary and cultural authority by standing as evidence of the club's dedication to its mission. Obviously literary selections might spur future spending by a membership persuaded of the club's ability to offer only the best. On the other hand, the editors also approached literary fiction pragmatically as one category of reading material among many. Accordingly, they measured submissions in this category with an eye toward the skill with which the author managed to address preconstituted desires and demands of readers. In dealing with literary fiction in this manner, the editors subordinated its usual status as a sign of the transcendent to its function as a device for providing education, self-reflection, the comfort of familiar truths, and the pleasures of imaginative absorption. In effect they treated literary fiction exactly as they treated cookbooks, reference books, gardening and self-help books, popular history books, and even those lavish volumes of photographs known in the trade as coffee-table books.

### SERVING THE SUBSCRIBER:

### THE GOOD COMMERCIAL BOOK

As the reader's reports piled up on my desk throughout the fall of 1986, I found it harder and harder to ignore the fact that, for the most part, the editors at the Book-of-the-Month Club conducted their business with their subscribers in mind. No matter how much they asserted, as Bill had, that their first allegiance was to the book itself, or how insistently they proved themselves to be preoccupied with the worth of the literary, they went about their daily business of reading most manuscripts by looking for those that would appeal to club members. This is to say, of course, that, in the end, despite the editors' absorption in the club's higher, literary mission, the organization was, finally, a business. More to the point, because the club was a consumer-oriented business, daily operations were structured fundamentally by the need to take account of both book buying and book reading. Since the organization was explicitly designed to prompt the act of purchase, the editors recognized that they needed to predict what sort of individual might want to buy the particular manuscript they were reading. At the same time, because they assumed that most book buyers were also book readers, they knew they had to imagine what a potential reader might be looking for in such a book. The very fact that they were constructing a mail-order catalog for a diverse range

{ *In the Service of the General Reader* }

of individuals necessitated tacit privileging of the multiple uses to which books could be put, which included simple ownership, display, gift giving, and, finally, different ways of reading.

A good commercial book was defined at the Book-of-the-Month Club as a volume that effectively met the preconstituted needs of the club's subscribers. The editors insisted, however, that a book must do this not merely willingly but responsibly and with considerable skill. The editors believed that books in virtually all genres sold in large numbers because they provided buyers with something they desired *and* because they managed to do so with striking originality, particular thoroughness, or unusual dedication. In according a certain priority to buyers, readers, and their interests, the club's day-to-day operating procedures construed editorial judgment itself less as a pedagogical mission of cultural uplift and more as a service activity in which the editor read on behalf of subscribers. The key assumption guiding editorial judgment in this representative mode was the notion that people bought books because they hoped to accomplish concrete goals through their purchase and through their reading. Here, for instance, are Phyllis Robinson's reflections on a dog training manual:

> Sound, sensible, and sprightly. What more can you ask from a guide to choosing and raising a dog? I like the way this book is organized. It begins by asking the prospective owner to consider what he wants in a dog and then goes on to discuss the physical, temperamental and behavior characteristics of various breeds. I can't think of a more helpful way to begin than by trying to match the individual's or family's needs with the dog's capacity to meet those needs. You want a quiet dog? Then don't get a terrier. . . . Often [the author] sounded so much like Gesell I wasn't sure whether I was reading about dogs or children! . . . This is certainly the book I'd turn to if I were shopping for another dog. It isn't cute, the author is not an unforgettable character. The advice is practical and solid and the emphasis is where it ought to be, on the dog.[28]

Clearly drawing on her past experience, Robinson imagined a potential buyer for the book in question. She conjured the image of an individual or family about to make the decision to purchase a dog and evaluated how well the manuscript under consideration addressed their needs. She judged the organization of the book sensible and solid and suggested that the information it provided was practical and, above all, usable. It should be pointed out here that she was actually matching her own sense of how potential dog buyers operate against the founding premise of the book itself. Because the two analyses matched in this case—she *could* imagine a family going about the decision in this deliberative, calculated, and very bookish way—she felt sure club subscribers would find much to like in the volume. Her judgment underscored the book's success at fulfilling the goals it had set for itself, and it suggested that the particular goals chosen by the writer were grounded in an accurate projection of the likely audience for the book. In effect Robinson's evaluative practice began with a form of social analysis rather than with the abstract assertion of certain critical principles.

All of the club editors tended to reject books when they felt that the writer in question had made a fundamental miscalculation about the potential buyer or reader. Although their reports suggested that they tried to evaluate a book "on its own terms," if they felt that those terms were at odds with what a buyer or reader would bring to the book, they recommended rejection. Evaluation was pegged very closely to a prior assessment of both buyer behavior and reader expectations. Here, for instance, are the comments of outside reader Dorothy Parker on a book attempting to combine two traditional genres: "[A] kind—of book that I almost always find displeasing for the reason that it is apt to be neither one thing nor another of its titular promises: neither a travel book nor a cookbook properly speaking. As a travel book, [X] is extremely flimsy, very little more than a sort of road map with accompanying notes: as a cookbook it is similarly sparse, frail, superficial, unadventurous, filled with the clichés of what people think of as Mexican cookery and very little else."[29] Like Phyllis Robinson, Parker tried to imagine the sort of people who might find such a book attractive. In the end, however, the portraits she drew proved unconvincing. She simply could not conjure the image of an audience that might need just this book. She continued:

Perhaps I'm being overly harsh: an American traveler who doesn't at all know that tragic land . . . and wants to know whether to turn right or left on the road from here to there might find it useful, though why such a traveler doesn't equip herself (or himself) with some other and better book I could not be brought to understand. And if an American home cook who knew nothing about these styles suddenly were seized with a desire to lay her hands on some basic recipes, well, here they are—but so also would she discover them in a hundred and one other sources, along with much else not contained in this book. Try as I might I can find no virtues here: the book doesn't offend so much as it leaves one deeply dissatisfied; and if it doesn't offend it's largely because it doesn't say anything worth saying. . . . Guides produced by the motor clubs are more useful to travelers than this, and innumerable other books and pamphlets provide a vastly more abundant introduction to the foods of Mexico. In sum, I'm afraid that try as I may I can find no significant virtues here.

Parker was saying that she could not imagine how the club would successfully match the features and characteristics of this particular book with the interests potential buyers would likely bring to their reading of the relevant catalog copy. Hers was at once a buyer- and reader-oriented view of the book she was evaluating even though she clearly made a serious effort to accept the book on its own terms. The book's terms, she suggested, were just not striking or unusual enough to prompt subscribers to buy it or to read it.

The editors knew that on occasion a book could do just that. As people deeply interested in books themselves, they recognized that they had often wandered into bookstores with no particular needs or aims in mind, picked up a particularly handsome volume or a peculiarly titled tome, and impulsively decided to buy it. In a situation like that, the book's presentation and execution had been forceful enough to create a desire, if not a need, that had not existed before. Parker herself implicitly recognized this possibility when she noted, "Even its appearance is impoverished: it's got up to look like an elementary textbook for the middle grades, and that, it seems to me, is a very poor inducement to anybody to lift the book off the rack." Even if she had wanted to override her own theories about why people tend to buy travel books or cookbooks, she could find nothing in this particular volume's layout, format, or conceptualization to justify the attempt to create an audience for it. In the end Parker ranked the book "poor" and flatly recommended against any further consideration.

It is worth comparing her judgment in this case with her reasoning and recommendation with respect to another unconventional volume, *Southern Food: At Home, on the Road, in History*, written by John Egerton.[30] Neither a standard cookbook nor a food memoir exactly, it was, according to Parker, "a gastronomical history of the American South." She further noted that "here is an attractive book, both an ambitiously researched account of the origins and vicissitudes of the cooking of the South and a popular ethnography and demography of the region." It also included a tour of restaurants and cooking establishments throughout the South that serve "down-home, traditional Southern dishes." Before elaborating any further, however, about the book's particular merits or demerits, she launched into the familiar and required meditation about audience. "You know better than I," she reported to the editors, "how large is the public enamored of all things to do with food, and not only with its preparation and consumption." She continued, "Perhaps publics, for I believe they run the gamut from readers of the late, irreplaceable Waverly Root, to the Annales 'school' of French historiography to Yale anthropologist Sidney Mintz's recent book on sugar—any attempt to see the world from the perspective of food. Though done with an entirely appropriate light touch that makes it all the more likely to reach a wider-than-expected audience, this is legitimate social history that can't be treated with condescension by academic historians."

Here Parker was constructing an image of the kind of potential buyer who might find this book intriguing. Not someone searching for recipes only, but an individual interested in the historical and social background of food traditions. As she put it, "This is a bookbook, not a cookbook—a book meant for *reading* (fancy that!) from beginning to end, it also contains recipes for dishes that bid fair to define what people usually mean when they speak of Southern cooking." The kind of familiar dishes that were dismissed as mere clichés and stereotypes of Mexican cooking in the previous volume were redeemed by their more literary treatment within a book that was defined by its own strong overall conceptualization and framework. Parker felt sure that the combination of the book's strengths would attract people like herself who would be fascinated by this total approach to food. She concluded, "And to make this wholly agreeable book still more so—and still more useful as a reference work, Egerton included a generous anthology by a host of writers (some 200 of them) on various aspects of Southern food and cooking. . . . This is a commendable book which I read straight through from beginning to end, skipping nothing, with lively interest and great pleasure. Strongly recommended."

As I encountered more and more reports like this one, it seemed increasingly clear that the search for good commercial books at the Book-of-the-Month Club was driven by the desire to find books that would readily appeal to a substantial group of potential buyers with particular needs, desires, and reading habits. Disinclined to judge those habits negatively or to try to change them, the editors and the outside readers worked hard to intuit what their subscribers' typical book buying and reading habits might be. They had to function as cultural analysts of book buying and reading behavior as much as they had to work as reviewers of particular titles. At the same time, however, the editors labored intensively to articulate for themselves what each author and manuscript attempted. But they did so always in the service of evaluating whether any given book addressed the expectations that their subscribers would likely bring to the catalog as a whole. Because the editors considered those expectations both predictable and essential to address, they worked hard to balance each monthly catalog in such a way that it would include the best new works in categories tried and true. In some cases the editors considered the categories so important to fill that commercial need overrode an individual editor's better judgment. Because they knew, for instance, that there were always people in the market for dog books, they aimed to offer at least one such title in every monthly catalog.

This imperative produced reasoning like that exhibited here in Elizabeth Easton's review of another dog book:

> There will no doubt be some engaging photographs of dogs . . . and I suspect a lot of color for $29.95—probably a very handsome book. It is quite a plug for the American Kennel Club, and there are chapters on the various groups of dogs. . . . Anyway, I'm somewhat ambivalent about this: I wouldn't buy it myself, but then I'm not probably a dog fancier. If I bought a dog book, I'd rather have something practical like GOOD DOG, BAD DOG. I suspect this boils down to whether or not we need a big dog book now, and how they have done in the past. . . . I'm not thrilled about this, but if we need a big dog book I guess it's all right.[31]

Had she been asked to evaluate the book in the abstract, Easton would likely have pointed to its particular combination of failings and irrelevancies and simply recommended rejection. However, because she knew that the monthly catalog was crying out to be filled, she made a more contingent judgment, suggesting pragmatically that the book would do well enough. Because she and her colleagues knew that dog books always succeeded with their membership, they were more favorably disposed to this volume than they might otherwise have been. Although they insisted that they would never buy a book they thought was truly bad, especially if the information provided was not up to their standards, the editors admitted that sometimes it was necessary to ignore reservations about mediocre books if they found themselves without a sufficient quantity of pet handbooks, say, or cookbooks or medical reference volumes. Thus did the club's commercial charter and its corollary respect for buyer demands operate to structure the evaluation process as a whole.

I should note here that in discussing "use books," a term frequently applied to intentionally commercial volumes of nonfiction aimed at specific audience needs, the editors also always asked themselves whether the book in question could be described successfully in brief catalog copy. In mail-order sales, the editors explained to me, books needed "handles," short conceptual tags that could be used to type a book quickly, to describe its probable use, and to identify its likely audience. Since their subscribers could not hold a book, leaf through its pages, muse over its contents, or generally weigh its costs against its evident qualities, Joe observed, they had to rely heavily on the copywriters' ability to convey this information in print and pictures. In most cases the *Book-of-the-Month Club News* could provide only a paragraph or two of description and a miniature reproduction of the book's cover as a way of giving the potential buyer information about the book's material character. It was imperative, therefore, that the book be "describable." The editors' observations with respect to this issue suggested clearly that the limitations of the catalog as a selling tool inevitably worked against idiosyncratic volumes that might attempt to defy familiar generic boundaries. Although a really surprising, very original volume could be sold successfully if the club was willing to commit out-of-the-ordinary resources to its presentation, more often than not the editors noted simply that the book could not be easily sold. They regretfully declined to buy the manuscript in question. Joe, Jill, Marty, and Robert told me repeatedly that books that did well in the trade often did not do well for the Book-of-the-Month Club. And that, they insisted, had everything to do with the fact that some books could be described simply and quickly while others could not.

## A BOOK IS MEANT TO BE READ

After weeks of taking notes about the treatment of commercial books at the Book-of-the-Month Club, it seemed clear to me that because the organization's primary aim was to find buyers for books, the editors understandably tended to select those that successfully demarcated a potential audience and presented themselves as volumes with an identifiable function and an easily described content. To a large extent buyer expectations were taken seriously at the club. However, the editors were not comfortable thinking of themselves only as booksellers. Most of the time they assumed that the buyers they were appealing to were also book readers. They thought carefully about the act of reading itself and about the many reasons people took up books in the first place. In their minds, books were meant to be read. Bookselling was a necessary precondition to reading. However, a desire to profit from a book's sale should not be the only reason for a book's existence. The importance of this assumption at the

{ *In the Service of the General Reader* }

Book-of-the-Month Club was made clear to me by the recurrent use of the word "crass" in reviews rejecting books that were too obviously commercial. When the editors used this term, they seemed to mean that the book in question had been too obviously designed as a moneymaker rather than as a legitimate volume providing a legitimate service for readers. Editor Pat Adrian described this sort of creation as "a book that is only an excuse for a book, that has flashy photographs, weak text, beautiful artwork. They're nonbooks, and they offend me." [32]

The editors encountered a perfect example of this sort of volume when they received a manuscript titled *The Rock Poster*. This elaborate book of full-color reproductions of ads for concerts and artists had been priced by its publisher at $85.00. It elicited nothing but laughter, however, when it was brought to the editorial table. In fact, very little was said about the book itself. The editors simply did not feel it was necessary to take the volume seriously. In reporting the results of the discussion in the weekly meeting report issued the next day, editor Jill Sansone wrote matter-of-factly, "There's just about every poster ever made in this $85.00 book; no." [33] The peremptory nature of the dismissal in this case suggested that a book was considered too crass for the Book-of-the-Month Club if it foregrounded too obviously its commercial function for its producers over and above the satisfactions it might conceivably provide for readers. The editors laughed uproariously at the ridiculous assumption that anyone might be willing to shell out close to $100 for a collection of reproductions of old rock posters.

Not surprisingly, the editors rejected another volume for virtually identical reasons. Titled simply *Coca Cola*, this particular book was a pictorial history of Coke advertising that had been beautifully produced by the corporation itself. The editors concluded quickly that they could not offer the book without appearing to plug the product. As Sansone summed it up in her report, "This book in BOM would be like an endorsement of the Real Thing. Handsome, fascinating, but we'll pass." [34] In this case the book conveyed too obviously what it was—a company-produced, promotional device.

The Book-of-the-Month Club editors' treatment of too-commercial books accorded well with their tendency to justify the business end of the operation by emphasizing what they thought of as their literary or cultural mission. They recognized pragmatically that they were in the business of selling books, yet they wanted to believe that, for the most part, people bought books because they wanted to read them and that they wanted to read them because they had particular objectives in mind. The editors were happy to oblige by searching for volumes that would fill those goals not only adequately but with a certain proficiency and skill. However, the editors would reject books that might prove to be commercial successes *if* those books foregrounded too crudely their status as commodities for sale on the market. They demanded that books declare their status as "literacy" objects, that is, as objects rendered special by the fact that they were designed to be read. As a consequence, such books had to display qualities conventionally associated with readability. Even commercial books meant primarily for display or gift giving had to exhibit the signs of the literary in the sense that they had to prove themselves obviously well conceived and well made. They had to call attention to the organizing intention behind them, the intention responsible for unifying their disparate parts.

All books at the Book-of-the-Month Club had to present themselves to the editors as "bookbooks." They had to call attention to their status as material objects unified organically by a singular purpose and organized seamlessly to accomplish a goal other than the one of generating a financial profit for those who had contributed to their production. Evident signs of actual authorship were very important, therefore. Such signs had to demonstrate persuasively that the book in question was a coherently crafted text rather than an automatically assembled, manufactured, machine-tooled object. However, those authorial signs also had to declare that "here is an author aiming to speak directly and distinctly to readers." Signs of authorship at the Book-of-the-Month Club conferred literary status, it is true, but they also always implied the necessity and inevitability of reading. A real book, according to the editors, was an object that called attention equally to its author and to its reader.

A review by Dorothy Parker once again effectively illustrates the importance of evidence of authorial craftsmanship at the Book-of-the-Month Club:

> The book at hand arouses longstanding negative biases in me: the imprint is that of a hustling house—more a marketing enterprise than anything else—whose list is pretty well known to me, as I'm sure it is to you. Moreover, I must say I'm deeply suspicious . . . of such slapdash, thin, random, sprawling, global anthologies. By this awkward term I mean simply the kind of book which marks off a quarter of the world . . . and goes on to paste up some samples of each, and thereby patch together a book. It's my idea of a book-like non-book, a pseudo-book, which afflicts the field of cookbooks with a chunk of merchandise that is

likely to disappear as suddenly as it appeared in the first place. Another "bright" idea blown away on the gusty wind of the next "bright" idea.[35]

What Parker wanted was not a miscellany assembled opportunistically from already available parts, but a volume woven seamlessly of the same thread and according to a singular, striking design. She expected that design, furthermore, to present itself as the emanation of a strong, imaginative author, a controlling intelligence aiming, above all, to communicate his or her thoughts to receptive readers.

Close to halfway through my year in the club's offices, as I encountered this reader's report and others like it, I was struck again by the persistent effects of the meaning attached to the literary. The editors seemed to require that even the commercial use-book, the meat and potatoes of the Book-of-the-Month Club's consumer-oriented operation, present itself as something other than mere merchandise alone. They demanded that books otherwise designed to be functional and to appeal to as many buyers as possible additionally exhibit signs that they had been created in a manner continuous with the highly valorized process of artistic or literary creation. Editorial expectations required that such books display the fact that they had been brought into being at the behest of a singular author who had been driven by a strong, organizing intention as well as by a foundational desire to be read by others. Books like these could admit to their status as instrumental manuals or practical guides to the accomplishment of mundane tasks and thereby highlight their orientation to reader demands. But they additionally had to mark themselves as book-books, that is, as texts that might also provide a form of readerly pleasure tied to the nature of their performance precisely as linguistic and literary acts. Commercial use-books were ennobled, finally, by their "good writing" and thus by their demonstrated connection, however tenuous, with the tools, strategies, and aims of education and art.

Robert Riger best captured this understanding of the intricate relation between commerce and culture as it was enforced at the Book-of-the-Month Club when he referred to the organization's typical product as "cultural furniture."[36] Although his phrase admitted that books were conceived at the club as functional objects, much like tables and chairs, it also revealed that books could not exist as material objects only. Because books were composed from language and were the creations of authors, and because language itself was inherently communicative, they were conceived specifically as objects-to-be-read, as tools ready to hand. Their object-status was redeemed by their connection to a higher purpose, the purpose of imparting at least the vestiges of instruction, education, and enlightenment to readers with a longing for something beyond the merely mundane. Nonetheless, such books were expected to serve their readers well. Books at the Book-of-the-Month Club, finally, had to present themselves as useful *and* they had to display the signs of having been marked by the transcendence associated with the literary and the cultural. They had to call attention to the fact that they were well written.

It is important to stress that evaluation and selection at the Book-of-the-Month Club were processes driven not by a simple hierarchy of value, with the literary and cultural placed always above the instrumental or the commercial. Had that been the case, the most literary book would have been the most highly valorized and the most frequently selected. Nor was the club governed solely by its privileging of reader expectations and desires. Were that the case, the editors would have weighed only the functionality of each particular volume and selected those that gave way most transparently before reader demand. Rather, these endlessly complex negotiations over the value of literary excellence and the need for commercial success suggest that evaluation and selection were guided at the club by the intersection of two axes of value. One axis measured the success of the writerly act of creation; it measured literary achievement according to preestablished aesthetic norms. The other axis measured a book's capacity to satisfy its readers' practical demands. Both axes, however, were equally essential to the definition of the operation. The editors' role was to calibrate the precise nature of the equation between these two forms of value with respect to every manuscript that crossed their desks.

Whereas the literary erred at the Book-of-the-Month Club by failing to make its transcendent insights accessible to the reader, the commercial erred most substantially when it spoke plainly and functionally to the reader but only of mundane things and, particularly, of debased monetary profit. The club's entire selection process was engineered to ensure that the one would be weighed against the other, that the reader's pragmatic needs would be balanced against authors' capacities to offer singular insight through the medium of a carefully tooled, heavily worked writing. Al Silverman's statement, I understood finally, had captured the peculiar nature of the club's operation. It was very much a business, but a business driven very much by a mission.

As the complexity and the richness of the Book-of-the-Month Club reader's reports—on everything from cookbooks to coffee-table books, from volumes of photography to literary biography—revealed to me the complicated and involved nature of the negotiations surrounding the selection of all volumes to be presented in the catalog, I understood better why the level of anxiety at the club was so high. A great deal was at stake. Not only were individuals' jobs on the line as a consequence of the management restructuring. So, too, was the very definition of the club itself as an institutional intermediary between readers and writers. If Time demanded that the club show a higher profit level or push its membership beyond the million mark where it had been stabilized for so long, the editors might well be asked to forgo their insistent demand that all books, even use-books and commercial fiction, be well written, that is, with a certain level of linguistic complexity and self-consciousness. And if they subordinated their consequent interest in literary excellence to reader demands, not only would most of them find the job less justifiable and less interesting, but so, too, would they abandon the constitutive mission of the Book-of-the-Month Club. The editors all understood this, although they perhaps would have explained it in a somewhat different language. However they articulated their concern, though, that concern intensified as autumn deepened into winter and change seemed to accelerate at the Book-of-the-Month Club.

## CHAPTER THREE

# The Intelligent Generalist
# and the Uses of Reading

MERGERS, MID-LIST BOOKS, AND GENERAL READERS

From September to February the editors reacted with alarm every time a new memo arrived from Larry Crutcher's office announcing another managerial addition to the Book-of-the-Month Club staff. The editorial group greeted each new employee with suspicion and regarded them all with a wary eye. Treated less as colleagues than as interlopers from outside, these individuals were considered harbingers of momentous change visited upon the club by alien forces. The threat they posed seemed to have little to do with Larry Crutcher's actual impact on the editorial operation. In fact, he proceeded cautiously. As far as I could see, book selection procedures remained largely intact throughout the fall and into the winter of 1986–87 and for some time thereafter. But the perception that things were changing fast persisted and even intensified as chill winds blew through the midtown canyons of the publishing industry. The internal changes at the Book-of-the-Month Club offices looked so ominous in part because they appeared to be mirrored by equally threatening changes within the industry at large.

In the preceding eighteen months or so, ten or more U.S. book firms had been sold or had merged with large publishing conglomerates. Perceived within the trade as a new wave of concentration following hard on the last merger trend that had played itself out in the 1970s, this shift in ownership occasioned particularly intense fear because so many of the transactions involved the union of U.S. houses with European and international conglomerates.[1] Two deals in particular generated anxious conversation and apprehensive speculation about the impact these changes might have on the character of U.S. publishing. In June 1986 British Penguin bought both NAL and Dutton, suggesting that the British firm intended to control a vast segment of the American trade and paperback industry from London. Then, in September, the German publishing giant Bertelsmann announced that it would purchase Doubleday & Company for close to $500 million. Bertelsmann was willing to pay such a high price, many in the industry speculated, because Doubleday's holdings included the highly successful Literary Guild. U.S. executives reasoned that Bertelsmann obviously hoped to extend its dominance of the book club field in Germany to the international scene by buying Doubleday. Since little actual information about the German book group's intentions surfaced, however, in the weeks following the announcement, rumors coursed through the industry and down the corridors of the Book-of-the-Month Club. If Bertelsmann had so much cash to work with, might the company empower the Guild's editors to outbid the Book-of-the-Month Club for the best, most important trade manuscripts? If they did, how could the Book-of-the-Month Club manage to remain profitable? Would Time respond by taking the club down scale? Would the editors be asked to bid only on blockbusters and sure bestsellers? Questions like these were whispered over lunches and in the privacy of individual offices throughout the autumn months and into the winter.

The situation proved so unsettling that the club's management decided to address formally the potentially changed publishing environment almost immediately after the Bertelsmann announcement. Only a week after Al Silverman presented his mission statement to his editorial staff, he made another formal presentation to acquaint the editors with a new strategic plan designed to consolidate and build on the Book-of-the-Month Club's traditional strengths. Alluding quickly to the tense atmosphere that characterized both the club and the industry at large, Al opened the discussion by observing that "soon, we're going to be in a whole new ball game."[2] In explanation, he pointed specifically to the NAL takeover, to the Bertelsmann transaction, and to the Dayton-Hudson corporation's announced decision to divest itself of the B. Dalton bookstore chain. While he admitted that, together, these developments would almost certainly lead to direct challenges to the Book-of-the-Month Club's control of the book club rights field, he suggested that they would also indirectly affect the club's ability to find the books it most wanted and needed. Silverman insisted, however, that the Book-of-the-Month Club would continue to do what it had always done best. It would continue to seek out "serious books for the serious reader." He encouraged his editors repeatedly throughout his presentation to "keep finding those books *you* like doing even in the middle of this new game."

Despite his offer of encouragement, Al acknowledged what many editors had begun saying to me in the weeks immediately preceding this meeting. He noted that growing international concentration within the industry was making it harder for the club to find good, serious books for its subscribers. Because the new global industry structure and its attention to the financial bottom line apparently favored blockbuster books that appealed to extremely large, international audiences of occasional readers, he suggested that fewer and fewer trade houses were able to publish the reliable, more complex "mid-list" books that fit the club's priorities so well. As a consequence, the club intended to adhere to this new strategic plan in order to ensure that a supply of serious, mid-list books would continue to be available for selection and distribution to its subscribers.

Within the world of publishing I knew the term "mid-list" had been used for most of this century as a kind of marketing and aesthetic shorthand. It had been employed to designate books considered neither avantgarde nor merely commercial in their literary pretensions and neither mass market nor narrowly targeted in their distribution aims. A mid-list book was generally construed as a book of sound quality created for a moderately sized, fairly specific audience of committed readers. I was not surprised when Al characterized the Book-of-the-Month Club's offerings as mid-list, since within the industry the term was generally used approvingly. I was wary, though, about the validity of Al's reasoning that the new mergers would destroy mid-list books, since I knew that for most of this century publishing industry analysts had been predicting the imminent demise of the mid-list book. The appearance of the bestseller list; the invention of the book clubs themselves; the creation of cheap, glossy pocketbooks; and the rise of the bookstore chains had all been branded by critics as the death knell of the serious mid-list book in the United States. Although each of these developments certainly exerted a definite impact on the trade, none had managed to wipe out publishing's mid-list completely. I had just attended a seminar in New York organized by the Center for Book Research, in which several industry experts argued that the audience for mid-list books had remained constant over the course of the last forty years while the audience for bestsellers had continued to increase. I wondered why this prediction was ritually repeated both within the industry and at the Book-of-the-Month Club. What was it about the serious, mid-list book that was so important to the trade generally and to the club more specifically? Why the intensity of the investment in the mid-list book and in the serious readers who were pictured as the mid-list book's ideal audience? What fear was being expressed when their demise was envisioned as something just over the horizon? Why did the Book-of-the-Month Club's fate seem so inextricably tied to the health of both?

In laying out the first two of the three strategies the club intended to adopt in order to maintain its characteristic list and publishing niche, Al predictably suggested that the familiar blend of the literary and the commercial would continue to characterize the club's offerings. However, in pointing to a third strategic aim, he introduced a new theme by suggesting that the club would strive to maintain its faith in its readers "as educated generalists." The club's subscribers, Al explained further, were neither specialists nor uninformed. Rather, they were intelligent generalists looking for the kind of rewarding book that would inform them at the same time that it would capture their imagination and entertain them. At the Book-of-the-Month Club at least, mid-list books were apparently also defined by the fact that they were pitched to generalists.

The interaction between these familiar modifiers, that is, between the idea of the serious and the idea of the general, suddenly seemed much more important to me. Although the phrase "general reader" had cropped up before in my research, I had paid relatively little attention to it, thinking it demarcated an uncomplicated, easily understood referent. "General" seemed only a casual synonym for some notion of the average reader. The concept of the serious reader had appeared more complex—did "serious" refer to reading frequency or to a particular habit of mind? I had simply glossed over the fact that as often as they referred to their subscribers as serious readers, so, too, did the editors refer to them as generalists. At this point, however, because of the weight Al accorded the idea of the generalist, I began to wonder how the constant coupling between the serious and the general functioned at the club to map the features and the terrain of the middle range of books that the organization seemed to claim as its particular publishing province.

In schematically laying out the strategic plan, Silverman noted that the club's first strategy to counter the new emphasis on mass market blockbusters would be an increasing effort to create its own books. Drawing heavily on books moving out of copyright and into the public domain, the club would attempt to compete with the chains by offering to its members volumes they could not find in chain outlets. Al observed that because few mall bookstores maintained any sort of substantial backlist, they inevitably failed serious readers. They did so, he explained, because serious readers refused to be confined to the latest bestseller or to the volumes advertised on *Donahue* or *Oprah*. Rather, they read seriously, which is to say frequently, deliberately, and for certain specific purposes. As a consequence their range extended beyond those few books marketed to the extremely diverse group of readers known as the mass market. The club would consequently attempt to remarket books that had done well for it in the past and seek to issue new editions of certain well-known literary or trade classics for which there was a constant demand. In a sense, Al suggested, the club would try to operate like a small, idiosyncratic bookstore oriented to the tastes of people who read regularly and widely on a broad range of topics. The club would continue to try to reach people with enough education to know that they had always wanted to read Ernest Hemingway's *The Old Man and the Sea* or Rachel Carson's *Silent Spring*. The books they would initiate would offer their readers substance rather than fleeting fad or fashion.

As a second strategy designed to counterbalance the first, Silverman explained further that the club would also seek to meet the challenge of the Literary Guild and the chain bookstores by competing with them directly on their own ground. Club officials would increasingly attempt to preempt their competitors by buying the book club rights to future titles of highly successful authors. As an example he pointed to the recent multibook deal with author Stephen King and alluded to another, as-yet unannounced agreement with a blockbuster thriller writer usually featured by the Guild. Additionally the Book-of-the-Month Club would announce *before* publication date an upcoming main selection that they suspected would do well in the bookstores and thereby extend to their members the privilege of acquiring such a "big book" even before it appeared in the stores. This admitted decision to compete more aggressively with the powerful chains and the potentially better bankrolled Literary Guild confirmed that the club depended heavily on its most commercial offerings to subsidize the more modestly successful titles on its list. It could not afford to concede the field of bestsellers to its competitors. What the club aimed to do was to absorb the ever-increasing costs of playing in this high stakes field by acquiring its characteristic mid-range books at a much lower price.

At the same time that Al alluded to the role of commercial books in subsidizing the Book-of-the-Month Club list, in his citation of the third strategy the club planned to adopt he returned again to the central importance of less commercial, more serious books at the club. To satisfy their readers' quest for "challenging" and "informative" books, Silverman observed, the club would turn to academic presses, which, he confessed, they

{ *In the Service of the General Reader* }

had tended to ignore in the past. Because academic publishers did not expect to make large sums of money on every title they published, they could issue well-made books designed for smallish groups of interested, intelligent, well-informed readers, the kind of people who constituted the heavy buyers at the Book-of-the-Month Club. Silverman added that since many of these small, undercapitalized houses did not submit their manuscripts for consideration by the club, the organization would be making a substantial outreach effort in the future to inform academic presses about the kind of things the club liked to offer. Al concluded that it was his hope that the club could acquire the kind of "good" books it needed cheaply from these new institutional sources. "However," he cautioned—and he underscored that "however" with a marked pause—"we have to be careful since some of the books the academic presses turn out are much too specialized for us."

I was surprised by Al's suggestion that the club would be looking to university presses in the future. Until that point I had only heard the word "academic" used as an epithet. When I had asked some of the editors what they meant when they referred to something as "too academic," they had replied that they thought academic books generally "boring" and "dry." Al's expressed worry in this situation suggested additionally that those perceived qualities might themselves be a function of the highly specialized, technical character of academic books. In turning to university presses, he suggested, the editors would have to be wary of academic books written for a small coterie of technical experts. Books like these were written at such a level of specificity that they lost the attention of generalist readers who had no need for such technical information. General readers, he implied, were after something else. Al did not go on to elucidate what those general readers wanted, because his staff nodded in agreement when he cautioned them about the specificity of academic books. As far as they were concerned, they already knew what he was talking about.

In leaving the meeting, I thought back to some of my earlier conversations with the editors. Recalling that the idea of the generalist had come up before, I even paged through some of my field notes to see if I had recorded notes about this. In fact, when I had asked Larry Shapiro to describe a typical subscriber, he had responded with the observation that this individual is "a generalist like me."[3] Furthermore, in the very first interview I had conducted the previous summer, Joe Savago had observed, "That's who we always hypothesize . . . the general reader." When I prompted him to expand, he mused, "A smart person who isn't a literary person but is a book lover who . . . can be tempted to stretch beyond just X amount."[4] His comment had been made in the context of our discussion of a recent club selection, *House of the Spirits* by Isabel Allende, which the catalog had presented as "accessible magic realism," according to Joe. He went on to note that the copy in the *Book-of-the-Month-Club News* assured club members that "although it's going to be a little weird and a little fey, you can read it." He continued, "You don't need to be afraid of it. It'll be a little easier and a little less weird [than García Márquez] for you. It's a very honest presentation for a hypothesized general reader."[5]

Joe's phrasing, it was clear from my notes, was not uniquely his. The term "general reader" had obviously recurred frequently in my early discussions, just as it had now surfaced in Al's elaboration of the strategic plan. This reaffirmation of the general reader's importance took on added significance in the waning weeks of 1986 because the anxious atmosphere heightened the sense that this reader's days might be numbered. Despite my skepticism about the impending disappearance of mid-list books, I was willing to entertain this additional supposition about the fate of the general reader because I also discovered at this moment that the term had been used regularly by the club's founder, Harry Scherman. The general reader apparently was a historically specific sort of reader, someone the club was explicitly created to address.

My research agenda mutated again as the Christmas publishing season launched into high gear. Somewhat less focused on the balancing of the literary and the commercial at the club, I turned my attention to the precise ways in which notions of the serious, the general, and the middle range interacted with one another in the course of editorial deliberations. I began to think of the editors themselves as certain kinds of readers reading at the club on behalf of others whom they characterized as intelligent generalists. But who, I wondered, were they?

## A SENSE OF DEEPENING CRISIS

As the holidays approached, I thought it clear that the ongoing upheaval at the club was exacting a heavy emotional toll within the editorial ranks. Ironically, the disarray proved helpful as I set about trying to give imaginary form to the club's general reader. Editorial anxiety and fear inevitably gave rise to innuendo, rumor, and worried storytelling. The editors' shared narratives proved illuminating because within them the specter of other readers and other tastes, all thought to be beyond the purview of the Book-of-the-Month Club, loomed large. The endless speculation about what was happening to the club was helpful because it tended to give con-

{ *In the Service of the General Reader* }

crete shape to the fate the editors most feared, to the kinds of readers and taste they thought outside the mission of the Book-of-the-Month Club. Specifically, by repeatedly evoking the threat of a less committed, less diligent reader, the kind of individual they feared Time, Inc., meant to force on them, they began to give more substance and weight to the image of the educated, intelligent, general reader they so revered and with whom they identified. As this individual emerged more clearly amidst the crisis atmosphere at the club, I also became much more sensitive to the ways he or she was invoked within club reader's reports. Sometimes, though, I found it hard to concentrate on those reader's reports and on my quest for the general reader simply because daily events proved so startling.

On January 13, 1987, Al Silverman and Larry Crutcher announced the departure of twelve-year veteran Lorraine Shanley. Although this departure was presented as a resignation and as Lorraine's choice, the fact that the memo announcing her departure noted that "she plans to explore a myriad of possibilities" and "isn't sure where her search will take her" suggested to some of the editors that she might have been asked to resign.[6] Hardly had the group had time to worry about the potential consequences of Lorraine's departure, however, when another bombshell exploded in their midst. Two days later, at the regularly scheduled editorial meeting, Editor in Chief Nancy Evans strode deliberately, and uncharacteristically late, into the already assembled gathering. Speaking even before she sat down, she blurted out that "since there has been talk, I want to announce this right away." Her words produced a palpable dread around the table. Apparently I was not the only one taken by surprise. All of the editors in the room sat up straighter, held their breath and stared at Nancy. Evans continued, "Later today, it will be announced that I have been named to head Doubleday Publishing." She rushed on with details about her duties and expressed her great regret at leaving a place she loved, almost as if to forestall her colleagues' reaction. She need not have bothered. Her words were met with stunned silence. After an awkward, prolonged pause, editor Eve Tulipan sighed heavily and spoke directly to Nancy, "Well, it's wonderful for you but a disaster for us." The mood lightened only when one of the other editors quipped, "Do you speak German?" Everyone laughed with relief at the insiders' reference to the new relationship between Bertelsmann and Doubleday. The laughter alleviated the shock, but it did not do much to dispel the sense of gloom that immediately resettled about the room. It seemed clear that Bertelsmann had already made a move to displace the Book-of-the-Month Club.

Evans's announcement was termed a disaster by virtually all of the editors because they believed that her departure exposed them to the Time management at a key moment. She had been well respected for her ability to make commercial decisions about potential bestsellers without giving up the quest for truly good books. As one editor put it, "She runs very effective interference between the editorial staff and the people at Time." In subsequent conversations the editors worried aloud about who would control Evans's replacement. Although they knew corporate structure specified that this should be Al Silverman's responsibility, some felt certain that Larry Crutcher would make the decision. They were bothered as well by the fact that an obvious in-house replacement was not available. Although Joe Savago, as Nancy Evans's assistant, should have been the obvious choice, it was evident to everyone that Joe had grown very ill over the course of the fall. Often absent from editorial meetings, his struggle to maintain his health was clearly occupying more and more of his time. None of the other editors, everyone agreed, possessed the stature or commanded the status in the organization to replace Nancy.

Evans's impending departure called attention to Joe's absence in a way nothing else had before. For the first time, people acknowledged publicly that he was very ill. Although I had suspected something was wrong, no one had said anything to me, and I felt that, despite our many conversations, I did not really know Joe well enough to ask. He certainly had not confided in me. In fact, I had worried constantly throughout November and December that I had offended him. I had written an academic article on the editors' treatment of serious fiction that featured many long quotations from Joe's own reports. When I gave him a copy of the paper, I waited anxiously for his response. It never came. Too apprehensive to ask him whether he had disliked the paper, I let the matter slide. I felt guilty for not approaching him directly. Finally, Jill Sansone, who was particularly close to Joe, told me of his deteriorating health in the context of a discussion about Nancy's departure. Ashamed that I had assumed that his preoccupation and distance had something to do with me, I finally called him to acknowledge his illness and to offer any support I could. He said he was willing to talk. "Why don't you come down to my office now?" he asked.

We had a long, quiet, sad conversation. Stunned by his angry talk of death and dying, I felt overwhelmed. He said he had not read my paper and probably would not. I told him I understood. "Keep going," Joe said, "I believe in what you're doing." With words, we stumbled around each other until, somehow, inexplicably, we both grasped almost desperately at a passing reference to the previous summer. We both had spent time at the beach, as we did every summer—Joe on Fire Island, I on Cape Cod.

Grateful for the distraction, we matched memory for memory. Dune grass, sea spray, the rank smell of hot sand, the shimmering play of light on a salt marsh at midday—these were easier, happier subjects. I think we were both relieved. But I also felt disconcerted and dismayed. For the first time I heard the guarded, slightly edgy tone of all our earlier conversations rendered dissonant now by the warmer, less circumspect pitch of this shared duet of memories.

The small rent in our professional facades necessitated by the gravity of Joe's situation exposed the distance between us. No matter how much I wanted to live under the illusion that Joe and some of the other editors had become my friends, his illness and their loving, pragmatic, day-to-day manner of caring for him exposed the ways in which my own friendship with all of them was profoundly limited *and* enabled by their generosity. In a sense, our conversation laid bare the debt that bolstered the knowledge I was developing of Joe, his colleagues, and their daily work. I felt the burden of how much I owed them. The fraught, compromised nature of the ethnographic relationship loomed large, not as an abstract, theoretical issue of the power differential usually inscribed in the relationship, but rather as the highly specific, personal matter of the responsibility I bore to Joe Savago, Bill Zinsser, Al Silverman, Phyllis Robinson, Maron Waxman, Jill Sansone, and all the others. I walked back to my desk profoundly disturbed. Weighted down with sadness, unsettled by an inchoate sense of shame, and troubled by the possible consequences of admitting my status as their debtor, I felt paralyzed by doubt. What *were* my duties and obligations now? I rode home that night shadowed by questions I could not answer.

Although I would like to be able to say that some event or revelation subsequently convinced me of the rightness of what I was doing, nothing so dramatic occurred. Nor did I suddenly see how I might fulfill my responsibility to those who were in some sense acting as my informants against the Time management. I simply boarded the train every morning, read report after report, and listened intently as the editors talked spontaneously with me about what was happening to the club. The fact that the editors were suddenly excluded from management decisions, as I had been, positioned us on similar ground. This structural situation, along with the sense that I was indebted to the editors, forged a much stronger identification with them. I gossiped with them every morning as if we were rebellious children sharing anecdotes and rumors about the activities of feared adults. Together we developed into fervent readers of signs. We scrutinized every memo, every overheard conversation, and every odd comment in the hallway for their implications and portent. We repeated the words of Larry Crutcher and even of Al Silverman. We examined them together, turned them over and over for their implications, and read them for what they could tell us about the fate of the Book-of-the-Month Club. Still, even though I was pushed by events to read *with* the editors at the club, my job was not on the line. They thought theirs were. Angry about the situation, they confided in me, I think, almost as a way to exact revenge.

Several weeks after Nancy's announcement, I found a sealed, unmarked envelope on my desk in the office services department. The envelope contained a memo that had recently been circulated to the editors along with an accompanying note identifying my confidant. The note, composed of only a few words, advised me, "Try this one for syntax and sense." This particular memo, which was termed a "Management News Bulletin," announced the appointment of a new director of Specialty Clubs and Club Development. It went on to detail the new official's responsibilities. After naming the individual, whose editorial credentials were not cited, an absence I knew everyone would detect, the memo observed, "This is an important role in the company, and crucial for a number of activities which we have identified as having growth potentials beyond what is currently being realized."[7] The last half of the sentence had been underlined heavily without additional comment. My correspondent assumed that I, too, would be appalled by the involuted sentence structure. The memo subsequently detailed who would report to the new director. Although individuals were named, they were referred to as "reports." I thought it peculiar that colleagues were referred to in this inanimate way. But when I got to the last paragraph, I could see clearly why the memo had been considered such an affront by my confidant. "We have been talking with several 'name owners,'" the memo went on, "about a joint venture Club." It continued, "One conversation, being led by Al Silverman, is presently hopeful. Al is providing concept; [the new director] will provide the deal structure."

In 1980s Manhattan, and in the winter after the Bertelsmann takeover, this language unmistakably evoked the world of high finance, insider trading, and corporate buyouts. In the editors' eyes it betokened the arrival of a world and a set of values as far removed as could be from the writerly universe of syntax and sense they knew so well. In the context of the club's particular crisis, the circulation of this sort of language within their midst portended for many the demise of the general reader and the rise of a blockbuster mentality devoted only to badly written bestsellers and film and TV tie-ins. The editors increasingly assumed that, like them, I would look upon this as an evolving disaster.

Shortly after Nancy Evans's hasty departure from the editorial chair, Larry Crutcher announced that Al Silverman would conduct the search for her replacement. Virtually everyone I spoke with termed this "a good thing." People expressed their relief spontaneously and suggested to me that Al would understand that what the club needed was another "editorial person," not "an MBA" who would talk about "growing the club" or who would write the sort of memo that featured words like "growth potentials," "concept," and "deal structure." What the club needed, the editors all seemed to agree, was a wordsmith, an individual who wrote elegantly and appreciated verbal excellence above everything else. Although they would be happy to welcome into their midst an individual who also understood that publishing was a business, they hoped that Al would find someone who would fit comfortably within their community, defined as it was by its primary devotion to the higher value of the word. Their repeated stories about the perceived linguistic insensitivity and incompetence of the dreaded "Time MBAs" once again served to underscore for them, and for me, the literary nature of their community and the importance of an attention to language in the books they selected and recommended at the club. In their minds the general reader was as interested in the quality of language used in a book as in the information, story, and delight it conveyed. And this individual was worthy of defense because so many other forces were conspiring to favor a more indiscriminate, less literate reader, the individual interested only in the latest bestseller because it had been discussed on the morning news shows.

It was virtually impossible to resist the collectively generated story that writerly values at the club were under attack. Subsequent departures exacerbated the sense of doom growing within the editorial ranks. But those departures also led to increased conflict and made all of us aware that significant dissension was developing among the editors about the implications of the ongoing management restructuring. Shortly after Larry Crutcher's announcement that Al Silverman would be directing the search for a new editor in chief, Bill Zinsser told me confidentially that he also would be leaving in the coming weeks. Although he took me into his confidence by telling me about his decision before it was made public, he revealed little about why he felt the need to go. He suggested, though, that "the winds of change" were blowing and that there was no longer enough satisfying work for him to do; the kind of special projects he had been in charge of were about to be curtailed as part of institutional streamlining.

He also wanted to get back to his own writing. I knew he had been work-ing on a book about the new writing-across-the-curriculum movement in schools and colleges, a subject we had discussed at length. That book be-came *Writing to Learn*.

Shortly after the formal announcement of Bill's resignation, a curi-ous interaction took place at one of the weekly editorial meetings.[8] This strange occurrence not only suggested that tensions were increasing, but it also gave me pause because it suggested further that not everyone at the club demonized the Time management as clearly as I had in my conversa-tions with Bill and with some of the other editors. It seemed clear that a few editors at least did not think very much was going to change at all. The interaction in question was prompted by a surprisingly long discussion of an odd coffee-table book titled *The Art of Giving*. Studded with lavish pic-tures, the volume chronicled gift giving by the rich. It was presented by Dividend Director Eve Tulipan, who communicated her distaste for the book even as she observed that she felt compelled to take it seriously since it was sure to do as well as its predecessor had. Despite her halfhearted de-fense, I was puzzled to see the discussion drag on as long as it did because the book was the kind of highly commercial, celebrity-oriented volume the group usually dispensed with rapidly. It was quite clear that a strong consensus developed very quickly against the book. Yet the editors seemed unable to reject it decisively. I wondered whether they were feeling pres-sure from Time about the need to take more books that would sell in large numbers. At one point Susan Weinberg spoke up and counseled rejec-tion. "There's not even one vote for it," she pointed out. "Not even Time would ask you to take it." I thought it odd that no one responded to her comment because it was obvious that everyone recognized that this was the first time Time's desires had been openly acknowledged at an editorial meeting. Her comment made explicit what had only been whispered be-fore. Her allusion suggested that Time might indeed be pushing for more commercial books, but still no one appeared willing to admit this. Finally the group reaffirmed its commitment to its traditional practices and dis-missed the book with the familiar "not for us."

The meeting was about to close routinely when Bill Zinsser spoke up. "I'm dismayed to hear Time mentioned in this meeting for the first time," he observed. "This [kind of book] is not what we are about. We can't think this way." His comments induced uneasy laughter from some and a loud "hear, hear" from others. I wondered what would happen next, since the editors had finally openly acknowledged in a semipublic way that they were uneasy about what was happening in the organization. Although I did not think Bill had intended to criticize Susan, her reaction suggested that she thought he had. She said nothing, however, and neither did anyone else. Susan told me later that day that she thought Bill's and the other editors' view of Time might be too harsh. She argued vigorously that she did not believe Time "had it in for the company" or that they were interested in "tampering with our mission."[9] She mentioned as well that she thought the anxiety and paranoia rampant within the editorial ranks were completely unjustified. The logic of Susan's comments made me wonder whether all of us had too easily branded Time the destroyer of the Book-of-the-Month Club. "After all," she argued persuasively, "we already do commercial books here. What's the problem?"

I puzzled anew over the nature of the editors' passionate investment in the intelligent, general reader. I thought, too, about my own increasing investment in the Book-of-the-Month Club's defense of such an individual. What were the editors so afraid of? Why had I unwittingly become, along with them, the defender of the general reader? Why the need to cling so insistently to the club's traditional mission? Why the heightened boundary work, on their part and on mine, to separate the club's goals from Time's? What was so disturbing, either aesthetically or socially, about the books and their projected readers that they feared Time would force on them? These questions sent me back to the reader's reports in the hope that they would tell me something more about the specific tastes of the general reader and simultaneously reveal why this individual figured so prominently in some of the editors' imaginations as well as in my own.

In looking at the Book-of-the-Month Club reader's reports this time around, I was struck even more forcefully by the fact that judgment was always conducted at the Book-of-the-Month Club in a category-specific way. Books were never compared across categorical lines. Rather, evaluation was tailored to preexistent understandings of particular genres and subgenres and to a consensus about their peculiar intentions, purposes, and goals. A good book was thought to be one that displayed its categorical essence with a certain flair and one that fulfilled its readers' expectations more effectively than most. Positive evaluations were tied to a title's ability to function for the editors as both a categorical representative and as a text that managed to exceed generic expectations.

An implicit theory of the practice of reading served as the foundation for the business of day-to-day evaluation at the Book-of-the-Month Club. Reading was not conceived as a unitary practice, nor were books evaluated according to a single set of criteria. Rather, reading was conceptualized as elaborated and wholly context-specific. Sometimes people read to be entertained; sometimes they read to be put to sleep; sometimes they read to find out how to eat; and sometimes they read to live other lives, to think other thoughts, and to feel more intensely. Books appropriate to one scene of reading would neither look nor sound like those written for others, nor would they capture their readers in exactly the same way that books that oriented themselves toward other readers might. To measure the success of any given book, the Book-of-the-Month Club editors evaluated not the features of the text alone but, rather, the precise nature of the fit between what the book offered and what its likely reader would demand of it. Still, success was never thought to be constituted by perfect fit alone. It was achieved when a book acknowledged the reader's expectations but pushed beyond them just enough to surprise the reading self. Serious books, it seems, both gratified readers' immediate desires and confirmed their sense of themselves as people willing to be expanded and challenged.

Good commercial fiction, for instance, had to be entertaining. As such, it had to be fast paced, easy to read, driven by good plotting, and peopled by engaging characters. Additionally, however, it had to provide the reader with an entrée into a fully realized world rendered with what might be called the viewpoint of an insider. Similarly, the editors demanded that popular history present its narrative coherently, but perhaps more significantly, they also demanded that it portray its account of the past as a comprehensible story about the actions of real people. It must educate without bogging down in irrelevant detail or vague abstractions; it must avoid the use of a highly technical vocabulary. Coffee-table books, on the other hand, had to be lavish, beautiful to look at, and surprising, according to the editors, but they studiously had to avoid too obviously "trashy" subjects. Health books had to address contemporary problems and concerns in a new light, but they could be neither too trendy and superficial nor too analytical and specialized. They had to be organized pragmatically and oriented to potential behavior change. The editors demanded, furthermore, that literary novels be verbally distinguished to be selected, yet they also required them to reveal a strong, intelligent, authorial presence that could guide readers in how to think about their own world. Genres, at the Book-of-the-Month Club, were treated always as functional contracts. They were thought to provide pleasurable experiences for their readers as well as distinctive, highly valuable goods.

The club's intelligent generalists, as they emerged from the reader's reports, were complex, fully realized individuals replete with recognizable intentions and goals. Treated with respect by the editors, they appeared as people who knew what they wanted from a book and who were fully cognizant of why they read. Daily practice at the club instituted a vision of the membership as discerning above all else. Because readers had some idea of what pleased them, the editors believed, they had a general sense of what they were looking for when they perused the club's catalog. This might only be a feeling that a new mystery would be just the thing to help them fall asleep during a particularly stressful week, or a more general sense that novels about women's lives helped them to reflect on their own. But because the editors recognized that people such as these turned to books for diverse reasons, those readers were categorized by the editors at the Book-of-the-Month Club as educated and well informed about bookish matters, as mirror images of the way they constructed themselves. The general reader was constructed somewhat ironically as a discriminating reader.

I saw more clearly why Time posed such a threat to the editors. The editors believed that many of the Time-Life books advertised on television were directed not at the Book-of-the-Month Club's cultivated reader, the intention-driven sort of person they prided themselves on serving. Rather, those books were aimed at a less knowing, more impulsive person, the occasional reader, in their view. The mail-order buyers of Time-Life books, the editors presumed, were the kind of people who could be seduced into buying an entire set of books on a single subject, such as the history of Western art or the various styles of gardening, because they were driven by the desire to assemble and display "knowledge" as an undifferentiated thing rather than as a focused and articulated body of information about a particular topic. The Book-of-the-Month Club editors postulated that unthinking, indiscriminate readers such as these could not be truly serious. Accordingly, they simply assimilated Time as a purveyor of books to this inferior class of readers to the already devalued constellation of commercial books, common readers, and unfocused reading aims that they relied on again and again to define who they were and what they understood to be valuable.

The editors produced their own knowing stance and that of the readers they served in opposition to a vision of desperately needy readers who, in their omnivorous need, were willing to consume promiscuously and haphazardly. Ever disdainful of the lack of focus and intention exhibited by this occasional reader, the editors valorized in opposition the determination, pragmatic intentionality, and instrumental focus of the person they called the serious reader. A powerful agency thus characterized this individual, but so, too, did a capacity to realize that agency in a range of differentiated ways. The serious reader was therefore also a general reader because he or she could take pleasure in and use a broad range of books as a form of self-realization. The serious general reader at the Book-of-the-Month Club was constructed, finally, in opposition both to exaggerated passivity and to a kind of constriction or narrowness. The editors assumed that general readers wanted to be hailed both as intelligent and as broadminded individuals, that is, as lovers of all kinds of books, as aficionados of the universe of print. It was not always easy, however, to find books that could address readers in this precise way. It was hard to find titles that both respected the generalist's intelligence and delivered something that she or he desired or lacked.

## IN SEARCH OF THE SUPERIOR MIDDLE

As I read through hundreds of reports and fleshed out the shape of the general reader they were written to serve, I developed a coordinate image of the editors as people engaged in a particular struggle. What the editors seemed to be doing over and over was attempting to wrest readable books from professional writers, researchers, and knowledge producers who, in the act of writing, were not simply attempting to address readers but who were also pursuing their own, sometimes individual, sometimes professional, objectives and aims. Some, who conceived of writing only as a means of economic support, sought only to maximize their audience by catering to the most widely shared sympathies and concerns. In the view of the editors, such writers failed to acknowledge the intelligence and capacity for reflection in their readers. Others, for whom the labor of writing was inextricably tied to professional practice, wrote to display expertise and to offer highly technical knowledge. They sometimes did not even seem to notice that they were writing something meant to be read by others. What the editors were after were those few, special offerings from people who could call attention to their particular expertise as professional writers and still speak to an audience of individuals quite different from themselves, individuals who did not possess equivalent expertise. Readable books like these offered something more than the recycled and the widely known, but they proffered it in such a way that it was comprehensible and useful to the non-expert and the nonprofessional. Inasmuch as general readers were constructed in opposition to too-passive, omnivorous, occasional readers, so also were they defined against the already informed, technical specialists.

While horizontal categorization figured prominently in day-to-day operating procedures at the club, certain principles of hierarchization crept into the process of intracategorical judgment. Although those hierarchies tended to be formulated as judgments about writing, they were implicitly grounded on social distinctions. The editors placed themselves and their subscribers somewhere between the ordinary, common reader on one hand and the highly trained, professional specialist on the other. Yet they tended to locate the former beneath themselves in a tacit social hierarchy while they tended to construe technical experts as their superiors in the sense that they acknowledged their greater command of a highly valuable commodity, knowledge itself. Still, the editors exhibited considerable ambivalence about the social status of technical experts, whom they sometimes seemed to resent precisely because they flaunted their skills too openly and displayed their indifference to everyone who could not make sense of their own highly technical observations. What they valued most, I thought, was the professional expert and technical specialist who could remember that knowledge and expertise were valuable only to the extent that they could be used by others.

As a way of exploring what seemed to be an implicit social theory of the proper relationship between writer and reader, I thought it might be useful to examine more carefully how the important category of popular history was treated at the club. Although many editors and outside readers reported on history volumes, the category was largely the province of one individual, Larry Shapiro, who had a master's degree in history from the University of California at Berkeley. He had decided not to pursue a Ph.D., he once told me, because he disliked most academic historical writing and could not imagine reducing his range of interests in order to produce it. Given his preferences and explicit rejection of the career of scholarly writer, I thought Larry might be able to help me understand the club's approach to popular history as well as the privilege it accorded to knowledge and information. I asked to talk with him about both. I found him extremely thoughtful and very clear about how good popular history had to be distinguished from academic history at one end and from superficial survey and chronicle at the other, the latter associated with the stripped-down, jingoistic accounts of the simplest kind of journalism.

Larry began by pointing out, "There's a lot of popular history, and popular history is at least partly written to entertain, to offer some of the reading values that fiction does, character interest and narrative interest, and information." Continuing, he explained that "what sustains people through a book are the entertainment values."[10] Popular history, clearly, had to couch the information it offered in a highly accessible form. It had to be merged with story. In a report that he specifically pulled out to show me, Larry observed, "Our people come out in large numbers for left to right narrative history."[11] His views, I recalled, had been echoed by outside reader Thomas Cooney, who also had once noted in a report that "to a general reader, the highest virtue of this history is likely to be its readability. It is simply but not condescendingly written, and its chapters and sections are organized with great skill to move deeply into subject matter and emerge into dramatic conclusions at major points of transition."[12] The popular historian had to respect the reader without abnegating his or her responsibility to serve as a knowledgeable and instructive guide. Joe Savago once wrote approvingly of Barbara Tuchman, "She is a master of readable, full and fluid historical narrative who is neither simple-minded (attributing events to a single, unequivocal cause) nor scholastically subtle (getting mired in the contradictory interpretations of a raft of professional historians. . . . History, her narrative tells us, is rich and dense with possibilities, currents and countercurrents, establishment voices and voices of protest."[13]

In our discussion Larry went on to suggest that despite the privilege the club accorded to story and the entertainment it provided for the general reader, the editors looked for something else as well. Readers wanted something more. As Larry put it, "When I qualify [the phrase] by 'good' popular history, I mean something which also has the weight and power to make you see things from a historian's perspective, that [which] good scholarly history offers. It shows you a way of thinking. It shows you a method. It gives you a sense of the way the historian operates." He continued, "And also, underlying its attractive surface [it] has as much research and as much thinking as good scholarly history is supposed to have. It's just not as apparent on the surface in popular history." The scholarly machinery, evidently, had to be submerged in order to allow the reader to focus in unobstructed fashion on what that machinery had produced—in effect, a certain knowledge of the past.

Larry continued by suggesting that at the Book-of-the-Month Club popular history was constructed as a hybrid. On one hand the editors required that it exhibit "comparative reading ease." On the other they expected it to aspire simultaneously to some of the characteristics and functions of scholarly history. Good popular history managed to make its reader at least somewhat aware that what the author offered was a vigorous interpretation and rendering of past events. As such, it called attention to the writer as an accomplished individual, someone who possessed special knowledge. Still, Larry cautioned, because scholarly history had forsworn interest in narrative sweep and vividly rendered character in recent years, it was extremely difficult to find books that could provide intellectual substance yet in an accessible way. Most academic books the editors reviewed were judged "dry" and "desiccated" because they favored statistics over persons, dispassionate analysis over engaging narrative, and abstractions over particularities. As Larry himself commented on a book that billed itself as a two-volume narrative history of America, "It's hard to imagine people reading this as narrative history. . . . The author is so dry, there's so little memorable anecdote, or felicitous expression, or noteworthy insight, that it would be like reading an encyclopedia."[14]

Curiously, as Larry spoke, his words evoked another powerful memory. I saw clearly, as if in a darkened movie house, the front yard of my childhood home, an image connected in my mind with a very specific scene of reading. It was the first day of summer vacation after the seventh grade. The late afternoon shade provided by the oak that towered over the house and yard made the surprising heat of the day bearable. I had just returned from the public library fired with a desire to know more. What I wanted to know in late June 1962 was why the word "communism" was always said with a sneer. I had been troubled that year during my class's first foray into world history by the account our teacher gave of the Soviet Union, which he insisted on calling "Russia." He had emphasized the coerciveness of Russian society, its lack of respect for individuality, and its demand for conformity. It was not as bad as China, though, where they demanded that you dress the same as everyone else and sweep the streets in the morning. Yet he also spent a lot of time on Karl Marx and a principle he seemed to be associated with, the idea that "from each according to his ability, to each according to his need." I could not understand what was wrong with this as a way to organize society. Determined to know more, I had checked out every book I could find in our small-town library on the Communist Party and on the history of the Soviet Union, and one on the Russian Revolution.

I never read any of those books through, though. Expectantly, I began each one, only to give up sometimes ten, sometimes twenty pages in, as the prose thickened, the detail piled up, and the print solidified into an opaque, oppressive wall. I felt frustrated and excluded. I still remember thinking it would be easier to read an encyclopedia. I also remember returning those books to the librarian feeling guilty that I had not managed to make them yield the knowledge they so obviously contained. Recovering from this peculiar reverie, I was struck by the fact that it had allowed me to identify with Larry's projected reader, the one who might be put off by a book's flat, toneless prose. For some reason I felt no inclination to justify or defend academic writers of history. The pressing desire to know, to learn what only others fully commanded, was still too imaginatively close at hand.

Returning to Larry Shapiro several days later, I questioned him even more closely on the subject of academic history. When I asked him to say more about how it differed from popular history, he mused, "I think you don't really need to be a writer to write good scholarly history." A writer, he added, is "someone who has a sense of audience." [15] Academic historians lack this sense of an audience, he explained, in large part because they write for people like themselves. Significantly, they write for other producers of history. When such people read, they are both determined and highly tolerant. They are willing to overlook and overcome infelicities in the writing and in the organization of a book because they have the technical expertise to do so. They do not need the same kind of writerly attention and guidance found in popular histories because, as specialists and colleagues, they already know. They share a large body of technical knowledge with the author and can interpolate when the prose is less than clear. At the same time, because such individuals read as part of their professional work, they do not require that the reading experience be pleasurable above all else. Academic professionals tend to construe the reading process as one marked explicitly by labor.[16] As Larry observed, "Academic history is rightly geared to problem solving and to debating the fine points of contrasting interpretations of data. It is oriented to the process of production rather than to the activity of reading."

Readers of popular history, Larry continued, are not so forgiving of dense prose and impenetrable jargon because they are reading in their leisure time at least in part for pleasure. They do not want to have to struggle to understand or lose the thread of a story for the tangle of abstract or analytical prose. Nevertheless, he insisted, these readers do want to be instructed. It might be said, he concluded, that popular history is considered "good" at the Book-of-the-Month Club "when it instructs its readers without abandoning its commitment to entertain them." In a sense, I mused to myself, the editors seemed to require that the writers of popular history seek common ground with their readers even while convincing them that the common is not banal. Hence, the powerful imperative to avoid the superficial simplicities and clichés of run-of-the-mill journalism. The trick was to provide bona fide knowledge without calling too much attention to the lack in the reader that motivated the desire for it in the first place.

I concluded that popular history at the Book-of-the-Month Club had to be readable, lively, and engaging, but, obviously, it could not be too light or superficial. It was required to take on an important subject, but it had to avoid the cliché. It was not cliché alone or stereotype merely that were inherently objectionable, however; familiarities and truisms could not be abandoned entirely. The editors were as stern in their disapproval of neologisms and professional jargon as they were of tired clichés. Rather, they required popular history to be informative and accessible at the same time. Above all, they demanded that popular history establish a close rapport between the writer and the reader. Its written style should explicitly position the writer between the superficial tabloid journalist, who dealt only in clichés and trivialities and courted the multitude, and the distant, dispassionate scholar, who called attention to his or her expertise through the use of a strange and difficult technical jargon while writing only for a small coterie of the already initiated.

The vision of a particular writer-reader relationship clearly prevailed at the Book-of-the-Month Club. Celebrated as respectful yet close, the ideal relationship was dependent on the precise social identity of the two participating partners. The editors' constant return to the importance of negotiating the proper relationship, in fact, emphasized the way their judgments about books functioned also as judgments about social matters. They thought good popular history was good not only because it displayed research in readable form but also because it addressed a reader who was distinct from the common herd and yet marked by a taste for the weighty as well as a penchant for learning. This social distinction was embedded in the very word, "banal," that cropped up occasionally in negative reports on books that were ultimately rejected. Historical etymology tells us that "banal" originally referred to a kind of compulsory feudal service that everyone in a community owed to a particular lord. The banal referred not simply to something possessed in common but to the common property of the subordinate. In denigrating the banal as the trite, the trivial, and the commonplace, the editorial system for evaluating popular history implicitly associated a tolerance for such familiarity with those who were socially inferior. Hence it was a system of social classification that implicitly acknowledged and feared the low social status attached to the common reader who desired a light touch and merely to be entertained. The typical subscriber to the Book-of-the-Month Club, its editors believed, wanted to be rendered distinct from this common reader. As a consequence, this individual turned to books that had been openly and deliberately selected—singled out—for their proximity to other, somewhat different books, those associated with the activities of professionals, who were themselves socially distinguished and elevated by their command of technical expertise. The intelligent, general reader was equal to an exchange with such high-status individuals.

In spite of the value attached to technical expertise, those who wielded it were not treated uncritically at the Book-of-the-Month Club. The editors revealed considerable ambivalence about books that foregrounded specialized competence in too obvious and untempered a fashion. Their impatience with opaque terminology and intricate, crabbed argument frequently slid quickly into resentment at an author's apparent refusal to take a reader's needs into account. What the editors seemed to detect at the heart of this refusal to consider the experience of the reader was a fundamental social arrogance and a feeling of superiority on the part of the professional expert for those who turned to him or her for advice. In dismissing a book written by such an author as "too cerebral, too intellectual, artistic, literary [and] special," for example, one of the editors heavily criticized a writer who made no effort to convey his knowledge in a clear and accessible manner. Others expressed irritation with academic historians' constant inability to recognize that the detail they themselves found so compelling would only bore the individual who had no knowledge of the intricacies of debate and discussion surrounding a given subject.

In commenting on a book that she had very much hoped to like, for example, Elizabeth Easton once wrote, "This is an exceedingly scholarly book, (the author, according to the publishers' blurb, is familiar with more than twenty ancient and medieval languages), and while the style is clear enough, it tells far more than the average reader cares to know about King Arthur." In finally rejecting the book, she concluded, "The author is a Professor Emeritus at The Claremont Colleges and this is no doubt a labor of love and enormous devotion. But it's not for the general reader." [17] Jill Sansone likewise lamented, "Great title, great idea . . . but its scholarly tone and format are off-putting. . . . I think the average reader (this average reader anyway) needs a little help getting through some of these historically significant theoretical points. A more popular approach written in a semi-lively tone would be more appropriate for our audience. I just couldn't get through this." [18] Similarly, in commenting thoughtfully about why a popular account of evolution failed, outside reader Suzanne Mantell pointed to the inability of the biologist in question to understand what a general reader might hope for in such an account. "I found this book to be dauntingly difficult to deal with," she reported. "The subject is tough, and [the author's] way of getting around that is to bend over backward to put things supersimply, which results in endlessly long, roundabout chapters that are difficult to get hold of." Significantly, she added, the book is "tinged by a smarmy attitude, and not at all gratifying (intellectually) to read. He relies heavily on metaphor and analogy to make his points, which rather than helping, makes the book all the more tedious." She concluded, "A popularizer he may be, and with a noble mission, but the book, in my opinion, thunks." [19]

The popularizer of professionally produced technical knowledge, it should be clear by now, was not considered an embarrassment at the Book-of-the-Month Club. The individual who could write tellingly and aptly and in a direct, lively fashion about her or his area of expertise was looked on as a dedicated, public-spirited translator. Similarly, the editors did not assume that the process of rendering technical information comprehensible to the nonspecialist necessarily gutted that information of substance or robbed it of its value. Complex ideas, they believed, could and should be formulated clearly for the vast majority of individuals who could not be involved in the process of producing such knowledge in the first place. The editors accepted without question that they lived in a world dominated by technical experts who monopolized the business of knowledge production. But they demanded that those individuals never forget that as experts they bore an important responsibility to communicate their knowledge to others. A good book was understood to be like a good teacher: authoritative yet respectful of students, knowledgeable yet personable, and instructive yet willing to participate in the fun. The editors' intuitive understanding of the desires that motivated the usual reader of popular history was powerfully delineated in their conversation and in their reports. It was so finely articulated that their words had evocatively summoned my own student-self, that girl who had longed for the book and the teacher who would recognize her desire to know and remedy the particular lack from which it derived without patronizing her.

The evaluative system in use at the Book-of-the-Month Club embodied a kind of social vision. The editors' judgments constituted a statement about the sort of relationship that ought to obtain between professional experts and technicians and the wider population. Embedded in the practical logic of their decisions was an implicit assumption that knowledge, information, and expertise ought to be the common property of all. The editors acknowledged that in a society as highly differentiated and complex as their own, not all individuals could expect to be producers of knowledge. At the same time they also demanded of those who managed to acquire special skills and technical competence that they exercise both with a certain amount of social responsibility and a commitment to the dissemination of their findings for the public good. In objecting to the insular focus and opaque jargon of so much academic and technical writing, they protested the failure of professionals to locate themselves within a broad-based community of generally educated peers. The editors objected to the tendency to foreground technical competence as a sign of social difference, as a mark of special group membership and resulting social distinction.

But even as they pragmatically supported the cause of the intelligent, general reader against the claim of professionals and experts to a private command of expertise—what Bourdieu has called a monopoly on cultural and intellectual capital—the editors simultaneously differentiated themselves and the general reader from that other reader who was characterized, above all, by a refusal to recognize the value of education and information in the first place. This individual they dismissed as part of the common populace, as someone who sought not substance but the empty pleasure of vacuous entertainment. A certain appreciation for seriousness and a recognition of the value of knowledge set the general reader apart from the common reader in the universe mapped out at the Book-of-the-Month Club. Despite the idealized relationship between expert and audience, this was still a class vision. When the editors looked for "trash" to satisfy the general reader's momentary need for "escapist entertainment," they looked for "class trash," in Joe Savago's words, books that displayed a concern for the language and an interest in conveying inside information at the same time that they captivated the reader with sensation, gossip, and an emotionally engrossing tale. Judgment at the club seemed both to enact and to depend on the familiar hierarchy of high, middle, and low.

Yet there was still something puzzling about the way editorial practices constructed this implicit social vision. While it seemed true enough that the Book-of-the-Month Club editors located themselves and the general readers they served in a middle space between common readers on one hand and legitimate technical experts on the other, there was also a way in which they construed themselves as superior to both. What gave the Book-of-the-Month Club system its unique character, I began to see, was the editors' pragmatic and resolute insistence not only in locating themselves and their subscribers in a middle space between two extremes but in celebrating the particular virtues of that space as well. With virtually every act of judgment, they positioned themselves above the common reader on one hand while they deferred on the other to the superior technical competence of the acknowledged professional expert. Situated between these two groups of readers, the editors compulsively demonstrated their conflicted sympathy with the interests expressed by both. What made their middle position superior to the others, in their view, was their own refusal to pursue one set of interests so single-mindedly that they completely neglected the equally valid other. To occupy the middle at the Book-of-the-Month Club was in fact to occupy a superior social position.

In assessing the merits of a book on Ellis Island, for example, one of the editors reported that "anyone whose ancestors entered America through this port will add their own emotional depth to this dry report." They will have to, Eve Tulipan added, "because the last part of the book does bog down in details about the composition of staff and other administrative details." She concluded, "The many photographs add a dimension of humanity to the book but I longed for a few human anecdotes to bring it all to life. . . . The subject is interesting but we should look for a more full-bodied treatment."[20] Embodiment and affect seemed to be crucial here. That is to say, reading pleasure at the Book-of-the-Month Club was somehow bound up with the emotional and sentient responses of a reader to a fully rendered imaginary world, even when that world was being treated factually. The editors seemed to associate reading enjoyment with the somatic and affective responses of the body to the experience of being transported by words to a meaningful and altogether human universe inhabited by people with similar needs and concerns. Although the club's editors clearly shared the values of a professional class of knowledge producers and associated themselves with its highly intellectual pursuits, they simultaneously identified with the more ordinary common reader, who was construed as one with few special skills but with desires to feel intensely and to be entertained and enchanted by a companionable storyteller.

It was the editors' split identification, finally, that produced their characteristic mediating project, which is to say, their search for hybrid books that managed to accomplish both sets of tasks. The Book-of-the-Month Club editors struggled to refuse the familiar categorizing that tends crudely to distinguish entertainment from education and sensual pleasure from cerebral intellection. While they valued learning and seriousness above all else, they did not approve of intellectual achievement if it enforced a distance from the pleasures of the body or hindered affective connection between people. In valuing books that were neither too void of intellectual content nor so dense and weighty that they made no provision for a reader's delight, they celebrated the individual who wanted to pursue enlightenment and entertainment at the same time. The editors distinguished themselves alike from those too closely associated with an unthinking body—readers unwilling to perform intellectual work as they read—and those who indulged in rationality and contemplation to such an extent that they denied the sentimental claims of the heart and the sensual demands of the corporeal. The Book-of-the-Month Club editors positioned themselves and those they served in a space *between*—between those who longed for sensations unclouded by reflection and those whose command of intellectual capital had produced nothing but disdain for anyone incapable of understanding their every word.

## THE MIDDLE TRANSCENDED/BOUNDARIES DISSOLVED:

### THE PLEASURES OF ABSORPTION

It is important to stress that the betweenness celebrated at the Book-of-the-Month Club was not simply a space produced by a social mediation. Rather, the middle was additionally defined by its association with a particular form of experience, a reading experience that was, above everything else, characterized by the pleasure it gave. The particular pleasure referred to again and again in reader's reports was always bound to a certain extent with a feeling of immersion, a sense of boundaries dissolved. This came through especially clearly in excited, positive reports where the breathless tone and the rush of the syntax always conveyed feverishly that the book in question had managed to captivate the editor completely. In these reports I could see the editor as writer, now distanced from the moment of reading, struggle to capture in words the intensity of having been filled up, overwhelmed, and almost drowned in the experience of another world. Here's Joe on Toni Morrison's *Beloved* more than six months before its publication:

> I don't want to throw around the word "masterpiece," not just yet anyway (even though I've waited over a week, since finishing BELOVED, to write this report) (a whole week), but I will declare that this is the most extraordinary, mesmerizing, soul-provoking thing I've read in a long, long time, the closest thing to "genius" I've run across in a long, long time—if it's understood that the brand of Genius I'm referring to partakes more than a little of the autistic. Think of Kafka, not his contemporary Mann.
>
> There's a story here, of course—this is a novel. It reaches back several decades before the Time Present of the novel, in 1872, but the novel BELOVED does not exist to tell that story, in any lucid and straightforward way, so much as to register the weight, the heat, the obsessional horror of that story in the life of its heroine, the former slave

Sethe. . . . The world of BELOVED is truly, awesomely, brilliantly, shockingly and movingly a World Unto Itself. If one of the platitudes about Literature is that it creates a completely realized world of its own, then BELOVED is Very High Literature—the creation, in extraordinary physical, domestic and emotional detail of the life of a strange and blighted household like no other, where the mystery and horror of the past lives on and colors with mystery and horror the life of the present. The novel isn't about something so much as it *is* something, a place of obsessional torment, of unshakable but also unfaceable memory, where one prays there may be a redemption as great as the suffering has been, which there may be, in the last pages of the book. In abstract, thematic terms—not really appropriate here, but begged for by the fable-like quality of the book—the book is about living, and not living, with what we have been and what we have done. . . .

People don't simply "sit," "walk," "look," "speak," in this book— every moment, every movement is observed with extraordinary, expressive vividness, every moment and movement "speaks" of the souls of the characters, who are made alive-to-each-other, waiting upon and hoping from and living with and for each other to a degree which bespeaks the clarity of Morrison's vision—she isn't "thinking up" these people, she is there, you are there, the strangeness of what goes on grounded in the inches-away immediacy of its realization. Let's do this one big, biggest.[21]

The intensity of reports like this one often grabbed me by the scruff of the neck. They captured my imagination. Forgoing diligent note taking, I often pulled out my address book and jotted down the titles of books I had not read, or made a note in my calendar to look for one that was scheduled to appear later that year. And I copied reports—endlessly—not always because I thought they would be useful when I began to write, but often just because they were so vivid. I wanted to have them with me later, after I read those books, to remember what Joe or Alice or Jill had said about them.

I loved the way the Book-of-the-Month Club editors talked about books and about reading. Once again, their talk conjured my past. The editors reminded me of the librarian at the Edward H. Bryan elementary school, a cheerful, helpful woman whose name I had forgotten but whose animated way of describing books I recalled with surprise and great pleasure. I remembered in particular the day she gave me *The Boxcar Children*, the first, long, "real" book I ever read on my own. I also recalled with an ache how she had steered me to those turquoise biographies of great Americans, my favorite among them the ones about Dolley Madison, Abraham Lincoln, and Susan B. Anthony. She had a way of drawing pictures with her words, of painting the vista that promised to open from within the pages of a book. The Book-of-the-Month Club editors sounded just as she did. Their windowless, book-lined conference room seemed awash not with sunlight but with the swirl of endless stories, strange places, and surprising characters, as did her small, silent library, squirreled away, up several stairs, behind the noisy multipurpose room. The vivacity and rich detail in their reports suggested that the books they described would be even more captivating than their words had been able to convey. I wanted always to go right from the report to the book itself. On more than one occasion I tracked down an extra copy of the galley proofs so I could read the book before it was published. I read *Beloved* this way. Books at the Book-of-the-Month Club, like books in that secret space of my grade school library, appeared before me as magical objects. In both places, reading seemed to exist as an uncanny pleasure, an act that was weirdly private but deeply social as well.

I felt intense satisfaction at encountering this view of reading again. The eagerness with which I approached interviews about the editors' understanding of reading belied the analytical stance I thought I had managed to maintain. I often reacted with enthusiasm as the editors talked. I felt that I knew exactly what they were trying to say when they responded to my request to describe how a good book made them feel. In their replies they often strained for the appropriate words, and our talk was always punctuated by certain metaphors and analogies. Former editor and judge Lucy Rosenthal admitted that she knew some people read more "coolly" than she did, but she insisted that what gave her the most reading pleasure was the experience of "inhaling" a book. Sometimes, she suggested, reading was even a violent experience. Really good books "mugged" her, she told me; they made her their "victim."[22] Al Silverman conceived of the experience in gentler terms but focused nonetheless on the way it seemed to suppress self-consciousness in favor of "communion" with someone or someplace else. In describing how he was "captured" by pleasure reading as a child, he noted that "it took me out of [my ordinary school] world into a world of imagination which I had never really experienced before, and to me it was like a wonderful wind that came over me. It had borne into me from unknown sources; it opened doors and opened up the air and began to give me a satisfaction that I had never had in my life before." He added thoughtfully, "So that was a shield for me, and it was a wonderful . . . it was . . . it was my Sancho."[23] This kind of reading, he told me quietly, is what the Book-of-the-Month Club is trying to provide for its readers. Joe Savago suggested that the best books gave you "that enthralling sense of immersion you get with a great raconteur."[24] "Swept away is what I want to be by a book," Lucie Prinz remarked, "carried off, made to feel intensely."[25] Although the metaphors and analogies differed, they always seemed to have a common theme. What gave the editors the greatest pleasure, I thought, was a feeling of transport and betweenness, a feeling of being suspended between the self and the world, a state where the one flowed imperceptibly into the other, a place where clear boundaries and limits were obscured. Good reading, as they described it, produced an awareness of the self expanded, a sense that the self was absorbed into something larger, not dissolved exactly, but quivering in solution, both other and not.

A "reader's book," as opposed to a "reviewer's book," at least according to the Book-of-the-Month Club editors, was one that forged temporary bonds between writer and reader. A reader's book functioned as a link between social worlds. The chords that linked those different worlds were the emotions and physical responses that the writer was able to evoke in the reader while regaling the reader with stories and mesmerizing him or her with strange facts and compelling information. The modality of reading privileged at the Book-of-the-Month Club emphasized both sense and sensibility, both affect and cognition. It mobilized the body and the brain, the heart and the soul. It was a mode of reading that stressed immersion and connection, communication and response. The editors saw their job, accordingly, as a process of balancing competing interests, of finding writers who could speak to more than a few like-minded peers. What they were after, the editors made clear, were books written by writers who had designed those books for readers, not for other writers. And those readers, the editors believed, wanted to take up the position of the enchanted child, the child who longed to be hypnotized by strange stories and fascinated by the relation of remarkable wonders compellingly told.

Perhaps this particular insight prepared me in an unexpected way for what happened next; it's hard to say. Between interviews I was reading through the entire run of the club's catalog, the *Book-of-the-Month Club News*, as a way of getting a better understanding of the kinds of books the club sent out. The exercise proved extremely tedious until I arrived at the years after 1950. I was roused from my sleepy, desultory note taking about a list of books from the 1930s and 1940s, which I found remarkably disparate and largely unfamiliar, by my pleasure at suddenly finding a wealth of titles I recognized. Here I found not simply occasional titles by well-known major writers, but fiction, popular history, nature books, and biographies, all of which I had read: *Kon-Tiki*, by Thor Heyerdahl; *The Dream Factory*, by Hortense Powdermaker; *Shakespeare of London*, by Marchette Chute; *Marjorie Morningstar* and *The Caine Mutiny*, by Herman Wouk; *Silent Spring*, by Rachel Carson; *Inside Africa* and *Death Be Not Proud*, by John Gunther; *To Kill a Mockingbird*, by Harper Lee; *And Quiet Flows the Don*; *The Keys to the Kingdom*; *Oliver Wiswell*; *Helen Keller*; *Gods, Graves, and Scholars*; *The Bull from the Sea*; *The Guns of August*—the list went on and on. Although I had devoured them all, I had not thought of them in years. Just reading the titles, however, brought back vividly not only the crinkly, plastic-encased jackets of every one of those books, as well as the details of their plots and the lives of their major figures, but flickers of the pleasures they had given me, echoes of the feelings I had had while reading them. Additionally, however, those titles evoked just as powerfully the odor, the light, the sound, and the exact texture of the room within which I had read them. I realized with a shock that I had read virtually all of them in a single year, my first year in high school, when I was bedridden in a body cast designed to remedy a severe case of scoliosis, or curvature of the spine. Those books came to me every month in a cardboard box filled and packed by Mr. Shymansky, the high school librarian.

The titles were charged with an electricity that surprised me. So, too, was the recollected name of Mr. Shymansky. I imagined him packing the box, fitting in the different books each month, and wondered how he had managed to include so many that had been selected and sent out by earlier readers and judges at the Book-of-the-Month Club. Perhaps he himself had subscribed to the Book-of-the-Month Club. Or perhaps the subscription had been registered in the name of our tiny town library, which had provided the base for the newly built high school's book collection. That would not have been unusual. Many rural and small-town libraries relied on the Book-of-the-Month Club as a distributor or book wholesaler. Whatever the explanation for the presence of that particular medley of books in the box, the effects they had had on me must have been extraordinarily intense.

The box appeared before me now in the same way my tree-shaded scene of reading and the grade school library had. And all of them melted away just as the club's own conference room did every Thursday morning. They dissolved, opened as a window onto a distant plain, each evoking other scenes secreted away in the books themselves. The box was no longer just a cardboard container, empty space filled with a jigsaw puzzle of bound volumes from the Book-of-the-Month Club. It teemed in my imagination with the same swirl of color, sounds, textures, and light evoked by those vague volumes on communism, by *The Boxcar Children* and the turquoise biographies, and by the editors' reader's reports and their exhilarating repartee in the editorial meetings. The box evaporated as a fog does, imperceptibly without announcing its departure, leaving only details of sound and sight and scent revealed with astonishing clarity.

But even as this vision of the box and its contents returned, complete with the memories of where it had once led, I also felt again the leaden weight of the body cast as it pressed against every desire, even the simple desire to turn over. I saw again as if from within that cast anchored to the bed those three small, high windows mocking me from across the room. I shuddered with recognition. The act of reading a book in those dark winter months, in that bedroom, in that bed with its hospital bars, had been a way to dissolve the plaster, to shatter its inflexible solidity, to fight back against its imprisonment, and to breathe the air of other worlds because I could not expand my own lungs deeply enough to take in my own. With sudden clarity I realized that this must have been the reading the editors had enabled me to recover in the offices and halls and words of the Book-of-the-Month Club. *These* ghostly books were the ones that shimmered just beyond awareness each time I heard Joe Savago, Phyllis Robinson, or Alice van Straalen launch into flight on the back of a book that had taken up residence within them only to explode outward onto something other. Perhaps I identified with the editors against the people from Time because I understood what they thought they would lose if they were asked to forgo books such as these. They feared they would no longer be able to read in this intense, profoundly personal way as part of their daily work. Their impending loss, I realized slowly—admitted only reluctantly—solicited my attention insistently because, in some odd way and for some peculiar reason I could not explain, that loss was one I felt I had already suffered. In imagining and fearing out loud what it would be like to be asked to read differently, the editors transported me back to a time before I had been so asked. Indeed I recognized in their book talk and in their particular way of reading what I took to be my own habits before they were confronted with the different, more analytical and critical approaches of the English classroom.

But hadn't I enjoyed, even desired the changes I was introduced to in those classrooms? What was wrong with being asked to read more critically? Hadn't I felt the thrill of learning how to make sense of "The Love Song of J. Alfred Prufrock" in the twelfth grade? Wasn't it satisfying to puzzle with others over the meaning of that red sun at the end of *The Red*

*Badge of Courage*? Wasn't the almost unfathomable richness and depth of Isabel Archer what made *Portrait of a Lady* so engrossing to read? Why, then, the sense of loss? And why the intensity of my antiintellectual anger seething just beneath the surface against literary critics, literary criticism, and academics? If books and book talk at the Book-of-the-Month Club were analogous to my own books in the box, that is, windows on fabulous, promising worlds, what now was analogous to the plaster cast? If I felt so exhilarated, indeed almost liberated, to hear people talk about reading and books in this way, what in my present professional life made it seem as constricting and as leaden as the flat, cold, lifeless plaster of that stiffened carapace? How did something that had once seemed so alive, so all-enveloping as those warm, plaster bandages had first felt, petrify, as they did, into a kind of rigid prison? Did the act of professional reading *really* feel so oppressive, so burdensome as the dynamics of my response to the club and its editors suggested?

I tried at first to dismiss my response as nothing more than nostalgia, a simple yearning to escape the responsibilities of adulthood and the worries of middle age. Indeed I tried to corral and control my identification with the Book-of-the-Month Club editors by disparaging my response as the result of a longing to recover lost childhood. Yet I also began to wonder what my university education in general and training in English studies in particular had to do with all of this. Why was professional, academic writing about books presented virtually without anecdote and affect? Why was so much of it so tedious to read? Why did academic literary critics show no interest in relating their own concrete experience of a text or in appealing to the emotional responses of their readers?[26] Why was it so clear to everyone else that "authentic literature" and "real art" were necessarily challenging and difficult to read, characterized always by complexity, intricacy, ambiguity, and irony? These questions kept returning. And as they did, I thought about how difficult I had found it to learn how to recognize the telltale traces of "the literary" and to value them appropriately. Indeed I recalled with still-acute embarrassment a moment in my freshman English class when my first composition was returned with an annotation that read something like, "Next time, try to write about a more significant book." Ayn Rand's *The Fountainhead* apparently was not considered sufficiently important for a college English class. At the time I did not fully understand why. I was mortified, though, by my transgression and especially by the fact that I had been fascinated by characters the professor clearly disparaged. I had completely missed the implications of Rand's so-called objectivist philosophy for the vividness of her characters.

In replaying the painful memory in the offices of the Book-of-the-Month Club as I turned the issue of my identification over and over, I recalled with perhaps a little less guilt my long-ago involvement in the headlong rush of Rand's plot, in the sexual play between Dominique Francon and Howard Roark, and in the intensity of their efforts to articulate their sense of duty to aesthetic principles and to the purity of their art. Somehow these concerns did not seem so romantic and shameful in this context, shored up as I felt by the respect for identification and emotional investment in fictional characters shown by the editors at the club. I felt freer to recognize that the adolescent who had read that book on the beach just as she was about to embark for college must have been searching desperately for models of the intellectual and the artist, examples of how to be independent, and rules for managing sexuality. Why, I wondered, did standard practice in English education seem to dictate disapproval of this sort of readerly absorption in supposedly bad books? What had been at stake in the effort to teach me and my peers about the preeminent importance of linguistic complexity and formal intricacy? And anyway, what was the point of teaching *explication de texte* to undergraduate freshmen who had no intention of becoming professional readers themselves? My professor always used the French phrase and pronounced it with a crisp, ostentatious French accent. Why? Why insist that undergraduates learn how to describe in great detail the structural organization of so-called superior aesthetic objects? What had been gained, finally, by teaching me precisely how to discriminate between "literature" and "middlebrow fiction"? The swift gesture of arrogant dismissal whereby sentimentalism, the middlebrow, suburbia, tract houses, and the *Reader's Digest* were offhandedly but nonetheless ubiquitously dismissed so as to clear a space for the more rigorous and "critical" reflections of Herman Melville, Henry James, Ezra Pound, William Faulkner, Wallace Stevens, and others had been a familiar, ritualized gesture in the classes I took as an English major. Chastened by this discovery that the life I had led before college filled my professors and the writers I was supposed to admire with disgust, I had dutifully positioned myself as their acolyte and worked hard to learn why these things were considered so suspect.

Clearly, I had been asked by that professional training to identify against myself, my family, and my past in order to construct myself as an intellectual, an identity that seemed all the more assured the greater the distaste it could express for the mediocrity of the middlebrow. But did I really want to defend the "warm-blooded," embodied sentimentalism and individualism of middlebrow culture against the claims of literary modernism, intellectual asceticism, and rigor? Was my identification with the editors and their readers a good thing? Or was it simply a way of fabricating a fictitious state of innocence, an earlier, more "natural" way of reading situated before a putative "fall" into a more knowing, hence compromised, way of reading? Did I really want to make a case for the validity of the reading experience that was celebrated and placed at the center of Book-of-the-Month Club editorial practices? Surely pleasure reading itself was also a way of reading, a historically specific manner of approaching books and interacting with them. What were the social and material conditions of possibility of this sort of reading for pleasure? How, when, and why were middle-class children taught that books were magical vehicles that could transport them elsewhere? What had produced a selfhood that felt like a form of imprisonment, an interiority at once empty and suffocating, requiring a filling up by fictional others and inspiriting air from outside? And was this way of reading really jeopardized by the spread of a critical, analytical professional form of reading? I wasn't sure.

❦

Winter gave way to spring, and the tensions at the club seemed to subside somewhat. Al Silverman made periodic reports to the Thursday morning editorial meetings about the progress of the search for an editor in chief. It was going very slowly, he always said, because they were being careful about the kind of person they hired. Eventually Nancy Evans departed for her new job, and Bill Zinsser left to write full time. Late in the spring I was told by several editors that the editor in chief position had been offered to someone who turned it down. Finally Al announced that he would be directing the club's editorial operation for the time being, with the assistance of Joe Savago and Jill Sansone. It was clear to everyone at that point that the job would not be filled soon. Jill was promoted to executive editor and appeared to do most of the director's work, since Joe was absent more and more. Alice van Straalen was also elevated to the position of general editor and asked to work on special projects. Robert Riger labored even more closely with the marketing division and the distribution offices in Camp Hill, Pennsylvania. Some thought he was being groomed to take over Nancy's job. Al and Larry announced two new initiatives, including a people book club (which would build, obviously, on Time's *People* magazine and market celebrity biographies) and a mystery book club that was intended to target buyers and readers of detective stories. This led to an increased work routine that produced considerable grumbling among the editors but little change in the way they read. I continued to attend meetings, lunched regularly with different editors, and scheduled follow-up interviews with everyone. Those interviews and lunches added to the material I had already gathered, but generally I felt I was turning up relatively little that was different or new. Gossip and rumor seemed to die down as well, and on the whole the club seemed to fall back into familiar routine.

Joe Savago died on Sunday, September 27, 1987. A memorial service was held two days later. Presided over by Al Silverman, the service was composed almost completely of Joe's own words read by his colleagues and friends. They read from his reader's reports for the club, and they read from his journals. I did not attend the service because I did not know Joe had died. I had returned to teaching full time and had traveled to the club that fall only one or two days a week.

The following Thursday morning, very soon after I arrived at the club's offices, Jill Sansone came to see me. Someone must have called her to let her know I was back because she appeared at my desk even before I opened my typewriter. She had something to tell me, she said. We went out to the hall, and she began by saying she was sorry that no one had called me. I knew immediately what must have happened. She said simply, "I should have called you. I know how you felt about Joe."

We talked a long time through tears and regret. She told me of the memorial service and gave me a copy of the typescript they had all read from. The readings were as sardonic and funny and high spirited as Joe always was at his best. I felt grateful that she recognized that I, too, would grieve for Joe. But neither of us could avoid the fact that no one had thought to call me. The train's plunge into the tunnel under the Hudson River that night seemed deeper and darker than it had before. Or at least I noticed it enough to remark on it in my field journal and to think about the river as the kind of divide that separated me from Joe, the editors, and the club. The fact that they had not called underscored the very real distance between us in spite of how close I felt to them. I wondered again about my responses to this year at the club. What had happened? Why did I feel so connected to them? Or perhaps more properly, why did I *want* to feel connected to them? Why the longing? And for what? Was the connection and identification I felt only an illusion produced by my own peculiar desires? And if it was, as my absence at that memorial service seemed to suggest, what did this portend for the scholarly ethnography I was trying to write? The questions were overwhelming.

I did not make a conscious decision to do something else. After Joe's death, though, I gradually withdrew from the club's offices. I resumed my teaching responsibilities and academic identity more intensely and turned my attention to the library. I buried myself in yellowing papers, old commentaries on the creation of the club, the oral history transcripts, Harry Scherman's papers, Dorothy Canfield Fisher's letters, and massive amounts of secondary material on publishing in the twentieth century. I pursued the early history of the Book-of-the-Month Club with a vengeance, I suppose, as a way of trying to explain my own more immediate history within it. I was attempting to calculate, I think, the costs and the gains of a history that had surrounded me, caught me up in its sweep, and deeply affected who I had become.

# PART TWO

## On the History of the Middlebrow

## CHAPTER FOUR

# The Struggle over the Book, 1870–1920

## MAKING ROOM FOR MIDDLEBROW CULTURE

In 1916 the Whitman Candy Company of Philadelphia marketed a Library Package, uniting a large box of candy with a small, leather-bound book. The promotional strategy clearly imagined the existence of discriminating buyers who might want to endow a gift of caramels and chocolate-covered maraschino cherries with the tony aura of high culture. Whitman obliged by offering its own product in conjunction with one of fifteen Shakespearean plays collected in a series called the Little Leather Library. Although the library had been conceived by publishers Charles and Albert Boni, this particular marketing device was the brainchild of their partner, Harry Scherman, a former copywriter in the mail-order department of the J. Walter Thompson advertising agency.[1]

Only one among many thousands of quixotic free offers in the long history of advertising, this particular coupling strategy might have disappeared into oblivion had Harry Scherman not gone on to create the Book-of-the-Month Club, perhaps the most influential book marketing scheme in American history. Viewed retrospectively, though, as the precursor of the Book-of-the-Month Club, the Whitman Library Package can be seen as Scherman's first exploratory effort to recast the very idea of the book in the service of selling more of them to the American public. Suggesting that the book was simultaneously a consumable, ephemeral commodity and a classic, permanent possession, Scherman's package shrewdly launched the Little Leather Library, which eventually sold more than 25 million copies through Woolworth's, drugstores, and mail-order sales. Its remarkable success enabled Scherman to embody the same hybrid understanding of the book in his subsequent Book-of-the-Month

Club scheme, an operation that united the traditional publisher's desire to issue singular, serious books with a serially oriented, magazine distribution format, itself driven by the quite different imperative to enlarge the reading audience as much as possible and to access it on a regular basis.

The Book-of-the-Month Club was astonishingly successful in the years following its 1926 incorporation because it insistently applied to the business of book production and distribution marketing principles and advertising practices generally associated with other industries. Those practices, which included branding and national advertising campaigns, had first been developed to sell products such as tobacco, soap, and canned goods.[2] In adapting those practices to the world of publishing, the club served as an important catalytic force in the ongoing reorganization of both literary and cultural production, a process that had gathered momentum during the last decades of the nineteenth century and into the early decades of the twentieth.[3] At this time the material and social forms of the country's slowly incorporating economy were gradually but insistently pressed on a book production industry notable for its continuing ideological, if not economic, dependence on a different model of production organized around the creative activity of a singular, autonomous author who was understood to be the initiator of the publication process. The challenge posed by the club and other like agencies to existing book production circuits exacerbated the ongoing fission of cultural production into the highbrow and the lowbrow, eventually necessitating the christening of a new category, the middlebrow, with the Book-of-the Month Club as its quintessential example.[4] The Book-of-the-Month Club proved surprisingly controversial—notorious even—in large part because those by-then familiar and seemingly innocuous marketing strategies adapted by Scherman to book distribution in reality posed a significant threat to the essential concepts and forms structuring the bourgeois literary realm, including those defining the book, the author, the reader, and the proper relations among them. More fundamentally, Scherman's strategies threatened to rework the very notion of culture itself as a thing autonomous and transcendent, set apart and timeless, defined by its very difference and distance from the market.[5] Scherman's distribution operation, as its much-imitated name suggests, instead envisioned culture as a material, time-bound commodity, topical, ephemeral, and, above all, destined for circulation.

In order to situate the Book-of-the-Month Club in its proper context, it is useful to summarize major trends in the history of the book over the course of the nineteenth century. During this period, contending parties struggled with one another over the proper way to conceive of the book, its distribution, and its use, just as they disagreed over the appropriate scenes and protocols for reading.[6] By the time Harry Scherman and the Boni Brothers enlisted the help of Whitman Candy to distribute the volumes of their Little Leather Library, two contradictory, competing discourses about the book had developed, and Scherman could deliberately appeal to both in an effort to challenge the crude oppositions structuring them and their relationship to each other. When he refined the strategy further to create the Book-of-the-Month Club, the surprising storm of protest it generated testified to the familiarity of the habit of cordoning off one kind of literary production from another, marking particular kinds of reading matter as appropriate only for particular kinds of readers and reading situations. This is not to say that publishers never mixed the kinds of books they published or that actual readers remained content with the sort of material deemed appropriate for them. Rather, by 1926 a series of relatively tight material and social linkages between particular kinds of writing practices, production methods, books, and readers had congealed into ideological habit, producing two quite distinct ways of conceptualizing the book.[7]

## BOOKS BOUND FOR CIRCULATION

The history of book production in the United States during the nineteenth century is, at least in part, the story of the growing prominence of what might be called the circulating book, the commercial book bound for exchange. The story is complicated and fitful, however, characterized by advances and retreats, innovations, and setbacks. To tell it quickly and in abbreviated form, as I need to do here, is to make its development look foreordained, inevitable, and easily explicable. In fact, a host of economic, social, institutional, and cultural factors had to come together over a relatively long period of time in order to produce a book conceived primarily on the model of the commodity, that is, as an evanescent object that could fulfill particular needs and desires and then be discarded.

This book was linked conceptually not with its author but with its potential reader or readers. Regularly associated either with the pleasures of leisure time or with the particular objectives of specific interests and occupations, this book was viewed as a utilitarian object, as a tool for accomplishing a concrete goal. Thus it could find its proper place in many different locations, including the workplace, the kitchen, and assorted conveyances such as the railroad or the streetcar. Since such a book was thought to be highly task-specific and thus lacking in long-term value, it required only the cheapest paper and bindings, including a soft cover. Often demonized by its critics for its tainted association with pleasure or the merely functional, this impermanent book was regularly dismissed by elite cultural critics as nothing more substantial than a bon-bon, as a "promiscuous eatable," in the words of one concerned literary voice.[8] Itself the result of vast social, historical, and cultural changes, this particular understanding of the book was both the product of and an important agent in the reorganization of the business of knowledge production at the dawn of a new, mass-mediated age.

Commercially oriented book production, of course, has existed at least since the advent of the printing press. The range, extent, and speed of that production was limited for a long time, however, by the manual nature of the printing process, by the high cost of paper, and by the limited means of distribution available to the first printer-publishers. Significant growth of commercial publishing in Europe and the United States only began to occur when changes in manufacturing more generally and in the organization of the market economy were consolidated and when complex technologies and new transportation methods enabled outreach to extended markets. As Alfred Chandler has shown so well for the United States, neither the structure of the standard business enterprise nor the character of distribution could change substantially while the economy as a whole continued to depend on traditional energy sources, that is, on the human body, animal power, and the wind. However much road building improved and shipping technology increased in sophistication in the early national period, the essential relationship between production and distribution remained unchanged as long as the transfer of raw materials and finished commodities was controlled by the physical limits of individual humans and animals.[9]

With the coming of the railroad, however, and the use of coal and steam, that relationship was transformed forever as a new potential for speed and extended distribution began to drive the entire process of production and manufacture. That change did not take place overnight, nor did it occur uniformly. But as the possibility of moving goods more quickly and efficiently to highly dispersed markets was recognized and seized, American businesses began to take on a different shape and character. As Chandler argues, "The new velocity of [manufacturing] output and flows encouraged the integration of several units into single enterprises. The managers of those new multi-unit enterprises were able to monitor the process of production and distribution and to coordinate the high speed, high volume flows through them more efficiently than if monitoring and coordination had been left to market mechanisms." [10] Characterized less and less, then, by its organization into two distinct realms, that of manufacture and that of distribution, the nineteenth-century economy slowly began to take on the appearance of a single system of endless circulation. Not only did raw materials and manufactured goods themselves circulate more rapidly, so too did the increasing quantities of information necessary for the coordination of the previously distinct processes of manufacture and distribution. The newly restructured businesses exerted enormous pressure, finally, on a system of knowledge and information production still tied in many ways to the individual person and to the human hand.

By the early years of the nineteenth century, the pen had long been outmoded as a technology of information reproduction and distribution. Still, newspaper, magazine, and book production continued to be weighted down by the ballast of a manually run printing press. As new technologies made their way into manufacturing, however, they were also adapted to the processes of print production and thus to the task of information dissemination as well. Hellmut Lehmann-Haupt and his collaborators on *The Book in America* have indicated that the creation of the paper-making machine, which produced a continuous web of paper, eventually led to the creation of the rotary press into which the web could be fed. That, in turn, led to the need for the stereotyping process that allowed the production of curved printing plates. Finally, the growing speed of the printing process as a whole called for the appearance of composing machines that could "produce a sufficient amount of set type to feed the hungry presses." [11] At that point the speed of information production, reproduction, and distribution was fully mediated by machine and thereby magnified substantially, dialectically enabling and fostering the market integration taking place elsewhere in the American economy.

These technological innovations were developed in part because businesses demanded faster circulation of banking and shipping information as well as news about relevant government regulations. To meet these needs, newspapers evolved rapidly in the United States, and there the new printing technologies were used most heavily. Cheap book production emerged in concert with the newspaper business since the creation of a regularly issued print vehicle necessitated that the channel of communication it opened be perpetually filled with material of interest to a broad range of readers. In addition to the commercially oriented information they carried, early newspapers vied for the attention of large audiences by printing fiction in serial format. When advantageous government postal regulations enabled them to send materials to a far-flung audience relatively cheaply, they pioneered what they called the newspaper supplement, complete novels printed on cheap stock, bound in paper and distributed through the mail.[12]

Very early in the process, however, the story paper entrepreneurs such as Park Benjamin and Rufus Wilmot Griswold at *Brother Jonathan* uncovered a major impediment to their scheme: the problem of finding enough material to fill their regularly issued pages.[13] Because they initially lacked the capital to pay people to write the fiction they wanted to print, they turned to piracy. When that led to opposition and efforts at copyright regulation, the story paper entrepreneurs began to experiment with other production arrangements. As Mary Noel, one of the first chroniclers of the cheap book business pointed out in 1954, "Only when they had gradually acquired a little capital and were prepared to pay well, did they discover that in authorship, as in more tangible things, demand expressed in dollars and cents created a supply. With capital came the 'hack,' who was as much a product of the Industrial Revolution as was the Hoe printing press."[14] In effect the story papers called into being a new kind of writer, an individual who wrote quickly, regularly, and according to the specifications of another.

Despite the ritual demonization of a writer like this as a hack, a move that shored up the dominant conception of the author as one who wrote independently and only when inspired, the cheap book business in the United States expanded fitfully throughout the second half of the nineteenth century and, in so doing, mounted a significant assault on traditional notions of authorship. It entered its second wave of growth in the 1870s with a more extensive distribution managed by middlemen such as the American News Company, which coordinated the distribution of cheap books to newsstands and dry goods stores. The cheap trade developed further in the 1880s and 1890s with the institution of paperback libraries and series of books pioneered by publishers such as Street & Smith, Donnelley, Lloyd & Company, George and Norman Munro, Frank Leslie, and Beadle and Adams. Aiming not only at widespread but repetitive sales, these publishers sought to open a permanent channel of communication like that pioneered by newspaper and magazine publishers, this time between themselves and book buyers, a conduit they then had to keep endlessly filled with a predictable supply of stories likely to interest consumers of previous titles.

As a consequence, these new word merchants transformed story production even further by contracting with a large pool of writers who wrote books regularly and repetitively according to editorial specifications by drawing on well-known material already circulating in the press and on the popular stage.[15] Significantly, these writers were not permitted to publish their stories under their own names. Such a practice would have made it difficult for series publishers to build up the repetitive demand they were seeking. Rather, writers' products were all ranged under a sign or trademark of the corporation, the publishing house itself. Sometimes they were asked to contribute tales for brand name series featuring a recurring character. Publishers hoped that multiple authors could pen stories about such characters quickly enough to generate repetitive and regular sales among a large public. At other times the stories of house writers were printed under a single nom de plume, in effect the name of a fantastic superauthor who turned out tales at a pace far beyond that of any human. The immensely popular stories of "Bertha M. Clay," for instance, were actually written to specification for Street & Smith by house writers such as William Wallace Cook, John Coryell, and Gilbert Patten.

Even now, writers like Cook, Coryell, and Patten are disparaged as mere "hands" laboring in literary sweatshops and "fiction factories." They are more appropriately seen, however, as something other than failed authors or as the denizens of a fallen world of inappropriately industrialized letters. To continue to construe them in this way is to naturalize a historically specific version of cultural production as well as to ratify the privileges of certain entitled individuals who were graced by virtue of their class status with access to literacy, who were endowed with the tools of writing, and who enjoyed material conditions that supported a certain kind of independently motivated creative activity. The new employee-writers like Cook and Patten ought to be seen instead as participants in the social diversification of authorship and in the evolution of a new prototype of cultural producer, that is, a corporate, prosthetically augmented, creative agent whose capacity to produce reading material was significantly expanded by social cooperation and by systematic integration into a carefully managed and controlled, mechanically assisted system.

What was called into being, in effect, through these new social, economic, and material arrangements was something akin to the prosthetic subject Mark Seltzer has recently discussed somewhat ambivalently under the name of "the body-machine complex."[16] This was a hybrid subject produced by the interpenetration of the biological and the mechanical, the natural and the cultural—what Seltzer terms the machine person or the naturalist machine. The moniker "Bertha M. Clay" was never equivalent to the name of a singular, individually embodied author. Rather, it operated more like a trademark.[17] It was a sign of a new form of cultural production whereby collectively and corporately produced goods were designed to circulate in a marketplace of ever-widening dimensions.

The force of the challenge these new arrangements posed to traditional notions of authorship and intellectual property was felt very soon after this kind of corporate writing evolved. In fact, even as proponents of a more traditional view of authorship were attempting to craft what eventually became the International Copyright Agreement of 1891, other cases were being litigated in ways that contravened the kind of author legitimated and protected by the new copyright act. As Michael Denning has already suggested, these other decisions tended to challenge the claim that stories were in any simple way the natural creations of an autonomous, singular imagination.[18] The issue was litigated through a series of contradictory and confusing cases concerning the Old Sleuth detective series written by Harlan P. Halsey, first published in George Munro's *Fireside Companion* and subsequently marketed as part of the Old Sleuth Library. Originally the stories in the series were presented to the public as the authorial work of the person Old Sleuth, since Halsey's name was never mentioned on the paperback books themselves. When several publishers, including Munro's brother, Norman, attempted to use the word "sleuth" in copy-cat series that also closely replicated the illustration of the frumpy detective that had been used to flesh out the person of Old Sleuth, the identity of this supposed storyteller became a matter for the courts. An early ruling enjoined Norman Munro "from publishing any stories represented to have been written by Old Sleuth, Young Sleuth, the Young Badger, the Author of Old Sleuth, The Author of Young Badger, or either of them . . . unless such stories were actually written by [Harlan P. Halsey]."[19] Thus Old Sleuth was legally understood to be Halsey himself or, at the very least, his unique authorial creation and therefore his property. In this case the claims of copyright law were reasserted and with them the view that stories were the creations and therefore the intellectual property of individual, autonomous authors.

However, when Halsey himself left Munro for another series house, Street & Smith, and began to feature Old Sleuth stories in the *New York Weekly*, the case was reopened. Decisions were rendered and reversed over the course of the next several years, and for the most part the issue turned on whether intellectual property rights were to be asserted over Munro's claim that his own trademark, Old Sleuth, had been infringed. For a time the courts haggled over whether the cover and title-page image of Old

Sleuth functioned as a trademark or as a mere illustration. Eventually the issues were decided in *George Munro v. Beadle* when the New York Court of Appeals ruled against Halsey, stipulating that George Munro had property rights in the name "Old Sleuth" and was therefore entitled to protection under the laws governing trademarks. The original author's creation was thereby granted autonomous status by virtue of the property rights and individuality invested in the trademark. No longer the possession of Halsey himself, Old Sleuth had become the property of the publishing house and its owner-manager who had first underwritten his appearance.

It should not be surprising that the kind of book that resulted from this corporate and collective process was often significantly different from the more unified volume conceived, penned, and edited by a single writer who thought of himself or herself as an individual communicating in a unique fashion with a series of discrete individuals. This commercial book was more like an ephemeral apparition, a temporary embodiment of cultural material in wide circulation at the time in other formats. Printed cheaply and distributed widely and rapidly, this book gave material form to popular common sense only to disappear shortly thereafter in favor of some new instance of this rationalized form of cultural bricolage. Denning has argued that the material that appeared in the dime novel and cheap library format was therefore an "unauthored discourse" in the sense that authorial voice was subordinated to the dominance of collectively generated plot and character.[20]

What developed through the course of the nineteenth century in the United States was a model of publication quite different from the one that had emerged first in eighteenth-century Europe. As part of that more traditional set of arrangements, publication was conceived of as a form of natural issue and property transmission, as the deliverance of an author's intellectual property to a receiver-reader.[21] As the beneficiary of those arrangements, the reader was expected to receive and revere that property above all else, to attend to its features and to make sense of it *as the author would have wished*. Alternately, this later system of cultural production conceived of publication as an endless process of circulation or cultural recycling, as a reformulation and ever-widening distribution of previously existing material. The success of the process as a whole was dependent on the regulation of the relationship among multiple and constituent parts, no one of which was more important than another. In publishing conceived of as an integrated and self-propelled system, the successful operation of that system was as dependent on the ability to produce and to marshal readers as it was on the capacity to recruit writers, find manuscripts, oversee the printing and manufacturing business, and to distribute books efficiently and widely. In this form of publishing the motor principle of the system was lodged not in the supposedly autonomous author but, rather, in the new linchpin of the system, the increasingly proactive editor, who was capable of initiating publication ideas and seeing them to fruition.[22] To facilitate the multiple acts of consumption envisioned and necessitated by the system, this new kind of editor found it necessary to think carefully about readers and reading. He needed to imagine why people read and what they read for, and then he needed to consider what factors influenced potential readers to buy books. What he demanded from his writers, finally, was a book deliberately designed for circulation, a book calculated to please its buyers, to yield to their desires, and to answer to their needs — a book readers could use.

It is worth pointing out that at the same time that the cheap book industry was expanding significantly and churning out more titles designed for mass distribution, the circulating book was being installed at the heart of another key literary institution in the United States, the public library. In 1876, in fact, at the centennial celebration in Philadelphia, where the American Library Association was founded, a new cataloging system was introduced by Melvil Dewey.[23] Prior to this meeting, the dominant system of library organization in the United States had been based on the practice of assigning each book a fixed location on the shelf, "generally according to the date it was received by the library."[24] Based as it was on the assumption that books were discrete and unique objects, the assumption driving traditional publishing's elevation of the author along with his or her individual creation, this system spatially separated volumes on related topics. It thereby rendered both the classification and research process tedious and difficult, if not virtually impossible.[25] It proved a particular obstacle to any reader who was interested in a given topic but who did not already know the titles of works or the names of authors relevant to his or her search. The system implicitly demanded, then, a highly literate, knowledgeable reader with significant familiarity with a small universe of printed books.

It is no coincidence that the history of the modern library movement began at this meeting in Philadelphia where Melvil Dewey first publicly described the new cataloging system he had designed for the Amherst Library, a cataloging system designed, above all, to facilitate book circulation. Based on his decision to divide printed knowledge into ten areas, Dewey's system was further grounded on the principle that those categories could be infinitely subdivided into more minute classes expressed by means of Arabic numerals. Books in his system were assumed to be in dialogue with one another; readers were conceptualized as people with prior goals and topical interests; and the business of knowledge production itself was conceived of as an infinitely expanding, always progressing enterprise. In a sense the Dewey decimal system might be considered the bibliophilic analog of the new organizational structures contemporaneously created by American businessmen in order to facilitate the integration of production and distribution systems and to foster the circulation of both goods and capital. Dewey's system enabled the ceaseless circulation of books by making possible increasing refinements of the cataloging process through subdivision and cross-referencing and by envisioning the possibility of many differently organized book searches on the part of different readers. Like cheap book production, then, the Deweyan public library was reader rather than author driven, and it was oriented toward increasing the circulation of books.

### THE LITERARY BOOK

Together, these institutions promoting the circulating book mounted a stiff challenge to that older discourse already alluded to, which defined the book quite differently. In this more traditional discourse the book was conceived of as the emanation of an author, as serious, as a classic, and as a permanent and precious possession. Characterized concurrently as a kind of verbal real estate, this book was considered intellectual or cultural property. Since its intrinsic value was understood to increase with age, such a book, it was thought, would endow its owner with the status and legitimacy associated with learning and the school. In this discourse the proper place for the book was the family library or parlor. As a dignified object, it required a design that would promote longevity; hence the need for high-quality paper, secure bindings, and hard covers. Reading was concomitantly conceived of as a matter of serious attention, as a duty and responsibility, and as an activity of reverential labor, albeit one that might bring sedate pleasure as well.

Although all the various components of this discourse had been articulated before the explosion of cheap book production in the 1870s and 1880s, that explosion generated an increasingly shrill yet more and more explicit formulation of this approved ideology of the book. In fact, troubled equally by the appearance, content, and method of distribution of cheap series books, trade publishers who thought of themselves as literary men ritually issued jeremiads about the demise of the book as they had come to know it, thereby specifying exactly what they thought a real book ought to look like and contain.[26] In 1887, for instance, in a letter to *Publishers Weekly*, Henry Holt composed what was an elegy for an older, more substantial book. He conjured the picture of noble days gone by, "when the favorite dissipation of many a substantial citizen, even in out-of-the-way places, was to drop into the book-store of an evening, look over the stock, and take home some book in a shape that would be a permanent possession in the family."[27] He continued, "Now most of those book-stores no longer exist, at least as book-stores. They are toy-shops, and ice-cream saloons with files of Seaside Libraries in one corner, and the substantial citizen, instead of taking home an occasional volume of Irving or Emerson or Macauley, or even of Timothy Titcomb or The Country Parson . . . takes home a toy, or a pound of candy or pamphlet copy of, the chances are even, some minor English author who, if he had to be reprinted in a book, would not have been considered worth reprinting at all." In his mind a proper book was the discrete creation of an identifiable, usually famous author, not one of many interchangeable stories filed haphazardly as an afterthought in the back of a dry goods store. Holt concluded his peroration with the observation that the new developments had contributed to "a great diminution . . . in the reading habit" and had destroyed the habit of buying substantial books.

Similar sentiments were expressed by the *New York Evening Mail* in 1880.[28] In commenting on the cheap book trade, the editors linked its growing prominence with what they characterized as the diminution of the dignity of literature. "When a book cost money," they observed, "it was something to be preserved with care, and guarded and cherished as a thing of value. Hence, the possession of handsome editions of good books was a matter of pride to their owners." Presently, though, they noted further, "books, even of sterling value, are read and thrown away." While they could agree that "this system of cheap books" brought good literature to those who would not otherwise be able to obtain it, the editors also worried that it inevitably devalued the worth of that literature. "The publication which may be bought for a few pence," they wrote, "however worthy its contents, is likely to be regarded like a newspaper, as something to be skimmed over and for-gotten." Admitting that the publication of cheap books was unlikely to cease anytime soon, they nonetheless pointed to "the advantages of buying the best editions that one's means will afford." In that way the volumes which are accumulated become one's personal friends, and literature will be considered, as in days gone by, a lasting thing of worth and beauty.[29] In the view of the *Evening Mail*, the value of literature was itself a function of the respect accorded to it, and that respect would not properly be expressed if literature could be obtained cheaply, taken lightly, or discarded cavalierly. Literature, in effect, was entirely dependent on the properly turned out and carefully cultivated book. Concomitantly, its value was understood to be a function of how dear it was, a condition that would perpetuate its rarity, exclusive readership, and limited distribution.

These two characteristic editorials make clear that as publishing was increasingly affected by the imperatives of a commodity system driven by the need to increase production and consumption, a discourse of protectionism developed among some cultural arbiters who saw the traditional book as an endangered species and reading as an art in danger of extinction.[30] They conceived of their cultural work, therefore, as a kind of missionary pedagogy and as a form of conservation. In the last two decades of the century they energetically set about constructing various cultural preserves designed to foster the right kind of reading. Although these preserves were established as safe spaces set apart from the commercial hustle and bustle of the workaday world, they were also carefully policed in an effort to produce the ideal conditions for the appropriate reading of "real" books. Foremost among these preserves, of course, was the public library, with its strictly maintained silence, but we might also include the public schools themselves and, in particular, the developing curriculum in English, which extended from the grade schools through the high schools and into the professionalized departments of the new universities. Both the circulation policies of the libraries and the tactics of the new literacy curriculum in the lower schools were designed to teach the American population not only what to read but how to read it.[31] The special concern of the upper-level English department was the identification, preservation, and dissemination of a narrowly defined category, the high literary or, more simply and colloquially, literature itself.

As Raymond Williams has shown, a radical restriction of the definition of literature occurred in Europe over the course of the eighteenth and nineteenth centuries.[32] Where once "literature" signified "polite learning," it was gradually narrowed to refer, first, to "all printed books," then to books of a certain "taste" and "sensibility," and then, more narrowly still, to imaginative or creative works of high quality. This latter restriction was effected, Williams remarks, "as part of a major affirmative response in the name of an essentially human 'creativity', to the socially repressive and intellectually mechanical forms of a new social order; that of capitalism and especially industrial capitalism."[33] In effect, the literary was counter-

posed as the prime instance of human creativity to the extreme specialization of work required for the production of commodities; to the constriction of language to a medium for circulating rational or informative
messages only; and to the reduction of social relationships to the simple
wage relation of capitalist labor. Criticism, he notes in addition, "acquired
a quite new and effectively primary importance, since it was now the only
way of validating this specialized and selective category" of the literary as
the product of everything most profoundly human and humane.[34]

Following Williams's early lead, Gerald Graff, Michael Warner,
Richard Brodhead, David Shumway, John Guillory, and Thomas Strychacz have recently attempted to track the parallel development of these
terms in the United States.[35] Although each looks at a different aspect of
the development of the literary field, and the causal arguments they articulate sometimes conflict, together their accounts at least suggest that a
similar restriction of the definition of the literary took place in this country over the course of the last several decades of the nineteenth century.
That restriction eventually produced the particular configuration of the
literary field that Harry Scherman and the Bonis acknowledged and de-
fied when they insisted on packaging Shakespeare with the chocolates.
Brodhead argues persuasively that the post–Civil War upper classes consolidated, in part, by identifying with particular practices of cultural production and consumption that were neither available to nor adopted by
the masses.[36] This led not only to the creation of great neoclassical museums, libraries, concert halls, and educational establishments in every
major American city but also to the establishment of a new "high literary zone" first identified with the *Atlantic Monthly*, *Century Magazine*, and
*Harper's*. Targeted specifically at an elite, highly educated audience and
demanding a highly polished and lengthy form of writing from their contributors, these magazines helped to produce a new version of literature
that was grounded in what Brodhead terms "a prior act of hierarchization and elimination." As he puts it, "This term [was] produced through
a stratification in which most writing, including virtually all popular writing, [got] marked as nonliterary and unworthy of attention . . . while some
other writing [got] identified as rare or select: in short, as 'literature.' "[37]

Modern criticism developed in the United States contemporaneously
with this production of a new high literary zone, according to Graff,
Shumway, and others, as Matthew Arnold's supporting ideas about literature as "the best that has been thought and said in the past" were imported,
interpreted for the American context, and then widely disseminated as a
"missionary view of literature." At first practiced in the form of a higher

journalism written by men of letters such as William Dean Howells, Barrett Wendell, E. C. Stedman, and George Woodberry, this form of criticism also made its way into institutions of higher learning just as those institutions were professionalizing on the model of the German university. In reaction to a form of highly technical research then being developed by philological scholars of the modern languages, generalist criticism in the universities elevated and revered this new, high literature as a repository of true human experience and spiritual values. They championed it as a key redemptive influence in a materialist age. Although generalist criticism enjoyed a brief heyday at certain key institutions in the 1880s and 1890s, including Harvard and Yale, it was eventually replaced by still another form of literary criticism grounded this time in practices associated with philological research.

This latter form of criticism was interpretive and was based on an even narrower understanding of the literary as a special kind of language use. Warner suggests, in fact, that modern critical practice as we know it developed out of a struggle for control of the literary between the older group of generalist critics and those attempting to establish English departments on a professional basis. The latter, he maintains, constructed literature as a "knowledge subject" simultaneously with their invention of critical labor as the philological business of scientific "inquiry, observation, reflection and inference." As Warner puts it, "Critical labor did not follow from the literary so much as it reinvented the literary."[38] It did so by rendering the literary as a kind of special opacity produced by complexity, subtlety, and intricacy of verbal organization, an opacity that demanded the hard work of the professionally trained, technically expert critic. Warner suggests, finally, that with the appearance of a fully established and organized literary critical professoriate around 1900, "great literature [had] become precisely that which [repaid] the attention of the specialist."[39]

Whatever the contradictions and tensions between these varying definitions of the literary, together they contributed to a particular discourse about the literary field that construed that field as a pyramid of literateness with the apex occupied by the best works of imaginative literature standing above the less good and the more mundane works of nonfiction, journalism, and popular writing. Whether the superiority of the literary was conceived of as a function of its special spirituality or its intricate complexity, literature was endowed with a quasi-sacred status. Concomitantly, criticism served the constitutive functioning of determining the very boundaries of the literary. "Literature" evolved, then, as an honorific term to be conferred by experts only on those works that rendered themselves distinct from the quotidian, the mundane, and the profane. As such, literary books resisted any instrumentalist approach to their contents. They were to be valued in and for themselves alone. Literature was not to be crudely "used"; it was to be appreciated.

## THE UTILITY OF BOOKS

The literary book developed in late nineteenth-century America at least in part to counter the influence and feared effects of cheap circulating books. Explicitly designed for rapid and distracted reading, those cheap books did indeed lend themselves to perusal in the interstices of daily life, that is, during commuting, during brief breaks from work, and at the end of a long and tiring day. They severed reading's traditional connection to religious and scholarly meditation and contemplation and yoked it as an activity to the achievement of more immediate effects, be they pleasure, the acquisition of information, or simply passing the time. Indeed, in the 1890s, curious Americans could purchase individual Diamond Handbooks from Street & Smith, one of the most successful cheap book houses, which would tell them how to write a letter, cook a steak, photograph animals, interpret dreams, or tell fortunes.[40] In effect, late nineteenth-century readers were given many more opportunities by the cheap book trade to purchase a book with the intent of treating it transitively as a utilitarian tool for the achievement of an immediate goal. In many cases readers of cheap books aimed simply to experience pleasure in its manifold forms, accompanied by diverse affective and somatic effects. Whether cheap fiction books were to produce the skin-crawling sensations of fear, the upwelling tears of pathos, the erotic excitements of romance, or the bated breath of suspense, they were picked up precisely because they *were* successful at moving the body and provoking the emotions.

Eventually the demand for this kind of fiction generated an intense debate within American libraries about the advisability of stocking such material for patrons. Various policies were designed to control the circulation of cheap fiction, including locked collections of suspect books and checkout polices that favored nonfiction over fiction.[41] At the same time a new genre of writing developed that was devoted to the issue of how and what to read. What is so ironic about this genre that aimed to promote the reading of literature and the classics is that it often did so not by linking those books with leisurely meditation and reverent appreciation but by associating them with a more instrumental view that emphasized the benefits they conferred on the reader. As a consequence, even these conservative critics of commercial books turned to the language of enterprise in an effort to characterize the literary book as an indispensable investment as reliable as traditional real estate. In their effort to preserve the connection between books and learning, these cultural missionaries inadvertently contributed to the slow process by which learning itself was conceived of as a transitive, utilitarian activity with concrete social effects.

Perhaps one of the most influential examples of the genre was the early volume written by Yale College president Noah Porter, *Books and Reading*.[42] The "Introductory" established quickly that Porter's advice was motivated by his own distress at the fact that the book environment had changed drastically. "Now," he wrote, "the minds of tens of thousands are stimulated and occupied with *books, books, books*, from three years old onward through youth and manhood. We read when we sit, when we lie down, and when we ride; sometimes when we eat and when we walk."[43] Readers need new direction, he concluded, not only because "bad books and inferior books are far more common than they once were," but also because "their poison is . . . more subtle and less easily detected, for as the taste of readers becomes omnivorous, it becomes less discriminating."[44] Porter aimed his advice not at the litterateur or at the scholar, but at "those earnest readers to whom books and reading are instruction and amusement, rest and refreshment, inspiration and relaxation."[45]

Beginning with the traditional discourse about the book as an embodiment of its author, Porter argued conventionally that "a book is always written by a man, and that it is never by any magic or mystery any better than its author makes it to be."[46] To read, he noted as well, is "to place ourselves in communication with a living man."[47] Porter further argued that to read was also to engage in a morally serious activity. As such, he intoned, it ought never to be indulged in aimlessly. "Passive reading," he lectured, "is the evil habit against which most readers need to be guarded, and to overcome which, when formed, requires the most manful and persevering efforts."[48] Explaining further, he noted that passive reading "is the natural result of a profusion of books and the indolence of our natures and our times, which desires to receive thoughts,—or more exactly pictures, many of which are thin, hazy, and evanescent—rather than vigorously to react against them by an effort that thinks them over and makes them one's own."[49] He concluded, "Almost better not read at all, than to read in such a way."[50]

The intensity of the figural language employed by Porter suggests significantly that it was not simply the possibility of inattentive reading that disturbed him. Rather, he was horrified by the specter of a self-indulgent reader who failed actively to engage the book being read. The fear of passivity and pleasure thus pushed Porter to sever his view of "serious" reading from its older, more traditional association with aristocratic and scholarly leisure and to connect it with a much more utilitarian, focused effort at information gathering. He argued explicitly, in fact, that a reader should approach a book with a fixed goal in mind because desultory reading excited the sensibilities and relaxed the power of attention.[51]

Reading, in Porter's view and in the view of many others, was clearly to be associated with a highly disciplined form of cognition and a practically oriented, utilitarian intellect. It was *not* to be associated with the sensual, somatic pleasures of the body or the fearsome power of the emotions. Thus the debate over books and reading was a heavily gendered debate in the sense that cultural conservatives always associated the threat of cheap fiction and passive reading with the dangers of "aimless," "indolent," and "ardent" femininity. This discourse recommending the worth of the serious, hardbound book might be seen as a prophylactic discourse unconsciously directed at halting the spread of a diseased literature and at preventing the proliferation of undisciplined reading, which might distract people from their right and proper business of extracting profit not only from the material and social world but from the literary world of words as well.

However vigorously the campaign against the illicit pleasures of distracted reading was prosecuted, the more traditional librarians and their theoreticians could do very little to halt the proliferation of cheap books and popular literature. Indeed, as Dee Garrison has shown, by the 1910s, attitudes toward mass-produced fiction had changed considerably among American librarians. Where once librarians had stressed their authoritative intellectual role and educational purpose, they began to emphasize the recreational function of the library and readers' rights to determine what they wanted to read. The reformers did not win easily, as the endless fiction debates at American Library Association meetings in the first decades of the twentieth century show. Eventually, though, a 1922 survey of thirty-three public libraries and state commissions discovered that although locked collections still existed, popular fiction was generously provided in open stacks in most libraries for the perusal of self-directed readers. As Garrison comments, by that point "overt paternalism [had been] discarded and the public library became a provider of best-selling fiction to Ms. and sometimes Mr. Mid-Cult."[52]

If the increasing tolerance of fiction helped to legitimate the goal of reading to produce pleasure, and the "how-and-what-to-read" literature advocated a vision of reading as a goal-directed activity, such conceptions were further underwritten by other developments in the publishing world. Indeed, a good deal of evidence indicates that a more utilitarian conception of the book as an object that could deliver specific goods had established itself in the first decades of the new century. In addition to the proliferation of fiction designed to produce tears, thrills and chills, and other forms of pleasure, more technical, textbook, and even trade houses issued many more nonfiction titles designed to impart highly specialized skills and to enable their readers to accomplish concrete goals. During this period, in fact, many specialized publishing houses began to appear that were devoted to issuing only law or business volumes, school textbooks, or medical books. Although the transitivity of most of these books was linked to their content, that is, to what they might actually convey to readers and enable them to do, a few irreverent entrepreneurs began to see that the book-as-object might be used to accomplish certain goals almost regardless of what it contained. They began to see that the very idea of the book and the cultural value attributed to it could confer status on its owners, who, in the publishers' unprecedented view, need not necessarily be readers. Potentially, then, every book sale could generate two forms of profit. On one hand it could generate cash for its publisher. On the other hand it could also produce perceived changes in the status of the individual who bought it because the more traditional discourse about the book had managed to associate the social prestige of learning with the particular technology for producing that learning in the first place, that is, with the leather- or cloth-covered book itself.[53]

This sort of logic is nowhere more evident than in the 1909 scheme concocted by the subscription house of P. F. Collier & Son to sell the Harvard Classics. The success of the scheme was predicated on the celebrity of Charles W. Eliot, president of Harvard University from 1870 to 1909.[54] Eliot's unprecedented fame as the country's foremost cultural critic was almost certainly a function of anxiety about the potential destruction of traditional culture in the wake of the transformations effected by rapid social change. For years, in fact, Eliot had advised countless board and committee meetings and spoken out regularly on educational matters. Among other things, he championed the cause of continuing education and supported the idea of evening classes and free lectures. He claimed most significantly, however, that every American should engage in perpetual education through the practice of self-guided reading. He even suggested that a five-foot shelf could hold all the books needed for a liberal education and that anyone could acquire learning through no more than fifteen minutes of reading a day. This sensational quantification of a process once treated as ineffable guaranteed Eliot notice in *Publishers Weekly*. Robert Collier learned of Eliot's views and decided to act on the economic vision they implied.

As his biographer, Hugh Hawkins, tells the story, Collier sent Norman Hapgood, a Harvard alumnus and editor of *Collier's Weekly*, to Cambridge to urge Eliot to select such a shelf of books. He stressed to Eliot that the derivation of the plan came from his own statements and "argued that the name of 'Harvard Classics' would spread awareness of the university into distant regions and small towns and that it would associate Harvard with good reading."[55] Evidently persuaded by Hapgood's utilitarian and profit-minded argument, Eliot agreed to be editor and secured the consent of the Harvard Corporation to use its name for the enterprise. For their part, *Collier's* set about advertising the classics widely, stressing in particular the transitive value of the books in constructing an image of the educated self. In one advertisement they even went so far as to suggest that fifteen minutes of reading a day would actually lead to a higher income. "Do you realize how much more *you* could *do* and *earn* if you gave yourself a real chance," they asked, "if for instance you knew the secret of fifteen minutes a day?" *Collier's* continued, "You can get from these 'Harvard Classics' the culture, the knowledge of men and of life, and the broad viewpoint that can alone win for you an outstanding and solid success."[56]

Although the selections in the first three volumes were chosen by *Collier's*, Eliot was responsible for the character of the series as a whole. Not only did he choose material widely acknowledged to be serious and often difficult, but he wrote an introduction to the library outlining principles for its use and a reader's guide suggesting different paths for study. In the end Eliot believed that the series advanced the cause of liberal education because it celebrated a nonutilitarian love of learning for its own sake.[57] However, his most vociferous critics disagreed vehemently. They charged that advertising by *Collier's* implied that the acquisition of a liberal education could be achieved without effort, indeed almost through the act of book ownership alone. As *The Nation* opined, "To give the multitude to understand that fifteen minutes a day solemnly applied to the task of working off the set of books, inch by inch, will transform anybody into a man of liberal education, is to turn the whole idea of our colleges into ridicule." The journal continued, "A final touch of grotesqueness is added when the five-foot shelf, instead of being vaguely indicated or left to the imagination, is expressly prescribed, and arrangements duly made to supply it, the same for all comers, through the familiar machinery of the subscription coupon." [58]

*Collier's*, it would seem, had diminished the ineffable value of learning and culture by lodging it too concretely in the tool that was its ordinary vehicle, that is, in the book as simple object, the closed book stored on a shelf, rather than the open book in the hands of an active reader. Their transgression was to objectify the book too thoroughly, to display too vulgarly its material and mundane character. In the minds of Eliot's many critics, who also included cartoonist Finley Peter Dunne, only the likes of Mr. Dooley himself could believe that books on the shelf conferred value and status, not to mention an education, on their owner. Utilitarianism, in this view, had been carried too far. Satirizing *Collier's* reduction of reading as a process to the simple fact of book ownership alone, Dunne let Mr. Dooley expose the apparent instrumentalism of this new bibliophilic logic with his enthusiastic justification to Mr. Hennessy of Dr. Eliot's plan. Indeed he assured his gullible listener that "[Dr. Eliot] realizes that th' first thing to hve in a libry is a shelf. Fr'm time to time this can be decorated with lithrachure. But th' shelf is th' main thing. Otherwise th' lib'ry may get mixed up with reading' matther on th' table. Th' shelf shud thin be nailed to th' wall iliven feet fr'm th' flure an' hermetically sealed." [59]

## BOOKS AS COMMODITIES

To the great regret of cultural critics like Dunne, Mr. Dooley was not the only American in the first decades of the new century to recognize the utilitarian value of the shelved book. A surprising number of articles appeared in magazines such as *Good Housekeeping* and *House Beautiful* proclaiming the decorative value of books. For example, Jane Guthrie observed confidently in a 1925 article in *Good Housekeeping* that "in themselves books are essentially decorative." [60] She continued, "Their very bindings hint repose, the welcome quiet hour in this rushing world of ours. Moreover, books are full of suggestion. . . . They are essentially feminine, too. They hint mystery, the alluring unknown." Although Guthrie attended to the matter of literary genre and content throughout her article, she did so only to make suggestions about what sort of books as objects might best be placed in the library, the drawing room, or the bedroom. Her goal was to match books to room function as well as to the inhabitants' changing aims and desires for reading. Significantly, though, books were especially feminine and therefore particularly powerful because they were not mere objects only. Rather, they were endowed with a halo of meaning and an attendant affect, and as such they could, like women, imbue a home with the sentiment and feeling so needed by modern individuals.

Guthrie made this clear in her discussion of what led to her insight about the evocative power of books. Observing that she understood the importance of home only "after fortune led [her] to make a home in many different places, from hotel rooms to furnished and unfurnished houses," she positioned the idea of "home" in explicit opposition to the rootless anonymity and lack of individuality in modern life, conditions that rendered existence flat and undifferentiated. Guthrie informed her readers that, in response, she deliberately sought to create the comfort, intimacy, and individuality of a true home, a home that was made rich with affect, memory, and emotion, through the careful display of meaningful objects like beloved books. Although she acknowledged that the decorator was usually responsible for giving a room its particular feel, in fact, her prose lodged agency and individuality most insistently in the objects themselves rather than in the decorator who wielded them. "Socially," Guthrie noted, "[books] have broken the ice in many a formal atmosphere and by a natural and even intimate introduction, provided a gracious and mutual admiration. How many awkward pauses they have tided over! They are a sort of smile and bow of acquaintance and good will to book-lovers who might otherwise long be strangers." [61]

The sort of thinking Guthrie employs here results from what is now commonly called the fetishism of commodities, a tendency to invest material forms exchanged on the market with certain naturally occurring, inherent properties. [62] That is to say, Guthrie writes about books as if the meaning she finds in them is a naturally occurring feature rather than the result of a long and complex social process of exchange whereby their value was set over and against value assigned to other commodities. Although the commodity form is itself thought to have arisen with the first appearance of capitalism and the market, and fetishism is thought to have appeared simultaneously, the process by which meaning and value were assigned to commodities became much more elaborate in the years following the initial, explosive success of the modern advertising industry. Advertising discourse, as it redundantly developed in mass market magazines during the years between 1890 and 1930, endowed objects destined for the anonymous market with all the distinctiveness and individuality of the producers from whom they had been detached in order to facilitate their circulation in the first place. [63] The industry managed this task though an artful manipulation of words, colors, and forms so as to provide a context within which each advertised commodity appeared. This context then functioned to create a semantic and emotional penumbra surrounding the featured object. The penumbra, the discourse suggested, might then surround any consumer who bought, used, or displayed that object.

In effect advertising discourse remade Americans into consumers and acquainted them with national name brands. It also managed to animate commodities with a second order of meaning and significance beyond the meaning that might attach to them by virtue of their capacity to satisfy certain basic human needs. In a sense, then, it conferred on commodities a kind of agency, a capacity to realize the individual's desires, if not to complete the individual him- or herself.[64] Accordingly, it was possible for the many millions composing the anonymous market to purchase mass-produced goods with the aim of marshaling them in combinations to create an individual style.

It is worth pointing out that in Guthrie's decorating advice, as in thousands of advertisements that appeared throughout the decade, individuality was no longer conceived of as a quality inherent in individuals but, rather, was construed as a condition that had to be achieved, that is, constructed or performed through the tasteful and judicious selection of commodities, in her case through the display of books.[65] The very commodities that many cultural critics believe robbed producers of their distinctive humanity thus can be seen to have also enabled the construction and performance of a somewhat altered form of individuality in those who bought and used such objects, that is, subjects positioned precisely as consumers. Because those commodities were not inert objects only but things shimmering with an aureole of significance and a kind of emotional weather, they could permit the realization of a form of individuality measured not by its achievements or its actions but by its emotional style, its disposition, and its manner of being. In effect this discourse helped to usher in a new and highly controversial form of subjectivity defined not in clear and abstract opposition to the object world but thoroughly and inextricably intertwined with it.[66] Thus Guthrie could conclude her piece, "Try [books]—working out personal needs according to space and position, and learn how *human* and interesting a room can be made."[67]

Guthrie's comments enable us to see the irony in the fact that as the book was more thoroughly objectified by a variety of marketing schemes and distribution mechanisms around the turn of the century, it was also more thoroughly endowed with an agency and individuality of its own. By suppressing its status as the product of a complex set of social actions associated with a determining act of authorship, this consumerist approach to the book foregrounded its capacity to bring about certain ends by virtue of its circulation in the market and its adoption and application by readers in the realm of everyday life. At the same time, it illuminated its status as an animate object endowed with a vitality and life of its own and hence with an agency capable of doing things both to and for readers.

We will return in future chapters to the complex subjects of commodities and consumer culture and to the social tension that developed between the partisans of what I have called utilitarian reading and professional litterateurs bent on preventing such an instrumental approach to books by valorizing literature as an end in itself. For the moment, though, I want to point out that the discourse of the utilitarian book was itself sometimes elaborated in explicit opposition to a more professionalized approach to books. In an article for *House Beautiful* titled "Books for the Home: A Selection for Both Merit and Color," for example, Margery Doud candidly advised her aspiring readers, "A well-known expert on interior decoration was stressing, the other day, the importance of books in the decorative scheme, and so, entirely *disregarding the austere library classification*, a new problem of selecting books by a color scheme presented itself."[68] Tackling this new classificatory problem herself, Doud offered suggestions about the best books in her own personal categories of the red, the green, the blue, and the gray. She is worth quoting at length:

> Blue pottery vases and bowls for flowers are most attractive, and certain blue books, placed not too far away, will repeat and emphasize the color. Among the lighter blues are Beebe's *Jungle Peace* and W. H. Hudson's *Away and Long Ago*, two books by naturalists who write beautifully and poetically. . . . With the darker blues are two of the most famous and desirable books in the world, Shakespeare in the Cambridge edition, and the *Oxford Book of Verse*. . . . In the new Concord edition, Joseph Conrad's tales of the sea are in rich dark blue. . . .
>
> If you would have a tranquil bedside bookstand in your guestroom, put there David Grayson's, *Adventures in Contentment*, those neutral tinted volumes, *The Amenities of Book-Collecting* and *Messr Marco Polo* and the little tan poetry of Christopher Morley, topping these off with a mottled pink and blue in the form of *The Monk and the Dancer* and *The Turquoise Cup*, by Arthur Cosslett Smith.[69]

Books could be categorized by color, Doud suggested, not simply because their bindings exhibited a particular hue, but also because that hue often expressed the mood or larger affect conveyed by the text itself. Like Guthrie, then, she was searching for a way to understand books as aids to emotional response and mood construction. Significantly enough, she repeated her distaste for the austere categorical scheme used by librarians. "Librarians," Doud continued, "have a dreadful way of thinking of books. . . . They have fallen into the very bad habit of mentally thrusting a nonresisting book into a class, just as a filing clerk inserts a bill into its proper pigeonhole." Continuing, she noted that "William James's most readable *Talks to Teachers* is pushed into the formidable 'philosophy' pigeonhole; Edward Yeomans's stirring comments on modern schools, called *Shackled Youth*, becomes a dismal 'social science'; and Pearson's *Books in Black or Red*, in which a clever author is able to embue a reader with his own exuberant enthusiasm for certain of his favorite books, is crushed by the ominous label of 'literary criticism.' "[70]

The striking oppositions that structure her observations in this passage suggest that what appears only as a rhetorical introduction to a piece on decorating is in fact a schematic social ideology and an evaluative map of book production and use. For Doud, the readable clearly cannot be formidable or philosophical; dismal social science cannot be stirring; literary criticism is ominous because it excludes the possibility of exuberant enthusiasm. In her opinion, then, academic or professional control over books refuses the aims and prohibits the pleasure of all who would read for the expression of sentiment or to experience intense emotional response. Her ultimate valorization of sensibility is accompanied and underwritten by a strong antiprofessional, antiacademic politic. In thus advising her readers what to do with books as objects, Doud is not simply commodifying literature and culture. She is also elaborating an ideology of personhood that conceives of individuality as a set of emotional states, complex, rich, and infinitely variable. That is why her algorithms for placing books attend always to color as an emotional quality, link that quality with the content of particular literary works, and thereby treat the book as a magical, talismanic object capable of creating a mood and state of mind for the desiring reader simply by virtue of its presence in a room.[71]

We shall soon see that this sort of person was installed at the heart of the Book-of-the-Month Club operation. For now, it is enough to note that the success of the club was a function of Harry Scherman's uncanny ability to concretize complex ideological sentiments like these in the very structure of his organization itself, in the advertising appeals he designed to sell his distribution system, and, finally, in the actual books mailed to readers throughout the United States. Indeed it should be very clear that a volume of Shakespeare displayed for its evocative allure and for the suggestive affect of its blue cover is not far removed from a pocket-sized, leather-bound Shakespeare offered as a bonus with the gift of a box of chocolates. Little wonder that Harry Scherman's Library Package met with immediate success in 1914. That package deftly combined otherwise conflicting ideas about the value of the book in a single object. As easy to acquire as a box of candy, Scherman's first volume of the Little Leather Library promised immediate gratification and pleasure on the act of consumption. Bound in leather, however, it surely would last, destined as it was to take its place beside the other volumes metonymically implied by Scherman's invocation of the term "library." Disarticulated, finally, by its very size from the troublesome intimidation associated with the great books of high culture, this miniature volume displayed its accessibility not to the high and mighty but to the little person, the average American. Scherman created, finally, a book aspiring middle-class readers could use, a utilitarian object whose very possession and display would create a nimbus of culture, thereby conferring a certain social status, even as it held out the contradictory promises of real cultural mastery and immediate gratification.

When Scherman offered all this and more to prospective members of the Book-of-the-Month Club in February 1926 in yet another innovative scheme that sold serious books as if they were ephemeral magazines, it soon became clear that he had done violence to older notions of the book as a precious object whose value was beyond calculation. The story of the early years at the Book-of-the-Month Club is the subject of the next chapter. It needs to be said here, however, that the significance of Scherman's contribution is intimately bound up with the creation of a new cultural constellation dominated no longer by the two clearly demarcated poles of highbrow and lowbrow culture and their attendant conceptions of the book as singular treasure or utilitarian tool. Rather, the club marked the appearance of a disturbing new nebula, the middlebrow. That nebula, as Scherman's efforts on behalf of the Little Leather Library and the Book-of-the-Month Club demonstrate, was not formed by the introduction of wholly new cultural material distinct from its neighbors at either end of the cultural hierarchy. Indeed the club included among its offerings both examples of high modernist fiction and sea yarns, mysteries, and adventure stories. The middlebrow was formed, rather, as a category, by processes of literary and cultural mixing whereby forms and values associated with one form of cultural production were wed to forms and values usually connected with another. Thus, as I will subsequently argue, the scandal of the middlebrow was a function of its failure to maintain the fences cordoning off culture from commerce, the sacred from the profane, and the low from the high. Scherman challenged this separation in many ways but most obviously by too openly selling Culture, thereby baldly exposing its prior status as a form of capital—symbolic capital, to be sure—but capital nonetheless. His organization proved troublesome, then, because it refused to perpetuate the distinction between two forms of value, one determined economically by the operations of particular interests in the market, the other understood to be fixed, universal, and transcendent. The Book-of-the-Month Club was threatening, finally, because it seemed to create a permeable space between regions otherwise kept conceptually distinct and because it challenged that double discourse of value that has served to ground the humanism of modern Western thought for some two hundred or more years.[72] To look at the construction of middlebrow culture by the Book-of-the-Month Club and at the howls of rage its transgressive posture generated among its many critics is to begin to understand the crucial ideological work performed then, and even now, by a transcendent and idealized culture embodied in the literary classic, bound in vellum and treated with reverence and awe.

## CHAPTER FIVE

# A Modern Selling Machine
# for Books

## Harry Scherman and the Origins of the
## Book-of-the-Month Club

### HARRY SCHERMAN'S MODERNISM

Henry Ford significantly accelerated the nature of American industrial production when he established the first automated assembly line in 1913 at his Dearborn, Michigan, facilities. That same year the first radio signal was beamed around the world from the Eiffel Tower, and Americans caught their first glimpse of modern art at the controversial Armory Show in New York. In the months after the show opened at the Sixty-ninth Regiment Armory, the bohemian regulars at Polly's, a basement restaurant at 35 MacDougal Street in Greenwich Village, discussed the works of Picasso, Matisse, and Duchamp and shared with one another their own artistic efforts to make sense of modernity.[1] In addition to Marsden Hartley, who had exhibited in the Armory Show, Polly's regulars included Max Eastman, Floyd Dell, Mary Heaton Vorse, Upton Sinclair, Gilbert Seldes, and Charles and Albert Boni, the proprietors of the Washington Square Bookshop, which was located upstairs. The bookshop itself drew crowds of young bohemians to the Village and later served as the birthplace of the Theater Guild.[2]

The group was joined regularly by an aspiring playwright who supported his dramatic efforts by working as a copywriter at the Manhattan advertising firm of Ruthrauff & Ryan. Although Harry Scherman shared the artistic ambitions of those who would later go on to define modernism in the American context, the group could not have known then that Scherman's characteristically modern accomplishments would be more closely related to those of Henry Ford and the engineers of that first worldwide radio signal than to those of the bohemian villagers. Indeed Scherman would create a characteristically modern business when he developed the

Book-of-the-Month Club, an organization that, like Ford's assembly line, installed speed at the heart of its operation in the interest of facilitating ever-faster circulation of goods, messages, and ultimately capital itself.[3]

As we saw in the previous chapter, manufacturers and entrepreneurs in many different industries had made concerted efforts in the final decades of the nineteenth century to reorganize distribution in order to keep pace with ever-quickening production. Indeed, there had been successes. No one, however, thought the problem entirely solved. As late as 1910 Thomas Edison observed that "selling and distribution are simply machines for getting products to consumers. And like all machines, they can be improved with great resulting economy." He complained, however, that "the plain truth [is] that these machines for distribution have made the least progress of all machines. They are the same in many instances that they were forty and fifty years ago. The average selling machine," Edison concluded, "has become unwieldy and ancient."[4] Edison understood that if the vast increase in American manufacturing output was not to doom the economy through the accumulation of an unwieldy surplus, new means for facilitating consumption would have to be found. His concern was felt even within the relative economic backwater of the publishing business. In 1913 *Publishers Weekly* announced that "the world is still looking for a publisher who will 'discover and invent' a new method which shall be practical and effective for the distribution of books of general literature."[5]

By that point the individual who would pioneer in the creation of a significant new book distribution method—a selling machine for the publishing industry—was well ensconced in the business that would itself help to bring about the larger revolution called for by Edison, that is, the advertising industry. In 1913 Harry Scherman was writing copy for Ruthrauff & Ryan. He was so successful that he was hired away within a year by J. Walter Thompson, perhaps the most prominent firm in the business. They asked him to guide their mail-order accounts. Only two years later Scherman joined Charles and Albert Boni in the application of methods he had perfected at Thompson to the business of selling books—not just any books either, but the classics of William Shakespeare. To make sense of Scherman's renegade willingness to treat books as if they were no different from other consumer goods such as mouthwash, automobiles, and oatmeal, it will be helpful to know something about his past, particularly his education.

Harry Scherman was born in Montreal, Canada, on February 1, 1887, to Jewish parents, Jacob and Katherine Harris Scherman. A native of Cardiff, Wales, the elder Scherman owned a general store in Montreal. Several years after Harry's birth, the Schermans apparently separated. Jacob returned to England, and Katherine moved with four children to Philadelphia, where she eventually worked for the Jewish Publications Society.[6] By his own account Harry developed into a bookish child with an early love for reading. He later attended Central High School in Philadelphia, considered one of the best in the city. At the time Scherman attended, Central was noted for its highly academic curriculum stressing classical languages and learning. Scherman finished at the head of his class in 1905.[7] When he was honored by the Associated Alumni of the school in 1960, Scherman observed that "Central High [was] the ideal institution in which to acquire a liberal education."[8] He acknowledged that at the time he was "torn over whether to be a doctor, or a lawyer, or an engineer, or a playwright, or a newspaper man." What he most remembered about his years at Central, however, were the men who taught him the classics. Among them he recalled "a smiling, rotund and somewhat red-faced Englishman, who should have been on the stage, he read Shakespeare so roundly and so well, and who could have excited a hod-carrier in everything Elizabethan, history as well as literature." Scherman added, "There was an equally wonderful crusader—that's the word for all of them—in Latin history and literature . . . who first taught us the rudiments of the language, and then got us really worked up about Caesar, Cicero, Virgil and Horace."[9] Scherman clearly had enlisted in his teachers' crusade, for his interest in the classics and in the value of a liberal education figured prominently in his later efforts to construct an appeal for the Book-of-the-Month Club.

The quality of Scherman's academic training at Central won him a scholarship to the University of Pennsylvania, at the time one of the only prestigious institutions of higher learning in the United States that would admit Jews.[10] Despite his penchant for Latin, Greek, and Shakespeare, however, Scherman enrolled in the newly organized Wharton School of Economics and Finance. His motives are now obscure, but they may have had something to do with the fact that both classics and English departments at that time were bastions of an elite Anglo-Saxonism and therefore inhospitable to all but those with the bluest blood.[11] Scherman dropped out of Wharton, however, completely unsure about the career he wanted to pursue. At the time he was continuing to develop his literary interests by contributing freelance articles to local newspapers and pondering the possibility of a career in journalism. He reenrolled at Pennsylvania in 1906, this time in the School of Law. In 1907 Scherman dropped out again. He moved to New York to be with his mother and siblings and accepted a position offered by family friend Lewis Lipsky, the editor of

*American Hebrew*. While reporting for *American Hebrew* on books, the-ater, politics, and New York social life, Scherman pursued his "first love," writing "social" drama.[12]

For a number of years thereafter Scherman struggled to find ways to support his creative writing and lived "on the edges of the theater," as he put it. He acquired his first experience in advertising when he wrote free-lance copy with his brother, William. This apparently led to a well-paying job with the Osborne Calendar Company, which Scherman took because he wanted to save enough money to fund a year of writing. As he later ob-served, this was "the usual self-deception that kids of that type have."[13] In-deed, once Scherman accumulated the savings he needed, he embarked on a rail journey throughout the United States and, according to Charles Lee, "[soaked] up the American scene, [spent] all his money, and [wrote] noth-ing."[14] Returning to New York and the bohemian literary life in Green-wich Village in 1913, Scherman took his second salaried job in advertising, this time at Ruthrauff & Ryan. Although he continued to turn out plays and stories that were promptly rejected by everyone, Scherman began to establish a name for himself in the field of mail-order copywriting. He later remarked, "I turned out to be particularly good in selling books by mail, and more or less naturally, because that was my interest." He attrib-uted his success to the fact that he had always "noticed particularly how people could be influenced to read books by what was said about them."[15]

Given such a comment, it would be easy enough to observe that at this point Scherman abandoned the ideals of liberal learning and forsook the literary life for the more modern occupation of influencing others to buy. While there is a certain amount of truth to such an interpretation, it does not adequately convey the intense nature of the double life Scherman was attempting to live. Debating the merits of the new developments in art, literature, and the theater with Polly's regulars at night, by day Scherman was attempting to sell books like *Power of the Will*, a "terrible" book in his estimation, "nothing but a self-help device." Yet Scherman was appar-ently untroubled by his efforts to operate in both the art world and that of advertising. Indeed he saw no reason why he could not rely on his more intellectual interests to help him in the daily business of writing copy. It is worth letting him tell this part of his story in his own words:

It just so happened that at the time I was tremendously interested in William James. In fact, after coming to New York, for several years I did the most intensive reading I had ever done, in fields I hadn't discov-ered before. So I was reading James's philosophy and his psychology, and just about the time this book [*Power of the Will*] came into the office. I was on James's chapters on the will. And so I wrote an ad. I threw aside the . . . book, because you couldn't pay attention to it, and wrote an ad that presented James's point of view. The ad ran and was a tremendous success. I think that in less than a year Pelton [the author] had sold by mail far more than he'd sold in the preceding twelve years.[16]

Already demonstrating an advertiser's understanding that a promotional scheme need have very little to do with the actual qualities of the product, Scherman did not operate on the assumption that the philosophy and psychology of William James were beyond the comprehension of ordinary mail-order customers. As a consequence he harnessed his own active intellectual life to the business of selling books, however different they might be from those he himself was reading.

During this period Harry Scherman also began courting Bernardine Kielty, an English teacher at a progressive school for poor children run by the Hebrew Sheltering Guardian Society. The school had assembled an impressive young faculty, including Harvard graduate George Cronyn, who taught art. A kind of literary salon developed around Cronyn, who managed to draw people such as Walter Lippmann, Kenneth Mac-Gowan, Hiram Motherwell, Philip Moeller, Josephine Meyer, and the Boni brothers—with Harry Scherman in tow—to weekly gatherings at the Pleasantville, New York, school. It was apparently there that Scherman and the Boni brothers first hatched their scheme to sell small leather volumes of Shakespeare.[17]

## THE LITTLE LEATHER LIBRARY

The Little Leather Library originated with the Boni brothers when they noticed that a cigarette company was giving away a free miniature copy of Shakespeare with each tobacco purchase.[18] This suggested to them that a slightly larger, leather-bound Shakespearean play might be widely marketed at the price of twenty-five cents. When they showed their dummy prototype to Scherman and Maxwell Sackheim, a fellow copywriter at J. Walter Thompson, Scherman suggested approaching the manufacturer of a product whose high cost might justify the inclusion of a premium. Having lived in Philadelphia, Scherman was acquainted with the Whitman Candy Company located there and felt that since candy was expensive, the company might see the sense in a premium.[19] When his successful appeal brought in an order for 15,000 leather-bound plays, the new partners had to scramble for the necessary start-up capital. They acquired this with the help of A. L. Pelton, the newly wealthy author of *Power of the Will*. Scherman resigned from the Thompson agency to become the president of the Little Leather Library Corporation and to oversee production. Soon the company boasted a library of sixty titles, all in the public domain, as Scherman later explained, "because we couldn't pay any royalties." [20]

Whether Scherman continued to long for success as a dramatist is unrecorded, but it must have soon become clear to him and to his partners that he was unusually good at the business of marketing books. His next step was to "take the Little Leather things down to Woolworth's," a shrewd decision, for the giant chain store ordered 1 million copies the following year. [21] Scherman later observed that "right down at the level of people who were five and ten cent buyers, you found that demand for really good literature." [22] He may or may not have been right about what prompted Woolworth's customers to buy so many miniature copies of the bard. It is certain, though, that in their eagerness to peruse the product, they created a considerable headache for Woolworth's, since they dirtied the books and contributed to what Scherman himself called the product's "spoilage." Still, Scherman was convinced that Americans from all walks of life wanted to read "really good literature," and it was this unshaken belief that underwrote every one of his later book distribution efforts. Scherman and Sackheim tried to sell the Little Leather Library Corporation three or four years later. When they could not, Sackheim suggested that they might want to avoid the expense of dealing with their middlemen, the book dealers and Woolworth's, by attempting to market their books directly through the mail. Their mail-order scheme was born on October 30, 1920, when the first ad for a thirty-volume set of classics for $2.98 was advertised in *Pathfinder Magazine*. [23]

In this new scheme Scherman and his partners relied on a combination of publication advertising and direct circularizing to reach all who bought only by mail as well as individuals who might never set foot in a traditional bookstore. To accomplish this Scherman created what he thought to be a new selling technique—he included a sample leather cover in the initial mailing. This cover was supplemented by a short letter that asked, "How much do you think thirty classics with this kind of binding and this size would sell for? Make your guess and then open the enclosed, sealed envelope." [24] The appeal suggests that the audience that eventually bought 30 to 40 million copies of Little Leather Library books was interested not only in economy but also in the idea of a library of classics, clearly a concept already associated with education and social respectability through the success of the Harvard Classics. That the cover device seemed to prompt sales suggests as well that the audience was additionally attracted to the possibility of owning an elegant and tasteful object. It seems clear that what Scherman was selling in this appeal, in addition to a series of individual and ephemeral books to read, was a collection of potentially permanent, respected, almost sacred objects—a set of things to own.

Despite his faith in the reading tastes of ordinary Americans, Scherman understood the talismanic properties attached to the book in the early decades of the twentieth century. This is made clear by some of the remarks he made to Columbia University's Oral History Project in 1956 when he attempted to explain to his interviewers how the Little Leather Library metamorphosed into the Book-of-the-Month Club, which differed from the earlier enterprise in that it managed to sell *new* books by mail. Scherman explained, in fact, that before the appearance of the Book-of-the-Month Club, it was generally thought impossible to sell anything but sets of classics by mail. He observed, however, that at J. Walter Thompson he had found that "we could sell types of books which it had never been thought possible to sell by mail—Conrad, Oscar Wilde, and so on."[25] He continued, however, with the crucial detail. They had to be sold as sets, and "expensive sets" at that.[26] The raw, unrefined quality of this upstart literature was apparently masked by the scent of expensive leather and the beauty of embossed bindings. Scherman would later christen such books "furniture books."[27] He understood that people bought the fine book sets, as they had bought the cheap Leather Library sets, not simply because they wanted to read them but also because they wished to display them as prized possessions. A set of expensive-looking books, it would seem, was equivalent to a set of the classics by virtue of the beauty, taste, and fullness of its presentation. Both sets, their purchasers undoubtedly hoped, would signify to visitors that this family placed a high premium on education, tradition, beauty, and taste.

What perhaps set Harry Scherman apart from many others in the publishing business was his utter lack of condescension for the buyer of furniture books. Although it would be easy to attribute his magnanimity to commercial self-interest and to portray his book marketing scheme simplistically as a typically perverse act of capitalist alchemy whereby authentic culture was transformed into an inert commodity, I think this would be a mistake. Scherman felt no superiority to those who wanted to own books because for him, as for Jane Guthrie and Margery Doud, books were magical objects. In his case they fostered not only intellectual passion and pleasure but financial success as well. Although Scherman would not have claimed as much, he was a perceptive social observer who understood keenly the rich cultural meaning attached to the book at a transitional moment in American history.

Like his advisers at Central High, he venerated the classics. However, as one educated rather than born to their acquaintance, he also understood the symbolic significance that those books held for people unaccustomed to living amidst them. Scherman's success at selling a variety of books was a function, I think, of his almost instinctual recognition of the mixture of awe, fear, desire, and promise the noblest books evoked for a population newly taken with the value and possibilities of higher education. Indeed, high school enrollment rates in the United States increased 650 percent in the years 1900 to 1920, and college attendance tripled in the years 1900 to 1930.[28] Although many of the graduates went on to careers in occupations that had little to do with books, the book itself became a symbol of all that they had acquired through their education. In spite of its greater accessibility and more frequent appearance in cheap, ephemeral form, then, the book as an abstract concept was further invested with symbolic significance by a generation of Americans desperately in need of markers to signal their accession to middle-class comfort and their command of middle-class refinement, achieved increasingly not by the accident of birth but by the rigorous process of institutional education and apprenticeship. A set of books bound uniformly and elegantly and displayed prominently in the home implied metonymically that education had been neither piecemeal nor haphazard but complete, organically related, and fully refined. In effect, those books were called into being by the proliferation of high school diplomas and undergraduate degrees, academic credentials attesting to a more widespread, more formalized, and more institutionalized acquisition of cultural competence. With the Little Leather Library Scherman offered his subscribers not simply a set of books but an opportunity to display the results of their hard-won progress through the still-new, national education system.

People of their parents' and grandparents' generations would likely have demonstrated their middle-class status by emphasizing their mastery of a complex code of manners, a competence that could only have been acquired at the time through long years of informal schooling in the proper middle-class home. As we have already seen, however, a transition had begun, and the individuals who would become Scherman's customers increasingly turned to a sophisticated manipulation of commodities and objects in order to signify their accession to comfort and respectability.[29] First instructed in the fine points of domestic and sartorial display by national, name-brand advertisers, this generation had been further tutored in the aesthetic of plenty by the popular, mass market magazines.[30] They were also instructed in the drama of consumer display by the appearance of dazzling movie palaces filled with mahogany, crystal, and brocade.[31] Increasingly, they idolized Hollywood stars as "leisure experts" skilled at the spectacular assemblage of a welter of consumer goods on glittering domestic stages such as "Pickfair," the home of Mary Pickford and Douglas Fairbanks.[32] Although the "consumer ethic," as Roland Marchand has termed it, would not appear in full bloom until the 1920s, with the appearance of concerted advertising efforts to promote the aesthetic of the ensemble, it is clear that during the first two decades of the twentieth century many more Americans were being instructed to speak of their achievements, their status, and their personality in the language of objects.[33] Self-consciously "cultural" objects such as the book were especially evocative symbolically because they carried a series of semantic entailments that spoke of their association with the learning, gentility, and contemplative leisure of that earlier era when manners, cultivation, and the signs of good breeding were so important.

Entrepreneurs like Scherman capitalized on the expansion of the educational apparatus in the United States by offering for profit cultural goods the system had taught its students to appreciate. Yet it is essential to note that they also dialectically helped to provide a guarantee of the value of the academic credentials vetted and conferred by the school system in the first place. Indeed these enterprises played an important role in defining the parameters of an extracurricular public space where school-derived knowledge might be further exercised. Without the appearance of such a space, without a public demonstration of the continuing utility of such knowledge in spaces beyond the classroom, resistance to the complex discipline called for by the school system itself might have been higher. In effect, by proliferating cultural goods and by expanding awareness of their availability, cultural commodities like the Little Leather Library provided both the occasion and the means by which individuals might display their continuing mastery of the strategies and dispositions their certificate supposedly measured, that is, their cultural competence. The precursors of middlebrow culture, then, helped to legitimate that competence by creating an arena for its sometimes routine, sometimes spectacular exhibition.[34]

At the same time, and perhaps even more significantly, by virtue of the particular marketing procedures they adopted, entrepreneurs like Scherman demonstrated that those strategies and dispositions were generalizable because cultural objects themselves were equivalent. Thus they established the efficacy of a particular relation to culture by first demonstrating the fungibility of cultural goods themselves. Salesmen like Harry Scherman, we shall see, sold culture as an abstract category of goods rather than as a series of wholly distinct and different objects. In the course of selling those goods they thereby established their interchangeability, their fungibility.[35] Subsequently, in instructing their customers in the fine points of exchange whereby the conspicuous expenditure and display of interchangeable cultural goods could be converted into enhanced respect, status, and material success, they additionally established those goods as capital—as cultural capital. They therefore helped to reinforce the liquidity of cultural capital in a society ever more dependent on advanced literacy, on the skills of reading, and on the capacity to mobilize and to control information flow.[36]

## MARKETING BOOKS: THE PROBLEM OF SINGULARITY

To flesh out this argument, it will be helpful to return to Scherman and his efforts to facilitate a constant, more regularized sale of books through the mail. The problems he encountered as a consequence of the first success of the Little Leather Library are instructive because they point to key obstacles to the establishment of books and culture as fully fungible property. In fact, Scherman soon recognized that a distribution system designed to sell only sets of classics was hindered by certain built-in limitations that restricted its expansion and placed a cap on its financial success.

The system worked, to begin with, because a process of conceptual abstraction had produced the category of "the classic" out of a relatively finite number of specific texts that had acquired a similar cultural value. Classics were classics because their supposed claim to legitimacy and worth had already been established by accepted authorities. They were therefore understood to have particular use-values. Precious as specific moral and spiritual guides, classics as a group gained symbolic weight from their association with those authorities—the clergy, the school, and the university—who had pronounced on their individual value. Classics were considered worth owning because they embodied so-called universal human wisdom and truth and could be called on in time of need for advice and guidance. Because such books were already understood to have particular uses, and because they subsequently had come to be associated conceptually with the sort of people who could afford to buy them, men like Scherman could successfully market the *idea* of the classic to those aspiring to demonstrate their status as well placed and well educated. He managed this by marketing the supposed benefits of owning the classics in the form of the object his publicity was actually selling, the elegant set of revered volumes worthy of a place of honor in the tasteful home. In effect, Scherman prompted multiple acts of purchase by exchanging the abstract idea of the classic with a physical object, in this case, a set of books. He thereby helped to codify an exchange value for the classic.

The abstraction of the concept was limited, however, because it referred to specific works of art whose status had been established by their continuing recognition and survival over a considerable period of time. This meant that Scherman's marketing success was both dependent on and limited by potential buyers' recognition of familiar names and titles within the set. Although the definition of "classic" might be stretched a little to include recent, ballyhooed titles that would strike a chord among targeted consumers, Scherman and his partners could not afford to venture too far afield for fear of sullying the purity of the category itself. Their ability to sell the set depended on its inclusion of particular titles, authors, and fixed texts. Sales were limited because the processes of reproduction and repetition on which an expanding exchange depended were themselves checked by the enterprise's too-heavy dependence on an abstraction that referred to a purportedly auratic art, that is, a unique, individual creation recognized for its inherent, essential, particular properties.[37]

Once a family had purchased the Little Leather Library, for instance, or a set of Conrad's or Wilde's novels, finite collections all, Scherman lost the benefit of their purchasing power to the producers of other consumer durables. The fungibility of the cultural commodity, in this case, was limited because the system as a whole was dependent on the prior operation of a different and very slow system for establishing value, that by which specific populations adapted particular literary and philosophical works to their daily use. Scherman could only expand the Little Leather Library of Classics and thereby sell more books to be exchanged for capital on his end and for status on the reader's end when another classic title was established in the public mind.

As a businessman Scherman refused to wait. He quickly realized that if his company was to maintain or increase its sales, he would have to find a way to sell new books because that would provide a perpetual supply of marketable objects and create the possibility of recurring consumer demand. Although he may not have attended the Wharton School of Finance for very long, he had clearly mastered modern economic logic and under-

{ *On the History of the Middlebrow* }

stood well that successful mass marketing depended on the ability to maintain consumer desire for an endless succession of entirely new products or at least for new variations and more stylish versions of familiar ones. The former project was more expensive because it entailed a costly publicity campaign designed to introduce a new product and to gather a following by convincing individuals of their need for it.[38] Consequently, innovations of style had already moved to the center of the consumer economy because they enabled producers to renew demand for products whose conceptualization, use, and value had already been established in the public domain. In toying with the idea of trying to sell a series of new titles rather than finite sets of established classics, Scherman was simply relying on standard thinking in the world of American business.

He soon ran aground, however, in his efforts to apply this logic to the realm of book publishing and distribution. As he observed in his Columbia interview, "Just one of the ideas we had—and we had a file of them—as something worth trying for the Little Leather Library Corporation, to keep its volume up, was the idea of selling new books by mail." He went on: "We had given considerable thought to this matter. We had been asked by a number of trade publishers to see about this. They knew how well we were doing for sets, and for older books. Now and then we would talk with regular publishers about selling new books by mail. But it turned out to be absolutely impossible to sell new books by mail, for the simple reason that the selling cost had to be charged against the single book. You'd never get a three percent response."[39]

Scherman was referring to the fundamental marketing problem that plagued the book publishing industry then and continues to do so today: how to design blanket advertising aimed at a mass market for a collection of entirely different, unique, and unknown objects. His comments simply repeat the common wisdom of the industry that financially feasible book advertising is an impossibility because the cost of a significant campaign has to be charged against single titles. This is the case, the argument goes, because each unique book appeals to its own unique audience, thereby necessitating a series of entirely distinct promotional schemes and campaigns. The mass marketing of books is limited, then, according to this logic, by the inherent specificity of each volume.

In his effort to capitalize on the vista of endless production and consumption promised by the idea of the new, the imperative driving the rest of the developing consumer economy, Harry Scherman had to confront the fundamental resistance of the book conceived as an individual creation to the processes of abstraction at the heart of the marketing, advertising, and exchange process. He had to confront the fact that the supposed particularity of the book prevented its conversion into a more fully fungible and therefore more marketable property. In order to continue to increase sales, therefore, Scherman knew he would have to learn how to sell new books as an identifiable category with recognizable uses for potential buyers. The problem was how to create an abstraction that would allow the endless repetition of individual instances of it without particularizing those objects too much. How could he demonstrate the value and uses of the new if every new thing was in fact unique and unknown? As he explained to the Columbia interviewers, "Now we had known as part of our established experience that you could sell individual books which might be called 'use books,' like *Power of Will* or *American Gardening*, things of that kind where there would be a broad market." "But," he went on, "you couldn't sell the new fiction, or new non-fiction books about which the general public knew nothing."[40]

Scherman believed that in the United States of the 1920s new instances of fiction and general nonfiction had not been established as "use books." He suspected that most Americans did not habitually fall back on abstract categories to make sense of the utility of many new book offerings. In other words, while they did think of some books as utilitarian objects—gardening books and self-help volumes, for example, were apparently understood to have clear functions and concrete applications, which enabled advertisers to write appropriate appeals for them—individual volumes of fiction and some nonfiction were not conceptually grouped into a category with recognized, culturally determined uses and value. This was the result, I believe, of the continuing, dispersed effect of the mutually dependent ideologies of the novel, of the writer as genius, and of the aesthetic as a transcendent entity, as an end itself. Together these ideologies constructed a vision of the literary book—and all others that aspired to its status—as the unique utterance of an autonomous individual who had composed from within, who expressed highly personal aims, and who therefore created a book chiefly valuable for its original content and idiosyncratic style.[41] The resulting utterance, the book, was irreducible to the utterance of any other and therefore addressed its readers in unanticipated and ungeneralizable ways.

Novels and their nonfictional relatives were, to put it baldly, simply novel, and as auratic objects they called for contemplative distance and reverent attention.[42] This ideology of the singularity of the book tended to work against the understanding that even aesthetically oriented attentiveness had its own functions and that even very different books sometimes

{ *On the History of the Middlebrow* }

performed quite general functions in people's daily lives. Real books, therefore, as opposed to the supposedly degraded, formulaic products of fiction factories and hack operatives, continued to be conceived as wholly incommensurate and resistant to absorption into a market system that was dependent on processes of abstraction and equalization. The fungibility and liquidity of cultural commodities like the book could not be demonstrated, then, until their particularity as singular utterances was subordinated ideologically to their shared and generalizable utility as certain kinds of consumer goods that might promote certain specific and highly valuable actions and experiences.

Scherman and many other publishing executives understood that the continuing success of trade books in a leisure environment increasingly dominated by radio and the movies depended on the publishing industry's ability to advertise its best wares broadly and to market them successfully. Some way had to be found, therefore, to generalize about the uses and value of books as an abstract category without reducing them to absolute functional equivalents of one another, as the cheap book industry apparently had, at least according to its critics. In attempting a solution, both Scherman and the trade resorted to the kind of logic the advertising industry had perfected to sell all sorts of different commodities. They turned their attention from the object itself and focused instead on consumers. They stressed what the object in question could enable consumers to do, to feel, and to be. The publishers began to emphasize how certain kinds of books could promote certain kinds of reading experiences for the buyer who was presumed to be a reader.

In the industry more generally, a great deal of attention was devoted at this time to pleasure reading. The concept was reconstructed and transformed from the morally corrupt, entirely wasteful activity envisioned by Noah Porter into a relaxing, self-enhancing pastime that might lead to the creation of "the book habit."[43] In fact, many commentators in *Publishers Weekly* and in the public affairs weeklies labored industriously to establish a positive connection between reading and pleasure, hoping thereby to send consumers to bookstores again and again to purchase new engines of emotional transport. However, it should not be surprising that even the most vigorous defenders of the pleasures of book reading could not ignore the more traditional link between books, education, and middle-class taste. No matter how hard they tried to privilege enjoyment and pleasure, these champions of the book returned again and again to its association with education and edification. As a consequence they always returned to the classics, suggesting that books whose value had been demonstrated over time would yield greater benefits than those promising only momentary distraction.

The pleasure-reading discourse stumbled over the residual reverence accorded the classics. It continued to maintain a distinction between one large set of books conceived as undifferentiated and equivalent—those that might promote mere pleasure and be discarded—and another set comprised of special, wholly individual volumes that would provide pleasure and edification and uplift. In returning to the conception of the book as a unique utterance with distinctive properties, they thereby limited the rationale for increasing book sales just as Scherman had done in marketing only classics in his Little Leather Library. Thus this discourse failed to establish an easily comprehensible and marketable conception of the new book as one with desirable properties and identifiable uses.

The quick success of the Book-of-the-Month Club, it seems to me, was a function of Scherman's solution of this troubling dilemma, the problem of how to market new cultural products widely, repetitively, and continuously without devaluing the idea of the cultural itself as a status category dependent on the presumption of the existence of a unique original. What Scherman confronted, in effect, was the contradiction between new forces of production and consumption and older ways of conceptualizing the results of literary processes of composition. We will see eventually that the club as an organization attacked the problem with a two-part strategy. First, Scherman himself found a way to market an open-ended series of books by emphasizing the benefits the single category of the new might confer on book buyers. Then, with the help of the people he hired to select his books, the club learned how to organize books into many different classes of objects, such as hammock literature, serious fiction, popular history, or adventure novels. Those objects were understood to provoke different kinds of experiences in readers. I want to look at the first of these strategies next and to reserve full discussion of the second for a later chapter.

## THE BOOK-OF-THE-MONTH CLUB AND

## THE MODERN, INTEGRATED CIRCUIT

Harry Scherman did not consciously think of the Book-of-the-Month Club as an answer to a historical conundrum. In his mind it was simply a merchandising scheme designed to address a commonplace problem in marketing, the problem of how to distribute goods in numbers adequate

{ *On the History of the Middlebrow* }

to an accelerated and ever-more-efficient production system. For him the problem was how to bypass traditional bookstores, which were concentrated in urban areas and on the East Coast, in order to sell more books to more people. In fact, in the original outline for the club, Scherman candidly observed that "the Book-of-the-Month Club will be a commercial enterprise and will be advertised frankly as such."[44] Although he noted as well that the operation would offer its subscribers "certain cultural advantages," it is clear that at this point he was driven primarily by the advertiser's belief that money could be made in book selling by enlarging the potential audience for books and by increasing that audience's disposition and opportunity to buy. As he explained in the original plan, "Booksellers don't begin to supply the natural demand for new books that actually exists in the public. They skim off the top-cream only. They sell books only to the comparatively few people who have the leisure, and who have formed the habit, of seeking out books to buy."[45]

Scherman's goal was to reach an entirely new audience for books by bypassing traditional publishing middlemen, their customary prejudices, and their conviction that books could only be sold in a series of individual transactions uniting a unique book and an individual reader who went to a bookstore with a particular author in mind. Scherman was certain that many more readers could be persuaded to buy if books were made more accessible to them. Reflecting later in life on the nature of the Book-of-the-Month Club's success, he suggested that it ought to be compared to the "mushrooming of suburban shopping centers," "the extraordinary spread of self-servicing," and "the immense rise of chain-stores multiplying their outlets weekly and monthly." Characterizing all of these as examples of "ingenuity displayed in the field of distribution," he noted that all aimed "largely at one objective—to making consumer goods more easily obtainable." "That," he concluded, "is the area where the invention of the book-clubs belongs."[46]

The challenge facing him in 1925–26, however, was not simply finding new mail-order customers. Rather, the point was to design a scheme that would not reproduce the booksellers' logic. Scherman had to find a way to ensure the regular and repetitive purchase of new titles churned out at an increasingly rapid rate by the trade. He had to design a scheme that would persuade potential book readers to buy more than a few individually advertised volumes through the mail. As he explained to the Columbia oral history interviewers, "That was the genesis of the Book-of-the-Month Club. Somebody had to take a group of books." But, as he further noted, getting people to buy a group of books about which they knew nothing was not so easy to achieve: "It couldn't be immediate, because people were not buying groups of books immediately; therefore they had to buy over a period of time. It therefore had to be something like a subscription. On whose authority, then? You had to set up some kind of authority so that the subscriber would feel there was some reason for buying a group of books, so that he'd know he wasn't buying a pig in a poke, and also that he wasn't buying books which were suspect."[47]

Scherman understood that he had to authorize the books he wanted to sell and he had to authorize them specifically as a group. In designing his advertising appeal he had to conceptualize the set of unknown and different books to be bought in the future as a single category of cultural commodities with a distinct identity and clear functions and uses. In short, Scherman had to find a way to abstract the idea of "new books" from the welter of different titles published monthly, and then he had to construct a rationale explaining why potential readers would be better served by receiving a range of new books selected by others on a regular basis rather than by relying on their own initiative to acquire individual titles to their liking in fitful, desultory fashion.

The solution Scherman designed proved to be disconcertingly successful. Its success can be attributed, I think, to the fact that Scherman's scheme both capitalized on the structural innovations of the Fordized economy and recognized implicitly that the relentless, staccato pace set by the inexorable production of an increasing number of goods and services caused great anxieties within the American population.[48] With respect to the publishing sphere, this meant that the increase in title output that had occurred in preceding years had presented readers with the daunting problem of how to winnow the mass of books published to a reasonable collection of a few titles to read. In response Scherman proposed to market not simply new books in general but "the best new books published each month." He promised to manage the flood of books for his customers and thereby acclimate them to the hectic pace of modern life. He proposed to do so by uniting an assembly-line distribution operation driven by the calendar and the clock with a selection mechanism designed to evoke the leisurely, disinterested deliberations of authorities whose province was the identification of classic works of literature and art that would stand the test of time. In joining these two quite different, even opposed mechanisms, he united a modern concern about time and timeliness with an older discourse about timeless value. He assured his subscribers that they could keep up with the tempo of modern cultural production without sacrificing their appreciation for distinction.

Scherman established the Book-of-the-Month Club as a subscription operation designed to distribute one book a month, both regularly and repetitively, to individuals who signed on as club members. Apparently he understood well the financial benefits of the economies of speed and regularity that structured the mass market magazine business. Regularized distribution was clearly designed to increase the speed of his stock turn, and predictable sales would enable him to gauge how much working capital ought to be invested in actual book production to avoid the problem of oversupply. Yet Scherman also knew that even the most sophisticated marketing organization would not survive if it could not design a successful appeal for its products. Thus he had to establish a particular identity for the new books he wanted to send out, and he had to persuade potential subscribers that these books had both uses and value. In effect, he had to give his new books a brand name and create consumer loyalty to his organization.

In an effort to accomplish this, Scherman stipulated that the books his subscribers received would be chosen by a "committee of selection" composed of "eminent experts" charged with identifying "the best new book published each month." The original outline for the club makes no mention of whom Scherman intended to approach, so it is clear that in the early stages of the club's creation he thought of the selection committee only as a necessary form of insurance, as a public relations testimonial about the quality of the product to be offered. The prior status of committee members as experts in the field of letters would enable him to confer metonymically the same high cultural status on the books they chose. Thus he did not offer Book-of-the-Month Club members a finite set of established classics as he had to the buyers of the Little Leather Library. Rather, he offered the generalized and highly abstract promise that his open-ended collection of new books, because they were the best, were sure to become classics. Any serious reader, he reasoned, would therefore be happy to acquire them for his or her home library.

In tying his operation to the distribution of new books, Scherman did not build in the kind of limits that had plagued his Little Leather Library scheme. Theoretically the Book-of-the-Month Club would never run out of books to sell or exhaust the desires and needs of potential customers as long as Scherman could persuade them that the regular acquisition of new books was useful in some way. Although it would take him months and a lot of tinkering to design his advertising appeal, it is clear even in the original plan that Scherman intended to sell his new books as a synecdoche for modernity. After detailing the bare bones of the plan, he noted grudgingly

that a particular objection to the plan might be raised by potential customers. As Scherman put it, "People may feel this will make reading too
cut and dried; that most people won't want to rely upon anyone to choose
books for them; each man wants to do his own choosing."[49] Although he
admitted the force of this traditionalist objection, which he would eventually have to address in detail, he concluded confidently that it could be
"easily offset" by appealing to a particular kind of reader who would feel
only relief at having his or her book selection managed by experts.

The Book-of-the-Month Club was designed not for the traditional
book buyer, Scherman observed, but for "the person who intends to keep
au courant with the best books, but who simply doesn't—through procras-
tination in buying." In this simple observation Scherman evoked the appeal of the modern with his use of a French expression calculated to con-
note the avant-garde and the stylish. Yet he also alluded simultaneously to
the frustrations created by modern busyness, including the habit of pro-
crastinating about just those sorts of activities people thought they most
ought to pursue. In offering the harried businessman and his busy wife
the chance to acquire effortlessly the best book published each month, he
was offering them a way to cope with the demands of the modern tempo
by placing in their hands the very embodiment of it, the new book. In
regularly acquiring this objectification of the new, these subscribers were
demonstrating to others their capacity to keep au courant, to stay up to
date, to be modern. Scherman thereby performed the requisite abstraction necessary to fit books to the demands of the modern marketing process. He constructed a generalized idea of the new book as one with particular relevance to modern life, whatever its subject, its approach, or its
genre, and he thereby ensured that he could sell new examples of the category endlessly without worrying too much about the particularity of any
one of them. Not surprisingly, most of his early advertising suppressed
the names of individual authors and titles selected by the committee in
favor of the prominent display of the brand name itself, the Book-of-the-
Month Club. In effect, he continued the historical process by which the
proper name of the singular, individual author was subordinated to the
trademark of the bureaucratic corporation.

At the same time, by referring to an older discourse about cultural value
with his use of the phrase "the best," surely chosen to evoke Matthew
Arnold's already famous dictum, Scherman insisted that his newly branded
books were also legitimate embodiments of culture, despite the leveling
his marketing process performed.[50] In effect, Scherman's operation was
profoundly hybrid, characterized simultaneously by its ties to a modern

economy of consumption and by its echo of an older, hierarchical society of inherited privilege and status. The basic apparatus of the Book-of-the-Month Club helped to convert books as cultural property into a more fungible form. By suppressing the individuality of any single book in favor of the general properties of the new, the scheme ensured that Book-of-the-Month Club books were largely interchangeable, at least with respect to their capacity to comment on the buyer's cultural competence and sophistication. At the same time, by stressing the fact that respected literary authorities had carefully read each book and pronounced on its high quality, the system insisted that the books were the genuine article—bona fide Culture—with all the requisite connotations of learning, refinement, and high social status. The lengthy ads Scherman designed to explain why potential customers might want to display their familiarity with the best new books therefore contributed to the codification of a set of equations whereby book display and book talk signified a certain kind of middle-class social status, increasingly convertible in a rapidly professionalizing society to career advancement and financial success.

The Book-of-the-Month Club, then, as it was initially envisioned in 1926, promised not simply to treat cultural objects as commodities, but even more significantly, it promised to foster a more widespread ability among the population to treat culture itself as a recognizable, highly liquid currency. Predicated as it was on an assumption of the inherent value of culture as a legitimate marker of social privilege, Scherman's operation continued to underwrite the fundamental logic of cultural distinction. At the same time, by proposing to make cultural objects such as the book more widely available, and potentially so to those without an inherited understanding of how to approach them properly, the club simultaneously threatened the scarcity and concomitant exclusivity of cultural competence and knowledge. Thus it posed a challenge to all whose social prestige and status was staked to their accumulation of rare objects and rarefied knowledge.[51]

The larger significance of Scherman's operation can be traced finally to his stubborn refusal to be bound by familiar shibboleths about the singularity of cultural objects such as the book. In a sense his early organizational efforts at the Book-of-the-Month Club might be seen as the material equivalent of Walter Benjamin's efforts to understand the implications of the process of reproduction.[52] Where Benjamin was able to offer in 1936 a theoretical explanation of how the technological possibility of reproduction fundamentally transformed the mode of existence of the cultural object, some ten years earlier Scherman had confronted in practical fashion the contradiction between a book still permeated ideologically by the aura of the work of art and a market process calling for infinite reproducibility and promiscuous, ever-expanding exchange.

Scherman's financial success was a function of his pragmatic recognition that truly open-ended exchange could not be achieved in the book industry with the reproduction of only a set of single titles. A reproductive process envisioned in that way still projected the theoretical possibility of a satisfied demand for any given title. Scherman aimed, rather, at the establishment of a permanent circuit of transit between the agencies of reproduction and a potentially infinite set of always-desiring consumers. His fundamental innovation was to focus on the circuit itself rather than on individual objects to be circulated widely through it. As a consequence, he understood that such a circuit could only be held open permanently by the assumption that an endless flow of new yet interchangeable goods might issue from it—hence Scherman's need to disentangle the notion of the new from the concept of the uniquely occurring. His contribution was to perform for the literary realm the strenuous ideological work of abstraction whereby a reworked conception of the new could be understood as amenable to infinite variation and repetition. In a sense his selection and distribution operation produced the new not as that which was distinct and singular, but as that which might be iterated, re-created repetitively and regularly in minute variation, the new now tied semantically not to the notion of the original but to the notion of a prototype. For Scherman's operation the value of this new cultural object was derived not from its unique conditions of creation or from the singular identity of its author but, rather, was vested in the social consequences of a buyer's display of it as the newest instance of relentless, unavoidable, modern change.[53]

Scherman was so concerned about establishing the permanence of the distribution circuit he was opening that in his first outline he stressed the fact that his customers would have no choice about the books they received. Not only would they be bound to accept the books that the club sent out, but they would be required to accept a book every month without respite. As Scherman sternly put it, "The books will not be returnable, nor exchangeable for others. He has to take what is given him. If he objects to the selection of the books by the committee, he can cancel his subscription."[54] His statement was the literary equivalent of Henry Ford's stipulation that "any customer can have a car painted any color he wants so long as it's black."[55] In effect Scherman was attempting to create an automated system that took the inexorable pace of Ford's assembly line one step further by attempting to regularize not only production and distribution but the more unpredictable process of consumption as well. He sought a mechanism whereby distribution could be converted thoroughly and automatically into consumption, thereby ensuring both the completion and the full integration of the market process. Scherman hoped to engineer a modern "selling machine" adapted to the requirements and peculiarities of the publishing industry.

The modern, Fordized character of Scherman's business enterprise consisted finally in its emphasis on circuits, circulation, and speed. I think it might plausibly be argued that Scherman's club was, in some ways, the organizational equivalent of the urban arteries and thoroughfares that Marshall Berman describes so eloquently in *All That Is Solid Melts into Air*. Arguing that what characterizes modernity more than anything else is the inexorable drive for development, leading to a "maelstrom of perpetual disintegration and renewal," Berman examines the way in which modern capitalist societies have both enabled and celebrated the necessity of movement and then deplored the consequences of the tempos thereby produced. He characterizes Georges Haussmann's Parisian boulevards as quintessentially modern inventions, as "arteries in an urban circulatory system," enabling "traffic to flow through the center of the city, and to move straight ahead from end to end—a quixotic and virtually unimaginable enterprise until then."[56] Like those arteries, Scherman's selling machine was designed to facilitate the flow of books not only from place to place (from publishing house to bookstore) but throughout the culture as a whole. In proposing to use every far-flung outpost of the U.S. postal system to sell his books, Scherman intended to establish a vast network for the incorporation of even the most isolated Americans into the nation's literary and intellectual life.[57] Scherman did not plan to stop, however, with the stationary network itself. He aimed, rather, to harness that network to the task of ceaselessly sending books along its many neural routes and ganglia. Like Robert Moses, creator of the Long Island Expressway and another important modern engineer discussed by Berman, Scherman strove to create "a system in perpetual motion" that would be characterized above all by the speed and relentless pace of its operation and by its level of internal and external integration as well.[58]

The Book-of-the-Month Club was nothing more or less than the application of the modern logic of integration to the realm of book production and distribution. What Scherman proposed to do with his organization was to adjust title production to a predictable level of consumption calculated through the device of the subscription system. Scherman aimed to produce only the number of copies he needed in order to supply those consumers who had been permanently integrated into the marketing circuit as regular subscribers. The judgmental process for selecting the titles to be circulated through that integrated system was, at this stage, largely a mechanism to ensure the regular acquisition of enough goods to keep the circuit open. With an astonishingly lame observation in the original plan for the club, Scherman dispensed with the committee that would soon elaborate a complex logic for categorizing books. He noted only that "as to the selection of books each month, that will be up to the committee. They may choose whatever book they want to recommend. The method for choosing it can easily be worked out."[59]

For Scherman, it mattered less what his new committee of selection chose or how they went about it than that they did so smoothly and regularly. In his mind the committee's real job was to process materials for the circuit and to give meaning to the brand name he proposed to attach to the new books he sent out. Scherman calculated that the Book-of-the-Month Club might do well in the contemporary context if the name itself could be made to address some of the complexities and emotional costs of modernity and yet continue to promote the idea of literary quality. When he finally set his mind to the task of hiring people to serve on his committee of selection, he was careful to go after literary celebrities with a particular kind of renown.

### THE COMMITTEE OF SELECTION AND
### THE MANAGEMENT OF MODERNITY

No record survives today of how Scherman and his partners decided on the five individuals for the selection committee, because no one connected with the club in its early days expected it to survive for more than a few years. Nor did any of these individuals leave notes or documents tracing their initial contact with the Book-of-the-Month Club. At the time, their participation in the enterprise must have seemed nothing more than a minor consulting job in the life of a busy, professional writer. Later, novelist and educator Dorothy Canfield Fisher, one of the individuals approached by Scherman, remarked that she knew most of the others who had been invited to participate. William Allen White, the well-regarded editor of the *Emporia Gazette*, had been a student of her father's at the University of Kansas.[60] She knew the newspaper columnist Heywood Broun because he had attended the Horace Mann School in New York when she served there in an administrative capacity after completing her Ph.D. at

Columbia. She was also acquainted with Yale English professor and editor of *The Saturday Review* Henry Canby and with columnist and author Christopher Morley because their literary activities had brought them into contact with one another in and around New York. Her observation suggests that Scherman and his partners selected a group of people who already knew each other in 1926. Apparently they also moved in the same social and professional circles. They did so, in part, because each occupied a somewhat similar position in the larger literary field. All had earned a reputation as professional experts who, despite an appreciation for literary distinction and excellence, were committed to the promotion of books in general and to the modern task of making culture available to more people.

Harry Scherman apparently approached Henry Seidel Canby first. Famous at the time as the editor of the highly regarded *Saturday Review of Literature*, Canby's authority to pronounce on the stature of newly published books was dually staked on his position as a Yale professor of English and on his previous work as the editor of the generalist quarterly *The Yale Review*. In fact Canby had left the academy to take up reviewing because he had grown impatient with the English professoriate's continuing refusal to treat American literature or to write about anything but the traditional English classics.[61] As he himself put it, "I began to think that live authors could be as interesting as dead ones."[62] Fascinated yet disturbed by the speed, fragmentation, and chaos of a modern world disrupted even more by the conflagration of World War I, Canby was committed to the idea of finding a literature adequate to the discontinuities and disorientations of the modern age.

Harry Scherman hired Henry Canby specifically as a reviewer and partisan of new books, as a new kind of literary professional who had an inherent interest in book selling by virtue of his commitment to promoting reading. Indeed the perspective and project of *The Saturday Review's* editor was apparently so compatible with the vision of Scherman and the club's founders that the magazine's editorial operation and the selection activities at the Book-of-the-Month Club were effectively merged into one. Amy Loveman, Canby's assistant at the *Review*, began by coordinating the mailing of submitted manuscripts to committee members. She progressed to performing the initial screening of those manuscripts and to dealing with the publishers themselves as the book club's representative. She eventually moved to the club offices, where she assigned books for initial review to a large pool of external readers, many of whom reviewed and wrote for *The Saturday Review of Literature*.[63]

Canby brought to the club not only his technical training as a specialist in the classics and the high literary, but also a thorough familiarity with the contemporary publishing terrain, a familiarity born of his responsibility to survey the entire field of book production and to identify all those titles in a range of publishing categories that stood out by virtue of their particular excellence. Thus he considered at the club, as he did at the *Review*, not only vast amounts of general fiction, including literary fiction, but mystery stories, poetry, biographies, autobiographies, books on politics and public affairs, histories, and books on science as well. Although the club's main selections would eventually prove less literary than the materials featured most prominently in the *Review*, it seems to have been Canby himself who was responsible for including experimental, avant-garde, and modernist literature in the mix of alternates eventually offered to club subscribers. Although Canby preferred the work of an older generation of writers, including Edith Wharton, Willa Cather, John Galsworthy, and Booth Tarkington, in part because he found the despairing cynicism and "amorality" of the modernists deeply disturbing, he was also keenly aware of the radical nature of modernist formal experimentation and acknowledged that this kind of stylistic play was often more closely attuned to the tempos and "deranged" sensibilities of the contemporary age than was the work of the writers he favored personally.

Canby was joined on the selection committee by bestselling novelist and popular educator Dorothy Canfield Fisher.[64] When Scherman approached her, she had already established herself as a well-regarded modern novelist who had made use of some of Freud's psychological theories in *The Brimming Cup* (1921), *The Homemaker* (1924), and *Her Son's Wife* (1926). Each of these novels had been treated as a peculiarly contemporary approach to troubling modern "problems" such as sexuality, gender relations, and feminism. Known also as the translator and promoter of Maria Montessori's educational theories in the United States, Fisher had recently become associated with the adult education movement as well. Indeed, her book *Why Stop Learning?* which discussed "the idea of mass education," correspondence schools, women's clubs, university extension courses, and the workers' education movement, was published in 1927, soon after the incorporation of the Book-of-the-Month Club.

In engaging Fisher, Scherman must have known that he was hiring a woman who had publicly disdained the glamorous literary life of New York for the hills of Vermont, which she had depicted tenderly in any number of sketches and stories. Over the course of the previous two decades, in fact, she had become associated with a kind of literary localism, characterized by folksy dialects, the expression of traditional values, and the depiction of close social connections. She often presented this localism specifically as an antidote to the abstractions and discontinuities of modernity. The complexities associated with Fisher's reputation marked her, then, as a female literary sage who could effectively mediate for her readers between the demands of contemporary life and an older, more stable, moral, and ethical universe. Scherman thought her interesting because she adroitly meliorated the disturbing consequences of modernity without resorting to simple, nostalgic escapism.

Although William Allen White's reputation was predicated less on his literary activities than had been the case with Canby and Fisher, like Fisher he was associated with the virtues of the local even as he was respected for his ability to take in the whole of the modern prospect. Famed as the editor of the decidedly midwestern *Emporia Gazette*, White was also considered a distinctively national citizen by virtue of his ability to comment on the U.S. political scene and because he had championed Progressivism and the interests of the middle class and had served as a prominent friend and adviser to Theodore Roosevelt. He was able to perform both roles simultaneously because the creation of national syndicates for news reporting made it possible to circulate locally produced opinion across the states to people troubled by the loss of regional specificity in the face of national name brands, standardized goods, and mass market periodicals.[65] In fact, White's fame had significantly increased when he published an emotional and moving memorial to his daughter, Mary, on her death in 1921. Filled with the deep sorrow of an ordinary father and loving detail about the unique qualities of a much-loved child, this column, which was circulated far and wide in print and on radio, probably did more than any of White's writings to establish him in the public mind as living proof that the modern world and the speed and abstraction it necessitated could do nothing to extinguish the special particularities and cherished idiosyncrasies that characterized actual individuals and everyday life.

In the context of a world growing apparently more anonymous, the Book-of-the-Month Club insisted on the continuing value of the personal and the local. This was achieved not only by virtue of the organization's name and its evocation of a homogeneous social gathering or by foregrounding the regionalist affiliations of some of its officials. It was also achieved through its portrayal of the selecting committee as a group of distinct individuals who offered their idiosyncratic, tailor-made recommendations to subscribers. This representation was particularly easy to manage with respect to the last two individuals who joined Canby, Fisher, and White on the committee. The considerable fame of both Heywood

Broun and Christopher Morley, in fact, had relatively little to do with what they did and everything to do with who they were. Both were well known as newspaper columnists, singularly interesting individuals who offered their opinions several times weekly on topics sundry and diverse.

Although personal bylines were by then common in American journalism and political columns appeared regularly on editorial pages, the phenomenon of the miscellaneous personal column written by a self-consciously idiosyncratic individual was a relatively recent innovation.[66] Pioneered by Eugene Field at the *Chicago Record*, George Ade at the *Chicago Record-Herald*, Finley Peter Dunne and Bert Leston Taylor (B. L. T.) at the *Chicago Tribune*, and Franklin P. Adams (F. P. A.) at the *New York Tribune*, this sort of column made a display of wit and satire as the rhetorical style peculiarly suited to the incongruities of modern life in a major city. As Carl Van Doren noticed in 1923, the columns were tightly tied to the urban metropolis in which they appeared and, as a consequence, were highly topical in subject and localized in reference. In New York, he noted, "they retail the gossip, promulgate the jests, discuss the personalities, represent the manners of New York."[67] Van Doren went on, "The great audiences which they have by virtue of their positions *they hold by their particular qualities. They are immensely personal.* They take the public into their confidences with whimsical candor."[68]

Heywood Broun's celebrity was a function both of his literary interests and achievement (he had published essay collections and two novels) and of his ability to comment trenchantly on a range of subjects, from sports to theater to local and national politics.[69] Identified most prominently in the mid-1920s, when he was approached by Scherman, as the intensely individual and eccentric author of a daily column said to be worth 50,000 readers to the newspaper that printed it, Broun was known as a passionate champion of liberal political causes. Shortly after he was named to the Book-of-the-Month Club's selection committee, he was forced into temporary silence by Ralph Pulitzer at the *New York World* for his impassioned and eloquent defense of Sacco and Vanzetti.

The title of Broun's column, "It Seems to Me," appropriately points to the significant nature of the innovation his work represented, that is, the invention of a magnified subject, an egregiously idiosyncratic individual, characterized not so much by special skills or actions but by the particularity of the opinionated views he held.[70] What was offered for public display on the op-ed page and in the personal column, therefore, was a print version of the spectacle of style, not style in the usual literary sense of highly crafted idiom, but style as the exhibition of a particular combination of syntactic components, whether drawn from the realm of fashion, home furnishings, cultural objects, literary taste, or even political opinion. In a society worrying about the potential destruction of an older form of individuality and distinction, the *World's* parade of monumental personalities enacted a kind of defense against the perceived abstraction and oppressive anonymity of the modern world.[71] It was the metropolitan equivalent of Dorothy Canfield Fisher's flinty Vermont realism and the logical correlative of Scherman's representation of his distribution machine as a club.

Christopher Morley's reputation was not unlike Broun's. Best known for his miscellaneous column, "The Bowling Green," which had begun in the *New York Evening Post* in 1920, Morley was also familiar to bookish audiences as the author of several volumes concerned with the book trade, including *Where the Blue Begins* (1922) and *Thunder on the Left* (1925). Identified generally as witty and even whimsical, Morley presented himself to the world as a buoyant man with wide and varying interests. Indeed, just prior to being approached by Scherman, he had been publicly characterized by Carl Van Doren as an individual made singular not by his special interiority but by his extensive, judicious set of personal tastes. Of Morley the public figure, Van Doren wrote,

> Seasoned in Oxford, he has the air of a man who has been reading old books and drinking old wine with old friends before a fire of old wood. His muse has haunted many libraries and has brought back many antiquarian treasures. At his pen's end he has the vocabulary of the Elizabethans, the idioms of the seventeenth century. A great deal of fine liquor, apparently, has flowed under his bridges. He knows where the best food may be obtained and ransacks ancient volumes for imaginary meats. He is a connoisseur of tobacco and understands to a nicety the conduct of a pipe. He talks spaciously of pets and children. . . . Mr. Morley has a robust feeling for life lived out of doors and a special taste for the sea and ships. . . . He has considerably enriched the imagination of his followers by laying a new stress upon the pleasures of eating and drinking, of playing and laughing, of collecting good things and living jovially among them, of preferring scholarship to jazz.[72]

Together Heywood Broun and Christopher Morley functioned for the Book-of-the-Month Club as specifically literary exemplars of a new, more modern subject. They were defined for the public not by their mastery and enactment of a unified social code of customs and manners but by the particular panache with which each displayed his own unique, wholly original taste. That taste was expressed not only in matters literary and cultural but also in politics, sports, food, and even clothes. The fact that Broun was known as much for his extreme dishevelment and his various sports enthusiasms as for his literary and political opinions, and that Morley's dandied aping of the dress of an upper-class English gentleman was seen as consistent with his anachronistic literary taste, points again to the growing propensity to conceive of all taste as of a piece and to understand the subject as constructed in and through its coordinated display.

As they were presented to the publishing world in 1926, the members of the Book-of-the-Month Club selection committee concretized a number of modern trends. On one hand, they functioned collectively as a bureaucratic subdivision in a larger system and contributed to the integration and smooth functioning of the operation as a whole. They engaged in the activity of what James Beniger has called "preprocessing," the identification and preparation of materials developed elsewhere for their efficient circulation throughout the system. They winnowed the huge mass of published manuscripts to a manageable few that could be fit to the gears of the distribution machine. To accomplish this they sometimes had to suppress their individual preferences in order to satisfy the tastes of the general readers whose collective purchasing potential drove the system to begin with.

At the same time, however, the judges offered their evaluative advice as singular, inherently critical individuals devoted to the pursuit of the distinctive and the unique. By discriminating among the many, by singling out only the best, they were thereby declaring their allegiance to an ideological formation constructed at an earlier historical moment that enshrined above all a notion of the autonomous, self-regulating, and self-determining individual. Such an individual, the ideology dictated, might express his or her self-same identity through writing, which he or she then offered in idiosyncratic form for publication. Through their own pursuit of the best such expressions, the Book-of-the-Month Club judges celebrated the possibility of rising competitively above the average, above the norm itself, a notion of social and cultural distinction, we will see in the next chapter, with continuing political support.

In somewhat contradictory fashion, though, Broun and Morley also modeled a new kind of individuality, the consumer subject discussed in the last chapter. In effect they demonstrated to club subscribers how to combine, in *bricoleur* fashion, an original literary taste with other individualized preferences for clothes, objects, food, and even opinions as a way of constructing the self. Decidedly not literary gentlemen of the old school, Broun and Morley insisted on the commensurability of the literary with everything else offered for sale in the marketplace. They exhibited, in embodied form, the categorical similarity—the fungibility—of virtually all cultural materials. For them the literary did not stand out as the apex of a simple, single hierarchy. In thus staging their own individuality so extravagantly, they demonstrated to Book-of-the-Month Club subscribers that an idiosyncratic selection of books (conveniently chosen from the organization's catalog), like everything else they preferred and therefore gathered to themselves, could be made to speak the language of subjectivity.

It seems clear that Scherman's financial success was in no small measure a function of his ability to ensure that this elastic agent, the Book-of-the-Month Club selection committee, actually held these contradictory logics in creative tension, fostering the operation of a consumer business on one hand while preserving the ideological reign of literary and cultural distinction on the other. Scherman succeeded not only because he created a better, more modern selling machine for mass-produced objects but also because he tempered the impact of his new machine technology by harnessing it to the goals of an older, essentially Arnoldian cultural project designed to seek out and to foster the idiosyncratic and the unique. Although not yet named as such, the middlebrow thus appeared in the form of the Book-of-the-Month Club as a way to think the contradiction between an older model of subjectivity and production and new cultural forces that both enabled and necessitated the construction of a subject capable of operating efficiently as a cultural relay or switching station, as one merely passing on or handing off eternally circulating goods and representations, which is to say, cultural capital. In treating the aesthetic object, the literary book, as one more tool to satisfy particular human needs, the club and other middlebrow agencies thereby explicitly threatened the sanctity, purity, and superiority of a culture conceived of as somehow beyond or transcending the profane negotiations of quotidian human existence.

In closing this chapter I think it worth pointing out that Scherman was able to create such a fruitfully contradictory operation because he personally experienced the contradictions his organization struggled to manage. Indeed, in his introduction to an economic treatise he published in 1938, *Promises Men Live By*, Scherman specifically addressed what might be called the ethical consequences of adopting the systemic logic he himself used to understand the book publication and distribution process. Speaking more generally about the point of view necessary for a proper understanding of modern economics, Scherman observed that since economic "science attempts to study . . . our complete living society, in which multitudinous millions of actions are interrelated one with another and are then succeeded by new ones, in a ceaseless round of change—it follows that the principal intellectual faculty the study demands is imagination."[73] He continued significantly, "and it must be of a high order." In calling for imagination of a high order Scherman intended that high to be understood quite literally. The economic imagination should not preoccupy itself with fleshing out the details of any single, particular economic transaction but must, in the mind's eye, seek to envision the entire network of relations and effects by which economic consequences were realized. It must adopt, in short, not the perspective of the individual but a wholly imaginary, bird's-eye view of the world.

And yet, Scherman also cautioned, even the most titanic intellect, the most creative imagination will inevitably falter and flag before this point of view. As he put it, "The imagination has a fatal weakness in that it tends—for relief . . . to abstraction and generalization, from which a great part of the acid reality of existence has been pressed, like a squeezed lemon."[74] In other words, the very abstraction necessary to encompass the whole set of relevant relations posed important dangers. Scherman understood that the systemic logic and perspective that was required of the imagination in order to take in the complexity of modern life effectively obscured the significance of individuals and singular actions that comprised the structurally related whole. He commented, "Almost every statement, historical or theoretical, which one reads upon economic matters is, in fact, a generalization in which are embraced countless real actions of unknown and unknowable human beings, sometimes extending over long periods of time." "The obvious danger," he continued, "is that, in dealing with these abstractions, one forgets to keep in mind the multiform realities *of genuine action* which underlie them."[75] Without sufficient attention to what he called "full-blooded human existence," the systemic perspective, Scherman feared, would only outline "mere *patterns of action*, a sort of desiccated life."[76]

We see here perhaps the key source of Scherman's success. Finding his professional feet in the advertising business, Scherman was modern enough to understand that a new world had recently been born and that it required both unprecedented forms of human response and extraordinary intellectual tools to take its measure. Yet he also sensed that such a world was profoundly unsettling not least because the speed of its relentless transformations and the complexity of its integrated forms tended to diminish the significance of individual experience and the importance of merely local action. Although he would not have used the word, he recognized the pain of what Marx called "alienation." He understood further that it was the source of an increasingly commonplace reaction to the abstractions employed not only by economists but by excessively scholastic businessmen, intellectuals, academics, and some politicians, specialists all in adopting the aerial perspective associated with systemic logic. As Scherman put it with respect to economics, "The average alert-minded person, meeting this study for the first time in classrooms and in books, feels instinctively that its material is, somehow, remote from his real experience. He is uncomfortable with its abstractions. He cannot understand them; and then, finally, in a sort of self-defense . . . he becomes contemptuous of them. He counts them dismal because he is finally worn out mentally, trying in some way to identify these cold abstractions with his own warm daily experiences."

The average alert-minded person of Scherman's observation, who longed for something other than the desiccated life offered by the schoolroom and who searched the fast-moving thoroughfares of modern life for the signs of warm-blooded, full-bodied, individual existence, was the targeted subscriber of the Book-of-the-Month Club. We will see in the following chapter that Scherman succeeded in capturing the attention of this subscriber, whom he called the general reader in opposition to elite specialists who spoke and read only the languages of abstraction, because he offered to integrate this individual into the modern adventure. He proposed to do so by showing him or her how to manage its relentless innovations and ceaseless change even as he also provided reassurance that such change constituted no challenge to tradition or to the significance of genuine human action, to the effectiveness of the activities of single individuals. Scherman's project was subsequently articulated in even greater detail by the members of the selection committee who themselves were driven by a wariness of abstraction and who privileged warm-blooded, individual lives in both their selections for the club and the various explanations and reviews they wrote justifying the logic of their preferences.

Harry Scherman's Book-of-the-Month Club was a canny material and ideological response to the troubling dilemmas posed by modern capitalism's compression of space and time through the rigorous implementation of economies of speed and scope. What it did so effectively was to negotiate the tension between an impending economic internationalism on one hand, conceived as au courant and modern, and a persistent localism on the other, a localism associated with the reality of ordinary, individual experience. Harry Scherman and his selection committee promised to make their readers up-to-date, modern citizens of a cosmopolitan culture through the agency of an organization portrayed deliberately as an intimate social group, as a club fully captured by the romance of the individual and the lure of the local. The middlebrow books delivered through the mail by the Book-of-the-Month Club carefully negotiated these contradictions, continuing to stress an aesthetic based on a psychology of the individual character even as they sought to represent the spectral appearance of new, disembodied forces that seemed to drive the economy, the culture, and indeed the entire social formation. While Harry Scherman's canny business sense was certainly crucial to the Book-of-the-Month Club's success, that success must also be attributed in the end to his unconscious yet nonetheless subtle understanding of the ideological dilemmas of the modern moment and to his remarkable ability to address them through a particular, innovative organization of the business of cultural goods production.

Harry Scherman *(painting by Joseph Hirsch)*

Henry Seidel Canby *(painting by Joseph Hirsch)*

Dorothy Canfield Fisher *(painting by Joseph Hirsch)*

William Allen White *(painting by Joseph Hirsch)*

Christopher Morley *(painting by Joseph Hirsch)*

Heywood Broun *(painting by Joseph Hirsch)*

The judges meet over lunch *(painting by Joseph Hirsch)*

Clifton Fadiman *(painting by Joseph Hirsch)*

Al Silverman

William Zinsser *(photograph by Skip Weisenberger, courtesy* New London Day*)*

Joe Savago

## CHAPTER SIX

# Automated Book Distribution and the Negative Option

### Agency and Choice in a Standardized World

## THE BOOK-OF-THE-MONTH CLUB

## AND THE LITERARY FIELD

When the Book-of-the-Month Club was legally incorporated under New York state law on February 11, 1926, no one hailed it as the significant commercial and literary innovation it was or predicted the organization's subsequent notoriety and success.[1] *Publishers Weekly*, in fact, printed only a short, cautious, almost laconic announcement introducing Harry Scherman's brainchild to the book trade. Although the club was described as "a plan of book promotion on an entirely new basis," the contributing reporter made nothing more than a perfunctory effort to describe the particulars of the operation.[2] Noting only that the book of the month was to be selected by "an unusual committee of critics and authors," the announcement added simply that "those who have accepted this responsibility are Henry Seidel Canby, chairman, William Allen White, Dorothy Canfield, Christopher Morley, [and] Heywood Broun."[3] At this point no one sensed that the creation of such a panel would set off a searching debate about the merits of literary advice, the appropriate forms for its delivery, or the consequences its reorganization might have for the American reader and reading public.

Even the club's owners, it seems, did not expect the organization to survive. They presumed that as a mail-order operation it would enjoy the usual short vogue, thrive for a few years, decline, and finally die out.[4] One of the firm's founding partners left only three years after the club was announced because he assumed that the depression-induced decline in its membership marked the beginning of its inevitable demise. As Scherman later acknowledged, the partners conceived of their enterprise "narrowly, purely as a business, like other specialty mail-order activities."[5] They had no premonition that what they had created would exert a significant impact both on the bookselling business and on the processes of literary production, circulation, and evaluation as well. Scherman was as surprised as anyone when the club generated intense publicity, spawned imitators, and sparked heated opposition only to survive intact for many years. He observed flatly in 1956, "We were shortsighted. . . . [The club] has become something of an institution, doing a special kind of job." Only then, with the perspicacity born of hindsight, could Scherman see that "the Club is one segment of an important field of activity—one that is relatively tiny moneywise, in the total economic picture—but of enormous significance socially: books both preserve and disseminate the best current thought of the time."[6] Although he did not say so, he ought to have noted as well that institutions like the Book-of-the-Month Club helped to define current thought as much as they preserved and disseminated it because they performed the role of gatekeeper; they selected the titles that would be most heavily publicized, distributed, and discussed.

The Book-of-the-Month Club did not achieve its status as an important twentieth-century cultural institution intentionally or by design. Neither did it manage this without opposition. Although the club's first appearance went largely unremarked in the book trade, it generated extraordinary interest among subscribers, who signed on at a rapid pace. Within the first year of operation the club had increased its membership from an initial list of 4,750 subscribers to 46,539.[7] This kind of growth might have gone unnoticed had Scherman's book club appeared merely an isolated and idiosyncratic phenomenon. Within an environment witnessing the growing prominence of experts of all sorts and a developing need for consumer advice, it did not. When the announcement of Scherman's operation was followed quickly by the emergence of five or six similar book clubs, including the well-placed and well-publicized Literary Guild, a disturbing cultural trend seemed to have been inaugurated. The first trickle of interested commentary soon swelled explosively into a flood of indignant if not vituperative protest. Indeed, the vehemence and persistence of the criticism directed at the book clubs is the best evidence that their appearance signified something more than the fact that a more efficient selling machine had finally been invented.

It is easy to understand why publishers and booksellers restively complained about the interlopers, interested as they were in preserving their own profits. But they were not the only ones who worried about the impact of the Book-of-the-Month Club. Scherman's scheme troubled just as many cultural critics and literary observers as it did the parties more immediately interested in the business of book production and circulation. Where the publishers and booksellers preoccupied themselves with the question of whether book club distribution would depress the bookstore sale of books, writers in the nation's literary monthlies and public affairs weeklies focused insistently on the likely effects that the Book-of-the-Month Club's selection and delivery process would have on American readers, on the quality of American literature, and on the activity of authorship. Frequently drawing an explicit analogy between American mass production and Scherman's assembly-line book distribution methods, these individuals fretted over the fate of the independent American reader and the nation's capacity to support something other than a mediocre, Fordized literature. Although the vogue for book club criticism waxed and waned over the next several decades, it did not reach its fullest expression until 1960, when Dwight MacDonald railed against the spreading "tepid ooze of Midcult" and identified the Book-of-the-Month Club and its judges, Henry Seidel Canby and Clifton Fadiman, as quintessential "yea-saying" representatives of Midcult, middlebrow culture that "pretends to respect the standards of High Culture while in fact it waters them down and vulgarizes them."[8] What became known as the book club wars began, then, as territorial disputes among business competitors but escalated rapidly into a wider conflict over the nature of literary advice, over the appropriateness of its rationalization, and over the effects its commercialization might have on readers, reading, and American literature itself.

In this chapter I look closely at how the Book-of-the-Month Club was established as well as at the ways Harry Scherman positioned it through advertising and publicity efforts. I also examine carefully the nature of the club's earliest procedures and operations in order to address the question of why the book clubs became embroiled in the debates about standardization then taking place throughout American culture.[9] I argue that although specific concerns about the health of the publishing industry and the larger literary field drove these discussions, they were also underwritten by broader, more widespread fears about the coming of machines and the fate of individual agency in a world growing more bureaucratic and regimented at every turn. The discussions were also informed by a profound gender anxiety prompted by the threat of women's changed social situation and by modern feminism. This anxiety made itself felt within the literary field as a form of deep distaste for the purported feminization of culture and the emasculation of otherwise assertive artists and aggressively discriminating readers.[10] However much they were welcomed by a population of middle-class consumers, the book clubs were greeted by their critics as a profound threat to independent American writers and readers, individuals gendered always as male and represented as endangered by the interminable flow of materials issuing from these new cultural agencies.

Although Harry Scherman's book club made every effort to distance itself from the most obvious forms of mass culture by deliberately evoking the aesthetically oriented language of high culture, his organization was criticized by cultural authorities who loudly proclaimed that they had detected the proverbial wolf in sheep's clothing. Scherman's insistence on wedding the Arnoldian pursuit of the best to the degraded form of the subscription coupon and the mundane activity of mail-order sales most offended his critics. By focusing on the complaints of those critics and the precise nature of their objections to the Book-of-the-Month Club, I specify just what was at stake in the effort to mark the difference between those who could discriminate between true culture and its imitation and those who could not and who therefore had to rely on the advice of others.

## THE INCORPORATION OF THE CLUB

Harry Scherman did not plan to challenge the traditional organization of the literary field in the waning months of 1925 when he perfected the organizational structure and operating procedures of his soon-to-be-announced plan to distribute new books through the mail. What he was after, by his own admission, was simply a more profitable way to sell books. Despite the fact that the Little Leather Library had apparently run out of marketing steam, it must have seemed an auspicious moment to launch another mail-order enterprise. Recent decades had witnessed the significant growth of leisure activities and industries and a substantial rise in consumer spending. Between 1897 and 1930, for instance, per capita annual income rose from $321 to $719. From 1909 to 1929, household expenditures tripled, with much of the increase accounted for by a rise in spending on consumer goods such as amusements, leisure pursuits, clothes, beauty aids, furniture, and automobiles.[11] In particular, household spending on books increased from $4.41 per household in the 1898–1916 period to $9.02 per household in the 1922–1929 period.[12] Scherman himself was convinced that the industrywide notion that only about 200,000 people bought books on a regular basis was ridiculous.[13] He had been persuaded by the initial success of the Little Leather Library that millions of Americans were eager to buy books but were prevented from doing so by the inadequate numbers and distribution of bookstores. Thus when he formally introduced his scheme in the original prospectus for the club, he stressed the fact that the "service" being offered would appeal to two "classes" of people. Not only would it assist those "who are anxious to keep *au courant* with the best of the new books," but it would appeal as well to those "persons who live in remote districts, where it is impossible to obtain books except with difficulty."[14]

The initial capital investment of $40,000 that created the Book-of-the-Month Club was put up by Scherman and his advertising partner, Maxwell Sackheim, and by Robert K. Haas, a Yale graduate and a vice-president at Chemical National Bank, who had recently purchased a controlling interest in the Little Leather Library. Haas was named president of the new organization, while Scherman was charged with responsibility for writing the club's advertising and publicity material and for supervising the day-to-day operation of the business. Haas later claimed that it was his idea to create a selecting committee to vouch for the new books Scherman's scheme was designed to sell.[15] Whether or not his memory was accurate, it is clear that in establishing the committee the partners had no sense that what they were creating would become the heart and soul of the Book-of-the-Month Club operation or that it would become the focal point of extended criticism. As I noted in the last chapter, the original plan for the Book-of-the-Month Club said nothing about how the selecting committee would organize and conduct its deliberations. Apparently this was because the committee had been conceptualized primarily as an advertising mechanism by men who thought of their organization in business rather than literary terms. The panel was chosen not necessarily because Scherman and his partners had any particular faith in the specific books the committee members might choose. Rather, they were hired because the business partners were convinced that their previously established status as recognizable figures with identifiable cultural standing would persuade potential subscribers of the integrity of the operation as a whole and of the likely quality of the merchandise being offered to them.[16]

Although Scherman and his partners had devoted little attention to the operation of the selection committee, they immediately began to adjust the conceptualization of their automatic distribution scheme in response to the concerns of the committee members who were hired. It was probably Scherman who recognized right away that a few of these literary experts were especially good at identifying aspects of the operation that might prove objectionable to publishers and the general public, two groups whose participation was essential to the success of the enterprise.

Even before the club was formally introduced to the public, therefore, Scherman and his partners significantly altered their plans in response to criticism leveled most insistently by Dorothy Canfield Fisher. These alterations implicitly acknowledged the difficulty of adapting Henry Ford's conception of automated production and distribution to the literary and cultural sphere.

Initially Scherman had proposed that the club identify one book each month as the best among all the volumes published in the last thirty days. That book would then be mailed automatically to all subscribers. Fisher objected immediately, however, apparently because she felt that such a procedure would focus the public's attention on single books rather than on the great many being published simultaneously. She was also sure that no single book could please all readers.[17] In her view, readers varied in their interests and needs, and reading was itself a rich, differentiated, multipurpose activity that required different books on different occasions. In responding as she did to Scherman's first plan, which would have functioned wholly automatically and treated all books as equivalent, Fisher identified the issue that would pose the biggest problem for the new organization in both an ideological and a financial sense, the problem of individual subscriber preference and choice. In fact, her objection foreshadowed the real difficulties the club would have in balancing the economic imperatives of machine automation and mass distribution with the cultural priority attached to individuality.

The partners responded immediately to Fisher's objection by allowing the committee to recommend more than the single volume offered as the book of the month and by writing into their initial plan the stipulation that subscribers might physically return any monthly selection they did not like for another recommended by the club. They did not permit those subscribers, however, the choice of receiving no book at all. Thus they installed a limited form of choice in the operation, albeit only at its end point. With even these modifications, however, Scherman implicitly acknowledged that books were in fact not identical and therefore not entirely fungible. They could not uniformly be compared with each other on a single evaluative scale. Readers were different. They wanted to read books for different reasons and on varying occasions. The Book-of-the-Month Club was probably successful, in the end, because Scherman proved adept at mobilizing the language and symbolism of individuality, choice, and agency while simultaneously taking advantage of the economic benefits offered by the principles of automation.

Because of these important alterations to the original plan, when the

{ *On the History of the Middlebrow* }

first "trial balloon" was floated in the *New York Times* on April 25, 1926, Scherman's copy emphasized both the automatic nature of the scheme and the fact that even though the books were to be issued like the numbers of a magazine, they were always sent "on approval."[18] Prospective customers were assured that because they could return the book automatically shipped to them "there [is] no chance of . . . purchasing books that you would not choose to purchase anyway."[19] Despite this insurance, what made the scheme most attractive, the lengthy ad insisted, was that it would enable its members to keep up with "the best of the new books" because it would prevent members from neglecting to acquire, "through [their own] carelessness," the books they always intended to read. Despite the promise to preserve the customer's initiative by permitting "the privilege of return," it was automatic distribution, in the end, that would counter passivity.

As Joan Rubin has shown so effectively, Scherman's advertising appeal addressed very modern anxieties about the effectivity and coherence of the individual self. "Why is it you disappoint yourself so frequently in this way?" Scherman asked. In this manner he spoke to readers who felt guilty about failing to organize their lives satisfactorily. Scherman admitted later that he was also deliberately evoking the fear of "backsliding." He appealed to the fears of recent college graduates who, in leaving their classrooms for the offices and corridors of American business, worried that they had forsaken the principles of liberal education and forgotten the value of culture.[20] The Book-of-the-Month Club's automation offered to its prospective subscribers a guarantee that they would never lose their facility with cultural capital. Club membership would enable them to demonstrate their awareness of the books and ideas that had been deemed most significant at any given moment. Such assurances were undoubtedly important to nervous, arriviste middle-class readers whose cultural competence had been acquired through formal schooling rather than through the more assured process of early and ongoing familiarization in the home.[21] At the same time, by allowing customer returns and substitutions, Scherman's scheme also promised potential members an opportunity to exercise their own knowing discrimination. At a moment when both the symbolic and raw economic value of conspicuous yet discerning cultural consumption was increasing dramatically, these were not insignificant offers.[22]

Surprisingly enough, not even Harry Scherman anticipated fully the degree to which his advertising appeal and book distribution scheme would strike a resonant chord among anxious Americans. When the first advertisements appeared, offering to send a prospectus about the operation to anyone who would return a coupon, only the most skeletal organization had been established to take care of the response.[23] Edith Walker, the club's office manager, later recalled that "at that time, we had no organization, other than myself, the three partners, two of whom were not actually active in the business, and one clerk."[24] Noting that she would "never forget that first Monday morning, when the three partners and myself opened the mail, wondering whether or not we had received even a single answer," she remembered that they knew they had a "going business" when the first envelope contained not only the coupon but a check for twenty-five or thirty dollars, an advance on the first round of books, which the ad had specifically not requested. The Herculean task of responding to the overwhelming return of the first coupons fell to Walker and Scherman, who then struggled mightily to fulfill the promises made in the initial ad and prospectus. Together they packed more than 4,000 copies of the club's first selection. Although Walker "swept up, acted as secretary and did most of the clerical work," within a year the Book-of-the-Month Club employed 46 individuals. By the end of 1927 the organization was composed of 86 employees, and in 1928 137 people worked in the club's Manhattan offices.[25] Harry Scherman's mail-order scheme was off and running.

## TEMPERING AUTOMATION

The organization prospered in part because Scherman and his partners understood the importance of attending to their customers. Walker acknowledged that policy was formed pretty much in response to correspondence from members. "We'd get five or six letters," she observed, "from people saying 'I don't want this or that, but can I do this?' We'd hash it over and think maybe it was a pretty good idea—let's let them do it." "Thus our policy was formed," she concluded, "and it went through many, many phases and changes over the years." At least at the outset, the policy changed frequently because it proved so difficult to identify a set of procedures that would work both financially and ideologically (in the sense that they would prove consistently appealing to subscribers). In particular, the partners had to struggle especially vigorously with the problem of consumer taste.

When Scherman and his associates had altered their original plan for automatic distribution in response to Dorothy Canfield Fisher's objections and made provisions for their customers to return physically any unsatisfactory selections, they had unwittingly created a mammoth problem for themselves in both bureaucratic and financial terms. Although their initial ad produced some 4,000 subscribers and led to the quick shipment of a book called *Lolly Willowes* by an unknown British writer, Sylvia Townsend Warner, the partners were distressed to find themselves swamped soon thereafter with returned copies. Since nothing could be done with the books at that point, they had to be scrapped at a significant financial loss.[26] The second club offering, *Teeftallow*, by the slightly more well known and well regarded T. S. Stribling, produced even more returns. Then, in January 1927, a near-disaster prompted the realization that something drastic had to be done if the partners' effort to build consumer choice into the operation was not to scuttle the fledgling organization entirely. As Scherman himself wryly put it, "The first book of 1927 was the one I pick as the one with which we had the worst experience of all. It was probably as a result of that book we changed the system radically. That book was *The Heart of Emerson's Journals*, edited by Bliss Perry. By that time we must have had about 40,000 subscribers—and that book just came back by the carload. The country didn't want *The Heart of Emerson's Journals*; they didn't want any part of *Emerson's Journals*. . . . It was probably around that time that we decided we'd have to be ever so much more liberal with the subscribers."[27]

The appalling sight of many thousands of copies of *Emerson's Journals*, abbreviated though they were, pouring into the club's offices at Fortieth Street and Eighth Avenue produced immediate action. In fact, that Emersonian scrap pile probably had much to do with the club's long-term success, for it led to an ingenious conceptual and operational innovation that adeptly negotiated the contradiction between the imperatives of an automatic distribution scheme and the need to preserve some measure of individual choice. Maxwell Sackheim turned the notion of choice inside out when he suggested to Scherman that a solution other than the obvious one could be found for the return problem. He suggested that the partners did not have to go so far as to extend to the customers the right to make positive choices every month in order to avoid the problem of returned books. Both he and Scherman understood that any alteration that would grant the initiative to the reader would never work financially because only a small portion of the club membership could be expected to order something actively in any given month. That solution would effectively dismantle the automated system they had so carefully set up and undercut the profitable predictability they had built into the operation.

Instead, Sackheim aggressively reshaped the notions of choice and action into circumscribed and reactive forms of behavior. He proposed to Scherman that they might extend to their customers the right *not* to get a book already chosen for them by the club's selection committee, a choice they would represent to the club on a coupon sent to them for that purpose. It is worth letting him recount the moment of invention: "I shall never forget the day Harry Scherman and I walked around the corner . . . where our offices were located, and I said to him, 'Why can't we notify subscribers of the book selected before shipping it to them, giving them an honest review of it and *tell them the book would be sent to them unless within two weeks they returned a certain form notifying us NOT to send it, or to send some substitute selection which we would also describe in this advance form?*' "[28] It is not hard to understand why Scherman agreed immediately to the alteration. Sackheim's ingenuity preserved both predictability and choice by relying on the fact of consumer inertia. Scherman must have understood instantly that a significant number of subscribers would almost certainly never manage to return the reply card and thus would constitute a relatively constant statistical base for book production and distribution. Even more important, however, he must have recognized that Sackheim's contrivance would create a highly useful feedback device in the sense that it would enable the club to calibrate the actual production of books to the early return of the reply coupon.[29] If large numbers of subscribers indicated initially that they did not want the monthly selection, the partners could curtail their production plans for it and thereby avoid the problem of oversupply. On top of that, the substitution requirement stipulating that subscribers had to accept at least one of the books recommended by the judges would preserve the automated flow of the distribution process since, in exercising the choice allowed by the system, the subscribers could not choose to receive no book at all. As a consequence, their initiative was entirely prepared for and contained within the automatically propelled distribution system.

When Sackheim's plan was implemented shortly thereafter, the partners still had not agreed on a name for it. Sackheim himself called it "the pre-notification plan." Others referred to it as "the automatic shipment plan." Still others dubbed it "the negative option," a name that eventually stuck and that is still used today not only by the Book-of-the-Month Club but by virtually every other time-oriented mail-order business. It is easy to see why. In effect, what Sackheim and Scherman accomplished with their negative option was the transformation of individual choice in the face of mass production and distribution into selection among a range of predetermined options. They constructed consumer action as a sorting or gatekeeping behavior, remaking the individual from self-propelled energy source into a kind of relay or switch, that is, into a device for the management and control of materials and information coming from elsewhere.

The activity Scherman and Sackheim asked their subscribers to perform was not unlike that performed by the selection committee members themselves as they winnowed the offerings of the publishing industry to a favored, selected few. Where the committee sorted and selected among materials presorted by publishers, the club's subscribers sorted and selected the further preprocessed materials offered to them by the club. I think it might be argued, therefore, that through the introduction of the negative option and the reply coupon the Book-of-the-Month Club was instructing large numbers of Americans in how to take up appropriate roles in vast, integrated systems for the production and circulation of both goods and information. It was teaching them, in effect, how to perform the kinds of work that would increasingly be asked of them by a consumer-oriented and information-dominated society, the work of sorting, representing, and passing on materials and information which, of necessity, circulated throughout the larger system.[30] The club modeled the idea of agency, then, less on the example of self-motivated, propulsive, physical action than on that of a cognitive or mental transaction, that is, a decision to respond in a certain way, to accept or reject options materialized from elsewhere and determined by others.

I think it important to observe here that Sackheim and Scherman's reformulation of choice did not render the Book-of-the-Month Club subscriber wholly passive, nor did it lead to a thorough abnegation of the self, as Joan Rubin has claimed. She has suggested, in fact, that "along with relinquishing book selection to experts, members surrendered to the club's 'automatic'—that is, externally-controlled—schedule of distribution: one book parceled out each month, arriving . . . unless the subscriber took the initiative of canceling it. The self-abnegation involved in that arrangement is apparent in a phrase that frequently appeared in the club's early advertisements: the slogan 'Handed to you by the Postman' highlighted the 'convenience' of the plan."[31] It seems to me, however, that the subscriber necessary to, and therefore effectively created by, the operational procedures of the Book-of-the-Month Club was not selfless but rather a transformed self, whose particular mode of realization was entirely integral to the functioning of the larger system within which she or he was incorporated. Having once agreed to be taken up by the system, subscribers could discriminate among the materials endlessly flowing from the Manhattan canyons of the publishing industry through the integrated network of the U.S. postal system, but they could not choose to stop that flow.

In effect, the self called into being by the negative option of the Book-of-the-Month Club was the "disciplinary individual" discussed by Mark Seltzer after Michel Foucault, that is, an individual absorbed into and replaced by the collective body of the organization, an individual whose agency had been prosthetically usurped and simultaneously enhanced by the machine and its organizational embodiments.[32] In choosing not to receive one book in favor of some other, the Book-of-the-Month Club subscriber was selecting among options that had already been programmed into the system by the organization itself. Even more important, however, the consequences of a possible refusal, the significance of that "no" carried out on paper, was itself contained by the system because the "no" was a limited "no"; it could never be a refusal of the system itself, whose external limits were thereby left intact. The possibilities for limited choice built into the Book-of-the-Month Club system therefore facilitated what Seltzer has called "the dream of directed and nonstop flow" that "forms part of the psychotopography of machine culture." The negative option, in sum, proved the perfect accommodation between the logic of machine culture and the residual ideology of the autonomous, independent, active subject in sovereign control and possession of his or her own will.[33] Despite the ingenuity of Scherman's adjustments, this accommodation did not satisfy all observers of the literary scene, some of whom objected vehemently and articulately to the kind of choice permitted by the Book-of-the-Month Club.

## THE BOOK CLUB WARS COMMENCE

Those objections were not voiced immediately, however. In fact, little opposition materialized at the club's start-up or during the first year of its existence.[34] The operation was initially well received because the partners had taken pains to avoid undercutting financially either publishers or bookstores in early publicity and ads. They stressed the operation's convenience, not its economy. Harry Scherman apparently also courted the editors of *Publishers Weekly* as allies.[35] He could successfully manage this because the arguments of his own publicity campaign could be taken up wholesale by *Publishers Weekly*. His claim that the Book-of-the-Month Club would enlarge the audience for serious books accorded perfectly well

{ *On the History of the Middlebrow* }

with the journal's own trade promotion efforts. Thus, in an article about the Book-of-the-Month Club as one such scheme, the editors asserted that "there are many people who would read at least one book a month if there was only some simple way of knowing what to read. It is such people that this unique service should reach, and as their interest in present day literature and the ownership of books is awakened, the bookstores should profit by the work of the Club."[36]

An important interactive synergy between the Book-of-the-Month Club and the larger industry was established in the early months of the club's existence. Determined to capitalize on any critical notice or favorable mention of their books in order to boost their sales, publishing houses touted selection by the Book-of-the-Month Club as evidence of the quality of their books. In so doing, they underwrote the club's authority and its claim that it was distributing the best book of the month, thereby legitimating its operation and providing additional publicity as well. Not content to wait passively for the club's "lightning to strike," publishers themselves soon began to court the favor of Scherman, the partners, and selection committee members by providing elaborate advance material about the books they were submitting for club consideration. Ultimately they would begin to tailor their acquisition and even the editing of their books to the needs, taste, and requirements of the Book-of-the-Month Club.[37] By doing this, they helped to establish the status, prestige, and power of Scherman's organization and tightened the integration of the larger system of book production as a whole. *Publishers Weekly* underscored the value of the club to the larger industry when it noted later in the year that clear evidence indicated that Book-of-the-Month Club selections actually directly stimulated bookstore sales, a fact the editors had gotten from Scherman himself, who tracked the performance of the club's first selections in the trade.[38] Their view was corroborated in the next issue by a letter from the treasurer of Doubleday, Page & Company stating that the sale of both *Teeftallow* and *The Saga of Billy the Kid* (the club's fourth selection) had increased significantly in the trade in the wake of their selection by the club's committee.

The early peace between the Book-of-the-Month Club and the trade was shattered finally when an apparently imitative scheme to sell books through the mail was launched in New York in December 1926. Although the Literary Guild had actually been conceived before the Book-of-the-Month Club was incorporated by Scherman and his partners, to everyone in the trade it appeared as just another imitation. Announced first in *Publishers Weekly* on December 4, the Literary Guild had been organized by

Samuel Craig and featured a selection committee that included chairman Carl Van Doren, Zona Gale, Elinor Wylie, and Joseph Wood Krutch. The Guild differed from the Book-of-the-Month Club, however, in that it proposed to publish its own editions prior to their regular publication in the trade, thus establishing itself as an outright competitor with the traditional publishing houses. The Guild's selection would be made from a set of specially submitted manuscripts rather than from the entire corpus of books published monthly, as was the case with the Book-of-the-Month Club. Although this first notice in *Publishers Weekly*, like that given Scherman's operation, was largely factual, the editors hinted somewhat ominously that they did not see the two distribution schemes in the same way. Noting that "the plan differs in some points from that of the Book of the Month Club," the editors observed that the Literary Guild proposed "to sell [books] below the retail price and to deliver in advance of trade publication date." "The Book of the Month Club," they added, "maintains the price which has been set for the trade edition and makes their selection from the entire published product of the publishers." [39]

What followed was as much testimony to Scherman's shrewd appraisal of the immediate field in which he was operating as it was to the disruptive potential exhibited by the book club phenomenon. Never for a moment, in fact, did the Guild enjoy the kind of honeymoon that had enabled the Book-of-the-Month Club to establish its presence in the trade. Craig's organization was attacked immediately for its price-cutting tactics, something Scherman had been careful to avoid. Indeed *Publishers Weekly* noted in its very next issue that "the general trade publishers . . . are not at all likely to look with favor on this plan," in part because they recognized that "the Guild is really opening a price war, which has always been the curse of the booktrade in every country." [40] Their martial forecast was accurate not least because the editors themselves fanned the flames of war. For the next year the pages of *Publishers Weekly* as well as the agendas of American Booksellers' Association meetings were peppered with reports on the controversy surrounding the book clubs. Eventually the association would go on record against price-cutting and putting books on sale before the date of publication. They also officially opposed the importation of "revolutionary ideas," a reference to the belief that the book club idea had originated in Germany. [41]

While it is unnecessary to chronicle every skirmish and counterskirmish in the battle that ensued, it is important to note that the massive publicity that resulted both helped the performance of the clubs and brought them to the attention of a broader audience. As a consequence the industry-based price war escalated quickly into a more general dispute about the effects of the book club phenomenon on the trade as well as on the entire sphere of American literary production. Scherman would soon discover that in spite of his careful cultivation of the trade, his organization had intervened in the larger field where the country's literature was publicly identified, defined, and evaluated, and thus he had to answer to those who thought of themselves as its legitimate guardians as much as to representatives of the industry itself. In fact, evidence suggests that even before the booksellers' and publishers' price war with the Literary Guild formally drew the Book-of-the-Month Club into the fray, Scherman and his partners had already become concerned about growing criticism of the club.[42]

During the previous November, Book-of-the-Month Club president Robert Haas had written to *Publishers Weekly* about the nature of the club's operating procedures. His communication was clearly designed to assure individuals in the trade that the committee's selection of the best book of the month was unbiased. His circular asserted, first, that no publisher or group of publishers held any interest in the Book-of-the-Month Club. All stock was held by Haas, Scherman, and Sackheim. Furthermore, Haas claimed, no member of the selecting committee had any financial interest in the club. He noted that the members "act with complete individuality and they agreed to act because they are convinced of the value of the idea." He also observed that the committee alone made the choice of the monthly selection without input from the directors and that the books were chosen by a voting system that ensured that even the committee members themselves did not know what books were selected until the votes were tabulated.[43] His observations were clearly calculated to reassure publishers that their books had an equal chance of being selected as the book of the month. They were also designed to reassure club critics that the selection committee's literary choices were wholly disinterested and therefore aesthetic in nature. In such reassurances began the club's long-preserved tendency to bracket its evaluative operation from its more openly commercial calculations and concerns.

Haas sent his letter to *Publishers Weekly* at about the same time Harry Scherman was apparently beginning to consider how best to respond to expanding criticism of the club. Although I have found no critical notices of the club before February 1927, there exists among Harry Scherman's papers at Columbia University a typescript titled "Report on the Book-of-the-Month Club after Seven Months of Operation."[44] The initial pages of the report attempt to explain the organization's early success, but the bulk of the manuscript is devoted to the "misunderstandings" it had provoked "in some quarters." As the report notes, the club "has occasioned a great deal of 'viewing with alarm.' " Since nothing was apparently published about the club beyond the positive material that appeared in *Publishers Weekly*, it seems likely that Scherman and his partners were concerned about the tenor of informal conversations, industry gossip, and possibly letters from friends. Indeed, Dorothy Canfield Fisher recalled in her own oral history interview that everyone who knew the judges, "all our *literary* friends, said 'You can't—you won't be allowed to give a disinterested opinion. That's a business concern, and a business concern has just one purpose and that's to make profits.' "[45] When juxtaposed with the seven-month report, her comment suggests that the nature and character of the club's selection process was beginning to prompt questions and to stir up negative commentary within literary circles even before the Literary Guild appeared on the scene.

Like Haas's letter, Scherman's seven-month report focused on the Book-of-the-Month Club's selection process, but it took pains to rebut an even more extensive complaint. Scherman admitted that "one interesting criticism aimed at the venture—interesting only because of the type of unanalytic thinking it represents—has come from some who regard this as another depressing manifestation of the 'standardising' of the American mind."[46] He continued with a summary of what was usually said: " 'What kind of people can these be who will allow someone else to choose their books for them? Pretty soon everybody will be reading the same books at the same time. They are setting up a sort of invisible censorship over us. How depressingly American!' " In answer to such criticism Scherman detailed the steps of the selection process. Emphasizing the fact that the committee members voted on the monthly selection, he asserted that the resulting "verdict of the committee is not set up as a pronouncement of some high court of opinion which it would be *lese majeste* to question." "Tastes differ," Scherman flatly asserted. "Any subscriber . . . who disagrees with the combined opinion of the committee, may exchange the book he receives for any other of the new books described." He asked, "How under these circumstances, is his choice among the new books limited?" To secure his point he noted further that the influence exercised by the committee was no more extensive than that exerted by book reviewers. There is no difference in the situations, he concluded, "except that the Book-of-the-Month club subscriber actually has a somewhat *wider choice* in practice and in addition actually *gets* the book or books that he wants to read."[47] His point was that without the organization's prosthetic augmentation of the agency exercised by the typical individual, potential book buyers often failed to obtain the very books they intended to read. Their vaunted exercise of choice often went for nothing.

Even as he was trying to address the problem of consumer preference and choice in operational terms, Scherman was gearing up to confront it as an ideological problem as well. This was necessary, I think, because it appeared generally true in the culture at large that the fate of the individual was threatened in a world upended materially, socially, and ideologically by the virtual triumph of machine production and mass consumption. Commenting further in the report on the charge that the Book-of-the-Month Club would ensure "that now a great many thousands of people are going to be reading the same book at the very same time every month," he countered with the defense that "presumably that's what books are published for." Bestseller lists, he noted, were designed to track just that phenomenon. In further addressing the charge that the book clubs would contribute to "a regimentation of opinion," Scherman argued that "every newspaper and magazine, by its very nature, gathers together its own group within our population and proceeds to work out some sort of standardizing of opinion and information upon these presumably helpless creatures." This was done, he observed, not only by Mr. Curtis, Mr. Hearst, and Mr. Macfadden but by "The Atlantic Monthly, Harpers, Scribners, and The American Mercury—they too, the 'highbrows' as well." He concluded, "all are engaged busily and deliberately in 'regimenting' the opinion of just as large a group of people as they can induce to listen to them."

Scherman's use of quotation marks around the word "regimenting," his repetition of the term "standardizing," and his extended parody of the horrified observations of his highbrow critics suggest that he conceived of his report as a response to a formulaic and familiar attack. In fact, even a cursory glance at the periodical literature of the 1920s will show that an extended debate about the impact of standardization on the literary realm did take place at this time. And as Walter Benn Michaels has shown, this more specific debate only extended discussions that had been carried on for years, first about the nature of democracy, and then about the consequences of machine production, mass distribution, and expanded commodity consumption. Parties to the larger debate as it was carried on during the first several decades of the twentieth century included the "Young America" critics Randolph Bourne, Van Wyck Brooks, Waldo Frank, and Lewis Mumford; the new liberal intellectuals clustered around *The Nation* and *The New Republic* such as Herbert Croly, Walter

Lippmann, Stuart Chase, and John Dewey; incipient literary modernists such as T. S. Eliot and Ezra Pound; and the myriad forces of the left avant garde that included Joseph Freeman, Mike Gold, Max Eastman, Matthew Josephson, Josephine Herbst, Alain Locke, and many others.[48] Although these cultural critics had their own agendas to pursue and differed significantly about the virtues of the new, machine-made, mass culture, most of them wondered about the impact of new technologies such as radio and film on the American population and remained intensely interested in the fate of the individuated subject in a world given over to what appeared as endless repetition of the same.

This larger discussion was so extensive and complex that I cannot provide even a simple chronicle of it here.[49] Instead I look more narrowly at the way the book clubs were caught up in the standardization debates of the 1920s, debates that focused generally on the Fordizing of America. With respect to the impact of this process on the literary realm, it seems clear that the debate was intensified by the 1922 publication of Sinclair Lewis's *Babbitt*. In any case, it spilled onto the pages of *Century*, *The Nation*, *The New Republic*, *The New Yorker*, *The Bookman*, and *The Saturday Review of Literature*, mainstream publications preoccupied with charting the dominant course of American literary production.[50] To that end the discussion encompassed a range of topics, including the nature of criticism and reviewing, the social function of literature, the benefits of reading, and the future character of the education system. Because hundreds of pages were devoted to these issues and because my concern is really with the criticism directed at the clubs, I can only hope to lay out the most basic parameters of the more general discussion here. The discussion is worth examining, however, even if only briefly, for it demonstrates that the conceptual structure of the debate dictated the terms within which the Book-of-the-Month Club and its imitators were received in wider literary circles. It also shows that what was initially troubling about the club was not the character of the selections it mailed to its subscribers. Rather, what most disturbed the literary scene was the very nature of the club's distribution process and the way that process threatened to remake active, discriminating readers and writers into passive, feminized consumers and effeminate poetasters.

For the most part the mainstream standardization debate of the 1920s was organized discursively around two opposed concepts. The abstract noun, "standardization," was used indiscriminately to refer to all those processes that were supposedly smothering American individuality through the proliferation of identical newspapers, magazines, books, and ideas in the modern world and through the creation of writers and readers as undifferentiated and regimented as military troops. In opposition, more hopeful prognosticators laid out a vision of a society of democratically distributed plenty filled with better-educated, better-read, more responsible citizens capable of performing the tasks necessary to the perpetuation of democracy. In updating the discussion of the role played by reading and culture in a democratic world by opposing the impersonal process of standardization to the democratically directed actions of responsible citizen-individuals, the debaters meditated on the consequences of "a gear and girder world" of interchangeable machine-tooled parts for a social formation predicated fundamentally on the notion of the autonomous, independent, intentional subject.[51]

Daniel Boorstin has suggested that the larger discussion of standardization was probably generated by a desire to comprehend the fact that Americans had recently been wrenched out of their older, geographically defined communities of proximate social distances and asked to think of themselves as mere integers in multiple, highly abstract "statistical communities." No longer able to conceive of themselves simply as inhabitants of given neighborhoods, churches, or towns, Americans were asked by policy experts and public discourse in newspapers and magazines to think of themselves as differentiated and assembled by their income, their intelligence, their size, their liability risk, their normalcy, and their deviance.[52] Prompted by tax policy, by insurance companies, by standardized intelligence tests for educational and military purposes, and even by the ready-made clothing industry to think of themselves only as abstract instances of recurring standard types, Americans understandably worried about what had happened to the heroic American individual, to the idiosyncratic, autonomous American self. Correlatively, they worried about how democracy would survive without its characteristic, constituent building blocks, its citizen-individuals.

The nature and extent of the worry about the American self is best summarized for my purposes here by a lengthy article that appeared in *Century* in June 1926, shortly after the first flurry of attention to the Book-of-the-

Month Club had developed. Although the discussion of standardization in "Take Them or Leave Them: Standardization of Hats and Houses and Minds" suggests that Boorstin's account of the debate's causes, along with more recent explanations offered by Walter Michaels and Mark Seltzer, is largely persuasive, it also reveals some important aspects of the standardization discussion that those explanations leave untouched.[53] In "Take Them or Leave Them," author Charles Edward Russell began by discussing several of the processes and actions that were typically grouped under the rubric of "standardization." What he was really after, however, was the long trail of consequences that might ensue from the implementation of any one of them. Although he discussed such particulars as the elimination of superfluous or redundant organizations, the creation of uniform machines, and the implementation of generalized standards of operation, at every turn he mobilized rhetorical figures and images to illustrate the ominous absorption of some individual into an undifferentiated mass. Asking "How many smaller companies have been combined into the great General Motors?" he complained, "Once flourishing corporations disappear from view into a system unified for efficiency and economy."[54] The end result of such a process, he argued further, can only be the creation of a single, unified system uniting all labor and all laborers. "What we are facing," Russell ominously predicted, "is a unified employer and a unified employment; all of us at work for one boss, and that not a man but a greatly efficient corporation."[55] Later eliding this vision of an oppressive, inhuman corporation with a self-propelling machine in perpetual motion, he laid out a dystopic vision of what could happen to the average American citizen were standardization allowed to proceed apace:

One might look forward to about A.D. 1956 and see a working population dwelling in a hive of a million standardized cubicles. Each worker sleeps in a standardized bed, at the foot of which is an open cabinet with stretched-out arms holding the man's clothing—standardized. A great gong outside sounds in the morning three strokes. Then a whistle blows; the bed sinks at the foot, rises at the head, and throws the man into the cabinet, whence he emerges completely clad. He has been dressed by electrical machinery—standardized. A little door in the cabinet pops open and thrusts out the man's breakfast, a standardized tablet of highly condensed nutriment. A great arm then grabs him by the collar and projects him into the street, where he falls into a line of men like himself, uniformed from top to toe and marching lock-step to the factory. . . . At six o'clock a tabloid dinner, standardized on the authority of Johns Hopkins University Medical Department and known to contain exactly what is best for a standardized stomach. From seven to nine, a standardized radio plays standardized jazz and furnishes to what is left of the cubicle-dweller's mind an assortment of standardized misinformation. After which machinery removes his standardized clothing and casts him into his standardized bed.[56]

Here the American worker was not even accorded the agency of the laborer deliberately working at least, even if only for an oppressive employer, nor was he granted the dignity of exercising a negative option, a decision *not* to accept the dietary advice of Johns Hopkins professors or something sent to him automatically by a modern business masquerading as a social club. Rather, he was submerged in the maw of some giant machine, enmeshed within it only as a component carefully integrated into a complex set of operations that seemed to proceed automatically without direction and without his consent. Russell's image was very close to the language of another critic who lamented that "we are victims of the machine. We have become a nation of copy-cats, with the same commonplace newspapers everywhere, the same movies, the same parroted phrases issuing from every throat. Chains of drug stores, groceries, filling stations, waffle parlors, lunchrooms, beauty dens. Cities all alike. Originality faces starvation."[57] Similarly, Russell might have voiced another's observation that "the one dead level" of the machine standard can only produce "a nation of automata. One hundred million Babbitts!"[58]

Russell's reliance on this familiar set of tropes suggests that the anxiety about agency, which Seltzer has identified as a recurrent problem for turn-of-the-century Americans, still plagued the national psyche more than twenty-five years later. Indeed, the 1920s debate about standardization and literary production might be seen, I think, as one more act in what Seltzer calls "the sublime melodrama of agency suspended and recovered." Seltzer's complete argument, which addresses the differences between market and machine culture, the logical contradictions of competitive and disciplinary individualism, and the centrality of the concept of agency to the literature of naturalism, is too rich and complicated to summarize here. What is immediately relevant for my purposes, however, is his claim that the advent of machine and consumer culture in the United States produced a profound panic about the status of the natural body in a world increasingly "made" in factories that produced not only durable goods and consumer luxuries but "character" and "men" as well. As Seltzer notes, "If turn-of-the-century American culture is alternatively described as naturalist, as machine culture, and as the culture of consumption, what binds together these apparently alternative descriptions is the notion *that bodies and persons are things that can be made.*" [59] Referring to David Macleod's argument that the regimented, character-building program of the Boy Scouts of America depended on a strategy for "replicating small units supervised by a promotionally aggressive bureaucracy," Seltzer observes that the Scouts' "character factory . . . standardize[d] the making of men, coordinating the body and the machine within a single system of regulation and production." [60]

Russell's *Century* ruminations effectively demonstrate, however, that the coordination of body and machine was not universally welcomed by Americans even in the 1920s. This kind of coordination promised for some only the fearsome prospect of human individuality both invaded by the intrusive machine and absorbed into the movements of its self-propelling, nonstop flows. In a world where the individual and the organic body were being increasingly replaced by the collective body of the organization—a situation figured in Russell's vision by the triumph of the supercorporation of General Motors, the experts at Johns Hopkins Medical School, and the invisible, universal boss of unnamed capital itself—some critics asked, "What remains of the heroic figure of the American self, the republican pioneer, or the fearless cowboy, wholly in charge of himself and the world about him?" In effect, they worried about the fate of will, intentionality, choice, and agency, the crucial ideological props of the independent citizen-subject in a machine-tooled world. As a former Ford employee put it in Stuart Chase's analysis of the problem, "Sure, if I'd tightened up nut number 999 myself any longer, I'd have become nut number 999 myself." [61] What worried critics like Chase and Russell was the possibility that adjusting the human to the requirements of the machine would transform the human into the machine.

But the slight hint of a gendered subtext in the Russell passage also points to a limitation in Seltzer's analysis. Although his argument is what I would call gender-sensitive, Seltzer does not make a concerted effort to explore how the anxiety about agency or the panic about the natural body that was characteristic of the period may also have been prompted by the changing status of women. As a consequence, it seems to me, his account misses one of the principal opportunities it opens up, that is, the opportunity to assess dialectically how discourses about specifically gendered notions of agency were occasioned not simply by economic developments or by technological and organizational changes—by machines and their bureaucratic analogs—but also by key social developments in the relative positioning of women and men. Russell's vision and related denunciations of the book clubs make clear, in fact, that the anxieties about agency, choice, individuality, and independence evoked by the prospect of standardization were themselves profoundly overdetermined. The autonomous male subject was portrayed in the standardization debates generally and in the specific discussions about the book clubs as threatened not simply by mechanical and therefore inhuman machines but, more ominously and as the consequence of an odd catachresis, by machines that appeared to be the result of some natural, organic, fertile force run wild. These discussions reveal that in spite of their mechanical status, machines were sometimes viewed through what can only be called gendered lenses that highlighted the processes of absorption whereby large, loose, amorphous organizations configured as eternally proliferating organisms overwhelmed or smothered distinct, singular, always male individuals.

This is evident in the gendered subtext of Russell's grim dystopia. To put it bluntly, women laborers are completely absent from the working population that he imagines will be in force by 1956. In fact, it is explicitly a man who is dressed, fed, and sent to work in lockstep with a line of other men. Significantly, however, the labor of reproduction that women traditionally perform has not been erased. It is now carried out not by individual women in the private sphere of the home but by the giant machine itself, which is, as a result, ominously feminized. Instead of the wives and mothers who once made beds, provided meals, laundered clothes, and ensured that their charges reported to their appointed places on time, thereby invisibly enabling their productivity, Russell's image of the future envisions those tasks being performed automatically and publicly by a giant, internally regulated machine that he portrays as a hive of a million standardized cubicles. In this hive, however, it is almost as if the power of the traditional queen, once concentrated in a single bee, has now saturated the entire system. Its very diffusion threatens the autonomy of men, who are presented as internal to that machine or hive, absorbed into it and subordinated to its systematic control. The nightmare vision specifically figures the threat of an amorphous, unnameable, unlocalizable force connected, however remotely, to the feminine and therefore powerful in its unlimited capacity for reproduction. This power seems to challenge the status of men as producers and creators precisely because their very existence is now explicitly shown to be dependent on the prior reproductive labor and power associated with women.

Machines appeared in the standardization debates, as they do in Russell's image, as authoritarian, repressive, and threatening to individuals seeking to assert their autonomy and independence. Similarly, in the debates over the book clubs, the bureaucratic organizations of the culture industry were analogized to such machines, and those machines were depicted as automatically dispensing an engineered product, stamping out one identical thing after another. However, despite the widespread emphasis on the automated, programmed character of the machine and on its capacity to impress that same standardized mark on everyone who came into contact with it, both machines and their culture industry analogs were also oddly identified with powerful, amorphous, organic forces that were imagined as submerging, inundating, or erasing all vestiges of individuated selfhood and its legitimate products.

## GENDER AND THE TRANSFORMATION
## OF LITERARY PRODUCTION

This connection, which seems to be made only tenuously in the Russell passage, often became more explicit in discussions of the book clubs. There, more intensely gendered metaphors were used during the 1920s and 1930s to demonize such organizations because they were churning out dubious cultural products at an alarming rate. In virtually all of their manifestations, these metaphors rhetorically constructed an opposition between the individual, independent reader capable of actively seeking out real literature and an undifferentiated mass of passive consumers who were satiated by their indiscriminate absorption of a wholly undifferentiated substance. Usually compared either to nonnourishing food or to food considered particularly distasteful, mass-produced culture was thereby doubly demonized by its metonymic association with those who would force-feed such food to their docile charges, that is, with women. As frequently as the book club critiques branded mass-produced, machine culture as anathema to the cause of art and to the fate of the deliberative individual, so too did they metaphorically connect such culture with the organic lack of differentiation associated with the feminine and the effeminate. By repeatedly associating new cultural agencies like the book clubs with the staples of a child's diet, and by linking the child's processes of indiscriminate ingestion to the mother, the critics of mass-produced art were metonymically evoking traces of what Peter Stallybrass and Allon White have called "the scandalous, grotesque body," the fertile, sexual body of the reproductive female, which has traditionally been used to demonize the materials and processes of popular culture.[62] Like the maternal body, with its earthy, material nature threatening to engulf everything from below, the popular classes and their bawdy, extravagant entertainments were constructed by such metaphors as a distinct social threat to the reign of recognized, legitimate authority. The book clubs, it should now be clear, were understood in precisely this way.

In the following passage, for example, in an article criticizing the book clubs, the author of "Books on the Belt" slid easily if incomprehensibly from images of conveyor-belt production to evocations of food associated with the authority and surveillance of mothers. "Have you had your book this month?" he queried. "If not, some club, league, guild, society, cabal, academy, mail-order house, or synod of presbyters has missed a chance. . . . For books are being made as accessible as milk on the stoop in this land of higher salesmanship, as compulsory as spinach. Thanks to the book clubs."[63] This association of suspect and authoritarian literary agencies with mothers was made even clearer in a letter written to *The Saturday Review of Literature* specifically criticizing the book clubs. The letter writer protested, "I am forced to accept Big Ben as a roomy, forced to partake of canned soups, radio, movies and censorship but I'll be consigned if I am going to have my books ladled out to me by literary cooks regardless of their professed or actual standing as critics, reviewers, or blurbsmiths."[64] After further detailing his criticism of the book club's selections as a "pig in a poke, all picked, packed, trimmed, deodorized," the letter writer concluded that he (undoubtedly *he*) would stick with bookstores. He added finally, triumphantly, and with a superior air, "No literary wet nurses for me."

As Stallybrass and White have shown, the natural, grotesque body has traditionally been figured as "a mobile, split, multiple, self, a subject of pleasure in the process of exchange," a subject, furthermore, that is "never closed off from either its social or ecosystemic context."[65] Thus, it has frequently been demonized in discourse by its connection with feeding pigs or nursing mothers, with acts of feeding and ingestion that are always portrayed as simultaneously pleasurable and disgusting. These passages from critiques of the book clubs suggest that opponents of the supposed ersatz culture spewed out by new and threatening cultural producers fell back on such familiar rhetorical tactics as a way of denigrating both the cultural organizations themselves and those who so enthusiastically consumed their output. Indeed, their rhetoric seems fixated on the processes of exchange at the heart of the book club operation, on the processes of mail-order distribution, and in particular, on the processes of "forced" consumption set in motion by the club's automatic distribution mechanism, the negative option notwithstanding. Hence the critics' characteristic emphasis was on the book club exchange as an activity dominated by the indiscriminate distribution of pabulum (the 1920s metaphorical equivalent of today's fast food) and on the correspondingly passive consumption of distasteful, undifferentiated, oozing substances. It seems highly likely, then, that the distant echoes of maternal force and infantile regression encoded in these references betokened the critics' deepseated worries about the threatening surge of social and material forces that posed a challenge to the survival of the separate, elevated, purified, rational, bourgeois, *male* body. What these critics seemed to fear was the "grotesque," thoroughly sexualized body of the reproductive female who threatened to subordinate men as her dependents.

This is not hard to understand in a culture suddenly grappling not only with machines but with the prospect of nonsubordinate women, women endowed with the official American rights of choice and voice—the vote—and at the same time liberated sexually as dancing flappers and vamps. Increasingly admitted to the public world of work through the portals of the much-expanded public education system, white middle-class women were also for the first time in a position to compete with white middle-class men for status, financial rewards, and cultural authority. And women of all classes were much more visible in public spaces such as department stores, the typing pools of corporate American business, and libraries as well as in elementary schools, the home economics departments of secondary schools, and even college classrooms. In the third decade of the twentieth century, then, it seems clear that masculine agency was as threatened by the effects of an increasingly visible, potentially uncontrollable and uncontainable population of women as by the tireless operations of self-propelled machines.

The interesting question, it seems to me, is why women and machines were discursively linked as a single threat within the field of literary production. After all, to describe a machine as an organic, fertile, maternal force run wild is counterintuitive to a certain extent. What, then, motivated the link? For that matter, why did the anxiety about women and machines boil up so intensely within the literary field in the first place? What exactly appeared to be so jeopardized by processes of machine production, and why was it asserted that mechanical production and reproduction necessarily feminized those who made use of the resulting products? More to the point, perhaps, what specific social and political effects were realized through the discursive work of gender in this context? When the book clubs were associated with mewling infants, unruly children, and

{ *On the History of the Middlebrow* }

their authoritarian mothers, who, by implication, was construed as the rational, discriminating adult, and why was this individual's appearance in the arena of public discussion so necessary and altogether reassuring?

A brief look at yet another intervention in the literary wing of the standardization debates can be helpful here. Although Young America critic Waldo Frank published this rambling, weird diatribe a few months before the Book-of-the-Month Club was actually introduced to the public and thus could not have been acquainted with Harry Scherman's selling machine for books, it is clear that he was worried about the threat posed to literature by related organizational efforts to make culture available to more than the educated few. Although he titled his article "Pseudo-Literature," the point clearly was not so much to define pseudoliterature itself as to reiterate, albeit somewhat hysterically, the definition of real or true literature. In so doing, Frank introduced into the discussion the figure who I think was behind a good deal of the expressed anxiety about the book clubs, their subscribers, and the products they dispensed, that is, the heroic, highbrow writer who "has traditionally addressed a minority in a minority."[66]

Frank set out by discriminating between "real" literature on one hand, which he significantly glossed as "the effect of creative thought and of creative vision," and on the other hand the "populous cordialities" of the "false" printed goods designed for "the mob" and "the mass."[67] Although he noted that "the printing press and the mock crowning of Demos . . . merely aggravated an immemorial condition," changes in the modern scene had made the problem worse, because "now . . . everyone is forced to read, the flood of words without creative source is stintless, and there are organized for it great armies of 'distributing agents,' of which an unconsciously servile group call themselves reviewers—even critics."[68] The problem was that an expanded and mechanized cultural production had made it necessary for the masses and the mob to rely on intermediary agents in order to decide what to read among the massive number of titles issued each month. As he put it, "The swollen plethora of pseudo-literature has perhaps lowered the visibility of the real through its sheer mass."[69] The point, evidently, was that the best writers might not get read.

Frank expanded on his initial definitions by suggesting additionally that where real literature was "creative" and thereby linked to a "creative source," its simulations were mechanically *re*produced (like print) and forced in an unending stream upon everyone, not by authors but by those new forces he called "distributing agents." Still, Frank insisted, and I think this rhetorical move was the crucial one, not even "the presence of hawkers and bawlers purveying printed goods to the mob" could alter the position of the unassailable figure of the true artist anymore than had "the deformation of the democratic doctrine into the myth that everybody is as good as everybody else."[70] Mass production could not obliterate the superiority of the true artist anymore than could Frank's own discussion of pseudoliterature. In fact, the very topic of pseudoliterature was simply a pretext for rhetorically introducing this other subject, the figure of the heroic artist, precisely in order to insist on his continued supremacy. Frank even counseled writers who might be longing for the kind of success enjoyed by Fannie Hurst that this was to hunger after the wrong reward. "For to have heard clear, even once, the word of God is to have heard it forever in all the calls of life." According to Waldo Frank, then, people ought to be reading the works of "the wooers of beauty and truth," the guardians of "the creative, the heroic, the religious spirit of true literature."[71]

In his mind the priestly acolyte, the graced subject, and the creative genius, along with his spontaneously created, unique work of art, were to be the salvation of liberal democracy. Correlatively, Frank opposed both to the mechanical, regimented universe of printed goods, to the world of the mob and the masses caught up unconsciously in the production and consumption of the identical and the same. What he seemed to be refuting, finally, was the implicit claim that forms of mass production and reproduction were in some way essentially democratic. At the same time he also insisted on the superior status of the creative artist at precisely that moment because he sensed that such an individual and all that he represented was suddenly vulnerable to strange and threatening new forces. In attempting to clarify why this might be so, he resorted to familiar gendered allusions and revealed if only obliquely who and what was really on his mind.

Despite his certainty about the conceptual opposition between creative genius and true art on one hand and repetitive mass production on the other, Frank noted that he was prompted to reiterate the antinomy by a troubling new development that he believed constituted a significant threat to the purity of his key categories. Acknowledging that "the gigantic reaches of pseudo-literature from the Hearst papers to Harold Bell Wright, *being allotted their proper place*, do no great harm," he warned that the status of true literature was more seriously jeopardized by "snobs" and "social climbers" who "desire culture even at the cost of thrills" and who are "aware of the term literature and want their share of it."[72] Mass culture and the mass audience, both in their proper place, it would seem, posed no problem at all. They did nothing to threaten the status of true creation and real literature because they were obviously so different.

But the kinds of products created and marketed to people who wanted only to surround themselves with the aura attached to literature did much greater harm. They threatened the distinctions he considered all-important. Although Frank provided no further details on the identity of the snobs and social climbers he disdained, his references and allusions were clear. He was thinking of those who aspired to the veneer of culture through participation in reading and culture clubs, an activity associated almost exclusively with women, and through the purchase of outline volumes; the latest, fashionable novels; and sets of classics, commodities associated predominantly with female buyers. He continued: "Their conception [of literature], of course, is derived from shallow study of the past. Incapable of recognizing the essence of an art, they dwell on its external traits and manners. And the contemporary writers who most flatter them are the emulators of these imitable parts. Such authors are competent in style, they are elegant, they reproduce in terms of up-to-dateness the forms and virtues of previous pioneers."[73]

According to Waldo Frank, then, up-to-date literary consumers and the people who wrote for them ignored the creative spirit of true literature and fastened only on its technical details, its outer shell. Consequently blind to literature's "independent body," its "primary creative stuff," they degraded the very name "literature" by repetitively producing only its imitation. Noting further that "it is precisely urgent that the name literature be not degraded," Frank informed his readers that "a confusion in words is the symbol of confusion in continents and souls." "Much of the dangerous condition of our time," he continued ominously, "springs from the fact that in the readjustment of social and spiritual forms, names [have] become the prostituted playthings of any fool or knave who wishes to mouth them."[74] According to Frank, therefore, the once pure form of literature stood in danger of being sullied by its association with effeminate poseurs who understood neither their own place nor that properly accorded to machine-stamped works that could only hope to ape the literary. What this form of cultural production threatened, then, was the very capacity to distinguish between the true and the false, the pseudo and the real. It threatened to usurp the prerogative of the real artist, the power to write, to create, and thereby to gain access to an audience.

In this case the knave who had taken the name of literature in vain was, not surprisingly, a woman—none other than "Mrs. Edith Wharton," who had presumed to publish a book called *The Writing of Fiction*, which made the egregious error of assuming that literature, like everything else, was to be made to order according to mechanical specifications. Comparing her volume to the newly fashionable cookbook, Frank noted that it "now reveals for even the most docile eye the vast, the complacently ignored abyss that can uprise between an art form and the creative spirit." He then closed his remarkable harangue with confident advice: "Let the reader run through these prim pages of technical details on 'situation,' 'character,' 'style,' 'fidelity to nature' . . . ; let him ask himself what all this has to do with the high sacrament of the word, which art and literature shall ever be. He will then need no critic. His own hunger for spiritual and aesthetic nurture should suffice to show him the difference between what he lacks and the straw food of fashionable letters."[75]

Despite the somewhat muddled progression of his argument, it is clear that in a world such as Frank's, true literature, the high sacrament of the word, was not a "made" thing. More like a religious truth than the fashionable product of technical labor, true literature required no handmaidens—neither distributors nor reviewers—to find its readership. Rather, it would stand revealed in all its virile glory before those truly worthy to receive it. It would do so because it was an original creation, the unique emanation of a heroic writer-artist, an individual dependent on no one but God and especially not on women who might claim, by virtue of their own capacities for reproduction, the fruitful power of prior creation.

I think Frank's strange commentary reveals the usually repressed fear motivating the characteristic slippage from the mechanical to the maternal in the book club critiques. In writing about the threat of a suffocating, maternal flow of always unsatisfying nourishment, what Frank and the others were imagining, so as to stave it off rhetorically, was the obliteration of the singular, individuated, adult subject and his literary apotheosis, the vigorous, virile, wholly original writer. Because the figure of the smothering mother, the Victorian titaness, as Ann Douglas has described her, was so unsympathetic a figure at a time when the boyish, bobbed flapper waif was the feminine ideal, the use of this trope made the survival of her struggling charge, the male writer, seem all the more desirable, necessary, and in the end, possible. I say possible here because I think that Frank and the others were really writing about their deep fear of a new and extraordinarily powerful system for cultural production, a system enshrining speed, repetition, circulation, and integration at its very core. That system, with its remarkable capability for linking production, reproduction, and consumption in an ever-tighter embrace, did away almost from the start with the very idea of origin, creation, inspiration, and source. It posed an enormous threat to the figure that stood at the center of an older system of production, the author who had first been endowed with property rights in his creations by eighteenth-century copyright and intellectual property law, which thereby recognized him as the source, the origin of his own work.

Women and machine production gave the lie to this fiction, it seems to me, because both insisted on and made visible prior production—on one hand the production that had embodied the author in the first place, and on the other that which provided him with the materials from which he had imbibed his language, his themes, and his form. By feminizing the new forces of production that so threatened individuated, male selfhood at this time—forces bound up with machine technology and coordinated organizational systems—cultural critics both motivated and effected the convenient and encouraging illusion that those forces and the kinds of subjects they called into being might be as easily contained and controlled as women were in a society where men traditionally controlled both the pen and the law.

The logic of Frank's article shows, I think, that the book clubs and other agencies for the organized distribution of literature and culture threatened, perhaps more than anything else, one of the key oppositional responses to machine-directed standardization. They thwarted the move to enshrine culture and the literary as the inherently redemptive expression of all that was most creative, independent, and original about the world of the human. In subordinating the aesthetic uniqueness of books to their equivalence as a certain kind of object, the commodity, they refused to recognize the literary as transcendent. At the same time, by positioning both writers and readers as little more than relays or nodes in a larger circuit directed by others, these new cultural organizations appeared to refuse the idea that some authors were more original than others and thus possessed a special power to single out those equal to their unique challenge. In absorbing both readers and writers into a vast, integrated system for the circulation of cultural commodities, Harry Scherman's selling machine threatened to cut the heroic author and his artwork down to average, standardized size. It threatened to deny his special qualities as a man among men. Frank Lentricchia has perhaps described this particular conception of artistic genius and individuality more forcefully than anyone in his discussion of Ezra Pound's notion of poetic virtu:

virtu as the goal of experiment; virtu as the discovery and expression of the very quality of individuality (in no two writers is it the same), the basis of an original ("self-reliant") writing and the reason of its persistence; virtu as bravery, courage, strength, and, in a word, *manliness* which has been obliterated by a feminized culture of the poetic commodity ruled over by Aunt Hepsy; that manliness the absence of which explains why literature in America is "left to the care of ladies' societies, and of 'current events' clubs, and is numbered among the 'cultural influences.'" [76]

For Pound, as for Waldo Frank, the high sacrament of the word was defined most fully by what it was not: the easy, sentimental effusions of a machine-tooled industry churning out cookbooklike products for the degraded pleasure and use of the generic Aunt Hepsy.

I think it should be pointed out here that however much both modernism and other avant-garde artistic movements sought deliberately to oppose the depredations of capitalist economy and the various material and social forces of production on which it depended, what they sometimes set up in opposition to those forces was actually an older model of the subject, the literary equivalent of the liberal individual, that is, the creative genius, the heroic poet, the romantic artist, "the author." Significantly, they maintained and shored up the difference of that individuated subject by constantly marking off his distance from the culturally devalued feminine, the force that apparently threatened to engulf and to reabsorb him into its undifferentiated flux and flow. Thus the critical move to judge, to discriminate, and to distinguish moved to the center of the larger modernist enterprise and saturated the literary field as it became ever more necessary to differentiate true literature from its ersatz imitation, to separate the serious artist from his mere hack follower. The authoritative status of the modernist high literary, it would seem, was increasingly dependent, then, on the practice of marking the critical difference between that conceived as the bona fide and the authentic and that which merely masqueraded as such.

Little wonder, then, that the vocabulary of the standardization debates ultimately proved inadequate to the critical project of demonizing and distancing the book clubs and other related purveyors of cultural products from literature's authorized proprietors. Sometime in the 1920s, in fact, a new word was coined that promised to bring under control this troubling liminal space of hybrid forms where the organic body of true literature was prostituted to the power of anonymous, systematized forces and sold to anyone with a few extra dollars. Although the terms "highbrow" and "lowbrow" had become part of common usage early in the century, the term "middlebrow" apparently did not appear until after 1920.[77] "Middlebrow" had not been listed, for instance, in the 1859 *Bartlett's Dictionary of Americanisms*, nor did it appear in the 1889 volume *Americanisms: Old and New*, by John S. Farmer.[78] Furthermore, in the first extended discussion of the notions of "highbrow" and "lowbrow" conducted by Van Wyck Brooks in 1915 in *America's Coming-of-Age*, the middlebrow made no formal appearance at all.[79] *The Oxford English Dictionary* traces the first appearance of the term to a 1925 article in *Punch*, which noted that "the B.B.C. claim to have discovered a new type, the 'middlebrow.' It consists of people who are hoping that someday they will get used to the stuff they ought to like."[80] The term had clearly moved into common parlance by the mid-1930s, however, when Margaret Widdemer published a piece in *The Saturday Review of Literature* titled "Message and Middlebrow," and Virginia Woolf used it extensively in a letter (which she never sent) to *The New Statesman* protesting a recent review of one of her books.[81]

In the next chapter I return to the book club debates from a somewhat different perspective in the hope of specifying in even greater depth why organizations such as Scherman's necessitated the demarcation of this new cultural territory of the middlebrow, that illegitimate quarter where authentic literature and true art were supposedly prostituted to alien and suspect powers. Specifically, I examine more carefully the nature of the nervous commentary that developed as the club and its imitators established themselves in the larger literary field. As the book club critique evolved throughout the 1920s and the 1930s, Scherman's judges became the lightning rod for criticism and displaced the distribution system as the most objectionable feature of the new organization. When this happened, the debate metamorphosed to a certain degree and took up new questions having to do with the nature of literary authority, the power of book reviewers and advisers, and the nature of their relationship to their burgeoning audience. By looking at these discussions in some detail, we should be able to see that the Book-of-the-Month Club and other related organizations devoted to broadening the sale of culture proved additionally disruptive of the literary field because they threatened to establish a semipermanent conduit between a new, mass audience and a small group of literary experts who differed substantially from those who had previously exercised control over the literary arena. The result of a larger economic and social transformation, the appearance of this new group of cultural mediators was symptomatic of the development of an unprecedented technical and managerial elite with extraordinary power and means to reach a potentially huge population. Finally, I examine how the arrival of this new class, of which Scherman and his judges were a conspicuous part, threatened to disrupt the order of the literary field and the larger public sphere as they had been understood in the past.

## CHAPTER SEVEN

# The Scandal of the Middlebrow

## The Professional-Managerial Class and the Exercise of Authority in the Literary Field

### CONFLICTING MODES OF LITERARY PRODUCTION

It should be clear by now that Harry Scherman's Book-of-the-Month Club did not intervene in the publishing business alone. Through its establishment of a committee of experts and its claim to send out the best book every month to its subscribers, the club additionally disrupted the established structures of literary practice and authority. Indeed, this latter maneuver generated the most intense attacks on the book club and its imitators, widening what had at first been only a trade war. Furthermore, it intensified the ongoing debate about the consequences of mass-produced standardization, especially within the literary field itself.

In creating his selling machine Scherman introduced into the literary field marketing strategies that had been widely used in other industries. Like those who sold Quaker oats and Pearline soap, he marketed books under the sign of the Book-of-the-Month Club in order to convince potential subscribers that his wares were reliable. By creating the brand name of the Book-of-the-Month Club, he committed himself to the promotion of products supposedly uniform in quality and to the suggestion that consumers themselves were fundamentally the same.[1] To make such a claim, however, in a society whose national identity was still intimately connected to its celebration of American individualism was highly problematic. It proved especially so for Scherman because he was working in an industry where products were still generated by a mode of production constitutively defined by valorization of an independent, autonomous creator.

By 1926 the general mode of production in the United States had been thoroughly transformed by the accumulated economies of speed and by the methodical reorganization of manufacture, distribution, and consumption into a single integrated and incorporated system. The literary mode of production, though, was still characterized by profound conflicts and contradictions.[2] Large sections of the publishing industry continued to be modeled after the imperatives of a mode of production in which individual authors with unique talents and training produced singular objects characterized by stylistic particularities and distinctive concerns. These individuals offered their products rather than their labor to publishing houses. Publication, in this view, was conceptualized as a linear process of natural issue and intellectual property transmission.

Other sections of the industry, however, had adopted the logic of modern mass production. They had installed corporate creation and managed distribution at the center of their enterprises in order to increase the flow of commodities for the market. Within this system, publication was conceived of as an endless process of circulation and cultural recycling, a reformulation and ever-widening distribution of previously existing material. Predictably, these operations were tarred with powerful epithets and dismissed as entertainment by champions of the author and the mode of production of which he was perhaps the defining element.[3] The category of the lowbrow was understood to include all standardized cultural objects that were generated through a corporately organized mode of production, including moving pictures, radio programs, and pulp novels. The space of the middlebrow was occupied by products that supposedly hid the same machine-tooled uniformity behind the self-consciously worked mask of culture. The evaluative geography of the high, the low, and the middle, it would seem, was mobilized specifically at this moment to control the temporal ascendancy of new, highly threatening productive forces.

To explain why resistance to some aspects of consumerist modernization persisted in the literary field is no easy matter. In effect, a mode of literary production lived on as residual cultural form, that is, as a form organized and developed at an earlier historical moment but surviving virtually intact into a rapidly changing present.[4] Generally, those associated with this particular mode of production claimed for themselves oppositional status; they cast themselves as the heroic resistance to a decline in the nature and the position of the literary, which they attributed to the appearance of collective production and mass distribution. In an effort to explore the sources and characteristics of this resistance, I look more closely at some additional objections leveled at the proprietors of middlebrow culture. My aim is to clarify the nature of the threat these new forms of production posed to a certain understanding of the literary field as well as to beliefs about the function that field performed in the larger social formation. Although a complex set of social and material factors surely contributed to the perpetuation of familiar relations between the kinds of authors, publishers, and readers that had come to characterize trade book publishing, it seems clear that the longevity of the system as a whole must be attributable in some fundamental way to the continuing ideological power of a particular understanding of print culture and the role of authorship and individual creation within it. Through a detailed investigation of the next stage in the book club debates, this chapter will attempt to specify in greater detail why these new distribution agencies seemed to pose such a threat to cherished ideas about the character and function of the literary field as a unique public space.

## THE ATTACK ON CANBY AND COMPANY

If Scherman and his partners failed to anticipate the extent of the opposition that would develop to their investiture of literary authority in a well-publicized selection committee, they could not have missed the early rumblings of the gathering storm that began soon after the first favorable notices of the club were recorded. Indeed a May 1926 editorial in *The Nation* explicitly addressed the phenomenon of literary selection committees and more generally took up the question of literary authority. The immediate occasion for the editorial, in this case, was Sinclair Lewis's refusal of the Pulitzer Prize for his novel *Arrowsmith*. The editors seized the occasion as an opportunity to applaud Lewis's principled stand and to ridicule the new fad of identifying "the best." Although their ostensible subject was the Pulitzer committee, their language suggested that the editors may have been thinking of Harry Scherman's committee of selection as well.

The idea of a literary prize is absurd, the anonymous editor wrote, "because of the capacity it assumes in a group of persons in a given year to decide which among several good books is the best."[5] The editorial continued:

When generations of critics are unable to agree upon a ranking of the poets, when as many opinions of a contemporary book are printed as there are reviewers to manufacture them, when nobody knows what literary virtue is anyway, how can three or five or seven gentlemen sitting in a room come to a meaningful agreement? Obviously they cannot, and anyone who has had the experience of being a judge on such a committee remembers compromises arrived at rather than preferences proclaimed. A's choice being obnoxious to B, B's to C, and C's to A, they end perhaps by agreeing on a fourth book that has nothing the matter with it—or nothing to recommend it. The absurdity lies after all in the assumption that there is one best book or poem, and also . . . in the rather pathetic faith of the public in the wisdom of judges.[6]

What is so striking about this particular passage is its offhand yet confident aside that nobody knows what constitutes literary virtue. It is odd, I think, because the statement was issued by a journal that published many literary reviews claiming validity for the judgments they offered and presuming to know something about literary quality. Value, it would seem, at least according to the editors of *The Nation*, was a matter of individual preference. While it is certainly true that *The Nation*'s reviewers and literary commentators sometimes disagreed among themselves about what great literature looked like, it is also possible to identify the magazine's general aesthetic position as one of cautious support for many forms of literary modernism and unambiguous scorn for the "light entertainment" that most Americans seemed to select for their summer reading. Despite their explicit emphasis on the individuality of taste, the editors of *The Nation* selected contributors who generally shared a common set of aesthetic assumptions. The fact that they obscured that commonality in the individualist language of A's, B's, and C's suggests that the notion of a generalized, centralized, and organized cultural authority was the problem. Cultural authority, it appears, was something to be questioned when it was claimed by others, but it was to be erased or denied with respect to one's self in the larger interest of asserting the power of individuality and the essential freedom of taste.

In fact, in an editorial titled "What Is Literary Authority?" published the year before, *The Nation* had effectively denied the need for such authority in the first place even while defending its own critical practice. Prompted to a discussion of the subject by the "remarkable growth in the quantity of criticism called for and produced in the United States," the editors asked the pragmatic question, "What kind of authority is it ever reasonable to expect?" Their answer was that all the clamorous American public could hope for was individual, "informed" critics with expertise in particular areas of specialization. They pointed out, however, that "mere information" did not a critic make, since it could not prevent him or her from offering mistaken opinions. After all, the editors observed, "in the last analysis there simply is no test by which a given person can be declared a perfect, unalterable authority on anything."[7] As evidence they cited the fact that "all the reading in the world could not save Dr. Johnson from being something of a fool when he came to discuss Milton, Swift, Fielding, and Gray. He was wrong about them all, for he atrociously undervalued them." Still, the editors averred, "he was a great critic."[8]

The obvious point here is that although the editors claimed explicitly that no test could be devised to identify unassailable literary authority, they took for granted their own capacity to determine that Johnson was wrong and that Milton, Swift, Fielding, and Gray were obviously and objectively great writers. The validity of their assertion, at least in their own view, was not a function of their particular expertise or their authority but of the inherent value of the great works themselves. As they put it, "[The Nation] believes that the main function of the critic is to assist the best books to take care of themselves."[9] Presumably, if such works were inherently the best, they would eventually be recognized as such by individual critics and by independent readers. By investing value in the textual object itself instead of seeing value as an attribution made by critics, the editors of The Nation could preserve their view of readers as independent individuals characterized by idiosyncratic tastes and at the same time explain the contradictory fact of critical congruence as a function of the inherent quality of given works. As a consequence, they could go on reviewing books and criticizing literary trends, believing that they were only facilitating discussion by publishing the independent ruminations of individual critics. Their strategic subterfuge hid the fact that they were actually helping to structure the larger debate and influence its course through the exercise of their own institutionally based power.

This convenient ideological maneuver was repeated again and again in the months following the founding of the Book-of-the-Month Club. In effect the club's critics attacked it for arrogating to itself too much cultural authority while denying their own competing claims to such power. In January 1927, for instance, only a couple of weeks after Publishers Weekly itself had come out against the Literary Guild, the trade journal published a detailed letter from bookseller Cedric Crowell, at that time also the chairman of the American Booksellers' Association Board of Trade, in which he took issue with most of the claims in the Guild's first prospectus. Although he was understandably exercised about the price-cutting issue, he heaped most of his scorn on the Guild's claim that its "distinguished Board of Editors reads the books and discards those you don't want and chooses those you do."[10] Crowell's complaint was driven by the same view of the independent American reader as that animating the editorial conception of criticism articulated by *The Nation*: "Does the Guild really mean to imply that the American mind is so stereotyped that it will be completely satisfied with the selection of the distinguished Board of Editors; that a book which appeals to Mr. X's sense of true literary merit will also appeal to all the other Misters of the alphabet? Does the Guild really mean to imply that the twelve books—six of them fiction—annually selected by its 'distinguished Board of Editors' can adequately cover for the intelligent citizen contemporary life in all its phases?" [11] Just as the editors at *The Nation* had questioned the legitimacy of the Pulitzer committee as well as the infallibility of a critic as universally recognized as Dr. Johnson, so Crowell questioned the right and ability of the Guild's editors to select books for others. In attempting to do so, he implied, they were stereotyping taste and therefore unduly controlling the exercise of independent aesthetic choice that would otherwise have been exercised freely.

Crowell assumed that two different readers would naturally have different tastes because each possessed a discrete individuality and unique sensibility. If people agreed, presumably, it was because the sheer quality of the work itself had overridden the particularities of their individual tastes. Interestingly enough, however, Crowell's language belied a certain anxiety about the viability of individuality. Indeed, by figuring his supposedly independent readers as alphabetic ciphers, as generic Mr. Xs and Ys, he revealed the familiar fear that the heroic American self, the autonomous reading subject, was nothing more than a hollow man, an empty vessel filled only with pabulum and propaganda imposed from without. The implicit threat evoked in his lament is the specter of a centralized authority determined to organize and to direct that already frightening mass of subjects, statistical persons only, each exactly like the next.

This sort of rhetoric was heightened considerably in February 1927 when Brentano's parodied the book clubs through its advertisement of a Choose-Your-Own Book Club in *The New Yorker* and in New York newspapers. Through the wit and power of satire, and by relying on an explicitly political discourse, the bookstore further tarred the clubs, if only by implication, with the loaded charge of "tyranny." Headlined "By Divine Right," Brentano's ad posted its own version of the Bill of Rights:

> The Constitution of the United States holds that all men are created equal and endowed with certain inalienable rights, that among those are life, liberty and the pursuit of happiness. Consequently we have formed a Choose-Your-Own Book Club Unlimited for all Americans, irrespective of race, color or previous condition of servitude, that they may:

1. Thru the bookstores of America have free access to *all books* for the *enrichment of life*.
2. That they may retain their freedom and liberty of choice in buying books.
3. That the pursuit of happiness may be theirs in the nearest bookstore.

To become a member of this Club, that is made up exclusively of men and women who are not content with hand-me-down opinions of eminent book jurors, one need only proceed to the nearest bookstore and purchase a book of his own selection.[12]

The tongue-in-cheek tone masks a certain shrillness suggesting that the Book-of-the-Month Club had not only meddled in the industry but had transgressed important ideological limits. The sustained invocation of nearly all the semantic counters circulating about the use of the signifier, "democracy," drew a stark contrast between the rational, independent, self-regulating adult confronted by a range of choices in a bookstore and the infantilized, passive dupes of the book clubs who were content with the hand-me-down opinions of eminent book jurors. Although the extremity of the rhetoric in this ad might reasonably be attributed to Brentano's commercial self-interest, similar representations appeared frequently in the supposedly more judicious columns of the literary reviews and in the public affairs weeklies.

The next entry in the war of words appeared in the March 5 issue of *The Independent*, where Ernest Boyd began his analysis of the book clubs with the claim that "the intelligent minority" need not concern itself with what was little more than a sordid "trade fight."[13] Unable to maintain this lofty position, however, he soon resorted to increasingly familiar political metaphors to castigate both the clubs and their customers. "The reader who takes advantage of this innovation in bookselling," he wrote, "will be adding to the process of standardization which has invaded every department of American life." "Soon," he continued, "a committee or a policeman will do everything for us short of drawing our breath. But that is hardly a matter that concerns the intelligent minority, which will have to continue as heretofore to do its own thinking and its own reading."

Like *The Nation*, Cedric Crowell, and Brentano's before him, Boyd was suggesting that book choices made by ordinary readers, that is, by non-club members, were free, independent, and uncoerced. By eliding the clubs with standardizing committees and policemen, whom he characterized as invaders of American life, he portrayed club members as defeated victims and the readers who did not join as actively resistant to an oppressive regime. He was thereby erasing the visibility, function, and power of the entire literary critical apparatus of which he was a part and which authorized him to speak in the first place. Boyd and those who shared his critical position conveniently ignored the fact that bookstore customers and bookstore owners had to find out about books somewhere, and that in accepting the opinion of a reviewer or a friend, they were also assenting to his or her authority. Even if they were resisting the authority of the book clubs, in so doing they were also acquiescing to a counterauthority exercised by others.

These few early comments about the clubs' intervention in the literary field establish clearly that what upset the clubs' opponents most was the fact that in recommending their preferences to a large group of people rather than to individuals, and in doing that as committees rather than as individuals, the book clubs' advisers were dangerously centralizing authority that was otherwise understood to be dispersed. Because such authority was conceived as dispersed, it was assumed that it was additionally open to disinterested, uncoerced, "free" assessment by others. As much as the book club debate, then, appeared to be about questions of literary value and in fact was part of a discussion of the impact of the machine and the standardization it made possible in American life, so, too, was it part of the nation's attempt to come to terms with the process of massification. The book club critics feared not only the massing of the huge, amorphous, uncritical audiences assembled by the new media but, equally, the unprecedented consolidation of highly centralized, commercially motivated cultural agencies aiming to address and to lead them. The book clubs and the literary experts they employed looked so threatening to their critics because they appeared to have the power as a cohesive and well-organized group to impose their own tastes on an even larger social body that itself lacked the critical capacity for assessment and the will to resist their influence. The book club debate originated, therefore, not only in fears about the loss of individual agency but also in the perceived threat posed by the creation of large enterprises for cultural dissemination and by the assemblage of huge audiences for their emanations.

The debate was premised on the largely unexamined assumption that such organizations usurped the power and prerogatives that had formerly belonged to individuals. Understandably, the critics of the book clubs accused these organizations of effecting the wholesale destruction of the untrammeled realm of rational inquiry, where self-regulating individuals freely decided their own views and eventually the fate of the civic community as well. In effect the critics were charging the book clubs with the destruction of the public sphere of critical discourse, an arena traditionally associated with literacy, print publication, and reading.[14] In making this charge, the book club critics were participating actively in a wider, international discussion of the problems associated with the centralization of cultural production. The book club wars were, in sum, a specifically American version of what we now call the mass culture debate.

## SAFEGUARDING THE PUBLIC SPHERE

In the United States, as elsewhere, the mass culture debate was touched off by widespread fears that the public sphere was being destroyed by the intervention of unprecedented cultural agencies with newfound power who acted only out of economic self-interest. At this historical moment, in fact, the image of the public sphere as the site of *dis*interested discourse was still so compelling that virtually all the parties to the dispute over the book clubs presented themselves as defenders of the public sphere. Before attempting to assess how an organization like the Book-of-the-Month Club actually intervened in this context, I want to look first at how the space itself was conceived both by the club's critics as well as by its proponents. To make sense of the intense fears Harry Scherman's organization provoked, it is necessary to understand the nature of the conceptual oppositions that underwrote the idea of the public sphere in the first place and to take account of the nostalgia and longing that invested it as a crucially important ideological space.

The key oppositions structuring the concept of the public sphere and ordering the book club debate in the United States were made especially clear in an anonymous essay published by *The Bookman* in April 1927. Despite an apparent preoccupation with the effect the book clubs might have on a somewhat narrowly conceived literary field, the article turned to the familiar language of American civic discourse to sway its reader. Specifically, it pitted the independent, rational, democratic subject against a vision of authority as centralized, organized, interested, and despotic. Titled "Has America a Literary Dictatorship?" this article focused on the selection committee of the Book-of-the-Month Club because, the author reasoned, "the hiring of critical and literary authority . . . immediately lifts [the clubs] out of the realm of purely commercial matters and brings them within the province of literature and the purview of criticism."[15] These two realms, the commercial and the literary, the author further asserted, ought to be kept conceptually and practically distinct. In his mind the literary world should remain pure, disinterested, and free from the exercise of undue influence. "Men and women of letters," he wrote, "who desire to obtain and retain a truly dignified and important place in the opinions of their discriminating contemporaries, the only contemporaries who in the final analysis can confer even a modicum of real fame—literary people, we repeat, whose ambition is authentic, cannot afford to tout themselves to the multitude as great, important, authoritative, distinguished, and altogether wonderful."[16] They cannot, he continued, not only because this would be to engage in "infernally bad taste," but also because it represented "a real attempt to standardize and to corral the authority to make literary fame," and by those whose rightful function was "to promote the spirit of *free critical inquiry*."[17]

The anonymous author left no doubt that he thought critical inquiry would otherwise be free if the clubs had not interfered. In specifically attacking Henry Canby, whom he characterized as "the heir apparent to the most authoritative position of critic in the field of American literature," he pictured the kind of state he thought the world of letters could be if Canby would only exercise his power appropriately. "By continuing to deal out the careful and independent criticism of which he has shown himself to be capable, and by gathering about him a number of untrammeled spirits, [Canby] might have enjoyed by general acclamation that authority which in the republic of letters can be wielded only by those whose opinions are individual and not dictated or warped by interest—in short, what great criticism has always been, the whole souled comment of a keen intellect dealing out judiciously from a ripe experience an interesting and informative comment upon books."[18] Canby's judgment, the author suggested, should be offered independently as the disinterested opinion of a rational individual, a democratic reading subject governed not by self-interest or idiosyncratic bias but by the pursuit of the objective principles of universal rationality. Such deliberation would promote, he argued, the free exercise of an equally rational judgment in the sphere of public discourse on the part of Canby's readers. In that case, he added, "when an author's book is accepted by the public, owing to an open discussion of its merits and demerits by reviewers, the public is then buying the book for *reasons*. The book's claim to be read has been successfully established in open court."[19] What was most objectionable about Canby's participation on the Book-of-the-Month Club's committee, he continued, was that the books were "to be accepted purely on [the committee's] authority." Discussion, disagreement, and difference were to be erased in favor of a final product only. "In other words," he concluded, "the rational process of reviewing [would be] entirely done away with for a series of private judgments arrived at in camera."[20]

His conclusion to this portion of the argument demonstrates clearly that he believed the Book-of-the-Month Club had introduced dangerous mediation into public literary debate. "Every right tradition of literature is outraged by this method," he wrote, "all the experience of critical tradition is disregarded." According to *The Bookman*, the problem was that the literary sphere, which should promote free public inquiry, had been colonized by insistently interested, commercially minded authorities not one whit concerned to justify their decisions but fully content to dictate only by virtue of their power. For the anonymous writer, disinterested rational deliberation about the intrinsic properties of important books was segregated from and defined diacritically as free by its opposition to the contingent investments and maneuvers of self-interested committees operating always to maximize various forms of personal profit.

The rhetorical figure of the disinterested, civic-minded reading subject was so potent at this historical moment that it even dictated the terms of Harry Scherman's early efforts to respond to his critics. Scherman wrote many letters to the weekly magazines and addressed the growing number of attacks on the book clubs in the pages of the newly instituted *Book-of-the-Month Club News*. What is especially interesting about his various defenses is the fact that they were formulated in virtually the same terms as those employed by his critics. The characteristic ideological framing of the issues involved is evident, for instance, in one of Scherman's important columns in the March 1928 *News*.[21] In this case, "What the Public Wants" was ostensibly devoted to explaining the difference between literary reviews and the "reports" contained in the club's catalog. Nonetheless, Scherman addressed himself to the larger issue of the committee's authority and worked diligently to redefine its purported usurpation of the public's right to choose. In explaining the detailed reports of books that had begun to appear monthly in the catalog, he admitted that "originally, as some of our old members know, the [selection committee] selected the 'book-of-the-month' and it went out to everybody [automatically] without any preliminary description." Although he noted that members could exercise "the individual power of veto" by returning the selection, he implied that he, too, felt that this system had not permitted enough freedom of choice at that point. He claimed that the reports had been instituted "as a natural extension of this protection to members against receiving a book they did not want or would not have chosen themselves." With this assertion Scherman signaled to his critics that, like them, he placed the highest priority on maintaining the individual reader's freedom of choice.

Scherman proceeded to explain the function of the reports and to urge his members to read them for their own benefit. In keeping with his emphasis on the priority attached to individual choice, he strategically represented the operations of the selection committee as the activities of a set of discrete and different individuals. He observed, "It is chiefly, however, in their own interest that we urge members to read these preliminary reports with care; the choices always represent the judgment of five, keen, open-minded readers; we can testify, who listen to their discussions; when they agree upon a book, by the law of averages alone, it ought to be worthwhile, for one reason or another. For they themselves have quite diverse tastes and, therefore, agreement in this company means something. But if there is one thing certain, in the world of books, it is that one man's meat is another man's poison."[22] Although this last observation seems to imply that Harry Scherman might have understood aesthetic value to be contingent upon an individual's particular interests, other data suggests that this was not the case. The early operating procedures utilized by the committee of selection indicate that Scherman and his colleagues also understood value to be an intrinsic property of books themselves. Critical agreement about the excellence of particular books was not the result of a congruence of interests or of the identity of multiple subjects but, rather, the result of a book's intrinsic merit and therefore of its ability to triumph over the contingencies of individual taste.

In the first few months of the Book-of-the-Month Club's operation, the committee members neither met nor deliberated collectively about the selection process. They voted in typical American fashion, in a veiled manner, as abstract democratic subjects, not as particularized individuals with specific histories and distinctive backgrounds. Scherman and his colleagues assumed that such a procedure would be adequate to the task because they presumed that any book receiving the most votes had to have been the best in the pool. They abandoned this procedure early, however, in part because they realized certain books were being selected with very few votes. As Scherman himself put it in his Columbia interview, "[The committee members] realized that it was impossible to choose any book without meeting and talking about it. They had to read the same books, and they had to sit and talk about them. It couldn't be done by mail or by votes or anything else. . . . There had to be a meeting and it had to be a regular meeting."[23]

Only a few months into the club's operation Scherman instituted a monthly meeting of the selection committee. At that gathering Henry Canby and company deliberated about a short list of books that had been previously winnowed from the month's output. By all accounts they talked with one another about their reasons for liking particular books until general consensus was achieved, a procedure that obviated the need to take a formal vote. Significantly though, according to Scherman, this discussion was not designed to replace the rational deliberations carried on by the larger public in the open arena but functioned, rather, as an instance of it. His subscribers, he assured his critics, were simply taking over where the committee members had left off. Thus when he ended his defense of his organization, he claimed that the reports on the monthly selection and the various recommended alternates were designed to describe the books accurately and to explain why the committee members had chosen them in the first place. Scherman asserted triumphantly and in the familiar language of American civic discourse, "What all this leads to is—the Book-of-the-Month Club and its [committee] defer gladly to your inalienable right to consult your changing moods in reading."[24] His final recommendation is worth quoting in full for the emphasis it places not only on individual diversity but also on the process involved in making choices:

> So—do, in your own protection, read these preliminary reports carefully; not only of the "book-of-the-month," but of the other books described. Weigh the reasons why the judges recommend each book; you will find them, we believe, good reasons, clearly stated. Weigh against them your present mood and your settled prejudices in reading (everybody has them and everybody's are different). The final decision should never be a hard one. For you know in general what you like and dislike. Above all, you know the sort of book you feel in the mood for at the moment. And, after all, it is a pleasant predicament always, none more pleasant—this choosing of a good book with which to spend a few hours.[25]

Scherman's direct address maintained the illusion that he was addressing a rational, deliberating subject, just as the committee members were explaining the reasons for their selections to other individuals who would then consider them rationally themselves. Furthermore, in rhetorically equating subscriber choice with judicious deliberation and implicitly analogizing his customer's selection process to that of debating an opinion in the public sphere, his column took great pains to obscure the fact that the club made its selections as an institution and that it was in the business of selling those choices to others on the basis of the authority it claimed for the selection process itself. Scherman insisted to the contrary that the committee members did not recommend books on the basis of their authority alone but laid out the rational reasons for their individual choices in the reports written for the *News*. Like his critics, Scherman refused to give up the illusion that individual choice in cultural matters was independent, entirely rational, and free of influence by external factors. Thus he reiterated a view of the public sphere as a space where individuals came together to converse freely and to deliberate rationally about the merits of everything from books to ideas to convictions.

Both Harry Scherman and his critics elaborated a view of the American public sphere not that different from that which was constituted in the eighteenth century with the first, early vision of a republican print culture. Michael Warner has shown, following Jurgen Habermas, that the notion of the public sphere was constitutively grounded on an equation between individuality, rationality, and disinterest. This occurred in the United States, Warner has suggested, when the public sphere was called into being dialectically with a specific, republican ideology of print that "elevated the values of generality over those of the personal."[26] This move was constitutively enabled, Warner notes, by a crucial but "covert identification of print consumption with the community of propertied white males," an identification that ensured that "the social diffusion of printed artifacts [among white men only] took on the investment of the disinterested virtue of the public orientation, as opposed to the corrupting interests and passions of particular and local persons," those others marked specifically and simultaneously by the difference of their bodies and by their illiteracy.[27] In other words, by marking all others specifically as "interested," it was possible to mistake the concerns, tastes, and opinions of white, male, republican readers as the expression and working-out of a universal public good.

Because of these equations, the language of public discourse was construed as impersonal, transparent, and general, and the paradigmatic public action was understood to be free and uncoerced republican reading.[28] As Warner has observed, "Society and the public acquired a positive — though unrecognized — identity in the transmission of print. The public was constructed on the basis of its metonymic embodiment in printed artifacts. That is how it was possible to imagine the public supervising the actions of officials even when no physical assembly of the public was taking place." That supervision was realized literally in the proliferation and widespread reading of pamphlets, newspapers, and broadsides. "In their routine dispersion, and in the conventions of discourse that allowed them to be political in a special way," Warner observes, "these artifacts represented the material reality of an abstract public: a *res publica* of let-ters."[29] The literary public sphere functioned, then, as the guarantor of American liberty and democracy.

When the book club critics invoked the vision of this highly abstract res publica, in opposition to a newer literary field that they characterized as dominated by centralized authorities for the promulgation of inter-ested opinion, they blithely ignored the ways in which they exercised au-thority, just as Harry Scherman had. Construing themselves in opposition to Scherman's organized experts as rational, dispassionate, deliberating individuals, they accused the club of disrupting the public sphere by intro-ducing wholly alien, commercial interest into an otherwise free arena. Since the public sphere of print discourse had been thoroughly commer-cialized for at least one hundred years by the time Harry Scherman arrived on the scene, just as it had been governed by publicly recognized liter-ary authorities writing for magazines such as *Century* and the *Atlantic*, one has to wonder what prompted this slippage from the language of literary value to that of civic discourse as well as the heavily nostalgic invocation of a universal rationality and dispassionate, disinterested discussion of the public good. To make sense of this, I want to consider more carefully what about the Book-of-the-Month Club's critical experts seemed so danger-ous at the time.

## MASSIFICATION AND THE POWER OF THE PROFESSIONAL EXPERT

In spite of Harry Scherman's attempt to deflect the charge that his selec-tion committee arrogated to itself too much cultural authority, a telling ambiguity in the organization's conceptualization of its advisory appara-tus soon crept into its internal discussions and its public pronouncements about itself. "The selection committee," in fact, gradually metamorphosed into "the judges." The latter title foregrounded the authoritative and quasi-official character of the committee, connotatively evoking an image of them as adjudicators handing down judgments from on high. Thus the increasing use of the term tended to repress the committee members' status as individuals, and at the same time it contested Harry Scherman's claim that they operated in representative fashion, making judgments that would otherwise be made by the subscribers. Although Scherman vig-orously tried to cloak his committee in the language of democracy and republicanism, the title "the judges" eventually stuck. Canby, Fisher, and the others became colloquially known as "the Book-of-the-Month Club judges" both within and without the organization.

The shift in terminology exposed something essential about the organization. In a sense it openly admitted that the Book-of-the-Month Club was to be driven by the tastes, opinions, and choices of an educated, professionalized, specialized elite. Significantly, however, as a way of squaring this troublesome hierarchy with a social climate newly worried about the fate of democracy in the post–World War I world, Scherman continued to argue that the particular expertise of this elite group was not to be exercised in its own private self-interest but was to be mobilized in magisterial, dispassionate fashion for the civic welfare of all.

This figure of the technical expert laboring in civic-minded fashion amidst a large, bureaucratic organization was not, of course, a Scherman innovation. As many have pointed out, what became known as the Progressive era in American history was at least partially defined by the growing domination of a new group of "scientific" professionals and technical experts, a group whose professional responsibility, it was thought, was to make its expertise available for pragmatic use in the public sphere. In Warren Susman's words, "The Progressive movement was certainly many things; but surely among them was a sense of revolt against politics itself in the interest of a managerial-oriented society, a government of trained and efficient experts who could make the system work to the profit of the whole nation and its citizens, a kind of neomercantilist view of the state and society directed by an elite of experts."[30] At stake in the debate over progressive reform was the issue of whether managerial elites could operate in disinterested fashion for the welfare of all. To the contrary, many feared that concentration of authority and power in centralized and specialized bureaucracies would lead only to the pursuit of special interests and thus to a contravention of the public will.

The issues raised within this larger discussion about the benefits and limitations of expertise were not unrelated to concerns articulated in the American debates about mass culture. Although the latter raised many questions about the moral and aesthetic content of mass-produced culture, a key concern was whether the culture industry could do anything but co-opt the public search for truth. Critics worried that movie producers, pulp magazine editors, radio broadcasters, and public entertainment moguls did nothing but disseminate endless examples of a thoroughly commodified and therefore degraded form of entertainment. Public debate about the role of consolidation and centralization in the mass media of the 1920s therefore centered about the possibility of preserving a sense of the public good in an environment increasingly dominated by highly technical and professional groups who controlled information dissemination and cultural representations as well.

As this new literature of critique attempted to make sense of the development of an increasingly industrialized and centralized cultural production, however, so, too, did it try to theorize the consequent assemblage of diffuse audiences. Those audiences were no longer characterized as the more cohesive "common people" or "public" or even as confinable "crowds" or "mobs," but as the more amorphous "mass." Like Theodor Adorno and Max Horkheimer, Ortega y Gassett, Walter Benjamin, and diverse others on the Continent, American critics of agencies like the book clubs were appropriately troubled both by the appearance of the new masses and by the fact that they seemed to be constituted in relationship to centralized authorities with new, more extensive control over both cultural production and distribution.[31] Although the different cultural critics did not characterize those in authority in the same way and therefore did not indict the same groups or forces for the same ideological crimes, they all felt that the public good was in danger of being usurped by small groups operating in their own localized self-interest and threatening to organize the masses for their own purposes.

These concerns were fueled by anticapitalist sentiments on the left, and on the right by anxiety about the long-term consequences of the Bolshevik revolution in Russia. At the same time, the imminent threat of Fascist governments on the Continent, all of which seemed to be adept at mobilizing the new mass media for their own coercive purposes, also proved troubling. However, while these forces were sometimes alluded to by mass culture critics in the United States, especially by those who were worried that cultural production was being commodified and transformed into capitalist art, the more immediate source of concern seemed to be the menace of the mob itself. Frequently, the debate appeared to be motivated most immediately by the massive demographic shift that had taken place in urban areas from about 1880 on.[32] Indeed the threat of an alien, clamoring hoard seemed to dominate rhetorically in much of the criticism aimed at the book clubs, the movies, dance clubs, and amusement parks. Apparently the great migration and massive immigration together with the increasingly polyglot cities they had produced had forced more individuals to encounter cultural difference. As a consequence, few Americans could avoid the feeling that the once-cohesive public sphere had been given over to angry social conflict in part because the public arena had been invaded by untutored, indiscriminate others incapable of exercising rational judgment or pursuing anything other than narrow self-interest.

Especially worrisome was the prospect that these alien, suspect others might be particularly gullible and therefore capable of being led by anyone with a capacity to reach them in large numbers. Accordingly, it seems that the fear occasioned by the assemblage of a mass audience characterized not by its shared participation in a culture of high literacy but by its marked difference from an abstract Americanness was directed not simply at the masses themselves in social practices such as the Palmer raids, strikebreaking, the regulation of alcohol and entertainment, and the imposition of quotas on the attendance of Jews at colleges and universities. In addition, those fears were directed just as vigorously at the agencies, organizations, and media responsible for amassing them in the first place into highly visible audiences and consumer publics. Hence the obsessive preoccupation with mass culture and agencies such as the book clubs. By configuring the literary field *as* the public sphere, and by insisting that this sphere normally brought together wholly independent individuals in free and uncoerced dialogue, the critics of the book clubs attempted to contain their fears of the masses these new agencies assembled by reassuring themselves that the familiar world they knew was not crumbling around them.

What proved especially troubling at this moment in U.S. history, then, was the potential for the establishment of a new social relationship, between a highly educated and specially trained elite on one hand and a vast, threatening, mass body on the other. The book clubs loomed ominously on the horizon because they seemed to give material form to this threat. They appeared poised to eradicate the deliberations of those individuals who constituted the public sphere, that is, disinterested, public-oriented, reading subjects. They threatened to replace them with the regimented actions of a thoroughly policed, wholly coerced mass of mindless automatons. The redundant emphasis on individual reading subjects in pieces such as "Has America a Literary Dictatorship?" accomplished discursively a feat the critics could not bring about in the social field. In effect, they shouldered aside and thereby denied the masses that loomed so threateningly on the modern historical horizon. At the same time, the repeated and respectful evocation of discussion, conversation, and debate among a collection of supposedly equal subjects dispensed with the troublesome issues of authority and differential access to the resources of literacy. Prior to the appearance of agencies like the book clubs, these essays insisted, both literary and political debate proceeded freely and rationally. At the same time, such debate was unencumbered by the intervention of self-interested parties devoted only to the sway of others for their own purposes.

This underlying fear of the mass can be made even clearer by comparing the kinds of representations we have seen thus far with the way chief Book-of-the-Month Club judge Henry Canby dealt with the relationship between the authority of the organization and the large population of potential readers it aimed to address. Canby believed implicitly in the value of public pedagogy and in the supporting role cultural institutions like magazines, newspapers, and even radio programs could play in the education of the general American population. Although he was not consistent and never managed to articulate a fully coherent defense of the Book-of-the-Month Club or other like institutions, he did argue intermittently for their potential as civic-minded tutors. He argued for an alliance between the capitalist culture industry and a trained, disinterested, elite who would use that industry to popularize knowledge and to extend the distribution of literature and art to a better-educated, more broad based population. In effect Canby began from the premise that, whatever else mass cultural production and distribution accomplished, it at least carried with it the potential for a more democratic address and greater inclusiveness.

Canby often went much further than Harry Scherman in defending the Book-of-the-Month Club's activities by picturing the judges as defenders of the public good against a snobbish, self-centered, highbrow elite who would reserve culture only for the privileged few. He fumbled around, in fact, in his editorial columns at the *The Saturday Review* for ways to justify the kinds of cultural fare offered to Americans not only by the book clubs but by the many other recently created organizations devoted to popularizing literary, artistic, and intellectual material. He was searching for a way to understand mass education by thinking democracy and standardization together. What is interesting about his tortured efforts to justify the work of the Book-of-the-Month Club is that they reveal a certain ambivalence about the enterprise and expose the extent of his failure to sustain rhetorically the equivalences he labored to establish. In fact his repeated return to the question of taste and aesthetic excellence demonstrates how difficult it was in the early twentieth century to cope with the implications of mass education and literacy for the traditional discourse on culture.

Although Henry Canby could eloquently defend the political justice of equality of cultural opportunity and of cultural standardization, he still could not give up his belief in the importance of certain aesthetic criteria or abandon the corollary assumption that mass literacy would eventually have to be followed by cultural remediation. In the end he returned always, as did his critics, to the issue of cultural authority. Canby differed from them, though, in his conception of the masses, which was not nearly as hysterical as theirs, a legacy perhaps of his Quaker heritage. At the same time, he retained greater confidence in the ultimate success of the Arnoldian cultural project for the general dissemination of sweetness and light. Though shaken somewhat, his faith in the redemptive power of literature and culture remained steadfast. Consequently, his condemnation of centralized cultural authorities was much less desperate because he did not feel as insistently the need to deny the very presence of the masses over whom that authority was to be exercised in the first place.[33]

In his February 12, 1927, front-page editorial for *The Saturday Review of Literature*, for example, Canby addressed the familiar "bogey" of his age, standardization. However, he self-consciously attempted to differentiate his view of it from that which had been taken by so many of his peers.[34] "They say of the America of 1927," he noted, that it is a nation "being fed a standardized education from standardized text-books by teachers so standardized that a breach of the conventions of doctrine may lead to penalties. . . . What they ask lies before such a country but a regimen of living and thinking in which no man differs from his neighbors, a civilization rendered colorless and flavorless through uniformity and inert through similarity of ideas." Canby noted that he intended to question this too-easy stigmatization of standardization. "The American public waxed and grew strong on standardization," he insisted, "on the standardization of the idea that life, liberty and the pursuit of happiness were the inalienable rights of all men. It grew to well-being on the standardization of the doctrine of work. It grew to literacy on the standardization of the thesis that education was the right of the masses and not the privilege of the few." He continued acidly, "Now that the masses are educated and the laborer is wearing silk shirts and buying Fords, we are alarmed lest the vigor of the country be submerged by the standardized knowledge and the standardized manner of living which have become the common property of the American millions."

In effect Canby was trying to give voice to a different definition of democracy. Resisting its equation with an atomized series of unique individuals, he was attempting to connect it to the generalization, spread, and extension of equivalent social and material conditions to all. Democracy, he suggested, was constituted by a community of people with equal opportunities. It was fundamentally dependent, then, on the process of standardization. Unlike his critics Canby did not erase all mention of the masses by constituting them in his discourse as individuals, nor did he demonize them when they did appear. In fact here, as elsewhere, he repeatedly represented them as "masses," as "millions," and as a "public" to be addressed in its collectivity. For him they did not conjure a vision of a regimented and hostile army whose existence had to be denied at all costs.

Nevertheless, having made such an admission about democracy and enabled the appearance of the mass on his discursive stage, Canby seemed almost to recoil in alarm at the consequences he might have unleashed, especially for the sphere of culture. "Conformity" in "democratic America," he noted, "is the price of respectability, and eccentricity is the deadly sin." Standardization of material and social conditions risks a concomitant standardization of beliefs, feelings, and desires. Where that might lead, he observed, to the "great peril of American culture," is to a state in which "a set of values emanating from the mediocre rather than the distinguished elements of the community" might be superimposed on it.

Comfortable as Canby apparently was with the standardization of certain political rights and even with the idea of a mass, he nonetheless could not tolerate the masses' preference for "unsubtle aesthetic and intellectual interests." Still, he argued, poor taste was not permanent. It betokened a "striving for the expression of unformed aesthetic and social desires" and thus "the possibility of developing standards of worth." As he noted, "False jewels, and rayon, and Books of Etiquette need not necessarily indicate anything more deplorable than an untrained taste." "What an opportunity," he exclaimed, "for the movie, for the radio, for literature!" And, he later added, for the book clubs as well.[35]

Here Canby joined his critics ideologically and parted company with them at the same time. Like some of them, he stitched the notion of democracy to the necessary guidance of an elite who could maintain appropriate standards. However, where Canby's opponents advocated the dispersed rule of a series of aesthetic and civic-minded critics, of individuals capable of simply pointing to the self-evident, revealed value of true literature, Canby valorized institutional forms as pedagogical leavening agents. Unlike his critics in the literary field, then, Canby refused to ban the masses from the cultural stage altogether. He willingly represented them in his discourse as the large, eager audience for these forms, as a people with familiar and comprehensible strivings. He seemed always to be able to identify comfortably with them as a group, and thus he exhibited little need to deny that they were out there by insisting always on their status as individuals. Henry Canby was willing to address, however imperfectly, the difficult question that his opponents' rhetoric sought to deny. He tackled the problem of how a relationship might be forged between those with power and the increasingly literate but equally and insistently visible masses, those millions materialized as consuming bodies, given insistent visibility and substance by what they wore, what they displayed, and what they consumed. Unlike his critics, who were appalled at the sight of millions of Ford-driving, silk-shirted Babbitts and who wanted nothing to do with either their materiality or their materialism, Canby was never pushed to deny his own cultural authority; he was never afraid of representing the other pole of the equation of power, the people over whom authority is always exerted. He understood their desires to be continuous with his own and therefore felt confident that they could be trained, elevated, and educated to the pursuit of rationality, beauty, and truth.

We might conclude from Canby's discourse that within its historical context the Book-of-the-Month Club's principal transgressions were two. On one hand the club too obviously foregrounded the fact that the exercise of cultural authority entailed a relationship with those who were socially suspect. On the other hand it contradicted the claim that cultural authority could be exercised in a wholly disinterested manner, since the club was so obviously a commercial, profit-minded venture. In opposition, the club's critics maintained an elaborate and important subterfuge. They insisted that the sphere of public literary discourse joined free, equal, and wholly autonomous individuals in the rational discussion of the merits of everything, from political ideas to the merits of a book. In their view the public sphere functioned by producing information, judicious deliberation, and ultimately a consensus freely arrived at. They construed the public sphere as uncontaminated by interest, that is, by particular, local concerns. They were able to do this because the individuals they envisioned were not embodied but rather imagined as abstract subjects defined by their rationality, their generality, and their universality. This abstract, universal, freely choosing reader was constituted, then, in explicit opposition to standardized consumer-subjects, to masses of bodies excessively materialized through the display of products by Ford, Arrow, Van Heusen, Helena Rubenstein, Frigidaire, and, of course, the Book-of-the-Month Club. Here, I think, in the materialization of the mass through commodification, we find the source of nostalgia for the traditional public sphere.

## THE THREAT OF COUNTERFEIT CULTURAL MASTERY

As we have already seen, Michael Warner has identified this peculiar state of disinterested abstractness, which he refers to as a kind of "negativity," as the characteristic feature of the eighteenth-century republican subject, the key inhabitant of the traditional public sphere. Indeed he claims that at a specific moment in American history the positive value of virtue as "the rational and disinterested concern for the public good" was constructed through a negation of the interests exhibited by particular, marked, material bodies. As Warner explains, women, blacks, Indians, the unpropertied, criminals, and various other subjects marked at once by their illiteracy and by their bodies, by "the humiliating positivity of the particular," were denied access to the public arena.[36] Warner concludes, "The posture of negation that served as the entry qualification to the specialized subsystem of public discourse remained a positive disposition of character, a resource available only to a specific subset of the community," that is, to white, propertied males, who were privileged to read.[37] Concomitantly, literacy itself developed as the quintessential mark of privilege, as that which had to be both acquired and mastered in order to demonstrate assimilation to and participation within the public sphere. Understandably, then, the literary field broadly conceived developed in the republican United States as the key social arena where individuals publicly demonstrated (or, perhaps more accurately, performed) their claim to social position and privilege and therefore to power.

In their vigorous invocation of the trope of the free public forum as a site for the interaction of rational and disinterested individuals, the critics of the book clubs insisted on their own abstract status as universal subjects. Thus they asserted their privilege even as they denied that the privilege of purported universality was exercised in their own interest. At the same time, they distanced themselves from those others who were marked at once by their resolute corporeality and materiality, by their lack of confidence in their ability to choose reading material, and, therefore, by their seduction by narrow, localized, interested groups, by undemocratic authorities. In the view of the book club critics, the clubs threatened to subvert rational public discourse because they usurped the agency of the traditional reading subject and proposed to substitute in its place the reduced, mechanic action, the negative option of a mere consuming automaton. The obvious question is why these defenders of this traditional view of literacy and print culture felt the need at this point in the twentieth century to insist repeatedly on the difference between themselves as active, rational, and free agents and those groups characterized allegedly by their passivity, by the pursuit of mere stimulation, and by their susceptibility to the propaganda of powerful organizations.

Although the explanation clearly must be complex, I think a significant clue can be found in the obsessive frequency with which these critics fastened on the modern materialism of the masses, on their repetitive purchase and use of standardized objects, clothes, and services, an apparently mechanized activity that was also oddly and insistently connected by the critics with the natural processes of the consuming body.[38] In fact this peculiar, almost contradictory linkage suggests that these defenders of traditional book culture felt the need to insist so fiercely on their own status as abstract, universal subjects and thus to reestablish their difference from the disturbing particularity of bodies because the engines of the thriving consumer culture had threatened to erode the corporeal differences that had previously marked the privileged from the powerless. If the millions who had once been identified by their particular bodies and by their linked failure to read could increasingly hide behind the managed facade of commodified and superficially cultured selves, how could one note the differences between statuses, abilities, and positions? How would one know who was to rule?

In a sense I am suggesting here that Fordized, silk-shirted, middlebrow Babbitts were so threatening because the uniform body of the machine-produced commodity threatened to erase the "natural" differences of organic bodies and thus to destabilize the system of corporeal distinctions that served as a basis for the allocation of privilege and power. The commodity, it seems to me, whether it was a car, a refrigerator, or a mass-produced book, at least potentially threatened to erase the distinctions whereby whiteness, maleness, and the command of both property and print were constituted as the absent conditions of privilege.[39] It threatened to enable millions to erase the marks of their subordinate embodiment with the standardized, uniform trademarks of incorporated American business.[40] Fences were necessary, then, to re-mark the difference between the rational and the embodied, between the universal and the particular, and between the abstract and the concrete as well as to cordon each off from the other. It was necessary, in short, to rehabilitate the mechanisms of subordination by insisting, first, on the continuity between the positivity and particularity of the natural body and the multiple, embodied particularities promoted by consumerism and, second, on the fundamental difference of both from the disinterested generality and universal humanity of the highly cultured, independent reading subject.

It should be clear now why the book clubs and other middlebrow agencies devoted to the marketing of culture as just another consumer product proved so threatening. In packaging and selling cultural objects as if they were no different from soup, soap, or automobiles, these organizations

{ *On the History of the Middlebrow* }

threatened to obliterate the fundamental distinction that underwrote this entire system of privilege, that is, the distinction between the material and the immaterial, between the particularities of the body and the universality of the intellect, in short, between the natural and the cultural. If culture was only one more material object, if it could be manipulated to produce the artificial facade of a made self, then it could no longer function as the special, unmarked mark of human distinction. No longer either transcendent or pure, culture as it was marketed by middlebrow agencies like the Book-of-the-Month Club was sullied by the particular terms of its embodiment and therefore exposed as just one more material form penetrated by interest, by the economic. Literacy and reading, furthermore, far from enabling the disinterested pursuit of the public good in a translucent sphere uncontaminated by the particularities of clamorous, concrete bodies could be enlisted in the pursuit of special interests. Books, as a consequence, could be constituted as mere propaganda and promoted as an instrument for welding bodies into an amorphous mass, into an ambiguously embodied collectivity all the more difficult to police because of its unlocalized, fluid character. The critics of the book clubs feared not so much engulfment, ingestion, and absorption by the spreading ooze of middlebrow culture as by the masses middlebrow culture apparently materialized in its scandalous address. This fear of engulfment in the late 1920s was overdetermined, I think, by the fact that both machine culture itself and the rise of the masses its various forms called into being—whether the consumer masses of the United States or the politicized masses on the Continent—threatened to obliterate the autonomous, self-regulating subject characterized most prominently by self-mastery and active agency, the particular subject valorized so insistently by high bourgeois culture.

The Book-of-the-Month Club and its imitators were troubling, then, not simply because they suggested that books, literature, and culture were manufactured objects. Nor were they disturbing only because they exposed the fact that cultural creation, dissemination, and use were as interested in and therefore as deeply bound up with the economic as was any other form of human activity. Certainly the book clubs accomplished both these things and, in so doing, they exposed the ruse by which bourgeois society had previously distinguished and isolated culture from the market. The book clubs thus implied that culture, far from fostering the triumph and the rule of natural excellence and universal good, might alternatively be enlisted in the naked pursuit of local economic interest. Cultural competence would not function as the indexical sign of natural participation in a universal human community—participation which, importantly, was theoretically available to everyone but in fact was denied to some because of their supposed irrational, subhuman status. Rather, cultural competence would function as a kind of devalued currency in an inflationary economy where anyone and everyone might command and display the signs of a counterfeit cultural mastery. It was the vision of a mass of such counterfeit subjects, men and women capable only of the reduced agency of the negative option and replete with standardized homes, clothes, culture, and views, that most disturbed Harry Scherman's antagonists in the book club wars. What they feared, above all, was the obliteration of the reading subject, the man of letters, the white, male, middle-class citizen of the bourgeois republic. They feared he would be overwhelmed by a mass of standardized automatons, culture consumers who might hide the telltale signs of their subordinate embodiment, the signs of their gender, race, ethnicity, and age, behind a facade of books, records, and artworks purchased scandalously by mail order and on the installment plan.

In the end the Book-of-the-Month Club's principal transgression may well have been its bald exposure and figuration of authority as a *social* relationship. The club's critics simply did not want to deal with the fact that massive public education and literacy efforts had dramatically altered the nature of the population capable of demanding information, entertainment, and enlightenment from the nation's cultural producers. Ironically, though, in dismissing the club by insisting that the real literary sphere joined only discrete and autonomous individuals in free, disinterested discussion, the book club critics not only erased the discursive presence of the more broadly literate masses on the cultural scene but also thereby inadvertently repressed knowledge of the fact that they themselves exercised cultural authority by wielding a particular evaluative and pedagogical machinery. As a consequence, they failed to take up the opportunity their competitors offered to them, that is, the opportunity to think clearly and to argue openly for their version of cultural authority against that proffered by Harry Scherman and the Book-of-the-Month Club judges. What they resisted above all, it seems to me, was any recognition of the fact that the appearance of the book clubs and other similar distribution agencies marked the beginning of a significant struggle over the control and organization of the larger literary and cultural fields. I want to clarify the nature of that struggle, finally, as a way of answering the question of what was at stake in the efforts to resist the coming of corporate production and mass distribution by a reiteration of the individual's privilege in the literary field and the public sphere.

A number of scholars have argued persuasively that through the first half of the nineteenth century, at least, the individuals who commanded economic capital in the United States also possessed a certain relationship to the intellectual and cultural tradition through their family's social position within the dominant ecclesiastical, educational, and cultural institutions. As a consequence, tightly knit elites in northeastern cities controlled both the economic and the legitimate cultural spheres until shortly after the Civil War.[41] However, as rapid industrialization and the immigration boom it fed on transformed the social environment in the last half of the nineteenth century, this older elite and its supporting intelligentsia mobilized to isolate itself from the unruly and troubling mobs newly visible in the shops, in the streets, in public squares, and at popular entertainments. Simultaneously, this elite also acted to educate the lower orders to its own refined tastes, values, and assumptions.[42] This led to the creation of a vast infrastructure for cultural pedagogy, including city museums, libraries, symphony orchestras, parks, and urban expositions.

As Paul DiMaggio and Lawrence Levine have demonstrated, however, the principal audiences for these efforts at cultural pedagogy came not from the immigrant masses, as some might have wished. Rather, they came from a burgeoning middle class, from newly emerging groups of nonmanual, white-collar workers whose jobs had been created by major transformations in the organization of production in the United States and who had been prepared for their innovative managerial, mental, and social work by the public education system.[43] As a way of demonstrating and augmenting their acquisition of educational and cultural capital, these upwardly mobile but highly insecure middle-class citizens flocked to the grand, neoclassical palaces for a thoroughly sacralized art and to the stately, neo-Gothic cathedrals of learning and high culture, which had been organized as nonprofit agencies designed to operate in the larger public interest.

It must be pointed out, however, that just as these new middle-class citizens clogged the corridors of new temples and palaces of culture, so too did they willingly buy many hundreds of thousands of new cultural products to display in their refined and proper parlors. Among the many things they purchased were chromolithographs, stereographs, pianos, parlor organs, bookshelves and bookcases, and as we have seen in Chapters 4 and 5, cheap series books and libraries of classics to fill them.[44] These products existed, as I argued earlier, in part because innovations in both production and distribution made them possible. It is equally important to emphasize at this point, however, that this expanded array of cultural commodities was made possible by a new sort of cultural entrepreneur who recognized the opportunities contained within the new technologies and who developed marketing operations to capitalize on them. The new cultural commodities were the brainchildren of men such as Frank Munsey, Cyrus Curtis, Edward Bok, S. S. McClure, and Peter Collier, all of whom started their own firms as speculative ventures with a small amount of capital.[45] They parlayed their initial investment into large profits on the basis of their intuitive understanding of new desires for cultural legitimacy on the part of families who had only recently managed to establish social standing by virtue of the whiteness of the collar worn by their principal wage earner.

Not surprisingly, perhaps, these enterprising businessmen felt little allegiance to the older cultural elite or to the values it championed. Thus a new middle-class profession of cultural entrepreneurship developed that was devoted to the business of commodifying and marketing taste. As it developed, its participants forged a new and distinct aesthetic constellation not so much out of simple deference to the tradition of high culture but out of a set of instrumental values connected more closely with their own economic self-interest. Culture, as we have seen, was less something to be offered for contemplation and study, to be valued in its own right, than a sign of achievement and a necessary token for participation in the middle class. Construed as fungible, then, culture appeared increasingly as a thing to be exchanged on the market for ulterior purposes. It was this form of culture, obviously, that was marketed so effectively by Harry Scherman and the Book-of-the-Month Club.

Like Scherman himself, most of the new cultural entrepreneurs were educated, but they had earned their social position and their access to education by virtue of their family's commercial activity rather than through the simple aristocratic inheritance of a joint economic, social, and cultural patrimony. Like Scherman as well, increasing numbers of the cultural entrepreneurs controlling the movie, radio, and entertainment industries in the 1910s and 1920s were the sons of immigrants who had entered the business of cultural production and dissemination as he did, because the field was wide open, because they calculated that they could make a profit on their investment, and because they empathized with audiences longing to demonstrate that they had arrived.[46] Scherman himself always professed a sincere and lifelong interest in books, culture, and learning, yet even late in life he was willing to insist that he really was the epitome of the "advertising man." Given such mixed motives, it is little wonder that Scherman and others like him appeared threatening to people who staked their own prestige on their disinterested ability to assist the best books and the universal values they supposedly embodied to take care of themselves. The book club wars suggest, finally, that in solving the problem of how to appeal to an audience otherwise captured by notions of individuality, autonomy, and free choice, Harry Scherman had threatened the security of those who insisted on the sacralized status of culture as a transcendent form distinct from the noisy, messy business of the marketplace, a form capable of ennobling all who came in contact with it.

Scherman muddied the crucial distinction between commerce and culture by commodifying not only particular books but the whole concept of Culture itself, rendered with a decided capital C. He challenged the labor of separation that warranted the bourgeois distinctions between the economic and the rational, the dirty and the clean, and leisure and work. He took that which, according to an older elite, was the natural patrimony of the disinterested man of letters and offered it for sale to everyone, including the lazy, the profligate, and the obtuse—in the language of the 1920s—to every Babbitt who could afford the price of subscription. Additionally, he threatened the purity of the culture he offered by equating it indiscriminately with mystery stories, adventure tales, biographies, and accounts of public affairs, all of which were sold in the same catalog beside the best book of the month. It is not surprising, then, that to his critics Scherman appeared a primary destroyer of essential distinctions. As Pierre Bourdieu has noted, "The most intolerable thing for those who regard themselves as the possessors of legitimate culture is the sacrilegious reuniting of tastes which taste dictates shall be separated."[47]

A question returns, then, about the identity of Scherman's opponents. Whose interests were served by these efforts to reconstruct the vision of a cultural and literary arena inhabited by the independent reading subject, an individual assumed to be operating in the service of the public good and fully capable of preserving culture in its own sphere, distinct and pure? People such as Stuart Chase, Ernest Boyd, Waldo Frank, Walter Lippmann, and the myriad reviewers writing for magazines such as *The New Republic*, *The Nation*, and *The New Yorker* cannot be easily assimilated into that older, aristocratic, Brahmin elite who had first been displaced by Scherman's precursors. In fact, like Scherman and the class of cultural entrepreneurs he represents, most of the book club critics themselves were the products of middle-class families who had only recently amassed the capital and the social standing to educate their children in the values of art, learning, and culture. Similarly, like Scherman, these men were not economically self-sufficient but made their living working for a salary within organizations that, like the advertising agencies where Scherman got his start, privileged the intellectual labor involved in creating the commodities peculiar to them, in their case, cultural commentary and critique. Structurally, then, the book club critics occupied the same position in the developing economy that Scherman did, yet they labored industriously to foreground their ideological and aesthetic differences from him. The obvious question is why.

To answer this question, it seems necessary to think clearly about the character and position of these cultural entrepreneurs as members of a new and distinct class fraction. Although many scholars have analyzed the development of an unprecedented professional, specialized, and technocratic elite in the years after the turn of the century, for my purposes the work of Barbara and John Ehrenreich has proved most suggestive. Their key argument about the larger group's ambiguous placement between, on one hand, their employers, corporate representatives of capital, and on the other hand, those they addressed as clients, largely salaried workers, many of whom labored with their hands, can be helpful in illuminating the kind of intragroup disagreement that cropped up within the literary field in the 1920s and 1930s.

According to the Ehrenreichs, the cultural entrepreneurs who began to appear in increasing numbers throughout the 1890s were among the first wave of a new group of workers in capitalist society that they have called "the Professional-Managerial Class." What particularly united this diverse group of technicians, managers, specialists, and professionals was the fact that its members performed some kind of intellectual rather than manual labor. At the same time, they functioned as salaried workers in public and private corporations ultimately funded and owned by others. Their appearance as a distinct group was enabled by the interaction of a series of complex social and economic developments. Large-scale transformations in the organization of labor, the accumulation of a significant social surplus (that is, workers rendered superfluous by a rationalized production process), and an intensified struggle between labor and capital necessitated the appearance of a group who could manage the resulting disruptions. A new managerial class evolved slowly, therefore, as a way of overseeing an increasingly diversified and segmented labor process as well as a working population growing more varied at every turn. The new managers and professionals were engaged specifically to address, to educate, to socialize, and to organize those whose labor was necessary to the fast-changing social formation. Set apart by their own success in school and by their consequent attainment of a highly specialized education, these professionals labored as managers and intellectual workers in a range of different arenas, including the literary field, seeking to replace more traditional, usually working-class forms of knowledge with the more legitimate, authorized forms they had been taught in the bourgeois-controlled institutions of the school and the university.[48]

In their schematic account of the emergence of this new group of intellectual workers, the Ehrenreichs identify three principal regions where new forms of labor evolved: corporate management and organization; civic and public institutional life; and the support structure for the developing consumer society. Although they acknowledge that significant differences characterized the activities of professionals who labored in each of these arenas, they argue nonetheless that those differences should be considered superficial in light of the structural position they occupied and as a consequence of the similar nature of the social function they performed. In fact, workers as diverse as corporate managers, engineers, museum curators, teachers, journalists, scientists, entertainment industry workers, and even writers of advertising copy served the organizations that employed them by educating workers of various sorts to think, to behave, and to desire in a way that was congruent with the interests of corporations and capital. Allied to a certain degree, then, with the institutions that immediately employed them by virtue of the fact that they utilized their expertise and technical skill on behalf of their employers, these new professionals were positioned initially in opposition to all those lacking expertise and congruent economic and cultural capital. The major function they performed, therefore, in the larger social division of labor was the elaboration and extension of bourgeois forms of knowledge throughout the rest of society. In effect they labored to reproduce capitalist culture and capitalist class relations.

The Ehrenreichs acknowledge that there were differences in how this role was overtly conceived, ranging from the concept of "policing," to "management," to "tutelage," and to "advice." Indeed many managers and professional workers did not recognize their work as ideological in nature or reproductive in function. Instead they insisted on their status as disinterested specialists laboring in autonomous professional fields who, by virtue of their training, could see more clearly, know more accurately, and therefore organize and manage for the benefit of all. The professional interests of these groups sometimes conflicted with the goals of their employers as they tried to establish autonomous control over their own arenas of expertise. As a consequence, professionals such as social caseworkers, for instance, occasionally identified *against* their employers and connected more intensely with the workers who were the recipients of their services. This occurred frequently as doctors, engineers, teachers, lawyers, journalists, and others attempted to consolidate their position as professionals, to define their work themselves, and to manage group accreditation and self-perpetuation. What they sought, in the end, was to establish their independence from those who ultimately paid their salaries.

In pursuing the right to govern themselves and to foster the autonomous development of their specialized fields of knowledge, these new professionals often began to distance themselves from employers they increasingly perceived to be self-interested in both political and economic terms. Accordingly they began to argue for their own superior claim to a position of social and cultural authority by virtue of their supposedly more disinterested, public orientation. As a consequence some professional experts, knowledge workers, and intellectuals actually envisioned a substantial "technocratic transformation of society in which all aspects of life would be 'rationalized' according to expert knowledge."[49] Their expertise and professional point of view, they claimed, would better serve the population as a whole. These early initiatives on behalf of professional autonomy eventually led some professional experts to elaborate a more extensive critique of the way capitalist interests dominated their own disinterested perspective. Thinking particularly of Thorstein Veblen, the Ehrenreichs allude additionally to Walter Lippmann and to the large contingent of so-called liberals housed at *The Nation* and *The New Republic*. Significantly, they conclude that "out of these continual skirmishes—over academic freedom, Progressive reforms, consumer issues, etc.—many in the [Professional-Managerial Class] were led to more systematic anticapitalist outlooks."[50] A certain ambiguity and ambivalence developed as the characteristic feature of the orientation of the professional-managerial class to its world of work. Situated perpetually between labor and capital, it repeatedly struggled with itself over how best to define its relationship to both.[51] It also struggled over the identity of its proper clientele.

From this conclusion the Ehrenreichs suggest that at least some of the internal debates carried out within various professions and in specific technical arenas or fields were the products of intragroup struggles between factions who differed significantly about the nature of their professional goals and about the role their expert knowledge was to perform. Competing groups of professionals quarreled, for example, over whether the subordinates they addressed were to be conceived of as an alien population in need of containment and control, as eager students seeking knowledge of their expertise, as mere client-consumers of their disinterested professional advice, or as innocents whose hearts and minds had to be won in the struggle with the forces of capital. They differed as well about how best to characterize the nature of the expert service they performed. Where some saw their professional work as a form of necessary civic policing on behalf of the dominant culture, disciplinary work designed to control those who would disrupt the social polity, others conceived it as a pedagogical social action on behalf of outsiders, that is, as a way of providing opportunities for parties heretofore excluded from reaping the benefits of the democratic way of life. Others saw it simply as a technical service that people could choose. Still others thought of their work as an entirely independent, radical critique of the very premises of capitalism itself. All of these variations, it seems to me, were clearly visible in the literary field of the 1920s when it was thrown into extreme disarray by the consolidation of new productive forces and by the insistent presence of audiences with very different forms of social, economic, and cultural capital.

## THE STRUGGLE TO DEFINE THE POSITION
## OF THE LITERARY FIELD

At issue, as we have seen, was the nature of the social relationship to be forged between newly visible and apparently alien cultural consumers on one hand and the new, integrated, corporate agencies for literary and cultural production on the other. Some, such as Harry Scherman and Henry Seidel Canby, argued that these profit-minded agencies could be harnessed to the project of educating people otherwise excluded from access to specialized knowledge. They envisioned, in effect, an alliance between the forces of capital and a new group of literary professionals who would direct these agencies in dispassionate, disinterested fashion for the benefit of all. Scherman and Canby used the language of democracy to argue that they were extending culture to those who might not otherwise have access to it. Others, such as Stuart Chase and Waldo Frank, were profoundly skeptical that such an alliance might work in the service of anyone but the corporate owners themselves. They argued, in opposition, that to remain uncorrupted, expertise would need to persist as wholly independent and autonomous. In fact it would need to remain the prerogative of individuals if it was to preserve a space for critique.

It is important to acknowledge in this context, then, that some of the opposition to both standardization generally and the book clubs specifically was elaborated as part of an emerging anticapitalist critique among professional-managerial workers in the literary field. In fact many of Scherman's critics objected to the clubs as an intrusion or penetration by the market into what they conceptualized as a previously free, uncolonized, natural domain, the domain of transcendent literature, culture, and art. Their objection to Harry Scherman's resolute materialization of culture as one more commodity among others grew in part out of their belief that artistic creation had the power to transcend the merely quotidian and the mundane and therefore could stand as the basis of a moral, ethical, and even political critique of the instrumentalism and utilitarianism embodied in capitalism. Setting their sights on their profession's capacity to identify works of high literary merit, which they believed transcended the specific conditions of their making, they were appalled by people like Scherman who failed to maintain the distinction between the material and the transcendent, the economic and the cultural. In criticizing new cultural middlemen such as Scherman, many participants in this debate about the autonomy of literature and art were implicitly making claims about the superiority of the literary field as an intrinsically oppositional space, as a public space set apart, beyond, or outside the market. Thus they portrayed it as the rightful home of the revolutionary avant-garde, a poetic cadre with the special expertise and sensibility to remake the world into a nobler, more humane, truly lettered place.

It bears repeating here that the criticisms of the Book-of-the-Month Club tended to link Scherman's failure to maintain categorical distinctions and to preserve the true purity of the literary with the simple existence of his advisory apparatus alone. The focal point of debate was the judges' position within a commercial, profit-minded organization. What was at issue was whether the process of book evaluation and recommendation should be organized in so instrumental a fashion in the first place or linked so closely to bookselling. The book club critics argued that reading ought to be guided by the more traditional and supposedly less coercive forms of expert advice offered by friends, neighborhood bookstore clerks, and, it must be said, "impartial" literary reviewers. The point to be made here is that these were the opinions of people laboring as reviewers, that is, as writers in a reconfigured literary field transformed by the appearance, first, of book review pages in metropolitan daily newspapers and, then, by the appearance of the weekly newspaper book review sections and magazines such as *The Saturday Review of Literature*. In fact, reviewing itself had been undergoing a process of professionalization for a number of years prior to the appearance of the Book-of-the-Month Club as the needs and demands of this new kind of periodical made it increasingly possible for individuals to make a salaried living exclusively as cultural commentators, columnists, and book reviewers. The debate over the advisory apparatus at the book clubs, then, can be understood as an intragroup struggle among similar but differently placed members of one section of the professional-managerial class, that fraction charged with oversight of the literary field.

Positioned as competitors by virtue of the different organizations they labored for, participants in the book club wars argued over their proper location and allegiance as key figures in the field, as arbiters who were instrumental not only in defining the idea of the literary and in identifying examples of it but also in producing belief in the value of such work in the first place.[52] Scherman's critics in fact occupied virtually the same position he did in the developing literary economy. They dispensed advice and opinions about cultural goods available on the market. However, their location within newspapers and highbrow magazines, which displaced and disguised their own institutional relationship to the advertisers and corporate owners that increasingly made their existence and social reach possible, enabled these reviewers to claim that they operated as individuals in an even more disinterested, civic fashion than did Scherman's judges.

It is evident, then, that the critics of the book clubs were alarmed by the implications of a direct connection between literary reviewers and an organization interested in selling books. They were concerned lest the quest for corporate profit infect the otherwise disinterested search for the literary. However, they did not recognize their own definition of the literary or their desire to associate themselves with it as a similarly interested endeavor. They did not see their defense of the literary, tucked away as it was between the lines of their criticism of the Book-of-the-Month Club, as an argument on behalf of their own authority and their right to control the larger literary field itself. It seems clear, though, that their criticism was driven at least in part by their unconscious concern that the club's power as an organization would enable it to usurp their role as cultural mediators, as arbiters of literary value and excellence. At stake, finally, in their quarrel with the book clubs was not only the question of who would control the literary field but also who or what would define the nature of the relationship between the field itself and the forces of capital so clearly involved in its transformation. In quarreling about the proper location and allegiances of those whose writings would establish the ground on which particular judgments were to be made, they were in fact debating what the proper role and function of literature, information, and culture ought to be in a twentieth-century world of commodities, capitalism, and consumption.

In the end the Ehrenreichs' analysis of the structural location of the professional-managerial class enables us to see that these debates about the book clubs, reviewing, and the position and function of expert literary advice were in fact a struggle to resolve the ambiguity and ambivalence of the literary professional's position between capital and labor. Especially at issue in the intrafield dispute was the question of where literary critics, advisers, and judges should labor and in whose service. Could a highly trained professor and literary critic like Henry Canby labor for a profit-minded organization like the Book-of-the-Month Club and still manage to recommend books that exhibited literary excellence rather than commercial possibility? Or, by surrendering his own disinterested concern for the public good to the corporation's desire to reach more readers, would he thereby foster the thorough commodification and devaluation of the public sphere? Equally at issue was the question of whether reviewing was to be conceived of as a process that facilitated bookselling, thereby augmenting an important capitalist industry, or whether it was an independent, consumer-oriented activity designed to serve the needs of aspiring readers. Or was it to be understood more abstractly and even more autonomously as a disinterested, almost sacred calling entered by those who saw themselves striving selflessly to realize the noblest human values through the identification of the larger culture's finest artistic creations?

Scherman and Canby, of course, argued that they extended culture's reach to new audiences, and thus they stressed the service-minded character of their business and pegged all of their operations to perceived reader demand. In opposition, their critics remained wary of the tastes of alien audiences whom they concretized and demonized as "the masses," and they suggested that critics ought not pander to them but should, rather, protect the literary by becoming its legitimate custodians. The debate about the appropriateness of the actions of the Book-of-the-Month Club judges was, finally, a debate about whether the professional book expert should be thought of as a salesmen and promoter, as a teacher and pedagogue, as a kind of cultural apostle with a special relationship to the divine activity of creation, or, more properly, as a leader in a politicized and redemptive avant-garde.

Most of Scherman's critics, of course, took up some version of the latter two positions, defending the supposedly superior status of the literary as a source of human knowledge. They maintained that their true allegiance was neither to the capitalists who employed them nor to the worker-readers they hoped to address but rather to the abstract principles constituting the literary field as a special space, a true outside, a place beyond the market and free from its instrumentalism and utilitarianism. They accordingly envisioned a role for themselves either as conservators of a revered cultural tradition, as missionaries in the service of a literature made sacred by virtue of its preservation of humane values in the face of capitalist reification and commodification, or they construed themselves as revolutionaries in the service of an alternate world yet to be born. In either case they positioned themselves clearly in opposition to the bankers, advertisers, and corporate owners who employed them or paid them through the aegis of a distant publisher.

Yet it must be said as well that in casting themselves always as independent critics capable of perceiving the truth and value inherent in real literary art, they equivocated about the source of their capacity to detect literary excellence when they saw it. They were never clear about whether it was their technical training, which might itself be extended to others, or some sort of inherent moral superiority that enabled them to see and to evaluate in a way different from the lay reader. As a consequence, their claim to authority over the literary field tended to be staked on their difference, on their distinction and distance from those who could not perceive as they did. Ironically, then, for many of them, disdain, disgust, and contempt characterized the attitude they adopted toward the population they supposedly hoped to reach with their efforts at enlightenment and education. Unable or unwilling to approach readers whose tastes and preferences differed so obviously from their own, they abandoned any who could not already attend to their trained commentary. Ever disdainful of popularizations, book chat, and book news, they deserted those readers who were on a quest after culture. They left them to the devices of other literary professionals whose orientation, for whatever reason, was more tolerant, less obsessed with the fate of literature conceived in a narrow sense, and more open to the search for books that could perform multiple functions for diverse readers. In a sense many of the Book-of-the-Month Club's critics took up an oppositional stance toward capitalism and the culture industry it funded, but they did so as members of an aristocracy of taste.

Additionally, in repeatedly foregrounding their status as individuals, the book club critics refused to recognize their position within a particular class or class fraction, that is, as part of a group of people with shared interests and investments. In effect they were indulging in a strategy that Stuart Blumin has identified as characteristic of the middle class more generally, the class, he suggests, that always insists that it is not a class. Blumin is referring to the phenomenon of the middle class's ideological privileging of individualism, its claim that an individual's social status and position is a function of his or her hard work, determination, and initiative rather than of any particular structural location within the economy. The book club critics' refusal to recognize the investments behind their own statements about literature and the state of cultural production was thus a highly characteristic move, the very act that enabled them to misrecognize the way they were implicated in the commercial system of production they so wanted to criticize. By insisting on their status as rational individuals and by characterizing their criticism as the disinterested search for the inherently and universally good, they refused to recognize their work as a defense of their own privilege, just as they refused to acknowledge that they were in fact trying to persuade others to adopt their particular values and views. In effect the book club critics ignored the way they themselves were embedded in the commercial system, and as a consequence they were able to maintain the illusory view of themselves as somehow special, different, outside, and beyond the market.

It might be said in summary, then, that most of the book club criticism was driven by deep suspicion about the corporations and class that owned and directed the productive forces in the United States, including the major newspapers and magazines that paid the salaries of the reviewers and critics who developed the critique in the first place. Consequently they labored industriously to establish their own distance from capital by insisting on the categorical difference between the economic and the cultural, between the market and art, and between out-and-out advertising and their own, supposedly disinterested advisory activity. Yet they could not identify easily with the larger population they were supposedly attempting to inform and to guide, in part because their own social position and identity depended on their ability as a group to legitimate their special expertise and therefore their cultural authority. That authority was therefore dependent in a crucial way on the differences between the critics and those they were asked to advise and to address. The assertion of that difference often realized itself in the form of moral superiority that thereby prevented many of them from thinking seriously about why they wanted to address and educate others in the first place. Accordingly they

demonized not only those who lacked their cultural competence and refined taste, the mass-produced, consuming automatons supposedly tied
to the book clubs, but also institutions like the Book-of-the-Month Club
itself to which such individuals supposedly turned in order to acquire, the
critics argued, a counterfeit version of the authentic cultural knowledge
only they themselves could provide. It is not hard to understand, then,
why middlebrow operations like the Book-of-the-Month Club looked so
scandalous. They were threatening to the extent that they foregrounded
the connections between culture and the market and to the extent that
they threatened to obliterate the distinction between those who were cultured and those who were not.

What was most scandalous, finally, about the Book-of-the-Month Club
was not simply its proximity to lowbrow culture. In fact, nearly all of its
critics admitted it was nowhere near as degraded as radio or the movies.
Rather, what was troubling was its failure to maintain the fences cordoning off culture from commerce, the sacred from the profane, and the low
from the high. The Book-of-the-Month Club was threatening because it
seemed to create a permeable space between regions and forces otherwise
kept conceptually distinct, a space that had to be mapped consequently as
the middle ground—as the middlebrow—in order to keep it under control. Crucially, the club exposed the fact that the middle ground existed
potentially as a colonizable space that was being surveyed and occupied by
new cultural authorities deeply involved with the activity of promoting the
distribution, circulation, and hence production of cultural goods. Their
interests and tastes, therefore, understandably looked very different and
highly threatening to those attempting to maintain their distance and that
of the literary field itself from the material forces controlling and structuring its operation. In representing these new authorities as dictators and
policemen, the critics of the book clubs sought to mobilize in opposition
an older vision of a political community of autonomous readers and independent cultural shareholders, each of whom singularly but unfailingly
would manage to confirm the hegemony of rationality, liberalism, discre-
tion, and taste.

We will see in the following chapter that in the years immediately after
the founding of the Book-of-the-Month Club Harry Scherman's judges
began to elaborate a vision of their own activities that was characteristically different from that offered by their competitors who were laboring
as literary journalists and, increasingly throughout the 1930s and 1940s, as
literary academics. In the process they began to construct a fairly consistent conception not only of the place and function of book reviewing and

reading advice in a rapidly professionalizing culture but, equally significantly, an informal theory of the book buying and book reading population and, finally, an aesthetics and pragmatics of book selection consistent with their view. As might be expected, given what we have already learned about Scherman and his operation, the Book-of-the-Month Club judges differed chiefly from their critics in their greater willingness to accept the interpenetration of the cultural field with the market. Consequently they tended neither to ask questions about the larger interests their activity served nor to demonize those who turned to them for advice, guidance, and support. They did not need to, we shall soon see, in part because the people they actually addressed were already positioned to hear their message; they already desired to be part of the professional reaches of the middle class. They took up their position as cultural mediators, then, with pleasure and a sense of mission that was not shared by their critics, who were deeply troubled by their own placement between capital and labor.

## CHAPTER EIGHT

# Reading for a New Class

## The Judges, the Practical Logic of Book Selection,

## and the Question of Middlebrow Style

### MIDDLEBROW CULTURE AS A SENTIMENTAL EDUCATION

Despite the extensive criticism of the Book-of-the-Month Club that developed shortly after its appearance, Harry Scherman's distribution machine proved to be surprisingly attractive to potential book buyers. From its initial list of 4,750 subscribers, the membership grew to 60,058 by the end of 1927, and in 1928 it increased again to 94,690.[1] By the end of 1929 the Book-of-the-Month Club sent books to 110,588 subscribers. The organization's success can be attributed to Scherman's managerial skill at adapting the fundamental principles of Fordism to the problem of book circulation. What he created with the Book-of-the-Month Club, as we have seen, was the organizational equivalent of a perpetual motion machine. His operation continuously processed new books for automatic distribution to a stable group of readers already transformed into consumers by the requirements of subscription.

It is equally clear, however, that the success of the club was closely bound up with Scherman's decision to tie his operation to the services of an elite group of literary experts. Whatever critics thought of the judges' decision to sign on with a profit-making establishment, the selection committee's offer to provide expert advice about the best books available proved attractive to large numbers of aspiring readers apparently stymied by the undifferentiated output of the fast-expanding publishing industry. In an effort to explain why the club's offer might have looked so promising to those who contracted to receive books regularly, sight unseen, I look closely in this chapter at the way the Book-of-the-Month Club judges operated as salaried, literary professionals. Such an examination will help to clarify why middlebrow culture developed as an essential component of middle-class life in the years between the wars. At the same time it will illuminate how this new commodity addressed particular conditions of everyday existence experienced by individuals within the professional-managerial class. We will find that in spite of Harry Scherman's and Henry Canby's professed interest in the masses, the club actually addressed people with at least some measure of economic and cultural capital and who longed for a more secure position as part of the professional elite. Indeed it will become clear that along with the books it distributed, the Book-of-the-Month Club sold two promises. It promised to make sense of the conditions of professional-managerial class life, and at the same time it promised to assuage some of the most glaring emotional costs of a life lived as a professional.

To accomplish this it will be necessary to make sense of the characteristic middlebrow ordering of the literary field. Thus I look first at how the Book-of-the-Month Club judges conceptualized the kind of literary advice they were offering and at the role judgment and evaluation played in that advice. Then I consider how they organized their critical activities and explore the unconscious logic that underwrote their evaluative practice. Finally, I examine the distinctive, affectively rich way in which they put that logic into operation. This is important because the Book-of-the-Month Club judges did not select the books they sent out to club members in dispassionate, wholly intellectualized fashion as the mere embodiment of some set of abstract ideological principles. Rather, they themselves responded to particular books with visceral emotion and accordingly recommended certain titles to their subscribers because they exhibited specific forms of pathos and passion—whatever their subject matter or form. As a consequence the judges foregrounded the role of readerly identification and empathy in the reading experience. For them, reading was as much an event defined by intense affective response and reaction as it was an act structured by desires for guidance, education, and moral counsel.

By exploring how the Book-of-the-Month Club judges sought to promote reading that accomplished certain pragmatic functions and exhibited emotional depths and affective range, I hope to clarify the nature of the habitus—a style of comportment at once behavioral, intellectual, and affective—that was being constructed for aspiring professional-managerial workers by the middlebrow culture they embraced so enthusiastically as their own. I suggest that in addition to seeing the Book-of-the-Month Club as an integral part of a new form of cultural production, we ought to understand it as well as an exercise in social training and pedagogy. The Book-of-the-Month Club taught its subscribers how to order the modern universe and how to parse its various domains. It managed this, however, because it first hailed them as subjects with pressing emotional needs and desires produced by their particular historical situation. Equally importantly, the club instructed its subscribers in the proper stance to assume with respect to the world, and it taught them ways of feeling appropriate to that stance. It modeled a distinctive middlebrow style. What I am after, as I have indicated in the Introduction, is the shape and feel of the "sentimental education" offered by the Book-of-the-Month Club to its many thousands of middlebrow subscribers.[2]

## BOOKS ARE FOR READERS

When Harry Scherman laid out his original plan for the Book-of-the-Month Club in 1926, he made it clear that he understood implicitly how the literary field was configured. He also demonstrated a canny sense of how his projected operation would likely challenge the traditional understanding of that configuration. Scherman suggested that he planned to create his committee of selection as a way of acknowledging the dominant view of the literary field as a special domain dealing with a category of printed objects distinctly different from all things commercial.[3] As he himself later put it, "Obviously, there would be suspicion that the books which would be presented to subscribers would be presented for *commercial* reasons." To counter that assumption, "there had to be some real assurance that the books that were going to be sent to them . . . were chosen for their *quality* as really desirable books. That necessitated a committee," he added. "The members of it had to be known to the public as completely disinterested people."[4] The original selection committee was established, therefore, to foreground the status of his books as literary objects rather than their role as commodities bound for circulation through the market.

After he hired Henry Canby, Dorothy Canfield Fisher, Heywood Broun, Christopher Morley, and William Allen White, however, Harry Scherman empowered them to do more than function as a concession to the dominant view of publishing. He asked them to provide something other than a mere testimonial to the quality of the merchandise offered by the club. In fact, he asked the committee members to make determinations about the quality of the merchandise itself, and more importantly, he asked them to determine their own criteria for making such determinations in the first place. Neither he nor his partners interfered in their deliberations. They left it to the judges to work out procedures and criteria for selecting the best book of the month. As I have already indicated, however, the committee had its own ideas about how to think about the literary field and about the nature of literary production. Consequently, only a few months into the enterprise, Dorothy Canfield Fisher and her colleagues urged Scherman to rethink some of the basic operating assumptions of the club.

As we have already seen, Fisher was instrumental in promoting reconsideration. She objected to the advertised premise of Harry Scherman's new organization, the idea that one book, better than all the rest, could be identified every month. She worried that promotion of a single title would obscure all the other worthy books published at the same time. And those books, she suggested, should not necessarily be compared with one another. Books were different, just as readers were different. Fisher conceived of her role at the club as a kind of scout on behalf of a variety of readers. She was attempting to match prospective readers with titles that would appropriately and effectively address their needs. Thus she urged Scherman to allow the judges to recommend more than the designated book of the month.

Fisher and the rest of the judges seem to have worried less about the commercial orientation of the Book-of-the-Month Club than Harry Scherman did. William Allen White, who expressed skepticism about his suitability for a literary undertaking when first approached by Scherman, wrote later in a letter to him that "now if I am worth anything to you it is [as] a mentor on that side of the merchandising operation."[5] Joan Rubin has shown that he often pronounced books "salable" and expressed concern about how the committee's more literary selections would affect the club's "business proposition."[6] Similarly, Christopher Morley's talents as a book promoter, which he displayed with great panache in his column "The Bowling Green," accorded well with the fundamental purposes of the Book-of-the-Month Club, which despite Harry Scherman's queasiness and organizational caveats, was commercial to its very core. Antiquarian and bibliophile though he was, Morley did not envision books as static, shelved, or cherished objects alone. For him they achieved their true vitality and dynamic promise only in the hands of active readers.

One of Morley's first literary successes was the novel *Parnassus on Wheels*, which chronicled the activities of a peripatetic bookseller devoted to making books accessible to ordinary people.[7] And at the end of *Ex Libris Carissimis*, a 1932 collection of his essays, he appended a list of his favorite books, which he troped as "Golden Florins." For him classics were not eternal treasures in some literary museum but value-bearing, circulating currency.[8] Morley also sought to familiarize the readers of his columns with something other than "the best books." He discussed all sorts of writers, major and minor; the latter category he justified by saying that "some of the most exquisite pleasures of print are to be found in pursuit of the smaller names."[9]

The Book-of-the-Month Club judges, like the organization they were hired to assist (and like Melvil Dewey, the cheap libraries, and the creators of the Harvard Classics), were devoted to the cause of the circulating book. In their minds the value of a book was not fixed once and for all at the moment of its creation but was established and reestablished anew in the process of exchange every time it made its way into the hands of readers who found particular uses for it in keeping with their own peculiar aims. Even Henry Canby, by all accounts the most literary of the judges, once observed that "the primary object of all writing about books is to give them currency."[10] This was especially necessary, he believed, in the bewildering and confusing modern age because people relied on books and literature to tell them how to make sense of the new forms of life that swirled so meaninglessly about them.

In fact, as I have indicated before, Canby left the professoriate to take up the activity of book reviewing because he felt that the conservatism of the literary academy prevented him from devoting his attention to the all-important task of searching out a literature appropriate to the modern age. "We are not concerned to know only whether Joyce's 'Ulysses' is inferior to Homer's or O'Neill's plays to the tragedies of Euripides," he once wrote. "Our chief interest is in interpretations not comparisons. We would know what these modern works . . . are good for, what are their defects, and how they might have been bettered."[11] Canby's turn to reviewing was motivated by his fervent belief that the general American public needed to discover a literature that might counter modern skepticism and materialism without turning its back on every aspect of modernity. "We shall listen to no philosopher or critic," he wrote, "who out of ignorance is afraid of the results of science, saying pooh! pooh! to the machines, and resorting to the seventeenth century or the fourth A.D. or B.C." He continued, "That life is out of control now is notorious, but it will never be brought back by cursing from a hill top. It is better to try to ride the machines than to pretend that they can be disinvented; wiser to guide a civilization than to oppose it utterly."[12]

In a sense Henry Canby continued to believe in the power and efficacy of words to address modern dilemmas. It was that faith, in fact, that caused him to worry so insistently about the difficulties of finding a literature adequate to the challenges of modernity in a world where so many more books were being churned out by faster presses and sped-up editorial processes at increasingly profit-minded publishing houses. As he put it, "Books are being published daily, and some one must tell the busy and none too discriminating public what they are worth—not to mention the librarians who are so engaged in making out triple cards and bibliographies and fitting titles to vague recollections that they have no time left to read." [13] Canby took up newspaper reviewing out of the conviction that "[the newspapers] alone . . . have kept pace with the growing swarm of published books." Without the reviews first placed on book pages and then collected in book supplements, he argued, "the public would have . . . only the advertisements and the publishers' announcements to classify, analyze, and in some measure describe the regiment of books that marches in advance of our civilization." [14] Henry Canby's commitment to regular reviewing and to the distribution goals of the Book-of-the-Month Club was a function of his belief that books could effectively provide the guidance modern people needed to make sense of the unprecedented rate and extent of social change they were forced to confront on a daily basis.

Adumbrated here, it should be clear, is an attitude toward books and, by extrapolation, culture at large that privileges the activities and objectives of circulation and use. Henry Canby was never driven simply by an overwhelming desire to identify the best that had been thought and said in the past. He was motivated by a mission to ensure the utility of books (and other cultural products) by getting them into the hands of people who might best understand them and apply the insights they contained. As he put it, "The best book is worth nothing at all if it never finds a reader." He noted as well that "good reading is a highly personal experience, whose quality depends upon the taste, the intellect, the imagination, and the sensitivity of the individual reader. Still he has to get the books. I find too little in histories of literature and criticism of how books get to readers." [15]

My point here is that just as Harry Scherman's desire to market new books in an endless stream prompted him to foreground the pleasures and uses of reading as an activity rather than to focus on the particularities of books as singular objects, so the judges' interest in book promotion and their matter-of-fact acquiescence to the market-driven nature of publishing pushed them to focus on the processes of book buying and book reading as well. In effect they installed readers and their differentiated reading activities at the center of their evaluative operation. Not all readers bought books, they knew, and not all book buyers bought books to read. Some books were bought as gifts; some were bought to be displayed.

Others were purchased as reference tools or as volumes intended to comprise a personal library. And still others were bought to be read through to the end. In their writings Henry Canby, Dorothy Canfield Fisher, and the others suggested that readers often sought different affective experiences in the act of reading, different relationships to the book they had picked up, and different ends as the goal of the reading process. Ironically, then, despite the larger advertising emphasis on the club's search for the single best book of the month, the judges began to elaborate a practical logic of selection that foregrounded not only the variability of readers and reading but also the variability of the evaluative standards used to find books for them.

Even Henry Canby's more narrow view of specifically "literary" books accorded with this larger perspective. Although he would continue to believe that the literary had a special role to play in what he called modern civilization, he considered its distinctiveness less a matter of quality and more a difference of kind, function, or purpose. The literary, for Canby, was not necessarily better than other sorts of books, nor was it universally useful. Nor did he believe that all instances of the category "literature" should be ranked along a single scale of value. Rather, Canby argued that, like works of sociology, psychology, general science, history, and biography, literary books appealed to particular audiences and performed distinct functions. They did so because all books concretized the experience of their authors and because different authors turned their experience to different purposes and goals. Books, like all forms of cultural production, according to Canby, attempted different things for different purposes and with different audiences in mind. Canby felt, therefore, that every book ought to be approached on its own terms if readers would do justice to it and get the most from it that they could. The reviewer's proper task, then, in order to facilitate appropriate connections between books and readers, was to clarify precisely what those terms were. The reviewer's job was to provide an adequate and informative definition of the book as a categorical object of a particular kind.

Canby's earliest collection of "essays in contemporary criticism" had been issued in 1922 under the title *Definitions* as a way of emphasizing the fact that he offered not a "sequence of chapters developing a single theme and arriving at categorical conclusions" but, rather, a series of essays, quite literally "attempts" to illuminate the multiple purposes, means, and achievements of contemporary writers in a confused age.[16] Then, as later, Canby did not consider his criticism an Olympian pronouncement issued from on high, measuring all works against a single, universal standard.

Rather, he viewed his essays as a series of attempts to open doors "through which both writer and reader may enter into a better comprehension of what novelists, poets, and critics have done or are trying to accomplish."[17] Such a mediating role was necessary, he believed, because the literary world had grown muddied as a consequence of augmented production and because the general business of evaluation and judgment had been thrown into disarray.

Henry Canby differed crucially from cultural critics such as Waldo Frank and Ernest Boyd in that he did not blame the much-remarked-on evaluative confusion of his era on the abandonment of standards altogether. He argued instead that standards had proliferated drastically. Observing that "one of the common complaints against this slipshod generation is that it has no standards," he countered, "not a lack of standards but a confusion of standards is our undoing."[18] And he well understood that such confusion profoundly unsettled the profession of literary criticism as it had previously been conceived. "Literary criticism," he wrote, "has become polytheistic and we worship at so many altars that we cannot ourselves name our literary religion."[19] For Canby the kind of religion of literature promoted by the modernists and the little magazines was a decided anachronism simply because the assumption of a universal standard on which omniscient judgment could be predicated was no longer possible.

The second most powerful judge, Dorothy Canfield Fisher, held views remarkably similar to Henry Canby's. In fact she insisted even more strongly than he did that literary judgments, evaluations, and descriptions needed to vary with their audiences and their objects. Nonetheless, because she believed that there was a fundamental continuity between literature and life, she treated all books as instrumental guides for living and argued that even fiction could enable readers to broaden their experience and to lead richer, more intense, and honorable lives. Similarly, she championed nonfiction titles when they strove to make their technical knowledge both accessible and useful to the general reader. She was known at the club for her interest in continuing education. Fisher was as aware as Henry Canby that readers differed not only in their interests and tastes but in their education and literary preparation as well. Accordingly, she conceptualized her role at the club as a promoter of many different kinds of interactions between books and readers, and she conceptualized her duty as a reviewer in a manner distinctly different from the way she thought of the activities of the traditional literary critic.

In a report on a book of poems by Marion Canby, for instance, she once expatiated at length on her understanding of the difference between book reviewing and literary criticism.[20] It is worth quoting several passages of her analysis, for they lay out clearly the thinking that was shared by all of the Book-of-the-Month Club judges, and they suggest that the judges were quite aware they were not functioning as traditional critics. "People of experience agree that one trouble with book reviews could be eliminated by firmly specifying at the head of each one . . . the kind of person for whom it is intended. One sort of review is written for actual readers of books, people of intelligence and taste not professionally literary in any way who, seeing a new volume would like to find a statement about it that gives them a fairly clear idea what is inside it and whether it is the kind of book they would be apt to find worth reading." Actual readers, Fisher suggested, were quite different from professional readers. Thus they needed something different from what was generally provided in literary criticism. Since the worth of a book was apparently a function of the content it offered to inquiring readers, a review ought to inform them about what they would find between its covers, and it ought to advise them if they would be likely to derive satisfaction or pleasure from reading it.

Literary criticism, on the other hand, because it was aimed at the professional reader, stressed judgment and evaluation rather than information and advice. Fisher suggested, in fact, that "the [literary] sort of review is intended, consciously or unconsciously, not at all for mere readers of books, but for other critics, and for professionally literary folk whose self-appointed business it is correctly to appraise and accurately to calculate the position of each new piece of creative writing, in relation with what has gone before and is likely to come after it in the history of literature." Evaluation and judgment, from her point of view, belonged to the province of the literary professional, whose job it was to provide a critical account of literary history and tradition. Fisher clearly believed that professional reading was organized differently from that practiced by the nonprofessional, and she obviously thought both entirely legitimate. She suggested, in fact, that "both kinds of reviews are interesting, worth-while and of value—but only when read by those for whom they are intended. Each kind is exasperating and disappointing when read by people who are looking for the other kind."

Significantly, Fisher concluded her report on Marion Canby's poems with the observation "that the reviews written for the Book of the Month Club News are of the first kind."[21] Like Henry Canby, then, who had abandoned literary criticism, he once reported, because he "had shaken off some pedantic ideas and no longer yearned to publish articles that only scholars could understand, which no one, not even scholars read," Fisher seems to have understood that criticism and the books critics tended to find valuable were closely bound up with the interests and concerns of a highly specialized, often heavily trained, and quite small professional audience.[22] Since ordinary readers could derive benefit from many different kinds of books, she suggested, the judges ought to concern themselves with more than the literary, and they ought to report accurately on the nature of those books for the club's subscribers. Although she was willing to include high literary titles on the club's list, she was as careful as Henry Canby was to ask herself whether a large, general audience might find a given title pleasing, compelling, or useful. If the judgment was no, she would argue vigorously for a report in the *News* that would characterize the book honestly and that would discourage readers who might not be up to its challenge or likely to find it interesting.

Of the April 1928 main selection, for instance, Elizabeth Bowen's *The Hotel*, the *Book-of-the-Month Club News* noted that "it is a book . . . that calls for a more than usually careful characterization to subscribers." The report continued, "It must be described, first, as a subtle book." Obviously hoping to avoid baffled or irate customers and a mountain of returns, the *News* cautioned its readers further:

> Those who enjoy writers like Joseph Conrad, Anatole France, Henry James—and to come closer to today—writers somewhat like H. M. Tomlinson, Willa Cather, Edith Wharton, will exult in it. It will yield its full delight, like an old and rare wine, only to those who take it in with an appreciative and unhurried attention. Those readers, on the other hand, who prefer the straightforward narrative—as exemplified by such novelists as Galsworthy, Tarkington, Bennett and innumerable others—while they cannot fail to appreciate the color and sparkle of this gem, may not be enthusiastic about it. If one is not in a proper mood, indeed, one may even find *The Hotel* annoying by reason of its subtlety, although this would be unfair to a deft piece of work.[23]

Similarly, the next issue of the *News* warned potential readers straightaway that Henry Canby had reported that *Mr. Weston's Good Wine*, by T. F. Powys, should be avoided "if you cannot endure symbolism" or "if the earthly humors of the all-too-human race, especially in the pursuit of love, shock you easily." In that case, the *News* concluded bluntly, "you are advised not to read it."[24] Apparently neither Canby nor Fisher had any compunctions about warning the club's subscribers away from books they thought distinct literary achievements yet esoteric.

The commentary of Henry Canby and Dorothy Canfield Fisher suggests that the judges believed the principal aim of the Book-of-the-Month Club was not to place books in the long sweep of literary history but to match readers with the books appropriate to them. Following from this premise, the logic of the evaluative system they established at the club in its early years developed three pointed concerns. The judges tried first to determine what sort of book they had before them. Then they attempted to understand why a reader might select this book rather than another. Finally they explored how best to describe that book to make its relevant features known to readers, who would approach it with previously formed expectations, desires, and needs. In the final analysis, despite their presentation to the public as authorities who could magisterially issue pronouncements on the basis of special literary expertise, the Book-of-the-Month Club judges developed an evaluative process that was thoroughly contingent and fundamentally reader driven. They tended to subordinate the critical act of literary judgment to the activity of recommendation. And recommendation, as they practiced it, was a self-consciously social activity constituted by their effort to understand and to adopt the point of view of their subscribers. Once they managed to understand readers' desires, needs, and tastes, they subsequently strove to match those aims to goods and authors already available in the public marketplace. In a sense the judges constituted themselves as social facilitators or mediators trying to foster connections between readers, books, and their authors. Thus they resisted taking up the usual critical distance and pose of superiority found in traditional criticism. More frequently in their daily practice they tried not to dictate on the basis of their own taste but sought to imagine themselves as the readers they aimed to address. Only after they had managed that act of imagination and identification did they turn to the monthly output of the publishing industry and seek particular books for particular readers.[25]

## THE PLANAR LOGIC OF MIDDLEBROW EVALUATION

Harry Scherman's judges conceived of their business less as a process of evaluation and judgment than as one of definition and sorting. Their job was to read all the books submitted by the trade, to imagine who might find such books interesting or useful, and then to evaluate how well particular books might satisfy those readers most likely to select them. Since the publishers had been instructed by Scherman to send many different kinds of books to the club, the judges quickly recognized that they could not compare apples to oranges or oranges to grapefruits. Not all books were literary books, and even literary books, the judges believed, varied considerably in form, function, and intent. As Canby himself observed, "There is—to take the novel—the story well calculated to pass a pleasant hour but able to pass nothing else; there is the story with a good idea in it and worth reading for the idea only; there is the story worthless as art but usefully catching some current phase of experience; and there is the fine novel which will stand any test for insight, skill, and truth." He continued, "Now it is folly to apply a single standard to all these types of story. It can be done, naturally, but it accomplishes nothing except to eliminate all but the shining best."[26] The project at the club, as a consequence, was to proliferate gauges and to multiply evaluative standards. The judges asked what every book was useful for. Even lesser books, with modest aims and intentions, they believed, deserved their readers, and those books could sometimes satisfy and serve their readers better than more ambitious titles.

In effect, then, Henry Canby and his colleagues treated all books that came to them as instances of multiple and multifarious types, that is, as examples of different classes or genera, each with its own peculiar functions and uses. "Is this serious fiction," they asked themselves, "or hammock literature?" "Is this a sea saga or a small woman's novel?" "Is it popular history or too specialized for the general reader?" "Is it literary criticism or literary biography?" Only after determining the category did they ask themselves whether a book was any good or not. Having determined that a particular title was a literary biography, for instance, they then asked themselves, "Is it a *good* literary biography?" "Does it fail as an entertaining yarn?" they similarly wondered. "Will it please readers who are partial to nature books?" To answer this latter question about quality, they additionally had to ask themselves what, exactly, characterized an excellent example of a particular kind of book. "What makes a good nature book good?" they wondered. "Is it the same quality or set of features that establishes the excellence of a biography or a work of serious fiction?"

The Book-of-the-Month Club judges focused on the diversity and variety of the literary field and on its ability to generate many different kinds of books with different features and different aims. In spite of Harry Scherman's ritual repetition of the claim that the club sent out the best book of the month, in practice the judges deemed this kind of absolute hierarchical grading an impossible and undesirable task. Their work, consequently, contested that hierarchical and pyramidal view of the literary field discussed in Chapter 4. Although they continued to recognize the existence of a special aesthetic category called Literature, which they rendered with a capital *L*, they also thought of the literary field itself as a universe encompassing all kinds of print productions. Accordingly, they differentiated books from one another on the basis of their differential functions and variable appeals to readers. In their view books were only comparable if they were of the same genus or type. It made no sense to judge a popular history lacking because its verbal style was undistinguished. Nor was it justifiable to eliminate a rollicking good story because its characters were superficially delineated. This is not to say that at the club the larger field was conceived as an open, free space, lacking in organization and structure. It was quite structured, in fact, but according to a different logic and in respect of different principles.

As a way of getting at that logic and its supporting principles, it might be useful to quote Henry Canby again on the variability of the literary as a special category unto itself. For although Canby continued to group most fictional texts under the sign of the literary, he also subdivided that body of texts on the basis of the functions they could perform for their readers. His comments here come from an essay about the difference between literary criticism and reviewing, a subject that concerned him throughout his career, as it did Dorothy Canfield Fisher. Criticism, Canby also felt, rightly concerned itself with literary values. Reviewing, on the other hand, which he believed properly functioned to inform readers about new books, needed to approach the question of value more flexibly. "It is sometimes necessary to remind the austerer critic," he wrote, "that there are a hundred books of poetry, of essays, of biography, of fiction, which are by no means of the first rank and yet are highly important, if only as news of what the world, in our present, is thinking and feeling. They cannot be judged, all of them on the top plane of perfect excellence; and if we judge them on any other plane, good, better, best, get inextricably mixed."[27] Canby, at least, was willing to judge books on other planes and thus to contest the very idea of good, better, and best judged on one set of aesthetic criteria. Fiction, for instance, could be evaluated for the news it provided of the contemporary world rather than for its linguistic craftsmanship. Canby continued significantly, "There is no help except to set books upon their planes and assort them into their categories—which is merely to define them before beginning to criticize." The crucial move in the evaluative practice of the Book-of-the-Month Club judges was not judgment at all but the activity of categorization, of sorting onto different planes.

The concept of different planes, it should be noted, constructs a vision of a print universe conceived of not as an organic, uniform, hierarchically ordered space. Rather, the print universe appears as a series of discontinuous, discrete, noncongruent worlds. Those worlds bring together readers with particular needs and demands and writers with special forms of expertise capable of addressing both. The role prescribed for the critic in a uniform literary world is that of Solomonic, omniscient judge. The disposition best suited to this more differentiated world of particular and locally specific purposes, desires, and goals is closer to that of a manager who has been charged with the smooth functioning of a complex system. The skills required of this literary manager—with the literary defined very broadly to include virtually all kinds of books and print—are more like those of the modern, professional librarian than the critic. Trained to bring together inquiring readers with the appropriate forms of technical expertise capable of answering their questions, the modern librarian is primarily oriented to the needs and tastes of readers. Relying on the card catalog and the innovations of the Dewey system of classification, this individual approaches the world of print not as a single universe but rather as a world of differentiated knowledge-production where language is put to multiple and different uses, where it is deployed differentially to describe and manipulate the world in highly specific, technically distinct ways.

Given this view of the world of print as a series of contiguous and equivalent domains, it should not be surprising to note that the category of Literature was treated by the Book-of-the-Month Club judges with a certain amount of ambiguity. On one hand the club's rhetoric about best books and future classics tended to evoke a sense of the literary as both sacred and transcendent, as the apex of all cultural achievement. On the other hand their day-to-day selection procedures and habits of description tended to construe the literary as only one more category among many. In practice, literary books were treated as books of a certain sort, as a special taste dependent on a high degree of education and familiarity with the complexities of literary history. The insight and enlightenment associated with the literary was offered at the club not as a superior form of knowledge but as a particular and peculiar sort with its own uses and applications, equivalent to yet different from other sorts of knowledge, such as knowledge to be found in works of science, political affairs, or history. Thus the judges' pragmatic approach to the larger literary field challenged the sacred status of Literature and contested its claim as the best that had been thought and said in the world. This does not seem particularly surprising when we consider that they lived in an ever-more-secular world impressed every day by the achievements of modern science and its supporting discourses, which foregrounded the material, the utilitarian, the technological, and the technical.

What I think we see at the Book-of-the-Month Club, then, is a disposition to structure the larger literary field according to a logic congenial to the emergent social group discussed in the previous chapter in connection with the debate over the Book-of-the-Month Club—the professional-managerial class. Increasingly educated to think of the world, whether mechanical, social, or natural, as an infinitely complex universe beyond the comprehension of single persons or even single points of view, individuals aspiring to membership in this group of workers were taught by specialized high school and college curricula to divide the universe into discrete domains and particular provinces, such as sociology, political science, the humanities, science, and history. They were asked to think of each of these areas as capable of being rendered comprehensible by highly specific and technical ways of knowing. Aiming to labor not with their hands but with their minds, these potential knowledge workers were asked to learn particular forms of technical competence and professional expertise and to use both to facilitate better description and manipulation of all that was encompassed by their own special domain. They were to convey the technical knowledge they commanded as specialists and professionals to people who were nonspecialists, to clients, consumers, or students in need of usable versions of such knowledge for pragmatic decision making and the conduct of everyday life.

The multiple planes of the literary field as conceived by the Book-of-the-Month Club judges, it seems to me, were structured according to this kind of logic, a planar logic that foregrounded the discreteness and particularity of domains and forms of expertise. This view also emphasized the pragmatic disposition of expertise and its fundamentally instrumental orientation in the service of a putatively general population. In effect expertise was constructed as a positivity in relation to a generality, the generality and lack exhibited by Harry Scherman's general reader, that individual who could not reproduce technical competence but who could, out of need and desire, recognize its claims, revere it, and make use of it for practical ends.

This parallel construction is evident in the way Harry Scherman presented his judges to the public. In fact, he did not simply present Canby, Fisher, Morley, Broun, and White as experts. He simultaneously stressed their orientation to the needs of the general reader. In the first prospectus issued for the club in 1926, for instance, he observed that the selecting committee consisted of "well-known critics and writers, whose catholicity of taste and whose judgment as to books have been demonstrated for many years before the public."[28] Then, beneath full-page portraits of each expert, he listed their professional credentials, stressing equally their special training and competence as well as their devotion to a broad, general taste. Of Broun, Scherman wrote, "His reporting revealed a rare critical and descriptive faculty which was fully developed when he became a columnist for *The New York Tribune* and afterward *The New York World*. Since then his comment upon things in general as well as upon the special fields of literature and the theater in which he has become an authority, has been followed by the intelligent with constant delight."[29] Furthermore, Scherman characterized William Allen White as "one of the most distinguished editors in America" and noted significantly that "in addition to service on many delegations and foundations, he is a writer of distinction in pure literature as well as journalism." He continued, "His admirable sanity, combined with a courageous and progressive attitude in all affairs involving the American mind, has won general recognition."[30]

The specialist and the generalist were locked together at the club and, more generally, within American culture at this historical moment, in a relation of mutuality, each serving the other. The specialist labored on behalf of the generalist, who in turn obligingly accorded the specialist respect, legitimacy, and ultimately authority itself. What the Book-of-the-Month Club sold, then, along with its subscriptions and endless stream of new books, was a social framework and cognitive map for understanding and organizing the world. In a social formation and economy increasingly driven by the need to generate, to distribute, and to control myriad forms of information and knowledge, the Book-of-the-Month Club performed the important role of acclimating the professional-managerial class and all who aspired to its status to the assumption that books and the experts who wrote them addressed the particular purposes of general readers. Less an innovative force in achieving national distribution of books than an exercise in social training and pedagogy, the Book-of-the-Month Club functioned more significantly, it seems to me, as a key cultural agency constructing the idea of the general reader, yet ironically modeling and thereby promoting belief in the worth of technical expertise and specialized knowledge.

The club promised such a membership the chance to keep up with the ever-advancing production of new knowledge as well as the opportunity to confirm its identity as educated and au courant. In a sense it assuaged an anxiety instilled by the increasingly specialized and technical curricula of the colleges and universities; it calmed the fear that once one had cut formal ties to institutions of higher education, one ran the risk of being left behind by relentlessly changing, highly specialized fields of knowledge. Although one's ongoing participation in a profession and its key associations would enable one to keep up with one's own field, all those other important fields of knowledge might grow increasingly opaque and incomprehensible to the flagging reader. Thus the Book-of-the-Month Club's many handbooks, outlines, guides, omnibuses, and popularizations helped to alleviate this anxiety and, at the same time, to produce a belief in the naturalness of technical knowledge and special competence as well as a sense that these could be translated for general readers who might thereby benefit practically from their advances and insights.

In dispensing its middlebrow cultural products, then, the club also recommended a particular orientation to those products and the culture they represented, a habitus suitable to a world organized and understood in this way. The club suggested that though knowledge and culture were the province of experts, they were valuable to the extent that they produced practical results and utilitarian effects for general readers. This was true even of fiction, they thought, which aimed sometimes to promote relaxation and escape and at other times to produce aesthetic pleasure. Both knowledge and culture were conceived, therefore, in utilitarian and pragmatic fashion. They were not valuable in and for themselves, according to the Book-of-the-Month Club, but for what they could do.

The middlebrow habitus or orientation toward the world that Canby and company taught was an instrumental one, finally, even when they were speaking about Literature with a capital *L*. Though the club began by appropriating an older, genteel view of culture and knowledge as higher forms of learning capable of ennobling all who came in contact with them, it did so in order to market those forms for its own profit, thereby refuting the notion that culture and intellectual inquiry ought to be thought of as finalities without purposes, as instances of the transcendent. The Book-of-the-Month Club extended its own pragmatic, utilitarian disposition to culture to those it addressed as subscribers by attempting to persuade them that a certain facility with the material contained in books could assure them of social success. Thus, while the club selected and sold serious cultural material and thereby continued to underwrite the notion of a higher, sacred culture of learning and art, it also invited its members to take up a relationship to that culture that was troublesome to those who saw themselves as its authoritative guardians.

For Henry Canby, Dorothy Canfield Fisher, and the rest of the Book-of-the-Month Club judges, all books, including fiction, achieved success and even greatness to the degree that they took up issues of everyday life. Value was also a function of a book's capacity to be used in pragmatic fashion to accomplish a particular end or purpose. The judges were wary of the dispassionate, highly intellectualized aesthetic distance associated with experimental forms of literary modernism and the highly academic criticism that had appeared to legitimate it. As a consequence, their guiding philosophy of book selection was less an aesthetic, in the sense of a philosophy or theory of art, than an ethos, a practical disposition or orientation to books that evaluated them according to how well they harmonized with a reader's moral norms, ethical standards, and expectations about pleasure. The Book-of-the-Month Club judges aimed to distribute more books to more readers not by seeking to elevate literary or aesthetic taste but by pursuing the possibilities of functional alignment, by attempting to match books and readers through a correlation of their most basic perceptual schemes for structuring "the everyday perception of everyday existence."[31]

This attention to the variability of readers and reading aims produced an evaluative practice at the Book-of-the-Month Club that was as attentive to minor works of crime fiction as it was to works aspiring to the status of great literature. Although Henry Canby and even Dorothy Canfield Fisher sometimes continued to insist on the value of the literary above all else in their nonclub writings, in their work at the club they treated books as a collection of categorically different objects, each category a subset with its own defining features, operative functions, and potential audience. Together the judges attempted to see the merit in a popular biography just as they tried to describe accurately the potential value in a work of free verse, a volume on foreign affairs, or a book on modern science. Although they continued to try to root out what Henry Canby called cheap vulgarity, none of them were very confident that they knew what that was in an age marked by extreme confusion. Thus they tried to follow the exhortation he had published before in *American Estimates*. Canby wrote, "Let us fight, then, in despite of time, tide, tendency, against cheap vulgarity in literature. But let us disclaim the reformer's easy distinctions as to what is to be saved and what damned." He continued significantly, "If the great first cause has foreordained a vital pictorial art to come from the comic strip, or a new literature from 'The Saturday Evening Post,' why let them come."[32] In an age of diversifying audiences, proliferating publications, and the destruction of sure and singular standards, Canby and company felt that it was essential for them as book experts to mill about in the crowd, to take for granted the muddle and confusion, and yet to keep their eyes open to all possibilities.

Not surprisingly, Canby and his colleagues produced an ecumenical practice at the Book-of-the-Month Club that enabled Harry Scherman's distribution machine to send out in 1928 alone Bernard Shaw's *The Intelligent Woman's Guide to Socialism and Capitalism*, Felix Salten's *Bambi*, Stephen Vincent Benét's *John Brown's Body*, Paul de Kruif's *Hunger Fighters*, and a book called *Whither Mankind?* edited by Charles Beard, which the *News* praised both because it represented "the ripest thought, upon a subject of interest, of some of the leading figures of our day" and because it exhibited "great readability."[33] In 1929 they sent out and retracted a book titled *Cradle of the Deep*, which had proved to be a hoax; *The Omnibus of Crime*, edited by Dorothy Sayers; *Kristin Lavransdatter*, by Sigrid Unset, who later won the Nobel Prize; and Walter Lippmann's *A Preface to Morals*.[34] In subsequent years the selection grew even more diverse as the club's judges moved away from their early predilection for serious fiction and toward a more self-conscious attempt to serve the full range of subscriber taste and to represent the varied output of the publishing industry. They increased the number of popular histories they offered and added more biographies, accounts of scientific developments and public affairs, and even medical manuals aimed at middle-class parents eager to implement the newest theories of child development in their own families.

In spite of the diversity of the Book-of-the-Month Club's list of main selections in the years after its founding, however, it is clear to anyone who examines those lists with care that one literary category did not make its way automatically to the club's subscribers. Literary modernism is conspicuously absent from the list of books the judges recommended as appropriate to a large general audience. This absence is usually read as evidence of the judges' aesthetic conservatism and of their retrograde allegiance to a set of genteel, nineteenth-century values. An examination of how they wrote about the reading experience itself and of a set of desires they seem to have brought to all the books they read suggests alternatively that their distaste for modernism was a symptom of their own very critical and quite modern reaction to a world that disturbed them as much as it disturbed William Faulkner, Gertrude Stein, Virginia Woolf, James Joyce, and even Edmund Wilson.[35] What they disliked most about the new fiction and poetry was that it seemed to encourage the cold indifference, disdain, and cynicism they associated with the modern era. The judges were much more comfortable with books that attempted to combat despair with sympathy and affiliation.

The Book-of-the-Month Club judges never formally articulated the set of values that underwrote their framework for evaluation. Even when they spoke to the interviewers for the Columbia Oral History Project in 1955 and 1956, they tended to speak about individual books and their specific reasons for selecting particular titles. Yet it is possible to tease out certain underlying patterns in the perspective they adopted not only to books but more generally to the world around them. Some of the most revealing comments they ever made were made about one another. When asked to suggest what they found most valuable about their colleagues, the judges pointed not to the acuteness of a mind or to the range of another's literary expertise but, rather, to an unusual capacity for feeling and empathy. A sustained interest in the qualities of individual persons and their potential for engaging the attention and concern of others animated the judges' fundamental approach to collegial relations as well as to books and even to reading itself as a socially significant practice. They sought out titles that would capture the regard of their readers and that would involve them in heightened emotional response.

Within the halls of the Book-of-the-Month Club, for example, Christopher Morley seems to have been appreciated for the manifold nature of his interests, for the intensity of his passions, and for his love of excess. In characterizing his colleague, Henry Canby remarked on Morley's "passionate gusto for experience" and observed further that "the excess in Christopher Morley is love of living, and by a natural transference of interest, every manifestation of intense living in others."[36] Significantly, Canby continued that "love of living as a passion is precisely the quality which this mechanical world of the twentieth century most often and emphatically lacks." He praised Morley's "capacity for mighty friendships, his wide-ranging curiosity, his red-faced indignations, his tireless enthusiasms" and speculated that his popularity was based on "a sound instinct for joy and pathos, sentiment and beauty, in the nobler varieties of humanity, which after all have their place even in a democracy of neurotics, schizoids, morons, and the emotionally unstable."[37] Whether or not Canby was right about the sources of Morley's general popularity, it is at least evident that Morley's intense interest in the emotive, affective quality of human life was one of the traits that recommended him to Henry Canby, Harry Scherman, and his other colleagues at *The Saturday Review of Literature* and the Book-of-the-Month Club.

This seems to have been the case with the other judges as well. Although Harry Scherman observed in his own Columbia interview that William Allen White tended too strenuously to avoid books that were difficult or obscure, he noted that his judgments were nonetheless useful to the club because he was attuned to readers' desires for compelling characters and involving stories. Similarly, Scherman's partner, Robert Haas, observed that Dorothy Canfield Fisher was the best judge in the early years because "she [had] the gift of putting her finger on the good elements in a book." [38] Although Haas himself did not suggest how she knew what those good elements were, a later judge, Clifton Fadiman, did comment on the personal qualities he believed were the source of her effectiveness at the club. "She has the freshest eye and the warmest heart of all of us," he observed. Significantly, he continued: "I think she tended to like books in which good came out triumphant; she was herself a lay saint, and a book that made an appeal to the heart and to morality made a great appeal to her, though perhaps those books weren't always the best books of the month." [39] Congruently, Fadiman described Henry Canby approvingly as "a scholar with the widest human sympathies, not a scholar of the study only." [40] A shared appreciation for what the judges called "warm-blooded" humanity, free-flowing sentiment, and intense affect, it would seem, was a privileged part of the taste or style cultivated at the Book-of-the-Month Club.

Although the judges could appreciate finely honed literary language, recommend serious efforts to communicate the complexity of world economics or foreign affairs to a general audience, and even promote the odd popular psychology book or mystery tale, the titles they commended with the greatest relish were often those that could be described in the words of Dorothy Canfield Fisher as "pulsingly alive, personal, human, and emotionally moving." [41] Even nonfiction books were scanned for their ability to infuse abstractions with warm-blooded humanity and the vitality of the individual life. Of an early nonfiction alternate recommended first in August 1926, Will Durant's *The Story of Philosophy*, one of the judges wrote, "Philosophy cannot be 'harsh and crabbed' when it is presented first as the ripening experience of remarkable men, next as an idea, and finally as a position freely to be criticized in the light of all we know." Significantly, the unnamed judge continued, "Spinoza in these pages becomes a man again. Giants like Aristotle and Kant become human, and Voltaire, in a brilliant chapter, is a dazzling personality who quite explains the world-wide power of his thought." [42]

What Book-of-the-Month Club judges demanded of the books they read, even popular histories and accounts of scientific discoveries, was a rich and elaborate realism of character. In the books they liked best, character was presented not as the simple function of ideas held or activities engaged in but as an emotionally specific way of holding the former and of participating in the latter. In their view a fundamental continuity and congruity between an author, a book, its evoked presences, and its readers made any reading experience truly worthwhile. According to the judges, really engaging titles were those that were as individual, as unique, and as deeply personal as their potential readers. Only books that revealed their affectively distinct identities by absorbing readers totally in their felt worlds were truly compelling. Thus the judges always began by attaching priority to the interests and emotional responses of singular individuals, and they maintained that the larger generalizations and abstractions of history could only be understood through the essential measure of individual human experience.

As Fisher once stated it in a review of *Tomorrow Will Come*, by E. A. Almedingen, "The difficulty in writing about vast cataclysmic episodes in history such as a great revolution is that the scale of the event is beyond the human." She continued, "And our imaginations are pretty closely limited, naturally enough, by human experience. Each reader lives his life within the boundary of what happens to him, himself. If he is unusually intelligent, he may follow mentally the narrative (which must by definition be impersonal) of the clash between forces greater than any individual: emotionally he can only gape blankly at the spectacle of a cosmic struggle." True understanding, Fisher implied, could not be abstractly intellectual; it had to be informed by empathy and by an appreciation of how, precisely, social change was humanly experienced. She liked this book, she reported to her colleagues, because it "made the Russian Revolution something more actual than what is read in a book or seen on a screen in a moviehouse" because it enabled the reader "to follow in realistic detail . . . the life led by one single human being who seems real to us, bring[ing] the whole melodrama of Russian history many degrees nearer to our understanding."[43] The choice of the word "melodrama" is crucial here, for it signals that Fisher, like the rest of her colleagues, conceived of history not as a distant spectacle to be taken in and explained or as a puzzle to be cognitively, intellectually solved. Rather, it was conceived of as a theater of affect, as a narrative to be imagined fully, to inhabit vicariously, and therefore to feel intensively as if it were one's own.

The particular habit of mind responsible for this kind of commentary was entirely congruent, I think, with the previously noted emphasis on the particular and the local, a subject discussed at length in Chapter 5. As

I suggest there, the judges exhibited an intense interest in the locally specific as a way of countering the abstraction and distance typically recommended as the only approach to the sheer, overdetermined complexity of modern life. Similarly, the judges seem to have recommended the value of the individual view and the intensity of the personal response as a counter to modern distance, cynicism, and despair. Canby, Fisher, and their colleagues treated the modernist abjuration of passion as a nettlesome piety and as a form of extreme and unnecessary asceticism. They were particularly wary of some champions of literary modernism who advocated a certain emotional stringency and intellectualism as the only riposte to the problems of modern materialism. Sentiment, in the vocabulary of the Book-of-the-Month Club judges, was not a singular thing to be avoided. Nor was the adjective "sentimental" construed as an epithet.[44] The judges praised books when they engaged the sentiments of the reader, with a strong emphasis on the plural here. The judges took delight in an extended vocabulary of human emotion and believed strongly that reading ought to generate a full range of affects.

Whatever else the club succeeded in dispensing in its early years, it seems clear that it communicated to its subscribers a deep respect for something that might be called middlebrow personalism. That is, the club constructed a picture of the world that, for all its modern chaos, domination by abstract and incomprehensible forces, and worries about standardization and massification, was still the home of individual, idiosyncratic selves. Those selves, the club's selections seemed to say, experienced the excitement and pain of the new in extraordinarily intense ways and responded to its conundrums with highly complex, even contradictory emotions. Although the club's judges promoted a kind of individualism, I use the word "personalism" rather than "individualism" as a way of marking the difference between their view of the human subject and those more dispassionate, highly intellectualized economic and philosophical conceptions of individualism usually thought to be at the base of American ideology. The individualism of the middlebrow subject, it seems to me, at least as he or she was constructed at the Book-of-the-Month Club, was an individualism of both affect and empathy. People felt—and they felt for others. At the same time personalism evokes the sense of being personable, of exhibiting an attractive and congenial affect, of being ingratiating and attentive to the interests and needs of others. The middlebrow subject, as I suggest throughout the last several chapters, was a subject oriented always to the gaze and assessment of others.

In keeping with this personalist habit of mind, reading was considered at the club as an event for identification, connection, and response. Although cognition and contemplation might enter into it, what made the experience most profoundly transformative was the act of experiencing something with greater force and fervor than one might be permitted in ordinary daily life. Accordingly the judges sought out books that would enable their readers to identify passionately with either fictional or historical characters, just as they promoted writers who could capture the attentions of their readers and prompt them to respond intensely to the peculiarities of the author's vision. A sense of absorption or connection, I think, was the state to be achieved through middlebrow reading. What the judges themselves valued and tried to provide for their subscribers was an experience of total immersion, a sense of being surrounded or embraced by a book, an act of deep reading, in the words of Henry Canby.[45] At the same time they sought heightened emotional intensity in that absorption, an experience of passionate response in literary engagement with another.

While undoubtedly an individualism, then, personalism as it was expressed at the Book-of-the-Month Club was a more social habit of mind than other forms of individualism, which tended to stress the atomism, autonomy, and independence of the singular subject. What the club's judges attempted to find, finally, for a membership that they insisted was extremely varied in its predilections and preferences, was a range of books that could alike scale modern problems to the measure of individual selves. Yet the reader was not to confront personal idiosyncrasy and particularity from a distance. Rather, she or he was to inhabit the parallel self provided by a book, to feel the way it vibrated both physically and emotionally in response to its own context, and to participate in a difference that was thereby rendered comprehensible.

The personalist ideal of connection and communion, it seems to me, was both a symptom of and a response to the isolation fostered by a modern, rationalized world carved up into discrete and different domains. Undoubtedly a further realization of the individualist and planar logic of the professional-managerial class, this personalism also functioned to counter the singularity of individuals and to meliorate their separation from one another by insisting always on their capacity for identification. At the same time, the emphasis on intensified passion and pathos counteracted the excessive rationalism and distance of the instrumental, utilitarian approach to life. It seems clear, therefore, that the affective component of the habitus constructed through this form of middlebrow reading was a way of compensating for the structural conditions and emotional costs of a professional's life. That life prescribed a pragmatic orientation to discrete tasks and tended to separate the professional from other professionals possessing other forms of expertise. At the same time, it separated her or him from those persons marked by even greater difference, that is, by their *lack* of expertise. Professionalism separated middle-class subjects from those considered beneath them in a social hierarchy. Deep reading, apparently, strove to counter the isolation produced by both kinds of boundaries.

The experience of sentiment in middlebrow culture functioned like a dream. It provided the occasion for the enactment of fundamental desires and wishes. What was desired was recognition by a literary other. What was wished for was attachment and connection to something beyond the self.[46] Indulging in sentiment enabled the reading subject to conjure momentarily the vision of a mutual, equable social relation constructed through the magic of narrative, character, and symbol and their capacity to promote identification and empathy in the reader. Thus the various components of the middlebrow habitus constructed by the Book-of-the-Month Club were never perfectly congruent with one another. In fact, the affiliative emotional style promoted by the club contradicted to a certain extent the differentiating logic it set forth. Of course the desire for affiliation was thoroughly dependent on the logic of discrimination. You cannot desire to reconnect things that have not previously been separated. My point is that though these aspects of the middlebrow habitus were mutually constitutive, they existed in a state of tension. Middlebrow culture may have prepared its subjects to take up a particular social position and to enact a specific social role, yet it may also have attempted to endow them with capacities to withstand the emotional costs of doing just that. Potentially, then, it might have encouraged habits of response and forms of desire that would place them at odds with some of the habits and expectations of their social role and location.

It is equally important to point out, however, that there may well have been limits to the kinds of connections and identifications the Book-of-the-Month Club judges could imagine or thought they could promote for their readers. This is extremely difficult to document systematically, but there is some evidence that the judges ruled out of consideration (especially as main selections) books and literatures that detailed the experiences of people thought to be too different from the white middle class that seemed to stand at the center of middlebrow culture. For instance, although the club occasionally recommended the works of writers associated with labor and the working classes, such as Clifford Odets or William Saroyan, their books were never accorded the legitimation of being made a main selection. One has to wonder, consequently, whether other, even more disturbing books were rejected as unacceptable to the membership even when they were being considered as alternates. Since none of the reader's reports from the earliest years of the club's existence survive, it is impossible to document precisely whether there were similarities in the kinds of books that were rejected. Still, a now-famous incident in the club's early history suggests that there may well have been at least tacit limits to the kinds of identifications the judges thought their subscribers could tolerate or enjoy.

In August 1939 Harper and Brothers sent a bound set of page proofs of a novel titled *Native Son* to the Book-of-the-Month Club.[47] The club's judges had already recommended novels and nonfiction focusing on "the negro experience in America," just as they had previously offered the works of African American writers as alternates. Never before, however, had they considered any of these for main selections. Several of the judges were impressed by Richard Wright's book, and they thought the time auspicious for promoting the work of what they called a "Negro writer." But they worried that a certain sexual explicitness, among other things, would offend the membership. Accordingly, the judges requested through Edward Aswell, Wright's editor at Harper, that certain changes be made in the manuscript. They wanted Wright to remove, among other things, explicit references to masturbation from a scene where Bigger Thomas and his friends watch newsreels about the beach antics of the daughters of the rich. Wright agreed to this change as well as to others (he removed all mention of a flirtatious Mary Dalton from the description of the newsreel, thereby softening his ironic depiction of the rich) and, in the process, significantly changed his portrayal of Bigger's sexuality. Surviving documents tell us little about the motives of individual judges, but they apparently informed Aswell and Wright that they hoped these changes would enable the book to reach a larger audience without offending the more conservative members within it. There were limits, apparently, to the kinds of identification middlebrow personalism could promote.

This is made even clearer by the correspondence between Dorothy Canfield Fisher and Richard Wright over the manuscript he originally titled *American Hunger* and which was eventually published in truncated form as *Black Boy*.[48] When Fisher wrote to Wright on June 29, 1944, the club had already asked Wright to shorten the manuscript significantly, and Wright had agreed in principle. Fisher was proposing further changes in language to Wright and additionally explored with him in a hesitant, apologetic tone whether he might consider suggesting in his epilogue that he had at least partly derived his passion for freedom from the basic traditions of the American nation. Fisher assured Wright that all Americans were not bigoted; some held fast, she wrote, to the principles of democracy and justice. For him to admit this and to acknowledge that "American" principles had somehow made their way to him even amidst the deep injustice he had to suffer, she added, would give succor to all those trying to hold their fellow citizens to principles of justice and liberty. Although Fisher's tone suggests that she was aware that Wright might be offended by her suggestion, her apparent understanding of and identification with whites active against racism seems to have overridden her compunctions about the request.

Wright replied subsequently that he had made the revisions Fisher had suggested, and he noted particularly that he had managed to use the word "American" at least once. He had not intentionally omitted it, he assured her, but simply had not thought to connect himself with specifically American principles because Negroes in the South were actively prevented from thinking that they stood on the same ground with white citizens of the United States. This was managed, he suggested, by the fact that most references to the national government and its principles were deleted from school textbooks in the South. He thought he had really derived his thirst for freedom from some of the writers who had critiqued the American nation, such as H. L. Mencken and Theodore Dreiser. Wright stuck to his own principled stand in his letter to Fisher despite the fact that he followed some of her suggestions. Undoubtedly those changes seemed small when the club could clearly ensure him a much larger audience for his book. After being selected by the club in 1940, *Native Son* sold 215,000 copies within three weeks.

These two interactions suggest, it seems to me, that the Book-of-the-Month Club judges may well have worried a good deal about what their subscribers could tolerate. In response they may have narrowed the range of literatures, experiences, and identifications that they offered to their middlebrow readers by rejecting books that depicted worlds too far outside the mainstream. Of course, it should be pointed out that this sort of winnowing and narrowing of the range of acceptable experience was undoubtedly also carried out at the editorial level in publishing houses themselves, in part because the people employed there had the same educational and social background as the judges. Together, then, the industry and the club may have acted to normalize certain experiences and a familiar range of legible emotion as appropriate to the professional-managerial class. In the process of promoting the kind of deep reading and engagement they believed their readers sought from books, the judges may well have acted inadvertently to control the extent to which boundaries between subjects could be dissolved or breached.

Ultimately, these multiple conflicts and contradictions raise a question about the function middlebrow culture might have performed and about the effects it might have had on the readers who consumed it so enthusiastically. Before broaching that difficult query, however, I want to return briefly to the topic of the club's rejection of literary modernism because I think a look at the grounds of that rejection will enrich our understanding of the affective experience middlebrow culture was seeking principally to avoid. Although this examination cannot provide an account of the full range of affects evoked by the Book-of-the-Month Club's many selections and alternates, it will at least tell us something more about the basic disposition middlebrow culture sought to foster in its reading subjects. We will find, I think, that under the leadership of Henry Canby the Book-of-the-Month Club judges tried very hard to steer clear of books that positioned their readers to feel certain negatively charged affects, including disgust, contempt, and shame. What they were after, finally, was a reading experience that promoted interest in an object or situation beyond the self and that dialectically evoked in the reader a sense of being recognized by another. This mutual regard in literary form created excitement, they believed, as well as hope and the possibility of commitment to the future.[49]

As I have pointed out, Henry Canby distinguished himself from people he thought of as "nay-sayers," that is, individuals who wanted to reject all of the machines and scientific advances associated with the modern era.[50] He was not, however, completely averse to cultural critique. He was quite aware of the fact that his society's materialism and utilitarianism was not a good thing, and in his evocative and elegiac personal memoir he looked back with keen appreciation for all that had been lost by the leap into the fast-paced world of the dynamo, the automobile, and the atom. Much of that memoir, which he wistfully titled *The Age of Confidence*, was devoted to tracing the distance between the discordances of the 1920s and 1930s and the era of his childhood, which he characterized as the "last epoch of American stability."[51]

It is worth a brief look at the way Canby evoked that lost world, for it was the source of his abiding interest in deep reading. Describing the peculiar serenity of his comfortable upbringing, he observed that the "feeling of a daily rhythm, in which each hour had its characteristic part, in a house where change came slowly and which was always home, nourished, if it did not create, the expectancy of our generation that the norm of life was repetition and therefore security."[52] Security, of course, sug-

{ *On the History of the Middlebrow* }

gests the image of the contented child held in reassuring embrace. Henry Canby's childhood was so reassuring and the expectations produced by the pressure of familial and community routine were so powerful that, forever after, he would find it impossible to welcome the interest and excitement of the future without feeling the grief of unalterable loss. He felt keenly the power of the modern era to propel the subject out of the reassuring hold of the social.

In fact he perfectly captured the sense of loss that pervaded all his reflections on his own era in an evocative and moving passage foreshadowing the disruption of the idyll of regularity by the forces of a more modern tempo. Attempting to describe the sensuous weight of a summer evening in the 1890s, he observed that "time moved slowly there, as it always does when there is a familiar routine with a deep background of memory." Canby recalled affectionately that the evening seemed "spacious" as a result. Even as he caught the experience of feeling securely grounded in a deep and rich expanse of familiarity, however, he chronicled its momentary disruption by the first harbinger of a newer kind of movement, a form of perpetual motion. "When bicycles came in and flocks of young people wheeled through twilight streets past and past again the porches where the elders were sitting," he observed meditatively, "it was the first breakaway from the home, a warning of the new age."[53] Although such motion was "then more like a flight of May flies round and round their hatching place," it would soon be transformed into the new rhythms of "a broken, excited syncopation, or the spondaic movement of boredom,"[54] motion insistently pressed upon a new era not by the fragile bicycle but by the more violent automobile and by the radio, the phonograph, the apartment house, and the activity of commuting.

There is a clear connection, then, between the security and stability of Henry Canby's early childhood and his subsequent search for deep feeling and a sense of continuity amidst the discontinuities and dissonances of the modern age. Indeed his ensuing valorization of the processes of identification and participation that might be achieved through reading was in part a reaction to the sense of isolation and loss produced by the distances and speed of the modern era. Canby himself understood this. In concluding his memoir, in fact, he evocatively described the sort of reading he had learned to love during that secure childhood. Surveying the literary geography of his parents' house, he recalled that one end of the family sitting room was presided over proudly by "a triple bookcase of walnut with scalloped trimmings of morocco leather below each shelf, intended to keep out the dust." Protecting the likes of Scott, Macaulay, Hawthorne, Longfellow, Dickens, the English poets, and its "foundation stone," the *Encyclopaedia Britannica*, this bookcase faced across the parlor another set of "deep shelves," which were, however, "hidden by curtains and by chairs" beneath the bay windows. "Hoarded" rather than protected there, according to Canby, was the "ephemera of the period," "yellow-backed novels, not so much hidden as withdrawn from the respectability of the room." Among the contents of those shelves, he remembered *Love in Orange Blossoms*, Rider Haggard's *She* (the only book he had ever been told not to read), Ouida, Marie Corelli, Anthony Hope, some Howells, Mrs. Humphrey Ward, and the earliest Sherlock Holmes. What is so interesting about Canby's treatment of these two literary provinces is that he refused to recognize the border between them. He liked the books in both sets of shelves and lovingly remembered the hours of contentment he spent reading many of them.[55]

In a complex and ambivalent evaluation of the significance of Sir Walter Scott, for example, whom he found in the walnut bookcase, Canby suggested that his own "deep reading" in Scott fostered in him a love for the *experience* of reading, regardless of the literary standing of the book capable of promoting it.[56] He acknowledged likewise that "from these romances so alien to our bourgeois Quaker town we drew an ethics for ideal conduct in emotional stress" and an "idea that we were to rush great-heartedly upon experience." Canby noted further that what Scott and his confreres conferred most importantly on readers of the 1890s was an ability to feel intensely.[57] As he put it, "We were all simmering with sentiment. It was precisely the sentiment that one could take over from Dickens or from Scott, according to temperament."[58] Strikingly enough, as the measured rhythms of his family upbringing forever impressed on him a longing for stability and security, so the intensity of this first acquaintance with sentiment and deep feeling created in Canby an inextinguishable desire to reexperience a particular kind of fusion with a book. Although he would go on in the chapter to register his substantial reservations about the multiple effects of this cultivated romanticism, a set of effects that included "the Spanish War, with its rather sordid imperialism, wrapped in guff about poor Cuba" and "the cult of Theodore Roosevelt," he evoked yet again, and with great appreciation, his "reading memories . . . of absorption in a book, earless, eyeless, motionless for hours, a life between covers more real than our experience."[59] Yet this experience of absorption was not to be an end in itself. Feeling was not to be indulged in for its own sake.

Canby valued from that time on a reading experience that swept the reader up in a wave of intensified emotion, overwhelming him or her, erasing any distance between author and reading subject. He continued, however, with observations about what that experience had made possible in the past. "Our reading," he recalled, "(ill chosen as it so often must have been) was neither drug nor irritant, neither revelation nor caustic. It was an extension without break of our own lives, and flowed back freely to become part of our own mentality." He continued, "For books to us were what the bards' chants were to the tribe—a recalling, an enriching, an extension of memory."[60] Henry Canby wanted to be recalled to the reassuring embrace he associated with his childhood. Books could evoke that embrace, and in so doing, he believed, they could enable the reader to project that memory of satisfaction into the future as a goal to be achieved. Memory and the sentiments it evoked were to be productive, then; they were to serve as a wellspring capable of nurturing the future.

The memory of satisfaction evoked by reading was extraordinarily important, according to Henry Canby, because the frantic pace of change in a world symbolized by the motion of bicycles, automobiles, radio broadcasts, and jazz tended to diminish the capacity to connect with what had come before in human history. He recognized modernity as a fundamental break, as a chasm opening between the past and the present. He also understood it as a condition of anonymity or distance created between individuals by the obdurate speed of disparate yet perpetual motion. Although his literary education at Yale endowed him with an appreciation for the complexities of specifically literary descent and equipped him with the perceptual capacity to identify aesthetic effects, Canby continued to value texts that yielded their fruits to the reader not so much through judgment or evaluation but through intense identification and participation. Reading, for him, was valuable to the extent that it intensified experience by promoting the transgression of boundaries not merely between individual selves but also between moments in human history.[61] Reading might serve as the bridge between past and present, as a traversible space between individuals otherwise separated by the conditions of modern life.

What Henry Canby disliked about literary modernism, then, was not its formal experimentation or its efforts to capture aesthetically the disjunctions of a syncopated age. Indeed, he could write sensitively about the linguistic play of Gertrude Stein and the strange temporalities of William Faulkner. He was not afraid of difficult texts, and he was quite capable of engaging in the strenuous reading required by modernist idiolects. He also perceptively detailed how these innovations arose as part of an effort to make sense of modern disorder. Yet Canby was distressed by the extreme distance between writer and reader that a highly idiosyncratic and demanding language like Joyce's created. He often interpreted the hermeticism of such a language as the product of an attitude of arrogance and dismissal, a move prompted by disdain for the ordinary and the commonplace and by a disrespect for the audience.

In a retrospective assessment of the literature of the 1920s and 1930s, for instance, he observed that "if there is one quality which the generation which called itself *the* literary generation and thought of itself as *the* generation lacked, it was the humility to recognize that 'in the beginning was the word' was not written for their guidance." He continued, "They dealt too much in words for each other and their ideas were often coterie ideas. They were clairvoyant but not clairvoyant enough to see the processes of minds less sensitive and less thwarted than theirs." Henry Canby disliked the contempt for all of American life exhibited by the experimentalists, and he was equally troubled by the disdain expressed by the new academic specialists for the students they were supposedly trying to address. He continued with the observation that "there was a certain arrogance in both literary and academic intellectuals which was admirable as courage, but not good for character, or for results. Humbler minds would have accepted the universe first, and then 'shot the works.' " [62] Although Canby could appreciate the achievements of the modernist narrative, he longed for a literature that would not contemptuously dismiss the world that gave rise to it; he hoped for one that, rather than push its readers away, would draw them in and invite them to participate in a joint project of reform and renewal.

Canby was also disturbed by the hollowness and the cynicism he detected in many modern stylists. "They write like sensitive typewriters," he observed, "operated by forces outside themselves." Continuing, he suggested that "they are sometimes intensely subjective, but find nothing inwards that does not shock, or confuse, or distress them." His further disapproval made it clear that he thought positive change could only come from individuals with rich internal resources. "They have no standards, no faith, no certainties, and this after the war and the depression is natural, but also no faculty of resting upon an inner confidence in their own existence as a soul and mind alive, reflective, philosophical against fate, and capable of pleasure in being and thinking in despite of circumstance." Canby concluded that what they had lost was "confidence in the possibilities of the state of being a man." [63] He put it most bluntly in another essay: "I had rather believe with the Quakers that all humanity is potentially good than run with these fellows who are obsessed with its imperfections. One conclusion is as scientific as another." [64]

Henry Canby did not disagree with the modernists' powerful critique of the instrumentalism and crass commercialism of the new, advertising age. As he put it, "After a little reading of advertisements and the stories written to accompany them, one's sympathies go out to Mssrs. Faulkner, Hemingway, et. al., who maintain that in spite of cosmetics all is not right with the world."[65] Similarly, he did not disagree with them when they argued that it was the special province of art to redeem the age by exposing its particular failings. He parted company with them, however, over how that was to be done. Renewal of the language was not enough, he suggested. Nor was a brilliant exposé of the special violence of the age. What was needed, Canby thought, was greater sympathy, a more strenuous effort to discover significance, a capacity to connect with others in the service of some larger good. Of Faulkner particularly he complained: he "has come out . . . and in the dry light of complete objectivity weighs his subjects for their pound or ounce of life with no predilection for 'ought,' with no interest in 'why,' and with no concern for significance. He is cruel and with a cool and interested cruelty, he hates his Mississippi and his Memphis and all their works, with a hatred that is neither passionate nor the result of thwarting, but calm, reasoned, and complete."[66]

It was the distance and dispassion Canby instinctively disliked. He believed that an art that produced only contempt, disgust, and shame in the reader could never do positive work in the world. It would only depress the reader further and turn him or her away from the project of renewal. What was wanting in a utilitarian and wholly instrumentalist age, he believed, was an appreciation for beauty and sentiment and a willingness to engage with others. Henry Canby believed implicitly in the worth of the individual human subject, and he understood that subject as one characterized most fundamentally by a capacity for warmth, passion, and commitment. Art, he believed, should promote precisely those qualities and feelings as a way of generating interest in the world.

Henry Canby preferred the modernism of someone like Vachel Lindsay, whom he characterized as "rapt, enthusiastic, fixed in his loyalties and his inspirations, . . . at the opposite spiritual edge from the intellectualism and verbal refinements of the modernists in poetry."[67] He suggested as well that the novel and the drama needed "to return to their age-long privilege of giving to the individual an intenser sense of his own reality in a society which is always trying to make him a number and a type." This is essential, he suggested, because "our modern societies require social control, they can subsist only by mass production, can be educated only by mass methods, can become civilized only by a beneficent standardization of the instruments of culture." He concluded decisively, "Literature and mystical religion, the first for the many, the second for the few who take their religion that way, will thus become the safeguards of such individualism as is essential if we are to socialize without depersonalizing the world. For it is the tiny flame of self-realization, self-respect, and self-expression kept alight by religion and literature which makes the individual worth collectivizing."[68] Sentiment, for Henry Canby, was not a sign of smug self-indulgence. Rather, it was a tool for promoting connection between an individual and her or his world, between an individual and another. He held out great hope that, in producing the affects of interest and enjoyment, acts of deep reading would transform individuals and push them to reconstruct the secure and reassuring hold of a welcoming community.

The Book-of-the-Month Club was devoted, finally, to an understanding of reading and writing as intensely individual yet oddly social affairs, as affairs of the heart as much as of the mind. Harry Scherman's judges attended carefully to the experiences and pleasures of reading rather than to the inherent properties and intrinsic value of books themselves. As Henry Canby put it, "Reading for experience is the only reading that justifies excitement. Reading for facts is necessary but the less said about it in public the better. Reading for distraction is like taking medicine. We do it, but it is nothing to be proud of. But reading for experience is transforming. Neither man nor woman is ever quite the same again after the experience of a book that enters deeply into life."[69] In the literary world inhabited by Henry Canby and his colleagues, the particular reading pleasures of immersion, interested investment, and recognition were construed as utopian because of their capacity to set desires in motion and their ability to incite hope in readers of books.

## CLUB MEMBERSHIP AND THE FUNCTIONS

### OF MIDDLEBROW READING

Who actually bought the books selected by the judges and sent out under the imprimatur of Book-of-the-Month Club? Were they the laboring masses, as the club's critics seemed to suggest, or were they already members of the middle class, as the judges' evaluative logic implies? And will knowledge of the demographic characteristics of the club's subscribers tell us anything about whether they were as intent on pursuing the pleasures of deep reading as the judges? Were the subscribers searching for experiences of immersion and connection, or were they more pragmatically focused on the particular contents of individual books? How many of them, in fact, even read the books themselves? Might the club's subscribers have absorbed the professionalist logic responsible for the shape of the selections as a whole just by reading the catalog? Or, in reading actual titles, might they have been deeply changed and influenced by the judges' preference for books that evoked intense affect? It is nearly impossible to answer any of these questions with any degree of certainty. Extensive data about the early membership of the Book-of-the-Month Club has not survived. Consequently, it is hard to know which of the contradictory impulses embedded in the organization's operations had a long-term impact on the club's subscribers. Still, because the questions are at once important and intriguing, and because some details about the club's members have been preserved in the oral history interviews and in comments by club officials, I think it worth a brief look at what we do know about the early subscribers to the Book-of-the-Month Club.

The best discussion of the first subscribers is contained in the Columbia University oral history interview with Edith Walker, who oversaw the process of acquiring new members. Significantly, Walker noted that the lists that worked best for her were "quality lists" with people who had "a better than fair income, some culture and [were] mail-order-minded." She added as well that "a mailing list of lawyers will surely flop. However, if I send only to members of the Bar Association, that's a different story. A compiled list of business executives, or people who own a fifty thousand dollar home, or those who own a Cadillac or live on a certain side of the street, never works. There is no selectivity in such lists. They have to have something other than a large income." [70]

Although it is difficult to say for sure exactly what that "something other" was, it seems clear that a significant portion of the club membership was composed of well-educated, economically successful individuals who also happened to place a high premium on culture and who were willing to spend both money and time on its acquisition and display. The very first list circularized by the Book-of-the-Month Club was the New York Social Register. Subsequently, university alumni lists proved productive. [71] Yet Walker's significant observation that only some well-positioned and well-educated individuals signed on suggests that the club may not have drawn well from those portions of the middle and upper classes richest in economic capital and therefore in control of financial institutions and the production apparatus. Rather, the club seems to have appealed to that fraction whose social position was based on its command of cultural and intellectual capital, on a certain acquaintance with the cultural tradition and a measure of specialized knowledge and expertise.

This sort of reader, in fact, may well have been Scherman's general reader, an individual once described by Henry Canby as "the average intelligent reader, who has passed through the usual formal education in literature, who reads books as well as newspapers and magazines, who, without calling himself a litterateur, would be willing to assert that he was fairly well read and reasonably fond of good reading. Your doctor, your lawyer, the president of your bank, and any educated business man who has not turned his brain into a machine will fit my case."[72] Although Harry Scherman claimed in his interview at Columbia that within the membership "there was an astonishing number, a good-sized proportion, found by Gallup in one of his surveys, of girls, secretaries, career girls," he also recognized that after the first few years the club "appealed very largely to university graduates, or people who weren't graduates but who had decided leanings in a cultural direction, and that these were youngish people, married people in their middle thirties—or early forties—who suddenly began to realize that they were more or less vegetating intellectually."[73]

Later the club appealed to a significant number of teachers and educators. Charles Lee reported, in fact, that a 1958 survey showed that 13 percent of the club's 500,000 members were teachers.[74] Of that 13 percent, 4 percent were elementary school teachers, 5 percent were high school or preparatory school teachers, and another 4 percent were teachers in colleges and universities. Similarly, in reporting statistics from surveys conducted in the years between 1947 and 1958, Lee notes that after 1949 only about 20 percent of the club membership had no college experience at all. Unfortunately he does not indicate whether the remaining 80 percent had graduated from college or attended for a few years only. Still, even with this spotty information, it seems plausible to suggest that the club drew its membership from the broad reaches of the professional-managerial class. Some of those individuals already commanded a certain amount of technical expertise—the doctors, the lawyers, the dentists, and the college professors. Their social position within this new class of knowledge workers was therefore probably fairly assured. Others, however, the more generalist elementary and high school teachers and those who lacked college experience, may actually have been aspiring to this class position or making an effort to establish a more secure hold on it. Positioned at the periphery of this new class by their only partial command of cultural and intellectual capital, they may have desired book club membership as a strategy for acquiring more of the knowledge they valued and as a way to display that knowledge publicly. What they wanted, it seems, was a way to

{ *On the History of the Middlebrow* }

demonstrate their worthiness as potential candidates for inclusion in the more visible group of managers and professionals.

It is impossible to determine whether other factors positioned a significant portion of the club's membership at the edges of this developing class or class fraction. No information survives, for example, about the ethnic composition of the Book-of-the-Month Club membership or about its religious preferences. Nor do we know anything significant about the race of the club's subscribers, although it is fair to say from a perusal of other documents like the letters to Richard Wright that the judges, at least, believed the membership to be almost wholly white. We do know that more women than men belonged to the Book-of-the-Month Club. Indeed, in the years between 1947 and 1958, female membership hovered around 60 percent. Although club officials tried to explain this by suggesting that wives joined for their husbands and families, it may also have been the case that women saw a book club subscription as a way to declare their membership in a class or class fraction where social status was generally pegged to public command of a professional position.

In any case, it seems plausible to suggest on the basis of this information that the Book-of-the-Month Club may have been engaged in the business of class consolidation in two distinct ways. It may have functioned to promote identification with the point of view of the professional-managerial class among individuals poised at the outer reaches of that group. Not yet possessing the extensive educational credentials that would certify their own command of technical expertise and professional authority, subscribers constrained by their gender, ethnicity, religious identification, or even by their race might have used the club as a way to add to their resources and to pass on to their children a certain attitude toward culture and education. In that case the implicit cognitive map and the tutelage in proper comportment offered by the club might have been even more important than any particular monthly selection. For those aspiring to inclusion in the ranks of the new professional elite, the club's middlebrow culture may have served as a complex pedagogy in subjectivity. In effect it may have functioned as a commercially available course in how to construct and manage a self appropriate to a fast-changing form of capitalist society, a society increasingly dependent not on manufacturing brawn but on the circulation of goods and both economic and cultural capital. Membership in the Book-of-the-Month Club may have served as a means, or at least a publicly enacted wish, to demonstrate one's support for the rule of knowledge, information, and expertise.

On the other hand, for the doctors, dentists, lawyers, professors, and managers who clearly composed a significant portion of the membership, the club's particular selections may have helped to consolidate their faith in a specific set of values and assumptions about the world. If we assume that some of them actually read the books they bought, perusal of title after title in a range of different categories, all of which insisted on the worth of the personalist subject and the importance of sympathetic identification between individuals, may have validated their desire to believe that the universe was not spinning out of control. Their reading may have assured them that their world was still centered—and centered in a way that they understood. At the same time, the club's emphasis on a characteristic middlebrow habitus and style may have offered subscribers like these the opportunity to consolidate, in the sense of firming up or redundantly emphasizing, their own sense of themselves as people with an assured and demonstrably successful way of negotiating change. It may have provided them with yet one more arena in which to adopt the stance or disposition of the knowledgeable subject, a person confident in the face of alterity and hopeful in the face of the unknown.

In the case of either kind of subscriber, it appears that the club very likely functioned to consolidate belief in the worth of technical expertise and the value of knowledge more generally. It may have operated, then, to manufacture consent to the rule of the expert and the specialist. It seems to have functioned as a key supporting agency in the construction of the hegemony of the new professional-managerial class.[75] Still, it is worth pointing out again that despite its reliance on a planar logic of organization and evaluation and its modeling of a characteristic middlebrow style, the Book-of-the-Month Club's approach to cultural materials exhibited important tensions. Those tensions, it seems to me, may have opened a space that enabled some subscribers to respond to the materials they acquired from the club in idiosyncratic and potentially discrepant ways.

Despite their celebration of culture, knowledge, and information, for example, the club and its judges also expressed an implicit ambivalence about the way those forms of expertise were to be exhibited. They only applauded experts who tried to marshal their technical competence in the service of others. The judges condemned and dismissed those who protected their knowledge by hoarding it within an arcane jargon available only to a few. Similarly, they excluded books that seemed to express contempt for those not in the know by pursuing insular concerns and issues of interest to only a small coterie of well-informed specialists. They praised popularizers who wanted to share their special expertise and who therefore offered it in comprehensible and manageable form to a general audience. It is possible that some subscribers may have been more influenced by the support for popularization than by the expertise it was grounded on. They may therefore have developed a sense that it was important to distribute knowledge broadly and to see to it that it circulated widely. This could have developed into an allegiance more dedicated to those dependent on the expertise of specialists and to their interests rather than to the interests of the specialists themselves. In some cases, when supported by influences from elsewhere in the culture, that may even have contributed to a subscriber's subsequent propensity to question the worth of expert knowledge itself and a capacity to see it as the agent of a highly interested bourgeois class. It may even have developed into the kind of anticapitalist critique that developed among some members of the professional-managerial class.

Similarly, a certain ambivalence was expressed at the club about the segregated and isolated worlds of expertise that made up the universe as seen by the professional-managerial class. On one hand the judges' logic of categorization and relative evaluation respected the segregation and autonomy of those various domains. On the other hand their constant search for sentiment, emotion, empathy, and the dissolution of boundaries functioned as a protest of the effects of carving up the world in such a way and as a kind of refuge from it. Neither like the class of people who employed them nor at home with those they were positioned to address, the professionalized subscribers of the club may have felt isolated in their little duchies of distinction and may have longed to connect with others on a level other than the abstract and intellectual. At odds even with their own colleagues by virtue of their need to compete and excel in their individual arenas, these new experts may have been constituted as much by their desires as by their privileged educations. To lose themselves in the heightened detail of a historical novel or the fully realized world of a fine literary biography might have provided vicariously a sense of being at home in a communal embrace that was hard to come by in daily life. At the same time, it may well have suggested to people who knew only one little corner of the world in any depth that unity of knowledge was still possible, that the world made sense in the end even if it had to be parsed according to the authority of the Book-of-the-Month Club.

The judges' characteristic emphasis on an affectively ordered personalism may have enabled some subscribers to use the books they purchased to question the advisability of separating science from philosophy, literature from medicine, music from mathematics, politics from art—pleasure from cognition. Similarly, it may have cultivated in them a strong and unsatisfied longing for connection and communion, a desire, too, that could have been encouraged and built on by other political developments in the period such as the successes of the labor movement, the increased movement of women into the paid labor force, or the incipient beginnings of the modern civil rights movement. Still, in helping to cultivate an intensely desiring subject—a multiple, mobile, and multilayered subject with porous, fluid boundaries open not only to others but to the object world as well—the middlebrow culture dispensed by the club may also have succeeded in producing a peculiarly modern subject, the subject-for-the-commodity. It may have contributed to the formation of an individual happy to take up a position crucial to the functioning of the growing consumer economy, that is, the position of a subject incomplete until he or she could express the self through an elaborated language of objects.

These multiple tensions and contradictions make it exceedingly difficult to describe in the abstract what sort of effects the Book-of-the-Month Club and the middlebrow culture it promoted had on subscribers. Individual subscribers may have responded to the contrary tendencies embedded in the general format of the club in different ways. The manner in which they took up middlebrow culture and made use of it in the context of their daily lives may have been significantly affected by the particular selections they made from among the club's listed offerings. Individual subscribers tailored their selections to their own interests. They may have reinforced the impulse to specialization by reading only popular history or public affairs, or in reading more eclectically they may have pursued a desire to see relations and connections asserted. Though the logic and assumptions used by the judges to evaluate many different titles exhibited the kinds of regularities I have detailed here, those thousands of books should never be reduced to a single set of schematic selection principles. The books themselves were internally complex, complicated, and often contradictory, and they were different from one another. As a consequence, it is exceedingly difficult to say with any confidence just how subscribers may have responded to the particular collection of books they received through the mail courtesy of Harry Scherman, Henry Canby, Dorothy Canfield Fisher, and the others at the Book-of-the-Month Club.

Still, the inquiry interests me because it raises a key question. What do people actually *do* with books? Can the idiosyncratic use they make of them actually counter or contest the dominant ideological tendencies others see in them? As a way of pursuing this inquiry further, I turn in Part III to some of the books actually sent out by the Book-of-the-Month Club. I reexamine some of the titles recommended by the Book-of-the-

Month Club in the late 1950s and early 1960s, titles that were passed on to me in 1963 by Mr. Shymansky, the Cresskill High School librarian. In effect I return to the questions I posed at the end of Part I. I attempt a provisional account of the hopes and constraints that those books, coming from an organization with this history, offered to me in the form of a middlebrow cultural endowment.

# PART THREE

# Books for Professionals

## CHAPTER NINE

# A Library of Books for the Aspiring Professional

## Some Effects of Middlebrow Reading

### A MORE INTIMATE HISTORY

My encounter with the Book-of-the-Month Club in 1963 had everything to do with the expansion of the professional-managerial class in the decade or so after World War II. I was part of a family that might otherwise not have been able to endow its children with professional aspirations. Although both my parents had attended college, my mother had been discouraged by her family from finishing her degree, and my father had only managed to complete his course of study in the new field of business administration with the assistance of the GI Bill. When he eventually finished, his degree enabled him to find positions in new industries associated with the postwar economy's structural need for a much larger group of people who could labor with their minds rather than their hands. As the child of such parents, I was taught to value books and to aspire to some form of intellectual work. I was a perfect candidate, then, for Mr. Shymansky's reading advice and for the Book-of-the-Month Club books he recommended. It is easy to see why I was so deeply affected by them.

In the years after the war, as more raw economic power was converted to the task of producing consumer goods in the United States, more individuals were required to manage the coordination of production with consumption. At the same time, many more professionals and knowledge workers were necessary to circulate the huge quantities of information so essential to an integrated consumer economy.[1] Like so many returning GIs, my father seized on the shimmering promise of white-collar work and eagerly took up the offer of a free university education, an education he could not otherwise afford. He pursued his degree in business administration at New York University's evening college and eventually parlayed his diploma into entry-level jobs, first in the booming television business and then in the fledgling civilian air industry. My brother and I were particularly proud of his connection to Capital Air Lines and to the glamorous and exotic business of air travel. We thought it marked us somehow as particularly well suited to the promises of the future.[2] We were, I suppose, but not so much by our father's starched white collars as by a whole set of changes in middle-class schooling in the 1950s. As baby boomers, we were coached incessantly in test taking by a new battery of achievement tests, lined up in college-prep classrooms, and goaded on by Sputnik-inspired fears that Russia would outdo the United States in technical proficiency, scientific achievement, and international political success if we American kids did not do better in school and aspire to a college education.[3]

By the time those Book-of-the-Month Club books arrived in my room, I had already been identified as appropriate material for accelerated high school classes by an ability to follow the rules, to answer appropriately when called on, and to produce the requisite assignments when asked. Although I read a lot on my own, what I read with enormous zeal were Archie comics, Nancy Drew mysteries (every one of them, and in order no less), *Seventeen*, various movie magazines, the Hardy Boys, and an odd lot of biographies from the Englewood Public Library. Apparently when I entered the hospital for scoliosis surgery in September of my freshman year, I already felt bound for college, for I was teased by the anesthesiologist after the first operation that I had bragged to everyone, as the gas took effect, that I was going to Barnard. Even then, I think, my brother called me a snob.

In any case I was thrilled to be singled out for attention by the school librarian, and so, during long, preternaturally silent mornings in a neighborhood deserted by my friends, who had swirled off as a group to the new high school at 7:45, I opened book after book and, in the words of novelist Richard Powers, "climbed down through the portable portals, everyone an infallible *Blue Guide* to a parallel place, unsuspected, joining the town and just at hand."[4] For me, reading was a lifeline, what Powers calls "narrative therapy" and "the cure of interlocking dreams." Fear and loneliness grafted me to those books and made of them routes to new worlds. For me, as for the past judges and the present-day editors at the Book-of-the-Month Club, those books rendered me "earless, eyeless, motionless for hours"; they left me feeling "swept away." Ultimately they left me with a passion for deep reading and enriched too, as Henry Canby had once been, by the idea that in the future I was "to rush great-heartedly upon experience."

Still, when my year at home was over, I was thrilled to be released from my private plaster prison. I returned to school and, with the kind of exuberant ingratitude only a child can afford, returned the last box of books to the library and decisively put them behind me. I remembered only the love of reading in the abstract. I cast about through high school and college for a way to fashion a life with books. My parents always thought I would end up running a bookstore, but for the longest time I could find no way to imagine a working life focused by reading. As it had for Henry Canby, then, teaching presented itself as the only solution, a solution, I have to confess, I took up somewhat grudgingly. The job certainly was not as glamorous as that of archaeologist or nuclear physicist or journalist, all professions I had tried on improbably and in fantasy at one time or another in answer to the question of what I wanted to do when I finished college. Eventually, when I wandered as an undergraduate into Dr. Russel Nye's university course "Literary Realism and Naturalism" and listened to him relate story after story about his own curious quest to unearth America's popular culture of the 1880s and 1890s, I realized for the first time that you could make a career of reading. College teaching was a job like any other. It could be aspired to and learned. At that point, like Henry Canby, and with no more of a call to teaching than he had, I "slipped" into the profession of academic English.

Only now, after years of trying to understand the differences between the high literature celebrated in those university classrooms and that earlier collection of books that had set me on this path in the first place, have I begun to wonder about the particular stories those middlebrow books told. What narratives of desire did they construct? What possibilities did they pry open in the future? What might they have contributed to my ability to be open to the example set by Dr. Nye? What exactly was the connection between middlebrow reading and the aspirations of an emerging professional? I return to Mr. Shymansky's boxes, then, and to some of the books they contained with new eyes and new goals. I want to open them again in order to examine some of the books I read in 1963 and 1964, all of which were sent out by the Book-of-the-Month Club in the years between 1950 and 1963. I want to do so in an effort to explore the possibility of a connection between the substance of middlebrow culture and the appetites, motives, and limitations of a new class fraction as it consolidated its control over the country's culture and defined, at least for a time, its purposes and direction.[5]

There is a problem, of course, in presenting myself as a representative here, whether of Book-of-the-Month Club subscribers or as a member of the professional-managerial class. I am well aware that it would be risky to claim too much for my readings either in 1963 or now, in 1996. To be sure, only a small percentage of individuals who read regularly with the Book-of-the-Month Club either held or went on to jobs as literary academics or professionals. Their reading may have been very different from my own, not least because their personal situation and needs may have been a good deal less extreme than mine. Additionally, they probably selected their own books from the club catalog without the mediating advice of an additional literary professional like the librarian who assisted me. At the same time, by virtue of my training and now long experience with the professional practice of interpretation, it may be impossible for me to access, recover, or reproduce the kind of reading I did in 1963 or that might have been done by professional people with no special expertise in the field of literature or in the business of reading. This is an imaginative exercise, clearly, born at once of a private need to remember and of the more professionally driven desire to understand what the particular mix of books sent out by the Book-of-the-Month Club over the years might have conveyed to its readers.

I offer the readings that follow cautiously, then—in a reflective spirit and in an experimental mode—as a story only about one middle-class girl's encounter with the literary field of the 1950s as it was surveyed and mapped out for her by the Book-of-the-Month Club and a school librarian. Much more research will need to be done to see whether there is anything in this encounter representative of others' engagement with the club and the middlebrow culture it dispensed with such self-confidence and alacrity during this period. Even that will be difficult, however, because few records survive from this period or others, either in club archives or elsewhere, that might tell us more about what individual subscribers actually made of the books they bought. Still, it is worth making a start, since spotty information does survive about the position of the Book-of-the-Month Club during the postwar years and about its relationship to its membership.

## THE BOOK-OF-THE-MONTH CLUB

### IN THE POSTWAR YEARS

The years after World War II were those of the Book-of-the-Month Club's greatest prominence, influence, and success. It was such a well-known institution that it was accorded extraordinary publicity and attention in a number of different venues. In 1947, for instance, the advertising industry publication *Advertising & Selling* featured "Why the Book Clubs Are Successful," an article by Maxwell Sackheim, one of the club's founding partners. The article focused in particular on the invention of the negative option, on the way it enabled the clubs to "capitaliz[e] on human inertia in building business" and on the potential adaptability of this key device to other business operations.[6] That same year the *Atlantic Monthly* featured an article by Henry Seidel Canby titled "How the Book-of-the-Month Club Began."[7] Obviously designed to provide the *Atlantic*'s readers with insight into the history of an admired enterprise, Canby's article openly acknowledged the usual criticisms of the club but went on to justify the good work the organization did on behalf of a larger cause. He wrote, "In all my experience as a teacher, a writer, a critic, and an editor, I have never had so satisfactory a sense of accomplishment in what our ancestors would have called the furtherance of good literature as in my more than twenty years on the Book-of-the-Month Club." He admitted that "I could have got more academic prestige, perhaps more intellectual prestige, if I had given all my time to a professorship or to the editing of a literary journal obviously not run to make money." "But," he concluded, "the conviction of superior long-term usefulness . . . remains."[8]

Despite Canby's own sense of satisfaction and the corroborating approval that came from other quarters, the book clubs' relationship to the bookselling industry remained unsettled as late as the 1950s, and this, too, contributed to extensive publicity. In fact, during the years immediately after the war a number of different questions were argued before the Federal Trade Commission (FTC), including the issues of whether the book clubs' cut rates were in restraint of trade and whether the dividends offered to new members were actually free. But even as these complaints were reviewed by the FTC and the courts, Harry Scherman and other club officials were honored at a dinner given by the Booksellers' League of New York on the occasion of the club's twenty-fifth anniversary. At that dinner in 1951 Scherman gave a long address explaining his thinking about bookselling and argued, once again, that club operations only increased sales throughout the trade. Evidently his opinion was shared at least by some, for in August of that year, in an article reporting the FTC action, *Time* noted that "privately, most booksellers admit that the clubs have often helped their business over the past 25 years."[9]

Eventually the clubs were exonerated of all charges after a number of different and contradictory decisions, including a negative pronouncement by the U.S. Court of Appeals for the Second Circuit in New York

City that peculiarly observed of the Book-of-the-Month Club, "We think it proper to note that, in the circumstances, the petitioner's practices, although they have been validly prohibited for the future, involved no moral impropriety." [10] Scherman apparently was considered a man of integrity even when his organization was under legal attack. The negative decision was finally rescinded in 1953 when the FTC relaxed its previous definition of "free" and thereby allowed the clubs to advertise as they wished.

At that point the Book-of-the-Month Club seems to have achieved a certain stature as a significant cultural institution. Indeed, only shortly thereafter, in 1956, the Columbia Oral History Project began the process of interviewing all of the principals in the organization. Four years later Harry Scherman gave an invitational address before the Library of Congress in which he estimated that, together, the book clubs had distributed more than 700 million books, "double the number of books in all the public and university libraries in the United States, plus those on the shelves of this immense institution." [11] While that fact may have been cause for celebration at the Library of Congress and prompted other large libraries such as those at the University of Chicago and the University of Minnesota to subscribe to the club, in other arenas it continued to promote grave concern. [12] That same year, in fact, Dwight MacDonald published his diatribe against masscult and midcult in *Partisan Review*, noting that "midcult is the Book-of-the-Month Club, which since 1926 has been supplying its members with reading matter of which the best that can be said is that it could be worse." [13] Apparently the club was so successful in establishing itself as a key cultural mediator in these years that it warranted renewed and even more vituperative criticism from writers such as MacDonald and Clement Greenberg and from the increasing numbers of literature professors whose cultural authority it challenged.

The postwar period witnessed significant expansion and diversification at the Book-of-the-Month Club as Scherman and his partners decided to build on earlier efforts to broaden the scope of the material they offered. In 1950, for example, they created the Children's Record Guild and then expanded further in 1954 with something they called the Music Appreciation Records. Designed specifically as "a kind of home university course in the appreciation of fine music," this venture drew on the talents of Scherman's son Thomas, who was the founder and conductor of the Little Orchestra Society of New York. In 1956 Scherman added the Metropolitan Opera Record Club as well. During the 1950s the Book-of-the-Month Club also added a Young Readers of America Club as a way of capitalizing on the sudden explosion in children's book sales fueled, of course, by the baby boom. Like others in the industry, Scherman hoped that the children he reached with his new books might subsequently develop into lifelong readers and book purchasers. Evidently, given the organization's overall success, he assumed that the club would be around for a long time, since, according to Charles Lee, a duplicate of the organization's subscription list was preserved in "a special bank vault in Northern New Jersey specifically maintained against the possibility of atomic destruction of the company's regular records."[14]

As I have already shown in Chapter 8, it is difficult to reconstruct a detailed picture of the club membership at any moment in its history. Drawing on the aforementioned report done by the club in 1958, Charles Lee's *The Hidden Public* gives the best account of who might have belonged to the club in the postwar years. Suggesting that "one outstanding characteristic of club members is that they are a very well educated segment of the population," the report noted that 68 percent of the members had attended some college and that "a large proportion of the members are members of the professions and are influential persons in their communities." The market researchers added that two-thirds of club subscribers were married, 65 percent were women, and 40 percent lived in communities of less than 10,000 people.[15] The average member was in her thirties, and 29 percent of the club's membership was drawn from the mid-Atlantic states, including New York, New Jersey, Pennsylvania, Delaware, Maryland, West Virginia, and Washington, D.C.

In 1958 my own parents were thirty-six years old. They lived in Bergen County, New Jersey, in a New York suburb of some 8,000 people. Neither were employed in the traditional professions, nor were they members of the club, in part, my mother suggests, because they considered themselves unable to afford the kind of financial commitment required by the Book-of-the-Month Club. Aside from this economic limitation, though, they were apparently much like the average members of the club. Club members joined, according to Dr. Ernest Dichter, who wrote "A Psychological Analysis of the Sales and Advertising Problems of the Book-of-the-Month Club," "primarily because it permitted them to state publicly that they were book readers and were interested in intellectual matters."[16] My mother made a similar statement by driving us every week to a library three towns and twenty minutes away. As I recall, no other family in our development made this particular kind of effort. So even if I did not officially receive the club's selections by mail, I was at least educated to value books and culture much as Scherman's subscribers evidently were. No wonder I fantasized regularly about the four free books I would choose if I could join the Book-of-the-Month Club. Small surprise as well that I responded with delight when my mother unpacked Mr. Shymansky's first box and stacked those weighty, gaily-covered volumes by my bedside table. I took my time paging though them. I examined their covers. I read their jacket blurbs and looked at their illustrations. Eventually, without knowing I was reading Book-of-the-Month Club selections and alternates, I began to read.

I cannot remember exactly what I read first, nor can I reconstruct the order in which I read those books. The titles I never forgot, though, and which even now I remember most vividly were *Gods, Graves, and Scholars*; *Marjorie Morningstar*; *Kon-Tiki*; *Advise and Consent*; *To Kill a Mockingbird*; *The Bull from the Sea*; *The Wall*; *Nectar in a Sieve*; *The Rise and Fall of the Third Reich*; *Shakespeare of London*; and *The Ugly American*.[17] These are the titles I can recall mentioning to others over the years or remember thinking about even before I became involved in this project on the Book-of-the-Month Club. But I also now remember receiving and reading from Mr. Shymansky (in no particular order) *The Guns of August*; *Fail-Safe*; *Hawaii*; *Black Like Me*; *Mila 18*; *The Making of the President, 1960*; *Lust for Life*; *The President's Lady*; *The Agony and the Ecstasy*; *A Separate Peace*; *Act One*; *Anatomy of a Murder*; *Please Don't Eat the Daisies*; *Day of Infamy*; *The Egg and I*; *The Old Man and the Sea*; *The Day Lincoln Was Shot*; *A Stillness at Appomattox*; *My Cousin Rachel*; *Death Be Not Proud*; *Cry, the Beloved Country*; and *Inside Africa*. That year I also read *Our Hearts Were Young and Gay*, *Rebecca*, *Oliver Wiswell*, several other historical novels by Kenneth Roberts, and *Cheaper by the Dozen*—Book-of-the-Month Club books all, but selected at earlier dates.[18]

Although I eventually want to consider some of these books individually and to read them again for what they reveal about my adolescent, preprofessional desires, it seems essential to look at them, first, as a middlebrow library. Indeed Dichter's research revealed that the typical Book-of-the-Month Club subscriber joined the club not so much to acquire any particular title but to begin the process of assembling a home library. When subscribers talk of books in connection with the Book-of-the-Month Club, Dichter reported to Harry Scherman and the other partners, "they show much more interest in and place more importance on accumulating an extensive amount and wide variety of books than they do on the single selections."[19] They joined, Dichter found, because the club enabled them to assemble their own personal library of books that they could be proud of and that they could present to their children as a hedge against growing social complexity and historical uncertainty. When Mr. Shymansky selected this particular group of titles, then, and sent them to me, he was doing nothing out of the ordinary. He was picking a few good books from a wide range of titles offered by the Book-of-the-Month Club, and he was passing them on to a bookish child who he thought might enjoy reading them for entertainment and education. It is worth pausing to think, then, about the kind of education this particular library provided in tandem with the particular pleasures it afforded.

## THE CLUB'S MIDDLEBROW LIBRARY

This time the boxes of books come from the Duke University library. As I unpack them, I notice, first, that virtually every one is well thumbed and heavily used. Many are stained with food and water, and virtually all have multiple, turned-down corners, marking pauses in past readings. Some have inscriptions from loved ones; others include nameplates and donation cards, suggesting that their owners presented them to the university as gifts. Many are reinforced with heavy canvas tape. Others are underlined and filled with college students' anxious notes and exhortations. A few even hide evidence of more idiosyncratic and imaginative readings. Page 24 of *To Kill a Mockingbird*, for instance, is exuberantly marked up with green ink. In fact, every *o* is filled in with green, and at the bottom of the page the happy artist has scrawled, "Pot is Good." This copy, number two of the four the university owns, is also heavily marked up by someone who obviously used it to give a dramatic reading or to construct a script for a dramatic presentation. The condition of this particular library of books suggests, then, that many other readers perused these pages at the same time I did, and even well after. In fact an old due-date slip indicates that this particular copy of *The Ugly American* was last checked out in 1992.

The books are additionally striking because so many are astonishingly long and consequently very heavy. *The Rise and Fall of the Third Reich* extends over 1,245 pages. *Marjorie Morningstar, Advise and Consent, The Wall, Hawaii, Stillness at Appomattox, Exodus,* and *The Agony and the Ecstasy* are all more than 500 pages. Perhaps Mr. Shymansky thought a girl with nothing to do and no place to go would have to be patient enough to wend her way through leisurely stories and nearly endless historical narratives. But when I compare these particular books to the rest of the material sent out by the club between 1950 and 1963 as announced in the *Book-of-the-Month Club News*, it is clear that the club exhibited a similar preference for very long books. Indeed, the club constantly admitted in their reports that, though their books were long, they were "exciting," "compelling," and "fast-paced." Of William Shirer's monumental tome on Nazi Germany, for example, the *News* acknowledged, "Perhaps *The Rise and Fall of the Third Reich* is too long (it must run to 500,000 words or more); there are sequences—for instance, in the material dealing with the outbreak of the war—where Mr. Shirer has so much to say that he entangles himself in a thicket of footnotes." But, the author of the report reassured subscribers, "these items do not . . . detract from the worth of the book as a whole. . . . It reads like a murder mystery (which, in a sense, it indeed is), and I found it gripping on almost every page." [20]

Whether this preference for length and obvious heft was simply another version of the club's long-standing interest in "bulk culture" or the product of the peculiar taste of the 1950s judges is difficult to say. Given the fact that a huge number of the books rejected by the club during this period were just as long as those they selected, it seems plausible that the phenomenon of the very long book may have been a product of the larger culture's effort to encompass and corral an ever-more-complex society apparently wheeling into incoherence in the post–World War II era. [21] In any case, what does seem clear is that this particular library of books suggests now, as it must have in the 1950s, that the world is an enormously intricate, rich, multilayered, and complicated place and, whether imaginary or actual, can only be adequately rendered through careful detail and at considerable length.

In this regard it is striking to note that many of these books are also bound with endpapers featuring maps and incredibly involved family trees. *Hawaii*, for example, provides two maps—one of the islands themselves and one charting "The Coming of the Peoples"—as well as genealogical charts of the relationships among the principal characters, who total more than two hundred. *Guns of August* provides maps of the western and eastern fronts during World War I; Shirer's book charts Hitler's "Bloodless" and "Military" conquests; *Kon-Tiki* sports a map tracking not only Thor Heyerdahl's balsa-wood raft but also the supposed routes of sweet potatoes and stone statues of pyramids as they made their way across the Pacific from Peru to Polynesia. Even *Shakespeare of London* tries to situate the reader within its internal world by locating in Shakespeare's London establishments such as Gresham College, Bishopsgate, The Globe and The Rose theaters, and the Royal Exchange. This library, then, like the 1950s-style elementary school classrooms I knew so well, with their heavy canvas maps on rollers almost impossible to work, tries hard to place its

{ *Books for Professionals* }

inquiring readers in successfully surveyed, fully captioned, and therefore comprehensible universes. Indeed, I recall poring over these many book maps with fascination and trying to enliven their flat, abstract space with the people and events about which I was reading.

Examining this library again, I am struck by how many of the books anxiously take on topical issues and current concerns. This is true even of the fiction. World War II is here in depth and endless detail; so, too, is the Holocaust. The books also focus insistently on "the communist threat" and on "the race question." Although the latter phrase is used most commonly in the books to demarcate the changing position of African Americans in the United States, it is also clear from this particular library that, at the Book-of-the-Month Club, the race question encompassed the problem of other dark-skinned peoples who occupied the "teeming" countries of India, China, and Africa. Although I did not see this at the time, these books seem to me now to be deeply involved in the ongoing project of reconstructing whiteness in the face of a threat posed by peoples who could no longer be ignored or fully controlled by the apparatuses of colonial administration and domination. While the books tend to mark a position on the race question that would have been called liberal at the time and exhibit a complexity I will come back to in discussing particular titles, it should be noted that they always presume a white, first world, relatively privileged reader, a person "responsibly concerned" about the "swarming Asiatic [and African] poor." [22]

When I compare Mr. Shymansky's small selection with the larger library chosen and sent out by the Book-of-the-Month Club, it is clear that topicality is the most insistent feature of both collections. In addition to the war, the Holocaust, communism, and race relations, the club's larger library features a tenacious preoccupation with the atom bomb and its consequences. It also shows fascination with contemporary advances in science, including the development of the computer, and with the changing nature of social relations, including work and the world of the corporation. Finally, it displays a slowly dawning concern with women's burgeoning unrest and growing ambitions. The Book-of-the-Month Club's middlebrow library, then, relentlessly advances the proposition that the first work of literacy and print is the business of making sense of the present-day world and its contemporary problems. Writing and reading in this view are exploratory tools of illumination, lanterns lighting the way under a lowering sky and in a universe darkened by uncertainty, confusion, and even evil. Indeed, in reading preliminary reader's reports and the *News* for these years, I am struck by how often phrases such as "our troubled times," "fateful events," "this uncertain period," and "our confusing age" recur. Clearly, the club's judges and its preliminary readers were disturbed by the world that surrounded them and were convinced that their subscribers were as well. As a consequence, the library they assembled for their subscribers is highly topical, attuned to the pressing problems of the 1950s, and pitched precisely to give voice to the profound anxiety of the age.

Still, the universe surveyed by the Book-of-the-Month Club is not marked by high seriousness only. In further comparing the books I received from Mr. Shymansky with the larger set recommended by the club, I am surprised to note that one very large category of books featured in the *News* is represented only minimally in the collection I read. Although the club clearly preferred books that took on substantial issues, whether in a contemporary or a historical vein, it also offered its readers large quantities of what can only be called light fiction. Neither weighted down by a concern with consequential, topical matters nor designed to provoke the reader to thoughtful reflection, this sort of fiction was offered to readers as a tool to while away the hours in happy diversion. Pleasure reading, it would seem, was as central to the club's mission in the 1950s as I found it in the 1980s. And this particular form of pleasure reading aimed to absorb the reader in the tastes, textures, and emotional tenor of other worlds. Regularly offered to readers as main selections during the summer months, this sort of material suggests that the club believed its general readers wanted to be entertained as much as they desired to be informed and instructed. Accordingly, they featured various entertainment genres, including titles such as *The Flower Girls*, by Clemence Dane, described in the June 1955 *News*. Billed as the kind of English novel "full of warmth, gaiety and energy" where the "characters enjoy good hearty meals and noisy parties and challenging humorous conversations," this novel was additionally described as a "romantic comedy" and "a spacious and delightful story, which cannot be read in an evening." Judge Gilbert Highet further reported to his subscribers, "We are meant to live with it, for a week or a fortnight." He concluded, "We shall enjoy this generous and warm-hearted novel most fully if we give it the same preparatory acceptance that we accord to a good play, when we sit down in comfortable expectation, and watch the lights dim, and see the curtain rise, and prepare to admire the bold energy of the adventurous hero, the quavering tones of the wily old magician, the dark rich cello voice and the glittering eyes of the enchanting but dangerous princes."[23]

Obviously this is the stuff of melodrama, and it played a substantial role in the mix of books sent out by the Book-of-the-Month Club in the 1950s. As much as the club's library was meant to provoke thought and to illumine contemporary problems, then, it was also designed to provide recreation and amusement. Literacy was as much about pleasure as it was about exploration and edification. Interestingly, though, this kind of material is virtually absent from the collection of books Mr. Shymansky provided for me. Although he sent humor books such as *The Egg and I* and *Please Don't Eat the Daisies*, the only fiction he included from the entertainment genres of the thriller, mystery, and romance was *Fail-Safe*, *Rebecca*, *My Cousin Rachel*, and *Marjorie Morningstar*, and even these tend to exhibit pretensions to social commentary. Perhaps he disapproved of nonliterary genres, especially those generally dubbed "women's fiction." Perhaps he thought them insufficiently challenging for a student who was already spending too much time out of school. In any case, the fiction he did send resembles the pleasure books in that they are long, diffuse novels with many characters, carefully rendered realistic detail, and lots of dialogue and action. However, what sets them apart is their marked tendency to take on serious issues in fictional form. *Advise and Consent*, a novel relentlessly packed with detail about the daily doings of the American Senate, focuses in part on the confirmation of a controversial secretary of state and his relationship to the Soviet Union; *Nectar in a Sieve* deals with poverty, colonialism, and the suffering of the Indian peasantry; *To Kill a Mockingbird* takes up civil rights and race relations in the American South; and *The Wall* and *Mila 18* both deal with Nazism and the Polish ghetto.

Mr. Shymansky, it would seem, thought I ought to learn even as I enjoyed myself. In this he was not all that different from the Book-of-the-Month Club judges themselves, for even when they touted pleasure reading and admitted that it had no redeeming value beyond that of its capacity to entertain, they exhibited clear nervousness about their transgression. In fact their presentation of entertainment reading was nearly always defensive in tone and almost furtive in its assertiveness, as if the judges were somehow looking over their shoulders, waiting for the reaction of disapproving elders. And the elders they imagined were clearly literary critics and English teachers, those professional readers of fiction feared equally in the 1980s by their successors at the club. It was the professional critic's preference for intricacy, subtlety, and complexity, the judges' worried self-justifications make clear, that had obviously come to dominate the literary field. These qualities dictated how new novels were supposed to be evaluated. Listen, for instance, to Clifton Fadiman introduce the thriller *Fail-Safe*:

Experience teaches reviewers to shun superlatives, especially cliché superlatives. But, because I know no simpler, no better way to put the matter, I am driven to one: *Fail-Safe* is the most exciting novel I have read in at least ten years. Not best; not profound; not a contribution to literature; not rewarding for its style. Just most exciting. But, let me add, not shallow either, not cheap, not tossawayable. It is the work of two highly intelligent men, Eugene Burdick and Harvey Wheeler. One is the co-author of *The Ugly American*, the other (true of Mr. Burdick also) an able political scientist.[24]

As if to forestall the carping complaints of literary critics like Dwight MacDonald, whom he can clearly imagine dismissing the book for its lack of profundity and for its workmanlike prose, Fadiman both admits the novel's literary failings and stresses its success as thrilling entertainment. Ironically, though, at the very moment he emphasizes the worth of sheer excitement, he reassures his readers of the intelligence of the book's authors and casually mentions their professional credentials. Even this book, he seems to say, though it makes no pretensions to literary value and seeks primarily to excite, is made weightier and therefore more justifiable by the authors' professional expertise in political matters.

The Book-of-the-Month Club judges, like Mr. Shymansky, apparently, found it difficult to abandon the idea that reading and books ought somehow to be connected with expertise, learning, and culture. A library was a library, after all, a place to seek information and instruction. Even when the judges recommended pure pleasure reading, they often fell back on qualifications, comparisons, and allusions that connected the book in question, despite its stylistic failings and lack of higher purpose, to more legitimate literary forms. Of Robert Traver's 1958 novel *Anatomy of a Murder*, for instance, Fadiman remarked it "is recommended not as a deathless work of literature, but as a wickedly quizzical melodrama of the law, perhaps less edifying than instructive. It is a lively, candid tale, blinking few of the less pretty facts of life."[25] Fair enough, it fails as literature. Clearly, not every book can aspire to the status of the greats. But then, having insisted on the value of melodrama in its own right, Fadiman performs an about-face and notes, "In its honest realism, its 18th-century masculine vigor, it may remind some readers of Smollett and Defoe." It is not literature, Fadiman seems to say, but it will remind the subscriber, who is anxious about wallowing in the thrills of suspense, of more legitimate literary forms. The Book-of-the-Month Club always wanted to have it both ways. It wanted to appeal to the general reader's desire for pleasure, entertainment, and titillation and, at the same time, to cloak itself in the highbrow garb of cultural significance.

If this sounds contradictory and more than a little tense in its efforts to balance competing criteria, it is. And that tension can be found throughout the *Book-of-the-Month Club News* and in the larger mix of books sent out between 1950 and 1963. It is even evident in the surviving preliminary reader's reports from the period. Taken together, these reports demonstrate that although everyone understood that they were looking for books that would, above all, be enjoyable to read, they also found it difficult to recommend titles that failed to flaunt some form of larger cultural significance, either stylistically, through a heavily worked literary language, or topically, through treatment of important or current subject matter. In fact, the category of books that proved most problematic at the club and resulted in more rejections by preliminary readers than almost any other form was that which they called "circulating library stuff," "women's fiction," the kind of "conventional costume parade" preferred by "the bosomier book clubs" and "rental library patrons." Cultural significance, it seems, was as gendered in 1956 as it was in 1926. Although the club was committed to serving its female members and to providing them with the kind of historical and romantic fiction they seemed to prefer, both the preliminary readers and the judges tended to complain about this material and selected only those examples of it that bordered on more acceptable genres. If a melodramatic storyline was not balanced by a vigorous realism or carefully constructed, literate prose, the book was rejected outright as run-of-the-mill and unworthy of Book-of-the-Month Club attention.

Not surprisingly, the club's conflicted obeisance to higher cultural value and to the pure pleasure of entertainment reading was played out graphically in the design and layout of the *News*. Indeed, the conflict often made the cover of the catalog virtually impossible to decode at a glance. Throughout the 1950s and even into the 1960s the *News* featured a reproduction of a well-known painting on the front cover. The cultural stature of the work was underscored by a detailed description of the painting on an inside page that included details about the artist, the work's composition and style, and its place in art history. Almost never, however, did the subject of the artwork have anything to do with the book that was being announced as the month's main selection. That selection was usually introduced, though, just below the reproduction. Frequently the book title was omitted in favor of a short, tantalizing blurb summarizing the subject matter in question. The placement of the description always made it appear to be the caption to the painting. More often than not, though, an odd dissonance was created because the topic of the book clashed with the tone of the celebrated artwork. The June 1957 issue of the *News*, for example, announced "a novel about modern American life" below an Honoré Daumier painting, "The Connoisseur," depicting a vaguely eighteenth-century gentleman contemplating a small version of the Venus de Milo. Inside the front cover the curious subscriber was further informed that this novel of modern life, *The Durable Fire*, had as its background "a struggle for power in a giant corporation" and that it also unfolded "as a tender story of a truly happy marriage." Daumier and the Venus de Milo were there, obviously, to link the club in the reader's mind with the supposedly eternal values of the high art tradition rather than with the topicality and frivolousness of this particular title. Neither avant-garde nor self-consciously challenging, this novel, the club's report made clear, was chosen to entertain. As such, perhaps, it required particularly vigorous propping up with familiar tokens of cultural esteem. In any case, in addition to contemplating the Venus de Milo, Daumier's gentleman conveniently lounged amidst open books, classical busts and urns, and heavily chiaroscuroed paintings in gilt frames.

Those cultural icons displayed on the front cover of the *News*, it seems clear, were the equivalents of Marchette Chute's Shakespeare, Mary Renault's classical Greeks, and C. W. Ceram's Egyptians, figures marketed to subscribers in the books advertised within. The presence of these subjects in the club's library, and in the smaller version of it offered to me by Mr. Shymansky, provided the authority and weight of cultural ballast. They counterbalanced the insignificance and superficiality of the literary worlds inhabited by people like Max and Rebecca de Winter, Marjorie Morningstern and her lawyer husband, and the characters in books like James Michener's *Hawaii* and Burdick and Wheeler's *Fail-Safe*. In a sense, they legitimated the library as a whole and provided fine cover for the more suspect pleasures associated with hammock literature and bestsellers.

### SHAKESPEARE OF LONDON:

### LONGING TO KNOW THE CLASSICS

It is difficult to know, of course, how much of this I understood consciously in 1963. I certainly could not have used the language I employed above to characterize the club if I had wanted to describe the attraction some of Mr. Shymansky's books held for me. I probably would have said

I read them because they sounded like good stories. But I did read at least some of them with a certain deliberate devotion because I thought their stature would enhance my own. I know I was entranced by the portal they promised to open onto the fabulous riches of culture and art. In fact, by the time Marchette Chute's *Shakespeare of London* arrived in my room that fall, promising to reveal the full, theatrical world inhabited by the famous bard, I already possessed my own, single-volume edition of the plays, illustrated by Rockwell Kent, prefaced by Book-of-the-Month Club judge Christopher Morley, and inscribed by my grandfather. I had known enough about the cultural value of the plays and the genius Shakespeare to request the book for a Christmas present the year before. "To Janice," my grandfather wrote, "May you find in many of these pages an inspiration to improve your English, that it may be a pride to you and a joy to others."

In paging through this book again, the volume I later used in my college Shakespeare class, it is clear to me that in 1963 my desires had already been informed by middle-class longings for the prestige conferred by familiarity with high culture. I was bent on surrounding myself with the aura of art and the status of the cultured self. In this I was not unique, I suspect, for by mid-century, at least, American public schools had already standardized a program in basic literacy grounded on the touchstones of a common cultural tradition. My grandfather's inscription implicitly recognized the centrality of Shakespeare to even the most elementary definition of the literate self, for he wrote not of the significance of the plays or of their extraordinary delineation of character, but of their language, which he held up as a model for emulation. Sentiments like my grandfather's, expressed so lovingly in so many other middle-class families, endowed many of us with the conviction that to present ourselves as educated individuals, it was necessary to know the classics.

These teachings about the value of the classics had been infused with added authority for me by the fact that they were most intensely prescribed by my sixth-grade teacher, Mr. Maw, who had arrived in our suburban town on exchange from England. He was both strange and impressively cosmopolitan, with his British accent and the way he wrote his European sevens. I was not the only one who copied his mannerisms. Perhaps we were willing to follow his lead because his constant railing about the cultural ignorance of American students tapped our worries about our country's failings and lack of sophistication in the wake of the Sputnik triumph only three years before. In any case, when he taunted us with the assertion that British students our age had already read Shakespeare, we were eager to prove we could do so as well. He had the school buy copies of *Romeo and Juliet* and *Hamlet* for every student in the class, and he set us to the task of reading the plays aloud and memorizing long passages from both. I can still recall which passages my best friend, Cathy Cheselka, and I memorized. In the spring we even boarded a bus and made a cultural pilgrimage to Manhattan to see Donald Madden portray the melancholy Dane. The combination of Mr. Maw's fastidious, refined demeanor and the authority he exercised without an iota of self-doubt must have been powerful indeed, for it induced a bunch of twelve-year-olds to sit through a four-hour play in language we could barely comprehend.

In any event, when Marchette Chute's own Will Shakespeare strode impressively into my imagination only two years later, he certainly came as one more lesson in cultural hierarchy. I wanted to know Shakespeare, to say I had read a biography of him, because of the cultural value that trailed beside his famous name. Chute was as conscious of the stature of her subject as I was. In fact she saw her task as one of counteracting the distance and abstraction that accompanied the usual hagiography. In her foreword to the book, she informed her readers that "this is an attempt to bring a very great man into the light of common day. It is an attempt to show William Shakespeare as his contemporaries saw him, rather than as the gigantic and legendary figure he has become since." "He was once life-size," she reassured me, "and this is an attempt at a life-sized portrait." [26]

As a way of tailoring the dramatic genius to the size of a general reader like me, she then filled her book with fine-grained detail about the Elizabethan life William Shakespeare must have led. As quickly as page 2, in fact, I learned that his father was a glover who sold his wares "just under the big clock in the paved market square," and that as an inhabitant of Stratford he would have been "fined if he let his dog go unmuzzled, if his duck wandered, if he played cards 'or any other unlawful games,' . . . [or] if he borrowed gravel from the town gravel pits." That sort of detail, of course, simultaneously underscored its ordinariness and its strangeness. It made Shakespeare's world both like and far removed from my own. As much as those facts helped to render Shakespeare in flesh and blood amidst the daily doings of community life, so also did they serve to shore up Chute's own authority as the researcher who had unearthed them in the New York Public Library. In the end those details functioned as markers of the continuity between Elizabethan England and the postwar America I inhabited, thereby providing mundane ground for propositions about the universality of great art. At the same time, they came to me as a form of specialized knowledge, the result of diligent research in documents found in a great library. Thus, even as the book sought to rescue Shakespeare from those who had "pull[ed] him away from the earth that had given him life," from the "scholars" who had "made him lord of the schoolrooms and the libraries," the very detail it marshaled so conspicuously to create the effect of a life lived on the ground, as it were, surreptitiously enhanced the value of scholarship and the authority of those whose particular business it was.

*Shakespeare of London* schooled me in the belief that cultural icons like the bard were as human as anybody else. Just as Harry Scherman's Little Leather Library edition of *Romeo and Juliet* had cut high culture down to manageable size, so Chute's biography unmasked the figure of the genius so as to convince me that Shakespeare, the man, was knowable by all. Ironically, though, to be known he first had to be embodied, enlivened, and inspirited by the assiduous work of a true expert. In the end the book enhanced the cultural status of the figure it wanted to humanize, just as it authorized the expert who could translate him for the general reader. With Marchette Chute's biography, then, as in so many other arenas, the Book-of-the-Month Club managed to have it both ways. It made culture accessible to the non-expert even as it emphasized and underscored the historic connection between culture and an elite group of experts with special access to its mysteries and intangible riches.

That a popular biography of Shakespeare taught a lesson in cultural hierarchy and emphasized the value of expert historical research is perhaps not surprising. But I wonder now whether the experience of living side by side with Chute's fully fashioned Will did not carry with it other, more personal connotations and subtle, long-term effects. For as part of a cultural pageant that Mr. Maw had designed, I had cross-dressed in the sixth grade as the bard himself. Where my friends masqueraded as Ophelia, Hamlet, and the ghost, and as Romeo and Juliet, Mercutio, and the nurse, a weird, cheeky hubris had inspired me to present myself in the guise of the writer who had imagined them all and set them about their affairs. I can still conjure the cloying smell of the theatrical glue my mother had found to apply a mustache and whiskers. I cannot remember why I wanted to be William Shakespeare or how I felt in the midst of the impersonation, but the act of identification seems consistent, if extraordinarily self-inflated, with my earlier efforts to imagine myself as Louisa May Alcott's Jo March. In homage to Jo and in imitation of her own efforts to make herself a writer, I had once fashioned a book out of loose-leaf paper, bound it with knitting yarn and a crudely illustrated yellow cover, and then attempted to compose a mystery story about a girl detective like Nancy Drew. I wrote only two pages, perhaps because I did not have the wherewithal to imagine what a girl might really do, what the shape of her future might look like. The only thing I was sure of was that she ought to drive a sporty roadster like Nancy's own. Did *Shakespeare of London* seem so impressive later because it promised to tell me what the course of a writing life looked like? Did I open it with anticipation after each interruption because I wanted to know more about how to make myself into a writer who could imagine the end to the story? Did I read it as an exercise in self-fashioning, however improbable the comparison it was based on?

I don't know. But it seems more than merely possible, for the nature of the other two books that were my favorites that year suggests that reading served as much more than a momentary diversion or as a course in middle-class self-improvement. Reading also enabled the halting work of what can only be called identity formation. Indeed, my memories of Marjorie Morningstar and of the archaeologists that peopled the pages of *Gods, Graves, and Scholars* suggest that Mr. Shymansky's books were so valuable and intensely loved because they enabled me to trace paths in imaginary futures, to try on the desires experienced by others, to think myself into new shape and form. Had you asked me what Herman Wouk's novel was about before I reread it two years ago, I could have recounted very little of the story, especially not Marjorie's capitulation to middle-class respectability. In fact I would have been very hazy about the details of the plot. What I could have recalled, though, were vignettes of Marjorie crossing a New York street at night and sitting in a cafe in Paris, a sense of her as independent and vaguely bohemian. I might even have been able to give words to the inchoate feelings the title evoked for me, a sense of exhilaration, the thrill of open-endedness and possibility. I surely would have told you that I loved the book and that I found Marjorie fascinating. About *Gods, Graves, and Scholars* I could have been more specific because I have never forgotten the figure of Howard Carter or the thrill of placing myself amidst the Egyptian dust and oppressive heat as the last boulder was rolled away from the final interior tomb of King Tutankhamen. I was mesmerized by moments when secrets were revealed. I was intrigued by lives devoted to the quest to know. What I was trying to do, I think, during that year of confinement, was to merge the emotional life of a girl like Marjorie with the cultural accomplishments of writers like Shakespeare and scholars like Carter, Lord Carnarvon, J. J. Winckelmann, and Heinrich Schliemann. It could not have been easy. The ambitions I was cultivating were open-ended, expansive—even voracious. But like Marjorie, I was a girl for whom such ambitions were not considered entirely natural.

Perhaps Herman Wouk's novel was as popular as it was among women and girls of the 1950s and 1960s because it captured with almost perfect precision the tensions and uncertainties of profound social change as it was about to erupt and explode. Those tensions and uncertainties course through the novel as a whole with almost excruciating intensity as Wouk relates every twist and turn in the life of the young woman Marjorie Morningstern while she attempts to fashion herself into the actress Marjorie Morningstar. Although Marjorie is eventually transformed by the story into Mrs. Milton Schwartz, the wife of a prosperous Jewish lawyer, most of Wouk's 560-odd pages are devoted to Marjorie's determined efforts to escape that fate and to make of herself someone more cultured and poetic, a woman more glamorous and independent than a suburban matron. The story sets in motion desires it ultimately feels it necessary to contain, but not before those longings have been laid out in such detail and with such force that they catch the reader up and enable her to participate in Marjorie's relentless quest to make of herself something different. There can be little doubt that this must have proved attractive in 1955 to women who had been fired in large numbers from their World War II jobs to make way for returning soldiers, as well as to their daughters in the years immediately afterward, who were being told that they were as essential to the fight against communism as their brothers. *Marjorie Morningstar* was a story for an unsettled age.

The tension in the book about the changing nature of women's aspirations is evident from page 1. The very first passages, in fact, vacillate back and forth, remarkably uncertain about what position to take on Marjorie's burgeoning desire. Significantly, that desire is shown to be both openly sexual and aimed at a world beyond sexuality, at a world characterized by work, professional accomplishments, and esteem. Although the novel's first pages spin out in sensuous detail a highly eroticized portrait of the seventeen-year-old Marjorie asleep on her bed, it does so in such a conflicted way that it grants the reader a position of extraordinary ambivalence about what it reveals. Wouk begins, in fact, in a distant, almost pedagogical voice intoning an abstract proposition. "Customs of courtship vary greatly in different times and places," we are told, "but the way the thing happens to be done here and now always seems the only natural way to do it."[27] The implication of the word "seems," of course, is that there are always other ways. Apparently we are to be told a story illustrating this lesson. We are meant to take up the distant view and to merge with this voice in order to become the ultimate judge of Marjorie's own courtship behavior.

Yet this voice gives way instantaneously to one whose point of view is much closer to what it describes and much more conflicted about what it sees. Ostensibly the third person narration is presented from the point of view of Marjorie's disapproving mother. But the details that are revealed suggest that there is another viewer as well, a concealed voyeur who takes great pleasure in Marjorie's dishabille. A feminist perspective suggests that the gaze is male, that Marjorie is displayed for the titillation of a leering male reader. But it also seems to me now that this other sight line may have granted female readers like me a view of Marjorie at a moment when she appears to have asserted herself sexually. This gaze may have enabled us to peer at ourselves as Marjorie and thus to think the unthinkable, that life might continue *after* premarital sex.

The passage begins, "Marjorie's mother looked in on her sleeping daughter at half past ten of a Sunday morning with feelings of puzzlement and dread. She disapproved of everything she saw" (3). However, the passage continues with a description that is as fascinated as it is critical: "She disapproved of the expensive black silk evening dress crumpled on a chair, the pink frothy underwear thrown on top of the dress, the stockings like dead snakes on the floor, the brown wilting gardenias on the desk. Above all she disapproved of the beautiful seventeen-year-old girl lying happily asleep on a costly oversize bed in a square of golden sunlight, her hair a disordered brown mass of curls, her red mouth streaked with cracking purplish paint, her breathing peaceful and regular through her fine little nose" (3). The snake, the red mouth, the sprawl, and the purple paint are all clearly meant to suggest some kind of sinful transgression. Yet at the same time Marjorie is caught sleeping peacefully in golden sunlight. What are we supposed to think? Has her suggested wantonness had no negative consequences? Are we to excuse such behavior? As we learn more about the nature of Mrs. Morningstern's disapproval, we are given a further hint about the extent of Marjorie's transgression, which is explicitly linked to shifting mores and changing times and subsequently explained away. "Marjorie was recovering from a college dance," we are told. "She looked sweetly innocent asleep; but her mother feared that this picture was deceptive, remembering drunken male laughter in the foyer at 3 A.M., and subdued girlish giggles, and tiptoeing noises past her bedroom. Marjorie's mother did not get much sleep when her daughter went to a college dance. But she had no thought of trying to stop her; it was the way boys met girls nowadays. College dances had formed no part of the courtship manners of her own girlhood, but she tried to move with the times" (3).

And the times, Wouk's wandering point of view suggests, are truly out of joint. Although Marjorie's parents desire only that she marry well to a Jewish boy who will provide handsomely for her, Marjorie, the story confirms, has other plans. She envisions for her future not only glamour but independence. The fact that her dreams are first revealed in the exuberant clichés of adolescent hope is perhaps what made the opening of this very long story so enthralling for young women wondering what the uncertain future might hold for them. It is worth quoting the articulation of her dreams in full.

> Since entering Hunter College in February of the previous year, Marjorie had been taking a course of study leading to a license as a biology teacher; but she had long suspected that she was going through empty motions, that chalk and blackboard weren't for her. Nor had she been able to picture herself settling into dull marriage at twenty-one. From her thirteenth year onward a peculiar destiny had been in her blood, waiting for the proper time to crop out, and disturbing her with premonitory sensations. But what she experienced on this May morning was no mere premonition; it was the truth bursting through. She was going to be an actress! [5]

It must have been her confidence and sure belief in her own destiny I found so electric and compelling. I am sure I thrilled at the way she played with her identity. If "wondrous resonance" or "stark elegance" were lacking in the name "Morningstern," then she would craft something else. Significantly, she would do it first in writing; she would simply inscribe a new self. Wouk underscores the importance of Marjorie's first willful act of self-fashioning by abandoning the characterless uniformity of print, scrawling her new name not once, but twice, in handwritten form: Marjorie Morningstar. Marjorie prints it hastily at first, but then, more carefully, more self-consciously, she almost draws it "in the small, vertical hand which she [is] trying to master" (6). Each *M* is rendered dramatically with three straight uprights and a confident, horizontal slash at the top.

Understandably, this was heady stuff. Hadn't my friends and I spent endless hours the previous summer experimenting with different ways to write our own names? In spite of the waffling in Wouk's narrative point of view, I *became* Marjorie. Clearly, however, not all of Marjorie's audience was made up of fourteen-year-old girls. Some were older, and some were already married themselves. But in a confused era, when prescriptions about feminine behavior were in flux, a story that relentlessly posed the question of what Marjorie wanted and followed her every move as she pursued it must have come as a welcome primer for a new, potentially more liberated age. And what does Marjorie want? "The finest foods . . . , the finest wines, the loveliest places, the best music, the best books, the best art. Amounting to something. Being well known, being myself, being distinguished, being important, using all my abilities, instead of becoming one more of the millions of human cows" (195). Marjorie wants what only a few years later would be labeled "having it all." Even more scandalously, she wants "children, sure, when I've had my life and I'm not fit for any-thing else any more" (195). *Marjorie Morningstar* suggests, at least at the outset, that domesticity is the booby prize.

Still, the novel is aware of how troubling are Marjorie's desires and how threatening her rebellion. Thus the only way it can allow Marjorie to pursue her goals is through liaison with a more accomplished, more powerful man. As a consequence we are given the dissolute yet disarm-ing Noel Airman — "Apollo," she calls him — both seducing Marjorie *and* pronouncing on the silliness of her desires. She will amount to nothing, he tells her, she is destined to become a Jewish "Shirley" wanting only a "big diamond engagement ring, house in a good neighborhood, furni-ture, children, well-made clothes, [and] furs" (173). The heir of Rochester, Heathcliff, Rhett Butler, and Maxim de Winter, Noel is even more ne'er-do-well than they. Yet he is also Marjorie's route to the bohemian world of Greenwich Village, the theater, and Paris as well as the ultimate occa-sion for the loss of her virginity. In fact after many pages of welling desire and tantalizing foreplay, Marjorie finally succumbs to the seduction and has sex with Noel. Surprisingly, the act is not rendered romantically but portrayed, rather, as something both distasteful and violent. "Then all changed," we are told. "It became rougher and more awkward. It became horrible. There were shocks, ugly uncoverings, pain, incredible humilia-tion, shock, shock, and it was over" (417).

It seems clear that we are meant to see this as the beginning of Mar-jorie's punishment, which is secured, finally, when she abandons her quest for a theatrical career and marries the boring, conventional lawyer, Milton Schwartz, who, knowing of her liaison with Noel, accepts her even with her "deformity," which is described as a "permanent crippling, like a crooked arm" (553). Some apparently read the novel's ending in this way. In fact, in introducing the book in the pages of the *Book-of-the-Month Club News*, judge John Marquand noted that "we are most unhappy when she begins to fall for the blandishments of Sodom's superficial but charming entertainment director." Marquand elaborated, "We hope against hope that she will not be seduced by Noel Airman, and when she is, we hope he will make her into an honest woman in spite of his flightiness and egocentricity. We wish she would not keep on loving Noel Airman, and are delighted when she throws him over." He concluded smugly, "There is something satisfying in our last view of her, years later, a gray-haired matron on the lawn of her suburban home, doing a solitary little dance with a glass in her hand when she hears her daughter 'Falling in Love with Love.' " [28]

That conclusion, it seems to me, is not so easily drawn as Marquand seems to think. Even Marjorie is permitted to pronounce on the capitulation that leads her to her suburban matronhood, and what she sees at her wedding is a "tawdry mockery of sacred things, a bourgeois riot of expense, with a special touch of vulgar Jewish sentimentality" (556). What Marjorie sees at the moment that she forgoes her adolescent dreams is that she is "Shirley, going to a Shirley fate, in a Shirley blaze of silly costly glory" (557). I remember thinking, "Not me." Like Marquand, I had wanted her to ditch Noel because he treated her so badly. But I also wanted her to get rid of him so she could concentrate on the theater herself. I wanted her *not* to abandon her dreams. I wanted very much to believe that she really was Marjorie Morningstar.

Was my reading idiosyncratic? I don't think so. The number of women who spoke to me warmly on the beach in the summer of 1994 because I was reading a copy of *Marjorie Morningstar* suggests that others remembered a book very unlike the one described by John Marquand. The title and book cover seemed to make me as approachable as pregnancy once had. "I loved that book," they told me again and again, just as others had once repeatedly shared stories of their own pregnancies and asked me when I was due. "My sister and I read it together." "My mother read it and gave it to me. We never stopped talking about it." As we spoke, I learned that most of these women had careers; they were people who had forged a place for themselves in the wider world. Could so many women have read the book, remembered it fondly, and wanted to talk about it to a stranger more than thirty years later if they had read it as a simple tale about the justifiable constriction of a woman's desire? Had all of them been satisfied by the disappearance of Noel and comforted by the house in Mamaroneck? I doubt it.

The last word on Marjorie's fate in the novel is not one of approval at all. Spoken by the one successful writer in the story who had once, long ago, desired her intensely, the words are stern and dismissive, and they grieve for what Marjorie had once been. Wally Wronken confides to his journal after meeting her years later that "she is dull, dull as she can be, by any technical standard" (564). What satisfaction, he wonders, "is there in crowing over the sweet-natured placid gray mamma she has turned into?" He prefers to remember her as she had once been, even recognizing "that she was an ordinary girl" and that "the image existed only in [his] own mind, that her radiance was the radiance of [his] own hungry young desires projected around her." As Nick Caraway remembers the green light at the end of Gatsby's dock, so Marjorie rises up before Wally Wronken as he writes—"in a blue dress, a black raincoat, her face wet with rain, nineteen years old, in my arms and yet maddeningly beyond my reach, kissing me once under the lilacs in the rain" (565).

Perhaps this last image of Marjorie in her blue dress, kissing under the lilacs, was the source of those feelings of possibility the title evoked for me over the years, the preservative behind that amber-tinted picture of Marjorie crossing a Manhattan street at dusk into the unknown. Perhaps I, too, preferred to remember Marjorie as she had once been as a way of encouraging myself to believe that my own future need not play out as hers had. It seems possible that many of us, like the women I met on a Cape Cod beach, read it as both a tutelary and a cautionary tale. Maybe we absorbed its hopeful longing for art, the theater, the excitement of the wider world, and the thrill of a freer sexuality as well as its warning that none of these are easily obtained, especially if you are a woman.

However strong the caution woven through its narrative of longing, I think *Marjorie Morningstar* was one of those experiences that taught me how to want. It built on my commonplace adolescent confusion about what the future might hold by helping me to assemble an elementary vocabulary of ideas and things that might serve as proper objects for desire. Despite its equivocation at the end with Marjorie's marriage, the book insisted through most of its 500 pages that a house in Mamaroneck would not do, and neither would a large diamond, an ostentatious wedding, or even conventional domesticity. What was portrayed with the most narrative energy throughout the long tale was the world of writing itself, a world associated with art and culture, with work, commitment, and a kind of hearty camaraderie. The book is striking, then, not for its misogyny and for its quite ordinary disapproval of all things conventionally feminine, but for the way it comes very near to recommending the traditional masculine world of ambition to women. Indeed it comes close to suggesting that girls, too, can desire openly, and not just sexually but in a manner more oriented to the external world, where meaningful and significant work are held out as the ultimate goal.

In this way, it seems to me, the needs of a particular class at a particular historical moment managed to assert themselves over the recommendation of traditional gender arrangements. As the new information economy was beginning to consolidate, it required many more workers to staff its institutions—those fast-multiplying schools, libraries, bureaucracies, and corporations devoted to the circulation of new forms of knowledge. Undoubtedly it seemed sensible, even if unconsciously so, to draw those workers not from the traditional working classes but from the untapped ranks of the middle class itself, from the hundreds of thousands of girls born after World War II. As one of those girls, I was encouraged to want by stories like *Marjorie Morningstar* and by television shows like "I Love Lucy" and "My Little Margie." They all encouraged girls to want more than had traditionally been accorded women in the past. What the middle-brow *Marjorie Morningstar* taught me to want in particular was the new professional's world of knowledge, culture, cosmopolitanism, and intellectual sophistication. At the time, I did not see that to command such knowledge was also to wield power over others who were themselves excluded from indulging in the very same desires.

## GODS, GRAVES, AND SCHOLARS:

### THE WHITENESS OF EXPERTS

*Gods, Graves, and Scholars* came to me less as an account of the painstaking labors of a particular group of professional specialists than as a further lesson in the vocabulary of desire. This book seemed to suggest, with its reverent delineation of the classical worlds of Greece, Crete, Egypt, and Mesopotamia and its equally fascinated account of the travel and adventure that had led to their contemporary rediscovery, that the limits of that cosmopolitan world need not be drawn at the boundaries of New York or even at those of Paris. Rather, they might expand outward to encompass the whole world, a world made exotic by remote islands and mysterious deserts. How I could have missed the fact that all of the travelers and adventurers in this tale were men, I do not know. It seems never to have occurred to me, since for months afterward I told anyone who asked that I wanted to be an archaeologist when I grew up. Identification was not gender-specific then or fully controlled by the underlying assumptions of the text itself. As I had become Marjorie Morningstar, so for a few hours did I fancy myself Heinrich Schliemann and Howard Carter, awash in sunlight and wallowing in the sands of faraway places and distant centuries.

What, in particular, made these figures and their work so attractive? Clearly it was the knowledge they sought, the significance of their labors, and the hardship they endured to accomplish their tasks. But all of these were rendered through C. W. Ceram's eyes, and Ceram saw in characteristically middlebrow fashion. He admired the archaeologists' expertise, but he found their accounts of their exploits boring. His book, he tells us explicitly, eschews "scholarly pretensions."[29] He further assures the reader who might be nervous about understanding this arcane profession and its remote subjects that he will "portray the dramatic qualities of archaeology, its human side." He continues encouragingly that he has not "shied away from prying into purely personal relationships," nor has he been "afraid to digress now and then and to intrude my own personal reflections on the course of events." What has resulted, he concludes, is "a book that the expert may condemn as 'unscientific.'" In a familiar middlebrow way, Ceram reveres expertise but portrays it as unduly stuffy, not quite attuned to the human scale. He will make accessible and engaging "the whole stirring history" of the archaeologists' "romantic excursions," which are usually "hopelessly buried in technical publications" (v). Ceram will show us how scholarship and expertise can give us access to the secrets of ordinary life; he will demonstrate how useful and human they can be.

He does so by offering what the general reader is commonly thought to want, that is, "dramatic story," personal relationships, and detail at every turn. We are given details about the archaeologists' lives, to be sure, as well as details about every expedition. But detail also figures significantly in the way Ceram presents the archaeological discoveries themselves. He offers the same illusion Marchette Chute had, that the world we occupy as readers is entirely continuous with the classical world inhabited by individuals long dead. Those individuals are now exhumed for us from the earth as mere bones, shards, and fragments, yet they are made to live again through the force of Ceram's imagination and through his use of a highly concrete language. Here, for example, is Ceram's evocation of what happened at Pompeii:

> Disaster began with a light fall of ash, so light that people were able to brush the powdery dust off their shoulders. Soon, however, lapilli began to come down, then occasional bombs of pumice weighing many pounds. The extent of the danger was only gradually revealed, and only when it was too late. Clouds of sulfur fumes settled down on the city. They seeped through the cracks and crevices and billowed up under the cloths that the suffocating townsfolk help up to their faces. If they ran

outdoors seeking air and freedom, they were met by a thick hail of la-
pilli that drove them back in terror to the shelter of their homes. Roofs
caved in, whole families were buried. Others were spared for a time. For
a half hour or so they crouched in fear and trembling under stairs and
arched doors. The fumes reached them, and they choked to death. [7]

Ceram revivifies the ghostly cities as he records their death. His personalism is as marked as Henry Canby's. It is not the distant, analytical
perspective of theory and research that he seeks but the earthly perspective of that man on the ground, the ordinary individual who feels caught
up in ominous natural events and the momentous historical movements
of his day. What Ceram gives in this book, then, are not only the living,
breathing archaeologists themselves in all the competitiveness and ambition he can imagine, but also haunting specters of history, those individuals who once created, built, inhabited, died, and were buried at Mycaenae,
Dendera, Luxor, Nimrud, and the Yucatan. He suggests with his homely
details about life in Pompeii and elsewhere, as Marchette Chute had with
her Elizabethan clocks, ducks, and gravel, that these distant worlds are
continuous with the reader's own.

Ceram instructs us explicitly: "This has become the archaeologist's
grandiose task: to cause to flow once more that historic stream in which
we are all encompassed, whether we live in Brooklyn or Montparnasse,
Berllin-Neukolln or Santiago de Chile, Athens or Miami" (20). I am sure
I must have added "or New Jersey, too." I wanted very much to feel myself a part of this "we" and its tradition, a party to its wisdom and riches. I
am sure I attended to his lessons with eager approval. Obligingly, Ceram
summed up his instruction boldly and with not an ounce of self-doubt:
"This stream is the great human community of the Western world which
for five thousand years has swum with the same flood-tide, under different flags, but guided by the same constellations" (20).

The patent imperialism underlying this statement announces itself
loudly now. However, in 1964 I was not attuned to such undertones. It
never occurred to me to doubt the truth of an assertion like this one. Nor
do I recall bristling at Ceram's matter-of-fact racism. What I heard was
simply more detail about Western civilization. In fact, in further exploring the nature of the relationship between the contemporary West and its
classical past, Ceram had observed quite unconsciously that without "our
heritage of five thousand years of history . . . we would be no different
from the a-historical Australian bushman" (18). He assumed that not one
of the readers who numbered themselves among his "we" would identify

with that primitive man in the bush. As if to ensure the impossibility of such an association, he expanded his point further with the observation that although "the white construction worker in an Australian city may never have heard of the name of Archimedes," he is necessarily better than any bushman because "he makes use of the laws formulated by Archimedes" (18). The bushman, clearly, is black, and the point of the passage is to align that blackness with primitivism so as to ensure that civilization and the West are understood to be white. And that whiteness, we are told, is expansive enough to include even the uneducated working classes, construction workers who labor with their hands. By virtue of the fact that they utilize calculations and methods traceable to the glorious Western past, presumably taught to them by experts who have real command of that knowledge, they are rendered superior to all people of color who, it is implied, have neither affinity for nor access to these traditions.

I see now why I could ignore the fact that all of the archaeologists and heroes in this tale of Western triumph were men. The book is deeply preoccupied with shoring up the identity of the white, cultured, Western reader. It is much more interested in policing the color line than in surveying the boundaries between classes or genders. What matters is the boundary between black and white, between savagery and civilization. Thus I could discount my own gender and that of the archaeologists about whom I was reading because Ceram took no pains to enforce the distinction between us. It was easy to roam imaginatively, then, to identify with these adventurers by taking up temporary residence in their bodies because those bodies were familiarly white. Our shared whiteness overrode any other differences between us.

Middle-class women's expanding possibilities, my reading of this book now suggests, may have been made possible at least in part by renewed anxiety about the activities of people of color and by ensuing efforts to establish and to maintain a clear border between white and black. The fact that my own identification as white was solicited entirely surreptitiously by this book ensured that my identification with the class of people who commanded the Western cultural tradition and positioned themselves within its stream was all that more effective. In reveling in the adventures and mysteries revealed by *God, Graves, and Scholars*, I wanted to see myself as a member of that class, a class constituted by its knowledge of the historical and cultural past and by its command of the specialized expertise necessary to add to that store of knowledge.

The book constantly encouraged and approved of that desire. More than anything else, Ceram's tale is a tale about the triumph of expertise, a triumph achieved slowly and progressively over time. Thus he begins with the first modern archaeological expeditions in Herculaneum in the mid-eighteenth century and moves from there to document the ever-more-systematic investigations of later scholars and researchers. The real heroes of the story, finally, are Lord Carnarvon and Howard Carter, the discoverers of the tomb of Tutankhamen, which represents, for Ceram, "the very summit of archaeological effort" (173).

What Ceram teaches is a belief in the efficacy of science and in the rightness of its abstract method. In fact, despite his earlier disclaimers about his modest, unscientific intentions and his disdain for the opacity of experts, Ceram's entire narrative is a hymn to the superiority of science and to its capacity to reveal the truth. Yet having said that, it is also essential to note that even his celebration of scientific expertise is tempered by that never-ceasing ambivalence characteristic of the middlebrow point of view. At the very moment when he relates the triumph of modern archaeological method, for example, the moment when Tutankhamen's sarcophagus is opened and the final coffin is exposed to air, he falls back, once again, on the power of the human detail. "There was something else on the coffin," he tells us, "that affected Carter and the others even more poignantly than the effigy" (197). It was, in Carter's words, "'the tiny wreath of flowers around the symbols on the forehead, the last farewell offering of the widowed queen to her husband. . . . They told us what a short period three thousand years really was—but Yesterday and the Morrow. In fact, that little touch of nature made that ancient and our modern civilization kin.'"

Ceram quotes this approvingly to prove that scientists, too, are human, and that they, too, are moved by love and fellow-feeling. He even allows Carter to speak again to demonstrate his point. He has Carter tell us directly that "'familiarity can never entirely dissipate the feeling of mystery—the sense of vanished but haunting forces that cling to the tomb. The conviction of the unity of past and present is constantly impressed upon the archaeological adventurer, even when absorbed in the mechanical details of his work'" (197). With odd relief Ceram adds flatly, "Carter really felt these reverent statements." He editorializes further, "It is good to know that the scientist does not deny the claims of the spirit."

It is hard not to hear this as reassurance specifically for the postwar age. Behind Ceram's humanized, flesh-and-blood archaeologists solemnly impressed by their connection to others across the space of thousands of years, one detects the shadow of other scientists, who lent their expertise not merely to the business of war but to the appalling work of mass annihilation. I cannot help but think that, whatever else its aims and intentions, Ceram's book was part of an unconscious effort to provide encouragement and comfort to a shocked population. He seems at pains to reassure himself and others that the long sweep of human history could not possibly be about to end, aided and abetted by dispassionate science. At times *Gods, Graves, and Scholars* comes across as a deliberate attempt to banish fears about the abstraction and arrogance of a scientific point of view that habitually forsakes the details of the singular and the individual in order to detect the patterns and rhythms of underlying structures. Like so much of the middlebrow library assembled by the Book-of-the-Month Club, it tempers its recommendation of professional expertise and its legitimation of technical experts with the insistence that neither are at odds with a preeminent, highly personal humanism—which I have called personalism—that simultaneously stresses the universality of spirit and emotion and the uniqueness of the individual. It bears repeating, however, that this humanism is fatally undermined by its implicit whiteness, by the assumption that people of color are not as civilized and, as such, are radically different.

In a highly unsettled age the middlebrow point of view could not be asserted in rigid, inflexible form. As a body of ideas about history, about the nature of knowledge, and about the character of human life, middlebrow culture was pressured by the upheavals of the time and forced to adapt to fast-changing social arrangements and political situations. Oddly enough it was often its conception of the person, its distinctly middlebrow personalism, that helped to underwrite its capacity for change. However, that personalism could also prove limiting, in part because a preference for the individual, the local, and the specific hindered the ability to see larger relationships and connections and sometimes prevented acknowledgment of the value of political movements. As a consequence, when middlebrow thinking attempted to take account of the demand for recognition by new groups, those groups were characteristically individualized, and newly recognized persons were cast in the position of noble unfortunates. They were seen as needy, disadvantaged people requiring the greater expertise and responsible compassion of their educated, more knowledgeable, and still always white brothers.

This emphasis on individualization is especially evident in another of Mr. Shymansky's books, one that proved particularly formative for me: Harper Lee's *To Kill a Mockingbird*. Reading it now, I am astonished by the book's complexity, which resides in the intensity of its efforts to articulate its understanding of individuality and in the rigor of its efforts to ensure that such an individuality might be recognized in all people, whether white, black, male, or female. If the book cannot finally imagine a world where the individuality of every human being is successfully secured, it nonetheless commits itself to establishing that a small group of extraordinary individuals can function as the guardians of the individuality of others. It suggests that those with special talents and abilities can function as a vanguard of insight, capable of seeing the individuality of those usually rendered invisible.

Harper Lee's novel aims for nothing less than the reconceptualization of women and "Negroes" as collections of individually different human beings rather than as categories of people rendered identifiable by certain common properties. In the end, though, it can only manage that task by modeling this newly recognized individuality on that of the white men who are presumed to be its most extraordinary exemplars. Although the book wants very much to be progressive about the subjects of gender and race, it fails finally to undo the fundamental equations that generally ensure that those with power are gendered male and tinted white. I want to look at Lee's novel in some depth, then, because I think it peculiarly revealing of the logic of a distinctively middlebrow individualism and because it fleshes out so fully the model middlebrow subject.

When I read *To Kill a Mockingbird* early in 1964, I was very much aware that the book was about race, racism, and white bigotry. At the time my intellectual world was as filled with the black and white images of television news programs as it was with characters from middlebrow books. The Kennedy assassination had taken up enormous amounts of time and emotional space soon after I returned from the hospital in November. But the months leading up to my diagnosis in July 1963 and my surgery in September of that year were also the months that witnessed the Birmingham riots, the bombing of the Sixteenth Street Baptist Church, and the March on Washington, all events I followed with my parents on the evening news. When I opened the covers of Lee's small novel, then, what flickered in the background were images of "Bull" Connor and his snarling dogs, firehoses trained on scrambling crowds, a bombed-out church and the four young girls who died there, and waves on waves of people marching to the Lincoln Memorial. Martin Luther King Jr. had just been named *Time* magazine's Man of the Year, and Lyndon Johnson had vowed to see passage of the Civil Rights Act. To a certain extent, reading this particular book was a way of participating in momentous events that always took place elsewhere and on television.

Yet I suspect that it was also the book's carefully delineated southern setting that enabled me to focus on other aspects of its story rather than on the issue of race relations alone. In fact, *To Kill a Mockingbird* has always been associated in my mind not so much with the events of hate it documents so carefully but with the single, monumental figure of Atticus Finch. The fact that the bigotry he quietly resisted took place in "The South" kept those events distant and significantly removed from the concerns of my own daily life. But Atticus was another matter. He appeared before me with strange force and immediacy. I still remember how peculiar his name sounded the first time I encountered it—at once as antique as the Penelopes and Jedediahs I found in the historical novels of Kenneth Roberts and as noble as the names in the Bible. For me the book was about Atticus. And Atticus was a reader.

I considered that the most important fact to know about him. I was also sure it explained his moral courage. In my mind there was more than a chance connection between the endless scenes of Atticus reading at night in a halo of light and his quiet determination to defend "the Negro," Tom Robinson, against charges that he had raped a white girl. Atticus was powerful because he suggested to me that certain consequences might follow from being a lover of books. Although I am sure I did not know the word at the time, Atticus Finch was my first concrete vision of what an intellectual looked and sounded like. He was also the first to suggest that bookishness was not merely a matter of being familiar with past cultural monuments but might, perhaps, be a way of functioning in a contemporary world in a responsible, socially committed way. It would be many years before I learned to question the grounding of this idea of responsibility in a prior notion of an elite with a special command of literacy and the expertise and power that followed from it.

Of course the tall, bespectacled man with the calm composure and unshakable moral convictions appeared before me through the eyes of his daughter, Scout. And Scout was no ordinary six-year-old girl. Not only did she possess a voice as strong as her tomboyish-sounding name, but she confirmed her remarkable independence by referring to her father by his

{ *Books for Professionals* }

first name as if he, too, was her equal. I marveled at his return of the favor, at the way he spoke to her honestly about everything, and at the way he refused to shield her or her brother, Jem, from the sins and hypocrisies of the adult community that surrounded them all. He appeared as extraordinary to me as he did to her. What Atticus seemed to promise Scout, more than anything else, was a way of being in the world, a model and vision for the future that most decidedly did not exclude her simply because she was a girl.

Lee's novel is as cognizant of the gender divide as it is of the line dividing black from white. Scout champs at the bit of femininity just as her father chafes at the rigidly enforced community strictures about the proper way to treat a Negro. She is appalled by the "starched walls of the pink cotton penitentiary closing all around her" (147) and thinks deliberately of running away. In 1964 I was heartened by her disdain for girlish things. The previous summer I had been perplexed and hurt when I was told to walk more sedately, "in ladylike fashion," because I was growing up. I wanted no more the life of what I called an Alice-sit-by-the-fire than did Scout. Together she and Atticus seemed to sweep clear a new ground, a ground Scout might occupy alongside her brother and her friend Dill, who proudly introduced himself to her with only two short sentences. " 'I'm Charles Baker Harris,' he said. 'I can read' " (13). Scout's world, like Dill's and Jem's, is as filled with books as it is with climbing trees, swimming holes, and old tires.

Make no mistake about it. The world of books and the intellect is gendered male in *To Kill a Mockingbird*. This is initially made clear at the moment Scout leaves home to encounter the public world for the first time amidst the desks and blackboards of the first grade. School is a bitter disappointment to Scout precisely because it cannot tolerate her independence. She is disciplined as much for her intellectual precocity as she is for fighting too exuberantly like a boy. The agent of that discipline, strikingly enough, is Miss Caroline Fisher, no more than twenty-one, with "auburn hair," "pink cheeks," "crimson fingernail polish," "high-heeled pumps," and "a red-and-white-striped dress." Scout remarks with disgust, "She looked and smelled like a peppermint drop" (22). Miss Fisher earns Scout's ire by humiliating her before her peers on the first day of school. Her transgression is that she reads too well. Expecting Scout only to name the alphabet she prints on the board "in enormous square capitals," Miss Fisher is stunned when Scout can read not only *My First Reader* but the stock-market quotations from *The Mobile Register*. She responds immediately with an incomprehensible prohibition. Miss Caroline Fisher tells

Scout that her father must not teach her anymore because it will interfere with the kind of reading officially prescribed for her by her school.

Scout is stunned. She knows Atticus has never consciously taught her to read. In fact, she tells us, "I never deliberately learned to read, but somehow I had been wallowing illicitly in the daily papers" (24). A licit, schoolbook literacy, here associated with feminine women, is abjured in this novel in favor of a more defiant, more virile literacy attuned to the immediacies of the daily world. Meditating on how she has come to commit the peculiar crime of reading too well, Scout continues:

> Now that I was compelled to think about it, reading was something that just came to me, as learning to fasten the seat of my union suit without looking around, or achieving two bows from a snarl of shoelaces. I could not remember when the lines above Atticus's moving finger separated into words, but I had stared at them all the evenings in my memory, listening to the news of the day, Bills to be Enacted into Laws, the diaries of Lorenzo Dow—anything Atticus happened to be reading when I crawled into his lap every night. Until I feared I would lose it, I never loved to read. One does not love breathing. [24]

From the first, then, Scout's reading and precocious intellectual life are associated with the world of her lawyer father. Although he has not deliberately taught her, he has shepherded her into literacy without concern for her gender or her age.

Significantly, Scout transgresses further later in the same day by showing herself capable of writing as well. Bored to death by Miss Caroline's cards with the words "the," "cat," "rat," "man," and "you" printed on them, she writes a letter to Dill. The fact that she writes in script enrages her teacher even more. This skill, we soon learn, was taught to her not by her father but by her family's cook, Calpurnia, who is first described to us in Scout's words as "all angles and bones" with a hand "as wide as a bed slat and twice as hard." Scout recalls that "she would set me a writing task by scrawling the alphabet firmly across the top of a tablet, then copying out a chapter of the Bible beneath" (25). "In Calpurnia's teaching," Scout adds tellingly, "there was no sentimentality: I seldom pleased her and she seldom rewarded me" (25).

Calpurnia's status as a stern and demanding teacher would be unremarkable were it not for the fact that she is black. Not only is she black, but she is constantly associated in the story with Atticus, who supports her authority, calls her a member of the family, and refuses his sister's subsequent efforts to dismiss her. At this point in the story, though, Scout hardly notices the color of Cal's skin, and she certainly understands little of its significance in 1935 in her small, southern town. She has no idea that Cal's skin color ought to have denied her the ability to read and prevented her from acting as a teacher to white children. However, *To Kill a Mockingbird* is the story of Scout's coming of age, and much of what she learns has to do with the complex power arrangements surrounding black-white relations. Eventually Scout discovers that Calpurnia's literacy is quite extraordinary.

The book wants us to approve of Cal's mastery of literacy just as we are meant to applaud Scout's special reading and writing skills. However, it is essential to note that the extension of literacy and recognition of Cal's individuality that seem to follow from it are conferred by authoritative, white men. Cal learned to read from a copy of Blackstone's *Commentaries* given her by Scout's Grandaddy Finch. Additionally, though Scout's and Calpurnia's reading may be associated in *To Kill a Mockingbird* with acts of transgression against traditional gender and race arrangements, when they do transgress, they do so with the encouragement of Atticus, a man who is presented to us not only as the most conspicuous reader in the story but as its social center and final moral authority. Described even by those who disapprove of his willingness to defend the Negro, Tom Robinson, as "a deep reader, a mighty deep reader" (174), Atticus comes before us as the model reader to be emulated and, ultimately, as the source of the book's own teachings about "Maycomb's usual disease," racism.

Curiously, as much as Atticus is celebrated as a wise and judicious lawyer throughout *To Kill a Mockingbird*, the source of his wisdom does not reside in his mastery of the abstractions of the law. His principles, we learn early, are much more homely. In counseling Scout he suggests to her that she will succeed in the future if she can learn a "simple trick." "You never really understand a person until you consider things from his point of view," he tells her, "until you climb into his skin and walk around in it" (36). Atticus advises Scout not that all people are abstractly identical but that they are particular individuals and, as such, the products of specific histories. He stresses that to understand how each individual sees, it is necessary to understand where he sees from.

In effect Atticus recommends a familiar, middlebrow conception of the person. His vision of the individual as singular and distinct is not far removed from Henry Canby's insistence that all human beings, even fictional ones, must be understood as "warm-blooded," embodied in unique, highly particular ways. Yet the book is also nervous about its investment in this notion, for it worries incessantly that seeing the individual as distinct and therefore as irreducibly different might jeopardize its commitment to redressing the limitations imposed on women and Negroes. The book is acutely aware, in fact, that arguments against racial bigotry, especially, are usually predicated on the idea of abstract equality. But the notion of abstract equality, a flat and universal sameness, is intolerable in the world of *To Kill a Mockingbird* because the book is driven by an equally powerful commitment to the idea of special talent and extraordinary gifts. It is torn, therefore, between the horns of a difficult dilemma: how to preserve its appreciation for singularity and uniqueness while, at the same time, conceptualizing a world where every individual's humanity is recognized and respected.

Significantly, it is Atticus who attempts to work out this conundrum for the reader in his summation to the jury deciding Tom Robinson's fate. But it is important that his reasoning is overshadowed and undercut to a certain extent by a feeling of inchoate dread that accompanies the book's narration of its framing plot, which is opened in the first pages of the novel, advanced only intermittently, and left unconnected to Tom's story until the final pages of the tale. This plot concerns a white man, the mysteriously different Boo Radley, who appears to threaten Scout, Jem, and Dill. At the end of the novel, Boo's killing of the person who actually tried to harm the children is covered up by Atticus and the town sheriff because they recognize that he did it to protect the children. Their success at protecting Boo is paralleled with their failure to protect Tom. This foregrounds, whether intentionally or not, that white men still possess the power to mete out justice and to confer rights and individuality on others and that they still do so selectively according to the color line.

Atticus's moral authority is nonetheless key to the logic of the book. It is connected to his ability to see individuals as distinct and different. Indeed he explains carefully to Scout that he is not defending a "nigger" but the individual, Tom, and that he is doing this not because of abstract principles but because Tom's case affects him personally. He does not explain how, although he admits that "the main reason" he is defending Tom "is, if I didn't I couldn't hold up my head in town, I couldn't represent this county in the legislature, I couldn't even tell you or Jem not to do something again" (83). At first it is difficult to discern why he reasons this way, but eventually we are led to understand that, for Atticus, authority is staked ultimately on the notion of responsibility, and responsibility is the special province of those with special talents.

This is established in what seems a gratuitous scene about the killing of a mad dog. The event is crucial because it provides the occasion for Miss Maudie to teach Scout and Jem about their father's extraordinary capabilities. When Scout and Jem are shocked to discover that their father is a crack marksman who can kill a wandering dog with a single, long-distance shot, Miss Maudie takes pains to explain to them why Atticus concealed his skill from them. "I think maybe he put his gun down when he realized God had given him an unfair advantage over most living things," she explains. "People in their right minds," she clarifies, "never take pride in their talents" (107). Singular "gifts," apparently, pose a problem to social equality. As such they must never be lorded over others. In Atticus's view, Maudie tells the children, such talents and gifts must be used modestly, in the service of others, and never in aggrandizement of the self alone. If Atticus did not use his talents for reading and reasoning to defend Tom, we are left to infer, he would be guilty both of dishonoring his gifts and of failing to fulfill his responsibility to those not so endowed. His particular responsibility, the trial scene makes abundantly clear, is to recognize and thereby to protect the individuality of those who cannot manage to protect themselves.

Atticus begins his final summation to the jury, in typical legal style, by dispassionately reviewing the evidence he has assembled. Almost immediately, however, he abandons his detachment and the sign of his professional status—he loosens his vest and tie and takes off his suit coat. Atticus speaks to the men on the jury personally, "as if they were folks on the post office corner" (215). Personal address, we are prompted to hope, will be powerful enough to overcome the prejudices of the jury and the abstractions of racialized, categorical thinking. Atticus's subsequent disquisition seems to provide foundation for that hope. He asserts, in fact, that the witnesses for the state "have presented themselves . . . in the cynical confidence that their testimony would not be doubted, confident that you gentlemen would go along with them on the assumption—the evil assumption—that *all* Negroes lie, that *all* Negroes are basically immoral beings, that *all* Negro men are not to be trusted around our women" (217). And that, Atticus observes, is itself "a lie as black as Tom Robinson's skin." "You know the truth," he adds, "and the truth is this: *some* Negroes lie, *some* Negroes are immoral, *some* Negro men are not be trusted around women—black or white." Atticus adds authoritatively, "This is a truth that applies to the human race and to no particular race of men."

With these comments Atticus seems to confirm the view adumbrated throughout the early pages of the book that human beings are different, that they are individual, and that they should be dealt with as such. Indeed his next remarks dispute the notion of abstract equality. Though "Thomas Jefferson once said that all men are created equal," he observes, "we know all men are not created equal in the sense some people would have us believe—some people are smarter than others, some people have more opportunity because they're born with it, some men make more money than others . . . —some people are born gifted beyond the normal scope of men" (217–18). People are individual and different, Atticus suggests, and some, he implies, deserve the position of authority and status they command. In effect he gives a familiar defense of middlebrow individuality and expertise.

Curiously, though, Atticus does an immediate about-face. He adds almost matter-of-factly that "there is one human institution that makes a pauper the equal of a Rockefeller, the stupid man the equal of an Einstein, and the ignorant man the equal of any college president. That institution, gentlemen, is a court" (218). Although Atticus concedes that "our courts have their faults, as does any human institution," he insists that "in this country our courts are the great levelers, and in our courts all men are created equal" (218). Here the justification of special talent and privilege seems to be withdrawn in favor of the assertion of the abstract principle of equality in a court of law. Significantly, this will compensate for a natural inequality that appears to be inevitable. But then Atticus wheels and turns one more time and abandons his entreaty to the principle of equality and appeals to the men as individuals. He concludes, "Gentlemen, a court is no better than each man of you sitting before me on this jury. A court is only as sound as its jury, and a jury is only as sound as the men who make it up. I am confident that you gentlemen will review without passion the evidence you have heard, come to a decision, and restore this defendant to his family. In the name of God, do your duty" (218). Atticus's halting, contradictory argument is the sign of the book's great uneasiness about squaring its defense of individuality and talent with its desire to recognize the humanity of all.

To no one's surprise, least of all that of Atticus, the men ignore clear proof of Tom's innocence and find him guilty. Despite the power of Atticus's personal appeal, they cannot overlook Tom's unpardonable sin—not the alleged rape but the fact that in his own testimony he expressed pity for his accuser and thereby placed himself above a white woman. The fact that the men fail to do their duty, as the book conceives it, only underscores Atticus's extraordinary nature and the fact that he has performed his and thereby fully lived up to his responsibilities. Although his moral act does not lead to Tom's acquittal, we are led to believe that it has contributed to social progress simply because the jury takes hours to deliberate. The implication is that Atticus's appeal to the men as singular individuals almost worked. In the future, social change will surely come through the responsible recognition of singular and distinct individuality.

No wonder I admired Atticus. He is presented in the book not only as an intellectual and as a witness to the individuality and humanity of both girls and Negroes, but also as the engine of social progress. But as I have already indicated, the denouement of the book casts a certain doubt on the efficacy of this personal approach to social problems. Soon after the dramatic trial scene, in fact, Tom Robinson is killed trying to escape from prison. Atticus suggests that despair led him to this desperate act. "I guess Tom was tired of white men's chances and preferred to take his own," he remarks (249). Whatever Tom's motivation, it is clear that Atticus's moral convictions and heroic performance of duty have been powerless to prevent the reestablishment of the racial status quo. In the end the black man is punished for questioning traditional arrangements of power. The punishment, it seems, will be extended even to Atticus himself. Bob Ewell, the father of the woman allegedly raped by Tom, vows revenge for Atticus's humiliation of him at the trial.[30] He attacks Jem and Scout. They are saved from certain death only when the two plots are finally joined and Boo Radley emerges from his hiding place, frees the children from Ewell's grip, kills him, and returns Atticus's children to him.

Significantly, Boo does not tell this story himself. His tale is pieced together by the sheriff and Atticus, who in effect speak for him. In the telling, Sheriff Heck Tate proves himself as adept at middlebrow logic as Atticus is. He will conceal Boo's heroic act not because he fears the town might misunderstand and brand Boo a murderer, but because he knows the unwanted attention will destroy Boo by "draggin' him with his shy ways into the limelight" (290). Because Tate recognizes Boo's peculiar personality, he empathizes with him, and because he empathizes with him, he becomes his protector. Although we are not told explicitly why the sheriff and Atticus can understand Boo so well, the very manner in which he is described highlights his color in extraordinary ways. Scout first reveals his presence to us by pointing to him. "As I pointed," she says, "he brought his arms down and pressed the palms of his hands against the wall. They were white hands, sickly white hands that had never seen the sun, so white they stood out garishly against the dull cream wall in the dim light of Jem's room" (284). Boo's color is stressed several more times as we watch Atticus and Tate make the decision to cover up his crime. We cannot help but wonder, then, whether the whiteness he shares with Tate and Atticus is not at least partly responsible for their ability to see the particular humanity in this otherwise strange and different man.

Are we further meant to take this ironically as Lee's sardonic comment on the true efficacy of Atticus's personalist approach to social problems? Is the familiar racist and sexist world restored at the end because Atticus's vision has failed? After all, these two white men only succeed in protecting the individuality of another white man. By the end of the story, in fact, even Scout herself realizes that although she feels "more at home in [her] father's world," she will soon have to enter the world of women, "where on its surface fragrant ladies [rock] slowly, [fan] gently, and [drink] cool water" (246). That ironic reading seems possible, but in the end, I think, we are meant not to judge these moral prescriptions about individuality wanting but to assent to their truth in concert with Atticus. Indeed the last words he pronounces in the story underscore the value of the by-now familiar lesson that Scout manages to derive from a book they are reading together. Half sleeping in her father's arms as he reads Seckatary Hawkins's *The Gray Ghost* to her, she insists that she has heard and understood the story it tells. "Yeah," she says, "an' they all thought it was Stoner's Boy messin' up their clubhouse an' throwin ink all over it. . . . An' they chased him 'n' never could catch him 'cause they didn't know *what he looked like*, an' Atticus, when they finally *saw* him, why he hadn't done any of those things. . . . Atticus, he was real nice" (295). Atticus confirms the wisdom of her assertion with his final pronouncement in the book: "Most people are, Scout, when you finally *see* them."

As *To Kill a Mockingbird* would have it, then, humanity and individuality are there to be seen. However, it takes the gaze of one with both knowledge and power, apparently, to recognize them and thereby to confer the status of personhood on those who cannot manage to establish it for themselves. For all its interest in empowering girls and Negroes, Harper Lee's novel finally assents to the rule of a learned and compassionate elite. Although we are led to believe that because this elite takes its responsibility seriously it might admit girls and Negroes to its bar in the future, it also implicitly suggests that such recognition will come only if both can remake themselves, as Scout and Calpurnia almost manage to do, in the image of a learned, white man. Indeed the very last two sentences in the novel provide inadvertent but poignant commentary on the welcome that might be accorded someone like Scout if she cannot successfully manage the masquerade. As Atticus leaves her room for the night, she tells us, "He turned out the light and went into Jem's room. He would be there all night, and he would be there when Jem waked up in the morning" (296). As we close the book, then, Atticus's gaze is trained not on Scout but on her brother, Jem.

I could not have told you all this in 1964. I certainly did not notice that it was the white man who was protected while the black man was lost. But I was dissatisfied with the novel's end. I remember thinking that Atticus's sentiments seemed a little too pat, a little too easy. I did not really understand how just *seeing* other people was going to corral Bull Conner's dogs or make James Meredith's road at the University of Mississippi any easier. Still, these were problems of "the South," a world where ladies rocked on porches and sipped cool water. They were easy enough to put aside, then, as other people's problems, and since I had no intention of ever finding contentment in sitting and sipping, I closed the book still admiring Atticus and bent on making myself in his image.

### THE REACH OF MIDDLEBROW DESIRE

Most of the books I read that year, as I turned fifteen, similarly celebrated the achievements of heroic men. Together with *Marjorie Morningstar*; *Gods, Graves, and Scholars*; and *To Kill a Mockingbird*, they tutored me about the value of a public world rendered significant by "serious" problems and "momentous" events. If they argued that this world had to be humanized and enlivened by the actions of individuals with extraordinary warmth and compassion, they nonetheless suggested that its compass could only be taken by people with broad knowledge and special training. What these books taught me to want, then, was a professional's power, a power lodged in books, honed in institutions of higher learning, and wielded in the name of greater knowledge.

The knowledge I wanted knew few limits. *Kon-Tiki* suggested that intellectual work might eventually take me to a place like the South Pacific, put me on a raft with a few other intrepid souls, and set me to proving a theory passionately held. *The Ugly American* suggested that I might actually understand why talk of dominoes and this strange-sounding country, Vietnam, with its even stranger-sounding cities, such as Dien Bien Phu and Hue, had suddenly begun to occupy so much time on the news programs I watched religiously. If the book was profoundly nationalist in its assumption that the United States was destined to bring its superior democracy to lesser states misguidedly enamored of communism, it also suggested that a commitment to the truth, to greater knowledge, might push one to criticize one's country constructively in the interest of greater global responsibility. Indeed the book's authors counseled me that "to the extent that our foreign policy is humane and reasonable, it will be successful. To the extent that it is imperialistic and grandiose, it will fail" (267). These sentiments provided fertile ground later for my participation in my generation's antiwar movement. But they also further reinforced my emergent professionalist aspirations with the exhortation, "We do not need the horde of 1,500,000 Americans—mostly amateurs—who are now working for the US overseas. What we need is a small force of well-trained, well-chosen, hard-working and dedicated professionals. . . . They must speak the language of the land of their assignment, and they must be more expert in its problems than are the natives" (284). I wanted to be such a person.

The books selected by the Book-of-the-Month Club and sent by Mr. Shymansky suggested that knowledge was so powerful, in fact, that it might even enable me to understand the inexplicable events that had shaped my parents' adult lives and the history of the twentieth century, that is, the events of World War II. I cannot recall a moment when I first learned about the war or the figure of Adolf Hitler. These events were part of the everyday texture of my childhood because my father's wartime picture albums documenting his years in the Air Force were always ready to hand. Every time I pulled them down from the front closet to admire the uniformed crew of his B-24 or to puzzle over the aerial photos of bombs dropping on German cities, my mother or father would haltingly try to explain why the war was fought, who Adolf Hitler was, and what he had done. But those events always still felt just beyond comprehension, unexplained, and inexplicable. Perhaps that is why I was willing to attempt a book whose narrative fragmentation I found very difficult—*The Wall*, by John Hersey. Maybe that is why I plowed through William Shirer's 1,250 pages of *The Rise and Fall of the Third Reich*. Rereading Shirer's daunting narrative now, I cannot imagine that I actually read the whole thing then. But I certainly wanted to, and even more, I know I wanted to say that I had. I suspect, in fact, that my desire to make sense of these most incomprehensible events of a generally baffling century was widely shared and the very thing that made Shirer's the most popular book ever sent out by the Book-of-the-Month Club. Even if the book was not fully read in every case, it promised those who ordered it, held it in their hands, paged through it, and perhaps made their way through only the first few chapters that a singular, dedicated man, armed with a relentless desire to know and an endless willingness to read papers, documents, letters, and books, could actually comprehend the incomprehensible.

When Dr. Waugh finally sliced through my cast with a tiny, buzzing saw in October 1964, liberating me at last from the house and that bedroom, I returned to school. Freed of my plaster armor, I felt terribly fragile at first and very small. I worried about girlish things—whether I could return to the cheerleading squad or what I would look like in a dress again. Mr. Shymansky's books already seemed an incidental part of a distant past, books that had provided only a stay against boredom, easy enough to forget, and certainly not worth mentioning to anyone. Their effects remained, though, steeling me for a future almost the way the bone grafts now straightening my spine enabled me to walk fully upright for the first time in two years. Although I was not aware of it, their powerful evocation of the riches to be found in the world of knowledge and expertise enabled me to dismiss those cheerful, cartoonish diagrams I found in my SAT booklet only a year later. Those diagrams claimed that girls with a certain SAT score would complete fewer years of higher education and make less money than boys with exactly the same score. I was determined that this would not happen to me. I wanted to be as familiar with a professional world as Atticus was and as authoritative as he seemed to be. I was determined not to take up my place on that porch Scout saw looming in her own future, nor did I want any part of the house in Mamaroneck next to Marjorie's. Books, reading, and the worlds they revealed were the hope Mr. Shymansky and the Book-of-the-Month Club gave me, the hope that I might breach the pink cotton walls of the feminine penitentiary.

For me Mr. Shymansky's middlebrow books accomplished many things. They staved off loneliness and peopled an imagination starved by enforced isolation. At the same time they preserved desire by delineating objects I might aim for at the very moment when I felt crushed by the necessity to contain every familiar want I had ever known, the desire to hang out with my friends, to ride downtown, to make the cheerleading squad, to go to a dance. Less immediately, perhaps, they surveyed, mapped, and made sense of an adult world. They described that world as one where the irreducible individual was a given, where knowledge was revered, and where expertise was to be sought after with intensity and a sense of purpose. They provided materials for self-fashioning as a result, and models to emulate. In the end they fostered my entry into middle-class selfhood and pointed me in direction of the professional middle class.

There were terrible costs, though, among them the repudiation of my gender demanded by the still-masculine image of professionalism. Indeed, I took my place in college classrooms where we read only a handful of books by women. As an undergraduate, the only female writers I read were the Brontës, Jane Austen, Emily Dickinson, and Edith Wharton. No Margaret Fuller, no Kate Chopin, no Gertrude Stein, no Djuna Barnes, no Virginia Woolf, and not even George Eliot. The women we read about—Carrie Meeber, Lady Brett Ashley, Hester Prynne, Caddie Compson, and Temple Drake—all seemed to meet an awful fate. Similarly, the way of reading we were taught required our subordination to an all-powerful text, whose flinty, virile power was always highlighted by its rejection of a feminine sentimentalism. It did not occur to me to ask what was wrong with sentiment. I was too intent on the goal of acquiring the particular form of technical expertise I found so compelling, expertise about literature and high culture. I wanted the authority that seemed to follow from knowing books and understanding how to read them. I wanted to command all that New York had once signified.

But I am also sure that I found Russel Nye's classroom so welcoming because he seemed to recognize that women read and that what they read were books by Susanna Rowson, Harriet Beecher Stowe, Mrs. E. D. E. N. Southworth, Laura Jean Libbey, Caroline Keene, and Margaret Mitchell. I chose his field of specialization, popular culture, at least in part because it promised a haven from the redundantly masculine world I had elected so unconsciously, a world whose highest accolades were reserved for writers who could display ostentatiously their refusal of all things soft, lush, mushy, and feminine. It now seems clear to me that my highly abstract dissertation managed to foster my entry into the middle-class and masculine world of professional competence because it also provided a transitional object in that its case study focused on the romance. It enabled me to cling, still, to a woman's world of haunted Gothic houses, terrified but plucky heroines, threatening heroes, and true love promised at the end.

But even as I wrote about Gothic romances as a graduate student, my view of them, their writers, and their readers changed. This happened because I was still reading and talking with other readers, women who directed me to their favorite books and who thus provided new eyes to see with, new ideas to think with, and new words to articulate both. Nancy Purcell gave me *The Bell Jar* and *The Second Sex*. Marsha Carlin introduced me to *Our Bodies, Ourselves*. Karen Butery told me to read Kate Millett's *Sexual Politics* and Elaine Showalter's *A Literature of Their Own*, and Sharon O'Brien introduced me to Nancy Chodorow's *The Reproduction of Mothering*. *Reading the Romance*, my own effort to explain the appeal of paperback romances, resulted from this reading. But I now think that it also grew at least in part out of grief for a willingly forsaken world. In some ways it was my unknowing act of homage to a universe I had rejected, a universe of women readers who managed to cobble together the planks, nails, nuts, bolts, joists, and beams necessary for self-fashioning from books and histories framed only to reveal the architecture of lives

{ *Books for Professionals* }

lived by men. The act of writing that book was my way of transforming Atticus Finch, the heroic reader of my adolescence, into romance reader Dorothy Evans, the woman I interviewed most extensively to try to understand why women found romances so compelling. It makes sense to me now why I chose the name Dorothy as her pseudonym. Dorothy is my mother's first name.

I do not want to romanticize the hope Mr. Shymansky's middlebrow books provided for a fourteen-year-old girl. That hope was not extended to everyone. The books successfully endowed *me* with a vocabulary of desire because my race and relative class privilege had already positioned me in such a way that I could imagine myself a member of their projected audience. The characteristics of that imaginary audience were dictated in part by the fact that the books had germinated in a culture driven by particular social and economic changes. Those changes necessitated the creation of new kinds of subjects with new kinds of desires and capacities. Quite simply, there was work to be done and not yet enough people prepared to do it. Middlebrow books performed the necessary ideological labor of drawing the precise outlines and purposes of professional-managerial class work, and they helped to imagine the interior life of the person that might make it possible. They modeled a form of subjectivity and structured desire in a way that was recognizable to readers like me precisely because we had *already* reaped certain benefits from the accident of our middle-class birth and the educational prerogatives that came with it. Perhaps it was the very intensity of the particular desires these books cultivated that prevented so many of us from seeing that the value of the knowledge and expertise they celebrated was dependent in the end on a prior act of exclusion whereby the alternative knowledges possessed by others were construed as ignorance or naivete or, even worse, as lack of ambition in the first place.

# AFTERWORD

The Book-of-the-Month Club continues to send books every month to hundreds of thousands of subscribers. It does so, however, as a changed organization with a quite different relationship to its membership and to a reorganized literary field. The much-rumored restructuring of the judges' panel took place in September 1988. At that time Wilfrid Sheed, Mordecai Richler, and Gloria Norris were asked to resign. In a *New York Times* article announcing the change, Al Silverman was quoted as saying that "the action positions us to meet the demands of the future." Elaborating on the nature of those demands, the reporter cited the words of the head of a large publishing house who observed that "the club appears to be trying to respond more quickly to submissions and apparently is seeking greater flexibility in decisions about main selections."[1]

Only two weeks later Time, Inc., announced that Larry Crutcher would succeed Al Silverman as chairman of the Book-of-the-Month Club. The *New York Times* reported the next day that the announcement was met with worry in the publishing industry. "Some publishing officials have expressed private concern that Time Inc. may be planning to clip Book-of-the-Month's editorial wings," the paper reported. "Whereas Mr. Silverman, who is 62 years old, and his predecessor Edward Fitzgerald, came up through book-club ranks, Mr. Crutcher, 46, came to the club in 1985 after serving as general manager of Fortune, as a vice president of Time Inc. magazines and as corporate vice president for financial planning."[2] Crutcher's magazine and marketing background signaled to the reporter in question, as it once had to Book-of-the-Month Club staffers themselves, that literary values were being forsaken for more commercial concerns.

After these two announcements the kind of speculation I had been party to throughout 1986 and 1987 spilled out of the club's offices and onto the pages of both the *Times* and the industry magazine, *Publishers Weekly*. Nearly everyone in the trade worried whether the judges would be replaced by people from within Time's own ranks, and they worried as well about the future direction of the club. Their suspicions that Time intended to make the club an even more commercially minded establishment were alleviated temporarily by the December 1988 announcement that authors Gloria Naylor and J. Anthony Lukas would become Book-of-the-Month Club judges. Their literary credentials encouraged some to believe that the club would not tamper with what the *Times* called "one of the most visible and important [positions] in the book industry."[3] However, when Al Silverman himself retired not long afterward, rumors developed again that the club's literary orientation would be altered fundamentally in the near future.

As the prospect of internal change had once pushed the editors to value more intensely the club's history and its apparent ability to balance the literary and the commercial, so too did the more public upheaval at the club prompt nostalgic efforts to measure its long-standing impact on the American book trade. The *Times*, in fact, published a long piece by novelist James Kaplan in its Sunday magazine that eulogized the club's longevity and literary and cultural stature and detailed the problems it was facing in a rapidly changing publishing environment. Kaplan opened his essay portentously. "The Book-of-the-Month Club," he wrote, "the name itself—upright and stately—connotes quiet afternoons on a hammock or evenings curled up by the fire with a good book. But these are strange times in the publishing industry, and days of turmoil at the venerable club."[4] Apparently, within the space of sixty years, the upstart organization that had been founded by Harry Scherman and then criticized intensely for its obsession with speed and sales figures had been transformed into a hoary literary institution and a commercial dinosaur. It had become outmoded, many thought, in what Kaplan called "the brave new world" of international media empires.

Referring to the fact that Time had recently announced that it would merge with Warner Communications, Kaplan suggested that "theoretically, this unprecedented corporate fusion makes it possible for a title to be published in hard-cover by Little, Brown (a division of Time Inc.), featured as a Book-of-the-Month Club main selection, reviewed in Time magazine, issued in paperback by Warner Books, made into a major motion picture by Warner Bros. and turned into a TV series by Warner Television." In this new environment the traditional printed book represented only one small stage in a larger integrated process designed to turn out corporate "product." The club's continuing attention to literary authority, to its modest but cultivated readership, and to the search for "serious" books seemed a quaint and highly impractical bit of antiquarianism in a world given over to the quest for media overlap and synergy.

Over the next two years the *Times* and *Publishers Weekly* reported regularly on personnel changes at the club. Most involved the appointment of people directly concerned with the increasingly difficult business of acquiring new members and with the marketing of the books themselves. Despite continuing assurances from within the club that the judges were completely free to make their own decisions about main selections, certain developments suggested that the alternate operation at least was to be guided by marketing concerns and overseen by the Time management. *Publishers Weekly* reported on January 20, 1992, for instance, that the club had restructured its managing units and was transforming the role of then editor in chief Brigitte Weeks. George Artandi, the recently appointed president and CEO of the club, announced the creation of a new managerial layer that would oversee both the Book-of-the-Month Club organization and the other specialty clubs. The restructured editorial department, headed by Weeks, would still read and process the manuscripts, but it would only make recommendations to management rather than choose the alternates itself. *Publishers Weekly* noted that "although the restructuring of Weeks's department was accompanied by her promotion to senior vice-president, indications are that her role has been diminished." The reporter continued, "Some observers interpret these changes as a reflection of management's perception of a lack of commercial acumen in the club's selections, evidenced in rival Literary Guild's walking away with many recent bestsellers."[5]

The reorganization did not produce the hoped-for changes. In September 1993 Brigitte Weeks was replaced by Tracy Brown as editor in chief. George Artandi was reported to have wanted "a really savvy publisher . . . closer to the business."[6] In an article discussing Weeks's "abrupt dismissal," one of the judges was quoted as saying that "marketing has a much stronger role than it has had in the past. The company is shifting away from being an editorial department-driven company to being much more strongly influenced from the marketing side."[7] Although Artandi himself disputed this, only a year later he finally dismantled the structure that Harry Scherman had created in 1926. On July 1, 1994, Tracy Brown announced the planned dissolution of the club's decades-old editorial board. No longer even referred to as "the judges," the group that had once been hired for its literary authority and asked to choose the best book of the month was summarily fired. Taking note of the change, the *New York Times*'s reporter observed that "the decision . . . brings to an end a venerable publishing institution that has become increasingly marginalized over the years, as the time between a manuscript's submission and publication has shrunk and market considerations have grown ever more important."[8] Newly dismissed judge Anthony Lukas was permitted to deliver the eulogy: "I have felt increasingly that the sales side of the scale weighed heavier and heavier. . . . I can remember many meetings in which I really learned about American literature, and these meetings became more and more anachronistic. We were conducting our meetings quite in a vacuum with little if any effect on the club's decisions."

The final epitaph for the club was recorded by the *Times* less than two years later. Headlined "Triumph of the Bottom Line," the April 1996 article commented on yet another corporate revamping and Tracy Brown's own dismissal.[9] Noting that the editorial department had finally been placed under the control of a newly promoted marketing director, Richard F. Schnable, the *Times* underscored the by-then familiar complaint that "the club has lost its soul to marketing strategies that push best sellers instead of the best writing, brand-name authors instead of risky new novelists." Acknowledging, however, that such changes were not unique to the club, the *Times* added that "the steadily growing influence of the marketing department is a story not only of the Book-of-the-Month Club, but also of the entire publishing industry, where it has become common for sales directors to shift across the house to positions as editorial directors and publishers."

It would be easy enough to underscore the *Times* epitaph and to offer these events as the final denouement of the history I have tried to tell here. In that case this would stand as a familiar tale of declension, as the story of how literary values have been subordinated to marketing concerns over the course of the twentieth century. Even more spectacular, this account of the apparent rise and fall of the Book-of-the-Month Club might be construed as one small scenario in the larger tale that has been indulged in again and again of late, that is, the all-too-familiar story about the decline and death of the book in a world of television, electronic computer games, and the Internet. Were I to conclude the club's history in this way, it could be read as an ironic tale about an organization hoist by its own petard. In this version Harry Scherman's hybrid effort to wed an Arnoldian cultural project to the advertising and distribution strategies of twentieth-century consumer culture would be presented as the victim of forces it had itself set it motion, doomed, in the long run, by its own financial greed and by the energy and creativity with which it had pursued the task of getting more books to more people. The implicit moral of such a story would be that the pursuit of a mass audience necessarily implies the simplification of cultural material to the lowest common denominator. Put even more baldly, such a story would proclaim that quality and value are a function of scarcity and that literature, culture, and art will only survive if they remain uncontaminated by the market and the right province of the aesthetically discerning and intellectually discriminating few.

Corporate buyouts, mergers, and the downsizing that inevitably follows are not unique to the publishing industry in the 1980s and the 1990s. When economic decisions like these are made, they have a corrosive impact on the day-to-day work of many and even more devastating effects on the lives of long-term employees who are fired in the name of long-range goals and the pursuit of profit. This trend, it seems to me, ought rightly to be questioned and deplored. But I am wary of ending this story about the Book-of-the-Month Club in the familiar moralizing way where opposition to certain economic and social practices would slide easily into the assumption that the cultural consequences of such decisions are always equally and necessarily pernicious. It is not at all clear to me that a publishing industry determined to sell more books of a certain kind necessarily harms the cause of literature or is contributing to the death of the book. After all, this industry that is increasingly preoccupied with the blockbuster bestseller is also a sophisticated user of niche marketing and, through the development of boutique imprints and specialized series, is also using its sales acumen simultaneously to target particular kinds of buyers in particular kinds of bookstores, those with a taste for so-called quality contemporary fiction and serious nonfiction. Comparative literacy rates and statistics are notoriously difficult to compute, but it is entirely possible that the size of the audience for self-consciously literary fiction has, and continues to remain, constant over the twentieth century.[10] What may have changed with the growth of the so-called bestseller mentality is the publishing industry's ability to design books that might appeal to people who ordinarily read only magazines and newspapers or who watch television. This industry that is now so focused on increasing sales could conceivably be promoting reading rather than contributing to its demise.

Harry Scherman himself may well have welcomed the kinds of changes Time, Inc., and Time-Warner have made to the club in the last ten years. Although he was deeply interested in writers, books, and readers and committed, finally, to the enlightening tendencies of culture, his early papers make clear that his search for the best books was a deliberate accommodation to the structure of the literary field at the time. His judges, as I have tried to point out, were hired to persuade people who thought the words "commerce" and "literature" were antonyms that there was no necessary reason why a sales-minded organization could not promote books of quality. Scherman thought of himself first as an advertising man and remained unembarrassed by the pursuit of profit. He may well have cheered in response to George Artandi's claim in that death-knell article in the *Times* that "the Book-of-the-Month Club is a major cultural institution, and in order to remain that way it has to occupy a significant part of the public mind." Scherman might well have approved of Artandi's further observations: "It is essentially a mirror of the marketplace. When you have as many people as we do, it's not an elite business. We sell people what they want to buy. I don't know if the club has changed. If it has, it has changed along with the rest of the country and its institutions." [11]

Artandi's comments might have suggested to Scherman that what we are witnessing as the twentieth century draws to the close is not the death of the book but its relentless transformation. Less the exclusive possession of a highly educated few, the book is more frequently produced as an engine of emotional transport for the many, as a means to intense and sometimes transformative pleasure, and as a way to participate in a common cultural ritual of the moment. Of course, to those worried about the ideological determinants of such rituals, troubled by the soporific effects of pleasure, wary of the seduction of being absorbed into a group, and disdainful of the experience and expression of sentiment, even this narrative is alarming.

It should be evident that I am not at all certain that the story of the Book-of-the-Month Club ought to be read as evidence for the simple decline of the literary in the twentieth-century United States, where the literary stands for all that is either politically oppositional or somehow culturally transcendent. It seems to me that the complex history of Scherman's organization and the conflicted nature of the literary material it sent out should caution us about drawing conclusions about the club's legacy that are too simplistic or without nuance. The club may have normalized and naturalized a class-specific view of the world through its book selection procedures and the particular body of material it sent out. At the same time, though, through its attention to and emphasis on the highly variable activity of reading, the club may also have empowered its subscribers to use those books in ways not entirely congruent with the ideological framework responsible for their selection in the first place. It seems fairly clear that the middlebrow books selected and authorized by the club helped to construct a dominant cultural form in the United States of the 1920s and 1930s, a form that was subsequently and redundantly promoted by publishing houses, libraries, schools, and even by Hollywood as it remade so many middlebrow books into feature films. Still, that new cultural dominant was riven and divided at its very core. What gave middlebrow culture its energy, power, and attractiveness were the tensions it managed to balance, the competing forces it was able to hold in solution.

On one hand the club underwrote and legitimated an ideology supporting the notions of special expertise and technical knowledge. On the other hand, by stressing the worth and necessity of popularization, the Book-of-the-Month Club and other similar middlebrow institutions also expressed resentment about the insularity and narcissism of professionals who claimed such knowledge as their special province. Although the club banked on the literary authority of its judges and therefore admitted that special literary expertise actually did exist, it made every effort to place that expertise in the service of nonprofessional readers, who had little reason to care about a book's intricacies of textual construction but who were manifestly interested in its ability to capture their attention, to promote an intense response, and to act as a form of provocation.

Similarly, the club exhibited a certain ambivalence about the organization of the domains of knowledge that made up the world for the professional-managerial class. On one hand the logic of evaluation at the club respected the separation and the relative autonomy of each of those various domains. History was different from science, the judges thought; science was different from literature; literature was different from public affairs. Information and knowledge in each of those domains, therefore, ought properly to be assessed and evaluated differently with respect to the special aims, interests, and investments operative in each. Different forms of knowledge and the experts who professed such knowledge were distinct from one another, and each had its own special validity or authority. Middlebrow culture, in effect, naturalized a world made meaningful by division and discrimination, a world inhabited by discrete individuals each made distinct from the next by his or her particular personality and distinctive form of expertise.

On the other hand the judges' and editors' quest for intense affect in the process of reading betokened a longing to see overturned the self-containment and isolation characteristic of a rationalized, bureaucratic, professionalized world. In their desire to promote a reading experience that produced heightened interest and investment in alternate worlds rendered in words, an experience that they described as one of absorption or incorporation, they construed the act of reading as both a protest against and a refuge from the highly segmented, professionalized world they otherwise recommended. The characteristic style of middlebrow reading and the ideology of personalism that aided and abetted it, at some level at least, offered a critique of the class-specific view of the world that middlebrow culture helped to underwrite.

Finally, the Book-of-the-Month Club surely acted to further the commodification of culture and, in the long run, to promote a new kind of consumer subject, who mobilized her or his literary taste as just another component in the construction and display of a self. Yet in providing an opportunity to develop and display a familiarity with culture for some who might not otherwise have inhabited an arena where they could do just that, the club may also have been acting to trouble at least a little the usually tight connections between social status, access to advanced literacy, and public command of a certain kind of taste. The books the club sent out often attempted to reign in the proliferating desire for command of cultural capital and subject status that changing economic patterns and educational practices had set in motion among more diverse populations. As in *To Kill a Mockingbird* or *Marjorie Morningstar*, they did so by trying to recommend the continuing normativity of the white, male, literate, bourgeois subject. It seems possible, however, that the effects of attempted narrative closure whereby authoritative male subjects like Atticus Finch or Wally Wronken were reinstalled as appropriate models for selfhood may have been overridden in the end by the contradictory material effect of extending an invitation to identify with them to a more diverse group of aspiring readers through the somewhat less socially exclusive mechanism of the marketplace.

Similarly, in helping to construct a subject who was not complete without the display of various kinds of goods, that is, the subject-for-the-commodity, the club may well have promoted consent to and thereby strengthened the reign of a consumer economy. Yet, at the same time, it may also have been helping to envision a subject not singularly tied to some unchanging essence but one more multiple, mobile, and fluid, a subject with more porous boundaries and therefore intensely intertwined with the object-world and distinctly receptive to the constitutive and transforming gaze of others. In concert with additional forces cracking apart the supposed coherence of the unitary bourgeois subject (like the diversification and hybridization of the population), middlebrow reading in particular may have nurtured a self potentially open to engagement with the social world in new ways, a subject not sealed off and autonomous but desiring and dependent, a subject therefore open to the possibility of fostering unprecedented connections and forging surprising alliances, such as those that fueled the civil rights movement, the women's movement of the 1960s and 1970s, and the gay rights movement after that.

The Book-of-the-Month Club's most important and lasting legacy may not have been the support it provided for the evolving consumer culture of the twentieth century or its role in fashioning would-be professionals for a society devoted to the generation and rapid circulation of information. Its more significant contribution may have been the encouragement it provided for another kind of subject—the reading subject—who does not approach only a few sacralized books as objects to be revered or fetishized but, rather, who uses all sorts of books as different and distinct occasions for reflection, meditation, contemplation, or pleasure. The Book-of-the-Month Club enjoyed its greatest success in an era when competing literary professionals were making claims about the essential superiority of a highly specialized way of writing and simultaneously developing a coordinate technical language for describing the many facets of the hard jewel of the literary text that resulted. It seems possible that the club's success might have been as long lived as it was because, in opposition to this reign of the fetishized text, its middlebrow judges may have managed to keep alive a vision of reading. In doing so they may have protected reading as a space between, a space neither ordered by the text itself nor controlled by the reader, but one born of that special act of ventriloquism whereby the reader speaks another's words in populated solitude.

In sustaining the kind of reading Marcel Proust has called "incitement," the Book-of-the-Month Club may have managed to preserve and thereby to endow us with a vision of a veritable Babel of readers, a vision like that which closes Italo Calvino's *If on a Winter's Night a Traveler*, where seven different readers energetically attempt to capture for each other exactly how and why they read what they read. Where one thinks of reading as "an itinerary of reasonings and fantasies," another sees it "as a discontinuous and fragmentary operation" prompted by the search for "confirmation of a new discovery among the folds of the sentences."[12] Where another asserts that "reading is an operation without an object" and declares the book "an accessory aid, or even a pretext," still another insists that "in my readings I do nothing but seek that book read in my childhood, but what I remember of it is too little to enable me to find it again." Most significantly, the Book-of-the-Month Club may have empowered us to remember what another of Calvino's readers insists on, "the *promise* of reading," its pledge to take us elsewhere, most particularly, to a future not yet known.

# NOTES

## INTRODUCTION

1. I tried to put this suspicion into words in an article written in 1985, "Interpretive Communities and Variable Literacies."

2. I was an English major at Michigan State University from 1967 to 1971. The major introductory courses at the time were "forms courses," which were designed to introduce students to the key literary genres of poetry, drama, the novel, and the short story. What we were taught in those classes were the techniques and methods of close reading and textual exegesis associated with the New Criticism. As Gerald Graff, Michael Warner, and John Guillory have pointed out, the New Critics tended to conceptualize literature as a specialized form of language use that called out for, and therefore justified, elaborate, careful, and highly technical strategies of reading.

3. Foucault, "Nietzsche, Genealogy, History."

4. See especially Bourdieu, *Distinction*. The reader will find as my arguments progress that this book has been profoundly influenced by Bourdieu's work.

5. Proust, "On Reading."

6. In elaborating the meaning of the term "sentimental education," used in his well-known essay on the Balinese cockfight, "Deep Play," Clifford Geertz notes, "Attending cockfights and participating in them, is for the Balinese, a kind of sentimental education. What he learns there is what his culture's ethos and sensibility (or, anyway, certain aspects of them) look like when spelled out externally in a collective text; . . . art forms generate and regenerate the very subjectivity they pretend only to display" (449–51).

## CHAPTER ONE

1. Silverman, "Fragile Pleasure." Silverman's essay first appeared in the Winter 1983 issue of *Daedalus*.

2. In 1985 the club employed twelve or so individuals as in-house editors. Although many of these people had other responsibilities, their principal task was to read manuscripts sent to the club by publishing houses. In most cases the club received these manuscripts about six months prior to their publication. In reading, the editors were expected to determine whether a book was good enough to be chosen by the Book-of-the-Month Club as a monthly main selection or whether it would be more suitable as one of the alternates offered instead. If the editors thought a book was selection material, they could pass that book on to one of the five judges employed by the club to make its official recommendations. If the editors felt a book was good but too specialized to attract a large audience, they would recommend its purchase by the club as an alternate.

3. Zinsser memo. Quoted with the permission of William Zinsser and the Book-of-the-Month Club.

4. The phrase "studying up" was first used, as far as I know, by Laura Nader in her article, "Up the Anthropologist." I myself have attempted to articulate my own sense of what is involved in studying up in "Ethnography among Elites." There I address some of the differences between the situation I was involved in at the Book-of-the-Month Club and the situation I enjoyed with the romance readers I interviewed for *Reading the Romance*. At the same time, I try to provide my own critique of some of the assumptions I made about my relationship to the romance readers.

5. This account is meant to refer specifically to the activities I observed and made sense of during 1985–88. Although the editors I encountered at the club may have used the procedures, assumptions, and judgments I witnessed at other times during their careers at the club, I do not want to generalize excessively on the basis of what I observed and understood then. As the reader will soon discover, the Book-of-the-Month Club was eventually integrated into Time much more tightly. I have no way of knowing, however, whether the practices and structures I describe here have or have not been altered as a consequence.

6. Savago reader's report, "*Contact*."

7. In using the word "distinction" here, I mean to evoke deliberately the work Pierre Bourdieu has done on the subject of taste and specifically his claim that taste operates as a game for establishing social distinction. To practice or to display one's taste, he observes, is to position oneself in a complex social hierarchy. As such, taste is deeply bound up with both social location and social trajectory, which is to say, it is intricately tied to the phenomenon of class in twentieth-century society. In constructing their own canon of recommended books, the Book-of-the-Month Club editors and judges, like literary professors, were involved in the practice of making both literary and social discriminations.

8. Several days before each meeting a list was issued to all editors of the books that were to be discussed. Each editor was expected to read all reports on these books before the meeting and come prepared to present the particular titles he or she had read.

9. For a discussion of the importance of public ritual both within social communities and to ethnography, see Marcus and Fischer, *Anthropology as Cultural Critique*, 61. There, for instance, they observe, "Rituals are public, are often accompanied by myths that declare the reasons of the ritual, and are analogous to culturally produced texts that ethnographers can read systematically. They are thus much more empirically accessible as the collectively and public 'said,' in contrast to the 'unsaid,' the understated, and the tacit meanings of everyday life."

10. Lamont, *Money, Morals, and Manners*, 233.

11. Shapiro interview, October 30, 1986.

12. All of the editors I interviewed had completed four years of university training, most at small liberal arts colleges in the northeast United States. Several had done graduate work as well.

13. In emphasizing the power and resistance of the Book-of-the-Month Club editors, I do not want to imply that the romance readers I interviewed previously

had no such power. In fact, they structured and controlled our interviews as well and, I suspect, resisted my questions in creative ways. In fact, it occurs to me now that because I was less familiar with their linguistic patterns and habitual ways of talking, I was probably less able to pick up on the nature of their resistance and their manner of polite acquiescence to my volunteered interpretations. In fact, I suspect now that they were often humoring me.

14. Gelman interview.

15. For a discussion of this issue, see my earlier article, "Book-of-the-Month Club and the General Reader."

16. Asher interview.

17. Waxman interview.

18. Norris interview.

### CHAPTER TWO

1. Silverman, "What We Stand For," 1. Used with permission of Al Silverman and the Book-of-the-Month Club.

2. Ibid., 2.

3. Book-of-the-Month Club subscribers exercise the negative option when they choose not to receive the monthly main selection. They make this known to the club on an advance form that they must return by a certain date to prevent the automatic shipment of that particular book to their home. This procedure was invented during the first few months of the club's operation, and since 1926 it has served as the basis of the club's entire mail-order operation. In Europe, Robert Riger has informed me, this way of organizing mail-order sale is called inertia marketing. For a full discussion of the moment of invention and the larger historical significance of the negative option, see Chapter 6, below.

4. Silverman, "What We Stand For," 8.

5. Savago interview, September 8, 1986.

6. Robinson interview.

7. My account here of the editors' treatment of literary fiction is significantly different from the preliminary account given in "Book-of-the-Month Club and the General Reader." There I placed much greater emphasis on the horizontal mode of categorization enforced at the club and suggested that literary fiction was simply treated as one among many different categories, not as the apogee to which all else aspired. At the time I was not fully aware of the editors' ambivalence about the literary or of their contradictory treatment of it.

8. Van Straalen interview.

9. Rosenthal interview.

10. Norris interview.

11. Weinberg interview, February 26, 1987.

12. Riger interview.

13. In an effort to develop a more complex conception of the way domination and subordination are maintained in the social world, Pierre Bourdieu has attempted to develop a more supple conception of class. As a consequence, he use-

fully distinguishes among several different forms of capital, including economic capital, symbolic or cultural capital, and social capital. In general, for Bourdieu, capital is defined as the different attributes, assets, or qualities of a person that can be exchanged for other goods, services, or position. Economic capital refers, then, to the quantity of material goods and income commanded by an individual, while cultural capital refers to competencies derived from education, familiarity with a legitimized cultural tradition, and modes of consumption. Social capital refers specifically to a person's social networks and connections. The class position of an individual in a network of domination is determined for Bourdieu not simply by his or her economic capital but rather by his or her command of all of the various forms of capital, by the manner in which these assets were acquired and are displayed, and by the overall historical and social trajectory of that individual. For the most systematic elaboration of Bourdieu's social theory, see *Outline of a Theory of Practice*. For two early explications and critiques of Bourdieu's thought published in the U.S. context, see DiMaggio, "Review Essay," and Elizabeth Wilson, "Picasso and Pate de Foie Gras."

14. Bill's chapter title was drawn from the main question on the reader's report form.

15. Zinsser, *Family of Readers*, 48–49.

16. Ibid., 49.

17. Silverman, "What We Stand For," 6.

18. In recognition of the fact that the Book-of-the-Month Club is an ongoing business that is very much dependent on the goodwill of the writers whose work it distributes, I have agreed to mask the identity of certain individuals when discussion of editorial opinion of their work might jeopardize such a relationship. I have done my best, nonetheless, to characterize the writer and the work in question so the relevant points about the nature of editorial opinion will be clear.

19. Mabry reader's report.

20. Sansone reader's report.

21. For a discussion of the way certain modernist assumptions about literature have dictated critical approaches to literary texts, especially in literary classrooms prior to the mid-1970s, see Tompkins, "Reader in History."

22. Asher reader's report.

23. The history of the relationship between realism as a literary form and a modern, bourgeois class of readers is, of course, long and complicated. Middlebrow culture, as I will show in Part II, developed partly as a reaction to the arrival of various forms of literary modernism, which both critiqued and exploded the conventions on which claims to realistic representation were based. In opposition, middlebrow critics and culture continued to assert the value of literary texts that specifically aimed to represent and thus to comment on the traditional social and material world. For an interesting discussion of the way some contemporary readers continue to value realistic fiction and to use it both to shape and to critique their own lives, see Long, "Women, Reading, and Cultural Authority."

24. Savago reader's report, "*Sport of Nature*."

25. The phrase "lay reader" was one Joe used constantly in discussion with me.

26. The converse also happens. In fact, a genre book such as a mystery or

thriller can break out and away from its usual fans by exhibiting unusual literary properties. This happened at the club with P. D. James, whose books were featured as main selections precisely because they displayed much greater literary complexity than most detective fiction.

27. The reference here is to the work of Judith Krantz and Barbara Taylor Bradford, two commercial writers whose books consistently appear on the bestseller lists.

28. Phyllis Robinson reader's report, *"How to Help Your Puppy Grow into a Wonderful Dog."*

29. Parker reader's report, January 5, 1987.

30. Parker reader's report, *"Southern Food."*

31. Easton reader's report, *"AKC's World of the Pure-Bred Dog."*

32. Adrian interview.

33. Sansone, "Report on the Editorial Meeting," 2.

34. Ibid.

35. Parker reader's report, *"Taste of Southeast Asia."*

36. Riger interview.


### CHAPTER THREE

1. See Whiteside, *Blockbuster Complex.* See also Coser et al., *Books.* For the immediate context, see Feldman, "Going Global."

2. The quotations here come from my field notes taken at the editorial meeting, June 19, 1986.

3. Shapiro interview, October 30, 1986.

4. Savago interview, July 8, 1985.

5. It is worth pointing to the complexity of the assumptions that Joe makes here about the club's subscribers. He assumes that at least some of those subscribers will have heard of magic realism, will know about García Márquez and the fact that he is considered "difficult," and will be a little afraid of trying him. Thus, he assumes, they will be relieved to be told that Allende will familiarize them with this valorized cultural commodity but in readily accessible form. Clearly, the reader he imagines is very much aware of books, critical opinion, and the configuration of the larger literary field.

6. Crutcher and Silverman, "Management News Bulletin," January 13, 1987.

7. Ibid., 17 February 1987, 1. Signed by both Al Silverman and Larry Crutcher, the memo circulated widely at the club. I had seen it already by the time it was given to me confidentially.

8. Editorial meeting, February 12, 1987.

9. Weinberg interview, February 12, 1987.

10. Shapiro interview, February 20, 1987.

11. Shapiro reader's report, *"Napoleon's Generals."*

12. Cooney reader's report, *"America."*

13. Savago reader's report, *"March of Folly."*

14. Shapiro reader's report, *"America."*

15. Shapiro interview, February 20, 1987.

16. My observations here have been much influenced by the account of academic writing and reading given in Brodkey, *Academic Writing as Social Practice*.

17. Easton reader's report, "*King Arthur.*"

18. Sansone reader's report, "*Christianity and Paganism.*"

19. Mantell reader's report, "*Blind Watchmaker.*"

20. Tulipan reader's report, "*Ellis Island.*"

21. Savago reader's report, "*Beloved.*"

22. Rosenthal interview.

23. Silverman interview.

24. Savago interview, July 8, 1985.

25. Prinz interview, October 28, 1986.

26. These meditations preceded the appearance of autobiographical writing within the academy in the mid-1980s. Associated at first with feminist scholarship and, to a certain extent, with the writings of experimental cultural anthropologists, this movement has exploded in recent years with the increasing use of the personal voice and the publication of autobiographies and autobiographical reflections by well-known scholars. For an introduction to some of the issues surrounding the appearance of this phenomenon, see Tompkins, "Me and My Shadow," and Nancy Miller, *Getting Personal*. On this trend in anthropology, see Tedlock, "From Participant Observation to the Observation of Participation," and Ruth Behar, *Translated Woman*. This last book was enormously important to me as I attempted to write more personally about my fieldwork.

### CHAPTER FOUR

1. Tebbel, *History of Book Publishing*, 3:288.

2. The standard reference on American business history is Chandler's *Visible Hand*. See, in particular, his discussion of James B. Duke and the sale of tobacco, 290–92. On the relationship between branding, trademarking, and the structural changes in the American economy at the end of the nineteenth century, see also Trachtenberg, *Incorporation of America*, 138. See also Strasser's more recent *Satisfaction Guaranteed*, especially her discussion of Crisco and Ivory Soap, 3–26.

3. I use the word "literary" here in its earlier, broader sense to refer to the larger world of print production that was thought to comprise virtually all kinds of writing in book form. During the period under discussion here, the meaning of the term narrowed significantly to refer only to poetry, fiction, and belles lettres.

4. For a discussion of the construction of the division between highbrow and lowbrow culture, see Levine, *Highbrow/Lowbrow*. On the appearance of middlebrow culture, see Rubin, *Making of Middlebrow Culture*. It should be noted here that Levine's positing of a kind of golden age in the United States prior to the 1830s or 1840s, when a common culture was presumably shared by all, has been deemed questionable. It is not necessary, it seems to me, to accept this proposition to see merit in his discussion of the process by which two, only loosely differentiated classes of cultural forms and behaviors were progressively distinguished from

each other, which is to say, reified as distinct and wholly different forms of culture. Similarly, it is important to note that Richard Brodhead, in a chapter on Louisa May Alcott in *Cultures of Letters*, has implicitly contested Rubin's argument about the dating of middlebrow culture. Brodhead suggests that Alcott's domestic fiction constituted a form of writing, a middlebrow form, different from the sort found in mass-produced dime novels and story papers and from the high literary writing appearing in exclusive magazines such as the *Atlantic*. While Brodhead's thesis is interesting, it seems something of an anachronism to me to use the word "middlebrow" to describe this sort of production when the term did not appear in popular discourse until the 1920s. It will subsequently become clear, then, that I am more sympathetic to Rubin's argument and that I myself use the term to refer to a historically specific organization of cultural production that appeared only in the twentieth century when cultural entrepreneurs wedded a particular notion of culture to the production and distribution apparatus associated with supposedly lower forms. For me, then, middlebrow culture is both a material and an ideological form. I have been much aided by Joan Rubin's exemplary work on middlebrow culture, and the reader will find certain convergences and similarities in our arguments, particularly in the way we both stress the hybrid nature of the Book-of-the-Month Club and the manner in which it mediated certain cultural tensions. The key difference is that where Rubin places a certain amount of emphasis on the ties between middlebrow culture and the older, genteel culture of the nineteenth century, I prefer to see the Book-of-the-Month Club as a profoundly modern institution. As a result, I think of middlebrow culture as an important modernist ideological response to the series of material, social, and institutional changes referred to as modernization (see Chapter 5, below).

5. In addition to Bourdieu on the connection between aesthetic value and social hierarchy, see also Smith, *Contingencies of Value*, esp. 30–53.

6. It is important to note that this was not the only period in which the definition of the book was furiously debated. On earlier debates in the eighteenth century, see Woodmansee, "Genius and the Copyright," esp. 443–48. For a discussion of different approaches to conceptualizing books and reading in an earlier period in the United States (a discussion, incidentally, that challenges Levine's postulation of a common culture prior to the appearance of high and low versions in the mid-nineteenth century), see Gross, "Books and Libraries in Thoreau's Concord." Gross's work suggests that two different tendencies have existed from the beginning in American book culture, a more democratic tendency toward diffusion and widespread distribution, and a more insular, hierarchical tendency to preserve the book as the province of intellectual and social elites. While this may well be true, it does seem to me that these tendencies were reified during the latter half of the nineteenth century and erected into two distinct sets of institutions and practices for producing, disseminating, and controlling books.

7. I want to stress here that I conceptualize "the book" as a historically variable form brought into being differently at different moments by a distinct constellation of material and social relationships. I do not think of the book, then, as a stable, unitary thing that has simply been produced and distributed differently at different moments. Rather, different social formations themselves have produced

quite different books. This premise is shared by many recent scholars working in the field now called the history of the book. For a useful introduction to the field, see Darnton, "What Is the History of the Book?"

8. Anonymous, *The Critic* (1884), quoted in Tebbel, *History of Book Publishing*, 2:504.

9. Chandler, *Visible Hand*, 49.

10. Ibid., 208.

11. Lehmann-Haupt et al., *Book in America*, 147. See also Madison, *Book Publishing in America*, 3–49.

12. For a full discussion of cheap book production schemes in the nineteenth century, see Tebbel, *History of Book Publishing*, 2:170–74, 481–510, 201–14. See also Lehmann-Haupt et al., *Book in America*, 129–30, 201–10, and Shove, *Cheap Book Production in the United States*. See also Reynolds, *Fiction Factory*.

13. Tebbel, *History of Book Publishing*, 1:242–43.

14. Noel, *Villains Galore*, 5–6.

15. For a discussion of the mechanics of dime novel production, see Denning, *Mechanic Accents*. The account given here is heavily indebted to Denning. For a full account of perhaps the most important of these literary "syndicates," see Abel, "Man of Letters."

16. Seltzer, *Bodies and Machines*.

17. For a full discussion of the trademarking process, see Strasser, *Satisfaction Guaranteed*, 29–57. See also Jones, *Copyrights and Trade-marks*, and Bugbee, *Genesis of American Patent and Copyright Law*.

18. Denning, *Mechanic Accents*, 23. I am largely recounting Denning's narrative here.

19. Ibid., and Noel, *Villains Galore*, 166.

20. Denning, *Mechanic Accents*, 24.

21. On the emergence of this publishing constellation, see Rose, *Authors and Owners*, and Woodmansee, *Author, Art, and the Market*.

22. On the appearance of the active editor and the transition to a mass market model of publication in the periodical business, see Christopher Wilson, *Labor of Words*, 40–62. On this topic, see also Brodhead, *School of Hawthorne*, esp. chaps. 5 and 6, and *Cultures of Letters*, esp. chaps. 3 and 4. See as well Mott, *History of American Magazines*, 2–34, and Peterson, *Magazines in the Twentieth Century*, 1–43. In addition, see Damon-Moore, *Magazines for the Millions*. My account of mass market magazines has also been heavily influenced by the work of Richard Ohmann, especially his two articles "Where Did Mass Culture Come From? The Case of Magazines" and "The New Discourse of Mass Culture: Magazines in the 1890s," both collected in *Politics of Letters*. Ohmann's work is more fully developed in his wonderful new study, *Selling Culture*, which appeared as I was completing the final revisions to this manuscript. I have not been able to take full account of his highly complex argument here.

23. On the creation of the modern library, see Garrison, *Apostles of Culture*.

24. Ibid., 4.

25. For a discussion of another ad hoc classification effort that preceded Dewey's more rationalized approach, see Zboray, *A Fictive People*, 136–55.

26. For a related discussion of controversy in book publishing at the turn of the century, see Christopher Wilson, *Labor of Words*, esp. chap. 3, "International Copyright and the Emergence of Progressive Publishing," 91. For further discussion of the ideology of the literary gentleman, see Coultrap-McQuin, *Doing Literary Business*.

27. Henry Holt, quoted in Tebbel, *History of Book Publishing*, 2:48.

28. Quoted in ibid., 2:502–3.

29. Ibid.

30. See, for instance, Rubin's discussion of the reaction of genteel literary critics to the explosion in book production after 1850 and to the kind of reading it promoted, *Making of Middlebrow Culture*, 23–25. She cites James Russell Lowell's extreme comment, "It may well be questioned whether the invention of printing, while it democratized information, has not also leveled the ancient aristocracy of thought. . . . It has supplanted a strenuous habit of thinking with a loose indolence of reading which relaxes the muscular fiber of the mind. . . . The costliness of books was a great refiner of literature. . . . The problem for the scholar was formerly how to acquire books; for us it is how to get rid of them" (24).

31. On the library, see Garrison, *Apostles of Culture*. On the relevant history of the American school, see Cremin, *Transformation of the School*. On the creation of the university English department, see Graff, *Professing Literature*; Vanderbilt, *American Literature and the Academy*; and Guillory, *Cultural Capital*, esp. chap. 2. On the related and parallel development of American museums, see DiMaggio, "Cultural Entrepreneurship in Nineteenth-Century Boston."

32. For a brief history of the word "literature," see Williams's entry in *Keywords*, 183–88. See also his *Marxism and Literature*, 45–54.

33. Williams, *Marxism and Literature*, 50.

34. Ibid., 51.

35. Graff, *Professing Literature*; Warner, "Professionalization and the Rewards of Literature"; Brodhead, *Cultures of Letters*; Shumway, *Creating American Civilization*; Guillory, *Cultural Capital*; Strychacz, *Modernism, Mass Culture, and Professionalism*.

36. Brodhead, *Cultures of Letters*, 157.

37. Ibid.

38. Warner, "Professionalization and the Rewards of Literature," 15.

39. Ibid.

40. Tebbel, *History of Book Publishing*, 2:499.

41. Garrison, *Apostles of Culture*, 18.

42. Porter, *Books and Reading*. On Porter and the Yale scholars, see Stevenson, *Scholarly Means to Evangelical Ends*. See also Garrison's discussion of Porter in *Apostles of Culture*, 71–72, and Rubin, *Making of Middlebrow Culture*, 18–19.

43. Porter, *Books and Reading*, 5–6.

44. Ibid.

45. Ibid., 16.

46. Ibid., 19.

47. Ibid., 20.

48. Ibid., 33.

49. Ibid.

50. Ibid., 33.

51. Ibid., 72.

52. Garrison, *Apostles of Culture*, 100. Garrison's statement contains an anachronism. As far as I can determine, the terms "masscult" and "midcult" were first used by Dwight MacDonald in "Masscult and Midcult."

53. In effect, these publishers had pragmatically learned to differentiate cultural from economic capital.

54. Hawkins, *Between Harvard and America*, 292–97. I have relied heavily on Hawkins's account in my summary here. See also Tebbel, *History of Book Publishing*, 2:530, and Wright, "Mammon and the Muse."

55. Hawkins, *Between Harvard and America*, 292.

56. *American Magazine*, February 1926, 195. I am grateful to Roland Marchand for drawing my attention to this ad.

57. Hawkins, *Between Harvard and America*, 295.

58. Franklin, "American College and American Culture," quoted in ibid., 294.

59. Quoted in Hawkins, *Between Harvard and America*, 296.

60. Guthrie, "Decorative Value of Books."

61. Ibid., 138.

62. For an excellent summary of Marx's ideas about the nature of the commodity and the kind of reasoning or logic it made possible, see Martyn J. Lee, *Consumer Culture Reborn*, esp. 3–24. As Lee makes clear, traditional left critiques of commodity culture, following Marx, conceptualize its establishment as, in fact, a declension, a decline in the independence, authenticity, humanity, and potentiality of the human subject. Recently, however, as Lee points out, a critique of this discourse has developed that both exposes its grounding in Marx's own fetishism of use-value and the concept of productive labor, and that attempts to open up a new inquiry into the history, significance, and effects of commodity culture. Lee conceives of his own book as an effort to explore the history of the commodity form. For another inquiry into the nature of the commodity and mass consumption, see Daniel Miller, *Material Culture and Mass Consumption*. In addition, see Appadurai, *Social Life of Things*. I will return to these issues in greater depth in Chapters 6 and 7, below.

63. Quoting the statistics of Daniel Pope, Roland Marchand has recently observed that total advertising volume in the United States increased from $682 million in 1914 to $1,409 million in 1919 to $2,987 million in 1929 (*Advertising the American Dream*, 6). Martyn Lee himself has observed, "Of course in the modern consumer marketplace the social meanings that attach themselves to commodities are, in the first instance, supplied by such institutions as advertising, marketing and similar promotional organisations. Without such institutions, commodities would be likely to confront consumers as alien objects devoid of cultural significance" (*Consumer Culture Reborn*, 17).

64. For an excellent and still-unsurpassed analysis of the way advertisements work, see Williamson, *Decoding Advertisements*. For a critique of Marx's notion of use-value, see Baudrillard, *For a Critique of the Political Economy of the Sign*.

65. For a discussion of the rise of consumer society and the role of manufac-

tured goods in creating identity, see Schudson, *Advertising, the Uneasy Persuasion*, esp. 147–77.

66. My account of the consumer subject constructed through these book-decorating schemes bears a distinct similarity to the portrait of the personality discussed by Susman in his highly suggestive and influential essay " 'Personality' and the Making of Twentieth-Century Culture," in *Culture as History*, 271–86. Susman argues that early in the twentieth century the dominant "character" model of selfhood began to give way to a new model of "personality," which stressed self-fulfillment and self-realization rather than the need to maintain equilibrium between the self and the social order through concepts of work, duty, and citizenship. He notes, "The new personality literature stressed items that could be best developed in leisure time and that represented in themselves an emphasis on consumption. The social role demanded of all in the new culture of personality was that of a performer. Every American was to become a performing self" (280).

Although I have been influenced by Susman's essay and by his important insights, I prefer the term "consumer subject" to his "personality" for two reasons. To begin with, I think the former is especially useful because it foregrounds the dialectical interdependency of consumer capitalism and a particular model of the individual subject. Thus the term stresses the fundamental interplay between culture and economy and works against the tendency to see culture as somehow above, if not outside, economy altogether. Second, I have steered away from Susman's notion of "personality" because it is now so linked in the theoretical imagination with its opposing term, the culture of "character." Although I think Susman's own account of the differences between these two models of the self is judiciously formulated and fully cognizant of the fact that both models present their own problems and contradictions, many subsequent adaptations of the terms have proved to be highly moralistic in nature. That is, as part of an ideological project to oppose consumerism and capitalism, various authors have presented the character model as if it were an intrinsically better model of the self, somehow more capable of adequately capturing the real depth of the human individual and its capacity for resistance to the instrumentalism of capitalist social life. Such a move, I think, remains captive of the very ideology it purports to analyze. It assumes the existence of depth and of the authentic subject rather than understanding both as particular historical productions. As a consequence, the notion of personality is demonized in a parallel and simplistic way by accusing it of superficiality, of vacuousness, of "banality," in the words of Jackson Lears (*No Place of Grace*). While I would not want to dispute the claim that the consumer subject is constructed through a highly managed display of discrete objects, I do think it problematic to assume concomitantly that the appearance of such a performing self *necessarily* constitutes a loss or decline in either individuality or authenticity. This model of selfhood, it seems to me, the consumer subject, the subject-for-the-commodity, offers different modes, methods, materials, and possibilities for achieving individuality that becomes less a function of a differentiated essence than of a unique combination of commonly occurring social materials. As a consequence, such a model tends to emphasize the value of fluidity, flexibility, and pliancy, thus constructing, *at least potentially*, a different sort of political subject, one perhaps more capable of adjustment and adaptability to the social presence of others. This, of course, flies in the face of the usual claim that modern capitalism has increasingly atomized human subjects and isolated them from one another, thus preventing political opposition.

67. Guthrie, "Decorative Value of Books," 139; emphasis added.

68. Doud, "Books for the Home," 192; emphasis added.

69. Ibid., 528.

70. Ibid.

71. I want to thank Carolyn Marvin for drawing my attention to the parallels between Doud's way of thinking about books and the use of talismans in tribal societies. This view of books was repeated and developed more fully by the Book-of-the-Month Club's judges, who also placed a high premium on emotion, feeling, and sensibility.

72. On the double discourse of value, see Smith, *Contingencies of Value*, 31–37.

CHAPTER FIVE

1. Bernardine Kielty Scherman, *Girl from Fitchburg*, 64–67.

2. On the significance of Ford's assembly line, see Beniger, *Control Revolution*, 298–301; Chandler, *Visible Hand*, 280; and Boorstin, *The Americans*, 422–28. See also Harvey, *Condition of Postmodernity*. Harvey comments, "What was special about Ford . . . was his vision . . . that mass production meant mass consumption, a new system of the reproduction of labour power, a new politics of labour control and management, a new aesthetics and psychology, a new kind of rationalized, modernist, and populist society" (125–26). My comments here are heavily indebted to Harvey's. In fact, I see this book as an attempt to modify Harvey's own efforts to provide a history of the aesthetics and psychology that developed concomitantly with modernization. Where Harvey concentrates on high modernism and then on postmodernism as the characteristic aesthetic forms of consumer capitalism, I suggest here that the historical account of this period is incomplete if it does not pay attention to the real cultural dominant of the period, the new middlebrow culture that was redundantly circulated to the guardians, managers, and technicians of this new society through the market itself, through schools, libraries, and other quasi-official cultural institutions.

3. The notion of the "modern" figures centrally in this chapter, as it does throughout the following two. It is, of course, not an uncontested concept. Even in the period 1880–1930 it was used by many different groups in different ways to give shape to the sense that the rapid economic, social, and cultural developments of the period were somehow distinctly different from all that had occurred previously. Thus the notion of a modern business was not necessarily related to what was referred to as modern art.

It should already be clear that my own understanding of what constituted a modern business has been heavily influenced by the accounts given by Alfred Chandler and James Beniger. Neither, however, makes any effort to relate economic or bureaucratic developments to changes in ideology or in cultural organization, an effort that has been made consistently within the traditions of Marxist thought. That tradition, it seems to me, can be helpful in trying to make sense of the appearance of the Book-of-the-Month Club and the phenomenon of middle-brow culture as long as one manages to resist the usual tendency to dismiss absolutely all forms of commercialized culture as essentially degraded, inauthentic, and ideologically suspect. The major challenge facing this project, it seems to me, is that of providing an account of the Book-of-the-Month Club's place in American economic history while yet articulating its complexity as a hybrid cultural form challenging the conceptual dichotomies on which the distinction between high and low culture, and that between the market and culture itself, was based. Only in this way, I think, will it be possible to do justice to the unevenness of the implications and effects of the phenomenon of middlebrow culture.

4. Quoted in Strasser, *Satisfaction Guaranteed*, 203.

5. Quoted in Tebbel, *History of Book Publishing*, 2:102.

6. For biographical material on Harry Scherman, see Charles Lee, *Hidden Public*, 20–25; see also the entries in *Current Biography, 1943*, 669–71, and *Current Biography Yearbook, 1963*, 374–77.

7. Charles Lee, *Hidden Public*, 19.

8. Harry Scherman, Speech before Central High School, Philadelphia, Pa., March 28 1960, Harry Scherman Papers, Material by and about Scherman, Manuscripts file, 4.

9. Ibid., 2.

10. See Wechsler, "Rationale for Restriction."

11. For a discussion of the history of English departments, see Graff, *Professing Literature*. For a discussion of the preference for all things English in literature departments, see Vanderbilt, *American Literature and the Academy*.

12. "Reminiscences of Harry Scherman," 1–38.

13. Ibid., 14.

14. Charles Lee, *Hidden Public*, 20.

15. "Reminiscences of Harry Scherman," 16.

16. Ibid.

17. Charles Lee, *Hidden Public*, 21; see also Bernardine Kielty Scherman, *Girl from Fitchburg*, 51–73.

18. "Reminiscences of Harry Scherman," 20.

19. Sackheim, *My First Sixty Years in Advertising*, 104.

20. "Reminiscences of Harry Scherman," 25.

21. Ibid.

22. Ibid., 28.

23. Sackheim, *My First Sixty Years*, 106.

24. "Reminiscences of Harry Scherman," 31.

25. Ibid., 33.

26. Ibid.

27. Ibid., 169.

28. Fass, *Damned and the Beautiful*, 124.

29. On the role of manners in nineteenth-century American society, see Kasson, *Rudeness and Civility*; see also Halttunen, *Confidence Men and Painted Women*.

On the role of commodity goods in American life, see Lears, *Fables of Abundance*, and Heinze, *Adapting to Abundance*.

30. In addition to Ohmann, see Garvey, *Adman in the Parlor*, and Scanlon, *Inarticulate Longings*.

31. May, *Screening Out the Past*, 155–65. I have also adapted the phrase "the drama of consumer display" from Harris, "Drama of Consumer Desire."

32. May, *Screening Out the Past*, 190–97.

33. Marchand, *Advertising the American Dream*, esp. chap. 5, "The Consumption Ethic: Strategies of Art and Style," 117–64. See also Bronner, *Consuming Visions*. On the connection between commodity production, consumption, and the modern need to develop skills in reading, see Schudson, *Advertising, the Uneasy Persuasion*, 156–61. Schudson notes, "For more and more people in the late nineteenth century and after, clothing came to be expressive and signifying. But so, too, did other material objects. Where buying replaced making, then looking replaced doing as a key social action, *reading signs replaced following orders as a crucial modern skill*" (emphasis added).

I should acknowledge here the notorious difficulty of dating the rise of the consumer economy. While many have argued that consumption only became important in the early twentieth century, there is also a growing literature in the field of material culture suggesting that domestic goods became increasingly important to the middle class in the mid-nineteenth century. See, for instance, Halttunen, *Confidence Men and Painted Women*. Given the persuasiveness of this work, I need to stress the fact that I am not suggesting here that consumer society was born only after 1880 but, rather, that in the period 1880–1930 significant changes occurred in the American economy and culture that foregrounded the role of the consumption of objects and their interpretive decoding in the daily life of more and more Americans. Reading, then, developed into an even more important and necessary skill not only because the ability to generate and to use information was increasingly essential to a professionalizing culture, but also because the interpretive, decoding habit it encouraged was generalizable to many other cultural arenas as well. Social and economic success was as dependent on the ability to read behavior, clothes, possessions, and taste as it was on the ability to read many different kinds of print documents.

34. I am drawing here on Bourdieu's account of the role played by the educational system in twentieth-century capitalist culture. He develops his account in the process of comparing modern cultures to so-called premodern ones in which symbolic or cultural capital tends to be lodged in particular persons by virtue of the accident of birth and inheritance. As he observes of such cultures, "When a society lacks both the literacy which would enable it to preserve and accumulate in objectified form the cultural resources it has inherited in the past, and also the educational system which would give its agents the aptitudes and dispositions required for the symbolic reappropriation of those resources, it can only preserve them in their incorporated state" (*Outline of a Theory of Practice*, 186). On the other hand, in a society with a developed educational apparatus, "by giving the same value to all holders of the same certificate, so that any one of them can take the place of any other, the educational system minimizes the obstacles to the free

circulation of cultural capital which result from its being incorporated in individual persons . . . ; it makes it possible to relate all qualification-holders . . . to a single standard, thereby setting up a *single market* for all cultural capacities and guaranteeing the convertibility of cultural capital into money, at a determinate cost in labour and time" (187).

35. Although the adjective "fungible" is now generally taken to mean "interchangeable," it was first used in the context of English civil law. *The Oxford English Dictionary*, in fact, cites an 1832 quote from Austin's *Jurisprudence* as its definition: "When a thing which is the subject of an obligation . . . must be delivered in specie, the thing is not fungible, i.e. that very thing, and not another thing of the same or another class in lieu of it must be delivered. Where the subject of the obligation is a thing of a given class, the thing is said to be fungible, i.e. the delivery of any object which answers to the generic description will satisfy the terms of the obligation." Clearly, any work of art considered to be unique cannot be fungible. That the singular status of cultural objects, the condition that ensured their nonfungibility, was perceived to be under attack around the turn of the century, can be seen from one of the quotations used by the *OED* itself to define fungibility. The editors note that *The Saturday Review* of 1886 commented, "A certain number of persons . . . do not . . . regard books as 'fungible', but exercise a choice as to the books they read." Harry Scherman, we shall see, challenged the first half of this proposition not by rendering all books absolutely equivalent but by organizing the print universe into different categories of books, that is, into a set of differential tools for provoking certain kinds of reading behaviors, experiences, and affects.

36. On the notion of liquidity in the realm of market relations and its relationship to questions of representation in the cultural sphere, see Agnew's important book, *Worlds Apart*, esp. 11-12 and 40-46. As Agnew notes, "The word 'liquidity' itself conveys the paradoxical sense of a pecuniary measure that clarifies and renders indisputable in one instance only to homogenize and render formless in another." "Money," he adds, "provides the standard by which values can be assigned in exchange. . . . 'Money is the purest embodiment of liquidity.'" It is my contention that it was the appearance of middlebrow culture, finally, that enabled academic credentials to function as the liquid measure of cultural capital. As Bourdieu notes, "Academic qualifications are to cultural capital what money is to economic capital" (*Outline of a Theory of Practice*, 187). On this point, see also Garnham and Williams, "Pierre Bourdieu and the Sociology of Culture," esp. 216-20.

37. The reference is to Walter Benjamin's classic analysis of the impact of mechanical reproduction on the nature of the art work, "Work of Art in the Age of Mechanical Reproduction."

38. This kind of advertising campaign is called the primary appeal. For a discussion of its importance to advertising discourse, see Ohmann, "Advertising and the New Discourse of Mass Culture," in *Politics of Letters*, 159.

39. "Reminiscences of Harry Scherman," 36.

40. Ibid., 37.

41. On the notion of authorship as an expression of personality, see Gaines, *Contested Culture*, esp. 42-83. See also Bourdieu's discussion of what he calls the "charisma" ideology of the work of art, which, he claims, "directs attention to the

*apparent producer*, the painter, writer or composer, in short, the 'author', suppressing the question of what authorizes the author" ("Production of Belief").

42. There is a certain inaccuracy in using this term here since Benjamin uses the idea of the aura to describe the artwork before the appearance of mass production. For Benjamin the aura of the traditional artwork follows from its singular occurrence in a specific time and place. Strictly speaking, then, one ought not to refer to the aura of a novel. I have, however, decided to employ the term here as a way of suggesting that the ideology surrounding the novel as a high art form in effect tried to preserve the notion that novels were distinct works of art even as the phenomenon of mass production was calling this claim into question.

43. See, for instance, Ted Robinson, "Book Habit," and Graves, "Humboldt College Plan."

44. Harry Scherman, "Original Outline of Plan for the Book-of-the-Month Club," 1.

45. Ibid.

46. Harry Scherman, Speech on book clubs, 2.

47. "Reminiscences of Harry Scherman," 38.

48. On this point, see Rubin, *Making of Middlebrow Culture*, 98–106. On the character of the modern tempo, the hectic pace of life it promoted, and the consequent anxieties it created, see Kern, *Culture of Time and Space*.

49. Harry Scherman, "Original Outline of Plan for the Book-of-the-Month Club," 3.

50. In *Highbrow/Lowbrow*, Levine has noted that "the Arnold important to America was not Arnold the critic, Arnold the poet, Arnold the religious thinker, but Arnold the Apostle of Culture" (223). For further discussion of Matthew Arnold's reception in America, see Raleigh, *Matthew Arnold and American Culture*.

51. The Book-of-the-Month Club's appearance, then, set in motion a process Bourdieu has identified as an inevitable development in the game of culture. He writes, "The opposition between the 'authentic' and the 'imitation,' 'true' culture and 'popularization,' which maintains the game by maintaining belief in the absolute value of the stake, conceals a collusion that is no less indispensable to the production and reproduction of the illusion, the fundamental recognition of the cultural game and its stakes" (*Distinction*, 250–51). Thorstein Veblen makes a similar point in *Theory of the Leisure Class*, first published in 1899. Although Bourdieu does not cite Veblen in *Distinction*, his analysis in fact reiterates, extends, and systematizes many observations about culture, taste, and consumption that were first made by Veblen. See especially his chapter "Pecuniary Canons of Taste," 115–66, in the Modern Library edition of *Theory of the Leisure Class*.

52. Benjamin, "Work of Art in the Age of Mechanical Reproduction."

53. Roland Marchand notes that during the 1920s, as part of an accelerated merchandising of style, advertisers undertook to promote modernity by educating the new consumer masses in a broad ideology of stylistic obsolescence based on the assumption that new goods enjoyed only limited usefulness. Marchand terms the relevant advertising work "the organized creation of dissatisfaction" (*Advertising the American Dream*, 156). It should be clear that in associating books with phrases such as "the au courant" and "the up-to-date" and in invoking the fear

of becoming a cultural laggard, Scherman was both relying on and contributing to this new discourse that helped to sever the connection between value and longevity, age, or permanence.

54. Harry Scherman, "Original Outline of Plan for the Book-of-the-Month Club," 3.

55. Quoted in Beniger, *Control Revolution*, 298.

56. Berman, *All That Is Solid*, 150.

57. In discussing the status of rural America in the period 1880–1920, Alan Trachtenberg has observed that "images of bustling, frenetic cities arose against a background of abandoned farmhouses and deserted villages, and many Americans pondered the change with regret and lament" (*Incorporation of America*, 115). "But," he continues, "these emptied places and impoverished regions were as much icons of incorporation as factories, railroads, and department stores. It was not that progress had passed them buy. The emptying itself represented a kind of integration." Trachtenberg notes, additionally, that "backward regions . . . represented easy markets for mass-produced goods. No place was so backward as to be out of reach of a railroad head and telegraph office, transmission belts which fed goods and information to country stores at rural crossroads." In effect Harry Scherman's distribution operation refined and extended this process of integration by connecting not country stores or rural crossroads to central networks but, rather, individual consumers themselves. In thus bypassing the troublesome bottleneck in the production/distribution system represented by the relative dearth of bookstores and insufficiently bookish merchants and clerks in general retail outlets, Scherman thereby increased the speed, regularity, and range of book circulation.

58. Berman, *All That Is Solid*, 306.

59. Harry Scherman, "Original Outline of Plan for the Book-of-the-Month Club," 4.

60. Fisher, "Book-Clubs," 209.

61. On the slow growth of academic attention to American literature, see Graff, *Professing Literature* (esp. 209–25); Vanderbilt, *American Literature and the Academy*; and Shumway, *Creating American Civilization*.

62. Canby, *American Memoir*, 252–53. *American Memoir* combined selections from Canby's two separately published autobiographical volumes, including *Age of Confidence* and *Alma Mater*, along with new material on his life with *The Saturday Review* and the Book-of-the-Month Club. Where possible, I have quoted from this volume because it seems to be more widely available than the other two. For a fine discussion of Canby and the other members of the committee of selection, see Rubin, *Making of Middlebrow Culture*, 110–43. I discuss these individuals in greater depth in Chapter 8, below, and comment there on how my interpretation of them differs from Rubin's. Here I concentrate only on the public reputations they brought to the club.

63. On the connection between the two organizations, see "Reminiscences of Amy Loveman," 522–38.

64. The best source on the details of Fisher's life is Washington, *Dorothy Canfield Fisher*.

65. Sally Foreman Griffith's biography of White, *Home Town News*, does a won-

derful job of exploring his resourcefulness in managing these particular tensions. See especially her chapter "Booster Nationalism," 187–210. See also Richard Brodhead's discussion of the 1880s and 1890s vogue for regionalism, *Cultures of Letters*, 107–41.

66. On the appearance of the humorous personal column, see Mott, *American Journalism*, 582–87.

67. Van Doren, "Day In and Day Out," 310. Also cited in Rubin, *Making of Middlebrow Culture*, 135.

68. Van Doren, "Day In and Day Out," 310; emphasis added.

69. For biographical details on Broun, see O'Connor, *Heywood Broun*, and Kramer, *Heywood Broun*.

70. None of the major columnists was a woman. For Rubin's account of Broun's and Morley's columns and of their significant emphasis on individuality, see *Making of Middlebrow Culture*, 133–43.

71. Henry Canby himself acknowledged this in an essay titled "Literature in America," included in *American Estimates*, where he discussed the new journalism and the personality column. "Furthermore," he wrote, "this rush of the anonymous ego to take refuge in rich, glaring personalities that write of the world as if it were still intimate, is an escape from science which has pervaded education with a consciousness of the abstract, immutable physical laws that take no account whatever of wish and ignore individuality completely" (24).

72. Van Doren, "Day In and Day Out," 311–32.

73. Harry Scherman, *Promises Men Live By*, x.

74. Ibid., xiii–xiv.

75. Ibid., xiv; emphasis in original.

76. Ibid.


## CHAPTER SIX

1. Charles Lee, "Book-of-the-Month Club," 31.

2. "Buy a Book a Month."

3. Ibid.

4. I am here paraphrasing comments Scherman made to the interviewers for "Reminiscences of Harry Scherman," 129.

5. Ibid., 363.

6. Ibid.

7. Charles Lee, *Hidden Public*, 30.

8. Dwight MacDonald, "Masscult and Midcult: II," 609, 592.

9. For two earlier discussions of the phenomenon of standardization and the controversies it generated, see Boorstin, *The Americans*, 165–244, and Michaels, "An American Tragedy."

10. I use the term "field" here in the sense elaborated by Pierre Bourdieu throughout his work but most especially in two essays, "The Field of Cultural Production" and "Field of Power, Literary Field and Habitus," both of which are included in *Field of Cultural Production*. For Bourdieu, "a field is an independent

social universe with its own laws of functioning, its specific relations of force, its dominants and its dominated" ("Field of Power," 164). Individuals struggle within fields for particular goods and rewards. Of the literary field, specifically, Bourdieu writes further:

> This field is neither a vague social background nor even a *milieu artistique* like a universe of personal relations between artist and writers. . . . It is a veritable social universe where, in accordance with its particular laws, there accumulates a particular form of capital and where relations of force of a particular type are exerted. This universe is the place of entirely specific struggles, notably concerning the question of knowing who is part of the universe, who is a real writer and who is not. The important fact, for the interpretation of works, is that this autonomous social universe functions somewhat like a prism which *refracts* every external determination: demographic, economic or political events are always retranslated according to the specific logic of the field, and it is by this intermediary that they act on the logic of the development of works. [163–64]

11. May, *Screening Out the Past*, 202; see also Berman, *All That Is Solid*, 299; Horowitz, *Morality of Spending*; Olney, *Buy Now, Pay Later*.

12. Olney, *Buy Now, Pay Later*, 13. There is very little specific information available about the nature of American spending on reading material or on reading itself prior to 1930. The two best survey articles on the subject, Stedman et al., "Literacy as a Consumer Activity," and Damon-Moore and Kaestle, "Surveying American Readers," contain few significant figures on either activity before 1929.

13. Charles Lee, *Hidden Public*, 24.

14. Harry Scherman, "Book-of-the-Month Club," 5.

15. "Reminiscences of Robert K. Haas," 952.

16. We will see in Chapter 8, below, that despite the apparent lack of attention to the literary preferences and aesthetic values of individual committee members, Scherman and his partners in fact hired a remarkably harmonious group whose preferences were surprisingly congruent.

17. "Reminiscences of Harry Scherman," 44.

18. Sackheim, *My First Sixty Years in Advertising*, 117. The advertisement appeared on p. 25 of the *Book Review*.

19. Sackheim, *My First Sixty Years in Advertising*, 118.

20. "Reminiscences of Harry Scherman," 120. Once again, in using such an appeal Scherman was apparently only relying on standard advertising practice at the time. Indeed, as Marchand shows in *Advertising the American Dream*, "what made advertising 'modern' was, ironically, the discovery of techniques for empathizing with the public's imperfect acceptance of modernity, with its resistance to the perfect rationalization and bureaucratization of life" (13). Interestingly enough, as evidence Marchand cites the 1930 observation of an executive at J. Walter Thompson that the inferiority complex has become "a valuable thing in advertising." Scherman apparently learned his lessons well during his own apprenticeship at the Thompson agency.

21. On the nervous, unsure relation to culture produced within the petite bourgeoisie by processes of cultural learning and acquisition that take place outside

the home and through formal institutions and agencies, see Bourdieu, *Distinction*, 318–46.

22. Neil Harris has come to a similar conclusion in his discussion of commodity culture in "Drama of Consumer Desire." There he writes, "In the 1920s, the flood of goods seemed impossible to dam; corruption could be avoided not by a refusal to participate in the great consumer drama, but by the exercise of choice and the determination of particular relationships between objects and individuals" (196).

23. In adopting the coupon approach to enable customer reply, Scherman was in fact simply employing the predominant form of copy-testing used in the 1920s. See Marchand, *Advertising the American Dream*, 75.

24. "Reminiscences of Edith Walker," 866–67.

25. Ibid., 873.

26. Later the club would be able to cut its losses on unsold and returned books by selling them to remainder houses.

27. "Reminiscences of Harry Scherman," 70. See also Sackheim, *My First Sixty Years in Advertising*, 119–20.

28. Sackheim, *My First Sixty Years in Advertising*, 119; emphasis in original.

29. On the importance of feedback operations to modern business as a key form of information control and therefore central to successful management of integrated operations, see Beniger, *Control Revolution*, 20. Beniger notes that "simultaneously with the development of mass communication by the turn of the century came what might be called mass feedback technologies: market research (1911) . . . house to house interviewing (1916), attitudinal and opinion surveys . . . large-scale statistical sampling (1930), indices of retail sales (1933) . . . and statistical-sample surveys like the Gallup Poll." It should not be surprising to note in the context of this discussion of the Book-of-the-Month Club's creation of its coupon-reply system that the club utilized several of these devices and even engaged George Gallup himself in the 1930s to begin polling on readers and reading behavior.

30. In addition to Beniger on the importance of information control, see especially Seltzer on the connections between sorting, representation, and machine culture, in *Bodies and Machines*, esp. 159–60. Seltzer argues that "the radical transformation in the thinking about programming and control from the 1870s to the 1930s that James Beniger has called 'the control revolution,' involved, above all, a rethinking of the problem of representation, communication, and information-processing: that is, the understanding of processes of representation—the always-material forms of information-processing—as production, and the understanding of production as processing, programming, and systemic communication" (159). He continues, "One reason why Maxwell's famous sorting demon (the hypothetical being that sorted fast and slow molecules so as perpetually to maintain energy in a closed system) seemed so paradoxical, at the time, was the basic difficulty in understanding sorting—information-processing—as work. And one reason why such a paradox now seems so commonplace is the basic difficulty in understanding work as anything other than as a process of sorting, representing, or programming" (ibid.).

In essence, I argue here that the Book-of-the-Month Club encountered opposition in part because of a similar inability on the part of its critics to recognize the activity of sorting materials and information distributed by others as a form of action, as the exercise of intentional activity, which is to say, as choice. For them, rather, choice was modeled on *physical* action, and its origins were located within the individual, interior self.

31. Rubin, "Self, Culture, and Self Culture," 790. Rubin backs off somewhat from her assertion in the revision of this passage for *Making of Middlebrow Culture*. See her remarks on pp. 100–101. Although Rubin is here discussing the first year's operation of the Book-of-the-Month Club, she suggests that subscribers could choose not to receive any book at all during a particular month. This was not the case. That innovation came considerably later, when the partners reduced the initial commitment required of the subscribers in response to the economic exigencies of the depression. By that point the organization was large enough and established on a sound enough financial footing to require only a portion of the membership to take a book in any given month.

32. For a harrowing portrait of an America dominated by its postal system, see Thomas Pynchon's novel *The Crying of Lot 49*, which explicitly takes up the consequences of a world dominated by the principle of Maxwell's Demon and poses the question of whether assembling and sorting information is work and whether, as work or labor, such sorting can ever accomplish the overthrow of the larger system. Through his exploration of the possibilities of conspiracy, Pynchon poses the question, in effect, of whether Oedipa Maas can stand outside the system or whether her opposition to it has already been predicted, taken into account, and therefore disarmed by the system itself. I am less interested in posing Pynchon's question about the Book-of-the-Month Club in particular or mass-distributed culture in general than its contemporary critics were, in part because it is not self-evident to me that we ought to strive to preserve the autonomous subject at any cost. I do think it important to ask, however, what kind of material gets sent through systemic channels like these and what kinds get systematically excluded.

33. See Seltzer's discussion of the importance of contract in market culture and its connection to the notion of the sovereign individual in *Bodies and Machines*, 71–74.

34. "Reminiscences of Harry Scherman," 127.

35. Although the evidence for this is indirect, I think the conclusion is warranted, given the fact that the materials in Scherman's files suggest that he was extraordinarily attentive to the various groups and factions in the publishing industry that might be affected by his operation. In addition, Charles Lee discusses the "alliance" between Scherman and *Publishers Weekly* in opposition to the price-cutting practices of the Literary Guild. See *Hidden Public*, 39.

36. "A Book a Month." The article does not make it clear where the internal quotation is taken from, but it must have come from one of Scherman's ads or press releases.

37. It is not possible to reconstruct from the documentary sources exactly when these sorts of connections and relationships were established, but they certainly were formalized at the time I conducted my fieldwork at the Book-of-the-Month Club offices. Not only did the club's many editors keep in close touch

with their counterparts at publishing houses through the use of the telephone and the business lunch, but house editors themselves sent elaborate packages of pre-publication material to club editors when they sent galley proofs of books to be considered for selection. In addition, the Book-of-the-Month Club editors frequently discussed the possibility of communicating with house editors about revisions to books that they thought would make them more attractive to a potential book club audience.

38. "Buying a Book a Month."

39. "A Publishing Book Club," 2146.

40. "Publishing Club Idea."

41. "An A.B.A. Page."

42. "Book Clubs and Book Shops."

43. "Details of the Book-of-the-Month Club."

44. Harry Scherman, "Report on the Book-of-the-Month Club after Seven Months of Operation." Two other mentions of the Book-of-the-Month Club appeared in *The Bookman* in July and September 1926 (pp. 623 and 119). Both only one sentence in length, the comments placed the club in the context of adult education and noted selection of *O Genteel Lady*!

45. "Reminiscences of Dorothy Canfield Fisher," 507; emphasis added. The implicit, taken-for-granted opposition between "literary" and "business" concerns, we shall see, developed as the crux of the matter.

46. Harry Scherman, "Report on the Book-of-the-Month Club after Seven Months of Operation," 5.

47. Ibid., 6.

48. On the early history of this debate about the relationship between literacy and democracy, see Warner, *Letters of the Republic*. See also Raleigh, *Matthew Arnold and American Culture*, and Levine, *Highbrow/Lowbrow*. Raleigh's analysis of Arnold's reception and influence in the United States is particularly helpful in this context, for he shows that the ideology of democratic individualism both warranted the extension of Arnold's project to America and posed innumerable problems for it. On one hand it underwrote the Arnoldian desire to educate all the people, while on the other hand it posed a threat to the survival of "the best that had been thought and said in the world." Of Emerson, perhaps America's first cultural pedagogue, Raleigh observes, "Although he was an ardent democrat, Emerson yet had the distrust of the untutored masses that Arnold had, and he warned: 'Leave this hypocritical prating about the masses. Masses are rude, lame, unmade, pernicious . . . and need not to be flattered, but to be schooled. . . . I wish . . . to . . . draw individuals out of them. . . . Masses! the calamity is the masses'" (10). On the Young America critics, see Blake, *Beloved Community*, and Hegeman, "Democracy of Cultures"; on the liberal intellectuals, see Seidman, *New Republic*; on the left avant garde, see Kalaidjian, *American Culture between the Wars*; on the entire social context of the period, see Ann Douglas, *Terrible Honesty*.

49. To date there is still no comprehensive account of the range of American opinion on the rise of mass culture. Several scholars have dealt with limited aspects of the reaction to the modern mass media at different historical moments, including Czitrom, *Media and the American Mind*; Marvin, *When Old Technologies*

*Were New*; and Ross, *No Respect*. As I was completing the last revisions to this manuscript, I received Gorman's *Left Intellectuals and Popular Culture in Twentieth-Century America*. I have not been able to take full account of his argument here. In addition, there is the still-useful anthology of thought edited by Rosenberg and White, *Mass Culture*.

50. "Babbitt" and "Main Street" were familiar rhetorical figures in these debates. In the August 1929 issue of *The Bookman*, for instance, Douglas Bush noted that "then came Mr. Lewis, and the revolt against parochialism and standardization was in full swing" ("Making Culture Hum").

51. For a discussion of the creation of a "gear and girder world" and the many responses machine technology evoked within the literary and artistic realms, see Tichi, *Shifting Gears*. For an earlier treatment of similar issues, see Marx, *Machine in the Garden*. In addition, see Nye, *Electrifying America*.

52. Boorstin, *The Americans*, 165–244.

53. Russell, "Take Them or Leave Them."

54. Ibid., 170.

55. Ibid., 171.

56. Ibid., 174.

57. Beffel, "Lost Art of Profanity."

58. Chase, "One Dead Level."

59. Seltzer, *Bodies and Machines*, 152.

60. David Macleod, quoted in ibid., 153.

61. Chase, "One Dead Level," 137.

62. Stallybrass and White, *Politics and Poetics of Transgression*.

63. Whipple, "Books on the Belt."

64. "The Bookseller."

65. Stallybrass and White, *Politics and Poetics of Transgression*, 22.

66. Frank, "Pseudo-Literature," 46.

67. Ibid.

68. Ibid.

69. Ibid.

70. Ibid.

71. Ibid., 47.

72. Ibid.

73. Ibid.

74. Ibid.

75. Ibid.

76. Lentricchia, "Lyric in the Culture of Capitalism." Although Lentricchia very usefully distinguishes the modernism of Robert Frost from that of Pound, notes the gendered quality of Pound's vision, and further suggests that Frost's version was more amenable to a larger, general audience, his admiration for Pound's form of critique is barely disguised. For an alternate account of Frost and other "popular modernists," see Abbott, "Modern American Poetry."

77. H. L. Mencken, for instance, in *The American Language*, dates the appearance of "highbrow" and "lowbrow" to 1905 (p. 206) but makes no mention of "middlebrow." Mitford Mathews, in *A Dictionary of Americanisms on Historical*

*Principles*, dates the appearance of "highbrow" to a 1908 article in *The Saturday Evening Post* (p. 804) and makes no mention of "middlebrow" at all.

78. Farmer, *Americanisms*; Bartlett, *Dictionary of Americanisms*.

79. Brooks, *America's Coming-of-Age*, 3–35.

80. Simpson and Weiner, *Oxford English Dictionary*, 9:741.

81. Widdemer, "Message and Middlebrow"; Woolf, "Middlebrow."


## CHAPTER SEVEN

1. Strasser, *Satisfaction Guaranteed*, 43.

2. For a discussion of the unevenness of both economic and cultural change, see Raymond Williams's exploration of the operation of dominant, residual, and emergent forms in *Marxism and Literature*, 121–27. I prefer Williams's formulation of this set of relationships to the revision of them developed by Terry Eagleton in *Criticism and Ideology*, even though I have appropriated his term "the literary mode of production" here. Eagleton, it seems to me, posits too mechanical a relationship between economy, cultural production, and ideology despite his explicit desire to avoid a kind of Marxist functionalism. Still, in using Williams's terminology it is important not to give the connotations of progress to emerging modes of production or to think of residual modes as simply retrograde and therefore conservative.

3. I have used the gendered pronoun advisedly here because, like Jane Gaines, Sandra Gilbert, Susan Gubar, Jane Tompkins, Nancy Miller, and many other feminists, I believe the ideology of the writer as literary genius was profoundly gendered. That is to say, writing was analogized as a kind of fathering of the work by means of the phallic pen. This ideology thus excluded the possibility that women might produce as authors. Consequently, writing women were represented as "lady amateurs," as "scribbling women," and as mere "local colorists."

4. In *Marxism and Literature* Williams defines the residual as that which has "been effectively formed in the past, but is still active in the cultural process, not only and often not at all as an element of the past, but as an effective element of the present." He notes further that "thus, certain experiences, meanings and values which cannot be expressed or substantially verified in terms of the dominant culture, are nevertheless lived and practiced on the basis of the residue— cultural as well as social—of some previous social and cultural institution or formation." See his argument, pp. 121–27.

5. "A Literary Main Street."

6. Ibid.

7. "What Is Literary Authority?"

8. Ibid.

9. Ibid.

10. Crowell, "Bookseller and the Literary Guild."

11. Ibid.

12. Quoted in *Publishers Weekly*, February 5, 1927, 490.

13. Boyd, "Writers and Readers."

14. See Warner, *Letters of the Republic,* and Habermas, *Structural Transformation of the Public Sphere.* See also Anderson, *Imagined Communities.*

15. "Has America a Literary Dictatorship?"

16. Ibid., 194.

17. Ibid.; emphasis added.

18. Ibid., 196.

19. Ibid.

20. Ibid.

21. "What the Public Wants," 4. It is interesting to note that the passages in this defense come almost word for word from Harry Scherman's "Report on the Book-of-the-Month Club after Seven Months of Operation." This suggests that the report may well have been written specifically in response to the increasing criticism of the book clubs.

22. "What the Public Wants," 4.

23. "Reminiscences of Harry Scherman," 64.

24. "What the Public Wants," 4.

25. Ibid.

26. Warner, *Letters of the Republic,* 108.

27. Ibid., 48, 108.

28. Ibid., 52.

29. Ibid., 61.

30. Susman, *Culture as History,* 92. On the relationship between the Book-of-the-Month Club and expertise in the Progressive era, see also Rubin's discussion in *Making of Middlebrow Culture,* 101–6. For an extended discussion of the connections between expertise, professionalism, culture in the Progressive era, and the middle class, see Bledstein, *Culture of Professionalism.*

31. For a discussion of this debate, see Leach, "Mastering the Crowd." See also Gorman, *Left Intellectuals and Popular Culture in Twentieth-Century America,* esp. chaps. 1–3.

32. See, for instance, Gorman's discussion of the way conservative critics of new forms of popular culture defended the old order against entertainment that pandered "to the base, physical passions and primal emotions of the public" (*Left Intellectuals and Popular Culture in Twentieth-Century America,* 20).

33. In fact we shall see in the next chapter that Canby did worry about the dangerous influence of elites. But he worried about "pessimists and doom-saying modernists" rather than the controllers of the new media and entertainment industries.

34. Canby, "Standardization," 1.

35. Ibid.

36. Warner, "Mass Public and the Mass Subject," 382. See also Berlant, "National Brands/National Body."

37. Warner, "Mass Public and the Mass Subject," 48–49.

38. See my discussion in Chapter 6, above, on consumption and references to the maternal body. My thinking on these issues has been much influenced by Warner's argument in "Mass Public and the Mass Subject," where he notes that

"minoritized subjects had few strategies open to them, but one was to carry their unrecuperated positivity into consumption. Even from the early eighteenth century, before the triumph of a liberal metalanguage for consumption, commodities were being used, especially by women, as a kind of access to publicness that would nevertheless link up with the specificity of difference" (384). I have also been heavily influenced by Berlant's argument in "National Brands/National Body."

39. It is important to observe here that I am not suggesting that commodities were in any way necessarily subversive. Clearly, access to commodities was itself differentially distributed by the hierarchical organization of labor opportunities, and therefore only some Americans could masquerade and hide their social origins behind a machine-made facade of cultural achievement. Neither do I want to argue, however, that as perhaps the key product of capitalist economies, the commodity carried within itself an inherent, natural essence that somehow enabled it to function as the inevitable bearer of capitalist ideas or ideologies. Rather, I want to insist on and attempt to map the consequences of the relative autonomy of the ideological sphere, a principle that enables subjects to say and do the unexpected with system-derived objects. My point is that the iterative feature of the commodity could be seized on to challenge the traditional capitalist ideological emphasis on the autonomy of the individual subject, a notion that was used to justify the independence of capitalists and therefore their right and ability to maximize profits within the market.

40. For a fascinating discussion of the representation of crowds in American advertising, see Marchand's discussion of the visual cliché of the adoring throng and the individual rising out of the mass in *Advertising the American Dream*, 267–69. He notes,

> In their visual clichés of adoring throngs, advertisers expressed one facet of their understanding of the problem of man in the mass. Constrained by their economic function to move masses of people to action, and dependent on the theory of economic progress through mass consumption for self-justification, many advertising leaders nevertheless contemplated the rise of the modern mass man with fear and contempt. Bruce Barton prized José Ortega y Gasset's *The Revolt of the Masses* and recommended it to acquaintances; other advertising leaders reiterated Ortega y Gasset's warnings about the threat of the tasteless masses to the citadels of high culture. Like other elites, advertisers tended to identify crowds with unruly mobs and to preach the virtues of the man who pulled himself out of the masses through special effort. Recognizing, empathetically, a rising public fear of submergence in mass conformity . . . advertisers frequently appealed to this concern by advertising products on the strength of their capacity to lift the individual out of the crowd. [268–69]

41. See especially DiMaggio, "Cultural Entrepreneurship in Nineteenth-Century Boston," 33–50; Jaher, *Urban Establishment*; Story, *Forging of an Aristocracy*; and Baltzell, *Philadelphia Gentlemen*.

42. See especially Kasson's brief but highly illuminating discussion of the struggle over Frederick Law Olmstead's Central Park in *Amusing the Million*, as well as Levine's treatment of what he calls "the sacralization of culture" (a term

first used by Paul DiMaggio) in *Highbrow/Lowbrow*, 85–168. See also Trachten-berg's still highly useful last chapter in *Incorporation of America*, where he discusses William Dean Howells's social and intellectual position and his reaction to the new, highly commercialized forms of culture. Significantly, Trachtenberg writes of Howells, "Whatever the reasons, the story papers expressed to him a mass consciousness at profound odds with realism, with culture itself. They stood as 'low' to 'high', and thus challenged Howells and others to their task of defining a level, a stratum of their own, a Central Park of the imagination, where civilized arts might be performed in the 'light of common day' upon a greensward of mea-sured and balanced views: a communal spectacle of a revived Republic. It was for Howells as for Olmstead a matter of 'civilization' or 'savagery': we read, or we barbarize" (200).

43. For an excellent discussion of the historical emergence of the middle class in the United States as a new category of nonmanual, managerial, clerical, and sales workers and of the theoretical problems inherent in trying to describe such a class "that binds itself together as a social group in part through the common embrace of an ideology of social atomism," see Blumin, *Emergence of the Middle Class*. See also his earlier statement of his approach to the issues in "Hypothesis of Middle-Class Formation in Nineteenth-Century America."

44. For an overview of consumption in the years from 1876 to 1915, see Schler-eth, *Victorian America*, esp. 141–67.

45. On Bok and Curtis, see Damon-Moore, *Magazines for the Millions*. On the popular magazines more generally and the men who directed them, see Schneirov, *Dream of a New Social Order*.

46. See Fine, *Hollywood and the Profession of Authorship*.

47. Bourdieu, "Aristocracy of Culture."

48. The Ehrenreichs first elaborated their understanding of the professional-managerial class (now often referred to as the PMC) in "Professional-Managerial Class." This essay was subsequently republished as part of a volume that included a number of responses to and critiques of their claim that the PMC was, in fact, a new and distinct class. Many of these critiques were based on a reiteration of the classic Marxist position that only two fundamental classes—labor and capital—with their distinctive relationships to the means of production, composed the capitalist mode of production. See Walker, *Between Labor and Capital*. The Ehren-reichs' claim for the necessity of revision to the classic Marxist model rests in part on their argument that, despite the fact that these intellectual workers are em-ployed in very different social fields, they are salaried individuals who work with their minds rather than with their hands. Thus, strictly speaking, they can be as-similated to neither capital nor labor. They labor for and in the interests of others, but they do so intellectually rather than manually. In addition, they perform cer-tain essential and quite similar functions. They address laborers and members of the working class as authoritative experts and attempt to replace commonsense, working-class forms of knowledge with legitimate bourgeois forms, ideas, and in-stitutions.

It is impossible for me to settle here, once and for all, the fraught, difficult question of whether the PMC is a distinct class, a class fraction, or a contradictory location within class relations. Still, I do want to point out that I differ with the Ehrenreichs in that I think that at least some professional-managerial class workers addressed other middle-class workers rather than laborers—in particular, those at the lower fringes of this expanding and ever-more-complicated class, people with a certain amount of either economic, cultural, or social capital who aspired to more solid, firm membership within middle-class ranks. Because of this, I think, PMC workers might be thought of as less engaged in the business of externally imposed class control or class formation than in that of class consolidation from within. In the final analysis, though, because even the most revered and well-paid professional experts do not finally control the means of production and thus, in some sense, ultimately labor for others, I think it makes more sense to consider them a particular class fraction rather than an autonomous class.

49. "Professional-Managerial Class," 22. The implication is that other members of the PMC did not feel themselves so completely at odds with capitalist society and were preoccupied instead with the more internal issues of how to design, structure, and govern the professions themselves.

50. Ibid., 23.

51. See Braverman, *Labor and Monopoly Capital*. See also Ohmann's discussion of the PMC in *Selling Culture*, esp. 118–74. It was Ohmann's work that first directed my attention to the connection between the Book-of-the-Month Club and the professional-managerial class. See his early essay, "Shaping of a Canon."

52. As Bourdieu argues, "Given that works of art exist as symbolic objects only if they are known and recognized, that is, socially instituted as works of art and received by spectators capable of knowing and recognizing them as such, the sociology of art and literature has to take as its object not only the material production but also the symbolic production of the work, i.e. the production of the value of the work or, which amounts to the same thing, belief in the value of the work" ("The Field of Cultural Production," in *Field of Cultural Production*, 37).

CHAPTER EIGHT

1. Charles Lee, *Hidden Public*, 30.

2. The concept of the habitus has been developed by Bourdieu in *Outline of a Theory of Practice* and in *Distinction*. Because of its complexity and a certain rigidity in the way Bourdieu understands its production, the habitus has been much discussed and criticized. It is best understood, I think, as a kind of behavioral logic—in Bourdieu's terms, ordered "schemes of perception, appreciation and action" (*Distinction*, 100). The habitus thus encompasses ways of seeing, ways of evaluating, and ways of acting. Such schemes characterize the activities of groups of individuals who have been socialized at a particular social location, itself defined primarily by its peculiar material conditions of existence. For Bourdieu, then, habitus is a function of *class* conditions. As he notes in *Outline of a Theory of Practice*, "The structures constitutive of a particular type of environment (e.g. the material conditions of existence characteristic of a class condition) produce *habitus*, systems of durable, transposable, *dispositions*, structured structures predis-

posed to function as structuring structures, that is, as principles of the generation and structuring of [subsequent] practices and representation" (72). A disposition, Bourdieu elaborates further, is itself a kind of structure that is the "result of an organizing action," and it functions consequently as a "predisposition, tendency, propensity, or inclination" to order the world and its constituent features and actions in a familiarly structured way (214). Dispositions, then, are exhibited partly as subsequent patterns of cultural consumption, appreciation, and appropriation. Bourdieu's point is that in gaining access to the world through language learning and early behavioral tutoring, the human subject takes up a particular stance to the world as an already meaningfully structured environment and that that stance is thereafter generalized in subsequent acts of perception and behavior.

Despite certain problems and limitations in the way Bourdieu himself applies the term, I have decided to use it here because I think it usefully captures the connections between unconscious logic or patterns of order and a range of behaviors and practices that are never indulged in randomly or completely controlled by the subject or solely the function of a given object or situation engaged by the subject. These multiple practices, including the behavioral, the gestural, the intellectual, and the affective, are ordered by certain transposable dispositions that are the historical product of life under particular conditions. Although Bourdieu himself tends to emphasize the gestural, behavioral, and especially the intellectual and aesthetic enactments of the habitus, I have added the idea of a distinctive affective practice or style because it seems to me that in addition to learning a distinctive way of ordering the world and one's behavior within it, human subjects also learn how to manipulate and negotiate an ordered language of affect, a vocabulary of feelings, and a set of rules for connecting those feelings appropriately to objects and situations. I suggest that as a quintessential middlebrow cultural institution, the Book-of-the-Month Club exhibited and recommended a distinctive habitus, characterized by a specific cognitive logic as well as by a particular affective style. It is important to note, however, that I do not believe, as Bourdieu seems to, that a habitus is singular and unitary and thus that all enactments of it are strictly analogous to one another. For me, a habitus is a complex formation, a set of components-in-relation. A given affective style, then, can be a response to the same conditions producing a characteristic way of cognitively ordering the world. As such, it is a component of the habitus thereby produced. However, that affective style may counteract the effects of those conditions, it may contradict them, or it may attempt to meliorate them. Consequently, that affective style can look as if it contradicts or counters other ways of enacting the habitus. However, because it is a response to the originating conditions and the logic or disposition they produce, I think it is still part of the basic habitus.

3. Harry Scherman, "Original Outline of Plan for the Book-of-the-Month Club," 4–7.

4. "Reminiscences of Harry Scherman," 41; emphasis added.

5. Quoted in Rubin, *Making of Middlebrow Culture*, 142.

6. Ibid.

7. Morley, *Parnassus on Wheels*.

8. Morley, *Ex Libris Carissimis*.

9. Morley, *Streamlines*, 130, quoted in Wallach and Bracker, *Christopher Morley*, 21.

10. Canby, "Exacting Art."

11. Canby, "Post Mortem."

12. Canby, "New Humanists."

13. Canby, *Definitions*, 199–200.

14. Ibid., 188.

15. Canby, *American Memoir*, 357.

16. Canby, *Definitions*, vii.

17. Ibid.

18. Canby, *American Estimates*, 199.

19. Ibid., 201.

20. Dorothy Canfield Fisher, review of *High Mowing*, by Marion Canby, box 26, folder 1, "Activities," Fisher Collection.

21. Ibid.

22. Canby, *American Memoir*, 278.

23. *Book-of-the-Month Club News*, March 1928, 1–2 (unpaginated).

24. Ibid., April 1928, 4.

25. Joan Rubin has been the pioneer in taking middlebrow culture seriously. My account, as a result, is heavily indebted to her work. I should point out, however, that our attitudes and approaches to the topic of literary criticism diverge significantly. In her account of the activities of the judges, Rubin acknowledges that she herself believes it important to maintain standards in the face of the judges' abnegation of them. She therefore holds them responsible for failing to teach such standards to their subscribers. In keeping with her assumption, Rubin evaluates the judges' activities by measuring the distance they had moved from the more responsible evaluation and pedagogy of the "true critic." Indeed, she accuses them of the "withholding, or underexercise, of critical authority" in their reports for the *Book-of-the-Month Club News* because those reports "tended to substitute narrative for evaluation, information for aesthetics" (*Making of Middlebrow Culture*, 102). I feel that her assertions are based on the familiar acceptance of the aesthetic as a higher form of human cultural production, of criticism as a higher moral calling, and on a view of standards themselves as in some way obvious, eternal, and universal. I would prefer to see all of these as contingent historical forms serving particular and identifiable social purposes. I want to suggest that the narrative and information supplied in those reports appeared there because the judges were searching for something other than the aesthetically excellent. Thus they *were* exercising critical authority, but in a form unrecognizable to those who insisted that authority be exercised only as criticism and in the exclusive service of literary and aesthetic values.

26. Canby, *Definitions*, 297.

27. Ibid., 298.

28. Harry Scherman, "Book-of-the-Month Club," 7.

29. Ibid., 6.

30. Ibid., 12.

31. Bourdieu, *Distinction*, 44. I am drawing here on Bourdieu's arguments about

the characteristic petit bourgeois approach to art and culture, an approach distinctly related to that of middlebrow culture.

32. Canby, *American Estimates*, 125.

33. *Book-of-the-Month Club News*, October 1928, 1.

34. For the full list of yearly selections to 1957, see Charles Lee, *Hidden Public*, 161–94.

35. Although no work by Faulkner, Stein, Woolf, Joyce, or Wilson was ever sent out as the main selection, the club's judges included many books by those authors among the list of recommended alternates. Frequently they marked these as titles for people with "special tastes."

36. Canby, *American Estimates*, 63.

37. Ibid., 64, 65.

38. "Reminiscences of Robert K. Haas," 972.

39. "Reminiscences of Clifton Fadiman," 561.

40. Ibid., 559.

41. Dorothy Canfield Fisher, report on *A Nation of Nations*, by Louis Adamic, box 26, folder 1, Fisher Collection.

42. "*The Story of Philosophy* by Will Durant." The summary of the book notes that "one of the Committee gives [the above] report of it."

43. Dorothy Canfield Fisher, report on *Tomorrow Will Come*, by E. A. Almedingen, box 26, folder 1, Fisher Collection.

44. Although the preference for the evocation of affect and sentiment among the Book-of-the-Month Club judges and the "sentimentalism" of domestic fiction in the nineteenth century are related, I do not think they are exactly the same thing. The sentimentalism of domestic fiction, it seems to me, is a complex of ideas and assumptions that construes deep feeling both as a gendered and as a Christian phenomenon. Tears were the signs of sentiment's presence, and the fictional conversion of men from the gospel of work to the ideology of domesticity was testimony to its effectivity. In middlebrow culture, sentiment is less singular, more elaborated, and it is conceived of as capable of producing a range of effects. Sentiment is more organized, rationalized, and instrumentalized, it seems to me, in middlebrow culture. On domestic sentimentalism, see Tompkins, *Sensational Designs*, and Samuels, *Culture of Sentiment*.

45. Canby, *American Memoir*, 92–93.

46. For a rich, extended discussion of an experience of reading that promoted connection and a sense of recognition by another, see Juhasz, *Reading from the Heart*. Juhasz writes beautifully about her passion for reading and notes, "I am lonelier in the real world situation . . .—when no one seems to understand *who I am*—than by myself reading, when I feel that the book *recognizes* me, and I recognize myself because of the book" (5). Although she connects this experience to the reading of love stories, both popular and canonized, it seems to me that she is describing the characteristic middlebrow way of reading that virtually all middleclass children of the 1940s and 1950s absorbed through their parents' oral reading of children's books, through schooling, and through the dominant culture of the time. But even this assertion is only an opinion, one that needs further empirical study.

47. For a chronology and discussion of this incident, see Arnold Rampersad's notes for the Library of America edition of *Native Son*, contained in Richard Wright, *Early Works* (New York: Library of America, 1991), esp. 911–14. See also his discussion of the Book-of-the-Month Club's intervention with respect to publication of *Black Boy*, in Richard Wright, *Later Works* (New York: Library of America, 1991), esp. 868–69. The decision by the Library of America to use the Harper proofs rather than the version Wright finally approved for publication has been somewhat controversial. For a discussion of the issue, see James Campbell, "The Wright Version," *Times Literary Supplement*, December 13, 1991, 14; Arnold Rampersad, "Too Honest for His Own Time," *New York Times Book Review*, December 29, 1991, 3, 17, 18; and James W. Tuttleton, "The Problematic Texts of Richard Wright," *Hudson Review* 45 (Summer 1992): 261–72.

48. Copies of Dorothy Canfield Fisher's letters to Wright along with some of Wright's replies are in the Fisher Collection. Wright's papers are at the Beinecke Library of Yale University.

49. My understanding and approach to affect have been much influenced by the work of Silvan Tomkins. For a useful introduction and selection of his work, see *Shame and Its Sisters*.

50. See his comments on the New Humanists particularly. I should point out that the reading of Canby offered here is considerably different from that provided by Rubin. She stresses his status as a transitional figure, negotiating a kind of truce between genteel culture on one hand and consumer culture on the other. She does, however, place considerably more emphasis on his qualities as a conservative Victorian, as a throwback to a more genteel age. Although I agree that Canby was a highly complex figure and that that complexity was undoubtedly produced by the fact that he came of age in an unsettled era, I see much more of the modern in Canby than Rubin does. In fact, his writings evidence a genuine appreciation for the advances connected with modern science and technology and a bona fide excitement at the pace of change. Although he was put off by the crudities of some forms of literary modernism, he also wrote passionately about the need for "a modern literature" and provided sensitive accounts of what writers such as Joyce, Stein, and Hemingway were attempting formally. I think Canby was actually an original cultural critic, neither wholly conservative and genteel nor simply avant-garde and politically left. He attempted to find a modern literature that might be equal to the complexities of the modern age, yet he also longed for a literature that could continue to provide a beacon of moral direction for confused readers. It seems to me that Canby and *The Saturday Review of Literature* deserve to be taken seriously as candidates for a full-scale biography and an institutional study. Obviously that is not what I have been able to offer here.

51. Canby, *American Memoir*, 13.

52. Ibid., 34.

53. Ibid.

54. Ibid., 29.

55. Ibid., 92–93.

56. Ibid., 95, 99.

57. Ibid., 95, 96.

58. Ibid., 97.

59. Ibid., 103.

60. Ibid.

61. Henry Canby's preferred mode of reading, it seems to me, is very much related to the kind of reading Robert Darnton has associated with the bourgeois readers of Jean-Jacques Rousseau and *La Nouvelle Heloise* in his important article "Readers Respond to Rousseau." Darnton has suggested that Rousseau and his readers pioneered a new form of reading that united the intensity of traditional sacred reading ("in order to absorb the unmediated Word of God" [232]) with the worldly desire to understand the modern universe and to know how to live in it. As Darnton notes, "This behavior expressed a new attitude toward the printed word. Ranson [a representative bourgeois] did not read to enjoy literature but to cope with life and especially family life, exactly as Rousseau intended" (241).

More recently, Richard Brodhead has explored the meaning of novel reading in the nineteenth-century United States and suggested that the state of absorption apparently beloved by all novel readers functioned to carry bourgeois discipline into the deepest recesses of the reading subject. As he puts it,

> A novel . . . is something "to get into": like the parent-child bond of middle-class disciplinary theory, the novel opens up a world-within-a-world with the power to enclose the reader within its projected horizons. The nature of this world in both cases is that it brings desires to intensified expression: it is deeply involving, "absorbingly interesting." Like the normative mother, the novel shapes the participations it arouses into a peculiar intimacy: it sponsors an intensely private relation that is still a relation, a going-out of oneself into intersubjective space (though in both cases that "mutual" space is really contrived by someone else). *And like* the mother's, the novel's intimacy is a tool for informing its "partner's" mind: since the power of an "absorbing" novel is the power to transpose its orderings into its reader's felt understanding through an invisible persuasion. [*Cultures of Letters*, 46]

Brodhead further suggests that, in its capacity to delineate alternate worlds, the novel also offered "adventure via the eye for the residents of [an increasingly] immobilized private space" (62).

While I agree with Brodhead that the kind of affective, intense, absorbing reading recommended by Canby did indeed work as a form of discipline in the way it helped to construct middle-class subjectivity, and that it functioned, furthermore, as compensation for the isolation of middle-class life, I place much more stress on the utopian longing for connection and social absorption at stake in this form of reading than he does. The desire to connect with others and to be caught up in a meaningful world, it seems to me, was as much the source of utopian social action in the nineteenth century as it was compensation for continued complacency. Additionally, because I place more emphasis on the contribution the reader makes to any text-reader interaction, I am much less sanguine about the author's ability to control the effects of a text or to discipline the reader in a predetermined way. Reading, it seems to me, is much more wayward than Brodhead admits. It also seems to me that hidden within Brodhead's indignance about maternal discipline is an unfortunate misogyny and fear of the maternal as well as a hidden assumption that a fully independent, autonomous, self-directing subject is a distinct and more authentic possibility.

62. Canby, *Seven Years' Harvest*, 14.

63. Ibid., 6–7.

64. Ibid., 131.

65. Ibid., 79.

66. Ibid.

67. Ibid., 47.

68. Ibid., 302–3.

69. Ibid., 180.

70. "Reminiscences of Edith Walker," 877–78.

71. Charles Lee, *Hidden Public*, 138, 149.

72. Canby, *Definitions*, 227.

73. "Reminiscences of Harry Scherman," 118–19.

74. Charles Lee, *Hidden Public*, 148.

75. Strictly speaking, it is not the hegemony of the professional-managerial class that is being constructed here. Rather, it is their authority as officially deputized managers that is being legitimated. They were to work, obviously, in the service of those who actually possessed power in capitalist society—at this point, the corporations and their largest shareholders.

CHAPTER NINE

1. These developments did not go unremarked at the time. In fact they were the subject of several books now recognized as classics in American sociology and political science. See especially Mills, *White-Collar* and *Power Elite*, as well as Whyte, *Organization Man*. All three of these books were alternate selections of the Book-of-the-Month Club. For the larger context of the rise of white-collar work and its impact on labor relations, see Braverman, *Labor and Monopoly Capital*, and Armstrong et al., *Capitalism since World War II*. See also Gouldner, *Future of Intellectuals*.

2. It seems odd to note that my father's job was in some ways analogous to that performed by the editors and managers of the Book-of-the-Month Club. Where they attempted to sell books to several hundred thousand "well-placed book readers" in order to promote broader consumption of books in the larger population, my father was employed by Capital Air Lines to facilitate the use of the commercial air industry by sports teams and media figures in the hope that this, too, would promote widespread air travel. As a result, he traveled a good deal with college football and basketball teams (in fact, this was how I first learned the names of most of the colleges and universities on the East Coast) and even with the New York Yankees for a time. For my brother and me, the real sign of our father's glamorous work was the fruit basket we got every Christmas from Mel Allen, "the voice of the New York Yankees."

3. In *Where the Girls Are* Susan Douglas does a wonderful job of discussing this larger cultural context and connecting it with the media consumption of those of us who grew up in the 1950s. It is important to note that inasmuch as I was an enthusiastic consumer of middlebrow books and culture during this period, I was also a great fan of the television shows, teen magazines, pop music, and celebrity idols Douglas discusses. In fact, in 1963–64 I was just as preoccupied with the Beatles as I was with Shymansky's books. About fifteen to twenty of my friends crowded into my bedroom on that Sunday night in February when the Fab Four first appeared on Ed Sullivan.

4. Powers, *Operation Wandering Soul*, 106.

5. I cannot recall every book that was in those boxes. Each title that *has* come back to me, though, as I have reflected on that year, I have discovered was selected by the club either as a main selection or an alternate.

6. Sackheim, "Why the Book Clubs Are Successful."

7. Canby, "How the Book-of-the-Month Club Began."

8. Ibid., 32.

9. "Cheaper by the Dozen."

10. Quoted in Charles Lee, *Hidden Public*, 83.

11. Harry Scherman, Speech on book clubs, 1.

12. My evidence for this comes from the copies of the club's catalog that I have recently examined. Borrowed from the Center for Research Libraries in Chicago, the copies of the catalog are variously stamped by the libraries at the University of Minnesota and the University of Chicago.

13. Dwight MacDonald, "Masscult and Midcult: II," 594.

14. Charles Lee, *Hidden Public*, 146.

15. "Audience Research Report."

16. Dichter, "Psychological Analysis," 3.

17. Ceram, *Gods, Graves, and Scholars*; Wouk, *Marjorie Morningstar*; Heyerdahl, *Kon-Tiki*; Drury, *Advise and Consent*; Harper Lee, *To Kill a Mockingbird*; Renault, *Bull from the Sea*; Markandaya, *Nectar in a Sieve*; Shirer, *Rise and Fall of the Third Reich*; Chute, *Shakespeare of London*; and Lederer and Burdick, *Ugly American*.

18. Tuchman, *Guns of August*; Burdick and Wheeler, *Fail-Safe*; Michener, *Hawaii*; Griffin, *Black Like Me*; Uris, *Mila 18*; White, *Making of the President*; Stone, *Lust for Life*; Stone, *President's Lady*; Stone, *Agony and the Ecstasy*; Knowles, *Separate Peace*; Hart, *Act One*; Traver, *Anatomy of a Murder*; Kerr, *Please Don't Eat the Daisies*; Lord, *Day of Infamy*; Betty MacDonald, *The Egg and I*; Hemingway, *Old Man and the Sea*; Bishop, *Day Lincoln Was Shot*; Catton, *Stillness at Appomattox*; Du Maurier, *My Cousin Rachel*; Gunther, *Death Be Not Proud*; Paton, *Cry, the Beloved Country*; Gunther, *Inside Africa*; Skinner, *Our Hearts Were Young and Gay*; Du Maurier, *Rebecca*; Roberts, *Oliver Wiswell*; Gilbreth, *Cheaper by the Dozen*.

19. Dichter, "Psychological Analysis," 21.

20. Gunther, "Great Book about Adolf Hitler."

21. This assertion is based on my reading of Book-of-the-Month Club preliminary reader's reports for the years 1950, 1951, and 1958. These reports are collected

at the Library of Congress and were donated to the library by Ralph Thompson, Harry Scherman's successor at the club. The library also holds a large collection of undated reader's reports, but these are primarily from the 1940s.

22. Fisher, "Report on *Nectar in a Sieve*."

23. Highet, "A Report."

24. Fadiman, "*Fail-Safe*."

25. Fadiman, "Selection for January."

26. Chute, *Shakespeare of London*, ix.

27. Wouk, *Marjorie Morningstar*, 3.

28. Marquand, "*Marjorie Morningstar*."

29. Ceram, *Gods, Graves, and Scholars*, v.

30. During his cross-examination of Mayella Ewell, Atticus establishes that Mayella had in fact tried to seduce Tom. Caught in the act by her father, Bob Ewell, she was then beaten by him. It is this humiliation that Ewell feels he must avenge.


## AFTERWORD

1. Edwin McDowell, "Book-of-the-Month Club Restructures Its Jury," *New York Times*, September 20, 1988.

2. Edwin McDowell, "Executive Shift at Book-of-the-Month," *New York Times*, October 4, 1988.

3. Edwin McDowell, "New Book-of-the-Month Club Judges," *New York Times*, December 2, 1988.

4. James Kaplan, "Inside the Club," *New York Times Magazine*, June 11, 1989.

5. Calvin Reid, "BOMC Restructures Managing Units; Weeks's Role Changed," *Publishers Weekly*, January 20, 1992, 10.

6. Quoted in "Book Club Replaces Its Editor in Chief," *New York Times*, September 14, 1993.

7. Quoted in Sarah Lyall, "An Editor's Dismissal Raises Talk of a Clash of Art and Commerce," *New York Times*, September 15, 1993.

8. Sarah Lyall, "Book-of-the-Month Club to End Its Advisory Panel," *New York Times*, July 1, 1994.

9. Doreen Carvajal, "Triumph of the Bottom Line: Numbers vs. Words at the Book-of-the-Month Club," *New York Times*, April 1, 1996.

10. For a clear articulation of this and related claims, see Stedman et al., "Literacy as a Consumer Activity," esp. 163–79.

11. George Artandi, quoted in Doreen Carvajal, "Triumph of the Bottom Line: Numbers vs. Words at the Book-of-the-Month Club," *New York Times*, April 1, 1996.

12. Italo Calvino, *If on a Winter's Night a Traveler*, trans. William Weaver (New York: Harcourt Brace, 1981), 253–59.

# SOURCES CITED

✿

## MANUSCRIPT COLLECTIONS

Burlington, Vt.
   Special Collections, Bailey-Howe Memorial Library, University of Vermont
      Dorothy Canfield Fisher Collection
New York, N.Y.
   Rare Book and Manuscript Library, Columbia University
      Harry Scherman Papers
         Scherman, Harry. "The Book-of-the-Month Club." Original brochure
         mailed to first interested subscribers. Material by and about Scherman.
         Folder D-III. Box 3.
         ———. "Original Outline of Plan for the Book-of-the-Month Club."
         November 24, 1926. Manuscripts file. Box 3.
         ———. "Report on the Book-of-the-Month Club after Seven Months of
         Operation." Material by and about Scherman. Folder D-III. Box 3.
         ———. Speech on book clubs, the Library of Congress. April 1960.
         Manuscripts file.
   Oral History Research Office, Butler Library, Columbia University
      The Book of the Month Club. Director, Allan Nevins. Interviews by
         Louis M. Starr, 1955.
      "The Reminiscences of Robert K. Haas"
      "The Reminiscences of Clifton Fadiman"
      "The Reminiscences of Dorothy Canfield Fisher"
      "The Reminiscences of Amy Loveman"
      "The Reminiscences of Edith Walker"
      "The Reminiscences of Harry Scherman"

## BOOK-OF-THE-MONTH CLUB DOCUMENTS
Quoted with permission of the Book-of-the-Month Club

### *Reader's Reports*

Asher, Marty. Undated. [Title and author omitted.]
Cooney, Thomas. "*America: A Narrative History*, by George Brown Tindall."
   December 1983.
Easton, Elizabeth. "*The AKC's World of the Pure-Bred Dog*, edited by Duncan
   Barnes and the Staff of the American Kennel Club." May 5, 1983.
———. "*King Arthur*, by Norma L. Goodrich." Undated.
Mabry, Robert. November 11, 1986. [Title and author omitted.]
Mantell, Suzanne. "*The Blind Watchmaker*, by Richard Dawkins." October 1986.

Parker, Dorothy. January 5, 1987. [Title and author omitted.]
———. "*Southern Food: At Home, on the Road, in History*, by John Egerton."
    January 5, 1987.
———. "*A Taste of Southeast Asia*, by X." Undated.
Robinson, Phyllis. "*How to Help Your Puppy Grow into a Wonderful Dog*, by
    Elizabeth Randolph Macmillan." Undated.
Sansone, Jill. January 9, 1987. [Title and author omitted.]
———. "*Christianity and Paganism, 350–750*, edited by J. N. Hilgarth." Undated.
Savago, Joseph. "*Beloved*, by Toni Morrison." January 1, 1987.
———. "*Contact*, by Carl Sagan." June 3, 1985.
———. "*The March of Folly*, by Barbara Tuchman." September 26, 1983.
———. "*A Sport of Nature*, by Nadine Gordimer." October 14, 1986.
Shapiro, Larry. "*America: A Narrative History*, by George Brown Tindall."
    December 27, 1983.
———. "*Napoleon's Generals*, by David G. Chandler." October 5, 1987.
Tulipan, Eve. "*Ellis Island*, by Barbara Benton." Undated.


*Interviews by the Author*

Adrian, Pat. December 10, 1986.
Asher, Marty. November 25, 1986.
Gelman, Steve. February 12, 1987.
Norris, Gloria. May 14, 1987.
Prinze, Lucie. October 28, 1986.
Riger, Robert. April 15, 1987.
Robinson, Phyllis. September 8, 1986.
Rosenthal, Lucy. September 2, 1986.
Savago, Joseph. July 8, 1985; September 8, 1986.
Shapiro, Larry. October 30, 1986; February 20, 1987.
Silverman, Al. July 2, 1986.
Van Straalen, Alice. July 1, 1986.
Waxman, Maron. February 19, 1987.
Weinberg, Susan. February 12, 26, 1987.


*Memos, Notes, Reports, and Publications*

"Audience Research Report." Index of Enthusiasm. March 1947. Audience
    Research, Inc., pp. 11–12. In the possession of the Book-of-the-Month Club.
    Lent to the author by Robert Riger.
*Book-of-the-Month Club News.* 1926–96.
Crutcher, Larry, and Al Silverman. "Management News Bulletin." January 13,
    February 17, 1987.
Editorial meeting. February 12, 1987.
Dichter, Ernest. "A Psychological Analysis of the Sales and Advertising
    Problems of the Book-of-the-Month Club." October 1948. In possession of
    the Book-of-the-Month Club. Lent to the author by Robert Riger.

Radway, Janice. Field notes taken at the editorial meeting. June 19, 1986.

Sansone, Jill. "Report on the Editorial Meeting of March 26, 1987."

Silverman, Al. "What We Stand For: A Message from the Chief Executive Officer." In author's possession.

Zinsser, William. Memo to the editors at the Book-of-the-Month Club. July 10, 1985. In author's possession.

## BOOKS, ARTICLES, DISSERTATIONS, AND PAPERS

"An A.B.A. Page: News and Notes of the American Booksellers' Association." *Publishers Weekly*, January 8, 1927, 130–31.

Abbott, Craig S. "Modern American Poetry: Anthologies, Classrooms, and Canons." *College Literature* 17, no. 2, 3 (1990): 209–22.

Abel, Trudy. "A Man of Letters, a Man of Business: Edward Stratemeyer and the Adolescent Reader, 1890–1930." Ph.D. diss., Rutgers University, 1993.

Agnew, Jean Christophe. *Worlds Apart: The Market and the Theater in Anglo-American Thought, 1550–1750*. Cambridge: Cambridge University Press, 1986.

Anderson, Benedict. *Imagined Communities: Reflections on the Origin and Spread of Nationalism*. Rev. ed. London: Verso, 1991.

Anonymous. Advertisement for Brentano's. *Publishers Weekly*, February 5, 1927, 490.

Anonymous. Advertisement for "Harvard Classics," Collier's. *American Magazine*, February 1926, 195.

Appadurai, Arjun, ed. *The Social Life of Things: Commodities in Cultural Perspective*. Cambridge: Cambridge University Press, 1986.

Armstrong, Philip, Andrew Glyn, and John Harrison. *Capitalism since World War II: The Making and Breakup of the Great Boom*. London: Fontana, 1984.

Baltzell, E. Digby. *Philadelphia Gentlemen: The Making of a National Upper Class*. Glencoe, Ill.: Free Press, 1958.

Bartlett, John Russell. *Dictionary of Americanisms: A Glossary of Words and Phrases*. 2d ed. Boston: Little, Brown, 1859.

Baudrillard, Jean. *For a Critique of the Political Economy of the Sign*. Trans. Charles Levin. St. Louis, Mo.: Telos Press, 1981.

Beffel, John Nicholas. "The Lost Art of Profanity." *Nation*, Sept. 22, 1926, 270.

Behar, Ruth. *Translated Woman: Crossing the Border with Esperanza's Story*. Cambridge: Beacon Press, 1993.

Beniger, James. *The Control Revolution: Technological and Economic Origins of the Information Society*. Cambridge: Harvard University Press, 1986.

Benjamin, Walter. "The Work of Art in the Age of Mechanical Reproduction." In *Illuminations*, trans. Harry Zohn, 217–52. New York: Schocken Books, 1969.

Berlant, Lauren. "National Brands/National Body: 'Imitation of Life.'" In *The Phantom Public Sphere*, ed. Bruce Robbins, 173–203. Minneapolis: University of Minnesota Press, 1993.

Berman, Marshall. *All That Is Solid Melts into Air: The Experience of Modernity*. New York: Simon and Schuster, 1982.

Bishop, Jim. *The Day Lincoln Was Shot*. New York: Harper & Brothers, 1955.

Blake, Casey Nelson. *Beloved Community: The Cultural Criticism of Randolph Bourne, Van Wyck Brooks, Waldo Frank, and Lewis Mumford*. Chapel Hill: University of North Carolina Press, 1990.

Bledstein, Burton J. *The Culture of Professionalism: The Middle Class and the Development of Higher Education in America*. New York: Norton, 1976.

Blumin, Stuart. *The Emergence of the Middle Class: Social Experience in the American City, 1760–1900*. Cambridge: Cambridge University Press, 1989.

———. "The Hypothesis of Middle-Class Formation in Nineteenth-Century America: A Critique and Some Proposals." *American Historical Review* 90 (1985): 299–338.

"A Book a Month." *Publishers Weekly*, July 3, 1926, 31.

"Book Clubs and Book Shops: The Book-of-the-Month Club States Its Position." *Publishers Weekly*, January 22, 1927, 274–75.

"The Bookseller." Unsigned letter to *Saturday Review of Literature*, February 19, 1927, 598.

Boorstin, Daniel. *The Americans: The Democratic Experience*. New York: Random House, 1973.

Bourdieu, Pierre. "The Aristocracy of Culture." Trans. Richard Nice. *Media, Culture and Society* 2 (1980): 225–54.

———. *Distinction: A Social Critique of the Judgement of Taste*. Trans. Richard Nice. Cambridge: Harvard University Press, 1984.

———. *The Field of Cultural Production: Essays on Art and Literature*. Ed. Randal Johnson. New York: Columbia University Press, 1993.

———. *Outline of a Theory of Practice*. Trans. Richard Nice. Cambridge: Cambridge University Press, 1977.

———. "The Production of Belief: Contribution to an Economy of Symbolic Goods." *Media, Culture and Society* 2 (1980): 263.

Boyd, Ernest. "Writers and Readers." *Independent*, March 5, 1927, 271.

Braverman, Harry. *Labor and Monopoly Capital: The Degradation of Work in the Twentieth Century*. New York: Monthly Review Press, 1974.

Brodhead, Richard. *Cultures of Letters: Scenes of Reading and Writing in Nineteenth Century America*. Chicago: University of Chicago Press, 1994.

———. *The School of Hawthorne*. New York: Oxford University Press, 1986.

Brodkey, Linda. *Academic Writing as Social Practice*. Philadelphia: Temple University Press, 1987.

Bronner, Simon, ed. *Consuming Visions: Accumulation and Display of Goods in America, 1880–1920*. New York: Norton, 1989.

Brooks, Van Wyck. *America's Coming-of-Age*. New York: Huebsch, 1915.

Bugbee, Bruce W. *Genesis of American Patent and Copyright Law*. Washington, D.C.: Public Affairs Press, 1967.

Burdick, Eugene, and Harvey Wheeler. *Fail-Safe*. New York: Macmillan, 1962.

Bush, Douglas. "Making Culture Hum." *Bookman*, August 1929, 591–95.

"Buy a Book a Month." *Publishers Weekly*, February 13, 1926, 519.

"Buying a Book a Month." *Publishers Weekly*, October 9, 1926, 1488–89.

Canby, Henry Seidel. *The Age of Confidence: Life in the Nineties*. New York: Farrar and Rhinehart, 1934.

———. *Alma Mater: The Gothic Age of the American College*. New York: Farrar and Rhinehart, 1936.

———. *American Estimates*. London: Jonathan Cape, 1929.

———. *American Memoir*. Boston: Houghton Mifflin, 1947.

———. *Definitions: Essays in Contemporary Criticism*. New York: Harcourt, Brace, 1922.

———. "An Exacting Art." *Saturday Review of Literature*, March 1, 1930, 32.

———. "How the Book-of-the-Month Club Began." *Atlantic Monthly*, May 1947, 131–35.

———. "The New Humanists." *Saturday Review of Literature*, February 22, 1930, 751.

———. "Post Mortem." *Saturday Review of Literature*, June 14, 1930, 1122.

———. *Seven Years' Harvest: Notes on Contemporary Literature*. New York: Farrar and Rhinehart, 1936.

———. "Standardization." *Saturday Review of Literature*, February 12, 1927, 1, 573.

Catton, Bruce. *A Stillness at Appomattox*. Garden City, N.Y.: Doubleday, 1953.

Ceram, C. W. *Gods, Graves, and Scholars: The Story of Archaeology*. Trans. E. B. Garside. New York: Knopf, 1954.

Chandler, Alfred. *The Visible Hand: The Managerial Revolution in American Business*. Cambridge: Harvard University Press, 1977.

Chase, Stuart. "One Dead Level." *New Republic*, September 29, 1926, 137.

"Cheaper by the Dozen." *Time*, August 13, 1951, 104.

Chute, Marchette. *Shakespeare of London*. New York: Dutton, 1949.

Coser, Lewis A., Charles Kadushin, and Walter W. Powell. *Books: The Culture and Commerce of Publishing*. New York: Basic Books, 1982.

Coultrap-McQuin, Susan. *Doing Literary Business: American Women Writers in the Nineteenth Century*. Chapel Hill: University of North Carolina Press, 1990.

Cremin, Lawrence. *The Transformation of the School: Progressivism in American Education, 1876–1957*. New York: Knopf, 1961.

Crowell, Cedric R. "A Bookseller and the Literary Guild." *Publishers Weekly*, January 29, 1927, 398.

Czitrom, Daniel J. *Media and the American Mind: From Morse to McLuhan*. Chapel Hill: University of North Carolina Press, 1983.

Damon-Moore, Helen. *Magazines for the Millions: Gender and Commerce in the Ladies' Home Journal and the Saturday Evening Post, 1880–1910*. New York: State University of New York Press, 1994.

Damon-Moore, Helen, and Carl F. Kaestle. "Surveying American Readers." In *Literacy in the United States: Readers and Reading since 1980*, ed. Carl Kaestle, Helen Damon-Moore, Lawrence C. Stedman, Katherine Tinsley, and William Vance Trollinger Jr., 180–203. New Haven: Yale University Press, 1991.

Darnton, Robert. "Readers Respond to Rousseau: The Fabrication of Romantic

Sensitivity." In *The Great Cat Massacre and Other Episodes in French Cultural History*, 215–56. New York: Basic Books, 1984.

———. "What Is the History of the Book?" In *Reading in America*, ed. Cathy N. Davidson, 27–52. Baltimore: Johns Hopkins University Press, 1989.

Denning, Michael. *Mechanic Accents: Dime Novels and Working-Class Culture in America*. London: Verso, 1987.

"Details of the Book-of-the-Month Club." *Publishers Weekly*, November 27, 1926, 2092.

DiMaggio, Paul. "Cultural Entrepreneurship in Nineteenth-Century Boston: The Creation of an Organizational Base for High Culture in America." *Media, Culture and Society* 4 (January 1982): 33–50, 303–22.

———. "Review Essay: On Pierre Bourdieu." *American Journal of Sociology* 84 (1979): 1460–75.

Doud, Margery. "Books for the Home: A Selection for Both Merit and Color." *House Beautiful*, February 1928, 110.

Douglas, Ann. *Terrible Honesty: Mongrel Manhattan in the 1920s*. New York: Farrar, Straus, and Giroux, 1995.

Douglas, Susan J. *Where the Girls Are: Growing Up Female with the Mass Media*. New York: Times Books, 1994.

Drury, Allen. *Advise and Consent*. Garden City, N.Y.: Doubleday, 1959.

Du Maurier, Daphne. *My Cousin Rachel*. Garden City, N.Y.: Doubleday, 1952.

———. *Rebecca*. New York: Doubleday, Doran, 1938.

Eagleton, Terry. *Criticism and Ideology: A Study in Marxist Literary Theory*. London: New Left Books, 1976.

Ehrenreich, Barbara, and John Ehrenreich. "The Professional-Managerial Class." *Radical America* 11, no. 2 (March–April 1977): 6–31.

Fadiman, Clifton. "*Fail-Safe*, by Eugene Burdick and Harvey Wheeler." *Book-of-the-Month Club News*, October 1962, 1.

———. "The Selection for January." *Book-of-the-Month Club News*, December 1957, 1.

Farmer, John S. *Americanisms: Old and New—A Dictionary of Words, Phrases and Colloquialisms*. London: Thomas Poulter & Sons, 1889.

Fass, Paula. *The Damned and the Beautiful: American Youth in the 1920s*. New York: Oxford University Press, 1977.

Feldman, Gayle. "Going Global." *Publishers Weekly*, December 19, 1986, 20–25.

Fine, Richard. *Hollywood and the Profession of Authorship, 1928–1940*. Ann Arbor: UMI Research Press, 1985.

Fisher, Dorothy Canfield. "Book Clubs." In *Bowker Lectures on Book Publishing*, 202–30. New York: Bowker, 1957.

———. "Report on *Nectar in a Sieve*." *Book-of-the-Month Club News*, May 1955, 2.

Foucault, Michel. "Nietzsche, Genealogy, History." In *Language, Counter-memory, Practice: Selected Essays and Interviews*, ed. Donald F. Bouchard, trans. Donald F. Bouchard and Sherry Simon, 139–64. Ithaca: Cornell University Press, 1977.

Frank, Waldo. "Pseudo-Literature." *New Republic*, December 2, 1925, 46–47.

Franklin, Fabian. "American College and American Culture." *Nation*, October 7, 1909, 321–22.

Gaines, Jane M. *Contested Culture: The Image, the Voice, and the Law*. Chapel Hill: University of North Carolina Press, 1991.

Garnham, Nicholas, and Raymond Williams. "Pierre Bourdieu and the Sociology of Culture: An Introduction." *Media, Culture and Society* 2 (1980): 209–23.

Garrison, Dee. *Apostles of Culture: The Public Librarian and American Society, 1876–1920*. New York: Free Press, 1979.

Garvey, Ellen. *The Adman in the Parlor: Magazines and the Gendering of Consumer Culture, 1880s to 1910s*. New York: Oxford University Press, 1996.

Geertz, Clifford. "Deep Play: Notes on the Balinese Cockfight." In *The Interpretation of Cultures*, 412–53. New York: Basic Books, 1973.

Gilbreth, Frank B. *Cheaper by the Dozen*. New York: Crowell, 1948.

Gorman, Paul R. *Left Intellectuals and Popular Culture in Twentieth-Century America*. Chapel Hill: University of North Carolina Press, 1996.

Gouldner, Alvin. *The Future of Intellectuals and the Rise of the New Class: A Frame of Reference, Theses, Conjectures, Arguments, and an Historical Perspective on the Role of Intellectuals and Intelligentsia in the International Class Contest of the Modern Era*. New York: Seabury, 1979.

Graff, Gerald. *Professing Literature: An Institutional History*. Chicago: University of Chicago Press, 1987.

Graves, C. Edward. "The Humboldt College Plan for Recreational Reading." *Publishers Weekly*, July 24, 1926, 244–47.

Griffin, John Howard. *Black Like Me*. Boston: Houghton Mifflin, 1961.

Griffith, Sally Foreman. *Home Town News: William Allen White and the Emporia Gazette*. New York: Oxford University Press, 1989.

Gross, Robert A. "Books and Libraries in Thoreau's Concord." *Proceedings of the American Antiquarian Society* 97, pts. 1 and 2 (1988): 129–87.

Guillory, John. *Cultural Capital: The Problem of Literary Canon Formation*. University of Chicago Press, 1993.

Gunther, John. *Death Be Not Proud*. Memorial ed. Preface by Cass Canfield. New York: Harper & Row, 1971.

———. "A Great Book about Adolf Hitler." *Book-of-the-Month Club News*, October 1960, 4–5.

———. *Inside Africa*. New York: Harper, 1955.

Guthrie, Jane. "The Decorative Value of Books." *Good Housekeeping*, January 1924, 47.

Habermas, Jurgen. *The Structural Transformation of the Public Sphere: An Inquiry into a Category of Bourgeois Society*. Trans. Thomas Burger with the assistance of Frederick Lawrence. Cambridge: MIT Press, 1989.

Halttunen, Karen. *Confidence Men and Painted Women: A Study of Middle-Class Culture in America, 1830–1870*. New Haven: Yale University Press, 1982.

Harris, Neil. "The Drama of Consumer Desire." In *Cultural Excursions: Marketing, Appetite, and Cultural Tastes in Modern America*, 174–97. Chicago: University of Chicago Press, 1990.

Hart, Moss. *Act One: An Autobiography*. New York: Random House, 1959.

Harvey, David. *The Condition of Postmodernity: An Enquiry into the Origins of Cultural Change*. London: Basil Blackwell, 1989.

"Has America a Literary Dictatorship?" *Bookman*, April 1927, 191–99.

Hawkins, Hugh. *Between Harvard and America: The Educational Leadership of Charles W. Eliot*. New York: Oxford University Press, 1972.

Hegeman, Susan. "The Democracy of Cultures: Transformations of the Culture Concept in Modernist America." Ph.D. diss., Duke University, 1992.

Heinze, Andrew R. *Adapting to Abundance: Jewish Immigrants, Mass Consumption, and the Search for American Identity*. New York: Columbia University Press, 1990.

Hemingway, Ernest. *The Old Man and the Sea*. New York: Scribner's, 1952.

Heyerdahl, Thor. *Kon-Tiki: Across the Pacific by Raft*. Trans. F. H. Lyon. Chicago: Rand McNally, 1950.

Highet, Gilbert. "A Report." *Book-of-the-Month Club News*, June 1955, 2–3.

Horowitz, Daniel. *The Morality of Spending: Attitudes towards the Consumer Society in America, 1875–1940*. Baltimore: Johns Hopkins University Press, 1985.

Jaher, Frederic Cople. *The Urban Establishment: Upper Strata in Boston, New York, Charleston, Chicago, and Los Angeles*. Urbana: University of Illinois Press, 1982.

Jones, Robert W. *Copyrights and Trade-marks*. Columbia, Mo.: E. W. Stephens, 1949.

Juhasz, Suzanne. *Reading from the Heart: Women, Literature, and the Search for True Love*. New York: Viking, 1994.

Kalaidjian, Walter. *American Culture between the Wars: Revisionary Modernism and Postmodern Critique*. New York: Columbia University Press, 1993.

Kasson, John F. *Amusing the Million: Coney Island at the Turn of the Century*. New York: Hill & Wang, 1976.

———. *Rudeness and Civility: Manners in Nineteenth-Century Urban America*. New York: Hill & Wang, 1990.

Kern, Stephen. *The Culture of Time and Space, 1880–1918*. Cambridge: Harvard University Press, 1983.

Kerr, Jean. *Please Don't Eat the Daisies*. Garden City, N.Y.: Doubleday, 1957.

Knowles, John. *A Separate Peace: A Novel*. New York: Macmillan, 1959.

Kramer, Dale. *Heywood Broun: A Biographical Portrait*. New York: A. A. Wyn, 1949.

Lamont, Michele. *Money, Morals, and Manners: The Culture of the French and American Upper Middle Class*. Chicago: University of Chicago Press, 1992.

Leach, Eugene. "Mastering the Crowd: Collective Behavior and Mass Society in American Social Thought, 1917–1939." *American Studies* 27, no. 1 (Spring 1986): 99–114.

Lears, Jackson. *Fables of Abundance: A Cultural History of Advertising in America*. New York: Basic Books, 1994.

———. *No Place of Grace: Antimodernism and the Transformation of American Culture*. New York: Pantheon, 1981.

Lederer, William J., and Eugene Burdick. *The Ugly American*. New York: Norton, 1958.

Lee, Charles. "The Book-of-the-Month Club: The Story of a Publishing Institution." Ph.D. diss., University of Pennsylvania, 1955.

———. *The Hidden Public: The Story of the Book-of-the-Month Club*. Garden City, N.Y.: Doubleday, 1958.

Lee, Harper. *To Kill a Mockingbird*. Philadelphia: Lippincott, 1960.

Lee, Martyn J. *Consumer Culture Reborn: The Cultural Politics of Consumption*. London: Routledge, 1993.

Lehmann-Haupt, Hellmut, in collaboration with Lawrence C. Wroth and Rollo G. Silver. *The Book in America: A History of the Making and Selling of Books in the United States*. New York: Bowker, 1952.

Lentricchia, Frank. "Lyric in the Culture of Capitalism." In *Modernist Quartet*, 47–76. Cambridge: Cambridge University Press, 1994.

Levine, Lawrence. *Highbrow/Lowbrow: The Emergence of Cultural Hierarchy in America*. Cambridge: Harvard University Press, 1988.

"A Literary Main Street." *Nation*, May 19, 1926, 546.

Long, Elizabeth. "Women, Reading, and Cultural Authority: Some Implications of the Audience Perspective in Cultural Studies." *American Quarterly* 38 (Fall 1986): 591–612.

Lord, Walter. *Day of Infamy*. New York: Henry Holt, 1957.

MacDonald, Betty. *The Egg and I*. Philadelphia: Lippincott, 1945.

MacDonald, Dwight. "Masscult and Midcult." *Partisan Review*, Spring 1960, 203–33.

———. "Masscult and Midcult: II." *Partisan Review*, Fall 1960, 589–631.

Madison, Charles. *Book Publishing in America*. New York: McGraw Hill, 1966.

Marchand, Roland. *Advertising the American Dream: Making Way for Modernity, 1920–1940*. Berkeley: University of California Press, 1985.

Marcus, George E., and Michael M. J. Fischer. *Anthropology as Cultural Critique: An Experimental Moment in the Human Sciences*. Chicago: University of Chicago Press, 1986.

Markandaya, Kamala. *Nectar in a Sieve*. New York: John Day, 1954.

Marquand, John P. "*Marjorie Morningstar*, a Novel by Herman Wouk." *Book-of-the-Month Club News*, August 1955, 1.

Marvin, Carolyn. *When Old Technologies Were New: Thinking about Electric Communication in the Late Nineteenth Century*. New York: Oxford University Press, 1988.

Marx, Leo. *The Machine in the Garden: Technology and the Pastoral Ideal in America*. New York: Oxford University Press, 1964.

Mathews, Mitford. *A Dictionary of Americanisms on Historical Principles*. Chicago: University of Chicago Press, 1951.

May, Lary. *Screening Out the Past: The Birth of Mass Culture and the Motion Picture Industry*. Chicago: University of Chicago Press, 1980.

Mencken, H. L. *The American Language*. New York: Knopf, 1919.

Michaels, Walter Benn. "An American Tragedy, or the Promise of American Life." *Representations* 25 (Winter 1989), 71–98.

Michener, James. *Hawaii*. New York: Random House, 1959.

Miller, Daniel. *Material Culture and Mass Consumption*. London: Basil Blackwell, 1987.

Miller, Nancy. *Getting Personal: Feminist Occasions and Other Autobiographical Acts*. New York: Routledge, 1991.

Mills, C. Wright. *The Power Elite*. New York: Oxford University Press, 1956.

———. *White-Collar: The American Middle Classes*. New York: Oxford University Press, 1951.

Morley, Christopher. *Ex Libris Carissimis*. Philadelphia: University of Pennsylvania Press, 1932.

———. *Parnassus on Wheels*. Philadelphia: Lippincott, 1917.

Mott, Frank Luther. *American Journalism: A History of Newspapers in the United States through 250 Years, 1690–1940*. New York: Macmillan, 1941.

———. *A History of American Magazines, 1885–1905*. Cambridge: Harvard University Press, 1957.

Nader, Laura. "Up the Anthropologist: Perspectives Gained from Studying Up." In *Reinventing Anthropology*, ed. Dell Hymes, 284–311. New York: Pantheon, 1969.

Noel, Mary. *Villains Galore . . . : The Heyday of the Popular Story Weekly*. New York: Macmillan, 1954.

Nye, David. *Electrifying America: Social Meanings of a New Technology, 1880–1940*. Cambridge: MIT Press, 1990.

O'Connor, Richard. *Heywood Broun, a Biography*. New York: Putnam's, 1975.

Ohmann, Richard M. *Politics of Letters*. Middletown: Wesleyan University Press, 1987.

———. *Selling Culture: Magazines, Markets, and Class at the Turn of the Century*. London: Verso, 1996.

———. "The Shaping of a Canon: U.S. Fiction, 1960–1975." *Critical Inquiry* 10 (September 1983): 199–223.

Olney, Martha L. *Buy Now, Pay Later: Advertising, Credit, and Consumer Durables in the 1920s*. Chapel Hill: University of North Carolina Press, 1991.

Paton, Alan. *Cry, the Beloved Country: A Story of Comfort and Desolation*. New York: Scribner's, 1948.

Peterson, Theodore. *Magazines in the Twentieth Century*. Urbana: University of Illinois Press, 1956.

Porter, Noah. *Books and Reading, or, What Books Shall I Read and How Shall I Read Them?* New York: Scribner's, 1871.

Powers, Richard. *Operation Wandering Soul*. New York: Harper Perennial, 1994.

Proust, Marcel. "On Reading." In *On Reading Ruskin: Prefaces to "La Bible d'Amiens" and "Sesame et les Lys," with Selections from the Notes to the Translated Texts*, trans. and ed. Jean Autret, William Burford, and Phillipe J. Wolfe, 113. New Haven: Yale University Press, 1987.

"A Publishing Book Club." *Publishers Weekly*, December 4, 1926, 2146–47.

"A Publishing Club Idea." *Publishers Weekly*, December 11, 1926, 2207–8.

Pynchon, Thomas. *The Crying of Lot 49*. Philadelphia: Lippincott, 1966.

Radway, Janice. "The Book-of-the-Month Club and the General Reader: On the Uses of Serious Fiction." *Critical Inquiry* 14 (Spring 1988): 516–38.

———. "Ethnography among Elites: Comparing Discourses of Power." *Journal of Communication Inquiry* 13 (Summer 1989): 3–11.

———. "Interpretive Communities and Variable Literacies: The Functions of Romance Reading." *Daedalus* 113 (Summer 1984): 49–73.

Raleigh, John Henry. *Matthew Arnold and American Culture*. Berkeley: University of California Press, 1957.

Renault, Mary. *The Bull from the Sea*. New York: Pantheon, 1962.

Reynolds, Quentin. *The Fiction Factory, or, from Pulp Row to Quality Street: 100 Years of Publishing at Street and Smith*. New York: Random House, 1955.

Roberts, Kenneth. *Oliver Wiswell*. New York: Doubleday, 1940.

Robinson, Ted. "The Book Habit: An Inquiry in Four Parts." *Publishers Weekly*, May 8, 15, 22, June 5, 1926, 1530–31, 1592–94, 1840–42.

Rose, Mark. *Authors and Owners: The Invention of Copyright*. Cambridge: Harvard University Press, 1993.

Rosenberg, Bernard, and David Manning White, eds. *Mass Culture: The Popular Arts in America*. Glencoe, Ill.: Free Press, 1957.

Ross, Andrew. *No Respect: Intellectuals and Popular Culture*. New York: Routledge, 1989.

Rubin, Joan Shelley. *The Making of Middlebrow Culture*. Chapel Hill: University of North Carolina Press, 1992.

———. "Self, Culture, and Self Culture in Modern America: The Early History of the Book-of-the-Month Club." *Journal of American History* 71, no. 4 (March 1985): 782–806.

Russell, Charles Edward. "Take Them or Leave Them: Standardization of Hats and Houses and Minds." *Century*, June 1926, 168–77.

Sackheim, Maxwell. *My First Sixty Years in Advertising*. Englewood Cliffs, N.J.: Prentice-Hall, 1970.

———. "Why the Book Clubs Are Successful." *Advertising & Selling*, August 1947, 38, 68.

Samuels, Shirley. *The Culture of Sentiment: Race, Gender, and Sentimentality in Nineteenth-Century America*. New York: Oxford University Press, 1992.

Scanlon, Jennifer. *Inarticulate Longings: The Ladies' Home Journal, Gender, and the Promises of Consumer Culture*. New York: Routledge, 1995.

Scherman, Bernardine Kielty. *Girl from Fitchburg*. New York: Random House, 1964.

Scherman, Harry. *The Promises Men Live By: A New Approach to Economics*. New York: Random House, 1938.

Schlereth, Thomas J. *Victorian America: Transformations in Everyday Life, 1876–1915*. New York: Harper Collins, 1991.

Schneirov, Matthew. *The Dream of a New Social Order: Popular Magazines in America, 1893–1914*. New York: Columbia University Press, 1994.

Schudson, Michael. *Advertising, the Uneasy Persuasion: Its Dubious Impact on American Society*. New York: Basic Books, 1984.

Seidman, Stuart. *The New Republic: A Voice of Modern Liberalism*. New York: Praeger, 1986.

Seltzer, Mark. *Bodies and Machines*. New York: Routledge, 1992.

Shirer, William. *The Rise and Fall of the Third Reich: A History of Nazi Germany.* New York: Simon and Schuster, 1960.

Shove, Raymond. *Cheap Book Production in the United States, 1870–1891.* Urbana: University of Illinois Library, 1937.

Shumway, David R. *Creating American Civilization: A Genealogy of American Literature as an Academic Discipline.* Minneapolis: University of Minnesota Press, 1994.

Silverman, Al. "The Fragile Pleasure." In *Reading in the 1980s,* ed. Stephen Graubard, 35–49. New York: Bowker, 1983.

Simpson, J. A., and E. S. C. Weiner, eds. *The Oxford English Dictionary.* 20 vols. Oxford: Clarendon Press, 1989.

Skinner, Cornelia Otis. *Our Hearts Were Young and Gay.* New York: Dodd, Mead, 1942.

Smith, Barbara Herrnstein. *Contingencies of Value: Alternative Perspectives for Critical Theory.* Cambridge: Harvard University Press, 1988.

Stallybrass, Peter, and Allon White. *The Politics and Poetics of Transgression.* Ithaca: Cornell University Press, 1986.

Stedman, Lawrence C., Katherine Tinsley, and Carl F. Kaestle. "Literacy as a Consumer Activity." In *Literacy in the United States: Readers and Reading since 1980,* ed. Carl Kaestle, Helen Damon-Moore, Lawrence C. Stedman, Katherine Tinsley, and William Vance Trollinger Jr., 149–79. New Haven: Yale University Press, 1991.

Stevenson, Louise L. *Scholarly Means to Evangelical Ends: The New Haven Scholars and the Transformation of Higher Learning in America, 1830–1890.* Baltimore: Johns Hopkins University Press, 1986.

Stone, Irving. *The Agony and the Ecstasy: A Novel of Michelangelo.* Garden City, N.Y.: Doubleday, 1961.

———. *Lust for Life: The Novel of Vincent Van Gogh.* New York: Grossett & Dunlap, 1948.

———. *The President's Lady: A Novel about Rachel and Andrew Jackson.* Garden City, N.Y.: Doubleday, 1951.

*"The Story of Philosophy* by Will Durant." *Book-of-the-Month Club News,* August 1926, 3.

Story, Ronald. *The Forging of an Aristocracy: Harvard and the Boston Upper Class, 1800–1870.* Middletown, Conn.: Wesleyan University Press, 1980.

Strasser, Susan. *Satisfaction Guaranteed: The Making of the American Mass Market.* New York: Pantheon, 1989.

Strychacz, Thomas. *Modernism, Mass Culture, and Professionalism.* Cambridge: Cambridge University Press, 1993.

Susman, Warren. *Culture as History: The Transformation of Society in the Twentieth Century.* New York: Pantheon, 1984.

Tebbel, John. *A History of Book Publishing in the United States.* 4 vols. New York: Bowker, 1972–81.

Tedlock, Barbara. "From Participant Observation to the Observation of Participation: The Emergence of Narrative Ethnography." *Journal of Anthropological Research* 47 (1991): 69–94.

Tichi, Cecelia. *Shifting Gears: Technology, Literature, Culture in Modernist America*. Chapel Hill: University of North Carolina Press, 1987.

Tomkins, Silvan. *Shame and Its Sisters: A Silvan Tomkins Reader*. Ed. Eve Kosofsky Sedgwick and Adam Frank. Durham: Duke University Press, 1995.

Tompkins, Jane P. "Me and My Shadow." *New Literary History* 19 (Autumn 1987): 169–78.

———. "The Reader in History: The Changing Shape of Literary Response." In *Reader-Response Criticism*, ed. Jane P. Tompkins, 201–32. Baltimore: Johns Hopkins University Press, 1980.

———. *Sensational Designs: The Cultural Work of American Fiction, 1790–1860*. New York: Harvard University Press, 1985.

Trachtenberg, Alan. *The Incorporation of America: Culture and Society in the Guilded Age*. New York: Hill and Wang, 1982.

Traver, Robert. *Anatomy of a Murder*. New York: St. Martin's Press, 1958.

Tuchman, Barbara W. *The Guns of August*. New York: Macmillan, 1962.

Uris, Leon. *Mila 18*. Garden City, N.Y.: Doubleday, 1961.

Vanderbilt, Kermit. *American Literature and the Academy: The Roots, Growth, and Maturity of a Profession*. Philadelphia: University of Pennsylvania Press, 1986.

Van Doren, Carl. "Day In and Day Out." *Century*, December 1923, 308–15.

Veblen, Thorstein. *The Theory of the Leisure Class*. New York: Vanguard Press, 1934.

Walker, Pat. *Between Labor and Capital*. Montreal: Black Rose Press, 1979.

Wallach, Mark I., and Jon Bracker. *Christopher Morley*. Boston: Twayne, 1976.

Warner, Michael. *The Letters of the Republic: Publication and the Public Sphere in Eighteenth-Century America*. Cambridge: Harvard University Press, 1990.

———. "The Mass Public and the Mass Subject." In *Habermas and the Public Sphere*, ed. Craig Calhoun, 377–401. Cambridge: MIT Press, 1992.

———. "Professionalism and the Rewards of Literature: 1875–1900." *Criticism* 27 (Winter 1985): 1–28.

Washington, Ida H. *Dorothy Canfield Fisher, a Biography*. Shelburne, Vt.: New England Press, 1982.

Wechsler, Harold S. "The Rationale for Restriction: Ethnicity and College Admission in America, 1910–1980." *American Quarterly* 36 (Winter 1984): 643–67.

"What Is Literary Authority?" *Nation*, March 18, 1925, 282.

"What the Public Wants." *Book-of-the-Month Club News*, March 1928.

Whipple, Leon. "Books on the Belt." *Nation*, February 13 1929, 182.

White, Theodore. *The Making of the President, 1960*. New York: Atheneum, 1961.

Whiteside, Thomas. *The Blockbuster Complex: Conglomerates, Show Business, and Book Publishing*. Middletown, Conn.: Wesleyan University Press, 1981.

Whyte, William H. *The Organization Man*. New York: Simon and Schuster, 1955.

Widdemer, Margaret. "Message and Middlebrow." *Saturday Review of Literature*, February 18, 1933, 433–34.

Williams, Raymond. *Keywords: A Vocabulary of Culture and Society*. Rev. ed. New York: Oxford University Press, 1983.

————. *Marxism and Literature*. London: Oxford University Press, 1977.

Williamson, Judith. *Decoding Advertisements*. London: Marion Boyars, 1976.

Wilson, Christopher. *The Labor of Words: Literary Professionalism in the Progressive Era*. Athens: University of Georgia Press, 1985.

Wilson, Elizabeth. "Picasso and Pate de Foie Gras: Pierre Bourdieu's Sociology of Culture." *Diacritics*, Summer 1988, 47–60.

Woodmansee, Martha. *The Author, Art, and the Market: Rereading the History of Aesthetics*. New York: Columbia University Press, 1995.

————. "The Genius and the Copyright: Economic and Legal Conditions of the Emergence of the Author." *Eighteenth Century Studies* 17 (Summer 1984): 425–48.

Woolf, Virginia. "Middlebrow." In *The Death of the Moth*, 180–84. New York: Harcourt, Brace, 1942.

Wouk, Herman. *Marjorie Morningstar*. Garden City, N.Y.: Doubleday, 1955.

Wright, Paul M. "Mammon and the Muse: President Eliot, P. F. Collier, and the Harvard Classics: 'Five-Foot Shelf.'" Paper delivered at the 1992 American Studies Association, Costa Mesa, Calif.

Zboray, Ronald. *A Fictive People: Antebellum Economic Development and the American Reading Public*. New York: Oxford University Press, 1994.

Zinsser, William. *A Family of Readers: An Informal Portrait of the Book-of-the-Month Club and Its Members on the Occasion of its 60th Anniversary*. New York: Book-of-the-Month Club, 1986.

# INDEX

176–77, 187, 202, 263, 281; and adult education, 178; as novelist, 178; and literary localism, 178–79; objections to Scherman's original plan, 192, 194–95, 264; and book selection process, 202, 267, 268, 269, 270–71, 278, 281; on book reviewing and literary criticism, 268–70, 273; on history writing, 282; and revision of Wright's *Black Boy,* 286–87

Fitzgerald, Edward, 352

Fitzgerald, F. Scott, 3

Ford, Betty, 36

Ford, Henry, 154–55, 174–75, 192, 372 (n. 2)

"Fordizing," 204, 244, 261

Foucault, Michel, 11, 198

Francis, Dick, 63

Frank, Waldo, 203, 218, 249, 253–54, 268; "Pseudo-Literature," 213–16, 217

Freeman, Joseph, 204

Freud, Sigmund, 178

Frost, Robert, 383 (n. 76)

Fuller, Margaret, 349

"Furniture books," 160

Gale, Zona, 199–200

Gallup, George, 380 (n. 29)

Galsworthy, John, 178

García Márquez, Gabriel, 94, 365 (n. 5)

Garrison, Dee, 144

Gay rights movement, 359–60

Geertz, Clifford: "Deep Play," 361 (n. 6)

General Motors Corporation, 206, 208

"General reader," 10, 91, 275–77; book club editors and, 22, 72, 95, 99, 101, 103–4, 106, 109–10, 112; Savago and, 73, 74–75, 93–94; Scherman and, 94, 185, 275; Canby on, 296. *See also* Readers

Genres, literary, 102

*George Munro v. Beadle,* 135

Gold, Mike, 204

*Good Housekeeping,* 147

Gordimer, Nadine, 36; *A Sport of Nature,* 72–75

Graff, Gerald, 140, 361 (n. 2)

Grayson, David: *Adventures in Contentment,* 150

Greenberg, Clement, 310

Griswold, Rufus Wilmot, 132

Gross, Robert A.: "Books and Libraries in Thoreau's Concord," 367 (n. 6)

Guggenheim Foundation, 49

Guillory, John, 140, 361 (n. 2)

Gunther, John: *Death Be Not Proud,* 118; *Inside Africa,* 118

Guthrie, Jane, 147–48, 149, 150–51, 160

Haas, Robert K., 191, 201, 281

Habermas, Jurgen, 234

"Habitus," 262, 388–89 (n. 2)

Haggard, Rider: *She,* 290

Halsey, Harlan P., 134, 135

Hapgood, Norman, 146

Harper and Brothers, 286

*Harper's,* 140, 203

Hartley, Marsden, 154

Harvard Classics, 145, 146–47, 159–60

Harvard University, 141

Harvey, David: *The Condition of Postmodernity,* 372 (n. 2)

Haussmann, Georges, 175

Hawkins, Hugh, 146

Health books, 102

Hemingway, Ernest, 293; *The Old Man and the Sea,* 92

Herbst, Josephine, 204

Hersey, John: *The Wall,* 312, 313, 317, 348

Heyerdahl, Thor: *Kon-Tiki,* 118, 312, 314, 347

"Highbrow" culture, 152, 218–19

High culture, 8–10, 37, 189, 190, 321

Highet, Gilbert, 316

History of the book, 128–29, 367–68 (n. 7)

History writing, 282; popular, 102, 105–6, 108–10, 279; academic, 105, 106–8, 110

Hitler, Adolf, 348

Holt, Henry, 138

Michaels, Walter Benn, 203, 206

Michener, James, 63, 74; *Hawaii*, 313, 314, 320

Middlebrow culture, 5, 357–58, 372 (n. 2), 372–73 (n. 3); opposition to academicism, 9–10, 12, 37; Book-of-the-Month Club and, 11–12, 16, 128, 152, 153, 183, 189, 259, 285, 297, 300; books and reading, 12–13, 284–85, 307, 351, 358–60, 391 (n. 46); and literary modernism, 15, 121–22, 288, 364 (n. 23); professional-managerial class and, 15, 262, 297, 351, 358; and cultural pedagogy, 15, 297; book club wars and, 189, 219, 244–45, 259, 310; emergence of, 218–19, 366–67 (n. 4); threat to systems of privilege, 244–45; middle class and, 261–62, 285; Book-of-the-Month Club judges and, 262, 277, 284, 285, 288; personalism and individualism, 283, 284, 336, 337, 359; sentiment in, 285, 391 (n. 44); *To Kill a Mockingbird* and, 337, 344

Middle class: and cultural value of books, 152, 161, 173, 248; and education, 161, 306; and cultural pedagogy, 247; and individualism, 258; and middlebrow culture, 261–62, 285; women, 331, 334; professional-managerial class and, 387–88 (n. 48); reading and, 393–94 (n. 61)

"Mid-list" books, 90–91, 94

Millett, Kate: *Sexual Politics*, 2, 350

Mintz, Sidney, 80

Mitchell, Margaret, 350

Modern art, 154

Modern era, 372–73 (n. 3); Scherman and, 154–55, 175, 184–86, 193; Canby and, 177, 265–66, 288, 289, 291, 293, 392 (n. 50); disruptions of, 177, 289, 291; literature and, 265–66, 293; advertising and, 376–77 (n. 53)

Modernism, literary, 3; middlebrow culture and, 15, 121–22, 288, 364 (n. 23); book club editors and, 70; book club selections and, 178, 279, 288; Canby

and, 178, 291–93, 392 (n. 50); and capitalism, 218; book club judges and, 278, 279, 283, 288

Moeller, Philip, 158

Montessori, Maria, 178

Morley, Christopher, 150, 177, 187, 263, 321; as public personality, 179–80, 181–83, 280; *Thunder on the Left*, 181; *Where the Blue Begins*, 181; newspaper column, 181, 264–65; *Ex Libris Carissimis*, 264; *Parnassus on Wheels*, 264; promotion of books, 264–65

Morrison, Toni: *Beloved*, 114–15, 116

Moses, Robert, 175

Motherwell, Hiram, 158

Movies, 357–58

Mumford, Lewis, 203

Munro, George, 134, 135

Munro, Norman, 134

Munsey, Frank, 248

Music Appreciation Records, 310

Nader, Laura: "Up the Anthropologist," 362 (n. 4)

NAL publishers, 89

Nancy Drew mysteries, 306, 323–24

*Nation*, 249, 252; and Harvard Classics, 146–47; and standardization debates, 203–4; and literary authority, 223–26, 227

Nationalism, 347

Nativism, 237–38

Naylor, Gloria, 352–53

"Negative option," 53, 196–97, 198, 309, 363 (n. 3)

New Criticism, 361 (n. 2)

*New Republic*, 203–4, 249, 252

Newspapers, 203; serial fiction, 131–32; personal columns, 180–81; book reviews, 254–55, 258, 266

*New Statesman*, 219

New York, N.Y., 21–22, 37–38

*New Yorker*, 29, 204, 226, 249

*New York Evening Mail*, 138–39

*New York Evening Post*, 181

New York Social Register, 295

Sacco and Vanzetti trial, 180

Sackheim, Maxwell, 158, 159, 191, 195–96, 201, 309

Sagan, Carl: *Contact*, 31–33, 42

Salten, Felix: *Bambi*, 279

Sansone, Jill, 97, 122; reader's reports, 43, 69–70, 71, 83, 110; and Joe Savago, 96, 123

Saroyan, William, 285

*Saturday Evening Post*, 278

*Saturday Review of Literature*, 204, 211, 219, 255; Canby as editor of, 177–78, 239, 240

Savago, Joseph, 117, 119; as executive editor, 29–30, 122; reader's reports, 30–33, 42, 43, 72–75, 114–15; and literary taste, 33–35, 61; and Time takeover, 49; and literary-commercial relationship, 58–60; on types of fiction, 60–61, 67; and general reader, 73, 74–75, 93–94; illness, 96–97; on popular history, 106; on "class trash," 112; death of, 123

Sayers, Dorothy: *The Omnibus of Crime*, 279

Scherman, Harry, 14, 22, 124; and Little Leather Library, 29, 127–28, 129, 140, 151–52, 158–61, 163, 164, 190–91; and general reader, 94, 185, 275; advertising background, 127, 154, 155, 157, 248–49, 357; marketing and advertising strategies, 128, 151–53, 157–58, 159–60, 163–66, 167, 168–70, 173, 193, 221; founding of Book-of-the-Month Club, 152, 154–55, 168–76, 187–88, 191; and cultural-commercial relationship, 152–53, 249, 254, 355, 356–57; and modern era, 154–55, 175, 184–86, 193; and books as consumer goods, 155, 160–61, 162–64, 165–67, 173–74, 375 (n. 35); and education, 156, 159–60, 161, 162, 193; as reporter for *American Hebrew*, 156–57; and book distribution system, 163, 168–69, 170–71, 174–76, 189, 190–93, 194–95, 196, 261; and selec-

tion committee, 171, 176, 177, 178, 179, 183, 191, 232–34, 235–36, 261, 263, 275–76; on book selection process, 171–72, 202, 232, 281; and subscriber choice of books, 174–75, 192–93, 196, 202–3, 231–32, 233, 264; *Promises Men Live By*, 183–84; on economics, 183–84, 185; critics of, 188–89, 231–32, 249–50, 254, 255; and returned books, 195, 196; collaboration with publishing industry, 198–99, 200, 271–72, 309, 353; "Report on the Book-of-the-Month Club after Seven Months of Operation," 201–3, 385 (n. 21); and standardization debates, 202, 203; and literary authority, 203, 233–34, 235; and conception of the author, 217; as cultural entrepreneur, 248–50, 254; and book club wars, 249; on club membership, 296; Library of Congress address, 310

Scherman, Jacob, 155–56

Scherman, Katherine Harris, 155–56

Scherman, Thomas, 310

Scherman, William, 157

Schliemann, Heinrich, 324, 331

Schnable, Richard F., 355

Schudson, Michael: *Advertising, the Uneasy Persuasion*, 374 (n. 33)

Science, 274–75, 335–36

Scott, Sir Walter, 290

*Scribners*, 203

Seldes, Gilbert, 154

Selection committee. *See* Book-of-the-Month Club—selection committee

Seltzer, Mark, 133, 198, 206, 207–8; *Bodies and Machines*, 380–81 (n. 30)

Sentiment, 283, 285, 294, 350, 391 (n. 44)

"Sentimental education," 263, 361 (n. 6)

"Serious fiction," 61, 69, 74–75

"Serious readers," 52, 73, 91–92, 103–4

*Seventeen*, 306

Shakespeare, William, 150, 151–52, 155, 158, 321–23

Shanley, Lorraine, 25, 26, 54, 95

{ *Index* }

Updike, John, 63
Uris, Leon: *Exodus*, 313; *Mila 18*, 317
"Use books," 81–82, 85, 87, 166
Utilitarianism, 254, 284, 288; in book
ownership, 147, 150–51, 152, 166

Van Doren, Carl, 180, 181, 199–200
Van Straalen, Alice, 43, 62, 119, 122
Veblen, Thorstein, 252, 376 (n. 51)
Venus de Milo, 320
Voltaire (François-Marie Arouet), 281
Vorse, Mary Heaton, 154

Walker, Edith, 194, 295
Ward, Humphrey, 290
Warner, Michael, 140, 141, 234–35,
242–43, 361 (n. 2)
Warner, Sylvia Townsend: *Lolly Willowes*,
195
Warner Books, 353
Warner Communications, 353
Waxman, Maron, 45, 97
Weeks, Brigitte, 354
Weinberg, Susan, 63, 100–101
Wendell, Barrett, 140–41
Wharton, Edith, 178, 270, 349; *The
Writing of Fiction*, 215–16
Wheeler, Harvey: *Fail-Safe*, 317–18, 320
White, Allon, 210, 211
White, William Allen, 176, 179, 187,
263, 264, 276, 281
White-collar workers, 305
Whitman Candy Company Library
Package, 127, 152, 158
Widdemer, Margaret, 219
Wilde, Oscar, 160, 164
Williams, Raymond, 139–40; *Marxism
and Literature*, 384 (nn. 2, 4)
Williams, William Carlos, 3
Wilson, Edmund, 279, 391 (n. 35)

Winckelmann, J. J., 324
Women, 148, 349–51; in book club and
standardization debates, 189, 208–9,
210, 212–13, 215–16, 217; book club
membership, 297, 311; employment,
300, 325; book club selections and,
315, 319; *Marjorie Morningstar* and,
325, 329, 331; *Gods, Graves, and Scholars* and, 334; *To Kill a Mockingbird* and,
337, 341–42, 346; authors, 349, 350,
384 (n. 3)
"Women's fiction," 317, 319
Women's movement, 359–60
Woodberry, George, 140–41
Woolf, Virginia, 219, 279, 349, 391
(n. 35)
Woolworth's stores, 159
Working classes, 285, 331, 387–88
(n. 48)
World War I, 177
World War II, 315, 325, 348
Wouk, Herman: *The Caine Mutiny*, 118;
*Marjorie Morningstar*, 118, 312, 313,
317, 324, 325–31, 359
Wright, Harold Bell, 214
Wright, Richard, 297; *Native Son*, 286,
287; *Black Boy*, 286–87, 392 (n. 47)
Wylie, Elinor, 199–200

Yale University, 141
Yeomans, Edward: *Shackled Youth*, 151
Young Readers of America Club, 310–11

Zinsser, William, 97; as executive editor,
22, 23–25, 26–28; *On Writing Well*,
24; and Time takeover, 28, 47, 54, 55,
56, 100–101; *A Family of Readers*, 64;
on book selection process, 64–65; resignation from the club, 99–100, 122;
*Writing to Learn*, 100